It was raw power given voice!

Rearing back its awesome spined and crested head, the icedrake roared—in challenge, maybe, or in scorn, and the sound that it made was beyond imagination, a cry of incalculable strength and majesty that made the air tingle and the earth shake. .

From the terror stamped deep into the wizard Gemmel's features, it was obvious that the dragon's power was not his to command. Yet despite that, he screamed out the ancient spell words, willing the nightmare creature to turn its wrath against those who sought to slay him.

And icedrake's jaws yawned wide, a frigid, blue-white cavern lined with ragged icicles, and it sent forth a smoky silver blast of unimaginable cold. It was a blast as silent as midwinter, no storm, no blizzard, no howling rush of wind; only the faint, brittle sounds of icy stillness which told of an end to warmth and life. . . . .

THE BOOK OF YEARS,
VOL 2

The Dragon Lord

The War Lord

PETER MORWOOD

DAW BOOKS, INC.
DONALD A. WOLLHEIM, FOUNDER
375 Hudson Street, New York, NY 10014

ELIZABETH R. WOLLHEIM
SHEILA E. GILBERT
PUBLISHERS
http://www.dawbooks.com

First Printing, June 2005
1 2 3 4 5 6 7 8 9

DAW TRADEMARK REGISTERED
U.S. PAT. OFF. AND FOREIGN COUNTRIES
—MARCA REGISTRADA
HECHO EN U.S.A.

PRINTED IN THE U.S.A.

The Dragon Lord

To Anne McCaffrey, Dragon Lady,
For all you are and have been,
And all you were, unasked:
This book. And much love.

Late October—early November 1985

Preface

".... by the style and tytle of an Empyre, and as soche held Domination over all those landes for nygh an hundred yeares.

Men full wys in War and Politickes do make assured declaration that, by enbuilden of great Shipes and ye subtleties and Wickednesse of ye Necromancer Duergar Vathach (ysenden hither by ye War-Lorde Etzell to make mischief), this Empyre did desyre and make essay to take enseizen of this lande of ALBA.

Yet by HEAVENES intervention are all preserved from soche sore Distress, for in Spring-tyme of this yeare did Droek Emperor of Drusul go unto his Ancestores, and since that his first-born sonne is dead before him and ye Succession thus ymaden doubtfull, ye Empyre now is rent by great Confusion whereas its Lordes do stryve each against ye other to have power and Mastery— for they are men of no Honor and shew not that Respect which all retainers owe by Duty unto their Lordes and which obligation demandes from those same Lordes unto their vassals . . .

Now it was yknowen unto all what reasones were engiven that LORDE ALDRIC of ye clan TALVALIN did journey to this Empyre: being full of Sorrow. Yet there are men whose wordes are recognised as Truth in all thinges, who do Declare that this LORDE did but execute a very certain Strategem commanded unto him by RYNERT-KING, and that small Honor if at all was done him by soche a Taske . . ."

Ylver Vlethanek an-Caerdur
The Book of Years, Cerdor

Prologue

Night and fog lay heavily on Tuenafen, and heaviest of all in the narrow streets of the port's Old Quarter. Nothing moved there save errant skeins of mist. Most of the houses were in darkness, their doorway lanterns shattered in the riots of the past few weeks. The few lamps which remained served only to emphasise the depth of shadows into which their light could not reach.

The horseman emerged from a silent swirl of fog that drew back like the curtain of an ill-lit stage: a black-clad man, astride a coal-black horse. Both were featureless silhouettes against the slow shift of gray, sable outlines lustrous with a sheen of condensed moisture.

The horse moved. Its hooves struck hollowly against damp-slick paving slabs, muted echoes slapping up and down the street between the blankly shuttered houses. Three paces only. Three heavy clanks of iron on stone; a blacksmith sound. Then silence once more as reins were twitched and the black horse stopped.

Its rider rose a little in his stirrups, turning warily from side to side. There was a tenseness in him, in the angle of his head and the set of his shoulders. For all his ominous appearance he seemed as nervous as a cat.

Somewhere close, a clock began to strike the hour and startled his horse into sudden, stamping movement. The sound of its shoes against the ground mingled with a crackle of invective as the rider's hands jerked back on shortened reins. Doubly betraying after those three un-considered steps of half-a-hundred racing heartbeats past, the noises made by man and horse rang clearly in the muffled quiet.

All too clearly . . .

Boots clattered at his back and a voice was raised in the harsh imperatives of command. The rider's heels kicked home and his mount plunged forward, away from the wan fog-filtered unlight and into the dark maw of a nearby alley.

There was an impact; the sound of something falling heavily to the ground; a muttering of satisfaction.

Then nothing but the noiseless movement of the mist . . .

1

King's Gambit

The Hall of Kings in Cerdor was an awesome place, a vast reverberant emptiness lined with pillars of stone to support the carven magnificence of its vaulted ceiling. Autumn sunshine slanted down through windows of painted glass to splash the tinctures of Alba's high-clan crests across a floor of tessellated marble. Flames danced and flickered in nine great hearths to drive chill from the air, but their heat could not thaw the ice which edged the voice of Gemmel Errekren.

"Do you know what you have done?" he snarled. The old enchanter was in such a passion as he seldom allowed to possess him, and the energies summoned up by high emotion swirled in lambent coils about his hands and the black, dragon-patterned stave they held.

A lesser man might well have flinched from the rage of such as Gemmel—and with good reason—but Rynert the King remained at least outwardly unruffled, sitting straight-backed and aloof in his great chair. "I do what must be done," he said calmly, "for the good of the state."

Portentous yet indefinite, such a statement might have sounded good in the ears of a councillor, but it failed to satisfy Gemmel. His teeth clenched so that cords of muscle stood out on his face beneath his beard, and the pulsing nimbus of his wrath grew more intensely visible.

"For the good of the state," he echoed in a flat sneer. "You give my son to the Drusalans and then you say it is for the good of the state . . . ?"

"Your foster-son, wizard. My vass—"

"*Enough!*" The Dragonwand in Gemmel's hands struck

once against the floor—a sharp, punctuative noise—and glowing shreds of power fluttered free like incandescent moths. "Don't *ever* quibble with me . . . !" There was an unsteady shrillness in his musical old-young voice which had not been there before. "Your 'reason' is no reason at all, King, and well you know it. No excuse— for all it can excuse so much . . ."

Rynert shot a glance towards the only other occupant of the hall, hoping maybe for support—but Dewan ar Korentin's face was as stony as the wall at his back. There would be no approval from that source.

The king's gaze returned reluctantly to Gemmel. "Explain," he said.

"Must I?" The enchanter was openly scornful, but Rynert chose—as he had perforce chosen all along—to ignore the lack of courtesy.

"Yes. You must. I am . . . curious."

"I wonder that you need be. Your . . . your reason has birthed too much misery down the years for any right mind to give or accept it without question. Save perhaps in matters of convenience . . ."

Gemmel's voice was lower now, introspective, as though he spoke mostly to himself, and there was a brooding shadow on his face which Rynert could see plainly even at ten paces distance.

"For it has created lies. Betrayals . . . And deaths. Oh, so many, many deaths! Both by the hand which holds a blade, Lord King—and by the hand which offers gold . . ." The enchanter's green eyes bored into Rynert's translucent hazel as though reading the secrets buried deep behind them in the hidden places of the king's mind, and Rynert dared not be first to break the contact for fear that by doing so he would betray himself.

"Yours is a reason I have heard before, *mathern-an arluth*—but the language was not Alban then . . ."

Only he could hear the whispered words; they were no more than a thread of sound, quiet as the metallic exhalation of a drawing sword, but they seemed to flay Gemmel with the lash of some reawakened shameful memory. Something other ears were not meant to overhear . . . but Rynert heard it.

"Once there was a village. Small. Ordinary. An Im-

perial village. And its people—small, ordinary people—
had committed some infraction of the Empire's laws.
They were being . . . chastised. I could have helped
them. I did not. Instead I asked why the soldiers were
doing what was being done; their serjeant told me that
it was for the good of the state and none of my affair.
And it was not. So I did nothing. Though it would have
cost me so very little of my power, even then. But my
son tried. And it cost his life."

The enchanter hesitated, as a man will when he rea-
lizses he has said too much, and shook his head before
staring again at Rynert. "I lost more than a son that
day. More than your mind can grasp, King. Much more.
I lost the ability to go ho— Everything. So do not use
that excuse to me again. Ever."

Rynert drew in a swift, ragged breath. He was not and
never had been a sturdy man, and now the heart within
his chest was jerking like the legs of a snared rabbit so
that it took all his small store of physical strength just to
conceal the fact. Anger, outrage and affronted dignity; all
these and more blended most incongruously with a pain
that went deeper than his own frail flesh. Gemmel's story
troubled him, touching a guilt which his own conscience
had failed to rouse, and reflected endlessly to and fro in
his mind like a candle poised between two mirrors; guilt
begetting shame, begetting still more guilt. . . .

"I am as you say, wizard. King." The word snapped
out, a verbal whiplash laid across the white-bearded face
before him, righteous anger that a man could hide
behind . . . "I must make such decisions whether I will
or not. The way of kingship is like a narrow path: it
must be walked alone."

Once more the studied, courtly phrases failed to impress. Gemmel was no longer angry, merely saddened
by his own ancient griefs—and he was a man very conscious of his own dignity, regardless of how he treated
that of others. So he did not follow his first impulse, which
was to spit the sourness from his mouth on to the stones
at Rynert's feet. Instead he gazed levelly at the slight,
crook-shouldered king.

Then turned his back and stalked in silence from the
hall.

Dewan ar Korentin broke that silence. Straightening from the wall where he had leaned, and watched, and carefully said nothing, he padded forward on soft-shod feet to where Ykraith the Dragonwand had notched the marble floor. "Statecraft," he muttered, looking at the damage. "Be careful, Rynert. It could well be the death of you." On Dewan's face was an expression close to that on Gemmel's.

"Then what," asked Rynert, not liking what he saw, "is *your* word on this?"

"You already know it. I warned you before about Aldric Talvalin and my protest is on record. Again I warn you—and again I wish it recorded. Do not play with him as you do with the other diplomatic games-pieces you employ. He is different, he is . . . strange. And his notions of honor are strange. Archaic, sometimes. Especially in the matters of duty and obligation."

"Qualms, old friend?" The smile which curved Rynert's thin lips did not quite fit. "I had not expected scruples from you."

Dewan's nostrils flared a little at that and he did not even attempt to mirror the smile. "Neither qualms nor scruples. Simple caution. And simple decency. You commanded him to perform what is a foul act for one of his rank—"

"A killing, foul . . . ? For that one? He merely does for me what he has already done for himself! I remind you, Dewan, that he is my vassal . . ."

"Vassal maybe, but he deserves better. Much better. I can speak as an outsider here: and I say that deceit may have its place, but that place is not in matters of Alban honor. It cuts two ways, Rynert. He owes you duty—but you owe him respect. And the situation seems just a little one-sided. May I remind *you*—with first-hand authority—that he was not named Deathbringer in idle jest. Perhaps . . . just perhaps, he will understand why you betrayed him—" he raised one hand to forestall Rynert's protest, "for I assure you, that is how he will see it."

"For his own safety's sake . . . !"

"For reasons of state, you said. Well . . . Perhaps he'll

accept it. Or perhaps not. But if not, Rynert, then I wouldn't wish to wear your collar. Not if you were king of all the world. . . ."

Perhaps deliberately, Dewan ar Korentin's accented voice no longer used the formal mode of the Alban language. There were some at court who would have regarded his addressing of the king in any other way as an insult, but Rynert was not one of them. He understood.

"It no longer matters, even if it once did," Rynert said dismissively. "The piece has moved; now I must watch how it affects play."

"Publicly. You must be seen to support your own decisions. But in private—as secretly as you sent Talvalin—could you not send me . . . ?"

"Dewan, you grow overwrought. Go away. Return when you feel calm again. And convey my compliments to your lady wife."

Ar Korentin stiffened, bowing acknowledgement of his dismissal with a marionette's rigidity, then strode towards the great double doors with disapproval plain in the arrogant straightness of his back. Rynert's voice followed him up the hall.

"But until you come back—feeling calm, of course—please regard your time and business as your own affair . . ."

Dewan halted, stood quite still for perhaps two seconds and then turned to face the king. Rynert had that suppressed brightness around the eyes and mouth which accompanies the concealment of a smile. Dewan watched it fade and felt uneasy even as he snapped through the punctilious movements of an Imperial parade salute. Then he bowed from the waist, Alban-fashion, and took his leave, knowing deep inside that there was an ugly wrongness about this whole affair.

But able to fathom no more than that. Yet . . .

Gemmel was waiting for him. Indeed, Dewan would have been more surprised had the enchanter not been there. "Wizard," he said quietly.

"*Eldheisart* ar Korentin," Gemmel retorted. If Dewan was taken aback to hear his old Imperial rank spoken aloud by such a man as this, he gave no indication of it. "Now do you believe?" the enchanter continued. "Was I so very wrong?"

"Not wrong—but not entirely right."

"How so? I lost one son to the Empire many years ago—I will not stand by and lose another for the . . . for the good of the state!"

"We should walk," said Dewan in a flat voice, his eyes indicating the sentries flanking the doorway of the Hall of Kings. None was obviously listening; in the presence of their captain they stood rigidly to attention and stared straight to their front. But they had ears even so . . .

Gemmel nodded once, minutely, and walked.

"Now hear me," ar Korentin began again, once he judged them a safe distance away. "Rynert has—"

"—Forefeited what little allegiance Aldric or I might have owed him!"

Dewan ar Korentin was a patient man and slow to anger, but his patience was rapidly wearing thin. Both hands came up to grip Gemmel's shoulders and if necessary shake him back to coherence, but something in the old man's expression suggested that anything approaching violence would be countered tenfold. He hesitated, hands in the air as he considered, then contented himself with a spread-armed shrug.

"Just once, wizard, try listening to someone besides yourself!" he snapped. Gemmel's teeth shut with a click, and his indrawn breath was an audible hiss; but Dewan pressed home his advantage in the relative silence. "As I was saying," the irony was if anything overdone, "*mathern-an* Rynert has granted me permission to go after Aldric. Into the Empire."

Gemmel lifted an eyebrow. "Tacit permission, of course. Nothing direct, and certainly nothing committed to paper . . . ?"

"Certainly not!" Dewan's sense of propriety was outraged by the suggestion. "This is of the utmost delicacy."

"So much so," the enchanter's voice was flat and nasty, "that your worthy lord might need to wash his hands of it at short notice. Mm?"

That possibility had not occurred to Dewan; but he had only to consider how Aldric had been—and was being—used, to realize that Gemmel was not making idle criticism. Yet he persisted: "Will you come with me? After all, Talvalin is your—your son."

"Foster-son," Gemmel corrected absently. "What you really mean is, will I come and help pull Rynert's political fat out of the Imperial fire before it flares into—Lord God, 'incident' wouldn't begin to describe it." The cold, clear emerald eyes transfixed Dewan like needles. "No. I won't."

The shock of that refusal could not be hidden, and ar Korentin floundered for several seconds before he managed to say anything remotely sensible. "So what do I do—go alone . . . ?"

"Not necessarily. *You* could come with *me*." With each emphasis the enchanter's long finger poked Dewan in the chest.

"What's the difference?"

"Between black and white. My way—you know and I know. His way—who knows who knows . . . ?" Gemmel was plainly recovering what passed for his sense of humor.

"All right," Dewan conceded. "Where do we go?"

"First, to the coast. By *my* route."

"And afterwards?"

Gemmel grinned a swift, vulpine grin which showed most of his teeth. "Restore all the marks of rank to that Imperial armor of yours. No. More than all. Exaggerate it. Promote yourself. It may be more useful that way than you think. But as for afterwards . . ." The grin flickered again. "Leave afterwards to me."

"This place is supposed to be secure—so how did it get in?" Both the harsh voice and the man who used it were out of place in this room of graceful furnishings and delicately muted colors. He was burly, florid and middle-aged, with a spade-shaped iron-gray beard, and he was encased to the neck in vivid scarlet-lacquered armor which was brilliant with the precious-metal geometric shapes of lofty rank. A sharp reek of oily metal hung about him—cutting discordantly through the fragrance of incense smouldering in a burner by the door—and leather creaked whenever he moved, as he did now in leaning forward to smooth an already-flat sheet of paper with blunt fingers. It creaked again when he twisted to stare at a tall, lean figure outlined by sunlight at the window. "I asked you a question."

The other man turned. "And I thought you were being rhetorical," he replied mildly, seeming undisturbed by his companion's brusqueness—although because of the glare at his back and the deep cowl which covered his head, no expression could be read from his shadowed features. "Set aside its delivery. Is it genuine?"

"Perhaps," the armored man conceded, turning the paper this way and that as if closer scrutiny might reveal some stamp of authenticity. "The codes were correct and the seals unbroken when it was found?"

"They were."

"Or so we must assume . . . But this translation," he slapped at it with the back of one hand, "is it accurate?"

"You wrote it. You translated it. You should know . . ."

"Most evasive." The armored man's chuckle was a dry sound, devoid of all humor. "But that's only to be expected." He set aside the enigmatic piece of paper and lifted the slim dossier to which it referred. Originally secured by wires, and by seals of both lead and wax, the folder's contents were plainly not meant for idle fingers to flick through.

As it was prised open once more, the man by the window left his place in the sun and walked lazily across the room. Each step was marked by the austere click of a long ash cane gripped easily in the fingertips of his left hand.

Flimsy sheets drifted across the table-top like the leaves of autumn; half-a-dozen pages in which—he knew—a man's life was laid open for inspection like something gutted on a surgeon's slab. "Impressive, is it not?" he asked softly.

There was no reply at first; each document was set out, carefully spaced and minutely shifted. Then, inevitably, one in particular was singled out for closer scrutiny. It was a portrait—or more correctly a likeness, for it boasted little in the way of artistic excellence. But its accuracy was uncanny, almost inhuman, for surely no human hand could capture tones and textures and nuances of color with such painstaking and subtle precision. It was as if the image in a mirror had been printed on paper.

"Impressive," said the armored man at last, "is scarcely adequate." He glanced up with a crooked smile, but as usual could discern no response to his comment even though by now he could see within the deep, dark hood.

There was only his own face, distorted and reflected back at him from the surface of a mask of polished metal . . .

The ash cane rattled slightly as it was laid down on the table; then gloved hands came up to throw back the cowl and burnished silver emerged from its concealment like a weapon being drawn. There was that same cold, impersonal menace; yet at the same time a very human satisfaction in the way the masked man purred, "I had sketches made. And distributed wherever they might prove useful . . ."

"Such as?"

"Every west-coast seaport which runs the Elherran trade to Alba. I have agents in them all."

"Of course . . ." The armored man nodded once, as if he had expected nothing less. His eyes were inexorably drawn back to those of the portrait: dark eyes, gray-green and icy as the northern sea in winter. Looking at those eyes, he had no difficulty in believing what he had already skimmed from the dossier about this young man. "Talvalin," he mused. "Aldric Talvalin. An Alban clan-lord. And you still think that Rynert sent this—betrayed one of his own?"

"I know he sent it." Now voice and mask were one, for there was something remote and terrible in that short sentence; and as the metal-shrouded face moved slightly, light slid sparkling away as though flinching from any prolonged contact with its surface. "I have known for two months now. And I have not found him yet."

"But that still leaves him loose in my . . . our . . . jurisdiction."

"Loose . . . ? I think not."

"What?"

"He may seem . . . loose, if you prefer the word.

Because we do not know his whereabouts. Yet. But he must leave us"—a quick gesture recovered the cane and stirred the papers on the table—"and we know where he will try. And then . . ." The leather-skinned fingers of his right hand spread wide, like a claw. The armored man looked at it, then at the mirror-blank masked face beyond. "Then we will have him and we will hold him. *Here!*"

The fingers closed.

2

Perfidious Alba

The beach edging Dunacre Bay was almost four miles long; it curved away below the Morhan Hills to the south-west, and out in a great shallow arc past the old fortress which gave the bay its name, off north and east towards the Ring Rocks and Sallyn Point. At low tide it was featureless and flat, admirable for walking and the exercise of horses; for then the surf-line—such as it was, except in stormy weather—lay seven hundred yards or more from the necklace of pebbles which divided sand from marram grass and bracken-covered dunes. The beach shelved leisurely out into the sea, and only those who knew this coast were aware of the sudden precipitous plunge as the sea-bed fell away into black depths which would grant access to ships of even the deepest draught.

Gemmel Errekren was one with such knowledge.

For all that, Dewan ar Korentin was not yet wholly convinced that the wizard knew what he was doing, no matter how well he claimed to know the vagaries of sea and shore. This very beach was an instance of his doubt. The tide was out, just at the turn; consequently there was a long, conspicuous walk before they reached the water and the safety of whatever vessel had been provided for their use. Hopefully the sentries on Dunacre's ramparts would think them fishermen, or crab-catchers, or gatherers of seaweed. Anything except what they were: two men creeping illegally out of Alba and even more illegally into the Drusalan Empire.

And maybe the sentries wouldn't see them at all, for though Dewan flattered himself that his eyesight was better than most, he was unable to penetrate the opalescent wall of mist and spray-spume which had rolled in from the sea just as their feet touched the sand . . . Again he glanced thoughtfully at Gemmel's back, as he had done more than once since the weather took its so-convenient turn for the worse; and again shrugged it aside as common sense took over . . .

In so far as any man could shrug under the burden which he carried.

Gemmel had insisted that they leave their horses stabled at the tavern and merely walk towards the shore, having hidden their baggage in that direction during the previous night. Unencumbered by the necessities of travel—he had elaborated, as he inevitably did—they would seem no more than two gentlemen taking their ease with a constitutional stroll along the beach.

They might have been unencumbered when they left the inn, thought Dewan wearily to himself, but they weren't bloody unencumbered now—though it was remarkable how Gemmel had contrived to foist all the truly heavy gear on to Dewan's broad shoulders whilst he stalked elegantly along with no more than his staff and an oiled-leather satchel of books. If he was such a powerful sorcerer as young Aldric Talvalin had insisted, then why couldn't he just wave that magic Dragonwand of his and make the bundles float out by themselves . . . ?

Even as he thought it, Dewan knew his notion was little more than nonsense. He had seen very little sorcery—although even that was more than enough—but it had made him aware that the Art Magic was as exact as any science. Certainly too precise to lift the weight off *his* back . . . ! He grunted, swore to himself as the unbalanced stuff he carried slipped still further to one side and hitched at it so ferociously that it continued to slip . . . this time down the other side.

"Wizard! Where's the bloody boat, wizard?" Gemmel showed no sign of having heard him, which was hardly surprising; the wind from the sea pulled Dewan's words right off his lips, tugged them to meaningless syllables and noise, then tried to push the fragments back down his throat.

And that was another thing—how the hell could any

fog remain so solidly in place when there was such a wind to disperse it? Any natural fog, at least . . .

It brought a recollection of the fog which had blanketed the battlefield of Radmur Plain: a fog created and locked in place by this same slender, scholarly old man.

As if sensing the trend of his companion's thoughts, Gemmel hesitated and half-turned with the shadow of a smile still crooking one corner of his mouth. "Oh, yes, Commander"—and although Dewan's shout had been lost on the tumbling wind, the enchanter's soft voice carried clearly and without strain—"I caused this fog as well. But note: it's a mere disruption of sight, no more. So I can spare more energy to secure it. Much more . . ."

The explanation, if that was what it was, told Dewan ar Korentin little that he understood; only that he need have no worries about being exposed on an open beach half a mile from any shelter by some vagary of the weather. It didn't reassure him; for his concern was not now so much with the possibility of betrayal, but with its consequences.

Mist or no mist, he still felt like some small black bug crossing a vast expanse of floor, with the same choked-back anticipation of a lethal swat coming out of nowhere. With one difference: he knew exactly where the swat would come from.

Dunacre . . .

His rank and position as Captain of the King's Guard—his *late* rank, he reminded himself, for it was certain that he had left it behind along with everything else but his self-respect—had given him access to such military information as the disposition of Alba's coastal defences; and while Dunacre was far from the newest of the south-eastern fortresses, it was by no means the weakest or most poorly manned. There were at least three wings of heavy horse stationed there—that much he knew for a certainty, because one of them had recently been stiffened by a training troop seconded from his own personal command, the Bodyguard Cavalry. And they were good. Very, very good.

Far too good for comfort in fact, especially when he was anonymously and illegally walking along a shoreline that was tailor-made for the kind of shattering Imperial style charge he had taught the Bodyguard to execute. And in the name of the High Headsman at Cerdor, "execute" was definitely the best word for it.

"As I said before," and this time Dewan shaped the words on his mouth so that Gemmel, still looking at him, could at least read them, "where's the boat? And how big is it?"

Gemmel grinned that toothy fox's grin of his, and enhanced it with a gesture of the Dragonwand which covered a thirty-mile sweep of open ocean. "Big enough," he replied. "And out there . . ."

It was not an answer with the sort of precision for which Dewan had hoped, but he chose not to argue. As he trudged after the old sorcerer, he was trying with little success to forget the many things he knew about the coastal citadels, uncomfortably aware of the truth in that old proverb about the dangers of too much knowledge. They were all matters of casual interest when read in the comfort of his quarters over a glass of red and some honeyed fruit, but became of pressing import here where their effectiveness was likely to be demonstrated in the most unequivocal manner.

Things like the powerful long-glasses installed—at his own suggestion!—to monitor the route of any potential invasion force; things like the awesome projectile batteries whose counterpoise petraries could launch flaming missiles which would cinder and sink any Imperial battlefleet long before shipboard catapults were close enough to make even ranging shots worth-while . . .

As if to add weight to his apprehension, the ghostly outline of a white painted tree trunk loomed out of the fog. Tall as the mast of a galion, it was identical to hundreds of others up and down the eastern coast of Alba: fall-of-shot markers for the shore batteries. Nor, guessed ar Korentin as he came close enough to see the grouped gouges scarring the wood, did it indicate extreme distance. He was entering the killing-ground, the area where a practised crew might hope to ignite their target with a single launch—and certainly to succeed in no more than three if they wanted to avoid a punishment detail. Once they were able to see what they were shooting at . . .

*   *   *

Dewan quickened his pace in an effort to draw level with Gemmel, who was striding out as though he was in very truth walking for the good of his health. Which, if he knew what Dewan knew, was an accurate enough assumption. Yet the old man seemed unconcerned—so unconcerned that perhaps he didn't know after all.

Dewan considered that possibility, then dismissed it as unlikely. In his opinion, Gemmel might not know everything even though he often seemed to do so. But without doubt, the wizard invariably knew a damn sight too much.

He was drawing as much breath as the weight on his back would permit to tell Gemmel a few home truths about the beach where he was so idly strolling, when the sorcerer turned abruptly and held up his hand. "Silence," he commanded. "Listen!"

Dewan could hear nothing at first but the hiss of wind and waves—and what was important about them? Then he heard something else and it was a sound made all the more immediate by nervous brooding:

The distant, dissonant clangor of alarm gongs.

Gemmel drove the Dragonwand butt-downwards into the sand with a spasm of irritation. Not anger, not fear; just irritation, such as a parent might feel at some child's act of pettiness. "So," he said.

"So . . . ?" echoed Dewan.

"So King Rynert has decided we are not to go our—my—own way after all. Despite all his assurances, of course." There was a dreadful calm contentment in the way Gemmel spoke, the cold satisfaction of logic proved.

"You mean to say—" Dewan knew that it was crazy to begin a discussion or even talk unnecessarily until they were both clear of this mess, but the words came tumbling out anyway, "—that Rynert had the choice of yea-or-nay right up to where we are now?"

"His representative had." Gemmel had already plucked the Dragonwand free and was walking rapidly towards the mist-wrapped sea, talking as he went. "The thin-faced gentleman I hoped was still asleep in the tavern."

Dewan could think of nothing sensible to say about that and kept his mouth shut.

"I decided not to point him out to you," the wizard

continued, "because if you recognised him, you might do something regrettable, and if you didn't then you might do something unnecessary. I thought we might shake him for long enough to reach the boat, but he must have marked our absence and made directly for the fortress. Probably didn't like our destination—after all, from this coast there's only one place we could be going . . ."

"But Rynert knew about that!"

"But did he tell his man? No. I doubt it." Gemmel's speech was growing staccato as his long legs raked over the ground, quick as a wading bird. He wasn't running, there was no need for anything so undignified just yet, even though Dewan had been for the past dozen strides. "Credit him with that subtlety. He didn't give instructions—not exact instructions. General, yes. But not exact. So he isn't responsible. Regrettable mistake. Nervous troops. Suspected spies. Not identified until afterwards . . ."

"Afterwards?" repeated Dewan stupidly. And it was stupid; maybe it was the running, or the shock of what Gemmel was telling him, because later he felt sure that in normal circumstances he wouldn't have uttered a word. But this time he did. And was flayed for it.

Gemmel stopped in his tracks with anger livid on his high-cheekboned face. "Compassion of God, must I draw diagrams?" That shrillness which Dewan had heard only once before was threading his voice again like poison in wine. "I had almost four years to kill the habit of idiot questions in my son!" His lips writhed back from his teeth in an expression which might have been many things but most definitely was not a smile. "My *foster-*son," he corrected himself with ponderous irony. "You had best learn it in the next four minutes, Dewan ar Korentin, if you want to survive the next four hours. Know this: you have crossed Rynert of Alba—so you are a dead man."

"But I have served him faithfully for—"

"Years . . . ?" Gemmel sneered. "And now you no longer serve him. Therefore you are no longer of use to him. So you are *dead!*"

That was a moment which Dewan knew would haunt

his dreams, should he live long enough to have any—
the moment when a sorcerer whose eyes blazed like
phosphorescent emeralds told him in tones which defied
doubt that he had been utterly betrayed. And betrayed,
moreover, by the lord for whom he had shed blood, lost
blood, suffered pain and gained his first-through-fiftieth
gray hairs. That he had been cast aside like a torn cloak;
that he was to be smashed into oblivion by "accident"
and by the men he had trained himself, so that the embarrassment of a difference of opinion would be snuffed
before it passed the bounds of simple gossip.

"If I live through this—" he began savagely.

"If any of us live through it, you'll have to take your
turn after my foster-son." Again there was a hard gleam
of teeth in the foggy light. "No. Call him my son. For
he is. And more than I deserve to regain, even though
I don't yet deserve to be called his father. Now run,
Dewan ar Korentin. Run as if your life depended on
it—for it does!"

They ran, a slop of wet and salty sand flying up around
their booted legs at each footfall. Somehow the mass of
gear across Dewan's back was lighter than it had been—
still as bulky, still as awkward, but no longer the same
crushing dead-weight. Gemmel's work? Or just ad-
renalin?

He neither knew nor cared—but he was thankful all
the same.

The wizard's voice reached his ears again, piercing the
sounds of wind and water, gasping breath and the thick
wet splat of running feet; but this time the old man was
not addressing him.

Gemmel was speaking to the fog!

Something—some *thing*—sighed over Dewan's shoulder and for one heart-stopping instant he thought that
Dunacre's weapon batteries had opened up on them.
Even shooting blind into the mist, those things were capable of setting the beach aflame from surf-line to shingle and in the process roasting any living creature on it.
But whatever passed Dewan had nothing to do with
human weapons. Or even with humanity at all . . .

The surge of energy which had passed him on the
wings of a hot wind tore open a tunnel in the fog that

was two men wide, one man high and ran straight as a spear-shaft out towards the sea. He could suddenly see parallel white bars of foam where waves curled in to break on the shores of Alba, and beyond them the small dark blot sliding swiftly closer which could only be the wizard's promised boat. Boat, not ship, was right.

Cockleshell was more right still.

Had he possessed more breath than that required for running, Dewan might have made some biting remarks about the vessel's size, speed and potential seaworthiness, not to mention passing comment on certain sorcerers who seemed to think that if something could float then that sufficed.

But all criticism was leached from his mind by the sound in the sky.

It was a huge rash of displaced air, as if something monstrous was falling from the clouds—and if Dewan's wild guess was correct, then that was no more than the truth. He flung himself bodily at Gemmel and both men went headlong onto the sand . . . and into a tidal pool already ankle-deep with chill salt water.

"What!" There was outrage and real fury in Gemmel's voice, so that if he had guessed wrongly Dewan didn't like to consider the consequences of his hasty act; but before the wizard could say more, everything was justified.

They felt the thump of impact through the ground beneath them a split-second before the fog flared incandescent orange and washed their backs with heat. The vast tearing roar of detonation came a full two heartbeats later, flooding the air with ravening noise and with the naphtha stink of wildfire. Greasy smoke boiled through the mist and the blast of fire which gave it birth thinned the concealing vapor even as its creator straggled to his feet.

Gemmel brushed uselessly at the mess of sodden sand which caked his clothing, shrugged and extended one hand to Dewan as the Vreijek hauled himself and his burden from the mire. Their eyes met, and in the wizard's there was true friendship for the first time that Dewan could remember. "Thank you, Commander," was all that he said. It was enough.

Dewan nodded once, then looked from side to side, spitting to clear his mouth as he surveyed the beach. There was more of it to see now than before the missile landed—too much more. "They must know this isn't a natural mist," he muttered, not so much talking to Gemmel as thinking out loud. "The wind would tell them as much. And," his gaze returned to the sorcerer, "I remember you told Rynert once how hard it was to stabilise such a charm." There was no accusation in his voice. "It's just the thing he would remember—and warn his dogs accordingly."

"Enough heat would burn off even a real fog," said Gemmel matter-of-factly. He was already jogging seaward again, moving more slowly now so that the noise of his own progress didn't drown the sound of more incoming shots—or whatever else the fortress commander might decide to fling at them.

Twice more they flattened against the beach, cuddling the gritty wetness of the shingle as if it was the softest feather quilt whilst the world around them was torn by fire. Gemmel's cunningly constructed shroud of mist was all but usurped by an acrid layer of black smoke which twisted in the wind and made them choke on its bitter reek—scoring throat and eyes and nostrils so that each lungful of air was an enemy.

Then there came another sound than that of airborne flame: the high, sweet scream of a cavalry trumpet. Gemmel bared his teeth and broke into a run again, aware that once more safety lay in speed. But ar Korentin did not move.

An instant later the wizard jolted to a splashing halt, shocked to a standstill as he heard a sword scrape from its sheath. "Dewan, no!" He was shouting the words even as he turned. "For God's sweet sake, no!"

Dewan's head jerked round and there was unconcealed scorn on his mustached face. "No? Then will they ride us down without a fight?" The eyes in that face were cold and flinty, an expression Gemmel had seen before. On Aldric's face. In Aldric's eyes. The eyes of his son . . . that were not the eyes of his son.

It was an expression that presaged violence.

"Don't kill!" The sorcerer's hand closed around Dewan's thick wrist and forced his swordpoint down with an inexorable pressure that made the Vreijek's thick brows lift in astonishment—forced it down until it grounded on the sand. "Don't kill," he repeated with a silky firmness brooking no questions. "They will be king's-men. Maybe *your* men. To kill would be . . . unthinkable."

"Then what will we—" Dewan hesitated, a wry smile twisting his tense mouth. "What will *you* do?"

"All that I must. Now get to the boat if you can. Move!"

Dewan shrugged his least-laden shoulder and returned the broadsword to its scabbard. "Your game, then," he conceded reluctantly, backing towards the waves so that his eyes could remain fixed on the place where the trumpet had sounded. A place hidden by drifting smoke and the remnants of the mist. A place right behind them. "Play it your way if you must—but remember that the blade is still here if you need it."

Gemmel glanced at Dewan and shook his head. "I hope not," he said, and walked swiftly onward with more words trailing over his shoulder and down the wind to ar Korentin's ears. "With any luck, I won't even—"

"—but you will!" The interruption was harsh. "Because our luck has just run out . . . !"

They came out of the smoke at a parade walk: a column of eight riders in skirmish harness. Eight—no more than a patrol. That was very like an insult, thought Dewan. Maces, swords, axes—but no spears. And no bows. So it was close work, then; someone wanted to be sure.

Over the whistle of wind in his ears he could hear the sound if not the sense of the red-plumed officer's commands as he waved his longsword overhead; it was a long-drawn, nasal singing such as cavalrymen use. And despite the threat, despite the menace, he felt something approaching a dark pleasure as the small formation swung from column to line of attack without the slightest ripple of excess movement. Perfect . . . He wondered if perhaps he had trained these men himself. Or some of them. Or none at all . . .

It was an idle thought, for what did it matter when they were about to try to kill him anyway?

And then they stopped. One horse snorted; another stamped, scraping at the sand with one forehoof as its head nodded up and down, up and down like a mechanical toy until the rider shortened his reins. There was silence now; all but the ever-present wind.

"Captain ar Korentin?" That was the officer again—a light, youthful voice contrasting sharply with his ominous appearance. A boy's voice. The entire troop was probably composed of such youngsters; men who had never trained under him, never served under him, never heard of him except as a name—and a foreigner's name at that—in distant Cerdor.

Very clever—and very wise, for if men of his own command had been ordered to take him Dewan knew that they would have disobeyed. Theirs was the old, old loyalty which King Rynert had so arrogantly flouted in his dealings first with Aldric Talvalin and now with Dewan himself; a loyalty based on the ancient Honor-Codes, born of obligations and duties between a lord and his retainers, and something which Dewan himself respected through nothing more than common courtesy.

"Captain ar Korentin, you must lay down your weapons!" The lad was trying hard to be officious, without much success. "You must come with us!"

"I must do *nothing!*" Dewan's parade-ground bellow slapped out across the beach, and he had the small satisfaction of seeing two troopers jump in their saddles with startled jerks so pronounced that even at this distance they were visible. "What I do is my own affair—and by the king's own leave!" That shook them even more. "And what I do now is no affair of yours!"

"You shouldn't have said that," muttered Gemmel at his back.

Dewan glared at the wizard, then at the soldiers, and clamped down on his anger far, far too late. Just because this officer was young didn't mean he was a fool as well. Such words out of his quarry's own mouth were a gift—and one which was put to immediate use.

"But it is, Captain; it is." The voice seemed older now,

harder and more sure of itself. "You are trying to leave this country in a most suspicious manner—that *is* my concern!" His sword gestured and the troop moved forward a little, closing knee-to-knee before halting for what Dewan knew would be the last time. The officer rose in his stirrups. "You-will-come-with-us-*now!*"

Gemmel laid a restraining hand on Dewan's shoulder and stepped in front of him to plant the Dragonwand upright in the sand. It was an action oddly reminiscent of the way in which an archer might drive home a palisade stake, and for the same reason—as a defence against cavalry. But Gemmel was no bowman and the reptilian spellstave was much more than sharpened wood.

"What of me?" the old man demanded, and though he did not shout Dewan knew from his own experience that the soldiers would hear him well enough. "I am Gemmel Errekren," the wizard said. A small fidgeting ran down the line of horsemen. "Do I not warrant a threat or two?"

There was no response. Either the troopers had not been told about Gemmel and were at a loss—or else they knew as much of his reputation as any other man in Alba. And that was sufficient to make anyone fall silent.

"Hear me well, for I will say this only once." A bleak serenity was lacing Gemmel's words as he closed the fingers of his left hand around the Dragonwand, just below the carven firedrake's head. Dewan felt a single pulse of power well out of the adamantine talisman, a pulse that clad his entire body in gooseflesh. There was a sonorous humming in the air and the sorcerer's hard voice sliced through it like a blade. "You are all meddling with forces which you cannot comprehend. And you are meddling with me. And I am subject to the human failing of impatience. So be warned. *Leave me alone!*"

His clenched fingers snapped open like the talons of a hawk and unleashed a great dry crack of thunder which sent all eight horses bucking and plunging madly across the beach. Two of the riders were unseated and slammed against the wet, unyielding sand inside all the dragging weight of their armor. Only one got up again. The remaining six wrenched their steeds back under control more by brute force than any skill; then, staring and confused as the animals they rode, they huddled into a poor copy of their original formation and sat quite still. The officer, one of the two fallen men, took an unsteady pace forward and tried to support himself with his sword—as best he could, for its unsheathed blade sank easily into the sand. His plumed helmet had been lost, and without it he was indeed the boy that Dewan had suspected—beardless rather than shaven, fair both of hair and of complexion. But now the fresh pink of his cheeks was darkened by a flush of rage and his voice held all the shrill spite of youth. "Ride over them!" he screamed. "Cut them down! Kill! Kill! *Kill . . . !*"

Whilst the soldiers hung back uneasily, Gemmel raked them with a dispassionate stare that ended disdainfully on the raving officer. Then he pulled the Dragonwand out of the beach as a man might draw a sword. "Oh, thou fool," he murmured. "Watch, and learn, and be wise."

Gripped in both the old enchanter's hands, the spellstave reared up to poise over his head like an executioner's blade. The wind from the sea died to a moan and thence to silence as if the world held its breath. And perhaps it did.

"*Ykraith,*" invited Gemmel softly in the stillness, "*abath arhan.*"

And the air went cold . . .

Dewan ar Korentin felt a shudder rack him as midwinter rigor bit with icy teeth at the exposed flesh of face and hand; he shuddered again—though not this time with the cold—as the remnants of fog turned pure white and tumbled with a tiny crystal tinkling to coat the beach with frost. Underfoot the sand crackled with the crisp noise of rimed grass on a freezing night, and puddles of sea-water snapped like sheets of glass beneath his weight. Breath hung like smoke on the unmoving, bitter air, then sifted down like snow to join the frozen fog.

"*Ykraith, devhar ecchud,*" said Gemmel; the words almost visible in the milky exhalation from his bearded lips.

They were whipped into nothingness by a sourceless gale which scoured the long beach clean of frost and

piled the million, million sparkling motes high above the
sorcerer in a vast inverted cone whose apex centered on
the upraised Dragonwand. It was a wind to cut the
breath from a man's lungs, a wind to flog clouds helplessly across the sky or raise a ship-killing storm. It was
a wind which all but tore Dewan off his feet.

It was a wind which had been given birth by the jolt
of energy unleashed by the spellstave, a jolt which sent
a solitary ripple scudding out across the surface of the
sea far faster than any arrow from a bow.

And yet it was a wind which scarcely ruffled Gemmel's beard.

The island was an uninviting place. Except for one small
inlet and an even smaller beach, it rose sheer out of the
ocean, rimmed by ragged talons of rock that tore wounds
of white surf in the dark and swirling water. It did not
encourage visitors; and nothing had disturbed its brooding solitude for months now, save the whisper—or the
storm-driven shriek—of wind through the mantle of veg-
etation that concealed whatever dwelt upon it from the
gaze of casually prying eyes. Not that there had been
any such for a long time; no ship had even come close.
Until now.

She was a deep-sea patrol vessel of the Second Fleet
and she was hunting pirates in the disputed waters of
the Thousand Islands group, south and west of Alba.
The *Ethailen Myl,* although that term was neither recognised by the Drusalan Empire nor used on their charts.
And pirates whose attacks, directed singlemindedly against
the Imperial convoys, suggested rather more than just a
taste for the most profitable victims afloat. It suggested
that they might be more than simply pirates after all.

For all her bulk, the warship came dipping delicately as
a swan around the headland and into the shelter of the
island's solitary cove. As her crew made ready to drop
anchor and to lower a boat for closer investigation—or
just to replenish the water-barrels—her commander up
by the stern batteries was studying everything most intently through a long-glass. So intently that when the
deck lifted beneath his feet, he did not look to see the
cause.

A ripple crossed the flat surface of the bay; its movement, a wrinkle on the oily calm of the water, was that of a current, or a breeze, or something monstrous moving rapidly beneath the surface. But though it was none of these things—for the water was sheltered and still, because the wind was from the south, and there was plainly nothing in the deeps alongside—yet it was in very truth something monstrous. And it swept towards the island far, far faster than any arrow from a bow ... .

So fast, indeed, that few afterwards could attest to having seen its passage through the sea, though there were many who could swear to seeing all that followed. It struck the beach and crossed it with a hiss of disturbed sand and gravel which many heard aboard the warship, even above the sounds and distractions of shipboard activity; and that crisp rustling of unexpected noise where no noise should have been drew the eyes of those on deck who should have been about their own affairs.

So it was that many saw the trees wave madly with a movement that, for all it happened with great force and at blinding speed, exactly matched the passage of a harvest wind across a field of ripened wheat; saw the shiver of the trees sweep up and up until it was no more than a tremor crossing the scrubby grass on the island's solitary peak; and saw the unexplained disturbance sink into solid rock as a wave sinks into sand.

Then there was time for gossip, time for speculation, time for such a falling-off in normal duties that the captain himself stalked to the rail of his quarter-deck and barked his crew back to work. But there was no time for that work to resume. No time for anything at all—

—Before the island of Techaur blew up ... !

It was a very little detonation, as such things were reckoned by those who survived them. Nothing like the blast—in living memory—which had flung a dozen small islands off the sea-bed near the coast of Valhol. But then the gods—or Heaven, or most appropriately the Father of Fires, depending on one's beliefs—had never really finished making Valhol ...

This, though, was another matter altogether.

A shock-wave of concussion slapped out across the bay, bringing with it shattered trees, lumps of red-hot rock and a steaming spray of gravel from the beach. The warship reeled and lost part of her rigging, but because—for various reasons—she had not been secured at anchor, she was able to ride out both the blast and the vicious twelve-foot wall of water running in its wake.

The island had lost maybe a hundred feet of height; most of that hundred feet was either smacking into the sea and raising columns of white water like good practice from a shore battery, or was still rolling skywards amid the dome-topped mushroom cloud of smoke and dust which reared above the abruptly-truncated mountain.

But it was the fire which flared around the abbreviated peak which most disturbed the warship's captain and was most instrumental in his decision to put several clear miles of water between himself, his ship and this place. A decision to leave it to the pirates, or the Albans, or the Elherrans—or anybody mad enough to want it. Because whatever else it was, this fire was not that of a natural volcano; one of his crewmen, who had seen Valhol's *Hlavastjaar*—that great rip in the world aptly named Hell's Gullet—had come babbling to him about the wrong way that this mountain was burning.

As if, the captain had wondered privately, there ever was a right way for stone to blaze like tinder.

But he could see exactly what the sailor meant: there was no thick spewing of honey-viscid rock, nor—save for the first explosion—any spray of ash and cinders. There was only that single intermittent jet of flame, so hot and white that it approached a shade of blue and so bright that it hurt the eyes even at this distance. He was not so foolish as to use his long-glass, but even unaided vision could see how the narrow flame sliced at the remnant of the mountain like a knife in tender beef. No, the captain corrected himself, like nothing so crude; this cut like the blade of a skilled surgeon, shearing with such precision that there might almost have been a mind directing it.

That was what frightened him most of all. The captain was a brave man—he would not have been commanding this police mission otherwise—but he truly did not want to meet whatever possessed that mind, and controlled that white fire.

For just a moment it was as if the sun had descended from the sky to poise in glory atop the ruined mountain of Techaur, and every man aboard the warship heard the sound which accompanied that glare of splendour. It was not the flat reverberation of another blast, nor was it the rumbling of falling rock.

It was a roar such as could only have been born in some colossal throat . . .

No orders were given by the captain or his under-officers; none were necessary. But someone flung the ship's helm hard over, heedless of the submerged reefs nearby, and with that strong southerly wind still tugging at her sails the patrol vessel reacted like a scalded cat, heeling about with foam creaming up from her long ram as she accelerated towards the open sea on no particular course except out and away from Techaur.

And from whatever being roared and flamed and dwelt there.

The plume of frost roiled and twisted as though imbued with some eerie life of its own, and a wan light glimmered deep within it so that each writhing contour was backed by a chasm of shadow; black rifts in reality where anything might lurk unseen. Strange shapes formed and faded in its turbulent depths, flitting in and out of the darkness like bats half-glimpsed at dusk.

There was no sound now from the soldiers; even their officer had ceased shouting. He—all of them—gaped wide-eyed at the fugitives they had been sent to capture or to kill. A simple mission that was simple no longer. There was not a man of the patrol who did not plainly wish himself elsewhere.

The crystals of fog constricted more closely together, forming the curves and angles of a geometry that had no place this side of madness. Even to look at it was to court vertigo and nausea. A harsh grin was etched into Gemmel's face as he used years of study to construct such nightmares as would make sleepers fear the night.

There was a thin, doleful note threading down the

wind, a monotonous reedy piping like a dirge played on
a solitary flute, and as if the whining melody had summoned them, things moved in the cloud. Amorphous ob-
scenities squirmed slowly in a tangle of serpentine limbs,
unclean creatures with a shocking suggestiveness in their
grossly deformed outlines. Dull yellow eyes glared down
at King Rynert's troopers with heartstopping malevolence and a perverse lust that went far beyond mere
hunger after flesh and blood.

A moment more of this, thought Dewan ar Korentin
queasily, and they must break. Or *I* will. His stomach
was churning, sending sour bile burning up a throat that
was already clogged and overcrowded by the beating of
his heart, and he was so centered on his own misery that
he did not see the ripple of disturbed water streak up
out of the southern ocean and lift clear of the sea with a
quick spume of spray that whirled up to join the writhing
horrors in the air.

And without warning—certainly without any bidding
from Gemmel—all movement ceased. The cloud hung
monstrous and immobile over its creator's head for just
an instant before contracting in a single spasm to a shape
that was unmistakable. Reason and logic insisted that
this too was an illusion conjured out of frozen water—
but neither reason nor logic had a place here, not from
the instant that ar Korentin glanced sideways and saw
the look on Gemmel's face change.

For a single beat he caught the remnants of the wizard's grin, mixed with an air of confusion that was almost
puzzlement. Then that had gone. And only the twist of
naked fear remained.

"Lady Mother Tesh . . . !" Dewan unconsciously
blessed himself at lips and heart. His soft exclamation
had been no oath, but a sincere prayer for protection in
this moment when all the defences of his scepticism had
been shattered and the very structure of his mind was
reeling under a shock that left him sick and giddy.

No matter now that he had seen something of this
sort before, even in the coolly unquestioning company
of Aldric Talvalin; still Dewan couldn't comprehend how
something so huge could remain airborne. Its flight, and

indeed its very presence here, made nonsense of everything he had ever been told.

Not that anyone had deigned to tell him much about dragons . . .

Rearing back its awesome spined and crested head, the icedrake roared—in challenge, maybe, or in scorn of the little scraps of humankind who cowered beneath the shadow of its wings—and the sound that it made was beyond imagination. Impossibly bass, unbelievably piercing, it was a noise like the rending of sheet steel and a music like the harmony of choirs, a cry of incalculable strength and majesty that made the air tingle and the earth shake.

It was power given a voice.

But from the terror stamped deep into Gemmel's features, that power was not his to command.

Yet as the dragon's silvery head swung down and around to regard him with great calm eyes that were the translucent blue of glacier ice, the wizard flung both arms wide in a greeting that was almost a salute. Gripped near its spike butt by his right hand, Ykraith the Dragonwand swept an arc through the cold, clear air and left a trail of pearly vapor in its wake. The stuff hung like smoke for a moment before sifting softly as snow onto the beach.

For a man so plainly frightened, Gemmel carried himself well and his studied arrogance betrayed nothing; only Dewan was close enough to read the truth in the sorcerer's dilated eyes. A sweat of exertion which had filmed his skin was frozen now into a cracked mask; each hair of his beard was as stiff as wire and his skin was crusted and crumbling like the time-fretted visage of an antique sculpture. If any vestige of his grin remained, it was now no more than the rictus born of hidden fear, and when he leaned on the Dragonwand it was the action of an old, old man, with an ordinary walking-stick. For Gemmel looked *ancient*.

And then he seemed to recover himself, straightening his back with a heave as though throwing off some ponderous weight. The semblance of extreme age faded and was gone as if it had never been, and once more Gemmel Errekren assumed the aura of an enchanter at the peak of his powers. Watching, Dewan wondered how much of that was real and how much just another illusion.

The icedrake hung above them on barely moving wings, gazing with huge patience at the small creatures whose efforts had called it into being and waiting for their reasons. The few seconds it had filled the sky seemed hour-long.

"Time stops," said Gemmel hoarsely, "as it stands still."

The enigmatic words meant nothing to Dewan, creating no answers but only questions. "What will—?" he tried to ask, but was hushed by a peremptory flick of the sorcerer's finger.

"Peace. Be silent. Be still." As if knowing he would be obeyed, Gemmel turned from the Vreijek and glanced towards the watching soldiers—fascinated like small birds before a snake. He raised Ykraith two-handed, the spellstave's dragon tip pointing towards the leisurely hovering icedrake. Its chill, remote eyes blinked once and it seemed to listen as the wizard spoke again, this time in a language which was neither Alban nor any of the Imperial dialects even though it had audible affinities with them all. *"Sh'ma, trahanayr,"* he intoned. *"Y'shva pestreyhar—y'men vayh't r'hann arhlaeth . . ."*

It was a strange tongue, jarring and glottal, somehow incomplete and yet somehow familiar, and with it Dewan guessed that the sorcerer was trying to assert his mastery over the summoning. Yes, trying, for by the tremor in Gemmel's voice he was still far from certain of success. Staring up at the great, graceful being, ar Korentin wondered apprehensively what its response would be—and even, in a dark and secret corner of his mind, whether an adverse reaction would hurt.

The thing which punched wetly between the bones of his left forearm did not hurt. Not for the age-long second after it struck home. *Time stops . . .*

But then it felt like the icy anguish of a razor.

Dewan flinched as it hit, clapping one hand to the wound as if that would do any good. His blood felt very hot as it washed over spell-chilled skin, and though he had been wounded many, many times before he still felt sick. Yet there was more offended outrage than anything else in his mumbled protest to an uncaring world: "But I was *sure* they didn't carry bows. . . ." Then he looked down, and saw the stub-shaft of the small steel dart, and knew he had been both right—and very stupid.

None of the troopers had had a bowcase amongst his gear. But they were Alban horse-soldiers and the paired *telekin* holstered either side of the high pommels were as much a part of military saddle-furniture as the double girths. It was a fact—one so obvious that only a foreigner, and one preoccupied with other matters at that, could be excused for the oversight. But Dewan's disgusted oath did not excuse himself, neither for forgetting about the Alban *telek* nor for failing to watch the youngster who commanded this patrol. Even before his shock-blurred gaze had focused on the missile's point of origin, he knew which of the men had shot at him. There was really only one candidate.

As if in confirmation, the young officer knelt on one knee and racked another dart from his spring-gun's magazine. The hard *click-click* of reloading carried clearly in the still, cold air. This time the weapon's stock was gripped in both his outstretched hands and he was squinting along it with one eye while the other squeezed shut in a demonic wink of aim. There was killing on his boy's face.

The *telek* steadied, unwavering now, and Dewan stared into its black bore for a time that seemed as long as the years of a man's life. Time enough to live—and time enough to die.

Time stops, he thought, and closed his eyes.

Preoccupied with his magic and with fighting his own fears, Gemmel had not seen the shooting. But he had heard that sound which is unlike any other—the meaty slap of sharpened metal piercing flesh. In that same long, long time which in real-time was less than half a second, he turned—registering another somehow significant double click even as he moved—and he *saw.*

Saw the levelled *telek* and the spurting wound, saw Dewan ar Korentin trying vainly to hold his own arm together, and saw not these things but another, older image. Not an injured companion, but a tableau which had haunted his most secret dreams for years. A sequence of inexorable events whose grim ending he was for ever helpless to avert. The inevitable conclusion which had taken away his son.

Gemmel saw, and knew, and ceased to care about himself. *"Trahan-ayr!"* he screamed, and above him the great white-armored wedge that was the dragon's head moved fractionally, expectantly, its eyes slitting like a cat's. *"T'chu da sh'vakh! TAII-CHA!"*

And the power which terror said was not his to command obeyed him.

The icedrake's jaws yawned wide, a frigid blue-white cavern lined with ragged icicles, and it sent forth a smoky silver blast of unimaginable cold. A seagull rash enough to fly too close tumbled from the freezing air and shattered like a bird of blown glass when it struck the beach. Yet the dragon's blast was itself silent as midwinter. No storm, no blizzard, no howling rush of wind; only the faint brittle sounds of icy stillness which told of an end to warmth and life.

King Rynert's cavalry went down like wheat before a new-honed scythe, men and horses together in one heap. There was not even the clatter of their gear, for by the time they hit the ground all had been sheathed and muted by an inch thick crust of snow.

Nothing escaped—except the slender object which whirred like a wasp as it flicked clear of the settling blanket of frost . . .

Dewan uttered a small noise like a cough. His mouth opened to make the sound and remained open as one hand tried to touch his chest. Then he toppled backwards like a felled tree and did not move again.

Without any further word or sign from Gemmel, it was over. The sky above the wizard's head was abruptly empty once more and the slowly warming air was as clean and clear as polished crystal. The soldiers and their mounts lay where they had fallen, moving sluggishly like sleepers in the grip of dreams. Gemmel spared them barely a glance; his concern was all for Dewan.

The Vreijek sprawled face-upwards, his spine bent at

an ugly angle by the bundle strapped to his back, his half-hooded eyes neither open nor truly shut. A ribbon of blood crawled from the corner of his mouth and dripped to the sand behind his head, and when Gemmel ripped open his tunic there was a mangled welt over his breastbone where the last *telek* dart had driven home. The wizard scooped it up and found the missile had been bloated three times as thick as normal by the layered ice which caked it, and its needle point was no more than a rounded stub of frosted metal.

But it had still hit Dewan like a hammer right above the heart, and there was a bluish tinge about the Vreijek's slack lips which Gemmel disliked most intensely. Ar Korentin was in the prime of his life, a strong, fit man—surely cumulative shock had not brought on . . .

Even as the thought formed, Gemmel was fumbling for a pulse with hands made clumsy by the cold which he himself had created, and when at last he found one he swore, viciously and with desperation; its fluttering was more a nervous tic than a pulse, too fast and totally irregular. Even as his fingers pressed down to confirm its presence the beat faltered, returned, faltered again once, twice . . .

And stopped.

No more blood dribbled from Dewan's mouth. The trickle of fluids from his torn arm ceased. He no longer breathed.

He no longer lived . . .

Gemmel's knuckles blanched as his grip tightened on the Dragonwand's adamantine surface; but he had learned during the past few terrible minutes that he could no longer trust the talisman to do his bidding. Its powers had passed beyond his control—and he suspected to his own great secret shame that he knew the reason why.

Ykraith dropped with an unheeded thud as his hand opened, and when it closed again it was to form a clenched fist which with carefully-judged force slammed squarely against Dewan's chest. Gemmel struck twice, then gripped his own wrist and began a rhythmic pressure with the heel of the free hand that was almost enough to break the bone beneath it. Almost, but not quite.

Push—push—push; fist, then pressure, then fist, then the firm steady pressure which tried to persuade Dewan's heart to beat again for itself. Again, and again—a hard task for two people, it was well-nigh impossible for one alone. Gemmel was panting now, breathless and sweaty with exertion and with the fear born of his own increasing despair.

Suddenly the bruised and battered rib-cage expanded with a convulsive jerk as Dewan's lungs wrenched in a whooping gasp of air. Gemmel felt the movement under his hands, and his fingertips sensed the drumming of a renewed heartbeat which pounded almost loudly enough to hear.

Ar Korentin began to breathe, and bleed, and live again.

The old enchanter, now feeling truly old, sat back on his heels and watched while his own heart-rate slowed and the sweat cooled on his trembling limbs. A little smile stretched his thin mouth thinner still as he realized that even without the Dragonwand, he had performed magic of a sort after all. Necromancy. Restoring the dead to life.

"I think," he whispered to nobody at all, "that makes us even."

After a short while he straightened, easing the kinks out of his spine, and cast a wary glance towards the other bodies which littered the beach. No worries there; they would be a quarter-hour or more just remembering how to use their legs. He squatted and slid the Dragonwand into the back of his belt, silently reminding himself for perhaps the hundredth time to buy or make the spell-stave some kind of shoulder-strap; then hunkered lower still and lifted ar Korentin from the ground.

There was no visible expenditure of effort now: only a smooth surge of strength that seemed somehow more than human. He cradled the big man's limp body in both arms as he might a child; as he had once carried his dead son; as he had once carried the young Alban warlord who was now his son. His own, most honorable son.

Gemmel laid Dewan gently athwart the stern of the boat; then he raised the sail, steadied the tiller and spoke the soft sibilants which summoned up an offshore breeze.

And though he was tired, unutterably drained and wearied by fear and physical effort and mental strain, he did all in the same abstracted manner—automatically, without thought.

For his thoughts were elsewhere now. They were out *there:* across and beyond forty miles of gray water, a distance too far for even a suggestion of the Empire's coast to shadow the horizon. All his thoughts, his hopes, his fears both real and imagined. Out in that far place. With the son who was not his son.

And he wondered if his son was safe.

3

Fire in the Night

Outside was dark and cold; an autumn night already edged with the oncoming winter. A scimitar moon cut fitfully through weak places in the overlay of rain-swollen clouds.

Inside was almost as dark, but within the small anonymous tavern the night was distinctly warmer. Flame-lapped pine logs burned slowly in a hearth of black wrought iron. Sparks glowed and spat; the blue, smoky air was scented with a sharp tang of resin; nimble shadows danced among the rafters. From one corner of the common-room came the protracted minor chords of a three-stringed rebec—each note nasal, penetrating, cruel as loss.

The few patrons sat uncomfortably around low tables, drinking from plain pottery cups and thus convinced that they behaved with the elegant austerity just now fashionable in the Drusalan Empire. Several looked back and the rest forward to days where a certain degree of luxurious excess was—or would again be—more socially acceptable. Their quiet conversation was overlaid with a falsely carefree tone which made the unease beneath it all the more apparent; and the source of that unease was not difficult to find.

He was dressed severely, all in black; and he sat alone with his thoughts and a redware cup of cheap corn spirit, bent over and staring into the amber liquid as if it contained the secrets of infinity rather than the oblivion which he had sought since sundown.

Uncertain of strangers at the best of times—and these were not such times—even a friendlier people than the sullen few who sipped and murmured well away from him would have been deterred by his appearance. He needed a shave, the pallor of his face throwing both a five-day beard and the bruise-dark shadows under his eyes into sharp relief, and his shoulders were hunched almost to the point of deformity by a *coyac,* a sleeveless jerkin of dense black fur. It made him seem not entirely human.

The number of empty jugs strewn across his table told of how long and hard he had been drinking, and by rights he should have slumped onto the floor an hour ago. But he had not; the quick, economic movements which filled and refilled his cup were still improbably sure and precise, and his icy gray-green eyes remained unglazed. That, too, was not entirely human.

There was a sheathed longsword lying on the table amid the clutter, its hilt within easy reach and its unsubtle presence a blatant threat to peace. The innkeeper had wanted to take the weapon from him after the first two jugs had been drained far too quickly, but he had been warned off in a grotesque mixture of stilted high-mode Drusalan sweetened by gutter Jouvaine, both threaded with an accent that had nothing to do with either.

Silver—a great deal of silver—had changed hands immediately afterwards, as if the stranger repented of his hard words. He spent the Empire's florins as if they had no value, and now was left alone to drink himself into a stupor since this had plainly been his intention all along—except that the stupor seemed as far away as ever.

Aldric Talvalin poured more spirit into his cup and gulped down half of the raw liquor with the wrenching swallow of someone taking a medicinal draught. It burned, making his nostrils flare and his eyes squeeze shut. Tears jewelled their corners, tears which were not born of mere maudlin drunkenness. Maybe tonight, if he drank enough, there would be no dreams.

Dreams. Memories. And within the dreams and memories, nightmares. Fear and fire and candle-light. Again they came, rising through the haze of alcohol which was trying to fog his conscious mind. It was an ill thing to jolt awake in the dark stillness of deep night, soaked with sweat and strangling in the sheets with the echoes of your own cry of terror in your ears. But it was worse by far to be awake already and to be jolted stone-cold sober.

Aldric sat as he had sat before, trembling all over, while the drink which should by now have laid him gratefully senseless on the floor became no more than an acid heat in his gullet. And still the dreams returned to haunt him.

Blood, and flame, and shrieking. Things that were, but are not: things that are, but should never be. Huge wings in a starlit sky. A tall tower stark against iron clouds, and a swirl of snow. Sobbing . . . Blue smoke streaming upwards, the incisive reek of heated metal and the sweet, sweet scent of roses.

Aldric dreaded his dreams, for they seemed always to presage only evil and bitter experience had proven the truth of that foreboding. His ringed left hand reached out to a crumpled thing on the table near Widowmaker's lacquered scabbard. It shifted as his fingers touched it, making a small, sere crackle. Once more he could smell roses. He had plucked this blossom from between the withered talons of an ancient corpse three months ago, standing at the heart of a burial mound in the Deepwood of the Jevaiden plateau. Now the rose, too, was withered: dry and dead, its baleful brilliance had faded to a more natural hue and the once-unwholesome richness of its perfume was diluted by time to a fragrance which was almost pleasant . . .

Even though it was dead, the Alban thought as he cradled the desiccated flower in the palm of his hand. Or *because* it was dead?

As dead as Crisen Geruath.

As dead as his own honor.

Although he had already contrived to send a note to Rynert the King—a terse, enciphered message of success at Seghar, delivered by the master of an Elherran merchantman—the task he had been set was still incomplete. There remained the messages locked by sorcery within his skull: proofs, he had been told, to Lord General Goth and Prokrator Bruda of Alban support, and confidences which might sway those overlords whose fealty yet wavered between one side and the other. Except that his part in the deaths of two other overlords made any meeting with these powerful men merely an elaborate form of suicide. Aldric had few illusions about Imperial judicial process; in all likelihood he had already been sentenced for the "murders" of Lord Geruath and his son. No matter now that had things gone otherwise it would have been Geruath himself whose introduction would have made any meeting easy.

Aldric had made his own decision after Seghar; the brutalities and the casual wickedness in that rotting heap of masonry had sickened him at last. He no longer cared that his tenuous hold on Dunrath remained subject to Rynert's whim, and had said as much. He was getting out of the Empire's sphere of influence as quickly as he could.

While he still could . . .

He should have been aboard the Elherran ship. Before God, the rendezvous had been arranged for long enough. And indeed, he would have been had not the sheer chance of an early morning canter led him to the crest of the ridge which towered high above Kenbane Haven, the only place along several miles of coast from which he could have seen the bay beyond the harbor wall—and thus the Imperial battleram which had come scything out of the dawn mist like a patrolling shark.

Kenbane had been one of five points of departure agreed in secret with Rynert and with Dewan ar Korentin. Now he wondered who else was privy to that supposed secret, for surely the warship's inopportune appearance was no coincidence? Even if it was, Aldric no longer cared. The threat had been enough.

But that had been almost two months past, near a Vreijek port many miles south-west of here. The passage of time, and the onset of the autumn gales, must surely have made even the Imperial fleet if not exactly careless, then at least a little less enthusiastic. He would see, when he tried again to leave. Tomorrow.

What profit in an enterprise, Lord King, Aldric rehearsed silently for perhaps the hundredth time, *when all chance of completing it is already lost?* Rynert probably had a hundred valid answers to that rhetorical question.

Or the single answer which was all a king required.

A young man had entered the tavern without attracting anyone's attention; indeed, had any noticed him at all, they might have been much impressed by the pains he took to avoid that notice. He was nondescript to a studied degree—dirty, tired, and with an air of boredom as though occupied by a repetitive and so-far-unrewarding task. The gaze with which he swept the common-room had more sleepiness in it than anything else. Until his eyes reached Aldric. And then the weary half-yawn which had begun to carve notches in the corners of his mouth stretched much, much further as it changed to a wide grin of self-congratulation.

The grin did not go unnoticed by the innkeeper at least, for he sidled up the counter to draw the young man's drink and to wonder casually—in the fashion of innkeepers—just what was tonight's cause for such obvious happiness, and did it mean a celebration?

"I think," murmured the young man, "that I may just have come into some money." He drank thoughtfully, savouring the fine vintage which right now he felt fully justified in ordering, and jerked with his chin towards the drunkard in black. "That one isn't a local, is he?"

No more than you, was what the innkeeper almost said aloud; but considering what this new arrival had just spent on a single bottle of imported wine, he thought better of it. And there had been something about the idly asked question which struck him as peculiar. Nothing he could pin down, but it had been there all the same. "Him, local? Not by a long ride in whatever direction you care to choose!"

"I thought not. You must have many travellers from the seaport coming in here to drink, eh?"

"No—too far for most, I fancy."

"Indeed . . ." Another grin split the young man's face. "Or too far to stagger back, maybe?"

The innkeeper laughed. "Something like that." Then he moved away to serve another customer and left the inquisitive young man alone with his wine, quite missing the intent expression which had settled on the dusty but no longer bored features.

Left in peace, the young man set down his cup with its contents barely tasted and began an unobtrusive study of this foreigner who didn't like to do his drinking in the port of Tuenafen. It had taken ten hours and forty taverns to reach this stage—that and a sizable outlay in undrunk drink. Now, however, the whole thing seemed as if it might be worth the effort. When the Vixen was pleased, she had definite ways of proving it.

The sketch she had shown him was a good one: detailed and probably most accurate. An excellent likeness of the man he was looking at. Not as alike as two peas in a pod, maybe, but close. Very, very close. Moreover he was in the right place, give or take the few miles to Tuenafen, and behaving—bar this unfathomable determination to get drunk—in the right way. It was enough at least to let the young man proceed as he had been instructed.

A beckoning finger summoned the innkeeper and brought him leaning confidentially over the counter, full of ill-disguised curiosity. *You can smell a juicy scandal in the offing, can't you,* the young man thought, keeping contempt off his face with an effort. *And you can't wait to hear all about it.*

"That foreigner"—he used the insulting Drusalan word *hlensyarl*—"is to stay here." There was a flat power in his voice which had not been there before.

"What?"

"Keep him here. Don't let him leave. I don't care how you do it—just *do* it!"

"But that sword . . . I can't!"

"I think you can." The young man straightened his back, squared his shoulders and shot a sidelong glance at the innkeeper. "Because if he isn't here when I get back . . ."

He didn't bother to complete the sentence.

Far steadier on his feet than he had any right to be— and far clearer in his mind than he would have liked to be—Aldric settled his bill with the innkeeper. For one who had tried at first to eject him from the premises, and then a little later to confiscate his sword, the man now seemed strangely reluctant to let him go. He fumbled more than usual as he made change from the fistful of florins which Aldric had slapped onto the counter, and as an apparent apology of sorts pressed a gratis bottle of wine into the Alban's hands.

Aldric turned it over and squinted at the letters etched on the green glass; then blinked twice, very fast, and tried again with the conviction that his eyes were tricking him. This "apology" was a bottle of sweet white Hauverne, *matherneil,* the Kingswine which changed hands in Alba—if it ever got there—for rising thirty marks a time. At first he said nothing, but with his free hand dug into the pouch at his belt and poured a shining, chiming stream of silver coins over the counter and on to the floor, no longer caring that *silver* was a mere courtesy tide where the Empire's money was concerned. In economic matters as in all else, Tuenafen was a part of the Empire. Let the useless currency buy something here, if nowhere else.

"For everyone," he said, a frown insinuating its notch between his brows as he concentrated on the slurring High Drusalan diphthongs; but the words he sought eventually fell into place. "Fill all the cups. And—" the bottle of Hauverne thumped onto the bar-top—"open this and bring two of yonder good glasses. One for me." His eyes locked with the innkeeper's as his left hand freed Widowmaker's shoulder-belt, and the slithering noise as the *taiken* dropped to battle position at his hip was like the sound an adder makes moving through long grass. "And one for you."

Whatever suspicions he might have entertained about the extravagant gift were silenced as his host first sipped appreciatively, then drank with every sign of enthusiasm and none at all of hesitation. Aldric smiled thinly and followed suit. The wine was remarkable; rich, fruity and as fragrant as honey. Its fumes rose to the Alban's head as the harsh corn spirit had never done—perhaps, observed the analytical part of his mind, because one was being drunk in the hope of its effect while brooding on the need for that effect, while this Hauverne was being drunk for the sheer pleasure of drinking it. If there was more than one road to oblivion, he thought, then this was the one he would choose. If he could afford it.

The tavern doors slid open then, and stayed open while the cold, cold night flowed in. Heads turned and a voice was raised in protest—but it cut off short as armed men crossed the threshold. Six of them, wearing crest-coats over light mail and with crossbows cradled capably in their hands. They fanned out to either side of the door with a crispness that bespoke drill and discipline.

Then stopped.

She glided into the common-room like an empress, wrapped in furs against the bitter air outside and with raindrops beaded on her high-piled auburn hair which flamed like rubies in the firelight. If the arrival of her guard—for such the soldiers were—had drawn a few eyes, then her own appearance summoned all the rest. Conversation ceased; the rebec's thin music fell silent; everyone stared.

She was well worth staring at, and knew it; easily as tall as any man in the room, her willowy elegance gave unconscious grace to every movement. Nobody in the tavern had seen her before, nor was such foreknowledge necessary to realize what she was. Either the pampered daughter of some high and noble house, wilful enough to travel the Imperial roads alone. Or a courtesan of the highest rank.

The young man at her side provided a stark contrast to her finery, for he was nondescript to a studied degree, dirty, tired—and not entirely unfamiliar to the barkeep, whose tongue licked at lips which had gone far drier than his cup of wine would ever quench. The two men looked at each other; one plainly apprehensive, the other with an air of malicious satisfaction and a confidence which he wore like a cloak.

When the woman snapped her fingers the innkeeper jumped despite himself, then emerged from behind his counter to bow judiciously low. Still unsure of her station, he preferred to treat her as high-born rather than make a dangerously insulting error. And there were the half-dozen troopers of her escort to reinforce his choice.

"You have rooms here." The fox-haired lady spoke

even that simple fact in a smoky contralto purr. "I wish to rest here. See to it."

If the innkeeper was startled by her decision to grace his establishment—which though clean enough, was certainly a class or more below where she would normally have chosen to stay—he concealed it well. Such an occurrence was rare, but not unheard-of; on any road there were those travellers who despite riches and importance—or maybe because of them—preferred for various reasons not to advertise the fact. His inn was only one amongst many which maintained two or three fine staterooms in anticipation of the day when Wealth might step through the door. As it had plainly done tonight.

It was not any innkeeper's place to wonder the whys and wherefores of it all, merely to make from it everything he could. Bowing lower than ever, the man went about his business buried in calculation—which had less to do with setting a fair price than with how much he could safely overcharge.

The lady and her companion made private conversation for a moment, mouth to ear; then the young man nodded, smiled slightly and went out, taking the soldiers with him to the unspoken but obvious relief of the entire tavern. Aldric watched them go, but found his gaze tending to slide back towards their mistress.

Mistress. His mind toyed caressingly with the word as he sipped wine and rolled the soft, sweet liquid over with his tongue. *Sweet.* The adjective in his native Alban—and the thought in his head—had nothing much to do with wine at all.

Granted, she was totally inaccessible. Granted, he had a failing for a pretty face and an attractive figure. Granted, that same failing had tripped him up more than once. And granted, finally, he was heading out of Tuenafen in the morning.

But he too could rest here for the night.

In the beginning there was fire, and a dream of fire; a dream of gazing down and down into the liquid seething of the world's hot secret heart; a dream of rumbling, almost subaudible sound and a dream of the smell of burning, incongruously slashed by a sense of unbelievable blue-white cold.

The great Cavern on the Island of Techaur, and a thing of power exchanged for his given Word. Granted for a promise made to . . . Made to . . .

Speak and say, kailin *Talvalin. Name my name.*

"Ymareth!" Aldric shouted the name aloud in his troubled sleep and so awoke, eyelids snapping back so that he stared straight up towards the darkness of the ceiling. Or at where the darkness should have been, for the ceiling was not dark any more. Light moved among the beams of rough-cut timber and it was not the light of dawn. Dawn did not flicker so; it did not roar beyond the shutters so; and it was not that awesome, awful amber.

Then there was awareness and full awakening, and the knowledge that this time his dream was real.

Aldric flung back the quilt from the narrow bed, rolling sideways to plant both feet square together on the floor—then clutched wildly at the wall as the whole room continued to roll around him. For just an instant, a few heartbeats, for the second which it took his naked skin to film itself in icy sweat, everything plunged sideways and only his fingernails gouging painfully into the plaster kept him from pitching onto his face.

There was a sourness in his throat, a queasiness in his belly and a pounding headache behind his eyes. He knew only too well what had caused *them*—but the bitter stink of fire, and the smoke which was making him cough? Steadying himself with an effort, Aldric crossed the room and flung the shuttered window open.

Heat slapped like a physical blow across his face and chest, the bellow of a fire out of control assaulted his ears—and mingled with that bellow was the squealing of terrified horses. To any ears it was a ghastly noise, but to an Alban horse-lord it was infinitely worse than that. "Lyard!" he gasped in horror, staring with wide, bloodshot eyes towards the stables where a solitary ribbon of flame was fluttering up its wall, a little insignificant thing no more than a handspan wide.

But the stable wall was wood—and the stable roof was thatch.

The Alban wasn't sure afterwards just how he managed to scramble into his clothes so fast; certainly there were straps and laces left undone, secured too loosely or too tight, but shirt and boots and breeches were all in place before the little flame had grown much larger. He thrust his *tsepan* dirk into his belt, wincing as its pommel nudged his nauseated stomach, then scooped up Widowmaker and made for the swiftest exit he could see. It happened to be the open window.

Betrayed by his wobbly legs, Aldric went over when he landed and rolled like a shot rabbit while dirk and longsword each went in different directions. Just after the bone-jarring impact came the nasty realization that in his present state he was as likely as not to have broken his neck. There was no time even to shrug.

A swift glance told him what had probably happened: the flames were billowing from an incandescent framework where the tavern's kitchens had once stood, and even in the instant that his eyes were on them they bridged the gap between courtyard and tavern proper. Thatch exploded like tinder, sparks and smoke filled the air, stinging and choking; a dense gray cloud rolled across his line of sight and something unseen collapsed with a tearing crash.

Where in damnation's bloody name is everyone? He saw them, someone, anyone, black silhouettes in the firelight, running about aimlessly or flinging meagre buckets of water. Some, more practical, were carrying their belongings clear of the doomed building.

No more time to watch.

Get the horses out!

All of them—can't let them burn.

Why won't it rain that deluge it's been promising all day?

The thoughts tumbled through Aldric's confused brain even as he ran towards the stable-block, staring apprehensively at that ribbon of flame which—in the few long strides which took him to the door—had expanded to a flickering yellow scarf tipped and trimmed with dark smoke. Confused or not, they were the last thoughts of any coherence he was to have for a long, long time.

The stables were built to a familiar Imperial pattern: tall sliding doors at either end of a broad, paved walkway which was flanked on each side by cedar-faced loose-boxes strewn with deep, comfortable—and fiercely inflammable—straw. The animals were normally free to move about in these; but tonight of all nights, someone had secured their headstalls to the iron holding-rings in the rear wall of each box. A spasm of anger shot through Aldric at this evidence of some groom's thoughtlessness; not so much because of the fire, and because his own task was immediately more difficult than simply flinging all the doors wide open, but for the simple reason that—tied up all night—none of the horses could reach food or water until someone came to release them.

It was simple; simply nasty. And had he the time, the "someone" responsible would be rooted out and made to dance for his neglect. Except that time was in very short supply.

Lyard knew his master and it was just as well. The Andarran's rolling eyes showed little but white, and he was streaked with the sweat of his terror and the foam from where he had champed uselessly at his halter; but he still allowed Aldric to lead him out at a steady pace, even though the flames of his own private hell skipped eagerly only a plank's thickness from his heels. Another minute, though. Another minute, and the big stallion would have pulped anybody in his path.

The pack-pony was next; Aldric flung the saddle-frame and then the boxes which contained his armor any whichway across the sumpter gelding's neck, then jerked aside hastily as it barged after Lyard directly as it was loosed. As it always followed Lyard—he coughed as smoke throttled what might have been wry laughter—but a damn sight more willingly than usual!

It was the other horses which were the problem, even though they weren't highly-strung, battle-schooled and consequently dangerous bloodstock like his Andarran courser, just a matched pair of carriage ponies and half-a-dozen riding hacks. But they were unfamiliar, and therefore risky. Scared, too; the laidback ears and bulging eyes would have told anyone that, even were they deaf to the piteous noises of fright. But it was just fright—not pain. Not yet.

Not ever, if he could help it!

The thatched roof caught as if hit by an incendiary just as Aldric went into one of the horses' stalls—and in that same second he slammed backwards and then down to the floor as if hit by a mace. It was close enough to the truth: the horse had lashed out in a paroxysm of fear and its iron-shod hoof had clipped his thigh, stunning the big muscle and tearing his heavy leather riding-breeches like paper. Another inch and it would have ripped flesh from bone and crippled him.

Muttering something under his breath, Aldric clambered back to his feet and cuffed at hindquarters which swung round to pin him against the partition. The horse flinched away—then thumped back, and stars inside his head joined the sparks already floating through the air.

Something—a dark outline against the fireglow—swam into view. No, some*one*. Aldric shook glowing motes from his eyes and the world snapped back into focus. It . . . he . . . was a man, big and broad-shouldered. One of the lady's escort? The man shouted something, but roaring flames made nonsense of the words.

"Get them out!" the Alban mouthed at him, enhancing his unheard words with mime, then returned his attention to the plunging horse. Its frantically jerking head had drawn the headstall's knot far tighter than human fingers could hope to loose, but—a knife appeared in his hand from the scabbard down one boot—there were other ways than untying . . .

No point now in trying to quiet the beast; it had gone beyond the stage where gentle words would have any effect. All he wanted now was to free the ropes which tied each horse—they would make their own way out faster than he could—and then get clear himself before the roof came in.

As if stimulated by his thought, the blazing thatch overhead creaked ominously and seemed to settle on its rafters while a drizzle of sparks percolated through the tight-packed reeds and straw. Aldric spared a single instant to glance up, then sliced his blade across the braided halter just as the horse threw all its weight into a final, desperate heave. The hemp went taut as wire, humming with strain, and the first touch of the razor-whetted knife jumped and skittered across its fibres. Then the edge bit home and it parted with a deep sound like the strings of a great-bass rebec.

The horse floundered back on its haunches as the rope let go, then wheeled to bolt headlong from the stable.

And Aldric sat down sharply, yelping with pained surprise as blood welled from the scar beneath his right eye, three years healed but laid open like an hour-old cut by the whiplash strike of the severed rope. He barely noticed the brief sting at the nape of his neck which might have been a spark. But was not.

As he darted from stall to stall, severing ropes and dodging horses as if taking part in some crazy rustic dance, he could hear the roof groan again as it settled further. Chunks of its structure fell away and the drizzle of sparks became a deluge, a torrent of burning fragments pouring onto the floor. A floor that, except for the paved walkway, was knee-deep in loose, dry straw. It ignited with the roar of a hungry animal and filled the confines of the world with fury. Heat washed over Aldric as he stumbled from the last stall on that side and into the main aisle of the stable, almost trampled as other horses—all the remaining horses—galloped past him on the way to open air and safety, and his mouth stretched into a tight grin. The trooper, if such he was, had been busy.

There was unknowing irony in the way that thought coincided with a rub at the sore spot on his neck—a rub which dislodged the tiny dart imbedded there.

He could see no trace of the man: too wise to linger in this incinerator, most likely. Aldric knew he would be wise to follow suit, for worms of smoke were already writhing from the wooden walls as they heated towards flashpoint, and the doorposts were already on fire. At each end of the building. The only other occasion whe62he had seen anything burn like this, it had been set ablaze deliberately.

His thought led nowhere; with this much straw about, no wonder the fire had spread so fast. But even so, the tavern wasn't full of straw.

That too meant nothing; it drifted across the surface of his mind even as he tucked his head down and sprinted for the nearest doorway. His legs were unsteady beneath him and once-solid objects were shimmering in the haze of hot light and smoke. Then all concerns and idle notions were swallowed in the vast rending as the stable caved in on itself. And on him!

The surge of heat made his senses swim as it consumed what little air remained, and a searing gale tugged at his hair as it funnelled through the blazing doorway; a doorway that receded down an endless corridor of fire even as he ran vainly towards it. He was conscious of the rush of movement at his back as something came scything down like a headsman's sword—

—heard the impact as it smashed between his shoulders like a giant's fist—

—saw the sparks exploding like a halo around his head—

Too late! You left it too . . .

And that was all.

"How did you find him in Tuenafen?" The man in scarlet-lacquered armor planted both his hands palm-downwards on the desk and leaned forward, his spade beard jutting pugnaciously. "How did you know?"

"I told you." Pinched between finger and thumb of a black-gloved hand, the scrap of parchment looked utterly insignificant and the writing on it was minute. But it afforded a certain degree of pleasure to the man who held it, for all that his glistening metallic mask concealed whatever smile might have curved his lips. Yet the smile was there, and plainly audible in the smug coloration of his laconic words: "I told you long ago—"

"Three weeks—"

"And now I too have been told."

"I didn't somehow think it was coincidence."

"I abhor coincidence." The masked man might have shuddered theatrically at the very thought, had he been prone to such gestures; but the armored man could see no tremor in the misshapen bearded face that reflected back at him.

"Of course." There was the merest touch of acid in his voice. "Except when you create it. I know." He straightened, pressed hands palm to palm and touched their steepled fingertips thoughtfully to the end of his hawk nose as he pondered a moment. "Now, Tuenafen." The hands clapped decisively. "The quickest route is by sea. I'll put a battleram at the disposal of your squad."

He stalked to the window and looked out, then turned back to the masked man who had not stirred from the highbacked chair in which he lounged with such elegantly irritating indolence. And the armored man smiled thinly. "*Teynaur* is moored in the estuary," he said. "Use her."

His smile widened as the masked man sat bolt upright, his lazy assurance gone in an instant. "*Teynaur . . . ?* But she's an—an augmented ship."

"Of course. Why not?" There was a long beat of silence. "Of course, if you don't like the idea, then let Voord go alone. Such things don't worry him—rather the reverse."

"To an unhealthy degree!"

"No matter. He is efficient—you employed that very word when he was sent to Seghar. Why—have you changed your views?"

"No." The reply was sullen. "He is still most capable, regardless."

"Good. Then it's agreed." The armored man gathered up his rank-marked helmet and settled it comfortably in the crook of one arm, obviously preparing to leave. Then he hesitated. "You want Talvalin alive?"

"Of course. Why?"

"So do I. And untouched. There is a distinct difference. Make sure that Voord remembers it."

"The wound is new. And he has a beard."

"The *beard* is new—and it isn't so much a beard as a need to shave. That's something I'm better qualified to know than you, my lady. But the wound was old when I saw it."

"When you saw it? When you thought you saw it—or when you saw what you wanted to see?"

"I saw what I saw. Look for yourself and then say I was wrong."

Paper rustled crisply.

"Close. Very close. This is an excellent likeness . . . of somebody. But is it close enough?"

"Close enough for me. I sent the messages last night and this morning: one by courier, one by pigeon. The usual."

"Without consulting me?"

"I saw no need; I thought you would approve."

"Never presume what I will or will not do. But yes, I do approve."

"And the Lord-Commander? What will Voord say?"

"Voord will be . . . very pleased."

It was surely a dream; a soft murmur of sound that droned like insects on a warm summer night. The sound took shape and became voices, a man's and a woman's. They ebbed and flowed, weaving patterns of words. But whatever language it was that the voices spoke, none of the words made sense.

The dream faded. His eyes remained shut; other than the slow rise and fall of his chest and the never-ending tic of pulses beneath his skin, he did not move. But with a swiftness that fell between one breath and the next, Aldric was totally aware of his surroundings.

There was softness above and below him; that was the yielding warmth of quilts, and it was comforting in its familiarity. Light surrounded him, for he was conscious of its brilliance beyond his eyelids. A faint taste of bitter herbs left a flavor like steel in his mouth, and there was a scent of flowers in his nostrils—the arid, delicate fragrance of dried blossoms set out to perfume the air. He opened his eyes to see them, to see where he was—

—and saw only featureless white, and knew that he was blind.

Sweat beaded on Aldric's skin and now he could not, would not move, even though each breath was coming faster and faster and the blood-pulse in his ears was running wild. *The fire!*

Memories crashed back into his brain: monstrous heat, smoke and flames surging in his wake as he fled for ever;

the roof coming down, the blow across his back and the midnight embrace of oblivion. The long fall into the dark which had never reached bottom.

A fall as black as blindness . . .

His skin was no longer beaded by perspiration, but slickly sheathed in it. Aldric could feel each droplet forming, running down his ribs, his jaw, his temples. What had happened could never, never have been so subtly selective as to destroy only his sight. Not that inferno. And if blindness was black, as the proverb claimed, then was this flaring whiteness—

Death . . . ?

With that thought came the great uncontrolled intake of breath which could only return as a scream.

Or a gasp; for in the same instant someone took the light bandage from his face and pressed a cool, moist pad against each eye in turn, and when they opened again Aldric's world lurched back to reality and equilibrium with a vertiginous jolt. The unborn cry became a hissing exhalation that trickled out between his teeth, for he was shamed by the sleek lacquering of fear that glossed his skin and by the—surely audible!—thudding of his heart. But the woman who sat by his bed and gazed down at him either did not or courteously feigned not to notice.

Without her furs and her guards and her imperious air, she looked very different. Her hair was unbound now, and in the lamplight which filled the room it was the deep rich russet of a fox's pelt. She was smiling.

"I thought . . ." he faltered; the admission was going to sound foolish, or cowardly, or both. "I thought that I was dead."

"Quite so. There was a time, indeed, when we thought that we had lost you." She spoke in the purring Jouvaine language and her voice was as Aldric remembered it: soft, throaty, surprisingly deep. A purr indeed. If foxes purred.

"Lost me?"

"Lost you," she repeated. "You were lucky—very lucky. The timber which hit you wasn't properly aflame, as you were running hard in the right direction. Otherwise you would never have got out."

"I should never have gone in," he muttered, deciding not to sit up as his stomach gave a little warning heave. His words, indeed his thoughts, were forming easily and that surprised him; he had been stunned before and the concussion had jumbled brain and stomach both. As she said: he must have been very, very lucky. He knew that he had certainly been something else. "Stupid—"

"Unselfish, courageous. You didn't have to stay after you freed your own horses—but you did, and you saved mine. That was typical, I suppose. You are fond of horses." Again the smile. "I know a little about Albans."

If she had hoped for some sort of reaction, the lady was disappointed. Aldric had never tried to conceal his nationality, because it was both difficult to maintain such a deception and immediately suspicious if discovered. His identity, though, now that was quite another matter. But the mere possibility of an ulterior motive behind her casual remark was enough to coil another worm of nausea through him, masked only by a smile of sorts to disguise whatever else might be read from his features. "Most people do," he replied carefully.

Or think they do. The words were on the tip of his tongue, but stayed there. For one thing, he was in no mood for opening his mouth more than was absolutely necessary, and for another this lady was his hostess—or so he guessed the lady to be, and the house around him, hers.

There could be nothing left of the tavern in which he had awoken last night, nothing at all. Of that he was certain. Even though he was very far from certain that it *had* been last night, or even the night before that. Aldric closed his eyes and shivered as he wondered how many days and nights he had really lost. And what had happened while they passed him by.

Who are you? Where am I? What is this place? What day is it?

The questions were all there, waiting—needing—to be asked. Banal questions, obvious questions, stupid questions. But all lacking the answers which he needed to start making sense of what was going on.

"You are plainly still far from well, *'tlei*," said the lady gently. "Sleep now. We can talk again later." Her hand was cool on his brow. "Sleep."

He slept.

He slept.
    He dreamed.
    He died!
    He woke. And woke knowing that he had been drugged, for this time he was wide awake and in full control of himself, his totally alert senses insisting on the fact and emphasising it with that faint metallic, medicinal flavor lurking under his tongue and at the back of his throat. It was a flavor he remembered, but had been unable or unfit to identify before; now it was unmistakably the after-taste of herbal soporifics. Mandragora, poppy—he was in the Empire now and the possibilities were endless, for the Drusalans had raised herb lore to an art-form and a science, whilst at the same time lowering it to a particularly unpleasant vice. Swallowing in an attempt to clear away the bitterness, Aldric realized just how very dry his mouth had become.

At least—his gaze slid left—there was an evaporation-cooled terracotta jug of water on a table near the bed. He rolled over and reached out, then hesitated momentarily with the thought of more drugs filling his mind. A brief consideration put paid to that idea; if he was to have been drugged, then he would never have woken up to worry about the fact. He ignored the cups to grip the jug itself, put the vessel to his lips and disposed of its contents in half-a-dozen rapturous gulps; stared for several seconds into the pitcher's brick-brown interior; then tilted it that few degrees further and allowed the last drops of water to patter coolly across his face.

Only then did the questions once more play follow-my-leader across the conscious surface of his mind. Who, and where, and when—and *why?*

There were various answers to that one, few of which were appealing.

But the lady . . .

She of the fox-bronze hair and the purring, feline voice. The lady had something to do with all this. Yes, all of it. The fire and the trapped horses. The grinding roar of falling timber and the shower of sparks before the lights went out.

And how in the name of nine hot hells did I survive?

Aldric's eyes raked the room, noting the understated elegance which plainly displayed the wealth and taste of whoever owned it—and by that intimation, owned the house as well. If it was intended to impress, then despite his cynical efforts to the contrary it succeeded. A quick grin bared his teeth as he saw those things which at first glance reassured him above all else; but it faded swiftly as comprehension of detail gave him cause for a deal of thought.

His saddlebags were set on a chair by the far wall. There was nothing wrong with that, although he was sure they had been opened and the contents carefully scrutinised. A garment of some sort—not one of his own—was draped across the linen chest at the foot of the bed, obviously meant for his use; well, his own clothes were either still packed away or in a smelly, smoky, unfit state unless someone had washed them. Or, he amended, caused them to be washed.

But his weapons . . .

Whoever was responsible for their disposition had known exactly what he—or she—was doing, for Isileth Widowmaker was not merely laid horizontally across a fine sword-stand of fumed oak as might be done by anyone who . . . what were her words? "Knew a little about Albans." Oh no. This was much, much more.

The *taiken's* weapon-belt had been wrapped closely around her black-lacquered scabbard in the interlacing style of *hanen-tehar,* as was proper for battle-furnished longswords; and his *tsepan* dirk had been placed on the cushion of a three-legged stool, then set close in beside the bed. It was an insignificant thing; but it meant that the honor blade was within the arm's-length of its owner which tradition and the Codes required.

His own weapons told Aldric that whoever he was dealing with knew more than he liked about his homeland, his background and quite possibly himself. And that they were confident enough to flaunt the fact.

He glanced towards the door, the speculation in that

glance born more of optimism than any real hope. If they—or he or she or whatever—were so sure of themselves, there might just be a remote possibility that the overconfidence could extend further. Into foolishness.

The thought was no sooner completed than he was out of the bed, Widowmaker scooped neatly from her sword-stand; and the scabbard had been shaken from her long blade before he paused long enough even to consider wrapping himself in the garment which someone had so thoughtfully provided.

It was a *cymar,* heavy and fur-trimmed, Vlei-style. The dense fabric was the color of autumn maples, the fur red fox; and it hung from Aldric's shoulders as loosely as a riding mantle. Clothing of any sort meant much more than simple modesty right now: in this potentially hostile environment his bare skin felt horribly vulnerable, and even a single layer of cloth could give an illusory protection.

Or should have done. If anything this sleeveless, side-slashed, open-fronted and monstrously oversized *cymar* seemed to emphasise with every movement that he was stark naked beneath it; which was subconsciously worse than having nothing on at all. Aldric glanced at himself and exhaled a soft oath. This was deliberate; and the robe had probably been selected with a deal of care to unsettle him so successfully.

Isileth's equally naked blade gave him more comfort; at least with the *taiken* in his hands, then armored, unarmored or newborn naked he could give a good account of himself to anyone, or any thing . . . no, *Thing.* His mind reconsidered that last, and an inward shudder raised the hair on arms and neck as he regretted tempting fate with such a thought. The events in Geruath's citadel at Seghar were still far too recent for such an idle jest, if jest it had truly been at all.

Smiling a mirthless smile, he very gently closed his ringed left hand on the door's iron handle and increased the pressure to an inward pull. Nothing happened. He relaxed a little, then pushed out. Again nothing. Tentatively he tried sliding it sideways.

Then shrugged with resignation and wrenched back with all his strength and weight behind it.

The door wasn't stiff, unoiled or jammed as he had allowed himself to hope. It was, as he had feared instead, locked and bolted top and bottom—and the jolt of his failed attempt to open it sent silver spikes of anguish into every joint from wrist to shoulder.

Aldric shrugged again, although this time it was really more of a suppressed wince, and would have sworn had swearing helped at all. Then as he considered the matter and flexed his arm to work the twinges out of it, he swore anyway. Gently—but with sincerity.

"Idiot," he muttered under his breath. "Should have known. Now after all that racket, who else knows?"

It was talk for the sake of hearing a familiar voice and nothing more. Despite his self-accusation, Aldric suspected—no, he was quite sure—that whoever wanted and needed to know he was awake knew it already. If he was a prisoner—or a guest, though to his knowledge not even the Drusalan Empire required that guests be kept under lock and key—then it was unlikely that the past few moments' activity would have gone unnoticed for long.

But who would notice? And who would they tell?

The Alban grimaced and recovered Widowmaker's scabbard from where his unsheathing flick had sent it; the *taiken*'s blade ran home with a steely whisper as he sank to both knees on the floor. Laying the weapon across his thighs, he sat back on his heels, drew the *cymar*'s folds more closely around his chest and composed himself to wait.

He did not wait long—and had not expected to.

Privately, Aldric reckoned that no more than ten minutes had passed from the first signs of life in his room to the series of metallic clicks as its door was unlocked. At the sounds he rose smoothly, swiftly and silently, and as he regained his feet and spaced them for balance his right hand tightened on the longsword's hilt, giving it that minute twist which freed the locking-collar. Widowmaker seemed to tremble with eagerness in his grip, like a poised falcon; she would leave her scabbard at a touch now, as blindingly quick as a striking snake.

And as deadly.

The woman in the doorway knew it. She stood quite

still, not in the least afraid if the smile on her full red lips meant anything; but she had been told, indeed, warned at some length, about how fast and dangerous this young man was, and she had taken note of that—as she now took note of many other things about him while her gaze swept with dawning speculation across his exposed-yet-tantalisingly-concealed and at last so very *alive* body. She had unashamedly drawn back the covers as he lay unmoving in drugged sleep, and had been mildly attracted to him then; but how very different this Alban looked now that lithe, powerful muscles slid and shifted purposefully under his tanned skin. Yes. Different indeed. For just an instant the hunger in her eyes was as naked as his body, beneath the *cymar* which she had spent a quarter-hour selecting from her brother's wardrobe. *And not a minute of that time was wasted.* She decided to treat this one with all the caution he deserved, and a little more besides. For the present, at least.

Aldric stared at her with eyes that were narrowed and watchful in a face which he had schooled to expressionless immobility. His whole demeanor was as poised and wary as a startled cat, ready to lash out or sidestep at a heartbeat's notice, because although a blurred and hazy memory told him that he had seen this woman twice before, it was only the first sight of her that he recalled with any clarity. She had been entering a room on that occasion too; but flanked by armed and armored guards.

Well, there were no guards this time. And that was her mistake, because if need be he could reach her and seize her, and lay the persuasive length of Widowmaker's bitter edge against her expensively scented throat before that throat could start to shape a cry for help.

And then, *then*—though the idea repelled him with its total lack of any honor—he could bargain for his freedom. With her life.

"You are awake." *Lord God and the Holy Light of Heaven, what a voice she had!* The fact was self-evident and made her words unnecessary; but their very triviality did something to ease the taut silence which clogged the bedroom's atmosphere like smoke.

"I am."

"Good." It was scarcely a conversation sparkling with brilliant wit. She hesitated, studied him from head to foot again with the same frank appraisal as before and nodded to herself. "You look very well . . . rested. And healthy."

Aldric felt uncomfortable under that stare. "I would feel more at ease with my clothes on, lady. Where are they?"

"They were foul. Stained, torn."

"—And mine. I asked where, lady, not what. I want my own clothes, not this—this horse-blanket." A very superior horse-blanket and one of considerable value, but that no longer mattered. Aldric knew he was trying to be ironically humorous, and knew too that he was not succeeding very well, for the emotion which his not-quite-humor concealed insisted on bubbling to the surface. That emotion was anger.

Anger directed at her, for the way in which his memory jarred with what he saw and heard. And anger which fed on itself as his uneasiness made itself manifest in an abruptness which was not the courtesy expected of a guest. Or was he a prisoner after all?

"My clothes," he repeated more quietly. Then, softly, "Please."

"Better." She said it with a sort of gratitude, not in the bantering tone of one who has scored a point. "Of course you realize, ' *'tlei,* that such a request can be fulfilled quite easily." The purring, husky tone was back in her voice and added a honeyed darkness to her words which had not been there before. She clapped her hands together twice and stepped to one side.

And a man came in: a man who made Aldric take an instinctive snap-step backwards through no more than simple caution. Not because of who the man was—just a liveried serving-man, no more—but what he was: huge. He stood head and shoulders taller than the Alban, and those shoulders were of a piece with the rest of him—bulky with corded muscles whose outlines were plain even through his clothing. He was the sort of excellent bodyguard whose presence alone was a weapon, the kind of man it would be wiser not to cross. And by the expression on his face, he had both understood and disapproved of the way in which his mistress had been addressed.

In his arms, precisely folded, were clothes which Aldric recognised: They were black, and leather for the most part—tunic and breeches and boots. But there was something else as well, and it was not leather but fur: a *coyac* of black wolfskin. Aldric stared at it and felt a small, strange, unaccountable roiling deep in the pit of his stomach. In his secret heart of hearts he had hoped. He had wished . . .

Of everything I own, I would as soon that one was burned to ashes. And the ashes scattered on the western wind.

And yet he could not think of any reason why.

With utter disregard for their neat folds, his clothes were dropped unceremoniously onto the bed, and one boot slid with a thump to the floor. The right boot, of course. It balanced upright for a moment, then toppled over. And a knife fell out of it with an accusing tinkle which drew all eyes.

It was Aldric who looked up first, with a feeling that despite their expressions of astonishment the throwing-knife's presence came as no surprise to anyone. The whole affair had probably been stage-managed from the start, as deliberate as the choosing of the overrobe he wore. Stooping, he set the boot upright again, picked up the knife and turned it over in his fingers once or twice, then unconcernedly returned it to the sheath stitched inside the long moccasin's laced and buckled top.

"Thank you." The remark was addressed to nobody in particular, and so neutrally voiced that it was impossible to tell if he was pleased, or amused . . . or blazing with anger.

The big servant glowered at him, and though he had known it all along, Aldric noticed as if for the first time the diagonal belt crossing his chest which was the shoulder-strap of a wide-bladed regulation army pattern short-sword. *So she has an escort after all,* he thought. *Of sorts. But one I could take easily. Just meat.* He met the other stare for stare and it was the bigger man whose gaze dropped first.

Not a flicker of satisfaction at the small victory showed

on Aldric's face, because he was growing more and more certain that someone, somewhere, was testing him for a purpose of their own.

But what was it?

"Get out." His command was so quiet that it was little more than an exhalation of breath. The servant hesitated; then, although it required a glance towards his lady and her nod of assent, he left without further protest and closed the door behind him as a good servant should. But the woman remained.

Aldric paused in the act of laying out his clothes on the bed and flicked a look towards her, then gestured with one finger. A little circle, drawn horizontally on the air between them. "Turn around, lady," he amplified, and waited until she had complied.

"I had not," she said to the wall, "expected a man of men who value honor to be also a man who threatens unarmed women." There was just a hint of disapproval in her voice.

"I didn't threaten you. Not even once."

"You did—and I saw you. You held your sword and you looked at me, and you wondered if maybe you might have to put the blade to my neck before you could get out of here. Oh yes."

"Was I so obvious?" Aldric made the concession sardonically. "Ah well . . ."

"I hadn't expected it of a guest in my house," she repeated.

This time Aldric said nothing. He dropped the *cymar* to the floor and drew fresh linens from one of his saddlebags, then busied himself working one leg into the tightfitting trousers of heavy cotton he wore beneath his riding-breeches.

"And I hadn't expected such a one to need long underwear."

The Alban froze, balanced on one leg with the other raised beneath him like a stork, half in and more importantly half out of the garment in question, and he blushed all over. Apart from his left leg from the knee downward, that "all over" was patently beyond dispute. His head snapped round and it almost certainly turned faster than the Drusalan woman had expected, for he caught the vestiges of an expression which later and calmer consideration insisted that he had not been meant to see.

She was looking over one shoulder and there was an impish smile on her lips. But in her eyes there was a glitter of truly malicious amusement. It wasn't honest good-humor, rightly created by her ridiculous, inaccurate but very apt observation. Oh God, no. It was a nasty wallowing in the undignified embarrassment which her words had caused. That wallowing, and the pleasure which stemmed from it, were stilled even as Aldric became aware of its existence—but the very fact that he had seen and recognised it troubled him.

"Not underwear, my lady. Trousers. Proper trousers." He hitched the trews up and fastened them firmly at his waist. "Try wearing combat leathers next your doubtless-so-tender skin some time," he continued waspishly, "then ask again about why I wear these. If you still have to."

Without further comment, or indeed further insistence that she look away since it was plain she had no intention of doing any such thing, Aldric finished dressing in clean clothes from the skin out. Somebody had been decent enough—if that was really the word he wanted—to shave him and bathe him whilst he was unconscious, so why not? Loose white shirt and knee-length hosen were followed by the black leather of breeches, boots and tunic. And then finally, unwilling to wear it but more unwilling still to let the woman see his reluctance, he pulled on the wolfskin *coyac*.

Its fur was as he remembered it on that rainswept day when it had first been pressed into his armored hands, as a payment for the death of a man who might at another time or in other circumstances have been his friend: deep, rich, warm, and redolent of the herbs which Drusalans liked to strew in their clothes-chests. Yet underneath it all was the faint reek of fire. And of spoiled, rotting flesh.

She watched in silence, impressed despite herself as he enclosed himself in a black that was made still deeper by the few points of contrast against snowy fabric or burnished brightmetal. On someone else it might have approached the melodramatic; but there was a melancholy about this man, an introspection and a brooding which stifled ill-chosen remarks at the source. Instead the woman said, "*Combat* leathers, Alban? Surely you don't . . . ?"

". . . intend to do without them, or my weapons? No. Not until I'm clear of this place. And much more confident of the company that I keep." His eyes met hers, feline gray-green and gemlike sapphire blue, each probing for reality beneath the façade of studied, obviously false ironic humor. "May I be entirely open with you, lady?"

"By all means." That sardonic undertone was not a pleasant thing to hear in any pretty woman's voice, and especially hers. Because she was so pretty. No—beautiful. Naturally beautiful; and expensively beautiful.

And she knew the power it gave her.

"I don't trust you, lady—I'm sorry, but there it is. I have what you might call a feeling about this whole affair, from the fire at the tavern to your apparent generosity. For which I thank you. But I can find no proof. Nothing I can hold, nothing I can be sure of. So I must accept your motives at face value."

"Now that is uncommonly kind of you." Her words were flat and the thought behind them vicious, but even though her tone scoured his ears like ground glass Aldric was glad he had made himself quite plain. At least he had proved that he was not quite as naïve as she might have thought. Though she was still so very, very beautiful.

"And if you did not accept, *hlens'l?*" It was the first time he had heard her use that particular Drusalan word amongst the smoothness of her Jouvaine, and it jarred. "What would you do?" Now she was mocking him, subtly but not so subtly that it passed him by.

"What would I do?" he echoed, picking up his *tsepan* with the ghost of a respectful bow, no more than an inclination of his head, before thrusting it through his snugly-cinched weapon belt. There was a moment's hesitation, as though he was considering his next words; and in that hesitation he lifted Isileth and looped her cross-strap across his shoulder, hooking it low so that the longsword rode diagonally across his back. Her hilt reared alongside his neck like an adder poised to strike, but for all her threatening appearance the *taiken* was being carried in peace posture. It was a courteous gesture and a compliment of sorts, one which would be understood by whoever had set the longsword on her stand with her straps wrapped just-so in accordance with lore and ritual.

But it was also an insult, one so subtle that only the same knowledgeable person would appreciate it—if "appreciate" was the right word with insults. For wearing a fighting sword like that, in the presence of a suspected enemy, proclaimed unconcern and disdain and announced *I consider you no threat* in elegant cursives clear as the noon sun to those who knew how to read them.

"Do?" he said again, almost tasting the word. The grin which followed was a pleasant thing to see, all white teeth and sparkling eyes—unlike the words which went with it. "Truly, lady, I have no idea. But I would ask you, now and later—do not press me into finding out. I doubt that either of us would enjoy the revelation."

He bowed from the waist and it was a false, theatrically elegant sweep of movement which was not an Alban obeisance and was therefore another insult to any who chose to regard it as such. "And now," Aldric lifted his saddlebags and hefted them into a comfortable carrying position on one shoulder, "I thank you for your kindness towards me and I take my leave."

"Leave, Alban?" Surprise and shock; if they were feigned, then she was as much a talented actress as she was a seductively beautiful woman—and it was undeniably for the latter reason that Aldric wanted to be out of her house, out of her city, out of her circle of influence. One of the worldly-wise savants of history had said: "It is a wise man who knows his own failings." Aldric knew his, only too well. "In the name of the Father of Fires, what are you running away from? Why leave so soon?"

"Because, lady, as you say: I am Alban. I want to go home. And if this is Tuenafen, as I believe, then there should be a ship to suit me in the harbor."

"I . . . think not."

Had her voice been amused, or mocking, or sardonic—or indeed, any of several things which Aldric had no desire to hear, then he might just have dropped the saddlebags and drawn on her. Woman or not, pretty or not. Beautiful or not.

But she sounded, looked, perhaps was, sincerely annoyed and regretful. Sufficiently so at least to still what was as reflex a fear-born action as the hunched and bristling back of a wildcat. A *kourgath* of the Alban forests.

But even then he had to draw in a slow, deep breath so that the thunder of his heartbeat would not come vibrating up to leave a tremor in his voice when he said softly, "Explain."

"There have been no ships in Tuenafen harbor these two days past. I'm sorry. Truly. Had I but known. With the blow on your head and the drags which my physician recommended, you were unconscious for almost three days and nights. Oh, Lord Father of Fires, if I had *known!*" Her expression changed, altering as the eddies of several consequent thoughts and considerations fled across it. "But after all," she said at last, "this is really for the best."

"Is it? What is?"

"You being here with me, and I in your debt."

"For those damned horses?" The foggy recollection of their earlier and rather one-sided conversation was growing much clearer. "All I did, lady, was to make a reasonable attempt at killing myself—and to no good purpose."

She tut-tutted at him and waved one finger in the air, as reproving as any tutor. "Not without purpose, I insist on that. Those horses weren't just damned, especially the carriage ponies. They were—are, thanks to you—damned fine, damned expensive and damned healthy. I owe you, Alban, yes. Say it is because of the horses."

"Lady, I don't understand what you're trying to tell me."

"If there was a ship in the harbor today, now, this very minute, and you went aboard to buy passage for yourself—oh yes, and for your *own* horses—then you would be wasting your time. Because you couldn't afford to. Not since the fire."

Though he made no sound and had not even formed the words with his mouth, Aldric's question was plain enough in his eyes for her to answer it at once.

"Your money is gone. All of it."

A chill like the touch of an ice-dipped razor slithered down the Alban's spine and he seemed to see the bars of a cage closing around him. But there was still one possible key that no one knew about. If only . . . He forced his voice to a flat calm. "How much damage was done? I . . . missed the end of it."

"Enought and to spare," she said quietly. "The tavern was gutted, burnt to a shell. Stables, kitchen, tap-room—and most of the guest-rooms too. Yours among them. Somehow your saddlebags weren't there."

Yes, they bloody were! He caught the snapping contradiction just in time; let her think she was playing him for a fool a little longer. But his saddlebags were invariably in the same room where he slept, even disregarding the presence of money; they contained the clean clothes and the razor which he needed first thing every morning. So who had moved them?

". . . they were found at last, and investigated—"

"Of course!" This time he did interrupt aloud, but his sarcasm seemed almost an expected response to her confession and consequently went unremarked.

"Investigated," she spoke with heavy patience now, "for some idea of who you were, no more. Because there was a stage when my concern was only to find some true words for your grave-marker."

Aldric stared at her and his mouth twitched slightly without completing any one of the dozen possible expressions which it might have formed—and not one of them an expression the Drusalan woman would have liked. But for her part she lifted both shoulders in an ostentatious shrug and let it go at that. Why start to worry now? the shrug said. You're still alive, aren't you?

"There was no money in the saddlebags, none at all. Nor in your pockets. If there had been, it would have been given to me for safe-keeping. And yet the inn-keeper kept insisting that you were rich. 'Free with Imperial silver,' were his exact words. Not any more, I'm afraid. Whatever wealth you might have had is melted

slag among the ashes of the inn. Now do you understand
what I mean when I say that I owe you?"

"I understand that I can no longer pay my own way
in the Drusalan Empire," Aldric returned a trifle frostily.
Either the silver in question *had* been destroyed—which
was unlikely to a degree—or it had been stolen afterwards to convey that impression.

"Quite so." She refused to be baited by his tone,
which was natural enough in the circumstances anyway.
"Until I repay my debt, you are my guest, Alban. Because otherwise—here at least—you are a pauper."

"Oh." That was all. Aldric set his saddlebags down
again and allowed his shoulders to sag. Not all of it was
pretence; everything was far too neat, far too obviously
planned in advance. And far too obviously planned for his
especial benefit, if benefit was quite the word he wanted.

But for all her pretended omniscience, the woman
didn't know everything. And in that lack of knowledge
lay his one hope and his one chance to get himself clear
of this mess before the cage was fully shut.

"I want to see my horses, lady; and to check that all
my gear is as safe as you assure me. And then I want a
look at the harbor anyway." It felt odd not having used
her name once, for all that they had spoken together for
so long; but then he didn't yet know it—nor she his.
Well, maybe that was for the best. Time enough for
names—even assumed names—when they were going to
be of some use.

"I'll have a servant escort you," she said quickly. Too
quickly for Aldric's liking.

"I'd sooner go alone."

"No!"

"No . . . ?"

"No. It would be too dangerous." He quirked one
eyebrow at that. "You are a foreigner. *Inyen-hlensyarl.*
And people are uneasy about foreigners right now."

His mind went back to the attitudes displayed in the
tavern common-room. "I've noticed that much already.
Why?"

"K'shva sho'tah, 'n-tach chu h'labech." "They fear you,
because they fear spies."

Strange that she could not trust the explanation to

Jouvaine, for all that they had spoken it comfortably up until now. Or maybe not so strange at all. In a strange country, inhabited by strange people, the strange becomes ordinary. Or at least acceptable. Without doubt he had found that to be true, in the Jevaiden at least.

"Why," she asked softly, as if the answer was obvious, "do you think that your bedroom door was locked?"

Aldric blinked once. He had planned to spring just that very question on *her* and glean what he could from the expression it provoked. But not now; indeed, it required an effort of his own will and facial muscles to prevent the position from being reversed. "To keep me from running away?" he hazarded flippantly.

The woman stared at him: Was that contempt he saw in her eyes, or was he just imagining it? "No," the denial was flat and toneless, "It was to keep everyone else out. Otherwise . . . Oh, Father of Fires, I don't know. Call it too much caution and let it go."

"Understood," Aldric lied, very reluctant to let it go at all. "Now. To stretch my legs and check my horses. The harbor?"

"Of course." She turned to leave, then hesitated and swung back with one hand extended. There was something nestling on the proffered palm, a thing of looped steel and silver, partially wrapped in snow-white buckskin.

The spellstone of Echainon.

And Aldric's heart came crawling crookedly back up his throat.

"This is yours. I kept it safe—as I would with anything belonging to a *guest.*" Aldric thought privately that she came down over-heavily on that last word, but passed no remark. "It's a beautiful gem."

Gem?

She had called it nothing more; the meaning of the Jouvaine word was plain enough. So the stone had somehow kept its own secret, concealed the eldritch blue glow which would have marked it as much, much more than just a gemstone. Even though he couldn't fathom how or why. Aldric's mind worked rapidly to make his position more secure, to explain away what she might have read from his eyes.

"Not even a gem, lady. Just semiprecious quartz, without intrinsic value even if it is a pretty thing. Of course, it *is* very old and there are those who would set a price on that."

The glibness with which the lies came to his tongue unsettled him. Almost as if someone—maybe the stone itself, for all he knew—was prompting him and guiding his reasoning for its own protection.

"But it's an heirloom of my family, nobody else's. I inherited it—"

Or stole it? The conjecture in her eyes was plain enough.

"And though nobody else might, yet I consider it to have some small worth."

His fingertips closed on the talisman, pincering it neatly off her hand and confirming repossession even as he bowed courteously to her. This time there was no suggestion of any insult; there was nothing insulting about a formal Alban Third Obeisance, even this abbreviated version. But the bow gave him opportunity to relax the muscles of his face, which felt as if they were cramping permanently into an expression of careful neutrality. Only the palms of his hands might have betrayed him with their light film of sweat, but the shaking of hands was Gemmel's custom, not his. "I thank you, lady."

The meaning of his hesitation was obvious enough. "Call me Kathur, Alban. Everyone does."

"Apt enough," said Aldric, allowing himself to smile. "Kourgath-*eijo,* of . . . south and west of here." Now it was Kathur's turn to smile at his small double witticism, both of them content with their exchange of lies. He had told her only that he was named for the lynx-cat on his heavy silver collar, and anyone with wit would realize that this was no more than a nickname; south and west took in a sizable slice of the Empire, as well as Vreijaur and the independent city states of Jouvann. An answer, in truth, that answered nothing.

Her reply had been as vague, thought Aldric as he took his leave. Kathur, indeed! So she had been named—or chosen a name—for the rich color of her hair. Because *en-K'thar* in Drusalan meant "the fox," and she had given him the feminine equivalent with its soft shift of vowels. *In-K'thur* meant no more or less than "female fox."

The Vixen.

4

The Hour of the Fox

Aldric reached out and gave the door a single firm
push. It swung inward, silently, and a broad bar of
dusty golden light speared past him into the gloomy stable, pinning his shadow against the deep straw on the
floor. He remained in the doorway for several minutes,
not moving, saying nothing, just watching the hard-edged
contrasts of sunlight and darkness and half-expecting
sudden movement.

More than half-expecting. Widowmaker was hooked
in battle position now, close in to his left hip on her
silver-plaqued weaponbelt, and his right hand had returned to her hilt after opening the door with a blurred
flick that was too fast and precise for accident.

His caution was not required, for slowly—as his eyes
became accustomed to the dimness within—they were
able to see that everything was in order. Exact order.
And that very neatness made them go narrow and flinty.

The horses were safe. The harness was safe (*good!*).
The pack-saddle and its armor-boxes were safe—though
doubtless carefully searched.

All safe. Everything he owned—except the silver
which would have taken him out of here at a time of
his own choosing. Yes, a selective fire indeed. Who set
it? Not a flicker of the sardonic thought showed on his
face for the interested scrutiny of the man who stood
nearby. The promised escort.

And the expected spy.

All of his suspicions were confirmed now; not that
they were meant to be allayed for long, or indeed at all,
by so transparent an excuse. But if the inn had indeed

been fired deliberately as the first step to getting him right where somebody—*who?*—wanted him, then it was an act of such casual ruthlessness as to take the breath away—the act of somebody who cared nothing for consequences. Or because of who supported them, didn't *have* to care. And that thought was the most frightening at all.

Aldric walked lightly inside and patted Lyard's questing muzzle as the big Andarran courser shifted in his stall, recognised the one man in this whole place he trusted absolutely and demanded attention. Aldric gave the black stallion an apple, autumn-wrinkled but still sweet, which he had filched from a fruit-bowl as he left Kathur's house, then for fairness' sake gave another to the pack-horse and crunched into a third himself as he scanned the stable building. His gaze swept over fresh bedding, noted new grain and clean water; he smelt the sweet and slightly dusty aroma which told him the place was well-aired and dry, and nodded faintly with reluctant approval, honest enough with himself to admit that he had wanted to find fault somewhere. He watched as the horses noisily consumed their presents, then walked slowly towards the tack set on a wooden frame at the far wall, turning his head to stare arrogantly at Kathur's servant.

"How far to the harbor?" He asked the question around a mouthful of fruit, deliberately rude.

There was no answer and Aldric tentatively considered repeating himself in Drusalan—even though the apple clogging his mouth could prove a challenge when speaking that guttural, slipshod language, especially when it was a language he had been at pains to prove he neither spoke nor understood. He decided not to bother. "I'll walk anyway."

He neither knew nor cared if he was understood, for as he spoke he stroked the flat of one hand casually over the elaborate, expensive tooled leather of his high-peaked saddle. More expensive than any footslogging or carriage-riding Drusalan could understand; his touch was that of a man sliding his hand across the naked body of a lover, and with reason.

He was still in control of his own fate.

The embossed pattern was a formal, elaborate and classic design for horse furniture, an abstract design of interlacing arabesques, and it would have required a more expert eye than existed outside two or three centers of scholarship—or else the systematic and absolute destruction of a plainly undamaged saddle—to discover the single welt which was fractionally thicker than all the others. Its very presence—*and* ensuring that nobody, not even Gemmel his own foster-father, knew of the discrepancy in the pattern—had cost Aldric three and one-half pound's weight of raw gold ingots. He had paid for the work two days after a particularly unpleasant conversation with no less a person than King Rynert himself, and had considered the metal well spent.

For within the slightly-too-thick-for-authenticity length of leather was a cylinder of parchment, rolled as thin as a goose-quill. A letter—and no ordinary letter, even on this far from ordinary mission for the king. Its very presence set the young Alban's mind a little more at rest. Let my lady Vixen say whatever she pleased about the state of his finances: he could afford to buy a rapid, secret passage after all.

Or a ship. Aldric thought a moment and consciously had to will the grin from his lips. Ship, nothing! The realization had not occurred until now. He could buy an entire merchant fleet!

For the letter was indeed very far from ordinary; it was credit scrip drawn on what Aldric had decided was the largest and wealthiest merchant guild in the northern Empire. A note of hand good—if need be—for thirty thousand Alban deniers' worth of bullion gold.

Despite what Rynert the King had opined on that subject, Aldric had been undisputed master of Dunrath and *ilauem-arluth* Talvalin for long enough—just long enough—to make good use of the fact. He wondered if anyone had yet noticed the guild-stamps in Dunrath's treasury which effectively depleted it by one-third; and had to resist the desire to laugh out loud.

Despite his reconfirmed wealth, Tuenafen made Aldric uneasy. Anywhere in the Western Empire would have had the same effect. Young Emperor Ioen and his rebellious Grand Warlord were heading inexorably towards an armed confrontation after the sudden and mysterious deaths which had struck the Imperial Court like a plague—or, as some fanatics proclaimed, the retribution of an outraged Heaven. The deaths had begun with Crown Prince Ravek, killed in a hunting accident which many believed was no accident at all, and had moved like a scythe in wheat through courtiers, councillors, advisors and ultimately to the emperor himself who was found dead—of poison, said some; of another sort of excess altogether, said others—on a concubine's couch in the Pleasure Palace at Kalitzim. And until their sudden demise, all had been puppets who danced most obligingly when *Woydach* Etzel pulled on the appropriate strings.

The emperor's surviving son, Ioen, had suddenly found himself thrust to center stage in a political drama for which he was totally unrehearsed; and that had raised certain suspicions about the passing of his father and his brother, for all that four years had separated their deaths. Not that the boy himself was accused; at the time of his accession to crown prince he was sixteen and hardly capable of such ruthlessness. But his guardian and mentor was: Lord General Goth was capable of anything he could justify—and recent months had shown him remarkably able to discover reasons for what he did.

Reports were rife of an assassination here, a kidnapping and imprisonment there and of skirmishes far more serious than the clashes between partisan gangs which Aldric had witnessed once or twice in other towns. It had already happened in Tuenafen, for the consequences were plain: broken windows, smashed doorway lanterns—and those as yet undamaged screened from harm by shutters or by grilles of heavy mesh. Minor streets were sealed by barriers and main thoroughfares had checkpoints manned by the city militia—armed men empowered to stop, search and if need be detain any who aroused their suspicions.

The atmosphere was tense, strained, brittle as thin ice, yet to Aldric's surprise people were going about their business in an ordinary way. It was only when he surreptitiously listened to a few conversations that he realized how false that first impression had been. They talked about what was happening in the Empire: the political divisions, the religious schism of the Tesh heresy—but always in roundabout terms that were vague, ill-defined and comfortable. "Dissent." "Difficult times." "Troubles." But never the obvious.

Civil war.

Almost as if by not naming the actuality, they could deny that it existed. But their laughter when it came was forced and over-loud, and they had an unpleasant tendency to follow strangers with their eyes while never looking fully at them. Aldric had caught such sideways glances more than once, out of eyes that flinched away directly his own gaze met them. And it made his skin creep.

Somebody, somewhere, had told him why, and it was a reason so ridiculous that he had given it no credence then. *Then.* Now, he wasn't so sure. His taste in clothes was the problem; his preferred black and silver garments apparently reflected partisan support—for *Woydach* Etzel the Grand Warlord, of all people!—and that, with his foreign air, was enough to influence any who saw him. No one in the Empire was neutral; either they approved of the way he dressed—or somebody, somewhere, would find him so provocative that he would end up knifed. Purely as a form of political statement, of course, and with no personal animosity intended, as if that mattered.

The fact that any political extremist attacking Aldric while Isileth Widowmaker rode openly across his back would find himself sliced in half—purely as a reflex defensive response, of course, and with no personal animosity intended, as if that would carry weight with an Imperial court—was small comfort. That was not the way to fade unobtrusively into any background.

But it would soon be Aldric's name-day, and he planned to be alive and healthy on that day to celebrate it properly. If that meant borrowing enough money from Kathur to buy himself new clothes, then so be it; after all, she did keep insisting how much she was in his debt.

In twenty-three days he would be twenty-four years old: a quarter century, near enough, although there had been many times when both he and others had doubted aloud that he would ever attain so venerable an age. It would be ironic, therefore—no, it would be downright stupid—if some fanatic with a belt-knife managed to accomplish what Duergar, and Kalarr, and Crisen (and all their respective minions) had failed to do, all because of an unfortunate choice of dress. *Light of Heaven*, the Alban thought as he mentally reviewed the list again, *were there so many?*

Then all of his random thoughts jarred to an abrupt, shocked standstill as he strolled around a corner and took in his first view of Tuenafen harbor—and the things that had got there before him.

Battlerams. Three of them, for the love of . . .

Feeling like a cat gone mousing in an occupied kennel, Aldric slackened what had once been an eager pace and shaded his eyes with one hand, scrutinising the anchored warships sourly and remembering his encounter with the *Aalkhorst*. That memory was anything but reassuring.

No, not three, he corrected silently as another predatory shape slid with heavy grace around the sea-wall. Four. Four fully armored first-rate ships-of-the-line, each of whose seven steel-sheathed turrets contained a chain-geared repeating catapult capable of reducing an enemy vessel to matchwood and drifting splinters. He knew; he had seen what they could do.

Aldric watched the new arrival as she came into harbor. Although long maneuvering sweeps had been deployed from oarlocks near her waterline, they were extended clear of the water and served only to give the battleram the look of some monstrous, malevolent insect. Only her spritsail was rigged. But that small white sail was puffed like a pigeon's breast by a wind from astern the ship, despite the offshore breeze which raised choppy ripples and sent them straight toward the oncoming bow.

It appeared that, despite the Empire's stringent legislation against sorcery, the fleet's requested waiver of such restrictions was still effective. This warship, and perhaps her consorts as well, had a witch-wind charmed into her sails. She could go wherever she pleased, whenever she pleased, regardless of the irritating vagaries of real weather; and she could do it far, far faster than any honestly propelled vessel could hope to match.

Now if only he could see whose side these brutes were on . . .

But they had stowed their sails, struck their colors and displayed no marks of allegiance anywhere on their reptilian hides. There was a nameplate clamped to the flank armor of the new ship's hull, but that was of little use for two reasons: firstly, it would require a knowledge of the Imperial fleet from coastal tenders up, to work out whether Emperor or Warlord owned any given vessel; and secondly——

Aldric couldn't read Drusalan. Oh, speak it—at least in the formal mode—yes; that was straightforward enough. But the language was written in a different alphabet from that shared by Alban, Jouvaine, Vreijek—for no other reason than sheer perversity, he thought sometimes. And they only wrote characters for consonants; vowels were represented by dots, bars and chevrons, nothing more.

At least the merchant guilds had more sense. A swift glance along the waterfront revealed what he had come to check: a painted wooden sign above a doorway which bore the same crest as his credit scrip—and as that stamped into a great many bars of Talvalin gold. The glance was very quick indeed, for Aldric could feel the escort/spy close up behind him, doubtless watching for anything worth reporting back—such as excessive interest in routes of departure from the Empire. Well, he would have little to tell apart from the fact that Albans were unsettled by the presence of the military. Since that held true for most Imperial citizens as well, it was not information with a great deal of use.

Until he knew more about the whys and wherefores of what had brought the warships here at such an inopportune time, Aldric considered that it might be prudent if he got off the public street and awaited developments somewhere more secluded. Kathur's house was one such place—indeed, so far as Tuenafen was concerned, it was the only place he knew.

There was a splash and a clatter of anchor-chain from

the harbor; sailors yelled instructions at each other as they secured the new battleram at her moorings and began to warp her alongside the others. Aldric looked incuriously towards the men as he began to retrace his steps, then at the ship itself. Dear God, but she was huge!

The salt-stained carapace of armor had been thrown open in many places now, and two crewmen emerged from a hatch to unclip the vessel's nameplate and carry it below. By now he was close enough to see the three uncial characters which spelt out the warship's name, and to catch a brief glimpse of the geometric patterning of vowel values. It meant more to him as abstract art than as a written word, and he was reluctant even to hazard a guess at how it would be pronounced aloud.

Something like *Te'Na'R,* probably.

In the early evening a bank of fog came rolling in off the sea, and as it overlaid Tuenafen with a damp gray blanket the deep boom of a warning gong began to throb up from the harbor. Sitting cross-legged amid the rumpled quilts of Kathur's bed, Aldric listened to its sonorous single note and sipped at a glass of wine he did not want or need, trying far too late to ignore the warm and silky skin which pressed against his own, languid and apparently sated at long last. He was acutely aware of a sensation which might have been his own shame.

Kathur rolled lazily onto her back and scored one long-nailed finger up and down his naked thigh, watching him intently through the tangled fringe of her copper-gold hair as she inhaled the sweet smoke curling up from burners near the bed. Something about his expression made her giggle drowsily. *"Ka s'lai immau-an, t' eijo?"*

"Nothing's the matter with me!" The denial came out far too hard, far too fast. "Nothing at all." He was lying, and they both knew it. Aldric did not look down; the Drusalan's bronze-and-milk-white body was a definite, indeed an all-consuming distraction to a mind which already had more than enough to deal with. And Kathur, following the latest fashion of the Warlord's court in Drakkesborg, had blended *ymeth* with her favourite bedroom incense.

Sex had not been his intention when he returned from the harbor; far from it. The sight of four Imperial battle-rams of an uncertain provenance, and all that they suggested, had squelched any such thoughts as effectively as navel-deep immersion in a bath of ice-melt.

It had not been his intention when she stepped out of her bedroom just as he walked past in the corridor outside, even though in fairness he had already entertained the notion of a visit once or twice.

It had still not been his intention even when he saw what she was wearing: a low, clinging, sidesplit robe that blatantly flaunted her full-breasted, leggy beauty—even in bare feet she was a handspan taller than he was—and whose rich, not-quite-transparent satin clung like a crimson second skin and made it enticingly obvious that there was nothing but Kathur and perhaps a touch of costly perfume underneath.

But when she had reached out without a word and enfolded his face in palms and fingers and bent forward to lay a kiss upon his mouth, his ironclad celibacy had become a thing of wind and straw. In itself and in its apparent brevity the most chaste of gestures, that kiss had yet contained a probing pressure of her tongue between his lips and then the swiftest promissory nip of teeth, hinting at pleasures undefined but yet to come. After such a kiss even the sternest Imperial *politark* would have torn his holy books and smashed his holy ikons and gone a-running after her.

No; up to that point, when temptation had become more than fevered flesh and pounding blood could bear, he could lay hand on heart and swear that it had not been his intention to bed the Drusalan woman. But it had been Kathur's intention all along. *She* had bedded *him*—and had done so most efficiently.

Efficiently . . . ? Yes, that was the only word for it. All the others—pleasurably, inventively, exhaustingly—were true enough, but faded into insignificance beside the icy technical brilliance which she had displayed in bed. As if following the steps of a complex but much-practised dance—*is that what rankles, Aldric?*—she had known exactly when and how hard to employ the em-

phases of tongue and teeth and nails and closely-
clutching thighs.

Riding aids, he thought cynically. But it was the de-
tached skill with which she had aroused him that would
not leave his mind—as if she had regarded his initial
reluctance as a defiant challenge to be overcome, nothing more. For just once, almost by accident amid the
sweaty squirming of their love-making, he had chanced
to stare for three full seconds straight up into her eyes.
That memory remained with him, and would for a long,
long time. Because there had been nothing in those eyes
but the spasmodic glitter of physical pleasure. That was
all. The rest was an emotional blank.

Even Gueynor, once of Valden and now mistress of
Seghar, had felt more for him than Kathur did—and *she*
had been paying for her own much-loved uncle's quick
and painless death. Something of which Aldric had not
learned until much later.

Efficiently. That was indeed what rankled, what had
created the tiny flutter of uncertainty beneath his breastbone. The flutter which might have been guilt at the
ease with which he had let himself be manipulated, but
which was much, much more. Suspicion burgeoning to
certainty that there was another purpose behind what
she had done to him, and for him, and only incidentally
for herself; a purpose that went beyond simple lust or
curiosity or—and he would have accepted the reason
gratefully, had it been true—boredom on a foggy afternoon.

With Gueynor or with Kyrin—*Kyrin, O my lady, O
my love,* the words came back to him again like a religious chant, *where are you now?*—he would have been
lying here, but cuddled together with a quiet affection
he would never feel for this Drusalan woman. Kyrin had
been right when once she had called him a romantic.
Because Kathur made love—and the word "love" was
itself a lie—like a whore; all was sensation, nothing was
emotion, because emotion and tenderness took time and
to a whore time was money. Aldric's mind flashed to the
first time he had seen her, that night when she stalked
into the tavern common-room in her furs and with her

guards to either side. He had thought then that she was either noble or a top-rank courtesan; now his opinion was more certain.

"Ai, irr'hem ymau tleiyan." The spiked fingernails coursed his spine. "Care killed a cat, my Kourgath. What's troubling you?"

He shivered—only a marble statue would not—and set his glass aside before suddenly-trembling hands spilled its contents all across his lap. Not, he thought with another luxurious shudder, that such an accident would inconvenience Kathur in the slightest. Not in her present mood.

"Dakkoyo-do, h'lau-ei," he said quickly, releasing himself from her embrace. "I told you: nothing's the matter. I was thinking, that's all."

"Ehreth kraiy'r hla, Kourgath-tlei. Then think about me." She made the suggestion in a voice like cinnamon and hot honey as she relaxed into an inviting sprawl of naked limbs. Aldric looked, and swallowed hard, and closed his eyes and took a deep breath—instantly regretting the last as a double lungful of dreamsmoke hit him, daubing rainbow patterns across the insides of his eyelids and through the echoing caverns of a suddenly all-too-spacious skull.

"Doamne diu!" he snarled softly. It needed no translation—one blasphemous expletive tends to sound very much like another—and Kathur laughed at him, then sprinkled another pinch of *ymeth* on the nearest censer. "Lady, stop that . . . !" Aldric began to protest, then turned it into a half-hearted shrug. "I'm not as used to this stuff as you are."

"But it should take your mind off those battlerams in the harbor."

"Battlerams?" His face was a masterpiece of innocent inquiry, a reflex reaction that was entirely wasted because her spy had been with him at the time and had apparently managed to make his report already.

"Battlerams," she repeated laconically.

"The Imperial military doesn't like Albans much," Aldric said, as if that explained everything.

"To the Black Pit with the military! I like at least one Alban very much indeed."

"Thank you, my lady. But . . . whose ships are they anyway?"

Kathur's mouth went very thin for maybe half a second and her heavy-lidded eyes flicked wide open, but Aldric, staring pensively at the crawling glow of sparks in one of the incense burners, missed it all. "Curiosity," she said carefully, "killed a cat, *hlens'l.*"

"Care, now curiosity," Aldric smiled, a smile as bright and false as paste jewels. "What have the Empire's proverb-makers got against cats anyway?"

Kathur didn't seem particularly amused. "And why the sudden interest in battlerams?" she wanted to know. "You've been fretting over something ever since you came back from the harbor. Tell me about it; a sympathetic ear might make you feel better."

"And sympathetic lips?" It sounded evasive even to him, and Kathur didn't deign to respond; she merely stared, and waited for an answer. Aldric met that stare for maybe a minute; then he gave up, lay down with his head cradled on crossed arms and told her . . .

Not what she wanted to know, but what he wanted her to know, which was not the same thing at all. Nearly— but not quite. He knew from previous experience that a carefully edited version of the truth sounded more convincing than the best-thought-out lie. And right now he had no honor-bound compunctions about misleading her. None at all.

"In the spring of this year," he began, "I was a passenger aboard an Elherran merchant galion. Unarmed, of course; it's well known that none of the Elherran vessels carry weapons. But we were attacked nonetheless—by a battleram. She was sailing under the Grand Warlord's crest and colors, but I doubt that had much to do with what happened. Her commander claimed that the galion was running contraband; we were somewhat shot up by then and in no mood to argue. But the marine cadre who boarded searched the Elherran from keel to mizen top without finding a thing. So did the *hautmarin* apologise for his high-handed action and offer recompense for the damage? Did he, hell! Arrogant bastard didn't give a damn!"

"Calm down, Kourgath. It doesn't matter now."

"No. Not now. Of course not. You're right. But can you wonder that I was . . . uneasy, shall we say?—when I found that pack of bloody commerce raiders in the harbor?"

"I don't wonder at all. But it's better not to wonder about what *They* do—not aloud in public anyway. *They* have many ears. And contacts in the most unlikely places." Kathur's lips curved in a small, cold smile redolent of many things, and she studied his face for a while as she toyed absently with the silver crest-collar encircling his throat. "You worry too much," she concluded, and her voice carried a mocking severity. "And about other people's problems. That's a bad thing. Positively unhealthy while you're still within the Empire's borders. So we'll have to find something to occupy that over-busy mind of yours. Something to help you relax."

"Other than *this!*" It was perhaps as well that most of the more subtle nuances of Aldric's intonation were muffled by his own right bicep, so that all Kathur heard was a real or feigned incredulity. That, and the widening of his one visible eye, was enough to make her laugh aloud.

"This, as you so coyly put it, is mere diversion. A pleasant way to . . ." her words faltered for the merest beat—an intake of breath as of something almost but not spoken that the Alban failed to notice—and then resumed smoothly, ". . . to pass the time. And also, if you want to view it so, a way for me to convey a little of my gratitude. And a way which you seemed to appreciate."

Aldric had heard reasoning of that nature before, and didn't much like to hear it again; but given the present circumstances, he forbore to comment.

Kathur nodded, rolled over in bed and reached for a slender silken cord which ran up and out of sight through a brass-rimmed hole in the ceiling; tugged it twice, then twice again, and lay back as if exhausted by the effort. Aldric had watched her, despite his other reservations enjoying the way her sleek body moved; now, as she flopped against the pillows, he hid a smile. "By the looks of you," he said virtuously, "shuttering those incense burners might be a good idea."

* * *

For just a moment Kathur glared at him, ready to be
angry if his baiting should be more than just a joke. She
had taken quite enough criticism of her private affairs
and conduct from her own brother—who didn't know
the half of it—without more of the same from this, this
hlensyarl who was no more than a part of her work. She
willingly conceded that he was both a better-looking and
a more enjoyable part than many who had preceded
him; but ultimately that concession changed nothing.

Her instructions had been concise, straightforward and
most certainly not open to other interpretations. *Find.
Identify. Hold.* They had been delivered twofold, as was
the custom; the first no more than a cursory cipher borne
on a pigeon's leg, but the second . . . Ah yes, the second.
That had been carried by no less than a weary, dirty
horseman in the yellow crest-coat of the Falcon couriers.
The very use of a Falcon had told her much about how
this mission was regarded even before she read what he
had brought her, sealed by lead in a leather pouch.

The whole thing had Voord's touch about it.

The arrogance which had employed a despatch-rider
forbidden to all but the Imperial Household; that sense
for the dramatic which had prompted the risky gesture.
And the arid, clinical precision of the prose which told
her in graphic—no, Father of Fires burn it, pornographic—
detail, what it was she would be expected to do. But
then, that was Voord's way.

He had always been fastidious, had Voord; excessively
neat in all that he did, no matter how perverse. Kathur's
mind unwillingly recalled the whimpering, agonized, ec-
static night of her recruitment by the Vlechan, and she
shuddered with revulsion at the memory even as conscious effort crushed it back down into the dark and
dirty part of her subconscious where it was confined.

Then he had been *kortagor;* now he was *hautheisart,*
promoted again at the end of summer for something
which even yet remained unspecified. What it might have
been, the Drusalan woman didn't know and would not
dare to guess . . . because if the rumours spoke the truth,
Voord was stranger now than ever.

And if so, then what did that make her?

The thoughts tumbled through her mind like images glimpsed on the flicking pages of a thumbed book, so swift as to approach the subliminal. And during those few seconds the Alban's one-eyed gaze remained locked with hers until at last she looked away, almost flinching from the expression on that part of his face which she could see. It was an expression Kathur had not seen before and would as soon not see again, for it seemed cynical, knowing and cold, and it made her feel truly apprehensive of him for the first time in their brief acquaintance.

No. More. It made her feel afraid.

And yet there was another side to the coin, another reason for her to be frightened which had nothing to do with any threat Kourgath-*eijo* might pose to her. Rather the reverse. There was a warm, delicious quivering within her that was more than the familiar aftermath of loving. Much more; she knew that sensation well enough to recognise that this was somehow different. It went beyond the physical, beyond a fever in the flesh and into something which she knew was impossible in so short a time. But which was also unmistakably true.

She was becoming involved.

It was a sense such as she had not felt for any man since . . . since a very long time ago. A sense of responsibility, a feeling that might in time become—Kathur shied away from letting the word form in her brain—love. It was a sense she neither understood nor wanted.

The idea of disobedience crossed her mind for the first time ever, and brought in its wake a nauseating spasm of terror. Disobedience would mean a reckoning later—with Lord-Commander Voord.

But if she obeyed, as she had always done before; if she followed her orders, as she had always done before . . . Then she would have to meet her own eyes in the mirror forever afterwards, and admit to the guilt and the betrayal and the dishonor she would see reflected there.

She was thinking the unthinkable. And she did not know why.

But had she thought to search amid the tangle of Aldric's discarded clothing, the Drusalan woman might have found a reason for such unlikely thoughts as those which troubled her so deeply. For there, concealed from sight in a tunic pocket yet close enough for her to touch had she known of its presence, was the spellstone of Echainon.

Had she known, and had she touched, she would have found the crystal's surface strangely warm against her skin. Not hot, not painful, but comforting as the sun on a summer day or the body of a lover in the night. And had she thought to listen she might even now have heard the song of the stone, a melodious humming half-heard on the outer edges of awareness; the sound never heard by concentration, only by chance.

Had she known, or heard, or touched, or merely looked, she would have found the crystal suffused with a misty blue radiance from the hair-fine spiralling of sapphire flame deep down at its core; and that above all would have answered her unspoken question as to the source of her strange thoughts. For the spellstone's light pulsed with a rhythm Kathur would have recognised at once.

It was the beat of her own heart.

Two men walked slowly through the twilight along a fog-bound road.

Slowly, for one was no longer so strong as his burly appearance might have suggested, and his face wore the gray, haggard look of a man recovering from a grave illness.

Slowly, because the other was white-bearded, old, and moved as if every one of his many years was a lead weight borne in the pack strapped to his drooping shoulders. He leaned heavily on the black walking-stave in his right hand—yet at the same time appeared to cringe away from any but the most necessary contact with it. As if the thing was hot and had burned him painfully, and was only awaiting its chance to do so again. There were beads of moisture on his forehead which had not condensed from the fog.

Suddenly—but with a note in his voice which bespoke resigned anticipation—he cried out and dropped the staff with a clatter to the ground. Both sounds were flat and dead, muted by the fog-thick air. He stared at the fallen staff with something close to loathing on his bearded

face, but made no move to pick it up. Instead he looked
wearily at his companion.

"Again?" asked ar Korentin. There was sympathy in
his voice.

"Again." Gemmel rubbed his hands together, trying
to soothe away the burning nerve-deep pain. "It keeps
on drawing power. On, and on. Never so much at once
as to do me lasting harm, always with enough rest between times for me to recover. And then . . . !" One
booted foot shifted as though he considered kicking the
fallen Dragonwand; then settled again as he plainly
thought better of the idea.

"Why? What does it want with so much power?"

"Your guess, Dewan, is as good as mine. And I don't
know. It no longer obeys me. You saw that on the beach
in Alba."

"Then give it what it wants," said Dewan savagely.
"Give it more than it can swallow. Choke it to death!"

"No! I think not. I have no idea what Ykraith's capacity for stolen energy might be—and I'm frightened to
find out. Because I might not survive the experience."

"Then . . ." The Vreijek hesitated, his brow furrowing
as he tried to make sense of the alien concepts of sorcery
in a mind not trained to its rules of logic, before committing his idea to the irrecoverable spoken word. "Then
give. Not much: just that little you say it always takes,
that it has always taken before, despite all you do to
prevent it. This time, don't resist."

"An interesting proposition."

"Try it. What have you got to lose?"

"My life, perhaps." With an open hand Gemmel fore-
stalled Dewan's protest—if protest it was, and not another untutored attempt to verbalise the workings of
magic. "But as you suggest—I'll try it. Because anything
is better than this. I daren't use the Dragonwand and
I'm growing afraid to carry it—but I can't just walk away
and leave it. Not here." He stooped to recover the spellstave, but in stooping caught an odd look of puzzlement
on Dewan's face and hesitated: "What's the matter
now?"

"A thought, no more. Before you volunteer the power

it so obviously wants, shouldn't you try to work out an answer to what I asked before? *Why?*"

Gemmel jerked his hand away from the Dragonwand as if it had changed to a venomous serpent, and the glare he directed at ar Korentin was equally venomous. "You contradict yourself as easily as my son!" he snapped. "Do . . . then don't do. Make up your mind!"

His earlier reply to that same question—that Dewan's answer would be as right or wrong as his own—was not . . . *quite* . . . true. Because Gemmel's mind's eye could recall the summoning on Dunacre Beach as clearly as if its colossal bulk was hanging overhead right now. A summoning whose form was not that which he had intended, but which was most shockingly appropriate to the name and nature of the talisman which he had used. A dragon. Summoned by Ykraith.

The Dragonwand.

Gemmel lifted the spellstave with his left hand—the one which didn't hurt—and stared at the design which patterned it from end to end as if seeing the inlay of adamant and gold for the first time. Or as if gaining a new insight from its shape. And he wondered.

Then in fear and hope, not knowing which feeling was the stronger, he supported the talisman's dark length on the palms of both his outstretched hands and built the structure of an opening-charm in the forefront of his mind. And let his power, that concentrated inner selfness which made him a sorcerer first and foremost, rather than a harper or a scholar or so many other things—although he was all of these and more—let his power surge through the opened channel into the fireshot dragon-shape that was Ykraith.

This time there was no pain. Only a sensation of warmth on his open hands, and a slight tiredness. That was all. Gemmel raised his eyebrows and turned to ar Korentin with the beginnings of a smile on his face. It was a wary smile, but for all that it was a smile which the Vreijek felt justified in echoing.

"Was I right?" he wanted to know.

"Well done, the untrained mind! Maybe sometimes I'm too subtle for my own good. Yes. You were right.

It didn't hurt me—and it didn't drain more than I offered, even though the channelling was wide open."

"So what use can it make of the power? Have you answered that yet?"

"I think so. Dewan, you know as well as I what this talisman is called; and where it came from. And what else was there."

Ar Korentin's jaw sagged slightly and his gaze jerked south and west, towards the distant sea lost in the mist and the yet-more-distant island lost over the unseen horizon. "Ymareth! *Vakk'schh ke'hagh trahann'r da?*"

"No, not awakening. It is awake already; indeed, it has slept lightly if at all since the day that Aldric took this," he patted the Dragonwand, "from the Cavern of Firedrakes on Techaur. That young man gained a deal more than he can imagine when Ymareth—"

The spellstave hummed softly, a vibration more felt in the air than heard aloud, and he fell silent. Both men stared at the talisman, Dewan with awe and wonder, Gemmel with anticipation. Neither was disappointed.

There was a soft, expulsive sound like that of a great breath held in too long, and white force burst from the crystalline flame of its carven dragonhead to hang like a captive star between them, bleaching the fog to silver upon which their shadows were smeared with the clarity of charcoal on new paper. A surge of power which even Dewan felt pulsed outward, an unseen ripple in an unseen pond. An instant later there was only the afterglow of a bolt of energy which had ripped through the fog with stunning speed and fled out of sight to leave the dull day duller yet. But both had seen the direction of its flight. South and west. Towards the sea and that which lay beyond.

"Lord God," breathed Dewan ar Korentin, with respect and disbelief all mingled with the oath.

"No," Gemmel corrected him, and if he smiled the sad smile which his voice suggested, it was gone when Dewan saw his face again. "Not 'Lord God' at all. Lord Dragon."

The island had never been an inviting place, not even in the time when it was lush and green with growing things. That time was long past. Now it was black and gray and desolate. What few trees remained more than a memory were charcoal stumps. All else was ash and blasted naked rock.

A thin plume of smoke drifted lazily from the island's solitary mountain, vented in gusts like exhaled breath from the yawning crater where once its tapered peak had been. But there was no other sign of a convulsion in the bowels of the earth: no black rivers of once-molten rock, none of the great bubble-pitted cinders flung out by such activity. There was only the aftermath of heat.

And an air of expectation.

As the short evening of late autumn drew night towards it like a cloak, a star began to brighten in the northern sky where no star should have been. As it brightened, so it moved, until this star that was no star was sweeping across the heavens in a glare of light that laid hard-edged black shadows behind wave-crests and fire-scoured rocks alike. Had any been insane enough to anchor in the island's bay, they would have seen the not-star descend in a great hissing parabola, dragging a tail of silver flame in its wake for all the world like a burning missile shot from some impossibly huge catapult, and they would have seen it plunge with unerring accuracy into the smoking crater, and they would have heard . . .

Nothing.

The silence was absolute; a silence that could almost be touched, as if it were made of heavy fabric. In the course of that long silence the true stars began to glitter in the void, a scattering of splintered diamonds strewn broadcast on a mantle of black velvet.

Ymareth reared from the throat of the hollow mountain with a whisper of iron scales and the single hard, bright clank of a talon striking stone. Wings blacker than the night were unfurled in the trembling air—a huge, leisurely stretching which could seldom be indulged in the confines of the cavern far below. The firedrake's head curved up and back on its great sinuous neck, between the canopy of the wings, and was still.

Ymareth waited for the dawn.

*   *   *

The shudder came from nowhere and from everywhere, a single jolt that was violent enough to bring Aldric's teeth together with a click. His eyes opened very wide, and had he been able to glimpse their pupils in a mirror he would have seen the drug-shrunken pinpricks dilate to huge black discs which were set fair to swallow all the gray-green pigmentation of the irises around them. But he did not need to see, for he could feel—and it was a feeling that he had known before.

Then it had been caused by his own nightmares, dreams strong enough to shock him from his own determined drunkenness. But this sudden surge of heat, as though hot oil was running through the marrow of his bones: this was stronger still. And he didn't even know the reason why.

But one thing he did know was that despite the sweet fumes of *ymeth* in his lungs, despite the strong wine coursing through his blood, despite what should have been a heavy lassitude in all his muscles and which was instead a tingling of urgency, he was in control of his own mind again.

And with that knowledge came the shameful awareness of something he had chosen to ignore, or to blame on other things. His own monumental stupidity! He had been duped, he had been dazzled, he had been trapped—and there had never truly been any excuse for it, though he had always found one.

His own failings. Lord God! They were vices that any man—his mind defined it sickeningly: any *honorable* man—should have ignored, as he might the pain of wounds or fear in battle. For the sake of nothing more than his own pride and private dignity.

Aldric felt the queasiness of self-reproach too long held in check come gurgling to the back of his throat like the dregs of bitter wine. His gaze shot to the silken cord which Kathur had pulled—twice, then twice again: a signal without doubt. But how long ago? Seconds? Minutes? Hours? No, a minute at the very most, for he could still remember that strange, reluctant softness stealing into the Drusalan woman's hard blue eyes just as she turned her face away from his. A minute? He flung himself out of the bed and scrabbled for his clothes.

Kathur rolled over and raised her head to stare at him. Without any surprise. She had been crying, and she was crying now, the great tears gleaming like gemstones below those sapphire eyes which Aldric would have doubted had the ability to weep. And on her face—that beautiful, imperious, wanton face—was an expression of aching loss and desolation such as the Alban had seen only once before.

Go now, Kyrin-ain. *The words were all said long ago.*

"So you know."

He stamped savagely into a boot and began to fight with its lacings. "Yes-I-*do!*" The last word came out on a grunt of effort. "And I should have known it long ago!" There was something very close to panic in the way he moved—and it was a panic only barely held in check, for when part of his shirt caught on something he took no time to work it free but simply jerked with all his strength. There was a quick rending noise and he swore viciously in Alban. As he tucked the ripped shirt into his leather riding-breeches, he turned a narrow watchful stare towards Kathur. "When will they come for me?" It was an idle question, and he had not expected an answer, but . . .

"At—at the Hour of the Fox."

Aldric lifted an unamused eyebrow. "How apt, dear Vixen. How bloody droll. And your own idea, I suppose?"

"No, I . . ."

"But that's—" he hurriedly converted the clumsy Drusalan reckoning in his head, "—ten at night. Two hours from now. So how was I to be kept here? By you? Or by . . ." His eyes flicked once towards the slender signal-cord, and his voice hardened. "Who did you call?"

"One of my servants." Kathur paused, but once she had begun the weight of her own guilty confession drove her into saying more. "My—my bodyguard; the man you met before."

"Ahh . . ." It was no more than an exhalation of breath, but it came out past an icy smile which grew fractionally wider once Aldric had lifted Widowmaker and looped her shoulder-strap over his head. There was a minute click as he thumbed the *taiken*'s safety-collar clear of her scabbard mouth. "Then I might just test a theory which crossed my mind when we met before. But only if he gets in my way. Because I'm leaving, lady. Now." A final glance about the room confirmed that nothing had been left behind—except for the large measure of self-respect which would take him such a long time to regain. Aldric turned to go, and then looked back. "Anyway, he's late. Just when did you expect him to appear?"

The bedroom door behind him was wrenched open, and above the sudden frantic clamour of alarms inside his head he heard Kathur's response quite clearly:

"Now."

Aldric didn't pause to marvel at that perfect cue. He convulsed sideways at right-angles to the line from his back to the doorway, and he did so with the thickness of a wolfskin vest to spare. Literally.

Something monstrous plucked a puff of black fur from the right shoulder of his *coyac* just as it wrenched out from underneath the blow, and he heard the *whutt!* of parting air as that same something continued down to smash into the floor.

It was a mace: a flanged, iron-headed horror on a haft almost as long as he was tall, and as it tore free of the floor with a groan of raptured timbers he could see that it was being wielded as easily as he might use a riding-quirt. This footsoldier's bludgeon was meant to flatten fully-armored men like beetles, and if it struck squarely against his unprotected body it would . . .

But that didn't make any sense! Kathur had taken a deal of trouble to hold him here of what amounted to his own free will, presumably to deliver him intact and healthy to . . . someone. So why was this hulking servant so set on smearing him across the floor? Jealousy? Never mind wondering why—he was trying to do it and that was enough.

Aldric flinched clear of another ponderous swing; this one ploughed through a dressing-table, stinging him with splintered wood and the perfumed shards of cosmetic jars. His eyes went cold. Long years of training took the place of an instinctive fear-reaction and his right hand flicked to Widowmaker's hilt, gripped, drew, and then faltered with no more than a double span of blade clear of the scabbard.

Yet completing that draw would have meant a certain kill.

Completing that draw would have extended into *achrankai,* the inverted cross, first of the classic *taiken* forms and a movement so ingrained by constant practice that it had become almost a reflex.

Completing that draw . . .

Would have whipped an unseen blur of steel beneath the servant's chin and down between his eyes. Would have opened his throat spine-deep and split his face asunder from hairline to chin in a single splattering instant long before he could have dodged or blocked. Or even realized what was happening.

Completing that draw would have solved many problems. So why not?

So why? Aldric shook his head as if dislodging a cobweb and looked again at Kathur. "Call him off, lady!" There was no fear in his voice, nothing that might have been prompted by cowardice but a faint, elusive undertone that might have been compassion. And yet the woman said nothing. "Do it! *Teii'aj hah, tai-ura!*"

Kathur returned the stare with blank eyes for just a moment, seeming not to notice his sudden perfect command of High Drusalan. Then she surveyed the tableau that was her shattered bedroom: all harsh light and shadow now, the bright corridor beyond the open door a stark contrast to the intimately dim interior. One of the gilded lamps had been upset, and the thick sweetness of its scented oil was another element of the nightmare which assaulted all her senses. She blinked.

And the stone of Echainon went dull. Perhaps it was the woman's sudden distraction towards her own possessions; perhaps it was Aldric's concern with survival more than personal honor; perhaps it was the weariness of a firedrake and a sorcerer in places far away. Perhaps it was none of these things. But when the stone's light died it was result, not reason, that was important.

Kathur blinked again—stared at Aldric—then said crisply, "Commander Voord be damned. Kill him."

A heartbeat's worth of utter shock slowed the Alban's

reaction, and maybe the man with the mace had been deliberately, deceptively clumsy in his earlier attacks. Because this time when the great iron cudgel moved, it moved far faster than it had ever done before.

And Aldric dropped on the spot.

If he had moved in any direction other than straight down the weapon would have caught him—and pulped him—somewhere along its horizontal arc; even then he felt a tug at his hair which was not the wind of its passing but the metal shaft itself. The mace-head had gouged deeply, uselessly, across the wall where he had been standing; but it would have gouged there anyway, heedless of the meagre resistance offered by his chest.

"You fool! Kill him now!" There was ugliness in Kathur's voice, the audible equivalent of that expression he had not been meant to see, and as he rolled to his feet with Isileth Widowmaker fully drawn at last, Aldric's lips curled back from his teeth in a snarl of almost animal intensity. It might . . . must . . . have been that wild scramble across the floor which lifted the pelt of the black wolfskin *coyac;* but for just an instant its fur was bristling across the Alban's shoulders as though it were a part of him.

And for that same instant—a freezing, burning, malicious and utterly dishonorable sliver of time—Aldric's mind was flooded with just one consideration: whether he could spare the fraction of a second needed for a snap-step right and the lashing backhand which would carve a memento of his company on Kathur's face that she would carry to the grave.

Then he squashed the notion, dismissing it. Because it was unworthy of a *kailin-eir;* because it was unAlban; because it was unTalvalin. And because consideration said he couldn't spare the time to do it after all.

The moon is only five days clear of new, dear Aldric. The accusing voice inside his head had Gemmel's intonation. *What would you have done had it been nearer full?*

Aldric exhaled through his nose with a sound like an angry tomcat's hiss. He couldn't have said against whom the anger was directed, and had no wish to dwell on it. Circumstances forbade that, for the servant was ready for him with the mace poised in what, had it been a sword, would have been middle guard center. He eyed the man's posture with a gaze that was still flinty with concentration but which had lost the gem-like killing glitter. It had leached out—or something was holding it well in check. Who or what, and why, he neither knew nor questioned. "Don't blame me for this," he said in the Jouvaine language, his tone almost regretful.

Then he moved.

Isileth Widowmaker thrust out as precisely as a pointing finger, in low line beneath all the blocks and parries that might have been made from mid-guard, and met only the slightest tug of resistance from firm flesh.

She drove deep, and twisted half around as she withdrew.

The big servant's eyes bulged from his skull and his mouth gaped wide even though he was too shocked to utter more than an unstructured whine. The mace was louder, clanking against the floor as his hands released it to scrabble at ruptured tissue. Then he too fell sideways to the floor. Aldric watched him fall, then flicked blood from his sword with a whipping, economic gesture and returned the *taiken* to its scabbard with an arid whisper of metal on wood. He was smiling.

Through the scarlet-shot gray mist of pain clouding his vision, the fallen servant saw that smile and knew the reasoning which lay behind it. His body, uselessly tensed against the follow-through that would finish him, relaxed. There would be no killing blow. He tried to smile in turn; only a small, twisted grimace, but enough to show that he understood.

He was meant to live.

Widowmaker would make no widow tonight. She had pierced the Drusalan's leg rather than his body, and had passed outside the bone to avoid the great blood-vessel which ran through the muscles of the inner thigh. It was a fierce wound, and one which the man would remember for a long time: the sort of injury which aches at the onset of damp weather. But he would be alive to remember it, and feel it ache. And he would recover.

Eventually . . . but not now. Now was for bleeding, and for hurting—and for realising that the dead do neither.

The man's smile went slack and crooked as his senses left him, but Aldric had seen the faltering expression and he nodded, once. His shoulders sagged a little with relief; something which had shown already in his smile and had been recognised as such. Relief at his own survival; and relief that Isileth Widowmaker, that ancient and sometimes wilful blade, had done no more than he intended her to do.

Kathur was still staring at him as he straightened his back, but now her eyes were blank and held as little emotion as the sapphire gemstones they so much resembled. Her mouth worked, trying to form words or maybe curses, but no sound emerged.

Aldric passed one hand across the ruffled fur covering his shoulder, and the action was not so much that of settling a disarrayed garment as of stroking something alive. He remembered, coldly and calmly, how he had wanted to mark this woman. To hurt her. It was like the memory of actions in a dream, without weight in waking life. There was a place for such behaviour, and a time, but it was neither here nor now. Seghar citadel under the Geruath overlords was both long ago and far away; but as a small shudder crawled through the Alban's body he realized that it was not yet long or far enough.

Inclining his head curtly towards Kathur the Vixen, Aldric walked from her room without a backward glance.

Thus he did not see the *telek* snatched from a hiding-place under the mattresses and levelled at his back.

Nor did he see the weapon waver and then drop from hands which were as powerless to squeeze its trigger as they were to stem a flow of silent tears. Had he seen, or had he heard a sob, it might have made some slight difference; or it might not. But he did not see, and did not hear, and it did not.

Somewhere in the too-quiet house a clock chimed the triple note which marked the turning of another hour. Unlike their Alban counterparts, Imperial Drusalan timepieces did not—indeed, by reason of the named hours, could not—strike a number; they merely drew attention to whatever image was indicated by their single ornate pointer. Aldric did not enter the room to look. He already knew as much as any Alban ever wanted to know about the clumsy, inexact system. But because he did not look, he did not know what hour it was. Or how much time he had to spare for making his escape.

Two hours from now, he had told Kathur. But he had slept a dreamsmoke doze with the sweet smell of *ymeth* in his lungs and her hands and mouth upon his body, and at the instant he spoke the words it had not been two hours but much less than one. And from the striking of the clock he had no time at all. Those chimes had signalled the end of the Hour of the Cat.

And the start of the Hour of the Fox.

Kathur's head drooped over the discarded *telek* and tears coursed down her cheeks, falling onto the weapon's polished maple stock where they humped on the lustrous wood like pearls of great price. She stared at their translucence as if she had never seen a tear before. Not such tears as these. She did not know why she wept, unless it was in fear. The cry of the distant harbor gong rang mournfully in her ears—a one-note song of warning—and Kathur knew she had good cause to be afraid.

Hautheisart Voord was not known for his tolerance towards those who had failed him. And as if her thoughts had power to summon demons, she heard soft feet in the corridor outside.

Kathur looked up, saw the flitting of shadows beyond the door and reached out with one hand for the robe of crimson satin which was now such an inadequate covering. She was wrapped in the flimsy garment as best she could contrive when the first *taulath* drifted like smoke into her room. In the space of a single intake of breath another had joined him: both clad from head to heel in a close-fitting charcoal gray that was almost black and which blended most unnaturally into the shadows near the wall.

Hooded masks left only a narrow strip of facial skin exposed—and their eyes, which to Kathur were like those of night-stalking reptiles. Those eyes stared at her, and for a moment it was not difficult to read the expressions flickering within them, for they studied—no, they consumed—a woman whose single garment exposed or emphasised far more than it concealed.

And a woman whose right hand gripped an Alban *telek* with every appearance of knowing how to use it.

The *tulathin* exchanged significant glances, but they did not come any closer. Nor did they say anything to her, although it was plain despite the masks that they had not expected to find Kathur alone. The wounded and unconscious man sprawled on the floor quite as plainly did not count.

Then there were more footfalls, and these were not soft—they were the firm, decisive steps of one who by reason of power and authority had no need for secrecy. No order was spoken aloud, but each *taulath* shifted with disciplined precision, flanking the doorway; they paused one beat, then snapped to attention and executed the rhythmic movements of a full parade salute. The hard smack of open palm on chest and thigh sounded like a premonition of Kathur's future. And then only if that future was kind.

A back-lit silhouette paused deliberately in the doorway for dramatic effect before crossing the threshold, and lamplight danced in sparkling motes from silvered rank-marks on a vermilion helmet as this third man turned his head slowly to survey the room. The helmet's deep cheek-guards, nasal and lowering peak effectively masked his features, but Kathur had no need to see his face to know who he was.

"Well, my dear lady." *Hautheisart* Voord spoke with a deceptive softness. "And where is he?"

Seconds crawled past, eon-slow, before Kathur could swallow enough terror for her acid-soured mouth to form the words of a reply. "Gone," she said. What else was there to say? "He realized—somehow—that he was being kept here." Then in mitigation, "But it was only minutes ago: I was able to hold him until then . . ."

Voord stared at her, saying nothing, eyes unreadable through the jagged shadows filling his helmet. "So. Then you tried to be clever rather than practical after all." Another dreadful silence. Then he turned, ignoring her. "Tagen, Garet, hear me: is the perimeter secured?"

"Sir!" The response was simultaneous, that of automata.

"Then go. Both of you. Trawl the nets and bring any

catch to . . . to the harbor. To *Teynaur*. And sail at dawn—whether I am there or not. Understood?"

"Sir!" Another salute and they were gone. Kathur watched their departure with resigned, sick despair in her eyes. The troopers were familiar to her: Voord's honor guard, men who accompanied him everywhere. The executors of his will. Their dismissal was an insult like a slap in the face. She was no threat. Nobody.

Nothing.

The street had been dark and silent, swaddled by layers of gray fog. A figure emerging from the shadows at the far side of the street had walked with quiet purpose towards the shuttered façade of Kathur's house; a house identified at last as the culmination and the goal of a long, weary quest. The figure was cloaked and hooded— nameless, faceless, sexless. But there was the merest suggestion of a sword's outline beneath the folds of that heavy cloak, and the faint scraping of metal that was the sound of armor.

Then the silent stillness was shattered like a flawed glass mirror by the quick hard beat of hooves on stone, and a man on horseback erupted from the stable entry near the house at near-enough full gallop. Before the hooded one could do more than flatten for safety against the nearest wall, the black horse's rider had gathered his mount and slewed it around in a metallic slither as iron shoes all but lost their grip on the slick pavement. Then man and horse were past and away in a swirl of sound and speed.

The figure by the wall straightened rumpled garments and still more rumpled dignity, stared for a few thoughtful seconds in the horseman's wake, then studied the blank house-front as if considering whether to enter and possibly become embroiled in whatever was going on there. A fold of the cloak was flicked aside; and now the presence of both sword and armor was more than mere suggestion.

Two gray-clad men flitted down from neighbouring rooftops, crouched warily for a bare instant and then flicked into the house through a front door that was plainly left unlocked for just that purpose. Unseen, unsuspected and concealed by the fog-dense shadows, an outline made vague and uncertain by the mantling of a too-large cloak watched with fascination—but wisely made no attempt to interfere.

Especially when a third man, helmeted and clad in full splint-mail, stalked arrogantly towards and inside the house.

"Give me that." Voord's right hand, gloved with sable leather and red-enamelled steel, was already extended palm uppermost as if a refusal was so unlikely as to be unworthy of his consideration.

But such a consideration had already passed through Kathur's mind with the speed and brilliance of a lightning-flash: not merely refusal, but *use!* Now, suddenly, without any hint of warning. The *telek* was already loaded and cocked, its safety mechanism disengaged, and the crook of her first and second fingers had already exerted three of the required five-pound pull. It would shoot on one pressure, and there was no need even to aim.

And the thought of that two-pound pull turned her belly sick. She could no more kill a human being—even one so patently inhuman as Voord—than she could turn the weapon on herself. And that was something which might be preferable to Voord's company in this next hour. The possibility and the chance of success were gone now, all gone; only acquiescence remained. Kathur's thumb secured the safetyslide; then she reversed the *telek* and laid it softly into the *hautheisart*'s waiting grasp.

His fingers closed, and with the weapon's bore pointing at her Kathur half-expected to feel a dart strike home even before she had let it go. But there was no dart. Instead Voord hefted the *telek*'s weight, and its sculpted stock settled as snugly into his hand as a falcon onto a familiar wrist. Carved and shaped for a right-handed grip, it fitted well, and he looked at it with something as close to admiration as any Imperial officer would grant to a thing of Alban manufacture.

"Very fine." He was speaking mostly to himself. "Yes. Very fine indeed. But then the Albans always were good at creating things to kill each other." His eyes met those of the woman and locked with them, like a snake with a sparrow or a weasel with a mouse, and though there was a smile on his lips it did not warm those eyes at all. "Tell me . . . does it work?"

Now the dart . . . Kathur's body spasmed in anticipation of the tearing impact and her eyes snapped shut in a useless reflex that was no defence at all against the death she faced. Only when nothing happened did their painted lids flutter open again, reluctantly; she was terrified lest any movement at all would invite the response she dreaded, but more terrified still to remain in the dark.

"I said, does it work?"

"I . . ."

"Does it work?"

Her gaze dared to tear away from the weapon's blank, black muzzle, but Voord's own eyes were as implacable. Whatever answer she gave would be the wrong one.

"Does it work?"

"Ohhh . . . dear God, I don't know!"

Voord's teeth showed briefly in a shark's smile. "Then let's find—" A soft sound at his back broke his words off short and he snapped around with the *telek* poised and ready; then both it and he relaxed. "Ah . . . You."

Kathur's servant tried to lean his weight on one elbow alone, unable to take his other hand from the hole which Widowmaker had left in his thigh. Regardless of how tightly those fingers were clutching his own flesh, blood still seeped slowly through them. He stared at the two by the bed, barely seeing them through his pain and not understanding what was going on. But he recognised one at least; and was full of shame. "M-my lady? I f-failed you, my lady. I failed. Forgive me . . ."

Commander Voord's head came round with the slow deliberation of a weapon-turret on a battleram, and his mouth formed the same silent *O* as the *telek*'s muzzle. The woman made no response by either word or gesture; she already knew how Voord's mind worked. And because she knew, she reached out with a crazy courage that was near to suicidal and clutched the *telek* by its barrel-shrouds. The *hautheisart* stared at her hand, and then at her face with the expression of one confronted by some noxious vermin.

"No!" Her voice was soft, her intonation vehement, pleading. "Don't. Even he saw no need—"

"He? Meaning the Alban. Didn't what?"

"Didn't kill. Not even in the heat of a fight. Because it wasn't necessary. And it still isn't . . ."

Voord's thin lips moved, stretching to a brief smile before once again forming that sardonic *O*. He blinked, lazily as a cat, and in that feline blink reminded Kathur for just an instant of Kourgath who had shared her bed.

"No need. For an Alban. No need for a man who can hide behind his oh-so-very-flexible code of honor. No need where any excuse will do instead, so long as it can be couched in the proper terms. Oh yes. It's easy then. But I too have been honored, lady, and in a better way. I have earned my honor, lady: I wear it for all to see. But I have no elegant little knife to let my life out if I fail. No. I must bear failure as I bear success. As I bear *these*."

His left hand reached up to touch the rank-marks on his helmet and on the high-collared black robe he wore over his red armor, and Kathur stared. Not at the *hautheisart*'s double bar-and-diamond worked in silver on black velvet collar tabs and scarlet steel, not at the jagged-lightning insignia beside it—for though the thunderbolt of the Secret Police served to frighten the ignorant, it was still no more to Kathur than the branch of service in which Voord held his command. As, indeed, did she.

No . . . She stared at his hand.

When she had last seen it, when it had last touched her, it had been slender and graceful like the hand of a musician, its contact soft as a butterfly's caress. Now . . . Now it was twisted, and crippled, and hooked like part of a military machine, a claw of distorted bone and sinew that was mercifully hidden by a leather glove. Now it was the sort of disfiguration which made men wince and look away and thank whatever gods they worshipped that they were still whole, untouched by war, or accident, or—whatever had done this.

"Yes indeed, dear Vixen. It is as I say. I wear my honor—whether I want to or not." The frightful talon lowered from her line of sight, but its presence, and its shape at which the concealing glove had merely hinted, remained in her mind and made her skin crawl.

Voord watched it crawl. "I suffered this, my dear, and so earned my present rank. Now I suffer the responsibilities of that rank. I am *Hautheisart Kagh'Ernvakh*. Concerned with internal security; espionage; counter-insurgency. And with the enforcement of—" a jerk of his wrist wrenched the *telek* from Kathur's grip, "discipline."

She flinched at the flat, vicious whack of the weapon's discharge, and shut her eyes again; but she could not shut her ears to a crisp, moist sound like a melon hit by a mallet, or the hollow thump of bone on wood as her servant's head was slammed back against the floor as if it had been kicked. Nor could she shut her mercilessly precise mind's eye to the image that was seared into it as if by red-hot irons; an image that she could still see now. An image that she would always see. The instant of a man's death.

He lay on his back, one hand thrown wide and the other still uselessly endeavouring to staunch the wound in his leg. But there was no longer need. And there would be no staunching of this latest wound, for it had already ceased to bleed. Blood and mucus was spattered across his cheek and forehead; his left eye-socket was a pit of oozing mush; a triangular chunk of his skull lay feet from where it had burst from the back of his head. But what expression could be seen on his ruined face was no more than faint surprise.

"Yes. It does work." Voord spared a glance for his handiwork, looked back at Kathur as if analysing her reaction and then at the *telek* with the beginnings of an idea that was as swiftly concealed as it was to blossom. "It does work indeed. And so do you, Kathur. Most of the time. Like another woman I once knew. But Sedna failed as well. As you failed this time—and by disobeying my direct command. You must remember in future. Punishment should aid your memory."

He made the weapon safe and laid it carefully aside;

then removed his helmet and dropped it to the floor, gazing at the woman with his head cocked quizzically to one side. Sweat-darkened hair was plastered flat against his skull, and there were shadows in the sockets of his eyes that were not created by any light or lack of it in Kathur's room. "The customary sentence is a bowstring—or impalement."

As the meaning of his words sank in, Kathur stared blankly at him and then slowly cowered away as comprehension dawned. The only sound to pass through her loose lips was an unstructured whimper of raw fear.

"Yet it could be said—in your favour—that you tried. You were told to keep him drugged and bound. But you still succeeded until . . . what was it you claimed only minutes ago? Then if there was a plea for clemency on your behalf, the sentence might well be commuted. Would you have me consider such a plea?"

Though Kathur did not, and in her extremity of terror could not make any coherent sound, Voord watched her with a sort of cold appraisal and nodded at last. "I am content. The plea is accepted." His hand reached out to stroke along her face and slowly down the rigid muscles of her neck.

The left hand. . . .

Kathur cringed within herself, but dared not let her revulsion show. Not even when that dreadful claw settled like a gross spider on her shoulder and then with a bitter, self-mocking sensuality smoothed the heavy satin of her robe aside. The garment fell free of its own weight and whispered down to puddle in crimson folds about her ankles, leaving her naked and shuddering before Voord's rapacious stare. Even then she did not move, did not attempt the classic cliché of one arm across her breasts and the other hand hiding her crotch; she merely stood with both arms hanging limply at her sides and her eyes lowered in a shame at her nudity that she had never felt with the Alban. She stood like a condemned prisoner facing the block, passively awaiting what fate chose to send her; and she heard the slow creak of leather as some effort of ruined muscle and tendon forced Voord's fingers open; and she waited for the degradation of its contact on her body.

There was no such contact. Instead the crooked fin-

gers clutched at the back of her head, tangling in the
locks of auburn hair, tilting her face up until Voord
could lean forward to kiss her on the lips. A faint scent
of some perfume such as courtiers used hung about him,
and his breath had been sweetened by the recent chewing of lancemint leaves. Other than that, he smelt simply clean.

And that was the worst of all.

Had he foul breath or his body a sour, unwashed reek,
Kathur knew she could have prepared herself better;
even though *Kagh' Ernvakh* had required her to seduce
enough men to know that it was those with dirty bodies
who had straightforward notions of vice, and the clean-
scrubbed sophisticates who were inclined towards what
even she thought foul, yet the contrast always shocked
her. As Voord shocked her. For though he was fresh
and pleasant in his person, his mind was warped and vile.

She could feel his kiss grow more intense, more passionate, and almost by reflex she responded with a pressure of her tongue against his lips. Then she felt his teeth
close, and felt the stab of pain, and tasted blood—her
blood—and knew that even though her "plea" had been
accepted she was still to suffer punishment after all.

Voord's left hand—talon—locked in her hair as Kathur wrenched away, and she jolted to a halt at the
length of his arm. He grinned at her, and there were
streaks of dark red on the white of his so-clean teeth,
and the glitter in his eyes was like nothing she had even
seen on any man's face in all her wide experience.

"Oh yes, my lady, dear Vixen my own, you *are* to be
punished after all. Surely you knew, surely you expected
it? Surely you looked forward to it as you did before?
And who am I to disappoint a lady?" He was struggling
with his own clothing as he gasped the words at her. "I
spare you the cord—but I think impalement is appropriate." He flung her face-downwards on the bed and
pinned her with one hand and his straddled legs. "Relax,
lady"—a weight of hot bare flesh and icy armor descended on her back and buttocks—you might even
enjoy it. But even if you don't," Voord shifted a little
and then plunged like a man riding an unruly horse,
"*I* will!"

There was a gasping interval of some few seconds.
Then at last Kathur began to scream.

In the street outside, a figure wrapped in a hood and
cloak heard the hoarse, outraged, anguished shrieks.
And wrapped the cloak a little closer and perhaps shivered in sympathy, and waited until the three men counted
into the house had become three men counted out of it
even if the waiting took this whole foggy night.

But did nothing else at all.

If it was stolen, then why only one and not both? Aldric
smacked pettishly at the butt of his sole remaining *telek;*
there was still no sensible answer to his unvoiced question, and perforce he set the matter aside yet again. Reining Lyard to a standstill, he stood in his stirrups to glance
back the way he had come, but could see nothing except
the mist, deepening to fog that darkened to blackness
and night. And yet . . .

He was certain that somebody was watching him.

It was gloomier here than he had expected. Oh, an
unlit city was as dark as any place not actually buried
beneath the earth had right to be, but Imperial cities
were not unlit. Not, at least, in normal circumstances.
But at some recent stage in Tuenafen's past, some political group had felt it necessary to their cause to smash
nearly all the doorway lanterns in the seaport's Old
Quarter.

Nearly all? They had probably destroyed the lot,
thought Aldric, and what he now saw were the very few
which had been replaced. Not that there would have
been many to begin with: most houses in this part of the
city were eighty years behind such modern affectations.
The architecture told him that much; above his head the
upper stories of both sides of the street leaned conspira-
torially together, so much so that in places one house-
holder could lean out and rap upon his opposite
neighbour's window. Even at midday they would block
out most of the light. Now . . . Now the effect was stilling
and claustrophobic. Ominous.

Aldric forced a smile at his own fretting, knowing
even as he did so that it would look more like a snarl.

Lyard shifted beneath him; the big horse was uneasy too, maybe uncomfortable on the smooth pavement which had been greased by a film of condensation, or because of his rider's mood, or simply because he too disliked the fog and dark and oppressive stillness. The courser's hooves clanked noisily—too noisily, thought Aldric—as he moved into the false comfort of the light from a surviving lantern, itself muffled by the watery yellow halo of fog which surrounded it. He was wondering if he could have spared the extra few minutes needed to load the pack-horse with his gear and—most especially—his armor. But the arguments he provided both then and now were specious, lacking the weight of conviction: bits of equipment and pieces of metal, even such metal as the battle harness given him by Gemmel, were things which could be replaced. Time lost now would be time gone for ever. Time which might well make the difference between . . .

What and what? There had been more than enough wasted time in the way he had spent the earlier part of the evening, enjoyable though that had been.

Aldric's gaze flicked from side to side, taking in what meagre detail he could see through the darkness and the drifting fog. Potential ambush points, escape routes and the like. *Escape routes!*—and myself none too sure of even how to get back to Kathur's house! His hand freed Widowmaker from where she rode obliquely across his back and secured the *taiken*'s scabbard at his hip before he gathered up the reins again and kneed Lyard forward. And if there was moisture in the palm of that ungloved left hand, then surely it was because of the foggy moisture in the air and no other cause at all.

Then . . .

A clock somewhere nearby ground harshly into life and began to strike for the hour—many, many minutes late, though Aldric at that instant was in no fit state to notice it. The sudden noise had shocked his highly-strung, already nervous mount and sent the stallion skittering sideways.

Towards the ragged granite facing of a wall.

Aldric saw the stonework loom out of the mist and spat an oath; then kicked his nearside foot out of its

stirrup-iron and up across his saddlebow before foot and
leg together could be crushed, and twitched back on
snaffle-bitted reins to get the warhorse back under control before his flank ground into the fanged abrasive surface. Lyard stopped instantly at the brief pressure on his
velvet mouth; nothing more was needed. His rider disliked and was loudly critical of the vicious metal used
by some who styled themselves horsemen to dominate
their steeds. Aldric had not time for such brutalities as
spade or curb or bradoon, and held that schooling was
of more value than the infliction of pain. His opinion
was justified now.

As he leaned forward to gentle the Andarran, and to
coax calm into himself as much as the horse, Aldric admitted privately that it would take just one more fright
like that—whether real or false—to send him wheeling
about on another route. Any other route but this one.
Yet to retrace his steps—a necessary evil, if he was to
reach the last junction he had crossed—would bring him
back to a certain high-walled courtyard which seemed
now, as it had never seemed before, an ideal place in
which to set a trap.

But it was not the only ideal place in Tuenafen.

As if summoned by the striking clock and the clattering of Lyard's hooves, boots slapped the wet paving-
stones behind him: many feet, running men closing on
him fast. And a voice: *"Dah'te ka' gh, hlens'l! Doch'taii-
ha!"* It spoke in Low Drusalan and its words were an
all-embracing order to stop, dismount, drop all weapons.
Surrender. And they were enough to send Aldric's sole
stirruped heel—the other still around his pommel where
it had been hooked clear of the wall—jabbing into Lyard's flank. The horse responded like a clap of hands,
snapping from immobility to a surge of acceleration towards the concealing darkness of the nearest alley.

Lyard's laid-back ears were barely tickled by the rope
stretched taut across its entrance, so precisely had its
height been calculated.

But it caught Aldric across the chest and plucked him
clean out of his saddle in a single uncoordinated backward roll, pitching him winded to the wet ground with
a flare of shrill stars inside his skull where his brain had

been. Black against the gray of the foggy night, a weighted net whirled down towards him, opening like a predatory spiderweb just before its mesh enveloped him in clinging folds.

Aldric flopped backwards onto the ground with the criss-cross pattern of the net-cords harsh against his face, and fury spasmed through him; fury at whoever had set this up, fury at the delay for which he and he alone was to blame and which had brought him to this, floundering like a landed fish in a Tuenafen street. Blind, crimson fury whose heat would not be quenched without the shedding of blood. His, theirs, anybody's!

Had Isileth been drawn he might have cut the net, might have butchered the men who even now drifted silently out of the shadowed fog, might have escaped . . . But the longsword was still sheathed, her presence a dull pain against his side where he had landed awkwardly on the loops and bars of her hilt. He could not touch her; and when some swine pulled on the drawline and the net tightened its embrace, he could not even move enough to ease the ache.

When they loosened off the mesh he kicked a few times, uselessly, and then gave up as heavy hands were laid on arms and legs to tie them up in what seemed an entirely excessive quantity of rope. Even to Aldric's dazed mind, coherent thought still fighting for precedence against the swirling sparks of mild concussion, all this care and consideration seemed overly elaborate. An arrow from the darkness would have been much more efficient.

And then as his wits began to trickle back and things fell into place, confusion was replaced by the beginnings of fear. He was to have been held in Kathur's embrace until he was collected by . . . someone. Her servant's attempt to kill him could be dismissed; it was not a part of the pattern. But now he had been captured and secured virtually unhurt. For someone.

Who? And why?

These men were dressed in gray; they wore hoods and masks; like *tulathin,* the Alban mercenary assassins. And that realization was as horrifying as any, for Aldric started to remember all the people—or the friends, supporters

and surviving relatives of people—who might pay the
sort of money *tulathin* demanded, just to have him
caught alive, unharmed and healthy.

Just to make his death their personal and very lingering pleasure. There were several such—too many for just
one man.

Despite the chill of the night a droplet of sweat
coursed down his face. They had taken all his weapons
by now, including the three hidden daggers which were
evidently not hidden well enough. And the spellband
with the Echainon stone set into it, which no more resembled a weapon than his crest-collar. They checked
that too, and the scar across his cheek, studying them
by the light of a dark-lantern and comparing all with a
sheet of paper one man held in his hand. Everything
was done without a surplus word or gesture, although
one cuffed him across the face when he attempted the
only action left open to him and tried to bite. It was a
petty gesture—on both sides—and the retaliation was no
reassurance. It was far too gentle.

"Close enough! He'll do. Take him."

A hood dropped over Aldric's head; no mere blind-
fold, it reeked with some soporific drug. He was growing,
if not familiar with, then at least accustomed to the off-
hand, casual employment of such things within the confines of the Drusalan Empire. It was as if, forbidden
sorcery except where the granting of permission was
convenient to those in power, men who would have been
enchanters had instead become apothecaries and chem-
ists, jugglers not of power but of poisons. As he breathed
the aromatic reek within the bag, Aldric's mind went
back five years to the last time he had smelt this smell.

Then . . . He was armored to the neck—Heaven and
the Light of Heaven alone knew where his helmet was—
and he lay flat on his back as he lay now, but instead of
stone pavement beneath him there was grass, and instead of gray *tulathin* looking down at him he could see
his brother Joren. There was concern on the big man's
face. Behind and beyond was the wreckage of an assault-
course jump; Aldric's horse was grazing unconcernedly
a little further on. And there was pain.

Pain like and yet unlike that he felt now—a grinding,

gnawing pain which worsened when he moved. Aldric tried to lift his head, but it seemed as though there was some great weight strapped to his brow, pulling him back and down. Someone—*was it Joren?*—leaned over him and slipped darkness firmly past his eyes. The same someone fumbled to hold that darkness shut beneath his chin. "I fell off," Aldric tried to say apologetically, "and I think I've broken . . ." The words in his head came out as no more than a drowsy mumble, but he made no attempt to correct them.

As the drug took effect, he did, and saw, and knew, nothing more at all.

5

Dragonship

Kathur lay where Voord had flung her at the last, after he was sated, after all that fevered, slimy, endless night. She was sprawled inelegantly across her bed—a bed which she would hack apart with her own hands if need be, rather than leave it and the memories it contained under her roof for one more day. And except for the bloodied, befouled, sweat-streaked tatters which had once been silken quilts, she was naked. Against her stripped skin she could feel the obscene pressure of the pillows which Voord had wadded into place to give support to and prevent retreat from his inclinations of the moment: beneath buttocks, beneath belly, behind head. And she wept.

Kathur's tears were not those of shame, even though she felt it for the first time now in five years as a first-rank courtesan; no, these tears were born of the harsh sobs which racked her, sobs which held more of frustrated rage than anything else. She had been terrorised, agonised, subjected to a cynical and systematic degradation, and she knew that there was no way in all the world that she could gain requital for it. The Drusalan woman dabbed a wincing hand at her mouth for perhaps the hundredth time since Voord's laughing departure; a mouth once mercly lushly full and the color of ripe cherries, but now puffed and split and bruised plum-purple. She felt that she would never be truly clean again.

There was a pallid light beyond the shuttered windows that told of oncoming dawn. Soon the house-servants would appear, with their mask-like faces which betrayed nothing of thoughts of disapprovals within, and their quick, capable hands which would tidy the aftermath of the night without any reaction to what they might have to touch. Just as they had done so many times before.

Except that now was not like all those other times.

None of those other times had ever left her feeling as she was feeling now. None of them had left a dead man stiff and cold on the floor at the foot of her bed. None of them had left the contents of a shattered skull soaked darkly into the rugs. None of them had left the foetid taint of death hanging on the air.

Kathur felt a churning looseness in the pit of her stomach and tried to close her nostrils to the reek, her mind to its source; rolling onto her side, she stared at the blankness of the wall beside the bed—stared anywhere, indeed, just so that she would no longer have to stare at the corpse with its smashed half-expression of surprise, or at the door which still gaped wide like the corpse's slack-jawed mouth, or even at the side of the room from which her snug and sybaritic world had been so totally torn asunder.

As she lay there, trembling, her skin slick with the icy sweat of nausea, her hearing seemed to grow uncannily acute and she could hear the most minute noises with utmost clarity. Noises distant: the tick of a bird's claws and the rustle of its feathers as it perched to preen on the sill beyond the window. Noises close: her heartbeat and breathing, and the whispering of silk disturbed by the rise and fall of her own rib-cage.

And the noises of soft movement at her back.

Kathur's heavy, drowsy eyelids snapped wide open and her very eyes seemed to bulge out of sockets that were no longer deep enough to contain them: sapphires inadequately bedded in a mask of carven ivory. For this was no sound made by a servant; they were quiet—but this was stealthy. Hope and horror fought for precedence in the half-dozen slams of her suddenly-racing heart. Because it might be Kourgath. Or equally it might be Voord.

Her head jerked up and around to look over the obstruction of her own shoulder, but flinched backwards in the self-same movement with a shrill small mew of terror, away from the glittering point of a sword which hung unmoving on the air less than a handspan from the fragile bubble of her eye. Had she sat up more abruptly— ! The very thought of what might have happened turned her belly sick again. Even now, the most minute forward thrust of that implacable steel and . . .

Her eyes focused beyond the weapon's point, and it was neither Voord nor Kourgath after all.

The intruder was cloaked, and hooded so deeply that the swathing of cloth resembled the cowl of a holy man. All that could be seen of the face within the hood was an inch or two of smooth chin; and it was impossible for even a gaze as experienced as Kathur's to read anything from that. But the thrusting-sword drew back a considerate inch or two, and its tip swung to one side so that it was no longer aimed quite so directly at Kathur's eye. The small motion which shifted it was accompanied by a dry metallic scraping, and that told her something at least. Whoever and whatever this person was, they wore armor.

"No noise." The figure's free hand moved across the hood's opening in a gesture which Kathur had never seen before, but understood at once: A quick, neat blending of the sign for silence and the threat of throat-cutting. She swallowed down a gullet that, though sore from screaming and . . . screaming, was still intact, and nodded hasty agreement while trying to fit a nervous smile onto a face which plainly didn't want to carry it. The cowl studied her. Nodded once in response. Then a finger jerked out at her with a suddenness that made Kathur jump. "And no movement."

Feeling like a mouse beneath the flight path of a kestrel, movement was the last thing in her mind.

As Kathur lay quite still, her anonymous visitor stalked about the room, dabbing inquisitively at things with the murderous point of that long sword, and despite the voluminous folds of the oversized cloak still contriving to move with all the mincing, lethal grace of a hunting cat. Kathur could see that it would take little provocation— probably none at all—for this particular individual to respond with a burst of killing violence. Whatever else the cloak concealed, it made a poor job of hiding tension, apprehension—and rising irritation. The dead man on the floor was inspected with no more than cursory interest. Until the *telek* dart which had killed him was found embedded in a panel of the wall.

"So." A glance—a sweeping glare from the blank blackness within the hood—studied distance, trajectory and penetration, and drew some conclusion from them all. "So, and so, and so . . . Did the Alban do this?"

The question snapped out harsh and clear after the muted introspective muttering of voiced thought, and again Kathur jumped. At first she did not answer, and for her hesitation was lashed by a volley of words in a language which she had never heard before. "Answer, damn you!" The voice returned to Jouvaine again, more heavily accented than before and using the most basic mode; each word's meaning was unequivocally clear now, and the speaker knew it. "Did the Alban do this—and if he did, why?"

Whatever patience there had once been in that voice was eroding fast, and as the cloaked figure took two long steps forward, it led with a levelled sword. Now not only accent but tone and timbre were impossible to ignore. There was something wrong about all three, something very wrong indeed, but still Kathur could not place what instinct said was obvious.

"Why, and when, and where is he? What is going on here?" The hood was pushed back, then shaken clear of its wearer's head.

And Kathur knew at last what was wrong. Except that it was *right*.

"I can't help but think," muttered Gemmel half to himself, "that *I* may have caused last night's fog."

"You . . . ?" Dewan ar Korentin flexed the big muscles of his shoulders and back in a huge yawn-and-stretch. Gemmel had been uneasy about entering a tavern and Dewan had given way to the old man's doubts; they had spent a chilly, uncomfortable night in some farmer's hay-barn, and now there were kinks in Dewan's spine which felt as if they would be there forever. He was getting too old for this, too old and too soft. Tonight, like it or not, wizard's objections or not, they were going to sleep in beds like human beings, not like rats in a rick. "Why say so? And why worry? It's gone."

Gemmel glanced at his companion and said something in a voice so low that Dewan made more sense from the movement of his lips. "I say so because I believe so—and I worry for the same reason. You saw what happened with this thing just as well as I."

Dewan looked at him, then at the Dragonwand, and grunted expressively. "I wonder what else you might believe, old man. And what else might happen because of it."

"That, friend Dewan, is something we may find out before much time has passed us by . . ."

The morning bloomed around them like a flower. Dewan had been right: the fog was gone, leaving in its wake a cloudless, chilly blue sky which toned through pastel shades of rose and saffron towards where the sun rose on their landward side beyond a screen of tree-clad hills. They were still very close to the sea, moving north-east towards Tuenafen Port on the Inner Coast-Road; the Outer Coast-Road ran a hazardous course along the crest of the limestone cliffs which marked the Empire's western boundary, and in rough weather was prone to lose stretches of itself to the hungry sea.

"*Yo!* Look there!" Ar Korentin pointed with the full length of his right arm towards the ocean—or more accurately, towards the black speck scudding across its beaten-metal surface. "Warship," he pronounced with such authority that Gemmel didn't quibble his opinion.

Not aloud, anyway; but the sorcerer reached into his satchel, withdrew a long-glass and studied the speck with it before uttering his agreement. "As you say: warship. And a big one. Bigger than I've ever seen before. Look." He passed over the long-glass. "What is it?"

Dewan squinted, and held his breath; the wizard's glass was more powerful than any he had used before, and just the beat of his own pulse was enough to send the magnified image dancing wildly about. It took him a few moments to fix the distant vessel in the circular field of view, and some seconds more to adjust its focus for his eye. Then he said something malevolent in his own language, something which provoked a raised eyebrow from Gemmel and suggested a certain familiarity with Vreijek oaths.

"Apart from that," he said, "what is it?"

"A battleram." Dewan's "of course" was unvoiced, but there all the same. "I should have guessed. Anything else would be too small to notice at . . . what, a mile-and-a-half?"

"Nearer two. He's bearing north. Out of Tuenafen?"

"There isn't another port on this stretch of coast that can take battlerams; not unless they've built one in the past few years and managed to keep it secret. Which," he slid the long-glass shut and handed it back, "I very much doubt."

Then he stared at Gemmel, guessing from the old enchanter's face that they were sharing the same thought.

"Aldric . . ." Gemmel said it first.

"We're too late."

"That . . . that depends."

"On what?"

"On whether he's aboard that ship; if he is, on who put him there. And on its destination."

"You know more about this business than you've let slip before, don't you?" Dewan accused, watching the sorcerer's reaction closely.

"More—but not enough. Rynert is very good at keeping secrets." Gemmel said nothing more for a while; he was watching the distant battleram dwindle beyond sight, and thinking unguessable thoughts about kings and conspiracies and other matters which were of importance only to himself. Then he glanced at the sky. The sun was well up now, though still concealed by the wooded high ground, and its glow was already giving a suggestion of warmth to the late autumn morning. "It's going to be a good day," he said idly, unslinging his satchel and taking a pack of biscuit and dried meat from it. "Breakfast?"

"Thanks." Dewan took a helping of the food; jerked beef like strips of leather, and twice-baked sheets of wheaten bread which both looked and felt as if it had been sawn from the trunk of a tree. It and the meat required as much effort to eat as if they had been in very truth what they merely resembled; breakfast was an exercise in chewing rather than a meal. "By the way," the Vreijek said after finally disposing of his first mouthful and washing it down with a swallow of black, bitter beer, "I'd sooner you said nothing more about the weather."

Gemmel squashed the beginnings of a smile. "Because it might be unlucky? I hadn't thought superstition would be one of your vices."

"Call it caution; I've grown very .. . . very cautious since I met you. And since the beach beyond Dunacre. The Valhollans have a wise proverb: don't praise the day until evening—"

"Or ale until it's been drunk. Pass the beer." He drank, and made a face. "This Hertan brew doesn't travel well, does it? Yes, I know the proverb you mean. It goes on and on rather. Don't praise a maiden until she's been married—and don't praise a wife till she's dead. Quite . . ." He laughed softly. "Well, I can praise my wife and will if you want to listen—but why that proverb in particular? You're not known for quoting things." He stared sharply at the Vreijek. "Especially words from Valhol. What made you think of it?"

"Just a thought. An idle notion. Nothing more."

Gemmel looked at him and smiled, and drank more beer, and said nothing at all.

When they stopped again the day hung on the cusp of noon; and with ill-concealed dismay Dewan surveyed a scene which he had not expected. For the past hour he had been praising the tavern where they planned to stop for a midday meal, and maybe rent the use of horses. Except that the tavern was no longer there. Oh, it had been until recently, and parts of its structure remained— but most of these were blackened, charcoaled wood and the rest were shanty reconstructions. Everything else was gone.

"So much for dinner," said Gemmel drily. "I still have some beef and biscuit—if you want it." He did not even trouble to feign enthusiasm at the prospect. Dewan made an expression of distaste and stalked across the seared ground to find out what had happened—also to ask what might be left that was worth raiding.

He found out rather more than he had been expecting.

Dewan supplied speculative details himself, when relating the innkeeper's story to Gemmel. Both men knew enough to make educated guesses whenever blank spaces in the secondhand story gaped too wide; and Dewan in particular was able to draw on his Imperial and Alban military service to suggest answers.

"It seems," said Gemmel around a mournful of excellent spiced beef stew—the tavern was making a determined effort to get back on its feet, and its more loyal patrons were chivalrously undeterred by the state of the place—"that we are going to Tuenafen regardless, and once there to find someone who can tell us a thing or three." He swallowed, and drank good red wine with an air of satisfaction.

"Find someone who might need persuasion, you mean." Dewan broke bread into his own portion, Vreijek-style, and sank a chunk or two idly with his spoon; then tapped for emphasis on the bottom of the bowl. "But if this is the work of *Kagh' Ernvakh,* both the finding and the persuading will be difficult."

"Kagh' Ernvakh?" Gemmel repeated the Drusalan words carefully; their literal meaning was clear, but what Dewan meant by them was a mystery to him. It was a mystery easily solved.

"The Honorable Guard. The Guardians of Honor. Translate it into Alban however you like, Gemmel—it still means nothing more than the Secret Police."

"Ah. And by 'persuading' you mean torture."

"Don't lose your appetite, old man." Dewan grinned briefly. "Persuasion covers more than you think: bribery, coercion, blackmail . . . I don't want to hurt anyone, any more than you do." He lifted another sheet of bread and stared at it thoughtfully, then ripped it across and across with unsubtle emphasis. "But if I must, then—"

"You will."

"Yes."

Gemmel wondered how sincere that threat might be; Dewan was not an Alban, and owed nothing to the Alban codes of honor. But then—if one was brutal and bore recent events in mind—neither did King Rynert. The wizard found that his mind was tending more and more towards considerations of honor and personal worth; towards how these might be valued; towards how his own honor might be weighed in the balance and found wanting. The thought was an uncomfortable one. If only it was possible to turn back time and undo past events . . .

For the briefest instant he found himself thinking about the great hold beneath Meneth Taran, and about the things which lay there. Then he dismissed the notion; that way was more dishonorable than to go on and try to recover what had been lost by his own efforts. Gemmel looked down at his own food—good beef and fresh vegetables, inventively blended with herbs and fiery spices—and despite the enticing aroma rising from the redware bowl he felt his hunger fade to no more than a faint emptiness. "So what is going on, *eldheisart?*" His use of Dewan's old military rank was no accident.

Yet the Vreijek was—or seemed—unruffled by it. "Someone wants Aldric Talvalin. Someone is prepared to pay a very large amount of money for the privilege— witness the presence of the battleram, which we both suspect might have him aboard. Or—or they have the rank to authorise such an action. And I don't know which would worry me the most." He drank more wine; not much, just enough to flavor his mouth which, if it was anything like Gemmel's, had the sour dryness of failure in it. "And *why* would they want him? I should have asked Rynert that much at least."

"What? The man who tried to have us both killed? What a waste of breath *that* would have been!"

"At least we know that he was taken from here alive."

"Yes—but how many days ago?"

"Two, three . . ." Dewan hesitated, a quizzical expression crossing his face. "Would Marek Endain know anything about it?" He threw the demon queller's name abruptly into the conversation; it had been Gemmel's idea to send the Cernuan after Aldric, as much to keep an eye on him as to help or protect him, and Dewan had acceded reluctantly to the idea—an idea which had seemed to him more full of risk than of use. But Marek's last report had been a garbled thing, full of wild surmise, which had ended with the information that he was now—

involuntarily—first councillor to the new Overlord of Seghar. And that the Overlord was a woman.

"Marek has his own troubles." Gemmel had read that last report as well, and had found it mildly amusing. The demon queller had been no more than a casual professional acquaintance, a sharer of scholarly interests, and to think of his rotund silhouette as the power behind any throne—no matter how small—was a notion which provoked a thin smile even whilst Gemmel's mind was occupied with more serious matters. Matters touching what even the Albans would regard as personal honor . . .

Dewan stared at him a moment, then shrugged to himself and drained his cup, throwing back his head to let the last fragrant drops flow into his mouth, and to allow the brilliance of the day to wash his face with azure heat. Then he choked.

And dropped the cup.

Its explosive thousand-sharded smash on the table right in front of him snapped Gemmel from his introspection, and he stared at the Vreijek with an expression that was half anger and half a fear that Dewan might have been stricken again with illness. But the big man's head was still tilted back, his mouth hanging open and stained to the chin with a dribble of red wine that hadn't quite reached its proper destination. Yet there were none of those signs which Gemmel had so feared: no shock of pain, no clutching at the chest. Only undiluted awe.

The wizard stared skyward in his turn. And remembered:

> . . . Long, long ago the firedrakes flew,
> And flaming flickered in the sunlit sky.
> But firedrakes fly no more within the sight of men . . .

Until now . . .

The sky was blue; pure, pale, late-autumn blue, unblemished by any cloud of black or white or gray. But across it ran a wisp of white, fine as a hair and so straight as to almost be a silver seam in the vaulting firmament. And at its uttermost tip, like the perfect barb of a perfect spear, was a minute black filament of darkness, mo-

mentarily flowing from cruciform to no more than a dark
scratch against the heavens with a rhythm that was the
beating of great wings. No one else had seen it. No one
else could have known what it was . . . except for Gemmel and Dewan. And neither of the two considered for
a moment that it could be other than . . . Ymareth.

"Splendour of God," breathed Dewan ar Korentin,
and there was much more than just an oath born of
disbelief in his reverent voice. He was now as Gemmel
had been then—years ago; lives ago.

As any man would be, possessed of an ounce of imagination or an ounce of romance in a soul no matter how
prosaic. Any man, any woman, any child would want to
see this wonder above all wonders of the world: a beast,
a creature, a being from the depths of legend of many
people, alive and magnificent in the clear cold air that
was scored by the vapor-trail of heat pouring from its
own mouth, glinting dark and glorious against the azure
arch of Heaven. Fifteen thousand vertical feet separated
it from its stunned audience of two, so that details were
indistinguishable through a haze of distance and the
glare of the noonday sun; Gemmel did not subject it to
the indignity of close scrutiny through his long-glass. All
of those who mattered knew already—that this was a
firedrake. A dragon. *The* dragon.

Ymareth.

And it was scything northward on the track of the
battleram which they had seen that morning, flitting out
of Tuenafen on the wings of urgency across the sea of
hammered steel. Not knowing that greater, darker wings
were driving in its wake.

"Innkeeper!" bellowed Dewan, "bring me the best
wine that you have left, and drinking vessels worthy of
it if you still have any!" The man did, and had, and
brought them all: tall, slender goblets of rock crystal and
burnished silver, stemmed so that they stood a foot
above the table's surface. The wine was golden Hauverne, *matherneil,* bottled in green glass; but Dewan
cracked the battle open on the table's edge with a single
snap of his wrist that sent both cork and bottleneck flying off to somewhere at his right-hand-side—then countered such brusque soldierly impatience with a mannerly

flourish worthy of a courtier as he filled first Gemmel's glass and then his own with the rich rare vintage. His grin, all white teeth and curling mustache as he lifted the goblet and stared at Gemmel across its rim, was filled with such pure, happy mischief that it stripped ten years from his weathered face.

"Drink hail and health, *purcanyath* sorcerer. To Aldric. And to aid unsuspected by all. Including, I think, the lad himself. *Hail!*"

Gemmel drank: once, twice and then to drain the cup. He began to laugh so hard that tears streamed from his crinkled emerald eyes. Or was the laughter only to conceal those tears which would have flowed in any case?

Gemmel didn't know.

Aldric's eyes opened sluggishly; there was a throbbing in and behind them, and he knew both instinctively and from bitter experience that if too much light startled that throbbing, he would be very, very sick. There was an acrid, vinegary sensation in his mouth and nostrils: the taste and chemical smell of whatever had put him to sleep—yet again!—and it occurred to him through a spasm of mild irritation which had nothing to do with the peril that he might be in, that he had spent the greater part of the past few days either drunk, or drugged, or knocked unconscious.

It was . . . undignified.

Aldric Talvalin was not a religious man; he had ceased to believe in the so-called benevolence of Heaven on the day his father died, and since that day—whether through an ostentatious grudge against deity or a private reluctance to be hypocritical—he had refused to cross the threshold of any holy house. But there were times, and this was one of them, when he had the distinct feeling that Someone was trying to make some sort of point.

Just now his whole sensory world seemed to be moving in a dozen quite illogical directions at once. Then things fell into focus—more or less—and sounds which had meant nothing bare seconds ago enhanced his realization of reality. His world—or at least his immediate surroundings—*was* moving. He could see the rolling of reflected light across a ceiling that was far, far too close, far closer than it had any right to be, and in his ears was a constant liquid rushing, blended with the multiple notes of half-a-hundred different creaks from wood and cordage. And he knew at once where he was. Or at least, he knew as soon as the narcotic clouds had cleared sufficiently from the dazed organ which did duty as his brain.

He was on board a ship.

With that conclusion, someone at the back of his mind broke into ironic applause. But it was true enough; he was aboard ship, and a ship not only under way but—if the sensations transmitted through his spine were any judge—moving at considerable speed. Flank speed, the Imperial Fleet called it, and Aldric thought to himself that Imperial terms of reference were all of a sudden highly appropriate, because the only vessel he knew of within several leagues of coast that was capable of such immediately apparent speed would be one or other of those he had seen in Tuenafen harbor.

An Imperial battleram!

The exhalation of breath which hissed out between his teeth was also a sigh of resigned defeat. So they had him after all—whoever *they* were. Kathur had won. Had the pleasures of her company been worth this and what was doubtless to follow? Aldric doubted it.

He had no need to move overmuch, or even to look around, to know that he was completely unarmed; completely helpless. That memory was clear enough, beyond the soporific fog: the hands which had stripped him of every blade which he carried, and which had sought out and removed the belts and laces from his clothing for fear they might become nooses or garottes.

Whether they feared that he would use such makeshift weapons against them or on himself had either not been clear or had been forgotten. Certainly if he was being carried to a lengthy and unpleasant death, then suicide whether in the form of *tsepanak'ulleth,* or something less formal but just as final, would be a preferred solution to be sought without delay. Certainly if he was *kailin-eir* of the old school, then they would have good reason to fear that he might kill himself and thus cheat them.

But he was not.

Aldric stared at the ceiling and admitted a fact which he had secretly known this long, long time: he would sooner live than die. No matter that it might well be true of most men, it was not true of Albans and especially high-clan Albans, *cseirin*-born, like himself. And yet unlike himself. "Where there's life, there's hope," Gemmel Errekren had told him once. Then, he had snorted in derision. Then, it had been the accepted and expected reaction. Then even then, it had been only a mask to the way he truly felt. Had he truly followed the beautiful, savage, bloody Honor Code of the *kailin,* how many times should he now have been dead by his own hand?

Too many. He remained alive through his own choice alone, and that was not cowardice no matter what might be said, or what had been said—though grant the truth, no man had yet been so in love with death to say it in his hearing. No. Cowardice was running away—not tactical withdrawal, but turning tail in flight whether that flight led to the woods or the hills.

Or the dark lands beyond the stab of a *tsepan*'s blade.

Courage was standing fast, setting to rights, taking the hard path. Courage gained and justified trust from friends and from companions—and from self. Aldric stared at the ceiling and grinned momentarily. *I must remember not to trust you near complaisant, pretty women,* he told himself sternly. *A most lamentable failing.*

Except where one is concerned.

But—his thoughts came back to present reality with a jolt—who commands all this? He could think of none among his possible enemies with such power and wealth and resource as had been so arrogantly displayed here. And there were not so many enemies, at that: the enemies of Aldric Talvalin showed a tendency to get themselves killed. But even so, a courtesan of the first rank as bait, the firing of an expensive tavern to close the trap, and the use of both a squad of *tulathin* and at least one battleram complete with crew and marine contingent! That bespoke either a disgusting private wealth, a stranglehold on someone with power and privilege—or power and privilege itself.

Power that involved politics, rank, status and an independently controlled unit of the Imperial military. Power that suggested the Emperor himself . . .

Or the Grand Warlord.

Woydach Etzel was one of the very few who fulfilled all the present criteria. He had access to a quite obscene amount of money—for which he had no need to account; he had the rank to discourage idle questioners; and he had the power necessary to maneuver warships like pieces on a gaming board.

So this was what a pawn felt like when a crown piece was hammered down on it and it was flung back into the box until next time. Except that carven bone and ivory felt no pain when the end came, whereas Aldric doubted he would be so lucky.

The cabin door rattled, then clicked, betraying the presence of a lock on the outside. It slid open and the young man who came in was wearing a marine's half-armor flashed with the single rank-bar of an officer-cadet—*en tau-kortagor,* in the Empire's cumbersome system of named ranks. Improbably enough, the young man was smiling. "Ah, good—you're awake." More improbably still, he was speaking in good—well, passable Alban. "No ill-effects, I trust?" Most improbably of all, he seemed genuinely concerned. Solicitude from such a source was so improbable . . . no dammit, so totally unlikely that Aldric thought his ears were playing him tricks, and he stared blankly at the pleasant-faced *tau-kortagor* until the question was repeated. Then, and only then, did he blink and shake himself back to some sort of sense.

"Ill-effects . . . ?" He too spoke in Alban, with something approaching relief after so long contending with Jouvaine and Drusalan. "None. None at all. So far. I'm fine. I suppose."

"Excellent. My name is Garet—on *Hautheisart* Voord's personal staff." He hesitated, as if anticipating a reaction, but the name was only one among many to Aldric and meant nothing significant. "And I've been assigned to your care. So—food?"

Aldric shrugged. His mind was still having difficulty in assimilating the situation, for he was not being treated as he had expected a prisoner of the Empire might have been. Far from it—except in one respect. For it was only when he shrugged that he realized—with a nasty start barely concealed—that he was still bound at wrist and ankle. He had spent so much time lost in thought, staring at the ceiling and wandering through his mind rather than exploring the narrow confines of the cabin, that he had not noticed the bindings until now. Unlikely as it seemed with hindsight, it was not so surprising after all, for they were not ropes but soft wide bands of woven silk, far beyond his strength to break but secured with such care that their presence was not a constriction of his limbs. Just an unsettling inability to move.

"What about these things?" He lifted them: snug, almost comfortable wrappings that were as secure as any wrought-iron shackle—and stared pointedly over his crossed wrists at Garet, who at least had the good grace to look uncomfortable.

"Oh—I, ah, I don't have authority to release you."

Aldric made a small, faintly disgusted noise which managed to suggest he had expected no other response, and that seemed to embarrass the cadet still more.

"But—but I could ask the *kortagor-ka'-tulathin* on your behalf. He brought you aboard, so he might just . . ."

And that small kindness was not something Aldric had dared to expect at all. Where there's life, he thought, . . . and lay back on his bunk to watch the play of light across that too-close claustrophobic ceiling. But he didn't dare to hope. Not yet.

The order to release him was not long in returning down the command chain from whoever authorised such things aboard this battleram; but it was an order wrapped in so many conditions as to negate its usefulness. Ultimately it was obeyed more in spirit than to the letter, as might have been expected about Drusalan orders.

His wrists and ankles were released, but he was not allowed on deck, and his left leg had been locked into an elaborate harness of steel and leather strips such as might be worn by one with a weakness in their muscles. Except that this was not meant as a support, but as a restriction; the hinging at its knee-joint was so tight that

each stride was reduced to a rolling, stiff-legged hobble.
He could walk, more or less, but his briefly entertained
notion of pouncing on someone was reduced to no more
than a wry joke. Aldric hadn't tried the experiment yet;
but someone, somewhere, had suspected that he might
and he could recognise the signs of being outmaneuvered yet again. The addition of a thumb-thick rope
leash which secured him to a bulkhead was downright
insulting.

Nevertheless, the food brought to him from the warship's galley went a long way to compensate for injured
dignity. No prison rations these: the various dishes were
uniformly excellent and another pointer to instructions
laid down for his continued well-being. There was a thin
soup; charcoal-broiled fish which he guessed was not
long out of the sea; meat and vegetables in a rich sauce
of herbs and cream; and a sharp white wine—cooled by
a water-jacket—with which to wash it down.

But like the over-elaborate security measures, the
food's very presentation was influenced not so much by
himself as by his reputation—or rather, by whatever
highly colored version of it had preceded him aboard. It
had certainly lost nothing in the re-telling, for every
piece of vegetable, meat or fish had been cut up in advance so that the only eating instrument he required—
and was given—was a kind of wooden spoon with
rounded, blunt fork-tines carved into it. The sort of thing
given to very young children, so that they couldn't possibly hurt themselves.

Or to supposedly lethal Alban *kailinin,* so that they
couldn't hurt anybody at all. The idea of a precaution
lest he try to take over an Imperial battleram with his
dinner service was so ridiculous that he sniggered himself into a fit of hiccups; although afterwards, as he ate,
Aldric reflected ruefully that if he was less well known—
or his reputation not so awesome—to whoever had arranged all this, then he might by now have had a chance
to get away. *Off a ship in open ocean? Be reasonable!*
Even so, it would have gained him a little more freedom.
Notoriety might be flattering to some of the people he
had met; he personally could do without it. And he won-

dered if the officer cadre of the Drusalan Empire had ever heard of the concept of a gentleman's parole.

The meal was good, and he was hungry. Those two facts led to empty dishes—and a stifled belch as Aldric lay back and composed himself for an after-dinner nap. It was not something in which he indulged given normal circumstances; but the thirty-odd pounds of strapping around his rigid, awkward leg was a constant reminder of abnormality. Besides which, he had eaten far too much.

Up on the command deck a sandglass was turned over and its turning was marked by a bell struck at the changing of the hour. Just after noon, thought Aldric drowsily: just after lunch. That makes it—the effort of thinking was such that he almost gave up—the Hour of the Hawk becoming, becoming . . . He yawned hugely and snuggled into the rolling, swaying, comforting embrace of the bunk as sleep overwhelmed him.

Becoming, he might have finished, the Hour of the Dragon.

It seemed that he had barely closed his eyes before they snapped open again, and he was jerked from an uncomfortable slumber by a sound that he had heard before: the clangor of an Imperial warship's alarm gongs sounding battle-stations. For just the first few seconds it was as if his strange, troubled dream had carried over to the waking world; then reality in the form of clattering footsteps outside and overhead gave the lie to such a notion. There was another clattering, harsher and more metallic, and the cabin's interior went abruptly dark as armored screens dropped over the two small, thick-glassed ports. Aldric found himself in twilight, his only illumination the wan trickle of daylight which filtered through shrouded weapon-slits in each screen.

It was no longer a dream—it was a nightmare, that same recurring nightmare of helplessness. Once more he was aboard *En Sohra;* once more the First Fleet flagship *Aalkhorst* was shearing down on him with white water boiling from her prow; once more he could only hope that she would turn aside.

And she did. The bunk beneath him heeled abruptly from the horizontal, its angle so steep that he all but tumbled off. A rushing of water filled his ears and the feeble light beyond the screened ports turned green and then black as the battleram in which he was an unwilling passenger executed a vicious evasive snap-turn. Aldric knew what was happening: he had seen such a maneuver before, from the outside—it *had* been the *Aalkhorst* that time—and he knew too that as the warship turned, part of her hull submerged under the sideways pressures of having her helm put hard over at speed. But Lord God! He hadn't known that such a turn could be so bloody *steep!*

Twice more the vessel lunged, and twice more Aldric dug his fingernails into the planking and tried to avoid being flung helplessly to the deck. Already there was blood on his face and a ragged gash at his hairline, as mementos of violent contact with one of the bulkhead uprights.

Then suddenly, between one rolling turn and the next, the watery light outside flushed a rich, rosy amber. Just for an instant: slower than the brilliant flicker of a lightning-flash, but much much faster than the blue-white skimmed-milk glow of a break in clouds crossing the moon. And the warship stopped.

Not dead in the water—there was too much momentum in her great bulk for that—but she lost way, ceased to be a vessel cutting through the ocean and became instead no more than a mere decelerating hulk. And Aldric could smell burning.

There was a dreadful stillness as if everyone aboard—officers, crewmen, marines, and even the ship herself—drew in a great breath and held it in expectation of something monstrous about to happen.

Aldric's barely-relaxed fingers tightened again as the battleram heeled—then clamped more convulsively still when the angle changed and he realized she hadn't heeled at all. She had *tipped,* her stern rearing out of the water as her beaked prow plunged down. He had never, ever watched a ship sink, much less had one go down beneath him, but he had heard it described and knew well enough what it was supposed to feel like. Like *this!*

The cabin door slammed open and outlined by its frame—indeed, clinging to its frame as Aldric clung to his bunk—was the young officer-cadet Garet. No longer friendly and no longer concerned—except perhaps for his own safety. Even—impossible though it seemed—no longer as young. Yet in the shadows of his close-fitting helmet his boy's face still seemed no more than sixteen, blanched white as bone with shock, or fear, or disbelief—as white as the knuckles of the hands which gripped the uprights of the cabin door.

"You!" He gasped the word, Drusalan now and guttural-harsh as only that language could achieve. "You—get on deck! Now! *Move!*"

Aldric stared at him and as if the officer's fear played counterpoint to his own emotions, felt the unknowing fear of the past minutes fade and freeze over until they were sheathed in an icy armor that was all dignity and pride and honor-born courage. Which was not the same as true courage at all, and Aldric knew that even if no one else did. But they appeared the same and that was enough. He slapped the brace on his leg with an irritable, careless gesture, as a man might swat at an insect he can't quite reach.

"I go nowhere with this. Remove it. *Now.*" And he spoke the words with studied malevolence in the highest mode of the Drusalan language that he knew, quite aware that the insult of implied superiority was a killing matter. Usually. "Well?"

Garet stared at him, gaped at him for half-a-dozen heartbeats—and then ripped the dress dagger that was one of his marks of rank out of its scabbard. Aldric thought that at last he had miscalculated, pushed a little too far, at last had overstepped the mark—thought that this would be a killing matter at any time, in any place.

The dagger point paused, glittering nastily in the cabin's subdued light, the silvery striations of honing on its cutting edges sparkling at him as the weapon trembled in an unsteady grip.

"I should gut you for that, *hlensyarl*," Garet whis-

pered. "And maybe I will. But not just yet. I have my
orders. Later . . ." He sucked in a deep breath, trying
to regain a degree of self-control. "But . . . but you're
going nowhere unless I have your Word. Your parole.
You do understand 'parole,' Alban, don't you?"

It seemed that he, too, knew how to use language for
subtle insult.

Aldric hesitated. Even though he had already considered such a possibility, and would have welcomed it half
an hour ago, things had changed. The warship seemed
under attack—*seemed,* he reminded himself—and he
might well have a chance to escape during any confusion
which might arise. But not if he was bound by an intangible thing that was harder for him to break than the
shackle on his leg.

His mind began to hurt with the swirling rush of variables: without his given Word, the brace would not be
removed; without its removal, his chance to escape was
nil; with his Word given and the brace removed, he
could not escape anyway. But locked up down here, with
iron about his leg, the only certainty would be of drowning if the battleram rolled over and began to sink.

"All right. All right . . . ! I swear. On my Honor and
on my Word, I do swear that I will not endeavour to
escape or yet take flight without permission granted by
those who hold me captive."

The cadet watched him coldly, his expression easy to
read framed as it was within the rank-barred helmet.
Tau-kortagor Garet was wondering, and not troubling to
hide his doubts, if the Alban's oath was worth more than
the exhaled air which carried it. Aldric returned the
stare with interest, and that interest was hatred.

"*So-ka, Drus'ach arluth'n.* My parole is given. Satisfied?"

The edge on Aldric's voice was as sharp as that on
the knife still aimed at his throat and slowly, slowly
Garet nodded. Just once. "I am content."

"Then," Aldric gestured with one hand, "take this
bloody thing *off!*"

The restraint fell away to the oak-planked deck with
a clatter that was very loud in the silence which had
settled on the warship, and as the bands of steel and

bullhide released their grip on his thigh Aldric felt the agonising tingle of blood as it poured back into vessels which had been constricted for far too long. He stretched the limb and flexed it, again and again; from hip to ankle it felt as if each muscle had been dipped in boiling brine, and despite Garet's ill-concealed impatience it was only when the leg felt and worked more as it should that Aldric nodded curtly and agreed to do as he was bid.

The inner belly of the battleram was much as he imagined a rabbit-warren might look to a rabbit: a maze of passages which branched off from one another, each low-ceilinged and constricted, each leading somewhere that was unknown to a stranger. He followed the *tau-kortagor*'s disapproving back along walkways, through heavy doors edged with greased leather that was obviously meant to keep water at bay—and always, always upward.

The Imperial warship was truly a huge vessel; doubtless she was not so monstrous as she seemed to him right now, but before God and the Holy Light of Heaven she had no right to be so big and so powerful and so armored and still defy the sea by floating on it.

Daylight through a hatchway hit him like a blow in the face and he flinched from it, shielding his outraged eyes with one arm. It was only the impact of the light from outside that brought home to Aldric just how dim it was on the lower decks where he had been confined. And he knew why, too: no lanterns. They had all been stowed away in case of fire.

So why, why, *why* could he smell such a reek of smoke and burning?

Aldric stopped in his tracks, suddenly afraid of the urgent summons, and equally suddenly there were two marines at his back, called up from God-knows-where or merely poised just out of sight against this very hesitation, ordinary troopers—if one could dismiss men so tall and strong as "ordinary"—and they hustled him inexorably through the hatch and out onto the open deck.

The sun shone down without heat from that sky of limpid blue which seems only to appear in autumn or winter, and Aldric shivered in air which by its very freshness felt chilly after the closeness of below-decks. Under the unsympathetic scrutiny of that bright, pale light, and despite the taint of smoke which stung his nostrils, he became aware of two things—and was disgusted by them both.

The first was his appearance, and the second was his smell.

He was wearing the same clothes as when he had left Kathur's house—clothes which since then had come into violent contact with a wet Tuenafen street—and they were filthy. Those same clothes, unchanged after the sweaty exertions of fight and fright and flight, and the capture which had brought him here, went beyond grime into foulness and the heavy stink of stale perspiration. Any Alban would have found such a state of affairs intolerable; to one so fastidious as Aldric, it was revolting. He felt his skin crawl as if it shrank from contact with his grubby shirt, the lank oiliness of his hair, the crescents of dirt under his fingernails. Light of Heaven, to have eaten a meal with such hands . . . ! He barely choked back the heaving spasm that would have spewed his late lunch all across the deck, and tried hard to think of other things. There were plenty such to think about.

For all that the air was fresh and at first cold, under its crispness was a strange medley of odours—even setting aside for a moment the aroma of unwashed Alban! Most powerful was the astringence of scorched cloth and wood; but under it was a warm, metallic tang reminiscent of the atmosphere in a blacksmith's forge. Aldric had smelt it before—but not in any forge.

The man who stalked across the quarterdeck to face him was close to raving; whether with fear or fury, Aldric didn't know. Most of the raving was in a Drusalan dialect which meant nothing—and given the few recognisable words which came through, ignorance was probably just as well. But inflection and tone conveyed enough for him to guess the gist of the captain's complaint, even before his language changed to something more intelligible. Yes, this was the captain, for all that wild eyes and a fear-pallid complexion detracted somewhat from the *hautmarin*'s rank-marks on his green and scarlet Fleet armor.

"Look at my ship! Look what's been done to my ship!

You! Alban! Damn you! What do you know about it, eh? Devil burn you black! What do you know about *that!*"

Aldric's escort seized him by the shoulders and wrenched him around, swivelling him in the direction of the captain's outraged, outflung arm. The warship's deck was a shambles: shattered yards, torn rigging and the charred shreds of what once had been its sails littered the vessel's planking and drooped wearily over the plates of its armored hull. An acrid film of thin gray smoke hung over all. And he saw for the first time what was on, what was all over, what was coiled massively around the semi-sunken turrets of the battleram's bow.

For just that instant, until he took a mental grip of himself that was as much a physical dominance of involuntary muscles, Aldric's lower jaw sagged just as far as that of anyone else aboard, because of all the situations he might have expected to face, this was the least likely. And of all the emotions he might have experienced, this was by far the most utterly impossible.

For it was *recognition!*

Because although he had looked at one before, spoken to one before, fought down his disbelief when facing one before, the last thing that he had expected in all this wide and wonderful world was to meet a—*the*—name-known and familiar Goddamn firedrake!

Except that here it was!

"Ymareth," he said, very, very softly. And perhaps his voice was not so quiet as he thought; or perhaps the firedrake's hearing was far more acute than he believed—or perhaps the huge glow of delight that rose within him was strong enough to carry clearly to its cause. Whatever the reason might have been, it didn't really matter. Because the firedrake heard him, or sensed him, or . . . something.

And it moved.

There was a dreadful languid grace in the way that the horned and jagged head curved back, elegant as an iron swan, but at the same time there was an arrogant flaunting of incalculable might and a pride that Aldric could appreciate. He heard sounds that he knew well, sounds that he recognised as if he had last heard them yesterday: a steely slithering of scaled coils and the slow bass surge of a vast respiration. The sounds of a living dragon.

As the ornate, elongated wedge of Ymareth's head swung towards him, Aldric prudently lowered his eyes— not merely through respect, for all that this huge being was deserving of such courtesy where many men of rank were not. As the firedrake's phosphorescent stare raked over all the men who lined the armored railing of the warship's quarterdeck, only one among them knew that he *had* to look away or be entrapped as much as any little bird before a snake. Aldric knew. No man born of woman could meet such a gaze and hope to walk away unscathed—or if the circumstance was wrong, hope to walk away at all . . .

The dragon exhaled gently and Aldric smelt again that harsh, clean furnace wind. The hot gust carried words in a voice that few had ever heard—a voice which held the sounds of steam and falling water, the sounds of stone-stroked metal and storm-waves on a rocky shore, the sounds of the sifting of blasted ashes. A voice that none save Aldric understood, and he only by virtue of the Charm of Understanding laid on him at their first meeting, months ago and miles from here.

"I give thee greeting, man. Well met, Aldric Talvalin."

Aldric shook free from the hands which held him and they fell away slack-fingered, the marines who flanked him struck dumb and witless by Ymareth's gaze.

He knelt, paused and then bowed forward to place his crossed hands against the deck and press his forehead briefly onto them in the Second Obeisance which he had given when he first met the dragon in the Cavern of Firedrakes on Techaur Island. Here and now it was perhaps not quite appropriate—Second Obeisance was properly due an equal or superior under the roof of his own hall and nowhere else—but overly elaborate manners were always better than insufficient, if sincerely meant. Then he sat back neatly on his heels and composed himself as best he could. Ymareth, watching in reptilian stillness, had not moved.

"Well met indeed, Lord Firedrake," Aldric returned; then, greatly daring, "But why—and how?"

Flame licked momentarily between the dragon's

parted jaws and Aldric flinched despite himself. He felt like a man walking a tightrope, balanced precariously between the perils of ignorance and that insolence which comes of importunate curiosity.

"Which first, O man—the 'why' or the 'how'? Thine is the choice." Insofar as it was possible to attribute human reactions to something so manifestly unhuman, Ymareth was amused and gently teasing. This was enough to make Aldric marginally bolder.

"Try the 'how,' my lord. I already know that Techaur and your abiding-place lie many leagues from here."

There was another quick spout of flame, that harmless incandescent swirling which Aldric had already come to recognise as laughter—and which he had already guessed was responsible for the state of the battleram's sails. Even though he was only halfway right . . .

"I am Ymareth. I am dragonkind. I searched for thee: I found thee. Such is our way." The dragon's head swung leisurely towards the sea, staring south along the now-vanished track of its passage through the upper air. "Yet verily, any task is made as nothing when there is a true guide with that searched-for. As was the Eye of the Dragon with thee, *kailin* Talvalin."

"The Eye of . . . ?" Aldric's voice trailed off with its question incomplete, for in his own mind's eye there was an image of Gemmel Errekren with the Dragonwand Ykraith in one hand and the azure-glowing stone of Echainon in the other. The spellstave's carven dragon-head had an eye already; but only one, and that an ordinary sapphire gemstone. Its other socket was empty. Then the wizard's hands came together, and when they parted the Dragonwand looked out on the world with two eyes, one of them alive and throbbing with the glow of its own internal energies. The Eye of the Dragon indeed!

And the self-same talisman which Aldric had carried these months past, in ignorance of the truth.

There were a great many things which he might have said, and probably an equal number which he should have said. But what at last came from his mouth was no more than a barely audible exhalation of, "Oh God . . . !"

Which served no real purpose whatsoever.

Ymareth watched him and again seemed to derive amusement from his confusion. Its thin-lipped mouth stretched back and back in a grin, that foxy smirk which Aldric had seen before; and though then he had thought it no more indicative of real humor than any other so-called "expression" on an animal's face, now he wasn't quite so sure. There was a certain precision about the way in which the firedrake's facial muscles moved which suggested that Ymareth was deliberately copying something observed and noted by its icy draconian brain, something which might be used to reassure the nervousness of humankind. If that was indeed the reason, it failed: there was no reassurance to be found in the shocking armory of fangs which the dragon's grin put on display.

"And the 'why,' Aldric Talvalin? Does 'why' not begin to pique thy curiosity?"

It did. So much so that for just an instant, just the merest breath of inattention, Aldric's gaze flickered speculatively upwards as the many possibilities of that *why* crossed his mind. And in that momentary glance he met the smoking amber mirrors that were the eyes of Ymareth. Truly the Eyes of the Dragon. Aldric's own eyes met them and locked with them. And were caught.

Time stops as it stands still. The voice was within his head, as Ymareth's had been—but this was not the dragon's voice at all. It was, or seemed to be "Gemmel?" Aldric's mind alone shaped the word, for his mouth and tongue could not. There was no reply—no repetition of the voice that had no place here, no reason to be here, and no reason to say what it had said, for all that the words were right and proper in the here and now. If here and now there was.

For time ceased to have meaning and reality ceased to exist. There was only himself and the two great glowing orbs that stared and stared and never, ever blinked. He was laid bare before their gaze: not naked *unclothed* but naked *without concealment,* stripped of the screens and shields men use to disguise the truth from one another. He was stretched out before the coldly burning scrutiny of the dragon, and what was there was all that he was. Without rank, without privilege, without title. Without anything to hide behind.

And he was ashamed.

He could see, as Ymareth could see, all the ugliness that was within him; all the unadmitted secret vice that might be indulged if only he dared to do so, all the carefully-forgotten sins that at one time or another had been indulged, all the things that any and all but the very purest carried deep inside, buried under manners and courtesies and outward show like the slimy life under a rock. Always there and known, but never revealed even to the closest of friends.

Until now.

The questions were not asked in any way that ears might hear or mind might comprehend; they merely formed, resolving from the gray mist of sadness that surrounded him. But once they had taken shape, they struck and flayed like iron whips. Questions which he could not answer—simple questions which in their simplicity probed with pitiless directness deep into his soul.

Aldric said nothing—and could say nothing—in his own defence. Guilt sickened him, rose choking in his throat, raised scars that would never heal. Then something snapped; he heard it snap, or felt it snap—a sound and a sensation like the breaking of a leash. And the world came back to him with a jolt.

Nothing had changed; he was still kneeling on the deck, straight-backed, sitting on his own heels. But his face was wet and chilled by the cold breeze. One hand came up—oh, so slowly—to touch the wetness. Tears. He had been crying, for no reason and for every reason. Because he felt dirty, soiled by having those things which were secret drawn out into the light of day, and yet at the same time he felt strangely cleansed as though that same drawing-out had purged him and somehow made him whole. Blinking the blur of unshed tears out of his eyes and dashing them away with his knuckles, Aldric focused on reality again. On the ship; and on the dragon.

Ymareth's huge head was right above him, an arm's length over his own, ponderous as the raw stone roof of the Kings-mound and as redolent of great age. He could feel the arid scouring of the being's fiery breath on his skin, and could smell the heated-metal tang of it. For the flames and the death they carried were so close now. And he was not afraid.

The fear had always been there, whether he admitted to its existence—tempering such an admission with mockery, as if to prove he wasn't really scared at all—or kept it locked away, nestled deep within him. Aldric had always imagined that fear of Ymareth as heavy and foreign and cold, a lump of ice-sheathed lead tucked underneath his heart; but now both lead and ice had been taken from their hiding-place and washed with dragonfire until they were melted and left not a trace behind.

"Know now why I came, Aldric Talvalin. Honor awakened me. Honor summoned me. Honor bound me as it binds you."

"Honor? What honor have I left? I threw it all away in Seghar long ago!"

"So say *ye*. I say *not!*" Flame gouted above his head— not the flutter which indicated humor but a blasting torrent of irritation that slapped heat down at him like a physical impact. There was an edge in the great voice, a steeliness like crossed blades; Ymareth was not accustomed to dispute. "Hear me, O man. I have such wings as may bear thee to thy liberty, if such is thy desire. Speak and say, will ye escape thus? Speak!"

Aldric closed his eyes, feeling his heartbeat quicken and the breath begin to catch in his throat. Escape? An hour ago, yes, and willingly. But now? Now he could not.

The dragon blinked once and he heard the metallic click of its eyelids clearly in the silence. "Speak," it repeated, more gently now.

"I cannot. I *must* not. I—" He looked up, deliberately seeking the dragon's eyes. "I gave my Word."

"The Word of one who by his own admission is without all honor?"

Aldric shrugged. "The right to keep a promise is all that I have left."

"So, and so, and so. Thou art more worthy than the Maker ever was, *Kailin* Aldric-*eir*."

To my eternal shame. Again Aldric heard the voice inside his head, and again it was not Ymareth but Gemmel who seemed to speak.

"To his shame," echoed the dragon.

Aldric listened, and heard, and at last a minute flower of understanding began to blossom in his mind. But it was a flower with somber petals, for the only meaning made possible by his understanding was such that his senses began to swim with the enormity of it all.

Ymareth's wings unfurled, dwarfing the Imperial warship, and Aldric realized with a jolt that which he had unconsciously known since he came out onto the deck: now that he could see the firedrake against a background of normality rather than within the Cavern on Techaur, it was far, far bigger than he had dreamed. Wingtip to wingtip, Ymareth's span was more than sixty yards; from nose to the flattened spade-shape which ended its tail—aerodynamic in section, like the horns and crest of its head—it was another forty yards in length. Weight . . . ? Enough to all but sink the bow of an armored battleram, more than enough to make flight impossible.

But then, everything to do with dragons seemed to be impossible: their speech, their intelligence, their flaming breath, their unnatural extra limbs—for surely it would be more right and proper for their wings to be like those of bats, an alteration of the forelegs—and above all the fact that at least one of these legend-bound creatures was alive and here before him, for all that logic said they could not exist in the natural scheme of things. Even though many men might desire dragons, the reality was overpowering. Inexorably the processes of Aldric's thought sheared away surmise, reducing possibilities one by one until only the last remained. If dragons could not exist in a natural world, but one at least unquestionably did, then . . .

Who was the Maker?

And the answer to that was such that Aldric could not bear even to let it shape within his brain.

"I go." Ymareth crouched low on tensed hindlegs, wings arcing up and up above the lean, scaled body until their uttermost tips met and crossed, then poised for the barest moment as the set of their membranes shifted to cup the air.

"Go?" Aldric asked the question hurriedly. "Go where?"

"From here. From this shell. They scarcely will forgive my flaming of their sails, for all that I bade them to stop ere harm befell. So. But the Eye will watch thee as it has watched aforetime. As I will watch thee, Dragon-lord. And I will know that which it is needful for me to know. Until that time, farewell!"

Ymareth's hind-limbs straightened like the throwing-arms of a catapult, flinging the dragon's armored bulk into a great bound towards the sky. An instant later and the wings swept down, their thunderous whack of displaced air ripping away what shreds of sail remained and all but blowing Aldric on to his back as they transformed that prodigious leap into true flight.

The battleram's deck kicked beneath him as it plunged still lower in response to the dragon's take-off thrust, then reared up past the horizontal as Ymareth's weight was abruptly removed. Great concentric ripples rolled away from the ram bow as it smashed back into the sea in a cloud of spray and creamy foam, mingling with the rings of disturbed water where the pressure of the drag-on's wings had slapped brutally against the surface. And then all was still.

There was only a rakish black silhouette in the sky, and the feather touch of that cold breeze from the north. It was a stillness that was all too brief: Aldric had barely risen to his feet, legs weak with reaction and knees sore from the impact of the oak-planked deck, before the two marines behind him shrugged off their firedrake-induced drowse and laid hard hands on his shoulders again. He glanced from side to side, looking at the troopers without really seeing them, and then relaxed in their grip without so much as a token twitch of either arm.

The warship's captain glowered at him, all of his ear-lier frantic anger quite gone now and replaced by a deadly control. He reached out one armored steel-and-leather hand, twisted up the front of the Alban's shirt and used it to lift Aldric onto tip-toe, almost eye-to-eye at last with the tall, lean *hautmarin*.

"It is as well for you, *hlens'l*," he said quietly—too quietly—"that I have my orders. Otherwise I would take great pleasure in supervising your protracted death. Oh, but I would. . . ." He said what he would do, in elaborate detail and at length.

Aldric stared at the officer, hanging in his grasp as limp and unconcerned as a kitten in its mother's mouth; stared at him and through him as if he wasn't there. Ignored him completely. He had heard all the threats before, more or less; some of them were original, indicative of a nasty mind, and some were commonplace. But all, because of those so-important orders, were just onion-scented air and the occasional passion-driven speck of spittle. Nothing more at all. In Aldric's mind right now were two words and two words alone, words which had nothing to do with threats or Drusalan naval officers, or anything so mundane as that. They were words he understood in the literal sense, but did not dare to recognise as a title. Yet. Words that should have been repeated as a question: *Dragon Lord?*

But once the *hautmarin* had run out of breath and invention, he let himself smile slowly and deliberately full in the officer's face. "Despite all that you say, shipmaster," and he used the civilian rank as a clearly understood insult, "all that you can do is write in your report. Yes?"

The Drusalan smirked. "No. Not quite. Take him below."

6

Recruitment

"That's the house," said Dewan. He didn't stop, didn't even slacken his pace, and most certainly did nothing so obvious as to point. But he sounded entirely certain and Gemmel was impressed.

Impressed not only with the results of his companion's ability to extract information—from people who often had not known that they were answering a question— but also by the house itself. Gemmel had tried to avoid preconceived notions of what they might find, but once he had heard that the woman they sought was a courtesan, his mind had replaced the word with all of its uglier alternatives. It was both unusual and uncomfortable: he was normally a most tolerant man.

But once formed, those preconceived notions had led to further misconceptions, errors that were now shattered like glass. None of the *sluts,* or *harlots,* or *whores* of his imaginings would or could live in such a dwelling; at least, if they were still to justify such names as his ungenerous subconscious had supplied. He altered the angle of his stride a fraction, intending to walk straight in—since surely gentlemen callers were familiar at this front door—but without apparent deliberate intent, Dewan was suddenly in the way.

"Not so hasty!" The Vreijek's voice was crisp and commanding, as it had been since first they passed through the Landwall Gate; Dewan could have donned the uniform and half-harness in his laden pack at any time, and not have drawn a second glance by incorrect demeanor. "Take this carefully, man. Remember the battleram. Somebody was here before us—if we're guessing right—and I want to make sure they're gone before we go barging in. So gently does it, eh?"

They walked on, idly curious about their surroundings and no more until Gemmel felt—*sensed* Dewan go tense. "In the stable entry. Don't *look!* One man. Minding his own business. Too much so, I think." There was the faintest whisker of hesitation in Dewan's stride, and Gemmel knew that violence and sudden death were being considered in that instant.

Then the Vreijek relaxed. He even chuckled—a deep, rich sound unusual right now for its incongruity. Now at last Gemmel chanced an over-shoulder glance at the source of such conflicting reactions—and stifled a laugh in his turn. "Ah," was all that he said at first, for all that there was a paragraph of meaning in his tone. Then: "He was minding his own business after all."

"His, and nobody else's."

The man Dewan ar Korentin had seen—and might have killed, had he not chanced that swift second glance— walked past them with no more than a nod and a muttered word of inconsequential greeting. He smelt somewhat of beer and he was busy fastening his breeches.

Gemmel watched him until he passed out of sight around a corner, leaving the street empty but for himself and Dewan. Then he turned a little, and his smile was gone as though it had never existed. "Now—do we stay here, or do we get this matter done with and out of the way?"

"I told you before, don't worry about it. You still talk as if I'm going to put someone's feet in the fire. I'm not."

"Unless you have to. And then you will."

"Not if I can get the information any other way, old wizard, old friend. I served with the Bodyguard Cavalry, not with the Secret Police. But I can still talk a good threat when I have to."

Kathur's head jerked up from the travelling-trunk she had been so frantically packing and turned towards the door of her room, a door that once again framed the back-lit outlines of intruders. Her eyes flickered from one man to the other, back and forth, and the garment in her hands slithered from its folds to hang in an untidy limp tangle like a wet flag. There was a hunted, persecuted look on her face, and it deepened to something near terror when one of the men took the single step necessary to bring him across the threshold; he was broad-shouldered, mustached, the younger of the two and the bigger in all but height, and he looked by far the more likely to hurt her.

Hurting had been very much at the forefront of the Drusalan woman's mind these past few hours. Hurting—and confusion, and misery, and regret, and all those other emotions that early yesterday she would have sworn that she was done with feeling. But now all of those lesser emotions were subordinated by an all-consuming fear.

To his credit, Dewan ar Korentin read her face and her eyes and stopped what he knew must be a threatening advance at once. "Gemmel," he said, using Alban, "best I think that you talk to her and I keep out of it. For now, anyway."

Gemmel shot him a quizzical, eyebrow-lifted glance, but followed the request immediately; he too had seen how terrified the woman was, and from the first glance had been appalled at how she differed from the description Dewan had cajoled from one of the local people. He was more appalled still by the all-too-plain reasons for that difference.

Only the fox-red hair remained unchanged; for the rest, although there was still an eroded beauty in her face and figure, it was masked by her expression and by the purpled tissue of a carefully-administered brutalising. Gemmel's mind refused to accept the lesser alternative of *beating,* because although what he could see was bad enough, the flinching, careful way in which she moved implied that worse was hidden by her clothing. Maliciously, sadistically, much, much worse. And to his own private shame both then and afterwards, the first words which left his mouth were an unjust accusation that he could only blame on shock and the cynicism of one who has seen too much cruelty to too many people to believe that even the most familiar might be incapable of it.

"Lady—did Aldric Talvalin do this to you?"

*	*	*

The battleram limped towards harbor; as she had limped heavily, leadenly, since her fiery encounter with Ymareth. Aldric, on deck and under guard, was limping too. Important prisoner or not, gentleman or not—both matters stridently if uselessly protested—he had perforce assisted the warship's crew to bring their vessel safely into port.

He had not known that the witch-wind enchantment was woven into the pattern and the fabric of the sails. He had not known that destruction of those sails meant destruction of the spell, and consequently of the battleram's ability to move at speed wherever her captain desired regardless of the vagaries of wind and weather. And he had not known—although he had suspected—that without the charmed sails at her mast and bowsprit, an Imperial capital ship became lumbering, ungainly and above all slow.

He knew it now, and the information had been docketed at the back of his mind for possible future reference.

Just as he also knew now—for it was engraved in every muscle of his body that hurt individually and collectively in a symphony of discomfort that would flare to real pain as they cooled and stiffened—how such a vessel must be propelled when the wind was in the wrong quarter for ordinary sails. By such aching muscles as his own.

Not muscles pulling oars, which he might have understood at once had not the lack of oarlocks along the battleram's armored sides denied any such notion. The ship's design was not that of a galley; and in any case her half-dozen close-maneuvering sweeps were too few in number for lengthy propulsion on the high seas. Instead there was some arrangement of shafts and cranks deep in her belly, enhanced by gears and cogs and wheels such as were so beloved by the Drusalans, which ultimately spun a seven-bladed thrust-screw at the vessel's stem. That much the captain had told him with a degree of relish as he was escorted below-decks to the drive chamber which ran almost the full length of the warship's keel and—he alone—shackled by neck and waist to ringbolts in the hull cross-members.

He had at first been advised, not ordered, to strip; and at first he had refused, thinking that it was just another attempt to humiliate him. And had continued to refuse until he saw the conditions in which he would be working. Then he had undressed quickly enough, down to the brief trunks which were the last step before nudity. He kept those. Albans were a modest folk, except in those situations where modesty was an affectation and which situations usually involved women—but he had been grateful that nothing warmer than the too-hot air was pressing on his skin.

That inferno of sweat and stink and nauseous motion would remain one of his choicest nightmares for a very long time. Not being slaves, the men in the drive chamber were not flogged as they worked; Aldric escaped only because of those wonderfully restricting orders. But they laboured achingly hard for all that, feet buckled into stirrup cranks that were like and yet unlike a treadmill, using the big muscles of their thighs and their body weight as well to turn the flywheel-weighted subshafts which led at last to the grinding, greasy main drive. After only a few minutes wrists and arms and spine and legs were all trembling with the strain of the incessant pumping push-and-pull, heads aching and giddy with the constant bending and straightening, hands flayed raw against the brace-bars for all that they were fitted with rotating sleeves against just such an occurrence; backwards and forwards, up and down again, and again, and *again,* hour after hour amid grunts and cries of effort, the constant squeak and clatter of machinery that was so wearing in itself and so unusual to one familiar only with the noises of a sailing-ship, the rush of water against the lead-skinned underwater hull and always in the background like the beating of a weary heart, the whap-whap-whap of the great rotating blades.

But it was over now and Aldric felt a certain glow of satisfaction, even of pride. Having been forced to the work and given no other option, he had done as well as any of the others who, he fancied, were more used to it. He had neither vomited nor fainted, although he had witnessed both, and he had completed his "shift," as the drivemaster-serjeant termed it, without flagging behind his fellows. Maybe he had been lucky, because he had been right below one of the shafts which drew cool fresh air from the open deck—by means of yet more bladed propellers, these turned by boy-sailors—but even so, that was not to say he would be in any haste to repeat the experience. Nevertheless it had crossed his mind that the underwater drive-screw at least preserved the integrity of the warship's armored shell, and that if there was another way than manpower to propel a ship in that fashion, it might well be worth a closer study . . .

It was then that somebody—some evil-minded bastard!—had sluiced him down with a bucket of icy fresh-drawn seawater all over his naked, sweat-scalded skin, and in the sudden horrific-becoming-glorious shock Aldric forgot everything else.

That had all been half an hour ago. Now, dressed in borrowed clothes and feeling at least marginally cleaner—if also hellishly tired—he stood on the battleram's fore-deck in the shadow of one of her weapon-turrets and watched as she was teased with a delicacy that approached art into a stonewalled holding bay little wider than the ship herself. Evening was approaching, and both his own vessel—he smiled wryly at that unconscious usage of the possessive—and the five or so others either in fortified docks like this or riding at anchor out in what seemed an estuary, were showing lights. That understatement scarcely described the hulking armored vessels which were illuminated like so many ocean-going mansions; or rather, like the floating fortresses they were.

"Alban?" It was *tau-kortagor* Garet again; one of the several men aboard who had treated him with markedly more friendliness since his unstinting efforts down in the warship's drive chamber. "You disembark here, Alban. *Teynaur* is going into dry-dock for repair after . . ."

"After what happened?"

"Yes." The expression within Garet's helmet might conceivably have been a grin. "You're being talked about."

"I can't say that I'm surprised. What do they say?"

"Do you want the polite version, or the truth?"

This time it was Aldric's turn to grin, even though the

expression looked stretched and uncomfortable. "If
that's the way of it, forget I asked. But . . ." He hesitated, knowing that he was about to presume on a tenuous bond of acquaintance—not even friendship!—which
probably didn't exist at all. "Where are we? And who
had me brought here?"

The questions seemed to make Garet uncomfortable;
at least he turned his head away as if fascinated by non-
events at the far end of the harbor, and Aldric could no
longer see his face. "The first I'm not allowed to answer," Garet said without looking back, "and the second, at my rank"—he touched a finger pointedly to the
solitary rank-bar at his collar—"I'm not allowed to
know."

Aldric shrugged. It was the sort of response he should
have expected, even if more courteously phrased than it
might have been; but a waste of time and breath for all
that. With a nod of acknowledgement to the officer-
cadet, he squared his shoulders and walked—not slowly,
but not especially fast—to a boarding-ladder where the
crew of the ship's cutter were waiting to take him
ashore. Ashore!

Lord God! Beyond the quays and the loading-cranes
that were commonplace on any waterfront whether military or civilian lay a sprawling structure that had nothing
whatever to do with wharves or warehouses. It was a
fortification, walled and turreted, gated and grim, and
its courtyards were alive with troops of horse and foot moving purposefully to and fro. Even to one accustomed to
such things it was an unnerving sight.

Teynaur had put into harbor three days late. This was
the first day of the tenth month, the first day of the
beginning of winter, and the evening sky was gray as
woodsmoke. Despite the many lanterns which bejew-
elled its massive walls, the crouched shape of the stronghold was ugly and ominous beneath that somber canopy
of cloud. Its spired turrets were stark against the lowering heavens and the banners which they bore—
indecipherable in the dusk—flapped listlessly from their
poles. There was no elegance in the place, none at all;
not even that austere grace sometimes born of pure

functional design. This looked like no more than it was: a fortress—and a prison.

Aldric stared out over the bows of the cutter and tried to keep real and imagined terrors under control. The sort of power involved here was appalling, and he could not imagine who would want him so badly that a fully-crewed battleram could be sent to bring him back. He fancied that he was soon to find out.

"Hlens'l?" One of the marine escort tapped him on the shoulder and proffered a leather bottle of the regulation pattern which all Imperial troopers carried as part of their equipment. If there was one thing Aldric would never refuse at a moment like this, it was a drink—even the notoriously rough, sour ration red. But at least it was cool in his dry mouth and warm in his belly and head; that was enough reason to gulp it down. He drank a little more, stifled a nasty acid belch—there was nothing but the wine inside him, and his stomach was complaining about both matters—then handed the bottle back and tried to snuggle deeper into the wolfskin *coyac* that someone had returned to him. While it didn't make him feel much warmer, it did make him wonder for just a moment about something other than his own imminent fate.

What phase was the moon just now?

Then the cutter bumped against a wooden jetty and he all but fell off the upturned barrel which was doing duty as his seat. The marines laughed, but not unkindly, and made observations about Albans and army-issue wine which Aldric preferred to ignore. He had in his time downed enough alcohol to float the *Teynaur,* and never before had he tasted stuff that was so obviously rented for re-cycling.

Two soldiers—regulars in crimson armor and full-visored helmets, not Fleet marines—came clattering down the steps of the jetty and lifted Aldric bodily, as if he was a sack of meal. He wasn't pleased. Directly his feet touched the lowermost step, weed-covered slimy wood but dry land for all that, he shrugged himself free.

"Thank you both, gentlemen," he said, "but I *can* walk quite well without you." For once he managed to achieve the right tone of injured dignity rather than dangerous rudeness, but that was not why the soldiers laughed—a hollow, metallic sound inside their closed helmets.

It was because, as Aldric discovered, legs that were both tired and grown accustomed to the constant motion of a deck found the immobility of solid ground a far from certain footing.

But he managed. Just.

The first two soldiers flanked him, presumably in case he did fall after all, but several more who had remained atop the jetty formed up behind and in front before setting off at an unsettlingly rapid march-pace. *Teynaur* was late, therefore he was late, therefore his presence was required at once. The Imperial *at once* did not leave room for excuse or further delay.

Their destination was one of the largest buildings within the fortress complex, and as they approached its door up a flight of broad stone steps, the sentries to either side of the door flung it open so that the little group could pass through without breaking stride. The sullen boom as it was slammed shut behind them had an unpleasantly final sound, but Aldric was given no time for reflection and little enough in which to look around.

This place might have started life at some time in the past as a palace or a mansion—before the military took over—and it remained a building where the high-born of the Empire would not look out of place. But there were no aristocrats in the handsome panelled corridors this evening: just soldiers, some in half-armor but most in tunics with both their arms full of paperwork. Even when the passages were briefly free of hurrying figures there was an air of furious activity, a tension which made the atmosphere tingle.

The boots of Aldric's escort awoke echoes in a vaulted hall as he was quick-marched through, neither pushed nor forced but simply hemmed about so closely that he either matched their pace of his own volition or had his heels trodden by the rearguard. They rounded another corner, entered a short, well-lit corridor which had only one doorway at its end and then stopped dead, for this passage was lined with soldiers.

These were big men in full battle harness, and their faces were uniformly blanked by the featureless closed visors of their helmets. There were six of them across the double doors, razor-edged gisarms carried at the port; but when two of Aldric's guards continued to advance, all of the sentries took a single well-drilled forward step—a step so precise and simultaneous that Aldric half-expected to hear the whirr of machinery—and levelled their spears, three at each chest. There was something cold, something automatic about their manner; something chilling. It was a suggestion that these men had their orders, and if those orders involved killing comrades-in-arms, then the killing would be done with dispatch and without a second thought. Only when the senior-ranked soldier of the escort spoke a password did the wicked points withdraw, and as if the word had set off a new series of signals, four of the gate-wards stepped aside while the remaining two threw all their weight into opening the ponderous bronze-sheathed doors.

The room revealed beyond the threshold was long, and low, and wide; lamps burned in sconces along its walls, striking reflections from the polished table which dominated the center of the floor, from the crystal goblets which rested on it—and from the gold-worked crimson armor of the twenty Imperial officers who sat along its sides and who turned as one man to stare at the intruder in their doorway.

Escort or no escort, Aldric froze in his tracks. At his back there was a rippling clatter of parade salutes, and only after they had been completed did someone give the Alban a much-needed shove between the shoulder-blades to send him stumbling into the conference room.

As he halted and straightened up a little, he eyed the officers dubiously—for their part, nineteen-twentieths of them regarded him with open curiosity—but at the same time he felt the stirrings of relief. There was real power here, the kind of power he had thought to find at the back of all—that of the Imperial military machine. Oh yes, Aldric knew the yellow metal bars and double diamonds of general-rank insignia when he saw them, and there were several right before his eyes. But he also knew the Emperor's crest of the eight-pointed star, and that was worked in precious metal on the temples of each man's helmet, resting on the table among the wine-cups. Emperor Ioen's supporters had no grudge against King Rynert's men—he had been assured of that, and it was one of the reasons which had brought him here to the Empire, what seemed so very long ago. Not caring who could overhear him, Aldric released a gusty sigh of held-in breath. Whatever he might hear from these granite-faced gentry would never be as bad as his imaginings.

There was one officer in particular who drew his eyes; the man was seated at the head of the table, gazing at him steadily, saying nothing, his only movement the slow *tap-tap-tap* of one index finger. His rank-marks were of a type of which Aldric had only been told and had never seen: the twin bars of commissioned rank, and over them a pyramid made up of three diamonds. All in bullion gold soft and pure enough to scratch with a fingernail. This was the most senior of all Drusalan military ranks, before political significance took over: *en-coerhanalth,* Lord General. But which one? With a perfunctory gesture of his hand the officer dismissed Aldric's escort— all but two who closed in to grip the Alban by wrists and biceps—before he rose and strode down the hall to confront his captive at close quarters.

He was a stocky man, this general—Aldric's own height, but with an already-broad build made massive by the armor which encased him. Though his grizzled beard and balding iron-gray hair were those of a middle-aged man, there was no dullness of age in the pale eyes which glinted below his heavy brows. Those eyes drilled through Aldric as if, like Ymareth's, they probed the innermost recesses of his mind. Except that this officer appeared more plainly to disapprove of what he saw there.

Aldric swallowed and refused to meet that piercing stare. Even without the guards, the other officers, the armor and the marks of rank, this man had a forbidding presence of his own. One blunt-fingered hand reached out, closed on Aldric's chin and lifted it up and back from where instinct had tucked it low over his throat. A finger of the other hand tapped—as it had done to the table—against the heavy silver torque of the Alban's crest-collar, and the general grunted softly to himself as if satisfied. That same finger touched lightly against the scar on Aldric's face, and this time the tone of the grant was displeasure at the wound's apparent newness. A moment more and the general turned away. "Release him," he said over his shoulder, and Aldric felt a muscle in his face tic involuntarily. Because the language of the order was his own.

Massaging his arms more for something to do than because they hurt—even though the sentries' grip had been tight enough to stop the flow of blood, and it tingled in his fingers as it returned to them—Aldric watched all the officers surreptitiously from under drooping eyelids. And the general who spoke Alban most of all.

"My lord," he said, cringing inwardly at the loudness of his own voice in the silence, "I thank you." He bowed a little, as was polite; then looked straight at the general, as was not polite at all, and tried not to care that his direct gaze might be considered insolent and dealt with as such. "But I would thank you rather more if I knew what the hell was going on!"

Nineteen high-ranked officers growled their displeasure—suggesting that each and every one of them was familiar with colloquial Alban—but the twentieth merely inclined his head. "Talvalin," he said. The statement was neither confirmed nor denied by so much as the flick of an eyelid, but he nodded again, seeming content. "Aldric Talvalin. Yes. Your file suggested that you might react like this." Aldric didn't miss the inference, delivered with all the subtlety of a battleaxe: *We know all about you, boy.* "And I," the bearded lips allowed themselves a thin smile, "am Lord General Goth."

At last. At long last.

Aldric did the most sensible and indeed the most appropriate thing he could in the circumstances—he knelt and offered Goth the elaborate courtesy of Second Obeisance that was due to him as senior officer here and thus technically lord of the place. It also gave him a chance to get his betraying facial muscles under control, so that when he sat back he was hiding behind a cool, inscrutable, half-smiling mask.

Goth half-smiled as well. "There is a proverb among my people, Aldric Talvalin. It refers to your people: 'Be wary of the Alban when he bows to hide his face.' Should I be wary of you, perhaps?"

Aldric shrugged; he doubted it. Doubted indeed if there was much this man had to be wary of, anywhere at all. Lord General Goth was third man in the Drusalan Imperial hierarchy, and paramount military commander— for despite its martial title, the office of Grand Warlord was more political than anything else; recent events had made that all too clear. Equally, or most likely more important, he was virtual father to young Emperor Ioen. Much as Gemmel was to Aldric, but for years longer. He was a man of honor, although it was Drusalan honor and more flexible than most Alban *kailinin* would have tolerated. Goth, in doing what he considered necessary for the good of the Empire, had been required to twist his vaunted honor almost beyond recognition.

"Then be seated, Aldric-*an*," the general invited. "Properly." It wasn't really an invitation at all, and Aldric did as he was told. "First," continued Goth when the Alban had settled himself, "I ask pardon for the means which brought you here."

Since the verb he used for "ask" was in an imperative mode, it seemed unlikely to be just a linguistic slip. That kind of accident was only made by such as Goth for its effect. So Aldric nodded and smiled, and made all the courteous little wordless gestures of one dismissing a paltry inconvenience.

Rather than an experience which had been terrifying at the time—he admitted this without hesitation, if only to himself—and which had still done little in the way of reassurance.

"Now, as to the reason for it all." Goth leaned back in his chair and made ready to talk at length; Aldric had seen such expressive body language before, too many times, for both Gemmel and Dewan were great preachers when the mood was on them. "You must realize, of course, that you were in what we regard here as debatable territory—most seaports must perforce be. . . ."

Locking an expression of polite interest onto his face, Aldric let five minutes of speculation and political theory wash over him. Either he had heard it all before, or he hadn't been interested in finding out about it the first time around. Then Goth said something which jarred him back to full awareness.

". . . and more than my men knew of your presence there."

Something of what he felt must have shown on Aldric's face despite his endeavours towards guarded neutrality, for Goth leaned forward and wagged a disapproving finger at him—a tutorial gesture much in keeping with his tone of voice.

"Come now, you didn't really think the goings-on at Seghar went unnoticed, did you?" He stared more closely, spade beard jutting pugnaciously. "Or *did* you?"

Aldric said nothing.

"Well . . . !" There was a deal of private opinion in the way that Goth exhaled the word, but he elaborated no further and instead lifted one armored shoulder in the beginnings of a shrug. "No matter now. But given the situation—and your apparent frame of mind—you would scarcely have paused for conversation had you been approached by armored regulars like those who brought you here. Besides which, their presence would have made my hand too plain. As I say, there were more eyes than mine in Tuenafen. So I was forced to resort to—shall we say, other means? Despite some opposition."

As if on cue one of the other officers got to his feet, snapped a perfunctory salute and began to address his superior in what Aldric could only think of as a polite shout—if such a thing were not a blatant contradiction in terms. Certainly it was very different from the muted voices at King Rynert's war council before the Dunrath campaign.

Another man rose, nodded to his equals, saluted his superiors and joined the discussion—if discussion was really the word for it, and Aldric was still not sure that it was. This man's oration carried more shouting and less politeness, so that the tapping of Goth's finger began again. Both speakers employed dialect, as Geruath of Seghar had done all those months ago—and for the same reason: so that the foreigner present wouldn't understand.

As indeed he couldn't. Aldric was curious to learn how they knew this fact; eager, too, to find out the other score or so of things which were perplexing him right now.

"Gentlemen," Goth said finally, his tone indicating a full stop to the discussion, "gentlemen, we voted on this matter when the plan was first proposed." He spoke Drusalan, and though the drawling accent which seemed to be a trademark of the military made understanding difficult, what he said was clear enough to Aldric. All too clear.

Plan? a voice was yelling in his mind. *Nobody told me about a plan!*

The first officer jumped up, scowling, and barked out a few words before making an indignant gesture in Aldric's direction.

"We have not been *forced* to anything," returned Goth. "This was a choice made by the whole council. And yes, Hasolt, I do remember your views at the time. Do you want to make your objections formal—a matter of record?"

"Kham-au tah, Coerhanalth Goth!" The officer glanced around the table, shot another unfriendly glare at Aldric and began to count off points on his fingers. *"Ka telej-hu, sho'ta en kailin tach; cho-hui k'lechje-schach hlakh t'aiyo? Teiij h'labech da?"*

This time, either because of his passion or because he no longer cared who understood him, the officer called Hasolt used Drusalan. Even without it Aldric could have taken meaning from his words and waving arms; and his complaint was one with which the Alban could—almost—sympathise. He had been led to expect a warlord, a *kailin,* and Light of Heaven alone knew what picture Hasolt had created in his mind. What he got, and what he was being asked to accept on the same terms, was a singularly scruffy *eijo*. A man who, as he said, could as easily be *h'labech*. A spy.

"Hasolt." Goth's voice was sharper now, and the officer fell silent. "That's quite enough. If you want to continue in this vein, then at least have the courtesy to speak so that our *guest* can understand. He may well wish to challenge you as a result."

Hasolt licked his lips, then bowed curtly and sat down; he was aware that he was in the wrong, but at the same time he was trying to retain some face by an air of respectful defiance. One thing was certain: he wanted no challenges from *eijin*. What Drusalans knew of the landless warriors was crude and melodramatic; it made them artificial, characters from a cheap play rather than the honor-bound self-exiled men they truly were. Seldom heroic, often villainous, always lethal. The perfect anti-hero. Not all of it was fact.

But not all of it was fiction.

Aldric suspected that Goth knew much more about his guest than he had confided to his colleagues. He wanted—needed—to know how much more; to know where the general had obtained his information. And there was one other question which, discourteous or not, seemingly cowardly or not, he had to ask.

"*Coerhanalth* Goth-*eir?*" The Drusalan glanced in his direction, eyebrows lifting in query. "Sir, what plan is this?"

"Ah. So Rynert didn't tell you after all? That was most remiss of him."

The reply sent an apprehensive shudder scurrying down Aldric's spine, and he felt his mouth go dry as the fear he had suppressed so well came flooding back. "Tell me? Tell me what? I was requested to deliver messages of—of some delicacy to Lord General Goth, in a place of his own choosing. Nothing more."

"Indeed." Goth steepled his fingers and stared at them in a very Rynert-like gesture. "Ah well." He seemed to come to some decision and looked past Aldric at the escort who had brought him from the harbor. "Return him his black knife," he told the escort leader, "then dismiss."

Aldric looked at the *tsepan* where it had been laid
gently—the soldier had either been warned in advance
about disrespect, or knew anyway—on the table before
him, and heard without hearing the clatter as the armored troopers took their leave. His *tsepan.* The Guardian of his Honor. A blade whose scars crossed his left
hand, scars he would carry to the fire. He lifted the
weapon gently, almost between finger and thumb, and
felt its black lacquer cool and comforting against his
sweaty skin as he pushed it through the belt which closed
his borrowed shirt-tunic. "General," he spoke Drusalan
himself now, for sincerity's sake, "again I thank you. For
returning my," the proper word eluded him, ". . . my
self-respect. But—what plan?"

"Was no mention made of certain favours you might
do for me—you and your sword?"

"I don't . . ." Aldric closed his teeth on the excuse.
Rynert's words were months in the past, but he had an
uneasy feeling that the king had indeed said something
of that sort. What was it? "If there is any favour you—
and Isileth—can do to further prove my friendship, then
I expect it to be done." A mere courtesy phrase to indicate cooperation with tacit allies, or so it had seemed at
the time. Now he wasn't so sure. "Suppose you hear
the messages?" he wondered at last, hopefully. Those
messages had been locked within his skull by sorcery,
and only those for whom they were meant knew how to
release them. Which meant they *had* to be important;
Rynert had said his messenger's rank alone served to
make them so, and Aldric was about to say as much
when a hollow, metallic voice spoke right behind his
head—where nobody had any right to be without his
knowing of it.

"Tell him, Goth—then perhaps we can get on."

It was probably impossible to get out of such a deep
and well-upholstered chair with quite the speed that Aldric managed then, but when he was as startled as he
had become in the past few seconds impossibilities
ceased to concern him.

The man who stood far too close for comfort at his
back was almost six feet tall, and though he was leanly
built there was altogether too much of him to enter any

room without someone as nervous as Aldric Talvalin at least suspecting he was there. Yet he had done so, with absolute success, and now stood with his arms nonchalantly folded as if proud of the fact. Grave and elegant in crimson and silver beneath the dragonsblood cloak of the Imperial military, he wore its hood drawn part-way over his head. But it was what that hood left exposed that started Aldric's pulse-rate jumping.

For it was a mask of mirror-polished steel.

There were far too many deeply-ingrained images from his memories of cu Ruruc and the demon-sending Esel in that tall, silent figure; enough, and more than enough, for him to jerk his newly-regained *tsepan* from its scabbard. Even though the suicide dirk was no fighting weapon, it had killed before—Overlord Geruath of Seghar, that had been, and at the hands of his own son. And anyway, it was all that he had. His own warped, miniscule reflection stared back at him from the surface of the mask. There was nothing else to read from that blank visage: no threat, no anger, no amusement. Nothing at all.

"Aldric!" Goth's voice was sharp with urgency. "Aldric, it's all right. This man is a friend." Tense seconds passed before the younger man relaxed enough to move from his attack-ready posture, and even then it was only to retreat on stiff, poised legs from an immobile would-be opponent. Not until Aldric was content with the separation space did he chance a single glance at Goth.

"If he's a friend, then make him show his face."

The masked head shook from side to side, just once, unspeaking but quite clear. No.

"He won't do that at your command, Aldric-*an*," the general said. "Or mine. This is Bruda. Prokrator Bruda, the other man your king commanded you to meet. *En Hauthanalth Kagh' Ernvakh*." Aldric stared, not understanding until the general elaborated further. "Call him Commander of the Guardians of Honor." Everyone caught the Alban's eyes flick from the glittering mask to the glittering blade of his own *tsepan*. "Or call him Lord of the Honorable Guard. He's Chief of the Empire's Secret Police."

Aldric returned the *tsepan* maybe a finger's length to

its scabbard and hesitated, glancing thoughtfully from the slender blade to Bruda's cold steel face; then he shrugged and slid the weapon home. "Secret Police." There was a world of unvoiced insult in the way he sneered the words. "So. Now I begin to understand."

"Perhaps you do." Bruda unfolded his arms, seeming quite unruffled by the display of open hostility. "And perhaps you merely think so." Snapping his fingers, he pointed in a single sweeping gesture to the officers who sat at each side of the table, and ended it with an over-shoulder jerk of his palm towards the door. "By my command," he said, "out." And that was all.

To Aldric's slight surprise they did as they were bidden at once, without question—and without a word of protest at the Prokrator's high-handed manner. That in itself told him a thing or two about the power of the Secret Police. But as he turned his head to watch them go, he caught his first glimpse of three men who stood silently in the lee of the doorway; men who by their appearance had nothing to do with the military conference but everything to do with Bruda. Only one he recognised: Garet, the officer-cadet who had been his gaoler aboard *Teynaur*. The others he had never seen before.

There was a man in armor, flashed with *tau-kortagor*'s rank bars like those Garet wore, and alongside them—also like Garet now, though they had not been there before—silver thunderbolt insignia which meant nothing to Aldric other than that Bruda wore them prominently at the collar of his robe. Whilst the third stranger was strangest of all, for he was a replica of the Prokrator himself, with a mask—this of red-enamelled metal etched with patterns that seemed to mean more than simple decoration—and a wide-shouldered scarlet over-robe stiff with matching silver-worked embroidery. Aldric's first impression was of some reptilian creature which only incidentally resembled a man; and it was an impression which refused to go away.

"My chief lieutenant, *Hautheisart* Voord," said Bruda in that resonant metallic voice of his, and Voord bowed with a courtier's grace. "I think you know his action squad already. *Tau'hach-kortagorn* Tagen and Garet."

Aldric looked steadily at the two officer-cadets, guess-

ing privately that such a low rank in the Secret Police
was far from low at all. Garet's profession of ignorance
had been no more than that. "We have met, yes—but
not socially. And without formal introduction."

A wintery smile crossed Goth's hard features. "We'll
be talking for a while yet; I think refreshments would
be in order. See about it, and bring Lord Aldric's gear
and equipment."

"All of it?" Voord's voice was plainly quite youthful—
and petulant—despite the hollow echoes of the mask.

"All. Do it. Now."

Aldric suppressed a smile; he had sensed from the
very first that Voord probably didn't like him much. The
reason didn't concern him, and it certainly wasn't going
to cause any sleepless nights since it was plain that as
Goth's "guest" he enjoyed a somewhat privileged position. The situation was one he was fully prepared to
use. Then his hearing plucked a familiar name from the
background mutter of conversation, and without thinking he echoed it aloud.

"Kathur?" Heads turned, and though he could see
only one face of the three that mattered, all were probably alike in their quizzical expression. "Then I was
right."

"Right about what?" Voord was the first to voice everyone's question.

"About the woman, Kathur—in Tuenafen. That it
wasn't a coincidence, when she and I . . ." He stopped,
embarrassed, but his meaning was clear enough.

"*Kagh' Ernvakh* regard coincidence as useful," said
Bruda, "only when we create and control it. At all other
times I dislike it intensely. Though it does seem that the
woman in question—"

"Went beyond her instructions rather," finished Voord,
and had his face been on show it would have been
stretched by an unpleasant salacious grin. "She was ordered to contact you, to keep an eye on you. The fact
that she chose to keep much more than an eye should
be a source of some amusement, *hlens'l*. It most certainly
was to me."

"Kathur wouldn't talk about—" Aldric burst out, and
was promptly silenced by a wave of Voord's hand. There

was something wrong with that hand, something horribly wrong.

"Kathur would," the *hautheisart* said with a nasty air of authority. "And did. After the proper persuasion. At considerable descriptive length. She gave you a very, very good report—one you should be proud of."

"Voord!" Goth really had no need for the added emphasis of a flat-handed slap against the table; that an Imperial Lord General had cause to raise his voice was emphatic enough. "I earlier had cause to warn *Eldheisart* Hasolt about insulting talk. Stop it. At once!"

Voord swung round on the general and, secure in his own power and the power of what he represented, paused just long enough for insolence but not so long that it was obvious. Only then did he salute. "Of course, sir. Immediately, sir. But these are merely facts related to me by one of my own agents. Sir . . ."

"Whether they're merely facts or your own opinions, Lord *Commander* Voord, be good enough to suppress them. Because regardless of your arm of service, Lord *Commander,* three gold diamonds outrank one in silver, and any *junior* officer can be broken by a *superior.* Do I make myself perfectly clear?"

"Eminently so, sir!" Voord was at attention now, and very likely sweating inside his mask. "But I would point out, sir, that this agent, this *woman* thought enough of the prisoner—"

"Guest, Voord, not prisoner. Guest."

"Thought enough of him to threaten me with a weapon later proved to be both loaded and lethal."

"And were you disturbed by this threat, *Hautheisart* Voord? Did it frighten you?" Goth's voice was silky.

"Frighten? Not for a moment, sir!"

"Then you were a fool. If you spoke to her as you have spoken to me, I'm surprised she didn't at least mark you just to teach you manners!"

"Lucky for her that she didn't."

Goth stroked his beard a moment and stared at Voord without troubling to hide his dislike. Then he smiled with a quick gleam of teeth and no humor at all. "But luckier for you."

It was perhaps as well that at that point the chamber doors were opened to admit several retainers. Most carried trays of food and drink, but two bore benches, on which were items that Aldric had thought he would never see again. His armor, left behind in Tuenafen—or so he had thought. His saddlebags and saddle, suggesting that just possibly Lyard had been transported here as well. It was not beyond the bounds of possibility. Then he saw what was tucked like an afterthought into the facial opening of his helmet's warmask; a cylinder of papers, bound with tape and sealed with the crest—he could see it even at this distance—of the Imperial Fleet. It had the look of a report about it; the sort of report that a warship commander might put in concerning certain irregularities on his last voyage.

Voord—Voord, Voord, Voord: where had he heard that name before?—stepped forward and plucked the scroll from its resting-place, snapping away the seal with his left hand. Aldric looked at that hand and shivered; something most unpleasant had happened to the *hautheisart* at some time, to leave him with such a claw, and it made his own few scars entirely insignificant. After only a moment scanning the sheets as they uncoiled from their tight roll, Voord nodded as if they had contained no more than he expected, glanced with his expressionless masked face towards Aldric and then laid them with a flourish on the table before Goth.

"Will you take wine?" Aldric jumped a little; the voice at his shoulder belonged to Bruda, who moved with uncanny silence for such a large man; the sight and sound of this sinister figure playing the courteous host— and playing it well—chilled him with a recollection of where he was.

"I . . . I would rather something with more strength, I thank you," he replied, cursing his jumpiness, cursing his shock-born stammer and taking refuge in slightly stiff formality. When he was offered Elthanek malted-barley spirit, he didn't for once pause a second to wonder how it had passed through the various blockades between its source and his hand. Instead he put the glass to his mouth, feeling and hearing its rim clink against his teeth, and let the liquid fire within it run down his throat to light a small, comforting furnace in the pit of his stomach. There he took another swallow; and a third.

There was a small metallic click behind him and Bruda removed his mask before helping himself to some food. Voord did likewise, and there was a third and more final clatter from the door as Garet and his companion secured it to keep unauthorised eyes from the faces of the Empire's Secret Police.

Aldric's eyes might well have been regarded as unauthorised, but special dispensation had left him on this side of the door so he stared his fill. First at Voord, he being closest—and also most likely to be annoyed by the scrutiny. The *hautheisart*'s features were those of a young man, sufficiently so to be remarkable when set against the markings of his rank. He was only a couple of years older than Aldric, most likely, and he looked thin, stretched, gaunt—although it was difficult to be sure about that, for there was armor beneath his patterned overrobe and it gave his body a bulk it probably lacked in the flesh.

Voord's hair was fine and washed-out blond, almost colorless; he wore it brushed straight back from a high, intelligent forehead that gave him a disdainful air. Hooded light-blue eyes returned Aldric's gaze with an apparent or well-played lack of interest—his mask, as was its purpose, had concealed an initial monstrous curiosity about the Alban's wolfskin jerkin, a curiosity born of reluctant, unbelieving familiarity. His whole attitude was one of studied indifference, and only his mouth was wrong; to match his languid expression it should have been full-lipped and decadent. Instead it was little more than a flaw in a clean-shaven face carved of white alabaster.

Bruda, for all his seniority in rank, seemed rather more approachable, more likely to make that small effort which bridges the gap from acquaintance to—however superficial—friendliness. It was a small thing, but one which experience had taught Aldric to regard as important. The Prokrator's face, that of a man in his early forties for all that he moved like one fifteen years younger, was . . . ordinary. Totally ordinary. Aldric was disappointed at first; he had expected drama, an angular jaw, high cheekbones, distinctive, icy eyes. Something to make this man look like what he was.

And then he realized that Bruda was *perfect* for what he was. Apart from his height, and there was nothing unusual about it for there were many who were taller, there was nothing about the Prokrator to hang a memory on. His features were regular, symmetrical; neither scar nor blemish nor any other distinguishing mark marred the smoothness of his skin, which in itself contrived not to be so smooth as to be worth remarking on. Even his sweeping mustache meant nothing, because mustaches could be shaved—or false. For all that he had the necessary eyes, and nose, and mouth—which themselves were neither large nor small nor irregularly shaped—Bruda to all intents and purposes had no face.

Aldric took another mouthful of spirit, fully aware as he raised the refilled glass that this and the ration red he had downed earlier were the only things in his stomach. He was equally aware how quickly that would make him . . . relaxed; and the prospect concerned him not at all. There was nothing now that would better his situation, and probably nothing short of an armed assault on the three officers could make it any worse. All of this hospitality hadn't fooled him; he knew the honeyed bait before a trap when he tasted it. The Alban *eijo*—for if that was what they wanted, that was what he would be—grinned on one side of his face with an expression he didn't trouble to complete, and drained the glass instead.

Made bolder by the alcohol which had already percolated into his system, he studied the discarded mask: those metal screens that were the public visage of *Kagh' Ernvakh*. Then he lifted the nearest—Bruda's—for closer inspection and looked up from his own face reflected back at him to meet the Prokrator's curious gaze. "Why?" was all he said.

"The masks? See for yourself. Status, and a mark of rank; secrecy, and somewhere to hide my face." Even Bruda's voice—and he was speaking Alban now—had no accent. No accent at all. Neither the underlying throatiness and sibilance of one whose first tongue was Drusalan, nor the nasal purr of the Jouvaine; not even any of the Albans' own regional colorations. The words emerged and were understood, but their source remained untraceable.

Aldric set down the mask and saw how even the lamplight seemed to shudder from its polished curves and angles. Or maybe that was just the slight movement of his own touch. "Yes. I see. All too well, I think."

"Bruda!" General Goth spoke from the head of the table, where he held a sheet of paper at arms' length with the plain wish that it could be held further still. "Bruda, read this if you would. The rest of you: Voord, Tagen, Garet, be seated. We should begin the business which has brought us here."

"Myself included, Goth-*eir*? asked Aldric, lifting his eyes from the steel mirror of the mask.

"Especially yourself. This concerns you—both as a man and as an agent of your king."

"Of course." If there was a faint edge to his voice, it was not directed at the general. "But have I a choice— whether to accept or to refuse involvement?" Even as he asked the question Aldric heard Bruda's soft, inhaled oath as the Prokrator read what a certain Imperial ship-commander had to say about a certain passenger aboard his vessel; and that inhalation told him what the answer would be. *Had* to be. And he was right.

Out of the three who might have given a reply, it was Goth who voiced it. "I regret not, Aldric," the general told him, but for all that there seemed to be little regret in the man's tone.

"Then I'd as soon not hear your plan at all."

"You misunderstand, *hlensyarl*," said Voord unpleasantly. "What the Lord General means is that you have no choice at all."

Aldric favoured him with a neutral glance. "We'll see. Afterwards. But for now," he deliberately turned his back on the *hautheisart* and inclined his head courteously towards the two senior officers, "whenever you wish to begin, sirs, I will be ready to listen."

"Our Emperor," said Goth, "has a sister; Princess Marevna. And she has spent the past two months under lock and key in the Red Tower at Egisburg."

"A princess," echoed Aldric in an odd, small voice. "Imprisoned in a tower. Yes. You did say, tower?"

"I did. The Red Tower. At Egisburg." Goth looked at him curiously, wondering just a little; but it was Bruda who tilted back his chair and hid the start of a smile behind one hand. He could see what way Aldric's thoughts were tending, and what their reaction might eventually be; and it was something which the sober, serious general might not like—even though it tickled Bruda hugely.

"It was her misfortune," that Prokrator continued, once his twitching mouth was under control, "to be on the wrong side of what is really a truce line (although nobody will ever dare to call it that) when yet another of those damned interminable so-called demarcation conferences—peace talks, if you really want to know—when yet another of those wrangles fell apart and the borders were closed. Marevna and her people were stopped well short of the frontier, taken into custody, and there they've been ever since."

Bruda pushed papers to and fro on the table, then flicked a glance at Aldric from under his lowered brows. "I don't know how Etzel's cavalry patrol came to be where they were at so opportune a moment. But I do know that the breakdown of the conference was engineered; I was there, and I saw it happen. Someone, somewhere, is playing a double game and when I find out who . . ."

"Knowing or not knowing does little to help the princess just now," Goth said stiffly. "She's a political prisoner and her continued well-being is the Emperor's responsibility."

Aldric nodded; this was a standard enough ploy. "What was the threat this time?" he asked blandly. There had to be a threat, there was *always* a threat.

"This." Goth set a tiny, elegant box on the table. Made of ivory, it was covered in a fine mesh of carving, openwork so that the red satin of its lining could peep through in contrast—the sort of thing in which a lady would keep her choicest gems. "This contained the letter by which Emperor Ioen was informed of his sister's abduction."

"And how many boxes did Grand Warlord Etzel promise to return the princess in, if her brother didn't behave himself?"

"Enough," said Bruda flatly, all his humor quite evaporated. "And he isn't bluffing. Never in all the years of the Sherban dynasty has any warlord made an idle threat."

"I can imagine," said Aldric. "Yes indeed." What point in making ferocious noises if the violence they promised was never carried out?

"For the sake of political balance it is vital that the princess be rescued," Goth was ticking points off on his fingers now, "and equally vital that the Emperor should have no connection with anything irregular."

Aldric looked at the general and fought back yet another crazy, humorless chuckle. Typical, he thought, that outright war was preferable to subterfuge. But then subterfuge of another kind had brought him here. As Goth explained further, he—Aldric—represented Alban support for the enterprise as no words ever could. An enterprise that was potentially lethal and which had at all costs to be resolved without unnecessary bloodshed. Neither side wanted a war if it could be avoided—but if it came, each would prefer the other to have started it.

"So then, my lord Aldric-*arluth* Talvalin," the general gave him his title for the first time, in much the same way any wheedling request is preceded by flattery, "what think you of our predicament?"

There was silence up and down the table; heads turned to stare at Aldric, waiting expectantly for his reply. And Aldric did as Prokrator Bruda had expected that he might.

He laughed . . .

"You mean—You mean to say that this is why I was dragged halfway across the Empire? For a story I might tell to children! Princesses and towers and wicked lords, by God!" He kicked back from the table, a jolting violent movement which brought Voord's honor guard out of their seats with swords half-drawn. "Sit down, you two!" the Alban snarled. "I won't bite!" Neither man moved, and he shrugged. "Then please yourselves. I no longer care."

"Aldric! Hear us out, man." It was Bruda now, the one man among the lot of them whom possibly he might listen to. That at least was what the Prokrator was hoping. "At least, listen to *me*." Bruda had not risen to his feet—had not, in fact, changed his posture in the chair at all. He radiated calm as a fire radiates heat, and when Aldric looked at him he caught the younger man's eyes with his own and held them for a moment, then gestured with his hand. "Sit down. Be still. Hear what we have yet to say—then be angry if you wish."

Aldric stared, glared rather, through eyes that had gone narrow and vicious, and the black wolf-pelt *coyac* covering his shoulders seemed for just a moment to . . . bristle? *No*, thought Bruda, *I'm imagining things*. Some inner prompting made him glance at Voord, and what he saw on the *hautheisart*'s already too-pale face made him revise his opinion. The ship-captain's report had been bad enough, but the implications of this were just too . . .

Then, very slowly and carefully, Aldric Talvalin resumed his seat.

He had been told many things already, Bruda knew, but not the unpalatable truth behind his being brought here. No one had yet decided how and when he was to learn that, but Bruda had once expressed the wish to be there when it happened. Now he was no longer so sure. He knew a great deal more than he had any right to know about this Alban clan-lord, but it was the way in which he and Goth and Voord had come to know such things that lay at the bottom of all. For all that it would be of benefit to the Empire which he served—and loved, though that was only admitted on rare occasions, in private, when he was in the maudlin stage of drink—the transfer of information had been a distasteful thing. Dishonorable. If there had been some other way . . .

But there had not.

Bruda was not *Hauthanalth Kagh' Ernvakh* for nothing. He commanded the Guardians of the Emperor's Honor, as old and respected a position as any in this young Empire, and to do so he was truly a man of honor and self-respect. Unlike Goth, with his plots and stratagems—and especially, unlike Voord. But very like the young man who sat bolt-upright not the length of his own ash cane away, sat and stared and dared him to try to make some sense out of his disrupted life. Aldric too was an honorable man; honorable not only as the

Albans defined the word, but also as the Prokrator him-self regarded it. He was consequently deadly—a whetted blade poised and ready to fall. But where? On his captors?

Or on the king who had so totally betrayed him?

"Aldric," said Bruda very quietly, "Princess Marevna was taken captive twelve leagues from the frontier. More than thirty miles inside hostile territory. So tell me—why is she held in Egisburg, a city only three leagues from the line?"

"Well within range of a mounted storm-column," ex-panded Goth.

Aldric looked from one to the other and whistled thinly through his teeth. " 'Here's your sister, majesty—come and get her.' And if the Emperor does send in a force—"

"Then the Empire will go up in flames from end to end. War, to justify the Warlord." Bruda leaned forward, his face taut. "Will you help us, Aldric? As your king desires?"

The Alban settled back into the padded embrace of his own chair and looked from face to face with hooded, unreadable eyes. His own mind was already made up—duty demanded it—but curiosity and alcohol were begin-ning to get the better of him. He wanted to know what these allies-to-be really were, beneath their eager, duti-ful, would-be heroic expressions that were concealed by masks of metal, and he knew a certain way of finding out.

"This whole affair," he said, no longer looking at any-one in particular, "is so twisted that merely trying to work through the basic permutations gives me a head-ache. And it stinks of intrigue. That's not a perfume I'm too fond of. So, just for your so-comprehensive records, king or not, duty or not—no, I won't." He allowed the small sounds of astonishment, anger or downright disbe-lief to fade away, then glanced bleakly towards *Hauthei-sart* Voord. "But I imagine you volunteered to change my mind. So. Convince me."

He had expected threats of violence, such as those uttered by *Teynaur*'s captain; what he had not expected was the exultant smile which stretched Voord's razor-cut mouth, a smile which sent a tiny shiver of apprehension across the Alban's skin. The pressures of the Imperial Secret Police, he guessed far too late, were likely to be more than commonplace. What could they be? Or promise? Or do?

He learned.

"The report from *Teynaur* is quite enough for this man to be handed over to the secular authorities on a charge of sorcery. That, however, would be time-consuming and ultimately a waste of our investment. In any case, mere straightforward death is no threat to a *kailin* of Alba." If drunk enough to tell the truth, Aldric would have differed with that opinion; but for once, and wisely, he kept his mouth tight shut.

"So instead," continued Voord, "I considered the dossier which we acquired. It gave me a means whereby this pride and honor—stubbornness, no more—could be turned to our advantage." He tapped one finger on the table and Garet slid a folder towards him across its polished surface. Voord opened it, flicked through the contents twice—an operation made clumsy by the bone and leather talon of his left hand—and extracted two fragile sheets.

"One: the steading of Tervasdal in Valhol." Aldric's head jerked up. "Two: the citadel at Seghar." A harshness darkened Voord's voice as he pronounced the name, and he arranged both sheets on the table with fastidious neatness, their edges parallel and just-so. Then he stared at Aldric. "And three: a certain very fine Andarran stallion, presently in the stables of this very stronghold. Kyrin and Gueynor and Lyard," he grated, all the mockery leaving his words as he slapped his right hand flat against the documents. "Do you really want to hear the details of what I have in mind?"

"You *bastard* . . ." All color had drained from Aldric's face, and his fingers were gripping the arms of his chair so tightly that the knucklebones shone ivory through the stretched skin.

"Think of everything your mind can compass, *hlensyarl*," hissed Voord. "And even then you won't have guessed the half of it."

Aldric came to his feet slowly—very slowly, like a man

oppressed by some vast weight—and only Bruda was
close enough and quick enough to catch the brief, bright
malice that glittered for a moment in the Alban's eyes.
He turned, shoulders sagging like those of a man broken
in body and spirit, a man with no defiance left, spreading
both hands helplessly wide as he bowed his head to
Goth. "The . . . my . . . sir, the decision is concluded.
When do we go?"

"Tomorrow," said Goth, "will be soon enough. First
you need clothing and armor."

Aldric waved one hand—a weak, indecisive gesture—
towards the bench behind him. "Armor I have already,
sir," he said.

"But not for Egisburg. Ride through that city's gates
in Alban harness and you would never leave again.
You'll need our cavalry equipment."

"I am keeping my own weapons." This time there was
a hardness in his voice which had not been there before,
an edge that left no room for argument.

Goth heard it and looked past him towards Bruda;
Aldric's peripheral vision caught the Prokrator's nod of
consent and also a hand-sign which meant nothing at
first. It was the sort of gesture he might have used himself, if signalling that something be increased, but here
and now it seemed right out of context—until Goth
spoke again.

"Prokrator Bruda concurs with your choice of weapons," said the general, and Aldric almost let his thoughts
be heard aloud. *Choice,* said his mind; *as if I gave you
any more choice than you gave me.* "But he also points
out that to warrant such blades you must also carry
high rank."

Aldric heard the clatter as Voord shot out of his chair,
knocking it over in his haste and this time didn't bother
to conceal the smile summoned by the sound—a smile
which widened to a grin of honest pleasure as the first
few words of an outraged protest were silenced by Goth's
upraised hand. "What . . . what rank, sir?" he ventured
at last.

Both of the senior officers considered for a moment,
but it was Bruda who answered at last. "A brevet of *en-
hanalth* should be quite sufficient," he said, accompa-

nying the words with a look which dared Voord to argue with him.

Voord did. "You can't do this!" he blared, all affronted dignity now. "You can't hand out such a high rank as if it was—"

"Voord!" Bruda's voice was sharp. "I just did."

"But . . . but that means . . ." Disbelief struggled with the reality of the situation and reality won. "He's superior to *me!*" Hoping that he was wrong, that this was perhaps some black joke played on him for his earlier foul manners, he stared at Bruda and then at Goth in the hope of seeing an eye twinkle or a smile begin to spread. Instead he saw the Lord General nod his head in agreement.

"Effectively, *hautheisart,* yes," Goth said. "He is superior." There was something about the way he said it which suggested that the superiority lay in more than merely rank, but Voord was past noticing subtle nuances of tone.

He flinched visibly at the general's words, for such a statement from such a source was not open to question— not after what had been said bare minutes earlier about the differences in their rank. But this was more important to Voord than even caution, and his next words were addressed, pointedly so, to his own commander. *"Prokrator Hauthanalth,"* he said, his use of Bruda's full style and title being for exactly the same reason that Aldric's had been spoken by Goth: to preface and emphasise a request. "Sir, tell me that I don't. . . . I don't have to obey his orders, do I?" The abject "please" was unspoken but patently obvious for all that.

On another occasion, or in a different situation, or even if Voord had not been so discourteous—no, bloody rude!—earlier, Bruda might have said what his lieutenant wanted to hear. Instead he too nodded, with finality. "I'll be the final arbiter, of course; not," with a significant glance at Aldric, "that I anticipate anything of the kind. But this is a step taken for protective coloration, so if *hanalth*-rank should by any chance give a command to *hautheisart*-rank before witnesses who might otherwise be curious, then *hautheisart*-rank will obey. Without hesitation or question. Is that understood?"

Pallid even at the best of times, Voord by rights should not have been able to grow much paler; but as Bruda spoke what little color there was drained from his face to leave it as white as chalk. An instant later he slammed his hand against the table-top—his maimed left hand—as if, needing in his rage to hurt someone, he resorted to the only person present he could hurt with impunity. Himself. It was a gesture redolent of such monstrous perversity that Aldric cringed inside as he saw it.

"*I will not!*" Voord's voice was shrill and tremulous, though it was impossible to tell how much of this was caused by pain and how much by fury. "I will take no order from that . . . that fatherless son of a whore, that—"

However much he might have been accustomed to abusing prisoners and subordinates, Voord plainly had had no previous experience of high-clan Albans. Otherwise he might have been more guarded in his choice of insult, or at the very least been sure of how close he was standing to Aldric Talvalin when he uttered it. Instead he made both of those mistakes simultaneously, and had not properly drawn breath to say more when the still-forming words were smashed back into his mouth by a fist that was backed by all the focused power of a swordsman's trained muscles.

Aldric's face had frozen over as Voord spoke, and long, long before anyone could cry halt he had swivelled at the waist in a half-twisting movement which put all of his upper-body weight behind the punch. It didn't quite lift the *hautheisart* off his feet, but it snapped his head back on his neck and staggered him so hard and fast that his feet shot from under him and he crashed to the floor amid a clatter of harness and weapons, with blood smeared on his face and chin from lips that had not so much been split as burst by the hammer-and-anvil impact between Aldric's bunched knuckles and his own teeth. As Voord's mouth sagged open and he gaped dazedly up at the Alban standing over him, splinters of one of those teeth gleamed whitely amid the blood.

"Sharp teeth," remarked Aldric to no one in particular. "Though I doubt that they're poisonous." He sucked the oozing, ragged skin across his knuckles for a moment 'to ease the stinging, took the hand from his lips and stared at the wound for a moment, then worked his jaws and spat a mingling of blood and saliva onto the floor a bare inch short of Voord's right hand. "But then, you can never be sure with snakes."

"Schii'aj!" The obscenity was a clumsily articulated shriek as Voord scrambled upright and slapped hand to shortsword hilt—then jolted to a standstill with the blade still sheathed. Again he had miscalculated where Aldric and speed and distance were concerned, for in the time it had taken him to regain his feet the Alban had sidestepped to the bench which carried his gear and had snatched up just one very particular item. Isileth.

The fur of the wolfskin *coyac* that Aldric wore moved like wind in a field of wheat. *"D'ka tey'adj, Voord,"* he said softly, ominously. *"Cho taeyy' ura."* The longsword in his hand was levelled at Voord's windpipe, so close that a handspan's worth of thrust would let his breath from it to mingle once and for all with the air; and that hand was far, far steadier than the hand of a broken and defeated man had any right to be. Far, far steadier than the hand of any man whose eyes glittered with such a force of leashed-in violence. Voord looked at the blade, at the hand, at the eyes, and knew that in the sum of these three things he looked at his own death.

"Stop!" Goth's voice, parade-ground harsh, slashed through the room and created for just an instant the necessary hesitation in Aldric which saved Voord's life. Neither the Alban *eijo* nor the Vlechan *hautheisart* had moved, but something—some tingling, vicious thing—was gone from the air.

"You heard him." Aldric did not take his eyes from Voord's face, nor his *taiken*-point from the man's throat; but at least he spoke instead of driving that point home. "You heard what he said. All of you. He is dead."

"No. He's too valuable."

Aldric coughed a single humorless laugh at that. "Valuable! You mean, he's an investment like me? Then, general, he should have invested a few seconds' thought in what he said before he said it!"

"But look at his face, man—look at what you did! Isn't that enough for one ill-chosen word?"

"No." Aldric sounded vindictive. "Not yet."

"Ach, let them fight!" Bruda's words drew everyone's attention, flying as they did full in the face of a superior's direct command. "But let it be with wooden foils. *Taid-yin.* I can see a sheaf of them yonder, in the Alban's gear.

"Or, at least," he amended after the silence had grown heavy but before anyone else could speak, "since Voord is as you say worth more undamaged—so are they both, general, so are they both—then let Aldric fight with somebody else. Anybody . . ." That was as much a challenge as a suggestion, but no one reacted by so much as the flicker of an eyelid. "You say to him, look at Voord. I say to you, look at him: right now he's wound up like a crossbow. He's dangerous. Lethal. And besides . . ."

Bruda settled into the padded embrace of his chair and propped his feet up on the table, crossing them casually at the ankles; and suddenly he no longer looked approachable. Instead, in that single languid motion he was transformed into all that an Imperial *hauthanalth* and a Chief of Secret Police should be—something arrogant; sinister; menacing. "Besides," and he tapped a folder cradled in his lap, "I'd like to see if he's really as good as they say."

"If you think for an instant that I'm going to entertain—" Aldric bit the words off short as *tau-kortagor* Garet stood up.

"You talk of insults, Alban—the sort of thing your honor thrives on. Have you forgotten how you insulted me, aboard *Teynaur?* Because I still remember even if you don't, and if you truly want a fight . . ." he spread arms sheathed in fine ringmail, "here I am."

Aldric stared at him; this was the same youngster, the same baby-faced cadet who had seemed almost friendly as the warship came into dock. And yet he was not the same. If this was Drusalan friendship, then it was as transient as snow in springtime. No matter, if that was so, he had no need of such friends.

And he knew that Bruda had spoken no more than the truth about him, because hide it how he might for the sake of manners and his own self-respect, he was taut and hot and trembling with fury inside. Angry enough indeed to fight with anyone. That was the cumulative effect not merely of verbal insults, but of being used and abused by these so-called allies, of being treated like a chattel, like something bought and paid for, like an inanimate investment—lord God! how that word burned like vitriol—rather than as a human being who could be and had been bruised in body, mind and soul.

But the cold, cold killing rage shuttered behind his eyes was still reserved for Voord alone. Widowmaker whispered back into her black scabbard and was laid gently on the table. Aldric uttered no redundant hands-off warning, because it was unlikely in the extreme that anyone would dare to touch the blade in Goth's and Bruda's presence, and they had too much sense to permit it . . . he hoped.

Garet had already selected a *taidyo* and was whipping the four-foot length of oak from side to side in what seemed a most experienced manner. It was unusual for anyone other than an Alban to be familiar with *taiken'-ulleth*, classical longsword play—his foster-father Gemmel was a notable exception, as in much else—and as he watched Garet's posturing Aldric wondered if this too, like so many other things, had been arranged; another test which had merely waited a long time before the proper circumstances for its employment arose. He didn't really care.

"I'm not allowed to damage you permanently," Garet said as he stalked across the floor, "but you'll remember how to address Imperial officers properly—next time you're able to say anything at all."

So was this set up by Voord? Aldric hefted one *taidyo* after another, seeming oblivious to the threats or at least selectively deaf. Then he chose one whose chequer-carved grip fitted his hands comfortably and tugged it from its canvas sleeve to test its weight and balance with a flex of his wrists.

Garet was still talking: threatening, boasting, casting doubts on Aldric's ability and on the worthiness of fighting with sticks. But Aldric knew these "sticks" of old, and knew—intimately—the damage they could do; on

an occasion, not so long ago that the pain of it had yet
been forgotten, a "stick" just like those they carried now
had snapped one of his ribs. That was why he laid his
own *taidyo* aside and buckled on the sleeves of his battle
armor—an action which provoked yet more scathing
comment from the already-mailed Garet and a certain
amount of muttered observation from the others present.
It didn't concern him; the long steel plates of the vam-
braces made a better shield against percussive impact
than the best linked mail-mesh ever made, and if Garet
was so inexperienced that he didn't already know that,
then he was likely to find out.

Lifting the *taidyo* again, Aldric raised it slowly in center line, low to high above his head, then equally slowly
across at the level of his eyes. It was *achran-kai* again,
the first and simplest form, but executed this time more
to check the fit of the armored sleeves than for any
other reason. Garet watched him, and Aldric could see
incomprehension flit across the young Drusalan's face.
Now that was very interesting—enlightening, almost. If
he failed to recognise an inverted cross in slow time,
then maybe—just maybe—he didn't know as much about
Alban longswords as had first appeared. And if that was
so, then . . .

Cramp suddenly stabbed at one shoulder-joint and Aldric gasped audibly as its silver bolt of pain bored down
the marrow of his bones. A legacy of being unhorsed in
Tuenafen perhaps, or of helping to propel the battleram
Teynaur to port; the reason was of no account. But
Garet had heard him gasp before he could silence the
involuntary sound, and had seen him wince.

"I'm better than you, Alban," the *tau-kortagor* said.
"I'm better because I'm faster, and I'm faster because
I'm younger. That's why I'm going to really hurt you,
Alban, and why there's not a thing you can do about
it." As he spoke he shifted into a stance that Aldric
recognised; it was one of the ready positions for duelling
with the long Jouvaine thrusting-sword, the *estoc*—a
weapon as different from the *taiken* as night was from
day.

Only then was he convinced; only then did he allow

himself a small, contemptuous smile, for only then was he quite sure who would win and lose. Who would be hurt—and who would do the hurting. Words came to his mind, heard or read somewhere far from here, a quotation from a play; not one of Oren Osmar's classics but something modern, terse and striving for the new ideal of realistic speech. The sort of laconic line that often sounded so wrong—and yet, just once in a while, so very, very right.

"Garet," Aldric said, "you talk too much."

An instant later, there was a *taidyo* lashing at his face. He didn't bother to block the cut—which was no true cut at all, but the kind of slash he might have expected from a man with a club—but merely sidestepped it without even bringing his own foil to guard. It was done with a studied lack of effort, and that was unusual for Aldric in such circumstances. The first rule—and the last—in any weapon-play was that to toy with an opponent of unknown capabilities was to invite disaster, and it was a rule he usually obeyed; yet now, though the opening for a devastating counter was there, he held back and instead merely grinned at Garet.

The Drusalan answered with a thrust—pure *estoc*-practice, that—aimed straight at the eyes.

Aldric said, "Idiot!" in a loud, clear voice that sounded almost annoyed, and did something he would never have risked with live blades unless in full armor. Enveloping the incoming point with a circular parry, he deflected it out to his left and then stepped inside the weapon's compass to snatch it back in again—pinned now in the angles of left upper arm and elbow. All that was required and all that he did was to make an edge-handed chop across Garet's fingers and a sidewise twist away.

The trapped weapon was wrenched from its owner's hand almost as if he had presented it of his own free will, and Aldric grinned again. "What was that you told me? That you're better?"

Prokrator Bruda clapped his hands slowly together in ironic applause, but whether it was at the swordplay or the dialogue Aldric didn't know. At least he had proved his point—and proved himself as well, both as a skilled

and as a restrained fighter. There was no purpose in
continuing this farce and he turned away to return the
taidyin to his gear.

Then a voice behind him said, "Garet." Aldric scarcely
recognised it as Voord's once-so-urbane tones; but then,
apart from a single shrill expletive he had not heard the
hautheisart speak since . . . since silencing him. He
looked back and saw the other escort—Tagen, was it?—
on his feet with one hand resting negligently on the pommel of his sword. Aldric tensed for an instant, then saw
that none of the attention here was directed at him. Instead Voord was staring at Garet over a bloodied ker-
chief that concealed most of his face, and though no
further words were uttered by that muffled, mangled
mouth, the young *tau-kortagor* seemed able to take
meaning from his commander's eyes alone.

Aldric too could guess easily enough what this little
tableau was all about. Having volunteered—if he *had*
volunteered—to punish this Alban upstart, ostensibly for
his own reasons, Garet was not going to be permitted
to stop. Not while he also fought on *Hautheisart* Voord's
behalf. Nor, Aldric fancied, would failure be well regarded; Voord did not look the sort of man who had a
forgiving nature.

Altogether more serious now, he bowed courteously
as he returned the captured *taidyo* to Garet's hand,
and was conscious of more attention along the conference table than there had been before. It was as if they
all knew that the next exchange would be more than
a mocking display of technique; and as if they knew
still more—something of which Aldric was yet ignorant.

That "something," whatever it might prove to be, was
already enough to raise the hackles on the Alban's neck.
"I will not draw this man's blood," he said, because it
was something that had to be said no matter who it
annoyed. If Garet had not been forced to this, then
maybe he would have had fewer scruples; but Aldric
had been King Rynert's—assassin? Executioner? Duty-
bound, honor-bound, reluctant slayer . . . Once. But
never again; not for any man.

He tried to think of some stratagem with which to end this matter quickly, before someone was hurt. Before *he* was hurt, since Voord wasn't going to be satisfied with just seeing a few welts and bruises. Not with his broken face to remind him of what Aldric had done.

They took guard again, but slowly now, warily and with a deal more care than the nonchalance of their first exchange, and the *taidyin* touched. Clack. Wood ran against wood, notched surfaces ticking as the pressure of wrists increased. There was a shuffling sound— someone's feet—and a moment's stillness. Clack. Another stillness, when nothing moved but mind and eyes. Then clack; clack-*stamp,* and Garet launched a cut—a proper cut this time, downward and diagonal to strike neck or shoulder, hard, fast and direct.

It was easy.

Aldric moved not back but forward, dropping to one knee, intersecting the arc of Garet's cut with his own *taidyo* as it whirred up and across. Gripped in both hands, his wrists counterflexing on the long hilt for leverage, the last six inches of the hardwood blade jumped from near-immobility to an unseen blur. And it hit squarely home within an inch of his aiming point—not on Garet's own weapon, to block, but on the Drusalan's tensed, extended forearm. To break. He shouted, once: *"Hai!"*

The mail that Garet wore was no protection, no protection at all; transmitted all the shock of the blow clear through whatever minimal padding was beneath, and even over the harsh rasp of oak against linked metal Aldric heard both forearm-bones give way.

Garet yelped thinly and released his *taidyo* to clatter across the floor, but before it had come to rest he followed it, crashing headlong to the ground as the follow-through accelerated down and all but tore the kneecap from his braced right leg.

He lay there, squirming and trying not to scream, while Aldric cat-stepped backwards with an expression of distaste stamped into his features. The other *tau-kortagor,* Tagen, barged past him and knelt at Garet's side to check his injuries. Aldric could hear his muttered curse quite plainly, for it had grown very quiet in Lord General Goth's great conference hall: quiet—and expectant.

"Well?" Voord asked it, his thick voice free now of all passion, anger or even interest.

"The arm is cleanly broken, lord; it should heal. But . . ." Tagen hesitated, and looked up at Voord before saying any more. "But he'll not walk without a stick, if he ever walks again."

"So. Small use to me, then. Why am I surrounded by incompetents?" he demanded of the air. No one troubled to supply him with an answer and he flung both arms wide in an exaggerated shrug of disgust and dismissal. The blood on his face was drying black. "At least they only ever fail me once. *Tagen, sh'voda moy: ya v'lech'hu, kh'mnach voi! Slijei?*"

"Slij'hah, hautach!" Tagen jerked his shortsword from its scabbard and rammed two inches of its point into the nape of Garet's neck. The injured man's eyes opened wide, all whites with just a pinpoint spot of pupil, and his mouth gaped silently; then his legs went kick-kick, kick . . . And he was dead.

Aldric forced his own bunched muscles to relax, quite sure that he was the only one to even react. That was worst of all, for in his innermost heart he had anticipated something like this and then dismissed it as beyond even Voord. It had been the "something" in the atmosphere which had disturbed him before they began to fight. He should have been on his guard, responded differently, not given Voord a reason to . . . to do what had been done. Then maybe a life would not have been wasted, spilled without purpose across the polished floor.

But what better way in all the world to impress a man known to be careless of killing—a man even nicknamed Bladebearer Deathbringer, by the holy Light of Heaven!— than to prove oneself more careless still. That was how Voord's mind had worked, even to the extent of having his own guard killed for the failure of losing a duel. Just to impress! It was appalling. But that was Voord, and at the last that was the Secret Police. And that was the Drusalans, for they had all connived at it, Goth and Bruda both, knowing what might happen—no, knowing what *would* happen—but saying not a word against it.

Aldric looked at them, and looked at the blood—dear God, so very little blood to mark a death!—and for once kept his thoughts entirely to himself.

7

Shadow of the Tower

"**I** often wondered why you had such an interest in *ymeth,*" said Dewan. He was trying to strike up a conversation again, for what felt like the hundredth time. Even an argument would be better than the gloomy silence which had settled over Gemmel since their interview—and "interview" scarcely described it—with the Drusalan woman who called herself Kathur the Vixen. If ever anyone talked too much, she did; and Dewan suspected that Gemmel's use of the dreamsmoke drug was no more than a contributory factor.

She talked, he thought idly, staring at Gemmel's back as they rode along on tired, hired horses. Well then, some of the men who had shared her bed must have been regular speech-makers, and it had all come spilling out, as unselective as an up-ended bucket. They had heard about the governor of Tuenafen; about the governor's son and his stableboy; about two of the seaport's magistrates and how they liked to relax after a hard day administering the Empire's justice. All of it had been fascinating in a small way, even though Gemmel obviously disapproved of most of it, and it would have been most useful had they planned to stay in Tuenafen and set up as professional blackmailers. But they had also heard about Aldric, and what *Kagh' Ernvakh* had planned for him.

Dewan had laughed, as he felt certain Aldric would also have laughed at the notion of rescuing a captive princess from a lofty tower. But the laughter had been of short duration and Gemmel had not joined it. This matter ceased to be a child's tale and a source of amusement when it involved a friend and the risk of that friend's death. And Dewan was well aware that Gemmel regarded Aldric as much more than a friend; he had heard the title *altrou*—foster-father—used by the younger man on more than one occasion.

The risk was greatly increased by a factor which Kathur had named several times: the Imperial officer called *Hautheisart* Voord. She had been Voord's lover once, and then his mistress, five years ago—for all that even then his tastes had tended to the exotic, rather than the conventionally erotic. Voord, Dewan had decided, was peculiar. But to be promoted *hautheisart* at the age of twenty-seven bespoke a mind and an ability that was out of the ordinary in much more than merely sexual preferences.

They knew now where that warped genius lay. Voord was a gamester, a gambler, a player of one side against another and both sides for himself. His games extended far back, beyond the death of old Emperor Droek and the division of the Empire. They continued through that division and right up to the present day: complex, self-serving and often murderous. Voord still played both sides, although there seemed of late to be a marked preference for one over the other—but Voord still worked hardest for Voord. There had been vague talk from Kathur about an attempt to control an isolated province on the Jevaiden plateau and transform it into an independent, neutral city-state—supporting and supported by the Emperor and the Grand Warlord both. It was a plan which had come to nothing for various reasons.

One of those reasons had been a certain Alban clanlord, sent there about his king's business and still ignorant of what he had upset.

Not that this was the first time Aldric and Voord had crossed paths in ignorance. Oh no. Voord himself had evidently talked far too much in bed in his younger days; presumably less mature, less confident—but quite certainly just as coldly cynical. He had talked about his first-ever great stratagem, originated solely by himself; the plan which had gained his first promotion, that long, long leap of one rank that so few men made—from *kor-*

tagor to *eldheisart*, and with it the transfer from infantry to secret police.

That plan had broken half-a-dozen of the Empire's notoriously strict laws against sorcery by its very inception, and was pushed through by—significantly—Grand Warlord Etzel's personal intervention. And no wonder he supported it; at that time the plan was certain to attract him, in his then-current uncertain position with the Imperial dominions at peace and questions being asked in the Senate as to whether the rank and title of Grand Warlord should in fact be done away with. It was a simple plan: the despatch of a man to a place, with instructions to create sufficient havoc for military intervention to be justified.

The plan which, four long years ago, had sent Duergar Vathach to Dunrath.

It was an operation which Kathur should never have known about, because it was a failure. That failure had done something to the way in which Voord's mind worked; it seemed now that failure was the worst sin in his canon and the one most drastically punished. But she had heard all about it—maybe because it was his first, maybe because despite its lack of success it had done no damage to his career—and maybe because in those days there had been no such thing as *sides* within the Drusalan Empire. Emperor and Warlord had been twin figureheads on the one ship, Dewan knew that much: he had been a part of it, and knew that the oneness was that of a puppeteer and his doll. But it explained Voord's openness as nothing else could.

Only fear had kept Kathur's mouth shut, and it had needed sorcery-assisted drugs—or drug-enhanced sorcery, Dewan was uncertain of precedence—to open it again. The great question now in his mind was: what would happen if, or when, Aldric found out? If he hadn't found out already. Either way, if he was still alive he would need help—all the help that they could bring to bear.

Gemmel rode on, sagging in the saddle and looking far from comfortable. He was usually a good horseman, certainly better than some Dewan had seen—although as an ex-*eldheisart* in the Bodyguard at Drakkesborg, he conceded that he was often over-critical—but right now the old wizard's mind seemed occupied by more than even the elementary, instinctive knee-grip and balance which kept him on his rented pony's back. Gemmel had been subject to broody periods like this ever since they landed in Imperial territory; indeed, ever since they had seen the white contrail of the dragon scratched across the cold blue vault of heaven. For the life of him Dewan could not understand why, because even he—unimaginative military crophead that he was—had been thrilled to the core of his being by the sight. It had not mattered that he had seen Ymareth before; in the Cavern of Firedrakes it had been somehow appropriate. Just—*just?*—one more strange and marvelous thing among so many other marvels. But in the open sky, with nothing to detract from its distant grandeur—although in truth, at two miles above his head it had been no bigger than a sparrow, and only the stately leisure of its wingbeats had shown it for what it truly was; that, and the condensing trail of heat from its mouth—-the sight of a dragon in flight was another matter entirely. Dewan's drinking of a toast to the great being's mere existence had been sincere, not mockery.

So what was wrong with Gemmel? Dewan looked at him again and wondered idly if it was worth-while wasting more breath in yet another attempt to cajole the old man into speech. Deciding not, he hunched himself deeper into the furred hood of his cavalry cloak.

There had been no dragon in the sky today—nor, for that matter, any blue sky for one to fly across. Only an overcast that was as gray and featureless as new-split slate. By the Alban calendar it was *Hethra-tre, de Gwenyer;* the Drusalan reckoning, for once, put it in more simple terms: the third day of the tenth month, and three days into winter. The year was winding down—and the weather just at present was trying hard to prove it. Today had started badly and grown steadily, malevolently worse, progressing from a nonexistent dawn lost in slanting rain, through a chill, and sleet, to a proper fall of snow. That at least was over for the present, but it had already transformed the countryside through which they rode into an ink-wash study; all light and

darkness, chiaroscuro. Everything was either black or
white, stark, toneless, without any subtlety of shading
beneath that leaden sky which was so heavy with the
promise of more snow. Dewan glared at it, and was answered as he might have expected by a quick flurry of
fat, soft flakes. And it was cold. The breath of men and
horses alike went smoking from their nostrils to drift
like skeins of fog on the bitter, barely moving air. Like
the breath of dragons.

Dewan ar Korentin wiped a crust of hoar-frost from
his mustache, itself become as black-and-white as the
landscape, and exhaled a soft oath on his next billow of
breath. *Cold,* he thought, watching the vapor twist heavily away from his face. *So cold.* His eyes abruptly shifted
focus as *something* drew their attention to the middle
distance. A movement, or a suggestion of movement; a
flickering, like a gnat's dance on warm summer air, caught
at the edge of sight. Except that this was by no means
summer, and whatever he had seen was no gnat. *There,
look!* No. It was gone again—if it had ever been there.
Dewan blinked; maybe it was a speck of moisture caught
on his eyelashes, or a bird—although he had seen no
birds today, they had too much sense to travel in such
foul weather—or maybe no more than a trick of his
imagination. He turned his head away, dismissing it.

And then snapped back, not believing, to gape as the
thing he was convinced he had not seen came scything
out of the low cloudbase like some monstrous bat with
a ribbon of black smoke scrawling like charcoal to mark
its line of descent.

Firedrake! Dragon! Ymareth . . .

Or—not Ymareth at all, for it was so *big!*

His fear was spawned by the thing's size and by the
steepness and the speed of its approach, for with wings
half-closed like those—Gods! too like those—of a falcon
stooping upon fieldmice, the dragon reached them in the
space of a single racing heartbeat. Too fast for evasion;
too fast even for prayer.

It slashed past, right to left, twenty feet above the
ground—and because they were both mounted, that was
a shocking less-than-twelve above their heads—in a
great rush of hot wind, moving far faster than any crea-

ture, even one born in legend, had any right to move. The thump of displaced air tore at their clothing, whipped up spirals of snow that melted even as they left the ground, and went whirling off in the dragon's wake as it climbed away, returned to its patrol height like the swinging of a pendulum by the awesome dive-created speed which had flicked it past them like a beast seen in a dream—or a nightmare . . . Huge dark wings, horned and crested wedge of head, armored serpentine body and a long, grinning, fang-crowded mouth whose trailing scarf of smoke brought with it the bitter reek of burning.

And the ponies which they rode went mad. Kicking and squealing, bucking and plunging, the animals tried to throw their riders, to throw their saddlebags, to flee in abject terror somewhere, anywhere, as far away from this airborne horror as their legs could carry them. The beasts' eyes were rolling crazily—all whites, as white as the foam which creamed on bits and bridles. And Gemmel, who had patently lost interest in staying mounted? He too had gone a little mad—Dewan could think of no other reason why he might be laughing.

Crowing with glee, the old man tumbled—very neatly, granted—to the ground, landing on his feet, and with a quick, casual gesture of the Dragonwand froze both of the fear-crazed ponies in their tracks. Only their eyes *could* move now; the rest, even to ears and tails, were struck still as equestrian statues in cold bronze. Dewan looked at the Dragonwand, then at the wizard, and thought *how very appropriate* to himself. He was too tactful—and wise—to voice the thought aloud.

But the dragon seemed to hear him; a quarter-mile away and three thousand feet up, the great wings beat once, twice, three times, accelerating its climb until it was rising almost vertically like a pheasant rocketing from cover; then no longer like a pheasant but as negligently acrobatic as a rook, it yawed, half-looped, rolled—then *twisted* snakewise in the air as no bird ever hatched from egg could do—and was coming back in the same instant.

The approach was slower now, a wide-winged glide rather than the previous attack dive, but no less ominous for all that. Dewan could see plainly that the smoke wind-dragged from its mouth was thicker now, denser, as if the fires of the creature's belly were fully alive. As if to prove the fact, the dragon's head vectored a few degrees off-line with a deliberation that reminded him nastily of a battleram's weapon-turret, and then—with a whistling roar which reminded him of nothing in or above or under the whole wide world—its mouth opened to unleash a gout of yellow-white flame, glaring and brilliant against the dullness of the day.

Dewan flinched at its brightness, and at the heat which slapped at him as if a furnace door had been flung open; but at the same time drew a breath of awe and wonder. If he was to die, then surely there were more squalid ways than this brief, bright glory. Another instant, and he was wondering at his own morbid turn of mind. The hundred-yard-long plume of fury faded and choked in a swirl of dark smoke and once more the dragon was upon them.

This time it moved slowly, so slowly that it barely maintained a flying speed. The great membranous wings flared and shifted to control the air which flowed above and below them, then scooped down at last in a great braking arc as Ymareth—if this *was* Ymareth, and Dewan was still far from convinced—rounded out its final descent and settled onto the ground with all the daintiness of a hawk returning to a familiar wrist, a delicate grace odd and eerie in something so huge. Dewan was reminded more of a cat in wet grass than a hawk. Except that this "cat" was one hundred and twenty-odd feet long, radiated a warmth that he could feel from where he sat—and right welcome it was, too!—and where the plate armor of its belly touched on patches of snow, those patches melted amid clouds of steam and fast-forming pools of water.

The dragon's head swung leisurely from side to side, considering them both: old man and young, mounted and afoot, shocked-silent and still chuckling. Its eyes . . . such eyes: pools of yellow phosphorescence which drew his gaze and held it . . .

NO!

That *would* have held it, had he not torn away with

an effort like that of lifting some great weight. His face darkened, flushed with blood that was not summoned by either of the contrasting stimuli of dragon-heat or winter-cold; it had been pumped there by a heart which the strain of looking away had provoked into a spasm of furious beats, a muffled drumroll which filled his ears and made his senses spin. It felt briefly as if his whole chest was about to split wide open to give the frantic organ room; then the hammering died away, and the world stopped swaying, and Dewan drew a normal breath again.

By that time the dragon had transferred its attention to Gemmel. The wizard stopped laughing at once and instead raised the Dragonwand before him as if to fend off the advancing head. Or to deflect the spell that burned in those great, glowing eyes. They regarded him, Dewan thought, with more than a touch of scorn—with what on a more human visage might well have been contempt. Then it spoke.

And Dewan understood what it was saying.

For all his years of service in the Imperial military, Dewan ar Korentin remained at heart what he had been born: a Vreijek. Not a Drusalan. It meant that he had been dismissed—more than once in his own hearing whether by accident or not—as a "mere provincial." It meant that he had never reached a higher rank than *eldheisart*-of-cavalry, and never would. It meant, too, that he was—though usually veneered by Imperial stiffness or Alban courtesies, both so studied that they cried out their falseness to all—one of a vehement, sensitive, imaginative race some said, inclined like peasants to superstition and who found the forbidden art of sorcery most attractive. It was much like what those same "some" said about Alban *eijin;* the stories were only partly true—or conversely, only partly false.

But most importantly, it meant that where a Drusalan or a Tergovan or a Vlechan—any of those who arrogantly styled themselves the Imperial races—might have retreated from the impossibility of comprehending dragon-speech into the ultimate, irrevocable refuge of madness, Dewan himself—after an instant's total nerve-shock, like that of a man jumping into a pool supposed warm but in fact icy—accepted what his brain told him as he accepted all else in this life. As no more than another facet of reality.

"I give thee greeting, Maker-that-was."

The words were within Dewan's head and understood there, nowhere else; because the voice itself, borne on a soft, hot wind, sounded no more like words than the hissing rumble of some huge fire. Above that nimble he heard the *click, click* as the dragon's eyelids shut and opened in a leisurely, insolent blink. "And this? In thy hands is it then a whip, a crop, a means to master such as I? I defy thee to dare use it so."

Gemmel looked from the dragon to the Dragonwand and back again; then lowered the spellstaff with a small, jerky, embarrassed movement. "I would not . . . I would not use it like that. You should know."

To Dewan's ears at least, he sounded somewhat ashamed. Just as he had done after he had assumed that Aldric had beaten the Drusalan woman Kathur so viciously when all sense, all logic—even a moment's pause for thought before he spoke—would have spared him that error. Not so much ashamed of being wrong, as of being obviously so before witnesses. What, wondered Dewan ar Korentin, could have the old man so preoccupied that he made such mistakes? The dragon? Maybe; because there was a tension between the two that Dewan sensed should not have been there.

"Why should I know, Maker? Upon thy word? Not so. Only the Masterword of Governance holds such weight with me. That—or the given Word of a man of honor. I am Ymareth. Dragonkind. Thou knowest well that which I am. In very truth, none should know it better."

Dewan watched and listened to the exchange sitting stock-still in the saddle of his stock-still horse, aware that he looked painfully obvious while he remained where he was and equally aware that directly he made the slightest move to dismount or in any other fashion become less obvious, he would only make himself still more so. He considered this; felt stupid; and stayed just where he was.

"Or perhaps," the dragon continued more softly, "I should know indeed, and should not have tried thee so, with denial and with doubt. We are of a kind, thou and I. There should be trust between us." Ymareth's great wedge head swung lower. "Why, therefore, is Aldric Talvalin held a prisoner by those who are his enemies? Know this, Maker: he is a man of honor indeed, for though I might have aided his escape out of this captivity he, having promised that he would not, did not. Think thou on that."

"Prisoner! Where?" For all his wish to avoid attracting attention, Dewan blurted out the question without thinking—and found himself staring down the dragon's throat an instant later.

"Aboard a vessel of this Empire's warfleet," Ymareth replied. "There at least I found him."

"Then I was right! Gemmel, I was right! It was that battleram after all—it must have been—"

"Dewan!" The wizard's voice was sharp with reproof. "Dewan, control yourself! How many battlerams are there in the fleet—in each fleet, for the love of Heaven—and how many possible destinations might each vessel have?"

Ar Korentin matched stares with the older man for a long five seconds; then looked away, subsided back into his saddle and closed his mouth.

Ymareth the dragon had watched this brief byplay with what might well have been dry amusement. "Maker," it rumbled softly. "Maker, if ye be yet so uncertain of this warship's abiding-place, why therefore do ye ride inland and from the sea where such vessels pass?" There was a knowledgeable mockery in the words. "Know this—the Eye of the Dragon sees much that is hidden, and mine own eyes can watch from such heights that the sight of men cannot know my presence. Even," the dragon neatly pre-empted Dewan's unspoken thought, "if they should have the aid of far-seeing lenses."

That suggested the sort of altitude which ar Korentin, still a Vreijek soldier at heart, preferred not to dwell on; he and his upbringing still had too much superstition about them for him to hear such things with anything like true peace of mind.

"And this I saw," Ymareth continued. "*Kailin* Talvalin was brought to a strong place that was filled with many soldiers. Time passed, and I saw speech among men who by their garb were of rank and power. There was a killing, to no purpose. Aldric Talvalin rides now with the soldiers of the Empire, clad in red even as they."

"To the Red Tower," breathed Dewan.

"To thy destination. Yea or nay?" Either Ymareth knew without being told, or was guessing—or was giving a command veiled as a suggestion.

"Aye, Ymareth dragon, Maker to made. But we know already of this matter concerning the Red Tower." Gemmel's voice was just the merest trace pompous. "And we travel there now."

"On these?" The dragon-voice inside Dewan's head was wholly sarcastic, no longer veiled by irony or allusion. "Then of a surety, thy need for haste must be small indeed."

"They were all that we could acquire at short notice," snapped the wizard impatiently, and it seemed to Dewan that he was speaking with the ease of long familiarity. Nothing else could explain such a casual approach to a creature which could roast him, or flatten him, or snap him in half as a man bites a biscuit. No matter, any of that—the implications behind it all were enough to lift the short hairs on the nape of ar Korentin's neck.

"But now there is a swifter way, if ye dare it." Ymareth did not elaborate further and had no need to do so. Verbally, at least. The dragon's wings spread out to either side of the bridle-path, enormous fingered sails more vast than those of a fully-rigged Imperial capital ship. Their silent invitation was plain, and chilling. Flight.

"What about . . ." Dewan's voice faltered. Sitting on one of them, the problem of the ponies was plain enough. Until he looked at Ymareth and at Ymareth's fanged, smoked-fuming mouth; and knew exactly *what about* the ponies. He was no Alban horselord, with a perhaps excessive love of that particular animal, but even so the prospect of, of feeding them to a dragon was enough to make his war-hardened stomach turn over.

"Take off the harness and all the other gear," Gemmel said dispassionately. "All of this must be done. Whether you like it or not."

"And would you be as quick with your orders if I was Aldric?" returned Dewan, his temper flaring up for an instant. It was an uncalled-for remark, known and regretted the instant that the words were spoken—directly it was too late to recall them.

"You're like him enough, Dewan ar Korentin. More than enough. You know how to hurt with words. Now—do it, and let's get this thing over."

Ymareth watched and waited with a dreadful patience, saying nothing, aware perhaps of how these men felt about the beasts they had ridden, aware that there was no place for words here and now. There was nothing to be gained by speech on either side; indeed, if the situation was looked at with the sort of honesty that was little short of brutal, this was a kindness. To abandon the ponies in this wilderness of scrub and snow and desolation would be to condemn them to a lingering death by freezing and starvation. Better the . . . what had Dewan's own thought been? . . . brief, bright glory of a dragon's fire.

So at least the Vreijek persuaded himself, as he loosened the cinch on the last saddle and lifted it away. As he lowered it gratefully to the ground a little way off—with all the gear strapped around it, that saddle was heavy—Gemmel's hand, feeling just as heavy, came down on his shoulder.

"Stay there," the wizard said. "You won't want to see this."

Dewan stiffened and looked up at the old man, while pity fought with contempt for room on his face. "You are like a king," he said softly. Which king was not specified. "You can command death by war, by assassination, by execution—but you'd as soon not watch it happen." Aldric had told him once about a killing before Dunrath; about how Gemmel, master of theoretical swordplay, had been shocked and horrified to see his theories put to practical use. This was the same. Dewan straightened up and shrugged the wizard's hand away, then turned around. "Maybe if you watched, if they *all* watched once in a while, you and they would be less free with such commands in the future." The ponies were still immobile, still frozen by whatever spell had been laid on them—as incapable of escape as prisoners trussed for the block. Or soldiers drawn up in line of battle. You've lived among the Albans for too long, he told himself, to be so concerned about the fate of a pair of nags. But still he gripped Gemmel's shoulder as the wizard had gripped his. "You gave the command, old man. It's only right that you should look at the consequence. So look. I said, *look!*"

He swung Gemmel around by main force just as Ymareth's huge head descended on its prey. At least the attack was merciful, for neither pony could have known what happened with each head chopped off at the neck like someone swatting the blossoms off dandelions. One instant they were alive and whole, and the next . . . not. Even the blood which gouted onto the snow was no worse than the mess which followed a successful hunt, nor the wet ripping noise of rending tissue any more dreadful than the sound of dogs at their meat. No, not dogs—cats. Ymareth ate with all the dainty fastidiousness of a feline—or a certain young Alban of Dewan's acquaintance.

There was a few minutes' digestive silence as Ymareth swallowed down the last fragments and considered their flavor. Then a lance of yellow-white fire billowed from its mouth, scouring away the last residue of blood and flesh from the dragon's teeth. Dewan understood now why it did not have the foetid breath of a carnivore; any stink was seared away by that cleansing gush of flame— which was just as well.

"Now," said Ymareth, and even though the words were unheard, forming as they did within the Vreijek's head, Dewan could detect a well-fed satisfaction in the dragon's tone. "Now, gather that which thee might need, and mount to my neck."

As he bent again to lift the pack of gear and armor to its accustomed place across his shoulders, Dewan hesitated and braced his weight against his knees until the pounding heartbeat in his ears had once more died to a murmuring of blood. A cold sweat had broken out across his forehead, and there was a hot throb of pain running down the very core of his left arm. For just a moment the world gyrated around him, mocking his self-imposed stability with its movement, and then grew still again. Dewan ground his teeth until his jaws ached and drew himself upright again with such a shudder as the Albans said was caused by someone walking across a grave. He no longer found that superstition funny. Not now. Dewan ar Korentin had begun to realize what it might be like to die.

For the tenth—or was it the hundredth?—time, Aldric swivelled half-around in Lyard's saddle to glance back at the men who kept him company. This glance, like all those others, made him feel no easier. It was certainly not the kind of company an Alban gentleman would prefer to keep—rather the sort of company that he personally would have made considerable efforts to avoid— had he the choice, which he hadn't. It was not Bruda, not even glowering Voord with his killer Tagen at his elbow, but the half-score of heavy cavalry who made up the honor guard for this group of staff officers and adjutants—the gold insignia were staff, the silver not— and thus gave credence to their supposed rank. Their armor was the foil lizardmail of *katafrakten,* and that in itself was what Aldric found unsettling, ridiculous though the feeling was. But he had ugly memories concerning *katafrakt* armor and about the demon-sending Esel who had filled such armor when he—it?—had been sent by Duergar Vathach to kill him. Those memories were only six months old—nothing like old enough for him to live easily with them. Not yet.

It was not merely the escort which disturbed him, for all that. Even granted that, apart from Bruda, he wore the most senior insignia of the little commissioned-officer squad, at the back of his mind Aldric knew that the bars and triangles and diamonds were only badges, only insignia which he had no right to wear. If put to the uttermost test they would be no protection. No protection at all. Even wearing the things made him feel uncomfortable.

At least the armor which in part bore those rank-tabs was comfortable enough. Senior officers, Bruda had taken pains to inform him, did not wear issue harness like an enlisted trooper. Their armor was tailored for

them with the same care as a fine suit of clothing—
indeed, with more care: unlike cloth, metal and leather
was unforgiving of careless measurement. It didn't
stretch . . . For all that what he wore now had been
assembled from available parts rather than forged especially for his limbs and body, it was—he conceded
reluctantly—as good a fit as his own beloved black *an-
moyya-tsalaer.* Right now, in very truth it was a better
fit altogether, for what with one thing and another he
had lost maybe twenty pounds in weight and it showed.
Alban full harness had a tendency to hang loose when
it didn't fit its wearer properly, and Aldric's harness
would have hung very loose indeed just at the moment.

This was red-enamelled, rather than lacquered black;
it was made of small plates and splints, but linked by
strips of mail rather than the lacing of lamellar; and yet
for all the differences, it was not so dissimilar after all.
Except for the helmet. The Drusalan officer's high-
crowned *seisac* had a peak, a neck-guard and cheek-
pieces like the war-mask of its Alban counterpart; but
everything fitted so much more closely that it was claustrophobic just to think about it. And it had a nasal. That
nasal bar had made Aldric squint for nearly three days
now, so that he was playing host to the mother and
father of all splitting headaches—although he was generous enough to admit that if he came out of this particular
venture with his head split by nothing more permanent
in its effect, he would be more than happy.

The roads were busier than Aldric had expected they
might be; either the Empire was in less internal trouble
than he had been led to believe, or its citizens were
making a laudable and convincing attempt at normal life.
Only one thing disturbed him a little, and that was the
reaction of ordinary folk to the military presence of
which he was perforce a part. He had seen something
similar before, in Alba, when he had ridden as an *eijo.*
But there, though timid, people had responded with no
more than cautious, courteous, mannerly respect. Here
it was just fear.

Not knowing the meaning of all the insignia splattered
in gold metal and colored enamel on his helmet, overrobe and armor, he was half inclined to ask somebody

on that first day of the ride to Egisburg. Then the inclination died. He was *hanalth,* and that rank was made plain by two horizontal bars beneath an inverted triangle surmounting a diamond made of two more triangles joined base to base. All in gold. And that was all he needed to know. All he really wanted to know. For the rest, whether they meant he was pretending to such rank in an élite, heroic regiment of cavalry; or in the political police whose action squads might execute a man for treason when his only crime was to empty rubbish wearing a ring bearing the Emperor's—or more likely the Warlord's—likeness still on his finger, thus insulting them by implication, Aldric had decided that ignorance in such matters was best.

But there was one matter in which he remained most interested, and moreover most secretive—it was not something he intended drawing to the attention of his companions. Once, twice, maybe three times he had sensed—and then seen—a mounted figure far off on the horizon. Maybe he was wrong, and maybe he was just guessing, but he did not yet need a scholar's spectacles and was still ready to swear that it was the same person every time. A long-glass might have confirmed that notion one way or another, but Aldric had none in his gear and though Voord carried one—a good one, Navy issue—he was the last person the Alban was going to ask. And maybe he *was* wrong, anyway; he could fathom no reason why a solitary rider would want, or dare, to shadow a column of heavy cavalry.

Aldric had once heard Gemmel use a word which described how he was feeling, and the word had stuck somehow in his memory. *Paranoia.* It was an odd, cumbersome, unAlban word, but once its meaning was explained it described exactly how he felt right now—how he had felt ever since the Imperial military had begun to take an interest in him. Nervous and suspicious of everything and everybody which didn't have an instantly discernible motive.

But why shouldn't someone else be riding this road? Egisburg was a large city and there were many more reasons to go there than—than his own. And any reluctanace to get too close to Imperial soldiers was scarcely grounds for suspicion; it was, rather, something to be applauded as laudable caution. For himself, he would as soon have the breadth of a province—at the very least—between himself and Voord at any time.

Except that he had given his word to help in this enterprise—given it not only to Goth and Bruda, who were only foreigners after all, but to Rynert as well. He was the king's man and it mattered not a whit that he had been pledging himself only in the very vaguest sense. A given word was a given Word, and a Word given was a word honored. Even if it did complicate his life exceedingly. He would hold to that Word to the best of his life's ability.

But he would have dearly loved a friend nearby—Gemmel, Dewan, someone, *anyone*—just to confide in now and then.

Lord General Goth had been right in his remarks about how close Egisburg was to the Emperor's part of the Empire—a distinction which he made clear with a sardonic smile that Aldric thought would have looked more at home on the jaws of a wolf. The Alban had *seen* a wolf grin just like that and he knew exactly what his thought meant.

By the straight Army roads it was two, or maybe three days ride from Goth's fortified headquarters; certainly no more. The journey would have been still quicker had they used the Falcon courier routes, but those of course were forbidden even to senior officers. And still more to those only pretending to such a rank.

Throughout that last long afternoon, four cold hours that were at one time crystalline clear and at another blurred by falling snow, Egisburg coalesced from a smudge on the horizon to the hunched, jagged reality of a city. Even then, it was only as evening folded its gray wings about them that they had their first clear view of the place which they hoped to enter—and leave—unseen and unscathed. Aldric sat up very straight in his saddle, aware that the sporadic conversation at his back had died away. It was scarcely surprising; but it did suggest that the reputation of the Red Tower carried a degree of weight even with the Secret Police.

There were larger fortresses in the world, he knew that—and had no doubt of the knowledge, having seen some of them. Datherga, Segelin, Cerdor, even his own hold of Dunrath was bigger than this; and they in their turn would be dwarfed by some of the Imperial fortresses, like the Grand Warlord's recently completed citadel at the heart of Drakkesborg. But for all their size, none of them could have looked so forbidding to intruders.

He had expected a slim spike of masonry, maybe something like that in the old story of the Elephant Tower which he had loved so much as a child, or like that which the holy men of Herta were said to build and in which they could hide from sea-raiders. The Red Tower of Egisburg was none of these. Somebody, once, long ago—at least two hundred years, if he was any judge of fortified architecture—had decided that they would build themselves a strong place here at the junction of two rivers. A "castle," as the Drusalans would have said. And this somebody had spent lavishly, unstintingly on the great keep that would be the core of his fortress; so lavishly that he apparently had no money left to do more. There were no curtain walls, no river-fed moat, no outer defences at all.

But there was the Tower.

From base to rampart it was two hundred sheer feet of worked granite, and its stones were sheathed in the thick glaze which gave the place both its name and its coloration: a deep, vivid crimson that was unpleasantly like the hue of fresh-spilled blood. It reared starkly against the iron clouds like the tower Aldric remembered from his dreams, distorted by an errant swirl of snow; and at the same time an amber ray from the setting sun stabbed from the west over his right shoulder and seemed to lick against the stonework. For that brief instant, until the rent in the overcast closed again, the tower glistened with a sheen that was almost sticky. Aldric would not have been surprised to smell the sweet, salty tang of new blood. And within his borrowed armor he shivered just a little.

The Red Tower's history was such that its name was used beyond the Empire as a threat to frighten naughty children. Beyond, but never within. Within the Empire, such threats frightened more than children. For within the borders of the Empire, the Red Tower's threat was real.

Aldric's guess had been right. It was to have been the most splendid, the most imposing and the most impregnable fortress in Drusul; and then the money ran out. No one but historians and scholars even remembered its builder's name now; he had been disowned by his infuriated family for committing the near-capital offence of squandering inherited wealth, and they wanted nothing more to do with him. He had died an unmarried, childless, nameless old man.

Eighty years passed, and the tower became a fortified residence for the hereditary Overlords of the rapidly growing new city-state of Egisburg, a place made rich by the traffic passing along its twin rivers and by the ironworks which were already passing into proverb. "As good as Egisburg steel" had been a token of approval more than a century ago. In those days the Sherban emperors had been more tolerant of autonomous city-states than they were now.

During the early decades of the Sherbanul dynasty's rise to absolute power—before the coming of the Warlords—it had become necessary to find a secure place where important prisoners, political hostages and "guests" of the Drusalan Empire could stay pending an ultimate decision on their fate. That decision could be a reprieve, or the signing of a favourable treaty— favourable to the Empire, naturally—or legal execution. Once in awhile it was just disappearance.

The Red Tower—which had acquired its name and its glazing when the city first declared its support for the Emperor ten years before, during that delicate few months when the second autocrat of the dynasty was considering who were allies and who enemies and what to do to each—was just such a place. Created as a fortress, finished as a home, it had all the necessary requisites and had been handed over to the then-current Emperor on the instant that his speculation passed from the cerebral to the verbal. Red being the preferred Imperial color (a fact made known to those who had chosen the tint of the glaze, and everyone was aware of it) the gift was accepted at once. Since then a considerable number of people had passed through the tower's lowering portals, and though most of them were accounted for in one way or another, there were still a score or so who had never been seen or heard from again . . . as if the somber crimson building had swallowed them. Yet in keeping with the façade of safe, comfortable accommodation for individuals of consequence—and since a few of them were indeed restored to their full rank and privilege with apologies of varying sincerity—conditions within the Tower were said to be little short of luxurious. And the guard contingent was supposed to be downright polite!

Dewan ar Korentin had told Aldric about this place over a drink; one of the many, many Imperial subjects which they had discussed in the short time available for Aldric to learn about them. He had said that a posting to duty in the Red Tower was regarded by most regular troops—and granted by their officers—as a kind of good-conduct award. That meant several things; most of all, that the attitude of the entire small garrison from its commander down tended to be somewhat lax. Quite apart from anything else, the construction, reputation and appearance of the Red Tower was such that it deterred all but the most determined escape attempts. Not that any of those had ever succeeded, of course—and for the same reasons, nobody should be mad enough to want to get *in*.

Except, reflected Aldric sardonically, that several otherwise rational people apparently were . . .

And somebody, somewhere, seemed to suspect as much. Why else would all the streets leading to Tower Square be blocked by army checkpoints? The soldiers manning them wore *Woydach* Etzel's crest and colors— Aldric was growing very tired of seeing that jagged four-pointed star disfiguring what he still regarded as his own clean black and silver, for all that he wore Imperial red right now—and they were turning away any who lacked the proper written authority to pass through their blockade, even those who, by the sound of their protests, actually lived in the sealed-off streets.

"What's the meaning of all this?" Aldric wondered quietly out of the corner of his mouth. "They can't be expecting us. Can they . . . ?"

"No." Bruda's reply sounded confident and unconcerned. "This is standard practice. A drill. A precautionary measure."

"Precaution against what?"

This time Prokrator Bruda made no answer.

There was a travelling fair in town: jugglers, musicians and acrobats—and knowing the Imperial Secret Police a little, Aldric guessed that some of them, the acrobats at least, were as likely *taulathin* as not. It was only a guess, because nobody had told him or even hinted that it might be so. But then, they probably hadn't told Lord General Goth either. The fair was keeping company with the more respectable and socially acceptable entertainments of professional storytellers and a theatrical troupe; altogether an expensive-looking show, drawn here for some festival or other to make the last few performances of the season before winter closed in, which had attracted more people than Egisburg seemed able to comfortably hold. One or two more strange faces would hardly attract attention; Bruda or whoever was behind this venture's planning must surely have known, and it explained much of the tight timekeeping involved.

For all the crowds, it proved easy to find lodgings; the cavalry escort were billeted at once with the city's garrison—for despite tensions among the politicals, there was no similar internal breakdown in the Army. Yet. That lay behind the arrogant ease with which they had travelled from Goth's headquarters, and was why the Lord General had insisted Aldric wear Imperial armor. It made him just another part of—the Alban sneered inwardly as the thought took shape—one big, happy army. And a part who was of such rank that he need not fear casual questioning; no military policeman or checkpoint serjeant would dream of questioning a *hanalth* of Armored Cavalry without a triple-thick, lead-lined, copper-bottomed damn good reason to hide behind. And if he had one, and was already so suspicious as to ask questions, then it was already far too late.

Officers of rank naturally did not live in barracks with

their men when there was better to be had, and in Egisburg there was much, much better. For all the teeming host of visitors, and regardless of the fact that they were the best in the city, there were still rooms vacant in the inns lying directly beneath the brooding shadow of the Tower. Vague, forbidding rumours of just who might be held in the citadel—and those rumours varied widely from the unlikely to the downright impossible—were enough to persuade all but the boldest and the wealthiest to seek rooms elsewhere in the city—anywhere elsewhere. Those who remained, other than high-ranking military officers, were men and women cushioned by money whose boldness was directly proportional to their wealth. And some were very, very *bold* indeed.

The explanation had come from Bruda, prompted by Aldric's voiced doubt that they would find anywhere to stay other than barracks and that he most certainly wasn't going to live and sleep in a place where his slightest error would show up like a candle in a cellar. They were riding easily through the crowded streets, letting the throng part before the horses in their own time rather than forcing a passage as they might have done; to do so would have been unnecessary, and obviously so. A casual drifting was much more natural in Egisburg's holiday atmosphere; as natural as the smile which it created on Aldric's face when he began to appreciate the citizens's cheery mood. It was the first such mood, and the first unforced smile, which he had experienced in far too long. More interesting still, the leisurely pace gave him time to overhear such of the storytellers as were close enough to avoid drowning in the background babble.

Aldric had long known that these professional storytellers were rather different from the Alban equivalent—like, for instance, the old man who had harped and sung at his *Eskorrethen* feast almost four years ago. *Four years ago this very month!* he realized with a slight start. Albans were conservative in many things, preferring the old ways to any innovation; that was not always a good thing, whether in the matter of literature or in wider world affairs. One might lead to a degree of cultural stagnation, but the other could be much more dangerous. Of

course, King Rynert's new approach—as typified by his
presence here—could be equally chancy. To Aldric!

That old man had memorised scores of old legends,
old stories, old folktales and even the old, approved way
in which to tell each one. But all, like their teller, were
old. However, the Imperial word for a storyteller translated literally into Alban as "one who makes tales which
entertain," and indeed they spent as much tune creating
new material as they did in learning the classics. It was
no accident that, though Jouvaine by birth and Vreijek
by inclination, the playwright Oren Osmar had produced
some of his most enduring and popular work under Imperial auspices. Even *Tiluan the Prince,* a play still widely
regarded as original, daring and controversial more than
eighty years after its first performance.

Not, of course, that such daring controversy touched
on anything to do with the Empire's policies; generations
of hard-working theatrical censors had seen to that, and
Aldric was not so naïve as to forget it. Still, it was intriguing to hear not only stories which he knew already—
though in a foreign language which required a degree of
concentration for him to understand—but also tantalis-
ing snatches of tales entirely new; although some of
these were familiar and popular favourites here, if the
noisy approval of their audiences bore true witness.

". . . As long ago as forever, and as far away as the
moon . . ."

". . . Know, O Prince, that between the years when
the oceans drank . . ."

". . . be sure that you return before the stroke of
midnight, for otherwise . . ."

". . . proud, pale Prince of ruins, bearer of the rune-
carved Black Sword . . ."

". . . the falcon struck thrice upon the ground and
became a fine young man . . ."

". . . I shall clasp my hands together and bow to the
corners of the world . . ."

Aldric was jolted violently back to an awareness of
his purpose in this city by a slap between the shoulder-
blades which observers—had their eyes been keen—
might have noticed struck him far, far harder than any
hautheisart had a right to strike a *hanalth,* no matter how

close their friendship might have been. But there was no friendship at all in Voord's grin when Aldric swung round with a stifled oath to glare at him. The man's thin, bloodless lips were stretched back far too tightly from his teeth; it was an ugly rather than an amiable expression, and both men knew that the other was meant to know it.

"There will doubtless be a time for sightseeing, *sir,*" the Vlechan said. "But later. Not now."

Drinking white wine from a flagon sunk in compacted snow to keep it cool, two Imperial officers sat in the otherwise deserted withdrawing-room of a fine tavern and regarded one another over the rims of their goblets. Two others were absent. *Hautheisart* Voord had gone out for an ostentatiously-announced walk, and if there was any ulterior motive behind his decision—coming as it did so closely on the heels of certain observations regarding sightseeing—not even Aldric Talvalin considered it worth commenting on.

Aldric himself, typically enough, had settled himself into his assigned room for some five minutes, then had gone looking for the tavern's bath-house. Bruda had shown no surprise; he knew the Alban people and their customs slightly, and this young man rather more than that. It was of course possible that Aldric was being subtly insulting, trying to imply that the company he was forced to keep made him feel unclean, but any insult so delicately subtle that it went unnoticed failed to be an insult at all. Instead Bruda and Tagen sat drinking their chilled wine, chatting about inconsequential matters in a relaxed way which would have shocked officers of a similar difference in rank who were unaware of the informal rank structure within *Kagh' Ernvakh*.

Aldric came in before the flagon was more than half-way empty, looking pinkly clean, still a little damp behind the ears and smelling the merest touch scented—in short, like any other officer of the Drusalan military on an off-duty evening. He was out of armor now and back into his own clothing as far as his pretence allowed; only the rank-flashed brassards on the upper arms of his tunic, and the wide embroidered shoulder-tabs resting

uncomfortably on the densely-furred *coyac* he wore over
it, gave any outward indication of what he was supposed
to be. The severe haircut inflicted on him before he left
Goth's headquarters was no different from that of any
other man, officer or other rank, and the overrobe bearing his other insignia was doubled carelessly over the
arm which carried his sheathed longsword. In the instant
of his taking a seat, that robe was flung casually across
the chair-back—and the sword leaned respectfully against
its arm.

"You should be wearing that," said Bruda reprovingly.

"The sword?" Aldric misunderstood deliberately, then
reached behind him and pulled the rank-robe further
down to make a better cushion for his head. "Or this
thing? Because you aren't wearing yours," he pointed
out with impeccable logic as he poured himself some
wine.

Bruda smiled thinly "Your point," he conceded without rancour. "But then again, I'm entitled to my rank;
I earned it. Yours is merely borrowed. So wear the robe
whenever you go out of this tavern: understood?"

The request was acknowledged—just—by a lifting of
eyebrows and wine-cup, and by the faintest of nods.

You do know how to be annoying, don't you? thought
Bruda. He said nothing of that sort aloud, and instead
turned back to Tagen and the conversation interrupted
by Aldric's arrival. "So—now that you've seen the
Tower, what do you think? Any ideas about getting in?"

"What?" Aldric sat up very sharply, flinched, swore
and shook cold wine out of his sleeve. He was none too
pleased by the import of Bruda's words; playing things
by ear was all very well in the proper time and place,
but this was neither.

Bruda's gaze flicked unemotionally from the spilled
wine to Aldric's face and back again in any eyeblink.
"Mop that up," he said, taking a drink of his own. "And
I wasn't talking to you. Tagen—you're from the hill
country. Opinions?"

"I think, Prokrator," said Tagen, after taking a moment to gather his thoughts, "that hill-climbing and the
Tower don't go together. No natural toe or finger-holds,
thanks to the glaze; and if you tried to hammer in a

spike you'd have the whole garrison out to answer your knocking."

"Conclusion?"

"As well try to climb a mirror as go up that bitch by normal means. Sir."

"I see." Bruda shifted in his chair. "Well, Aldric: no comments yet?"

"No. Not yet." There was more on Aldric's mind right now than being sarcastic; and granted, that did make a change.

"Sir?" said Tagen in the voice of one struck by a sudden thought. "Sir, I might be able to get a grapnel on to one of the parapets."

Glancing at Tagen, Aldric opened his mouth to say something like, "What, ten-score feet straight up, and in the dark?" then closed it with a snap as the *tau-kortagor* idly flexed one arm and gave a hint of the heavy muscles hidden by his sleeve.

Yet Bruda did say much the same out loud—although not scornfuly but with regret. "Not even your strength could manage that feat, Tagen," he said.

"Oh, not throwing it, sir." The man laughed a little, flattered that his commander had given such a possibility sympathetic thought. "No, I was thinking of a cross-bow."

"You'd have to pad the hook," said Aldric. "Those things must be noisy when they hit stone. And you'd have to get it first time. Could you?"

"Not first time—not in the dark. Nor second, most likely. But I could promise third or fourth."

"By which time the—what was it?—the whole garri-son would be out to answer your knocking, eh?" Aldric echoed Tagen's own doubt softly and the Drusalan grinned, amused by the word-play.

Bruda was not amused. He set down his goblet with a sharp click that drew all eyes and turned it slowly around and around as silence fell. "Well done," he said acidly. "You're skilled at picking holes, Aldric-*erhan*." The Alban "scholar" suffix was more an insult than any-thing else, the way he used it now. "But let's hear some-thing positive for a change."

Aldric stared at the two Imperial faces . . . hard faces,

foreign faces—and knew quite well that he was taking a
risk even to voice his thoughts aloud. But he did, at last.
"Try sorcery."

The door opened and Voord came in as if on cue.
Or as if he had been listening outside. "Sorcery?" The
hautheisart's voice was disbelieving. "Alban, you deserve
credit for sheer gall at least—thought little enough for
wit. To recommend the use of the Art Magic to a Chief
of Secret Police must rank among—"

"Look at the warships of our so-gallant fleet, dear
Lord Commander Voord!" snapped Aldric, "Then tell
me more about how magic is forbidden in the Empire!"

"So you know about the Imperial proscriptions, then,"
observed Bruda unnecessarily.

Aldric stared at him a moment, and nodded; who
didn't, for Heaven's sweet sake? They were only the
most viciously penalised edicts ever to appear in a legal
statute book, and they had been stringently enforced
ever since their inception fifty years before. Enforced,
that is, except where raw power could command them
to be set aside.

"If you know, then perhaps you could also suggest
where I might find a sorcerer?" Bruda continued in a
voice of deceptive sweetness. "Vreijaur, perhaps? Or
maybe even Alba?"

It struck Aldric then that Bruda might not be quite
as sober as he had first appeared. "Your lieutenant has
already pointed out that you are Chief of Secret Police,"
he returned flatly. "As *Hauthunalth Kagh' Ernvakh*, you
tell me."

There was a chilly pause, then Bruda threw back his
head and laughed with a harsh bark of mirth which startled Aldric considerably. "All right," he said, still grinning, "I will. There." One hand pointed to where Voord
was leaning against the door-post looking enigmatic.
"That's your wizard."

"*Him?*" Aldric was, and let himself sound, insultingly
incredulous.

"And why not?" smirked Voord. "Where better to
practise secret arts than in the Secret Police? We all of
us have our little vices. I already know some of yours,

and this is one of mine. You might find out what the others are some day, *hlensyarl.*" His smirk went thin and nasty. "Or they might find you."

"My personal staff are men of many talents, Aldric," said Bruda. It was impossible to tell if the fact pleased him, but somehow Aldric fancied not. "Many talents—and various."

"So it would appear." The Alban poured himself more wine, and flavored the inside of his mouth with a minute sip. He met Bruda's eyes and held them with his own. "I'll remember that."

"Yes. Best that you do."

"Prokrator," cut in Voord, "I was a little late. What are *we*"—all Imperial officers together, he implied, and no play-acting foreigners—"discussing?"

"The *tulathin* and the Tower," said Bruda, and hesitated. "Well, would magic be of use?"

"Perhaps . . ." Voord's voice tailed off as he realized he had over-filled his cup and concentrated on bringing it unspilled to his lips, where a long draught brought its contents to a safer level. Only then did he lower the goblet and nod slightly in agreement. "Yes, perhaps indeed."

"Prokrator *hauthanalth,* this is scarcely evidence of careful planning!" From the tone of his voice, Aldric was not so much surprised as angry; annoyed that a plan which in its earlier stages—the "acquisition" of an Alban representative—had seemed geared to the fine tolerances of an expensive machine, should now have degenerated to speculations over wine. And after another half-second's consideration, he said as much aloud.

"Careful planning?" echoed Voord before Bruda could say anything. "But it is, Talvalin. It is. All of these 'speculations' as you call them, have been aired before."

"And advance reconnaisance? You all talk as if you were seeing this Red Tower for the first time!"

"Most of us are; but it was carefully surveyed by one of my agents not long ago. A single man, rather than a group—attracting less attention that way, and preserving what he learned in his head rather than on paper, for the sake of secrecy."

"So much secrecy that I see no evidence of what was learned. Who was this so-called ag—" His words cut off as he realized what the answer would be.

"Garet."

He was right. "Oh," was all that Aldric said in response to Voord's statement, but inside his mind was in a whirl. It was ridiculous that so delicate an enterprise should hinge on the knowledge of one man, and that such knowledge should be carried only in the fragile vessel of that man's mind. It was so ridiculous that Aldric felt suspicion plucking at his hackles yet again. Learning that Voord—of all people—had a fondness for sorcery was one reason; and enough reason to make anyone suspicious without anything to bolster it. But that discovery was beginning to nudge other, deliberately suppressed and now half-forgotten memories into place. Memories from Seghar.

"What plan for us, then?" he wondered aloud, knowing that he was almost too elaborately nonchalant. "Do we climb ropes like *tulathin*—or spiders—or such vermin, or do we—"

"Walk in through the Tower's front door?" Bruda finished Aldric's question for him. "Yes, in fact we do. A bold approach. I have all the proper written authorities: genuine for the most part, where we could get them. Otherwise carefully forged."

"Walk in," repeated Aldric softly. "Just like that."

"Exactly so. What could be more realistic? And any other response would be suspicious in itself." He caught Aldric's sceptically lifted brows; could hardly have avoided doing so, for the expression was not hidden at all and he could scarcely have missed it. "Oh yes. You're forgetting, Aldric *ilauem-arluth* Talvalin, that we all— you too!—are senior officers of the finest Army on the face of the earth. Important people, man! We'll pay our respects to the garrison commander later this evening, and to any . . . high-ranked guests he might have. Because he knows we rode in today, and he would be shocked by the breach of protocol if we failed to walk in tonight."

"I hope you're right, Bruda. Indeed I do. For all our sakes." Aldric stood up and settled Isileth Widowmaker's cross-strap comfortably on his shoulder, then her scabbard to his weapon-belt. The longsword had come in with him; had leaned her hilt on the arm of his chair as a loving dog will lean its nose; had not, in fact, been allowed to stray more than an arm's length away since she was returned to him, even though it was considered most unmannerly to carry a battle-furnished—and thus threatening—*taiken* when to do so wasn't necessary. But those were manners for Alba and among Albans; here, in Aldric's view, the sword's presence was necessary. Very. And would continue to be so while Voord hovered in the background.

Then he glanced at Bruda, nodded and lifted the rank-marked black and silver overrobe from his chair. "Satisfied now, *sir?*" he asked with a thread of good-humor in his voice.

"Reasonably, *hanalth.* But the rank-robe is crumpled; it could do with a pressing. See to it before you wear it on the public street."

"Yes, *sir!*" Aldric snapped a neat half-salute for Bruda's benefit, turned to leave the room—and found Voord blocking his path.

"Just where the hell do you think you're going anyway?"

Aldric hesitated, considering the flavors of the various responses he could make; then shrugged and put a sort of smile on his face as he brushed past. "Sightseeing," he said. Then he dusted an imagined smudge from the black fur of the *coyac,* where Voord's arm had touched it. "And to have a look at the moon, if the sky's clear enough." He sank the last barb with an unsubtle malice, sure of the Vlechan now. "I'm tired. But you know what they say. 'A . . . change is as good as a rest.' "

"Be back by the Hour of the Cat," Bruda advised Aldric's receding back.

Aldric turned sufficiently to see the Prokrator's face, then said, "You mean by eight of the clock, of course. Although midnight would be as appropriate."

"The Hour of the Wolf? Far too late! Why do you—"

"Voord might tell you. But I doubt it." Aldric smiled again, the smile of one who knows a secret, and left.

*   *   *

Because of clouds and darkness there had been little
sensation of flight; but there had been every sensation
of great speed and Dewan's face and hands were numbed
and stiffened by the icy wind which had scythed past
them. Only his legs were warm, where they forked the
dragon's armored neck. But for all the discomfort, and
all the—he would not give the word more than an instant's consideration, even though he knew it was
correct—all the terror, Dewan ar Korentin would not
have missed this experience for half the gold in Warlord
Etzel's coffers.

No, not for *all* the gold, because every once in a while
the silvery gray blanket above, beneath and around them
had parted, and he had seen the fires of countless stars
mirrored by the lantern-lights of human men far, far
below. It was impossible to guess the speed of Ymareth's
flight, but the thinness of the cold air and the difficulty
he had in breathing it told him that he was at least as
high off the ground as the mountain-peak he had climbed
for a wager long ago. Why the air should grow weak,
Dewan didn't know; but he was intelligent enough to
conclude that if he felt now what he had felt then, and
the only similarities were altitude and cold, then one or
the other was responsible. And he had been equally cold
sitting on a horse, so . . . Perhaps the richness remained
near the ground, where there were more men and beasts
to breath it.

"Egisburg," said Ymareth's voice inside his head, and
with the word the dragon tilted onto one wing and began
a lazy, spiralling descent. Dewan's ears popped as they
were filled with the rich, thick lower air, and he swallowed automatically to relieve the pressure; but he was
no longer thinking vaguely scholarly thoughts about the
composition of air at different heights above ground
level.

Instead he was gaping like the stupidest backwoods
peasant at the sight which came drifting up towards him
as he sank through the clouds towards it, knowing that
he was gaping and not caring who else knew. *Egisburg,*
Ymareth had said. The single word, the name, could not
begin to do justice to the great strew of luminescent

jewels which were spread out below him. Oh, Dewan knew what they were, and what their colors meant: the lamps of the city, yellow for the most part, bright and steady where their source was oil-fed lanterns, duller and flickering for live-flame torches. There was a cluster of sapphires—someone's house-lamps, glazed in blue glass; there emeralds; and there rubies. Further away, slipping beyond sight as they glided down and thus narrowed the angle of view, Dewan caught a brief glimpse of the wealth and reputation of Egisburg: the amber glow of her furnaces, near the silver ribbons that were the confluence of the city's two rivers. Now and again there would be a harsh glare where some ironmaster worked late into the night, and the cold wind brought with it a faint, faint reek of charcoal smoke edged with the acrid bite of white-hot metal. It smelt of . . . dragons.

The dragon beneath him banked over and away from the myriad glitters of the city, and Egisburg slipped smoothly out of sight under Ymareth's wing and body as it turned toward the darkness beyond the city boundaries in a search for somewhere safe to land.

How can even a dragon see in this? Dewan thought wildly. The thought was stifled an instant later as he learned just how a dragon could see after dark; for the billow of flame from Ymareth's jaws was as hot and white and brilliant as a lightning-flash, and threw the scudding ground below—and not so far below, at that— into a sharp-edged relief map worked in black and silver-white.

Arrogant, Dewan thought then, but not careless. Who'd be out on a night like this? And who'd believe what they saw if they saw this? And who'd believe *them?* If they were stupid enough to mention anything so linked to sorcery within the borders of the Empire!

Ymareth's flight curved around, leisurely and slow; Dewan felt the shift of muscles under his gripping thighs as they adjusted the set of the dragon's wings, and then he felt those same muscles flex like cables to drive the wings forward and down in the final landing maneuver he had watched earlier this same extraordinary day. The dragon's mailed spine kicked up at Dewan's unarmored one, a sensation reminiscent of taking an assault-course jump bareback, and settled beneath him. Movement ceased.

And they were down.

Dewan climbed from Ymareth's neck—"dismount" was scarcely an adequate description for such a height as was between him and the ground—and walked away like an old man, very stiffly and carefully, his legs locking at the knees with every stride. He was aware that by rights he should still be frightened, or shocked, or at the least startled; but he knew equally well that if asked he would admit only to exultation and great wonder.

Ymareth, crouched huge and impossible in the broken moonlight a few yards from the Vreijek's back, watched him even though the man was unaware of such a scrutiny. "He is as one who has looked upon the face of his god," said the dragon softly, privately, for Gemmel's ears alone. "Seldom has this form given such joy." Yellow-white fire danced lazily in fanged jaws, but there was no threat in the gesture; only satisfaction and a great, gentle amusement.

"I did not teach you blasphemy," returned Gemmel a touch sourly. "And you aren't a god."

"I did not say so—that was thy word. But now that thee makes mention of it . . . ."

"Don't!" It was only after his twitchy, nervous response that Gemmel realized how he was being teased. Almost affectionately so, if the word applied to dragons.

"Thee taught me the appreciation of humor, Maker. So enjoy the jest."

"I taught thee—you—so that you would better understand humankind. Not to make jokes. Stop it."

"Not at thy command. Not now." Ymareth's mind-heard voice hardened, became severe and almost reproving. "Thou art no longer worthy of such obedience. Not now. In the future . . . Perhaps. But know: the Dragon-lord is he who refused escape and safety for his honor's sake. Remember it, Maker-that-was."

Gemmel ignored all the strata of implication in the dragon's speech, as much because he was unwilling to consider them just now as for any other reason. But he looked into the dragon's eyes, as few men might have done, and after several moments smiled. "Then I commend myself to the future," he said simply. "But what has been done, has been done—and what I must do, I will do. Ymareth Firedrake, I am *lonely*. You know my mind as none other, yet not even you can dream of such loneliness. Always, always alone. And my son the Dragon-lord, with the face of the son of my blood; surely that is a bitter jest of the Darkness."

"So thou namest now a jest of the Darkness. Of Fate. Of whatever name thy choice desires. But a jest—such as those I am forbidden. Is that justice, Maker?"

There was logic in the dragon's reasoning. *Do as I say,* thought Gemmel, dredging up a phrase from years past, *not do as I do.* "Your pardon, then," he said, as he had never thought he would. "For my lost honor's sake, I commend thee to the Dragon-lord Aldric Talvalin. My fosterling. My son. Guard him. Aid him. Keep him safe."

"All those and more." Ymareth spread great, dark wings in a stretch, and yawned like a cat so that for just one instant Gemmel was gazing right down the dragon's throat. Fire slumbered uneasily within it. "But tonight is an ill night for watching; the heat in yonder city makes confusion against the cold air."

"What if . . ." Gemmel began to say. The dragon looked at him—nothing more—but the wizard fell awkwardly and immediately silent.

"There is the Eye of the Dragon," said Ymareth. "Thus he is at once within my notice—and thine also, if it is thy wish to spend again a little power. That power which the Eye has stolen betimes, these few days past, so that I at least might see."

Gemmel looked from the Dragonwand to the dragon and remembered the stinging hurts which he had suffered willingly or not; and he might well have become angry had not Dewan's voice slashed through the chill night air like a razor.

"Now what of the Dragonwand, Ymareth, Lord Firedrake?" Gemmel, listening, would have doubted Dewan ar Korentin capable of such delicate courtesy as the mannered form of Drusalan which he now employed. But though he listened, the wizard did no more and

passed no comment either then or at any other time.
"As if in a dream," continued Dewan, "I remember that
Aldric Talvalin gave his promise that the gift of a talisman of power would be returned to its rightful owner
and its rightful place. Yet I see it here. So then, what of
the Dragonwand?"

Ymareth's eerie, terrible, beautiful head turned slowly
as if surprised to hear such words from such an unlikely
source. So far as black and steel and goldbright scales
could hold the expression, there was warm pleasure on
the dragon's face and in its phosphorescent, unwatchable
eyes. "It is fine that thee cares for such a matter here
and now. But be assured, Dewan ar Korentin," and
hearing his name from such a source made Dewan shiver
slightly, as it had made Aldric shiver before him, "that
I am in no haste or eagerness; for such is not required.
Be at thy ease. *Kailin-eir* Talvalin gave his promise. That
is enough. He promised its return when all was accomplished and that time is not yet. Though he knows not
yet whose will he does, he knows full well the meaning
of what he does. Ykraith Dragonwand is a part of that."

Though Dewan could sense the needle of an insult
somewhere, buried deep, he was unsure if the dragon
had meant deliberate hurt by it or merely a goad to
Gemmel "the Maker"—a title which to Dewan had
many facets of significance—who had become, in the
phrase which he had overheard, "Maker-that-was." He
turned, slowly, no longer speaking half over his shoulder
as he had done when first trying to come to terms with
so many enormities, and deep inside himself Dewan—
ex-Eldheisart of the Bodyguard, king's confidant, warrior's friend, wizard's acquaintance and now most impossible of all, dragon's rider—felt himself dwindle into
insignificance.

"Ymareth," he said, dropping from the formal mode,
"this is near the heart of the Drusalan Empire. Aldric,
Gemmel and myself—we are three individuals against a
mighty realm. What can *you* do?"

A gush of fire from the dragon's jaws threw down
stark shadows beyond the trees of the small hollow
where they had landed: a billow of pale, cool flame that
was the dragon's laughter. "O ar Korentin," the words

forming within his head had an aura of chuckling about them, fluttering like an alcohol flame, "if thou art within a mile of what I ·can do, ask again. If asking is required . . ." Then the flickering amusement died away, fading like a morning mist in sunshine. "Enough. For all the darkness it is but evening yet, however these Drusalans calculate their hours of night and day. Best therefore that I not remain. From thy words, good ar Korentin, I do not exist within the boundaries of this Empire. That makes me sad. But for all my sadness I would as soon give no priest of this land a conflict of belief. Yet. Later, later they will see, and know, and believe indeed. I go. But remember," and had the words been spoken rather than heard within the confines of their listeners' heads, they would have been lost in the sounds as Ymareth prepared to rise once more into the air, "remember that I watch by Dragonwand and Dragon's Eye. Be aware of aid uncalled-for. Farewell!"

The downward slap of air all but threw Dewan off his feet, for all that he was expecting something of the sort. By the time he had wiped powdered snow from his eyes, the dragon's lean black silhouette was no more than a scudding disruption of the cloud-occluded stars; but it mattered little to Dewan that he could see no more than a dark razor-slash interrupting the jewelled twinkle of the winter sky. He stood in silence and he stared, his head tipped right back on his shoulders, and he did not move from that position until Gemmel reached out to lightly touch him on the arm.

"So," the old wizard said, "how much do you know of me now, Dewan?"

The Vreijek's unwinking gaze shifted from the stars and that which flitted across them to Gemmel's bearded face, blinked twice and came to focus. Dewan smiled then, very gently. "You are not Dragon-lord. Not Maker. Only Maker-that-was. You must explain those titles to me, Gemmel."

"Soon. You have said what I am not—what else?"

"A—a wizard. And a scholar. A man wise in many arts. And the foster-father of, of my friend."

"Then Aldric is your friend . . . ?"

"Yes. Because he speaks the truth—at least to me—

as only a friend can do. Because we talk as equals. And
because we can insult each other!" That last was accompanied by a laugh, but Gemmel had been reading between the lines all along and needed no signal to
understand. In the Alban culture, and especially among
the high clan *cseirin*-born, any men who could swap insults had to be friends. Otherwise one of them would
be dead.

"Then tell me," Gemmel purred, "what has he told
you of *en-altrou* Errekren, old Snowbeard his sorcerous
foster-father? For he must have told you something,
surely?"

"Enough." Dewan looked at Gemmel with a clear-
eyed gaze that even in the darkness suggested much
unsaid. "He told me that you lived beneath *Glas'elyu
Menethen.* I laughed at him then, but he insisted—so is
it true: *under* the Blue Mountains?"

Gemmel nodded, and at that starlit acquiescence
Dewan swallowed audibly before he dared continue to
speak. But when he did, the words began tumbling out
with all the excited eagerness of a boy maybe a quarter
of the Vreijek's real age—a boy Dewan might once have
been, and a man he might yet have been, before or without the Drusalan Empire and its military service. "Under
the mountain—Lord God! Under Thunderpeak."

Gemmel had not said so—had not used the name at
all—and at the back of his mind he began to wonder
just how much—knowledge and guesses both—Aldric
had told Dewan when they were both just drunk enough
to exchange confidences. He knew that the younger man
made friends quickly and thoughtlessly, in the way that
often led to hurt on both sides. And hurt to third parties
as well.

"He said that you travelled as well, great distances to
many countries, before you came to Alba—"

"Came *back* to Alba, Dewan," the wizard interrupted
softly. It was enough to put a slight hesitation in the
flood of words, and a thoughtfulness as well.

"You had a son. He . . . died."

"Yes. Long ago."

"You told Rynert the King, that day in Cerdor when

you found out about . . . how Aldric had been given to the Empire."

"I told him that my son died. But not how he died; nor who killed him; nor anything about the consequences of that killing. I told him only what you heard yourself. That I had lost a son—and much more than a son." Gemmel shivered. He looked around him and fixed his attention on a tree stump left by some woodcutter earlier in the year. "I'm cold, Dewan," he said. "Cold . . . and I'm beginning to hate the dark. We'd both be better for some heat and light."

Without waiting for agreement—or disagreement, or warning, or anything else—he raised one hand and pronounced the Invocation of Fire. A pulse of force gathered around and then sprang from his fingertips, pale as a dying candle, so weak that daylight would have made it no more than a half-sensed haze in the air; but for all that, the snow beneath its track flashed from white solid to white steam with no intervening stage as liquid. Then it hit the stump: a core of unseasoned wood wrapped in spongy, sodden rot and topped off with more snow. There was a sound like the crack of the world's biggest whip . . . and the stump burned as hot and clean as holly dried for kindling.

"Better," said Gemmel, and scooped up a little snow to ease the blisters rising on his hand. That small discomfort was well worth it. Heedless of lingering dampness, he dropped his small pack to the ground in the lee of a clump of bushes and sat down on it, stretching chilled feet gratefully towards the blaze.

Dewan looked at him and drew breath as if to say something; then thought better of it and sat down in his turn. "Now. Tell me. And tell me first of all: who killed your son?"

"I . . . I never knew his name. But he was the uncle of the now-*Woydach*."

"Etzel's uncle?" Dewan stared at the fire, not understanding at first; then, still staring at the fire and remembering how it had been created, understanding all too well. "Oh God. *That* one! The one who was—"

"Burned. Roasted alive where he sat on his horse and

laughed at my dead son. Killed by magic, Dewan. Killed by me."

"Then *you*—you're behind the Empire's edict on sorcery!"

"The Grand Warlord's edict—but yes, I am. I, and the thing I did."

"Fifty years ago," Dewan muttered, thinking aloud and not meaning to; then he considered his own words and turned abruptly to face the wizard—literally, for now he was staring carefully full at Gemmel's face. It was white-bearded and careworn, but Dewan was giving it more than the casual glance that was usually already colored by preconceived assumptions concerning wizards—and those who called themselves wizards. It was an old face only until Dewan tried to set a value in years on "old"; and then it wasn't quite so venerable after all.

A man in his fit and healthy middle sixties. Too fit and healthy for such an age. Old enough—and yet not old enough. Aldric had said how much like himself Gemmel's son must have looked; but when they had first met, the Alban was already twenty years of age and probably seeming older through the fright and grief he had experienced. Either Gemmel had been a father in his teens—not impossible, but unlikely given how strait-laced his morals could occasionally be. Or Dewan's arithmetic was at fault—which was equally unlikely in this case of simple addition.

Or something was not what it seemed.

"Gemmel?" There was a damnable tremor in his voice when he spoke, but the wizard gave no sign of having heard it. "Gemmel, how . . . how old are you?"

"Older than I was yesterday. But not so old as I'll be tomorrow." That there was no smile with the words chilled Dewan more than the snow-melt soaking into his clothes. "It's all a matter of time. And time is something I always had plenty of. Except now. Now I have far too much!"

Dewan felt his skin start to crawl beneath his furs, his armor and his damp clothing, because he had a feeling—no, he *knew*—that he was about to hear things he didn't want to, yet equally didn't want to miss. He wished Aldric were here, with that healthy streak of cynical humor which was just what Dewan needed right now. Because Dewan, ex-*eldheisart*, ex-bodyguard, ex- all the rest, knew something else with absolute certainty.

He was terrified.

But not so terrified as to get up and walk away. Gemmel was gazing at the star-shot sky as though searching for something—the return of Ymareth, perhaps; or perhaps not. It was more as if he searched for that something beyond the sky that neither of them could see, a something that only he might hope for.

"I should have spared him," the wizard said at last, "because by then his death was needless. Too late to save my son. Too late to bring him back. But I killed: in rage, in grief . . . in vengeance. Because I had the power to do it, there, then, at once—and because I wanted to, more than anything else in all the world."

"There's nothing wrong with vengeance, Gemmel. Look at Aldric. Look at what he did—and with your help."

"Oh yes, with my help. And with what motive? Why did I do all this?" There was a dreadful bitterness in Gemmel's voice, a shame and self-loathing which to Dewan had no business there. "I had my reasons. I always have *my* reasons long planted and long in growing. But now they're coming to full flower and I'm afraid the price will be too high. I'm afraid I'll lose my son again." Gemmel took a deep breath and held it, then let it slowly out and smiled and shook his head. "And no, Dewan, you're wrong. Because there's everything wrong with vengeance—at least, for me. It can only be forgiven if it's right, if it's expected, if it's the proper thing to do. The Alban High Speech has seven different words for 'revenge,' did you know that? Seven words, each with its own proper circumstance for correct usage. The taking of revenge is an Alban's heritage, Dewan. It isn't mine; never has been. I was wrong to do it. It cost me my . . . my honor. And Ymareth knows."

"Ymareth? Was that why—"

"Yes. Why it holds me in amused contempt—for being less than those to whom I was and should have remained superior. You heard it. I am no longer Dragon-lord. Ymareth respects only honor—an intangible thing which cannot be bought or forced; a fragile thing which must be earned and held, no matter what the price of its holding. I lost mine fifty years ago; I haven't regained it yet."

"Oh, I . . . Dragon-lord I understand," Dewan managed at last, "for all that it's one of *Woydach* Etzel's titles too." Gemmel glanced towards him, raising an eyebrow, but said nothing more—plainly waiting for the rest of the question, because what Dewan was trying to say had to be a question. And it was. "But what about . . . What about—*Maker?*"

The wizard smiled. "Another title. Concise; descriptive; accurate. And true."

"True!" Anticipating something, being absolutely sure of it, was not at all the same as having it confirmed. "Then you *made* . . . ?"

"Yes."

Dewan had promised himself that he would do nothing foolish, nothing which might compromise the carefully cherished dignity which gave him a screen to hide behind. So he didn't spring to his feet, nor did his mouth drop open, nor did he swear. But slowly, very slowly in keeping with that dignity, his right hand moved to touch himself over the heart and above each eye in the old Teshirin blessing. "Father, Mother, Maiden," he whispered, "be between myself and harm, now and always." He kissed the palm and closed the fist and only then said, "But why would you make a dragon?" in a voice whose steadiness surprised even himself.

"Because I wanted to." The laconic answer paused on an upward tone, so that Dewan stayed quite still and perfectly quiet and waited for the rest. "And because it was appropriate, and because I could."

"Appropriate?" the Vreijek prompted, speaking as a man might walk when all beneath his feet was made of blown glass and tolerance.

"There are world— . . . Places where armed guards are right and proper, and places for high walls; places for fences made of wire with fangs like roses, and for wires with—with lightning running through them. And there are places for threads of light hotter than the sun in summer, threads that can cut and kill. But here . . . Here I *wanted* to have a dragon." Paying no mind to the burn-blisters already mottling his fingers, Gemmel gestured at the fire and it flared up more fiercely still. "Not just to guard gold—you've seen the Cavern on Techaur, of course?"

Dewan nodded. There had been far more than gold in it, but he doubted now that Gemmel meant silks or costly perfumes or any of the other things that he, Dewan ar Korentin, would have thought worth guarding against theft.

"Then you'll know what I mean when I say that anyone not *sent* there with specific instructions would probably steal whatever took their fancy. Or try to."

Again the Vreijek nodded. Dewan could remember his own hands and those of Tehal Kyrin, reaching out as though of their own volition to touch, to hold, to lift—and perhaps to take. Only Aldric's cry of warning had stopped them; and later events had shown what would have happened had they completed the attempted theft. He did not know, and did not ask, how Ymareth the dragon had been made, quite well aware within himself that he would neither understand nor really want to know. Dewan knew quite enough already to know he wished to hear no more.

That was not to say his education stopped there and then, for as Aldric had warned him—five, six, seven months ago?—with a slightly drunken grin of good-fellowship, once started on a topic of conversation Gemmel Errekren would pursue it until either it was explained to his own absolute satisfaction or, more usually, his audience rose in rebellion to silence him or leave. Right at the moment, Dewan decided that his own wisest course was to sit quietly and listen.

"What can a person do to control something," Gemmel said, "when its power is such that even the possibility of its falling into the wrong hands is an unthinkable nightmare?"

For all that the question sounded merely rhetorical, Gemmel paused so long that it seemed he was waiting for an answer, an opinion, a guess. For something. Dewan provided one, and even then his quietly ventured, "Secrecy?" was more to end the dragging silence than because he thought he might be right.

Gemmel shook his head in a jerky way that was more emergence from a dream than denial—but denial it was, all the same. "Not secrecy. That seldom works. Few things can be kept a secret for long. Either the secret is discovered independently, or it's betrayed by spies and traitors, or by idealists who think equality of information should be restored. And throughout the course of history, Dewan, such great secrets have usually been weapons of one kind or another—ways to kill, not ways to cure. One country learns how to heal a terrible disease, and they give the knowledge to all; let that same country discover how to reduce a city ten times the size of Egisburg to dust and cinders in a single flash of light, and they try to keep it to themselves. Fear, do you think? Or shame? No matter. Not once such countries start to think of success in war not as 'win' or 'lose,' but in terms of what number of dead will prove acceptable. Acceptable, Dewan, not intolerable . . . ."

Gemmel gazed for a long time into the dance of flames, as if seeing something else entirely in the incandescent shift of embers and the crawl of sparks. Then he looked up again. "The Albans place great store by honor," he said. "And no, I'm not patronising you, Dewan. You're not Alban, not even by marriage, so I can say things to you that I couldn't—or wouldn't—say to Aldric. Honor—call it the extent to which a person can be trusted—is a measure of that person's worth. Of their personal ability—their power, if you like—to keep things safe. An oath, a promise, a secret; even a piece of gossip. But such power can be directed out as well as held in. As magic. A person of much honor is also a person with the capability—and no more than the capability, mind you—for considerable magical skill. But in Alba, the concept of honor has developed in such a way that using magic is no longer consistent with the reputation of an honorable man."

"Which is why Rynert has sent Aldric to do his dirty work!" concluded Dewan savagely. "Because one way or the other, no one will think the worse of him!"

Gemmel applauded, making that simple gesture of striking his hands together something laden with irony. "Well done!" he said. "Except that Aldric's capability is because of, rather than a lack of, what Rynert the King is pleased to define as honor."

"And Ymareth recognises it."

All the sardonic humor disappeared from Gemmel's face and Dewan wished that he had kept his mouth shut. "Yes," the wizard said, and all the old bitterness was back. "I instilled a respect for honor in Ymareth when I made it. Not a respect for me, myself, the Maker, but for—. For what I was. I knew that *then* nobody could take the dragon from me. Because I had given it intelligence, the ability to judge and to reason. That was why cu Ruruc couldn't—" He bit the words off short and blinked, but he knew that Dewan was watching him.

"Gemmel," the Vreijek said, and he spoke very softly now, as if trying not to give offence. Or fright. "Gemmel, there's a time and a place for all things. This is the time and place for truth. Total truth. Nothing hidden. What I think already, what I guess, is likely far, far worse than anything you could tell me, and look—" he spread both arms wide, shoulder-height, and in the heavy furs he wore over his armor he looked more like some big, friendly bear than ever before, "—I still have my sanity. If I was going to go mad, don't you think I would have done so long ago? I doubt that you told Aldric any of this; but credit him with wisdom and an open mind at least. After four years of your tuition, maybe . . . ? So. All of it. And on *my* honor, if you can trust such a thing given by not even an Alban-by-marriage, what you say will go no further without your leave."

There was another silence, broken only by the crackling of the fire—and by another small sound which at first Dewan could not place. Suspicious, he laid hand to sword-hilt and scanned the clearing's perimeter for intruders; then turned very slowly back to Gemmel. Because the old man was crying.

Dewan ar Korentin was a military man and a king's bodyguard, a good drinking companion—but not someone overly familiar with emotion. For that reason, and they both knew it, he had never been a particularly good husband to Lyseun his wife. All the love in their marriage had been one-sided and at times he was glad they had no children. But not now. Now he wished they had

had as many as his own parents, for then he might have had some inkling of what to do. Gemmel was crying, yes—but not as old folk will, or like a child. Instead he wept like a young soldier Dewan had once had in his command, years ago in Drakkesborg, who had committed some offence—the details were forgotten now, but it was nothing important: against a barrack-mate, probably, petty theft or a discovered lie—and instead of the small penalty his crime carried he had been wholly, unconditionally and unexpectedly forgiven for it. Dewan could only do now as he had done then; he sat quietly, neither offering useless sympathy nor, equally rude, ostentatiously pretending that nothing was amiss. He simply watched, and waited, and said and did nothing, but was there all the time—a burly, amiable-if-needed presence who took no offence and gave support merely by that.

At last—only a matter of a few minutes—Gemmel sniffed vigorously like a man suffering a drizzly winter cold and nothing more, then scrubbed his face with both hands and rammed their knuckles into his eye-sockets hard enough to bruise. "Thank you, *Eldheisart* ar Korentin," he said, not looking at Dewan's face.

"You know how to laugh as well," Dewan said, and left the rest of the proverb incomplete. *No one should laugh until they know how to cry.* It was Valhollan, something he remembered from talking to Aldric's lady: Tehal Kyrin. A lady who should never have been sent away, he thought. Had I known then what I know now of Rynert-King, I would never have agreed to it. More— I would have opposed it to the limit that my place allowed. Beyond. But that page is written. *And rewritten;* it was a notion which gave birth to a thin smile, but notion and smile were born for himself alone.

"Yes," said Gemmel, "I know how to laugh. But not honestly—only at the foolishness of this world, or at the simplicity of humankind—" and no matter what he had said, Dewan felt something curdle inside him at the way the wizard chose his phrasing, "or at my own cleverness. I thought I was so very clever, Dewan—so cunning, to use the king's wishes for my own ends. Remember those messages I locked into Aldric's head before he left Cerdor for the Empire? Support, and aid, and all those other things. Well, they weren't alone. I put something there for myself as well."

"Maybe you shouldn't be telling me this," Dewan said nervously.

"All of it, you said. So: all of it. You saw the Grand Warlord when you served with the Bodyguard in Drakkesborg, yes?"

"Yes. Many times—"

"And close? Near enough to see well?"

"*Yes!* But what has that to do with—"

"Patience. Listen: learn. He wears different uniforms for different ceremonies; of course he does, I've checked and I know he does. But one thing never changes; you must have noticed the one piece of regalia which never leaves him, the one kept closer even than an Alban keeps his *tsepan?*"

Dewan *had* noticed; though his facial muscles were under full control and did not so much as twitch, Gemmel saw the involuntary dilation of his pupils in the fireglow and nodded as if the Vreijek had agreed on oath in writing.

"En sh'Va t'Chaal!" The Drusalan words came out on an exhalation of gray vapor, seen as much as heard, and Gemmel nodded once again.

"As you say: the Jewel of Green-and-Gold Ice. A cumbersome name. Where does Etzel wear it?"

"At his throat—it clips as a centerpiece onto whatever collar of office he might require. But why ask? You've seen it yourself—haven't you . . . ?"

"No. Not for . . . a long time, and then not as a piece of jewellery. But I'll describe it for you and you can tell me if I'm right. And then I'll tell you what it really is."

"What it *really* . . . ?"

"Oh yes. Because it's not a gemstone. And never was. It's a million times more valuable than that, especially to me." Gemmel's hands sketched a quick outline on the air. "Oblong, about so by so—one by one-half palms—and two fingers thick. Transparent, but tinted slightly by the green at its core and the mesh of gold filaments surrounding that core. Three of its edges thick with gold studs, like sunken beads. And cold enough to take the skin off an unwary hand.''

"You *have* seen it, Gemmel—or something very like it. Yes, that's *t'Chaal* as I remember seeing it. But you forgot the frame."

"Frame?"

"Yes: gold filigree, crusted with emeralds. The jewel-not-jewel is mounted in it."

"Of course—because of the coldness, and because of the way that it's worn. I see."

"And what is it, if it's not a jewel? Tell me that."

"It's . . ." Gemmel hesitated, seeming reluctant to take the final step. "It's what my son was carrying; what I lost when he died. And what Aldric will try to steal for me."

"What!"

"That was the last message I locked into his mind, because I thought—the way people and events were explained at that time—that he would be in no danger. No real danger. Then everything went wrong. At Seghar. When the killing started. And even after that I thought he would have been all right, because he would return to Alba rather than risk himself on a venture gone sour. And he must have tried—God, how he must have tried!"

"Until Rynert handed him over."

"Because of those rotten, stupid, petty messages? Because he was determined to prove his support for the Emperor, to show how far he would go, how many loyal vassals were willing to sacrifice themselves for his cause. And because we knew the truth behind it, he tried to have us killed! Just as what I put into Aldric's mind is going to get him—my son—killed again . . ."

"Not if we can reach him first—that's why we came here, Gemmel. But you said that you would tell me, and you're trying not to do it; *what is t'Chaal?*"

"It's a primary control. A circuit." Just one glance was enough to show that Dewan understood no more than the thing's importance. "It's a key, Dewan, a gateway for me to control the lightning which will . . . It's my road home."

"Home?"

"You know—or at least you guess. Aldric does and

you've spoken to him. Because when you learned for
certain of my hold in the mountains, you said 'under
Thunderpeak.' A name I hadn't mentioned even once.
Meneth Taran: The Mother of Storms: Thunderpeak.
That place has had something of a reputation for years
now. And Aldric surely told you what he saw beneath
it . . . within it. Didn't he, Dewan?"

"He hinted. That the mountain itself was . . . hollow.
Filled with lights. And power, incalculable power—the
very air sang with it. But there was something else."
Dewan's voice faded into silence and he stared at the
fire as though hoping for inspiration or for strength before slowly raising his eyes to Gemmel's face. The old
man's expression had not altered by even the flicker of
a muscle; it remained as neutral as an unwritten page,
not prompting for a reply, just waiting. And
Dewan finished at last, in simple, undramatic words that
asked neither for proof nor for denial.

"Aldric said he . . . He thought it was a ship."

"He was right. My ship. A ship that once could sail
between the stars. Because I am now as I told the dragon,
Dewan. Alone. And very far from home."

8

Heartsease

Aldric stopped smiling directly the common-room door closed at his back. A smile was not the sort of expression he felt like wearing right now; raising his right hand and holding it in front of his nose, he could see—as if he needed visual confirmation—the tremor in the fingertips, The hell with that! He was trembling all over, because saying those few words to *Hautheisart* Voord had brought on as bad a fit of reaction-shakes as anything he had done these past few tense days. He leaned back against the door and closed his eyes; not in an attempt to eavesdrop, even though the conversation he had primed and left behind him would be well worth listening to, but merely to let the hammer of his heart drop to something like its normal rate. There would be no eavesdropping through that door anyway—it was oak plank three fingers thick and hadn't even shifted in its frame as his full weight was leaned upon it—but likewise there would be no hearing Aldric as he drew in huge gasps of breath. Stupid to provoke such a man as Voord—utterly crazy. But just as crazy to let him think that *everyone* was ignorant of his private dealings.

Straightening again, Aldric glanced at the long black and silver rank-robe draped across his arm. Bruda was right, of course. It was badly creased, too badly for a man of—or assuming—high rank and dignity to wear it on the public street. Not that Aldric cared overmuch about the dignity of the Imperial military, but if it likely gave the lie to what he was pretending, then best follow what had been suggested. He stopped off at the doorway

to the servants' hall and handed the garment over with
a few suitably terse words of instruction.

Then he made his way quickly and quietly to his own
room. No matter what he might have said to Voord, no
matter that it was still something like twelve days to the
full moon, he was not going outside with the wolfskin
coyac on his back. The jerkin made him feel uneasy. At
another time, in another place—and most certainly with
another coat—he would have laughed at the notion of a
garment having such an effect on a hardened cynic like
himself. Except that he was no longer quite so cynical
as he once had been, particularly where this black wolf-
pelt was concerned. He had seen enough. More than
enough, far too much.

Even thinking about it was more than Aldric could
tolerate in his current frame of mind; with a convulsive
wriggle of his shoulders he squirmed out of the *coyac* as
if it had suddenly become something filthy. And maybe
it had. He held it by the scruff of the collar between a
reluctant finger and thumb while he stripped away its
embroidered shoulder-tabs, then pushed open the door
of his room and threw it from the corridor haphazardly
onto a chair, not caring if it caught there or slithered to
the floor. The thing had served its purpose, as a provocation and a flaunting of supposedly-hidden knowledge; let
Voord make of it whatever he would and explain it
whatever way he could, Aldric had no intention of wearing it again.

Without the wolfskin's weight across his shoulders, it
was as if an equal weight had lifted from the Alban's
mind—a strange sensation, like the removal of a foul
smell or the healing of slight nausea, or the dismissal of
a . . . presence.

He glanced just once at the bundled darkness where
the *coyac* crouched, half on the chair where it had
landed and the rest dangling limply like something newly
dead. Then he deliberately turned his back on it and
went to his saddlebags to take out an object which was,
to his present way of thinking, far more wholesome: the
Echainon spellstone; or the Eye of the Dragon. Whatever its proper name, it was a blindfolded eye right now,

for the crystal was still wrapped in its covering of fine white buckskin. Aldric bounced it once or twice on the palm of his hand, wondering why Voord—who had certainly either searched his gear in person or had its contents reported to him in detail—hadn't made some comment. Or even stolen it outright.

Maybe. . . . Just maybe. . . . Loosening the lace which held the pouch of buckskin shut, he pulled it away and the stone lay in his hand. Completely clear, completely innocent, completely without any flaring luminescence pulsing from its heart. It was now as it had been with Kathur the Vixen, and by inference as it also must have been with *Hautheisart* Voord: nothing but a man's luck-piece of crystal or quartz, set in wrist-loops of polished steel and silver so that it could rest elegantly on the back of its owner's hand.

Or nestle in his palm. Though they were not to know that, and would not have realized its significance even if they had.

Aldric gazed down at it and felt his mouth stretch into a smile that wanted to do more—wanted to grin, to chuckle aloud, to open wide and shout with laughter. But he did nothing of the sort, knowing full well that such behaviour would have provoked all the questions which the stone had so far avoided. As he fitted it snugly to his left wrist and pulled up the cuff of a glove to cover it, Aldric saw—briefly, just enough to prove the dormant power was still there—a single twisting thread of azure fire at the crystal's core, minute and fragile as a human hair, yet bright enough for that one instant to splash his shadow harsh and black behind him on the wall and ceiling.

Then everything was dark again, a darkness held at bay only by the shuttered oil-lamp hanging from its chains above his bed. But now it was a comfortable darkness; more comfortable than it had been this long, long time. Too comfortable, perhaps.

The snow was no longer falling when he stepped outside, and the sky had cleared enough for a faint scattering of stars to show—but the air had become icy. Aldric was not overly concerned by that; he was warmly booted, jerkined and gloved and even the—freshly pressed!—Drasalan rank-robe was of the hooded, quilt-lined winter-weight issue. Dressed so, he could appreciate and almost enjoy the bite of the crisp, clean cold.

Even had it been damp and dismal, he would scarcely have noticed; and not at all after the first five minutes, for that short time was all that he required to walk briskly from the tavern to the square—and the festival—and the storytellers.

It wasn't the eaters of fire or the eaters of swords who interested him; not the jugglers, the acrobats, the singers and players of instruments. The storytellers alone drew him like a moth to a candle-flame. Aldric eased through the crowds towards them—and *eased* was right, for dressed as he was it involved no effort. The first and only pressure of his hand on an arm or shoulder drew an immediate backward glance and his rank-marked clothing did the rest.

He listened, fascinated, regretting that he could spend so little of his time with each, intriguing snippets imping-ing on his hearing as he moved to and fro. The gloves were off now—perforce, for like so many others he was munching on a sheet of unleavened bread which had been split and stuffed with sliced, spiced meat. Remov-ing his gloves had been a necessity, what with the hot juices running down his fingers, but the Echainon stone remained no more than a handsome clear jewel . . . with just the tiniest, half-seen strand of blue deep down inside it. Like a flaw, he thought to himself.

". . . a sage," said one storyteller, "with a slight flaw in his character."

Appropriate, said Aldric's mind. ". . . and then," said another further on, "the Bridge of Birds lifted above Dragon's Pillow." Two tellers and but a single tale. Al-dric smiled; he knew that story and liked it well. Each storyteller—all of them—had a raised seat, half-ringed with benches for their audience. Every bench was full and beyond them the fringe of casual listeners who had to concentrate if they wanted to hear every nuance of their chosen story, and who tended to hear distracting phrases from half-a-dozen others anyway. Only paying audiences were beyond the range of interruption. Obvi-

ously enough: the spacing was based on professional eti-
quette, consideration, courtesy among . . .

Then Aldric's head jerked around, his smile vanishing;
for what he had just heard had to be more than accident,
more than just a tale. There was an uncomfortable coincidence between certain memories and the words.

". . . the dragons confer honor where *they* will."

He could feel his hackles lifting. Maybe this *was* coincidence, but it was still too close to what had happened
to him, and to what Ymareth had said to him, for him
to ignore it safely. Once he had traced her voice above
the background babble, the speaker was easy enough to
aim for: a stocky, middle-aged, matronly woman whose
silvery hair was pulled straight back from her forehead
and held there by a bronze clip, and who wore an unmistakable suit and overmantle of turquoise velvet. But
more important, and more noticeable even than her own
appearance, was the embroidered design on each sleeve:
a dragon, crawling from cuff to shoulder.

Moving closer, Aldric waited until she had finished
her tale of dragons. *Dragons again.* Call it a dragon in
the Empire, call it a firedrake in Alba; call it anything
at all, my lady—just tell me why, why, *why* one came
looking for *me!*

There, she was done. Aldric thumb-flipped a coin towards a nearby drink merchant, lifted two of the wooden
tankards from his counter, had them filled with the pale,
frothy local brew of beer and then made straight for the
woman who spoke with such authority of dragons.

"Your throat must be dry, lady," he said in careful
mid-phase Drusalan, proffering one of the mugs of beer.

She hesitated, lifting her eyebrows at him and at his
rank-tabs and at his gift; then with the merest ghost of
a shrug she accepted the drink, said, "You're right, commander," in an accent he had never heard before and
took a healthy swallow. After a second or two she
smiled. "But until now, I hadn't realized just how very
right that was. Thank you." The woman bowed politely
and Aldric almost echoed it before remembering his supposed character and snapping a half-salute instead. "I'm
Aiyyan ker'Trahan; and you are . . . ?"

"Dirac. *Hanalth* Dirac." No lie, for the Drusalan form

of his name was common enough and besides, Aldric wasn't about to give the Alban equivalent—with or without a surname—to anyone whose business it was to remember names and events and the stories that went with them.

They made a strange and unlikely pair, subject maybe for a story in itself: a storyteller and a soldier standing drinking beer together in a city square which might have been deserted for all the notice either of them gave the crowds. Aldric did most of the talking, hedging his way like a cat on eggs between one non-specific and another—as non-specific as he could manage and still hope for a useful reply. About dragons, about honor and more warily yet, about the forbidden Art Magic.

Aiyyan watched him all the time he spoke, and the night-dilated stare from beneath her brows was far too shrewd for the Alban's peace of mind. Those green eyes reminded him of Gemmel, and like Gemmel the lore-woman seemed able to read beyond the outward meaning of his words and to study the unvoiced truths within.

"So . . ." she said at last. "I *see*." Aldric felt that she did indeed, far more so than he had wanted; and he was already regretting his own rashness. "Commander," Aiyyan's voice was much softer now, much more confidential, "these are hardly subjects for discussion in the public square. Especially since you chose to come here wearing *those*." She flicked a quick, disdainful gesture at the insignia which glinted in so many places on his dark clothing. "Undress uniform doesn't fade unnoticed into many backgrounds, does it?" Then she grinned, a flash of teeth that lit up her entire face. "But I make my living from—such subjects of discussion and I'd like to hear more. Lots more. Safer by far if we talk later, in private. Over another drink, maybe. Either there—" she nodded sideways to where a painted tavern sign caught the lamplight, "or . . ." The woman considered in silence, then came to some inward decision. "I have a small library in my home, commander, dealing with"—again that brilliant grin—"those subjects. Especially the winged, fire-breathing ones. You'd be a welcome guest on your next leave; I find your interest most refreshing."

"Lady, my thanks for the offered hospitality at such

brief acquaintance, but . . . ." He was trying, and failing, to keep a back-note of apprehension from his voice. "But this is urgent!"

"Indeed?" She glanced at him, looking hard and deep, and her eyes narrowed as once more she looked beyond the apparent to what truth might lie behind it. Not merely his words this time, but the whole man himself. And she saw. Now all the badges and the marks of lofty rank could not conceal the fact that this Cavalry *hanalth* was in all probability no older than her own second son—and most likely younger, at that. But there was an air about him, not merely an expression in the eyes and face but the whole set of his body, that spoke of . . . Not fright exactly; Aiyyan corrected her own thoughts even as they formed. More of unease. He looked—and now her storyteller's mind inserted coloration that was all too apt—like a scholar who had found logic in something unbelievable. As if he had just found a way to prove that twice two equals five. Or three! "We really must set aside the time for a lengthy talk, Commander Dirac," she began to say. And then stopped saying anything, since it was plain that he was no longer listening.

Instead the commander was staring off and away over her shoulder, not quite into the distance, for big though it was Tower Square could scarcely boast a view that would qualify as distant, but certainly *at* something, with an intensity that was disturbing. Aiyyan broke eye-contact just long enough to shoot a glance over her own shoulder, then turned back with the beginnings of a new respect and wariness in her own face. She had thought that this young man was interested in legends which his peers considered either peasants' fare or slightly distasteful— hence his nervous secrecy—but she had not for a moment thought that there might be something more. Now she wasn't so sure.

Already the young *hanalth* was backing away, his mind quite plainly on his own affairs once more. The focus of his gaze flicked back to her for just an instant, and in that instant he saluted her, grinning as she might have done herself on a would-be witty exit line. Except that his grin, his tight-lipped baring of white teeth, lacked the essential quality of humor. "Lady, about what I said: this is more urgent still!"

And then he was accelerating away.

"Ker'Trahan steading, commander," she yelled after him with all the power of a voice that had been trained for song and public speaking. "Beyond the Great and Lesser Mountains and through the valley . . ." Aiyyan ker'Trahan closed her mouth around the unfinished sentence, knowing that to continue was a waste of breath. She looked from side to side and felt the slightest tremor of embarrassment as she met the interested—if somewhat bewildered—stares of the new audience who had begun to take their seats around her. A scarcely-formed notion of following the *hanalth*—just to see what happened; all right, call it nosiness!—took no further shape as she sat down and composed herself with a toss of her silvery head and a sweet storyteller's smile. One after another they named favourite tales: classics, rarities, her own work.

Aiyyan pushed the strange young officer and his most un*hanalth*like interests right to the back of her mind. But not out of it entirely; he was far too interesting a potential story-character for that. Then she drew breath, nodded at her audience, and began:

"Lessa woke, cold . . ."

What Aldric had seen, and what Aiyyan the storymaker had seen, was a man on a horse. But no ordinary man, and no ordinary horse—that, of course, was the problem.

He was an exhausted man on a lathered horse and—though neither of them knew it—he had ridden through Egisburg's North Gate at a hard-gallop less than five minutes before. His long yellow overmantle—splattered now with the parti-colored mud of two provinces and an independent holding—bore embroidered crests at chest and cuffs and in the center of the back: stylised blue gerfalcons, with gold-feathered wings. They were the unquestioned markings of an Imperial despatch-rider, one who might at a moment's notice be commanded to ride at a pace that involved two hundred miles between one dawn and dusk along the roads of graded dirt that were forbidden to all but those who wore the Falcon badge.

This horseman had the look of one reaching the end of such a mission: a messenger with seventy leagues and a score of weary mounts in his wake across the Empire. Both his sweat-stained appearance and the jingling cross-belt hung with warning bells attracted curious glances—mostly from those who would have done better to mind their own business, but in at least one case from one who was determined to profit from the chance which had let him see this new arrival in the city.

The Falcon courier was a source of murmured speculation; and several of those who murmured then cast would-be knowing looks towards the black silhouette where the Red Tower reared into the night sky. There could be, they ventured, only one reason for a Falcon to arrive in Egisburg in such a state and at such an hour. And that reason was the Princess in the Tower: Marya Marevna an-Sherban.

Without exception, they were both wrong and right at once.

Such a suspicion had flickered across Aldric's mind when he first saw the rider walk his stiff-legged mount around the swarming mass of people in the square. But then he had seen him halt, reining in the horse with the gentleness of skill and consideration. And that was when the second possibility took shape. His own presence in the city—indeed the presence and the purpose of the whole small group—could be another and equally viable reason for a Falcon to ride tonight into this of all the many cities of the Empire. There was no chance of getting through the crowds fast enough to intercept the man, even had he been prepared to try. Instead Aldric made his impolite and over-hasty goodbyes to Aiyyan the talemaker—privately determining to hold her to her offer of hospitality sometime in the future—and began the process of returning to the inn where Bruda and Tagen and Voord awaited his return, and the striking of the Hour of the Cat. Damned if that rider didn't look as if he was waiting for someone! Or something.

A clock chimed somewhere at the perimeter of the square, and Aldric's head twisted on his neck to see it and to read what hour showed on its face. Then he relaxed a little; the half-mark of the Hour of the Dog, and seven o' clock as Albans reckoned time. But he didn't relax completely because that still left an hour for the courier to set everything wrong before a "deputation of officers" arrived at the Red Tower's gate. When a convenient space presented itself at his elbow, Aldric shouldered himself clear of the people in Tower Square and, throwing the assumed dignity of his assumed rank to the Nine Cold Winds of Hell, he began to run.

And because of that precipitate departure, he quite missed the courier's contented glance at the selfsame still-striking clock, and the leisurely way in which he shook his tired horse to a walk.

Another clock was striking for the same hour as Aldric approached the inn. Wondering vaguely and with no real interest why the Empire failed to regulate its public timepieces more correctly, he slackened his pace. Somewhat out of breath—a breath that fumed white in front of him as he gasped it in and out—and stickily warm despite the freezing night, he tugged with both hands at his rumpled clothing. Right now, Bruda's sarcasm he did *not* need—not when at the same time something fatally unpleasant might be brewing in the Red Tower.

Ahead of him a door opened; snapped hurriedly open to release a fan of yellow lamplight sliced by a fast-moving shadow, and then as hastily jerked shut. For some reason that was no reason at all, Aldric swivelled sideways and faded into the darkness between two buildings. It wasn't exactly suspicion, and it wasn't quite wariness. But it was enough to put him where he couldn't be seen, without a pause to think about it.

Softly set-down footsteps approached and passed; and Lord-Commander Voord's distinctive profile passed him by, back-lit by the tavern's courtyard lamp. No matter that he was already near-enough invisible, Aldric flattened himself against the wall at his back and wrapped anticipatory fingers round Widowmaker's hilt. Nothing came of it and Voord strode on, but to Aldric's senses, heightened by perception or deepened by suspicion as they were, he strode too quietly for so early in the evening. Later, perhaps, and it might have been no more than an innocent wish not to disturb, but now—to Aldric at least—each step seemed furtive, stealthy . . . And worth further investigation.

Closing the black-and-silver rank-robe right up to his throat and flipping its deep hood over his head, Aldric waited for a count of ten before venturing back onto the street. By then Voord was a good thirty yards away, and hard to see except when he was silhouetted by a paler background. Aldric took note of it and was careful not to make the same mistake himself.

Voord's progress made him smile thinly at the *hautheisart*'s arrogance; the man had taken not the slightest precaution against detection or pursuit, and stalked through the streets of Egisburg as if he owned them. And a jolt of sobering thought suggested that he just might. Aldric, by contrast, slipped quietly from shadow to shadow without being overly obvious about it. At least he was wearing his own moccasin boots rather than the heavy military issue; even the quality-controlled officer's pattern made tracking by ear a simple undertaking. Had Voord done the same, then in all likelihood he would have been lost before the end of the first narrow street.

Eventually the Vlechan halted. Then—and only then—he swept the street with a glare that had been signalled whole seconds in advance. Without even trying to glimpse his quarry's doings, Aldric was already hidden snugly and quite out of sight around a corner—holding his breath, and listening with the good ears that God had given him.

He heard first a soft, staccato tapping and then the slither of a heavy wooden door sliding in well-waxed channels. Aldric was sufficiently quick-witted to memorise the pattern of the tapping; and sufficiently cautious not to risk a rapid glance around the corner until the slithering sound was repeated and, more importantly, punctuated with the solid thump of a closing door.

There was nobody to see. As he had guessed, Voord was inside whatever door had just opened and shut. *But which one?* Aldric silently debated for a few seconds whether to move closer or not. Then had the choice made for him.

Don't!

Voord came out again, very fast, and Aldric wrenched himself back out of sight with equal speed. The Vlechan had been inside for only a matter of minutes—and what sort of time was that to spend on a secret which involved use of the Falcon couriers? Other than asking Voord himself, there seemed just one way to learn the answer.

No. There were two. Either he could go back, confront Voord and hope that Bruda could pry more than well-turned lies from his subordinate; or he could learn it himself, in the same way that Voord had done. Whether the *hautheisart*'s source would be amenable to repeating himself was something Aldric might well learn within the next few minutes. *You're an idiot,* he told himself. Silently he agreed. There was really nothing else to do.

By the time he reached the door Aldric had his course of action planned—more or less. It wasn't sorcery, and in a way he wished that it was; there would be fewer variables that way. It was just a virtuoso display of daring and impudent nerve. Holding in a deep breath to calm himself—*calm? now there was a joke!*—he reached out with one gloved and slightly meat-spiced hand to firmly rap the door.

"Keii'ach da?" The voice might have been muffled by thick timber, but its tone was plain enough: suspicion, pure and undiluted. Voord had come and Voord had gone, but no other visitors were expected.

Aldric paused, counted ten and then rapped again more loudly. More irritably. More in the fashion of a man kept waiting five seconds of which four were a compound insult. He sifted through his mind for what he intended to say—which was obvious enough to that same mind—and the form in which he meant to say it, which was proving somewhat more elusive. Whoever was on the far side of that as-yet-unopened door would have to be impressed by and convinced of his authenticity within two sentences and without credentials, or he would never be convinced at all. And then it would be killing time.

And still the high-mode diphthongs eluded him . . . Aldric had of necessity used Drusalan as a first language for almost a month now, except for those rare occasions when he could employ Jouvaine or—luxury!—Alban. And therein lay the problem. For during that almost-month, apart from one or two anger-fuelled lapses he had been careful to avoid just such phrasing and construction as he was now pulling from his memory; because spoken by inferior to superior, the High Speech was a blood insult. And in all the Empire, there was nothing more inferior than a rankless Alban.

"Is it thy intention that I stand here until the dawn?" he snarled at last, pitching his voice low and loading it with all the arrogance that he could summon. Not that High Drusalan in its augmented mode required much in the way of tone to make it arrogant. Aldric breathed deeply once more, with a studied, calming count between inhalation and speech, then spoke again. "I grow impatient with thee, man!" A good octave below its normal level, his voice sounded fierce, gritty—and strained, observed part of his mind. Aldric mentally commanded that part to keep quiet. "I command: open, or there will be blood spilt!" *You're committed now, so say it all!* "Voord commands! And I warn: I have finished speaking!"

He hadn't known quite what would follow that— whether the door would inch back or jerk open all at once. In the event it did neither, but slid smoothly to one side without any apparent haste. Playing this game by instinct, and ignorant of whatever rules might govern it, Aldric knew he didn't dare risk losing the initiative. Which was why, instead of stepping forward and inside directly there was room to do so, he stayed right where he was and let the lamplight come to him.

It worked: he heard a soft oath from inside, and as a cold smile skinned lips back from teeth he knew why. Because of his appearance. Pale from nervousness and shrouded in black from head to heel, there would be only the barest suggestion of humanity about the face revealed in the stark lantern-glow. Any other points of reflected light came from metal; the black, glinting hilt-guards of a sword, and rank-insignia so immediately impressive that even to consider it might not be genuine would feel like the beginning of a crime.

And there was always the possibility that this dark figure really was *Kagh' Ernvakh* Commander Voord, of evil reputation. That thought in itself was quite enough.

"You grow wise—at last," Aldric observed bleakly, and with those comforting words he stepped across the threshold, staring unblinking at the man who had opened the door until he bowed very low and slid it shut again. It was the courier; no longer wearing his distinctive robe, Aldric still recognised him by the heavy mustache swept halfway across his face. "Better," the Alban said, Voord-style. Haughtily. "But your manners need mending. Take care that I don't mend them for you—because my way leaves scars." That too was in keeping with what Aldric had guessed of Voord's reputation; but so much so that when the courier flinched from the threat, it made him feel uncomfortable. He was here to gather information, not to terrorise.

But there was a crossbow in the corner of the little room, a weapon covered less than adequately by a length of cloth. It was both spanned and loaded, its threat such that Aldric-"Voord" favoured it and then its owner with the lift of disapproving eyebrow before dismissing them both with a shrug. "What's your message?" he demanded, resorting thankfully to an easier level of speech but retaining his air of arrogance by the simple expedient of keeping his back turned.

"Message, sir?"

"Message, idiot!" Aldric let it snap out, knowing well enough how any officer of rank, let alone Voord, would treat a subordinate who did no more than echo his questions. "Are you deaf? Or merely impudent?" He half-turned and slapped one leather-gloved hand with loud significance—he had no time to be subtle—against the menacing jut of Widowmaker's hilt. "Because if impudence is your problem, be assured I have a cure for it!"

The courier drew in a noisy breath to deny the allegation; and lost his chance as the man he knew as Voord swung round on him at the first sound of inhalation. "Yes?" the officer said nastily; there was a handspan of blade clear of his sword's scabbard now. Then, nastier still and most unpleasantly perceptive: "Who else was here tonight?"

Usually the weatherbeaten color of old brick, the courier's face was shades paler already; and at this question it blanched as near to bone-white as such a complexion ever could. He was caught off-balance by every alternative he could choose: repeating the question to gain time would merely further aggravate this already all-too-angry *hanalth,* and a refusal to say anything would have the effect, whilst lying to a man who most likely knew it all, chapter and verse . . . In the end he told the unvarnished truth, for safety's sake—and that was worst of all. "Commander Voord," the messenger faltered wretchedly.

"Yes? What?" Aldric rasped the reply, deliberately misunderstanding.

"No, lord. N-not you. Another . . ."

"Another *what?*" Aldric let his tension vent itself in feigned impatience. "By the Father of Fires, I'll gut the man who gave a fool this mission!" His raging stopped abruptly as he decided it was "time to understand," and he repeated, "Another?" in a voice so soft it barely carried across the room. But the courier could guess what thoughts must now be tumbling through "Voord's" mind.

Aldric stared at him and allowed a released breath to hiss slowly out between clenched teeth. "There was someone else? Pretending to be me?"

The courier nodded.

He instantly regretted it, for the back of one black-gloved hand lashed him across the face. "And you believed him." Aldric let the words come out without inflection, but inside himself he felt sick; delivering that backhand slap might have been in keeping with the part he played right now, but it was not in keeping with the way he had grown up, or with the company that he had kept, or with the Code that still wrapped around his life more closely than he knew. How closely could one play a role like this before it became reality? Aldric was frightened of learning such an answer.

"You believed him," he repeated—not a statement, but an accusation of guilt. "And so you told him what should have been for my ears alone. And you let him go. But you kept *me* standing in the street!" Aldric let the feigned outrage drain from his voice, only to replace it with an equally feigned and equally realistic note of suspicion which edged each word like a razor. "Yet you didn't think to mention this previous visitor. Was that because you hoped I wouldn't know about him? Was that it?" He purred the last, soft and cajoling, letting it fade into silence. Then: "ANSWER ME! *F'KAAHR, SCH'DAGH-VEH!*"

Terrified by the intangible thing that was the reputation of the Imperial Secret Police, and more particularly by the less intangible and all-too-widely-known reputation of *Hautheisart* Voord, the courier fell to his knees and spilled everything he knew in a tremulous whimpering which was all mixed up with pleas and abject apologies. The very sound of it was enough to clench Aldric's stomach into a nauseous knot. He had killed men in the past, but he had never—until now—driven any man so far down the road of absolute fear. It said more than he had ever wanted or needed to learn about what Voord was really like, and about how skilfully Aldric had simulated him. For just one self-loathing, disgusted second the Alban was within a muscle's twitch of walking out. Then the preliminary babble of excuses came to an end and the true message began.

And Aldric, too, felt the icy touch of terror . . .

It was a plan of sweeping concept, of elaborate construction, of ruthless simplicity; and it reeked of Lord-Commander Voord.

As he filled in the details of the instructions which the courier relayed to him Aldric began to understand a great many things more clearly. Why so much time and money had been expanded to lay hands on him and bring him to Egisburg; why Voord had allowed himself to be overruled with so little protest from one who was—and it could scarcely be denied even now—of considerable standing and high rank. It explained, too, a reason behind the small annoyance which had troubled Aldric as he had left Kathur's house in Tuenafen as far behind him as he could—even though his own stupidity hadn't given him the time to leave it as far behind as he might have wished. The apparent theft of one of his paired *telekin*. Most people, he had discovered, knew at least a little about Albans: about their fanatical adher-

ence to an outmoded Code of Honor, their suicide
daggers . . . and about the spring-guns which were in
their modern fashion as typical an Alban weapon as the
taiken had been in the past.

Let such a weapon be found close by Princess Marevna's murdered body, and its mate found bolstered at the
saddle of the King of Alba's envoy, then no court of
justice anywhere—at least within the borders of the Drusalan Empire—would require or search for any other
evidence than that set out before them.

For this was first and last a plan involving murder.

Aldric considered and rejected the daintier term "assassination," because he refused to let it dignify what he
was hearing. There was no daintiness here. He wondered
when and why and how the plan had first been mooted,
and at whose suggestion, and realized that though the
message was for Voord alone he could trust nobody
now. He dared not fling what he had discovered in Bruda's face, for was Bruda not Voord's superior, and as
likely implicated as not?

But the basic idea was so *simple!* Trial was what his
mind continually returned to, for Aldric knew that in
other circumstances even he would more than half believe that King Rynert would have someone murdered
for political advantage. He knew, if certain suspicion was
knowledge, why the last emperor had died so suddenly:
and there were bound to be other informed sources than
himself. Dewan ar Korentin, for one. That the big bear
of a man who had become his friend should soon think
him capable of murdering women made Aldric's blood
thicken in his veins. And Dewan would believe, because
he knew the ruthless rules of expedience as well as any
and he had been present when Aldric swore on his Word
to do what was necessary to aid the king.

Marevna, alive and imprisoned in the Red Tower, set
pause to the continued strife within the Empire that
brought a wary peace to Alba; the peace which lasted
only for as long as the Imperial armies were turned inward. While the princess was held by one faction as
surely for the behaviour of the other, cooler heads than
those of the military might prevail, and could lead to
ultimate agreement that such leashed-in force might bet-

ter be expended in bringing the benefits of unity within one Empire to those not yet part of the greater whole. Annoyingly, aggressively independent Alba, for one. But Marevna dead and entombed with her ancestors at Kalitzim would be no bargaining counter for any side to use. Unless by the manner of her passing.

A simple appeal to simple emotion would be all that *Woydach* Etzel's faction needed; it was he who stood to gain the most, he most likely who was behind this plot—and certainly he who would know how to make best use of such a Hell-born opportunity. Aldric could hear the speeches in his head already: not the mannered rhetoric of Osmar's plays, but the fieriness of words intended to lash up a frenzy of grief and thus create a common cause. Revenge!

That was something which Aldric knew all about. A thirst for "justified" vengeance was a thing of frightening intensity among individuals, and none were better qualified to admit it than himself. He had felt it; had seen its blue-white burning in Ykraith the Dragonwand; had seen it burning just as hot in the blue eyes of Gueynor Evenou, now Overlord of Seghar. And such an emotion running unfettered through an already militaristic empire was not a thought he cared to dwell on overlong.

But another thought drifted, settled and took on solid form. *Seghar,* said the thought. *This has happened to you once before. To play the scapegoat, betrayed by a blade that was yours and could be no-one else's.* That was the time when Crisen Geruath murdered his own father and used Aldric's *tsepan* to do the deed. Almost forgotten voices linked Voord's name with Seghar, and with Crisen; the details were long lost, but the connection had been made. It was enough.

More than enough.

Then the farther door slid open and another man came in, saying as he entered, "Serej, has the Commander—" He and his voice stopped in the same instant. Aldric didn't know him, had never seen him before, and it was plain from his expression that this lack of recognition was returned. More words made it plainer yet: "Who in the Fires are you—and what are you doing here?

Aldric didn't have to be watching to know that the

courier—Serej?—had jerked himself backwards and was now staring from one to the other with shock-widened eyes. And he didn't need sharp ears to hear the soft obscenity born of sudden realization.

"He said that *he* was Voord, Etek."

"I've worked with Voord bef—" Again his words were cut off short—and Etek himself was within a finger's thickness of the same fate—as Aldric, without even the warning of an intaken breath, flicked hand to hilt and whipped Widowmaker's already-loosened blade clear of her scabbard and straight out into the first cut of *achran-kai* all in the one sweeping arc. Only a slight knowledge of Alban swordplay and the spasmodic quickness of the fear of death saved Etek; for while the first had given him an inkling of what to expect, only the second was fast enough to evade the terrible gray steel that blurred through space his throat had occupied a split-second before. Wisps of his beard drifted in the *taiken*'s wake, razored off without so much as a tug to show where hair and wicked edge had met.

His own army-issue shortsword came from its own sheath in the same instant as his sidestep, lifting frantically to block the downward second stroke of the inverted cross as it descended on a line running right between his eyes. At the last moment his block changed to a glissade deflection, and as metal shrieked and sparks flew from the point of contact Etek's eyes bulged with the discovery that a square impact from this intruder's blade would snap his own in half.

Serej the courier picked his moment, then lunged towards the loaded crossbow propped against the wall. All he had to do was reach it, point it and pull the trigger. Serej's hands were already reaching out when he half-heard a scuff of soft boots before that noise and all else was drowned in the sound of a shout.

"Hai!"

Aldric had caught the courier's move, and had broken contact with Etek's blade for long enough to spin right around before facing him again. It was movement so unexpected that Etek did nothing even though for just an instant he was offered the target of an unprotected back, and it was so swift that he had no time to use his chance before that chance was gone again. But Aldric's turn was still enough to let him cut, just one; it licked out at full force—savage, graceful and perfect.

Serej the courier continued on a lunge gone loose and uncontrolled, and it ended as he slapped down full-length against the floor. Momentum skidded him a little further forward, close enough for his outstretched right hand to reach the waiting crossbow . . . even though he no longer had a use for it. The impact of his fall had parted the last few tissue adhesions in his sheared neck—and as his body stopped, his head rolled free.

Aldric knew that the man was dead; had known it halfway through the arc of the cut, when he felt the crisp-to-yielding jolt along his arm as Isileth the Widow-maker made another. He had held no malice for the man and felt the anguish of his killing burn within him; but all of his attention was refocused now on Etek and he forced the hurting down, back from the distracting *now*. There would be more pain before he was finished here; and he would have to finish quickly, for this man had already survived two strokes more than he had been expected to. The clangor of steel was a sound which always drew unwelcome attention, and the sooner such a sound was curtailed the better.

Aldric seemed to hesitate an instant, shifting his feet and his balance; his grip on the *taiken* shifted fractionally. Then he feinted one—two—*three* . . . And the third was not a feint at all. He heard the strike go home and jerked himself to one side, away from the vivid spurt which burst out of Etek's chest like wine from a new-tapped cask. It was a jet as deeply, brilliantly, ominously crimson as . . . as a rose which Aldric had once known, and it was as thick as his thumb and as long as his arm before its arch turned downwards and broke into drop-lets. They spattered against the floor with a sound like rain, a color like rubies, and a smell like a slaughteryard.

Etek looked down at the spread of gaudy stain across his shirt and tunic, at the pumping of his own heart's blood and at the pale-faced young man who had drawn it from its secret places with his blade. He tried to say something—witty, angry, a curse, a denial of death or a protest at this theft of his life, something which might be remembered for a little while. It came out only as a blood-flecked exhalation and sounded like *"h'ahhh . . ."* Then his knees buckled and he fell down, and was dead.

Aldric held that last accusing stare long after Etek's eyes had glazed—trembling, telling himself that he had done only what had to be done, that these men had been enemies, that the responsibility for choosing death had been theirs and not his; that he didn't care at all. But he did.

The days were gone when he could have pushed a killing from his mind, dismissing it as no longer of importance once the act was done, and he was glad of it. The alternative to *feeling* was to have none, to have as little concern or conscience as the weapon itself. Widowmaker would eat *his* life as readily as any, with another hand about her hilt. That change had come with awareness of what he had always secretly known, that there was an obligation to the killing of another living thing beyond the swing of a blade or the squeeze of a trigger. It was remembrance. He stood very still with the new-copper stench of warm blood in his nostrils, looking at his dead; and feeling lost. *Not yet twenty-four, and how many corpses now?*

He knew the answer: the number, and in some instances—not many—the names as well. There were some who might recite such a bloody list with pride in the skill it showed; and there were some who might think that he had done the same in the past. When he remembered . . . But that was not a recollection Aldric made proudly. He was humbled by it, and ashamed of it—humble that he had lived while they had died, filled with shame that without his hand they might live yet. But there was *self-defence*, and there was *expedience*, and there was *necessity*. Three words which were all that any killer needed.

They left a taste like vinegar and ashes on his tongue.

A storyteller finished, smiled acknowledgement to the courteous bows of her audience as they left and sipped at a little more cold beer to soothe her throat. The story just concluded was one of her own and no effort to tell, linking as it did like a chain—or a mesh of mail, for it might lead off in several directions at once—with other of the tales she told. Tales whose characters were as well known to her as her own family and friends.

Aiyyan's smile broadened at that, for often enough those characters *were* her family and friends, their quirks observed and embellished with humor and with love. It was a fault of hers. No, not a fault, a privilege which those who wove tales from the joint webs of imagination and experience were well allowed to exercise.

She had met several such potentials in the past day or two: that scholarly man whose fiery enthusiasm suffused everything he turned his considerable mind towards; the woman with the string of riding-horses—Aiyyan had bought one and left herself with an option on two more—and the string of anecdotes. And that twitchy young *hanalth* with the dragon fixation . . .

Something, some *thing* made her look up towards a sky which was half dark and flecked with stars, half gray with another band of snow-laden cloud. And she saw . . . She would have seen nothing on a cloudy winter's night, had that night been other than what it was: festival. Ordinarily this great city was a dark place after sunset, freckled only sparsely with the lanterns hung outside the houses of the wealthy—or the loosely moralled, which was often one and the same. But now, tonight, on this holiday, Egisburg was lit as brightly as anywhere in the Drusalan Empire—even Drakkesborg or Kalitzim—and the glow of all that extravagance reflected dully from the surface of those lowering clouds. Not enough maybe to increase the light in the streets below, but enough that their no longer totally dark surface formed a pale backdrop to . . . things in the sky.

There were two such: one was the Red Tower, and its hard-edged outline sent an unsummoned shudder up from Aiyyan's imaginative soul. There was a brooding about that dark fortress, and an expectancy which was enough to make her glad that in the morning she and her new horse—or maybe horses—would be leaving this city and returning home before the winter closed on them completely. But the other thing was smaller than the Tower, and blacker than the Tower; it was a scrap of lightless nothingness, a rent in the clouds that was blacker than black and as lean as hunger.

And it sailed through the night sky at twice the Red Tower's height above the Red Tower's topmost turret!

Aiyyan stared until small glowing motes began to swim before her eyes, and then she stared some more. She watched until the—all her mind would shape was *what I daren't believe I'm seeing,* in case giving it a name would somehow make it disappear—the winged creature drifted out beyond the gray of the clouds and across the starlit heavens. Even then she could still follow it, for those cold star-fires blinked briefly out as the great dark shape sliced between them and the world.

Another of the sparks which danced in her vision expanded, putting forth a long bright tendril that as swiftly died again. Aiyyan released a breath that was more than half a sigh; had she not been watching—what she knew now that she *was* watching—she might have thought that quick straight scratch of fire across the sky to be the track of a falling star. Except that no starfall that she had ever seen before had swirled and plumed and choked in smoke as this had done.

"Ohh v'ekh!" said Aiyyan ker'Trahan, and put a deal of feeling into it. *"M'nei trach'han kelech-da?"* Oh yes, Commander Dirac. I see now. I *see . . .*"

She did indeed: something she had always wanted to see, since the first tale she had ever made about them. A dragon.

But having seen this one, she wasn't sure that she wanted to stay for more. Huge and powerful though *her* dragons were, there was still an underlying gentleness in them; and she had felt nothing of the sort in her brief glimpse here. Another long talk—with a little more forthrightness in it!—with *Hanalth* Dirac would prove enlightening, even educational, but Aiyyan had no desire now to wait in Egisburg to find out for herself the answers which he had hoped to learn from her. It was not fear— a daughter and mother of soldiers, Aiyyan wasn't particularly subject to that—but it was most certainly caution, for once she started thinking about him again in connection with what she had seen, the storymaker began to notice little oddities which at the time had gone unregarded. Most important was his speech; its accent had not been that of Drusul, nor Tergoves, nor Vlech. And if he was not of the Imperial races, then he was a provincial. And if he was a provincial, then there was no way in the world that he could possibly wear the *hanalth*'s bars and diamonds. Her own sons had been in the Empire's armies, the younger just released from his term of service, and she knew of the unofficial—but rigidly enforced—restrictions on promotion.

So why *was* he wearing those rank-tabs? Aiyyan didn't want to know. And because she had been speaking to him, and been seen speaking to him, she wanted to be away from Egisburg before whatever he was brewing boiled up in her face. The doings of the great, the not-so-great and the downright notorious had a way of hurting all around them, innocent bystanders most of all.

Aldric walked slowly and steadily along the street and along his own shadow, flung far in front of him by the leaping flames behind. Those flames cleaned away the final remnants of what he had done, but he did not look back. Instead he ignored the fire and pushed it from his mind; but he did not and would not push aside the two whose funeral pyre it was. The two whom he had killed. "Serej and Etek," he said softly—recalling the names, the faces, the men. Because forgetting would be to kill them twice.

What to do? Stay or run? He had thought about both sides of the problem, even though all along he knew that he, what he was and what he tried to be had only one choice that could rightly be made.

There would be no point in running anyway, because somewhere in this city—whether in Voord's or Tagen's or maybe even Bruda's hands—there was a *telek* which was the undoubted match of that weapon seen by all too many people bolstered at his saddle. An unusual accoutrement for a cavalry *hanalth*—though apparently not so unusual as to be forbidden by Lord General Goth—it would have been noticed, remarked upon . . . And would be remembered. With its mate still unaccounted-for, then whether or not he was there to take the blame at once Princess Marevna would die tonight—and even if

he fled, that would be explained in such a way as to
compound and confirm his already apparent guilt. It
could not save him, and it would not save her.

By the same token, there was nobody he could safely
tell: in this Imperial city everyone was a potential enemy,
a potential informer ready and willing to betray him for
no reason other than what he was, if that was discovered.
Hlensyarl and *h'labech,* foreigner and spy: the Drusalan
words were probably interchangeable, even more so
when the foreigner was wearing a uniform and a rank
to which he was most certainly not entitled.

It left the conclusion Aldric had reached at the very
beginning, when Serej the courier had first outlined this
dirty little plot: to rescue the Princess—it was still a cliché, but he no longer laughed at it—but to rescue her
on his own terms. Properly. At least he had a slight
advantage now; he was forewarned of treachery and
knew to expect it, while They—whoever *they* might be—
were unaware of his knowledge. He hoped.

"One day, Aldric," he told himself, "all this is going
to get you killed." It was like something Dewan ar Korentin might say; and there would be those who would
presume that his reason and his choice lay with what
else Dewan might say. Because of Dewan, and Gemmel,
and the king—yes, even the king—and all those others
who would mutter and look askance if he did his duty
so well that he had the death of an innocent woman on
his conscience. But that was not and never had been his
reason. It was simpler and more straightforward than
that, a reason which would have made him continue with
this rescue even if by running now, at once, as far and
as fast as Lyard's legs could carry him, he would avoid
all the consequences of his failure.

That reason was the self-respect which men called
Honor. Drusalan though Marya Marevna an-Sherban
might be, and sister of the lord of a state that one day
might be at war with his own, yet he was still bound to
help her to the best of his ability. *Honor-bound:* a term
used lightly now, but when it was meant sincerely it
bound as tight as chains of steel. He had the right to
fight for it, and the right to die for it either on another's

blade or on his own. The *tsepan* he now wore hung from his belt in the Drusalan military manner was a constant reminder of the oath which he had taken—an oath which he might put aside as he might put aside the black dirk, but one whose existence he could never forget while the white scars on his left hand's palm remained.

Aldric looked down at that hand, at the place where the scars were hidden by his glove—and its fingers clenched into a fist at what he saw on the wrist above the black leather cuff. There was a flame within the spellstone: tiny, spindle-shaped, and throbbing in time with his own pulse. Its appearance was familiar: the slitted intensity of a cat's eye.

Or the Eye of a Dragon.

Aldric's head tilted on his shoulders and he flung back the rank-robe's hood to stare straight up at the night sky; just as, elsewhere in the city, a storyteller was doing at this same moment. He saw what she saw; but in his case there was no momentary hesitation before acceptance, no beat of disbelief. He knew and recognised at once. *Ymareth.*

Not knowing the power of the dragon's eyes at night, but quite willing to believe that one way or another the great being was watching him, Aldric drew himself up straighter and offered the shadow in the sky the courtesy of an Alban crown salute. No matter that it was incompatible with the uniform robe he wore, no matter that such a token of respect was rightly due the king alone; Ymareth the dragon had done more for him than Rynert, and had shown him more kindness in its reptilian way than the king had ever done in his. The dragon hung against a sky half-snowclouds and half-stars, and vented a brief, bright lance of fire. It was a signal, a reminder and an encouragement needed now if ever that Aldric was not entirely alone in this city full of enemies.

And after all was done, once the princess had been freed—*oh, such confidence, Talvalin!*—and he had discharged his present obligation to the man whom he called "Liege" and "King" and "Lord"? What then?

Aldric didn't know.

*   *   *

"Did you see that? Gemmel, did you see it?"

"So you're talking again. Well, thank you for that much, anyway."

The soldier and the sorcerer stood together on a low ridge near the road which led down and across the river-plain to Egisburg's great gated walls. They had been set down something like two miles from the city—a negligible distance in fine weather, or even now had it been daylight and they able to use the roads. But it was not, and they had not, and the cautious slog in darkness through snowfields where drifts had sometimes risen to six and eight feet in height like frozen white ocean waves had taken the best part of an hour. It had been accomplished in total silence on Dewan's part, except for grunts of effort and the occasional heartfelt oath. His mouth had closed at Gemmel's final revelation and he had not spoken to the old man since; perhaps no longer sure that "man" was a proper term of reference.

"I . . . All right, yes I am. I must. I've known you long enough before, before—"

"Before I gave you honest answers to your questions, and you found that you didn't like the sound of truth after all?"

"I—I found it hard to swallow."

"Like the man who ate the cart-horse," Gemmel said, and grinned. It was the old grin and the old Gemmel, and Dewan felt a deal more easy in his mind to see it. "You mean that flare in the sky? A falling star."

"That was no star, falling or otherwise!"

"Good. Then we can agree on something. Would you also agree that we should abandon this excessive caution just for once, and use the road?"

Dewan looked along the road for as far as he could see in both directions; which wasn't far at night, but far enough to make sure that there was no one else in the area. It wasn't so much using the road so close to the city that concerned him, but the chance of being seen emerging from concealment by someone who might take an interest in the question *why?* "All right," he said. "All clear. So come on." He floundered through another drift, noting with absent irritation that Gemmel waited until he had done so before following him through the already-broken ground. "I must remember, Gemmel, wizard, *friend,* to let you take your turn in front some time," he growled, slapping snow off his furs and clothing.

"As you wish," said Gemmel, reaching the road— which so close to Egisburg was not merely paved, but also kept reasonably free of all but the heavier falls of snow. "Then I'll lead from here, shall I?" He walked off down the road.

Dewan watched him for a few seconds and in those seconds, with snow still in his hands, the Vreijek fought a noble struggle with his own sense of dignity, the inadvisability of what he was considering—and the potential satisfaction that a well-aimed, tightly-squeezed and accurately hurled snowball would bring.

Then he dropped the still-loose snow and dusted off his hands, and set off after Gemmel without another word.

Aldric returned to the inn without making any detours; he avoided the square and its distractions and therefore didn't see one storyteller in particular gathering her gear together in readiness for a rapid departure from a city which had lost all its attraction for her. Most of all, Aldric wanted to get back and behind a locked door before he met someone who might pass comment on his appearance. He hadn't checked, but there was most likely drying blood about him somewhere; he had enough intimate experience of killing swordplay to know that its traces were hard to avoid, even when one was the winner.

The entrance hall of the inn was empty, and he was glad of it for though he might be calm and in control right now, he doubted that he could remain that way if he came face to face with Lord-Commander Voord. Later, perhaps, but not just at present. He closed the outer door noisily behind him, deliberately signalling his return to any interested ears and knowing that any such would be listening for *his* return alone, since from what he had seen of Voord's departure that worthy had not— supposedly—left the building. He would be back by now, of course. Aldric cast an eye towards the inn's big case-clock in its alcove by the stairs and hesitated, surprised. Barely half of an Alban hour had passed since he had flinched into the shadows and out of Voord's sight as the man stalked out into the night. A half-hour—or a quarter, Imperial! Then walking leisurely as seemed his custom, it was likely that Voord himself was not long through this very door—much more quietly, of course. That was a piece of luck indeed, and probably just as well.

Unintercepted by whoever might have remained in the withdrawing-room to finish up that flagon of chilled wine, Aldric reached the door of his own upstairs room without incident and put out one hand to open it. Then he paused, looking at the hand with his head quirked quizzically to one side. As he had done earlier, he raised it level with his nose and stared. It was steady, as steady as it had ever been, and not even the vibration of his pulse was enough to shake the black leather-skinned fingers. *Am I growing used to murder, then?* he thought somberly. It was not a possibility which held much appeal. *Or is it something else entirely?*

Now that was likely indeed, for the thought of doing something worth-while at last—the rescue of a prisoner rather than the assassination of someone never met before, like those two in Seghar, would be enough to calm anyone; or at least to fill them with an excitement that was a deal more wholesome. Aldric threw open the bedroom door, noting absently that it was darker than before because someone—a servant perhaps, or simple lack of oil—had reduced the lamp to a mere glow of flame.

Once inside he turned, pushed the door shut again and ran its heavy deadbolt into place. There: all secure! And then he stiffened because something, somewhere was not quite *right!* Without moving, he analysed the brief glimpse of the room which he had caught as he crossed the threshold: the furniture was unmoved, the shuttered windows as he had left them, his gear untouched. Other than the reduced lamp, nothing had changed. Until, moving only eyes that were rapidly adjusting to the gloom, he saw it and in that instant every alarm inside his head went screaming off at full pitch.

Lying down the geometrical center of the bed, dividing its mattress in two precise halves, was a sheathed sword. Jouvaine pattern, said some dry index of his mind through the warning jangle which filled it. *Estoc* thrusting-sword. But it was not a weapon he remembered seeing carried by any of his companions in this rescue party—even though it was familiar, somehow. More: there was a presence in the room, a living person somewhere, hidden, waiting. All the muscles and the sinews of Aldric's body tensed and his right hand flexed for the grip of Widowmaker's hilt.

But before his fingers closed on it, the sword was plucked away from his hip by knowing hands—knowing, because while one gripped the *taiken*'s scabbard with the lift-and-twist which unhooked it from the weapon belt at Aldric's waist, the other unclipped one end of the cross-strap which passed over his shoulder. It passed over his shoulder now like a snake, slithering with the sound of a viper on parchment as the whole weapon was wrenched clear of his hand with frantic speed.

A voice spoke in his ear, a voice from so close behind him that he could feel the warm breath carrying every word. How did that happen? he raged inwardly. Nobody gets that close if they mean mischief! And then: but what if they don't?

"Stand still," the voice said. "Just answer me this: What is a woman that you forsake her, to go with the old gray Widowmaker? This Widowmaker!" The *taiken*'s gray star-steel blade clanked once inside its scabbard as the chape grounded on the floor, and Aldric's eyes went wide as he stared for a long moment at nothing at all, swallowing once or twice, trying to clear his gullet of the hot throbbing constriction that was surely his own heart, pounding halfway between his mouth and its proper place. He did not hear the longsword clash against the floor; all he heard was that voice.

And all he said in answer to its question was, "Kyrin?" He turned then, expecting to be wrong, expecting to be cheated yet again by his own imaginings; but he was right this time and he was not cheated now, because it—she—was Tehal Kyrin after all.

All the tension drained from face and body, but was

replaced by a shuttered, enigmatic, unreadable expression very far from that which the Valhollan had been expecting. "Lady," he said, giving her the ghost of a bow, "one moment." Then he walked quietly across the room and adjusted the lamp until it flooded them both with light. "Yes. Lady, your . . . your eyes are as blue as I remember them; your hair is as fair." He did not move to touch her. "And you have troubled my dreams both waking and asleep this six months and more, Tehal Kyrin, Harek's youngest daughter. But lady, why talk to *me* of forsaking and of Widowmaker?"

He held out his right hand for the weapon and Kyrin took the three steps forwards that was just enough for her to lay it gently, respectfully, on his outstretched palm. The fingers closed, reaffirming possession, gripping tightly, and rotated Isileth Widowmaker so that Aldric was staring at her past the longsword's looped, forked guards. "This has been true to me, lady; I trust her and she returns that trust. It—*she* has not yet left me for another. I did not, will not forsake. I did not and w-would not forsake you. That choice was yours and you made it. You alone."

For just a hurt heart's beat there was a look in Kyrin's eyes which Aldric had seen before; he recognised it, for he had caused it now just as he had caused it then, so many painful months ago: a look as if he had reached out and struck her across the face. After a moment she drew breath, and with it seemed to draw on some reserve of inner strength, enough at least to meet him stare for stare past the black steel of Widowmaker's hilt.

"Aldric-*an*," she said, pronouncing it as salutation and as valediction, using the honorific rather than the affectionate form and with her Valhollan accent emphasising its vowel-shift all too plainly. "Aldric-*an*, you've lived for too long with this cold mistress. I travelled far to find you, to be with you again. Foolish, with an uncertain reception waiting at the end of all. Or maybe not so foolish after all. Now that I know how it is between us, I can leave again—and this time be at peace within myself. Did you flatter yourself that yours were the only troubled dreams, the only sleepless nights? There were times when I lay awake in the darkness, alone, when I wondered if I had done right or wrong. Not wrong to go with Seorth; there was no wondering about that. Not after I learned that he and Elnya had been married within a month of my . . . My supposed loss, when my uncle's ship foundered off the Alban coast. Have you ever found yourself an excess number, Aldric-*an?* Discovered that you were one too many under your own roof?"

"But you said . . . !" Aldric burst out, stopped himself, considered. Then, accusingly: "You showed me a letter."

"Which you couldn't read. You only guessed at what it meant and because of . . . I'm sorry. There was a deal of deception with you unknowing in the middle. I said things I didn't mean, things that weren't true, because— because I was afraid. Afraid of them, afraid of all the power they had and afraid for you. I told them and I told you what they wanted, because I knew that even you couldn't turn *no* into *yes,* and you'd have come to harm if you tried. Because you would have tried, Aldric, *Kailin-eir* Aldric *ilauem-arluth* Talvalin. I know you, knew you well enough for that. As I thought I still knew you." Kyrin forced herself to stay wide-eyed, staring and arrogant, because she knew that just one blink would be enough to let the waiting tears go free.

"Kyrin." She looked at him and the *taiken* was no longer between them; it had been lowered and was hanging slackly in his hand—as near to being flung aside, perhaps, as it would ever be. "They, Kyrin? Who are *they?*" He asked it, but was already sickly certain that he knew the answer.

"Dewan," she replied without hesitation, "Dewan and the king." Then she saw the muscle start to tic along the renewed scar beneath his eye and caught a stifled gasp between her teeth and knuckles. "But they promised that they would explain—they would tell you everything, their reasons, their need . . . After I was gone. Everything! They *promised* me."

"Words—that's what promises are. Sometimes, made with honor, they're worth the having. But mostly they're just breath with a little sound in them. So what did you say that *they* wanted to hear so much? What did you tell us all?"

"That there was no love between us. Nor ever had been. Dewan asked me and he wanted to hear *no,* so I said *no.* But . . ."

"But?"

"But I should have had the courage to tell him the truth. To say *yes.*"

Aldric's hand came out slowly towards her face and she didn't move a muscle, braced in case he . . . The leatherclad fingers touched gently along the line of her cheekbone in the old caress, and stroked at a stray tear which had escaped all of her efforts.

"Truth, lady? *Yes?*"

"Truth. Then. Now. Always." Then she saw the change in his face, and most especially in his eyes, and began to be afraid again—not of him, now, but for him as she had been before. "Aldric, you're *cseirin*-born. High-clan. They would never allow . . . You can't fight tradition with a sword!"

Softly, thoughtfully, almost to himself: "You said that once before."

"But it still holds true!"

"Not now. Not for me. Not after what I've had to . . . Duty, Kyrin. Obligation—it's a two-edged sword. Our proverb cuts both ways. It's the sword to fight tradition with, because after what I've done, what I'll yet do—though before the Light of Heaven, it's more for myself now!—for Rynert the King, he owes me. He owes me honesty at least! No deception—and no broken promises. And afterwards . . . afterwards we'll see about tradition and the sword, my lady. This sword. This old gray Widowmaker."

He laid the longsword down, delicately, respectfully, on the bed beside the *estoc* which was Kyrin's own, which he had seen her wear a score of times; which he had recognised and yet not known.

"Then it was you," he said, wondering now that he could have been so dull as not to realize.

"Where?"

"On the road to Egisburg. Following. I thought I saw someone once or twice; and I thought I felt a presence, a watcher, many times. How?"

"Dewan ar Korentin," she said and confused him

more than ever. "He and a Drusalan woman he told me to find."

"Kathur the Vixen!"

"Kathur the bitch-fox," Kyrin corrected, sweetly vicious. "Yes. She told me enough to get here. Because when I came to Alba, looking for you, you were gone—some mission for the king. But Dewan sought me out, met me secretly and used words like *decency* and *betrayal* about something which the king had done. He didn't approve; and he had already told Gemmel. The sorcerer. Your foster-father, Aldric? Is that true?" Aldric nodded silently and waved her to continue. "But he told me this: 'Look for him; find him if you're able, help him if you can—and stay with him if he and you both want each other still. With my blessing for all it's worth. And tell him that I'm truly sorry.' "

"Dewan said *that*?"

"He told me to tell you that the old bear is getting far too old; and blind and deaf and stupid, because he should have been half wise enough to ignore the *no* when what he really heard was *yes*."

"Kyrin-*ain*, I say yes as well. And I always will." When he put his arms—those killer's arms—around her and held her close, it was like a dream. There was the scent of her hair, the cool smoothness of her skin, the warmth of her lips and the simple nearness of her being there—but unlike so many other dreams there was not the bitterness of waking. "Lady," he whispered—*O my lady, O my love*—"I missed you far more than I ever knew till now. I prayed you would come back, somehow, some day. And death strike down the first man who comes between us again . . ." He kissed her again, gently and then fiercely, hungrily—and she was as gentle, fierce and hungry and they were both trembling in each other's arms, for it had been too long, too long, six months that had been a lifetime apart.

And a fist hammered on the door, making them both jump and shattering the moment. "Get yourself armored up and neat, dear *hanalth*, sir," came Voord's voice, edged with a sneer scarcely blunted by the thick timbers through which it passed. "We leave in ten minutes for the Tower!"

Silence. Then: "Who was that?" It was Kyrin's question, but when she glanced at Aldric's face she knew that she needed neither a name nor indeed an answer. Because for just an instant she had caught a glittering of pure hate in his eyes such as she had seldom seen before.

"Death strike the first man who comes between us," he repeated. "If Hell or Heaven hears my prayers and curses, I hope that one is answered." Then he took a step away from Kyrin and shrugged out of the military rank-robe, flinging it across the bed in a businesslike, no-nonsense manner which could never be confused with stripping for more pleasant purposes. "Did you understand him?"

"I don't speak Drusalan."

"Damn . . . What he said was *hurry up*. None too politely, either, burn his snake's skin black. Anyway—" he jerked with his chin at the racked armor near the wall as he tugged off his own, too-Alban outer clothing, "Could you, please?"

Kyrin hesitated just a second, still confused, then began scooping metal and leather officer's-pattern harness from the frame beside the window where she had come in. There was no sign even now that the shutters had been disturbed; but then Tehal Kyrin's talent for subtle burglary had never really left her. When coupled with a lithe, slim build and a natural gymnastic ability, hunger made an excellent trainer of thieves.

"What are you doing tonight that's suddenly so important?" she wanted to know, kneeling beside him to tighten the buckles of armored leggings with long fingers which had a distracting tendency to wander. Those fingers told her that despite his outward air of calm, Aldric was thrumming inside like a full-drawn bow. Part of it had to do with her, but the rest . . . It wasn't fear, not even the flash of anger which she had caught from the corner of her eye. Just simple, plain excitement!

"I didn't believe it when I heard at first; so you won't either, most likely. But it seems that the princess . . ." Between grunts and oaths and struggles with intractable red-enamelled splint-armor, he managed to get out an edited version of the story. "But that apart, they can't know what I intend."

His voice was muffled by the scarlet arming-tunic he pulled over his head in mid-sentence, a heavy thing of quilted cloth and leather with thick padding at the shoulders where the hauberk's weight would lie, and as his face emerged from its neck-opening—tangled with laces and nearly the tunic's own color with exertion—there was an expression on it which told Kyrin that he had had an idea. No—an *idea,* dammit!

"Just for now, let's forget most of what they don't know and concentrate on one aspect—*push*—which even I hadn't thought of until a few moments ago. God, that's more comfortable!" He held out both arms so that she could buckle on the laminated defences running from knuckles to elbows and wiggled his fingers amiably at her to prove to them both that his hands could still move freely. "Because since you're here,"—Kyrin looked up and arched a disdainful eyebrow—"this is what I want you to do."

9

Patterns of Force

It was snowing again as they left the inn; dense white flakes from a dense gray sky falling vertically, steadily, heavily past that dark tower brooding over the city. Hooded and cloaked, gloved and booted, muffled as tightly against the weather as any of the others, Aldric still stopped short and unwrapped enough of his helmeted head to see the fortress better. Oh, he had seen it before in clearer air and better light, but never while walking towards its gate with the intention of going inside the belly of the beast. That knowledge put rather a different interpretation on what he saw.

It was huge, and sinister as a hungry animal. A great dark block of stone set down square in the middle of the city, eyed with lamps and fanged with the iron spikes that fringed its drop-gates, it was an evil building both by appearance and by reputation. As he drew closer, Aldric saw nothing that might alter such a judgment.

They were four armored men flanked and followed by eight more: an honor guard found by the squad of cavalry who had ridden with them. Black and scarlet, silver and gold, the soft swaddling of fabrics and the bright, hard glint of pigmented metal all stark against the fallen, falling snow. Few were on the streets to remark on their appearance, for the festival was running down, its momentum gone on this last night of holiday; it was somehow appropriate that this foul weather should have come to force the revellers indoors—there to talk, to reminisce, to drink and to become drunk against the sober thought of winter closing in.

Aldric was uneasy, made guarded and wary by what

he knew and what remained undiscovered; his nerves were drawn to a fine pitch, tingling almost to the snapping point, and he was sensitive as never before to other sounds, reactions, feelings; emotion hidden well or ill. He could sense something about them all, and not merely because his mind had told him such sensations should be there. Bruda, Tagen, Voord. All of them. And they could probably feel just the same surrounding him. So long as they dismissed it as mere nervousness and nothing more! For under his rank-robe, pushed through his weapon-belt and out of sight but within quick reach of his right hand, was a *telek*. His own *telek* from his saddle holster, its drive-spring and action greased and checked, its rotary cylinder freshly loaded with eight lead-weighted steel darts. He carried it now in the certain knowledge that he would surely need the advantage given by this missile weapon.

Because he was equally aware that someone else's cloak concealed the other one.

Hoofs beat for just a moment behind them, dull and muted in the snowfall silence, striking in the measured cadence of a slow walk. Not one horse: several. Then as suddenly the sound was gone. No one turned, for no one was so very interested. But Aldric, expecting to hear just such a sound, smiled quickly to himself within the shadows of the rank-flashed Imperial helmet and then composed his face again.

Bruda had not merely made encouraging noises about the power of his forged pass authorities: they worked. Presented at the Red Tower's perimeter wall, they drew a clashing full salute from the sentries on guard within the shelter of the great gate-arch. It was acknowledged in the approved manner—Aldric half a watchful beat behind the others, to see what was done—with right arm snapped up to chest level, forearm horizontal and crooked in, palm downwards. And nothing more than that. He was—they all *were*—superior.

The soldiers both at the gate and those met with increasing frequency as they crossed the Red Tower's grounds—pairs of men, Aldric observed, and always one of them with a crossbow slung at his back—gave them the respect of further salutes but showed no other interest. Visiting officers, staff, flag or line officers; they were all a common enough sight around the Tower, brought sometimes by curiosity while they were in the area, and sometimes on more businesslike errands. Whatever the reason, their presence was not worth noticing other than as something more needing a salute.

At last they reached the Red Tower's gate, yawning to receive them, jagged above and below with the drop- and rising-shutters which gave it that look of unappeased hunger. Aldric stepped into the shelter of its lowering outerworks and threw back his hood, stamped a time or two to rid himself of loose snow and looked about him with a deliberate curiosity. He had decided that trying to hide such interest would appear more false than indulging it to the full, so he indulged.

For all that this place was known as a comfortable residence where noble guests could be invited to stay without fear of their leaving without permission, the first sight of the maw of its gate said *prison* in black-letter uncials too big for any mistakes. The famous red glaze did not continue beyond the outer cladding, except for the big six-sided tiles which paved the floor, and that gave Aldric, already far from comfortable with his private image of this building as a ravenous devourer, the unpleasant notion that he was standing on its tongue. The walls were built of gray stone, cut and dressed in massive blocks a score of tons apiece. Gray and huge. It was not the cold, but an errant uncalled-for memory which raised gooseflesh all over Aldric's body. The memory was of a tomb which he had entered: an ancient tomb, made of such monstrous stones. The tomb of one who had been dead a long, long time. This place had the same feel to it—of things long dead and better left to sleep out the rest of eternity undisturbed. Breath drifted from his mouth and nose, and he realized that he had been holding it this few seconds past. For no reason other than his own imaginings. Or, maybe not.

He could hear Bruda's voice in the background, but saying little of interest—only the conventional courtesies of rank to absent rank by way of a very junior noncom. "I convey by you respectful greeting to the noble commander, and desire that he permit us . . ." And so on. It certainly wasn't enough to account for the low-intensity warnings sounding intermittently at the back of Aldric's mind. But neither would they stop.

There was heat in his left hand and he knew that if he chanced to roll back the cuff of his glove, this whole place would be flooded by the blue-white glare of the Echainon stone. It was fully active now—through no desire on his part—with waves of heat that rose and fell with his pulsebeat and a sensation of contained force that he was certain the others could feel as well. Yet there was no sign of any such reaction. Either they couldn't feel it—or they were hiding the fact that they could. Either way, what was going on?

The *eldheisart* presently commanding the Red Tower's garrison was scarcely an imposing figure when at last he appeared, for all the neatness of his indoor-duty tunic. He looked more like a uniformed innkeeper than a soldier—fleshy around the waist and jowls, a man who enjoyed good food and drink—and Aldric wondered how much that might be due to the very special guest housed here.

Certainly there had been nothing in the least soft about the other troopers and officers whom he had seen; for all the relaxed and casual way in which they carried out their guard duties, they had struck him as a capable and dangerous group of men. More dangerous, indeed, *because* they were on duty here, rather than in spite of it. "A reward for good conduct" was how Bruda had described a posting to this garrison—which suggested that all the hard-eyed men inside and outside Egisburg's Red Tower were here because they were better than their comrades. Better at the soldier's trade of killing; for their look was not that of men whose superlatives lay in the gentler arts.

Then Aldric overheard something which made his heart start to race, but which at the same time had him forcing a sardonic smile off his face before it became too obvious. He had been standing a little off to one side while Bruda and the garrison commander made polite small talk over little glasses of some locally distilled spirit. It was as colorless as water, cold, heavy as oil and reeking of juniper, and most unusually where any alcohol was concerned, Aldric had found it vile. Mixed with something—anything!—yes, perhaps, but not neat. Unfortunately the others were swallowing both their small measures and the refills at a most affable rate and with every indication of enjoyment. That obvious disparity was making him look different and had most likely prompted the plump *eldheisart*'s remark; that, or the fact that by the look of him these hospitality-cups were far from being his first drink of the night. No matter.

What did matter was that Aldric heard him sniff through a red nose and then say quite plainly, "He seems a little, well, young for a *hanalth*. Don't you think, Commander?"

That had made him nervous, but it was Voord's equally audible reply which almost made him laugh out loud, for all the sincerity of its insulting tone. "That little bastard—your pardon, sir—doesn't wear the thunderbolts right now, but he's with *Kagh' Ernvakh* all the same. And he's here about Princess Marevna." It was a spur-of-the-moment improvisation which was almost worthy of applause, because when it was recalled later in the light of events that Voord still thought were yet to come, the few words of that remark and the poorly hidden detestation in it would point yet another finger at the "murderer" of the princess.

Right now, however, it served the more immediate purpose of diverting the *eldheisart* from any continued interest in a guest who might have just turned into a venomous snake, if the portly officer's reaction was anything to go by. And so far as Aldric was concerned, that was entirely to his liking.

The stairways inside the Red Tower were all wrong, for a fortress. They were far wider than they should have been and they didn't spiral to inconvenience an attacker's shield-arm. Surely even in the Drusalan Empire the basic practicalities of defensive architecture hadn't been overlooked? Of course, all those years ago the purpose of the building had been changed; it had ceased to be a fortress and had become a residence for the Overlords of a notably wealthy city-state. Lords who would wish to flaunt that wealth with the construction and the decoration of broad, high halls, lofty windows and—*yes, all right,* Aldric conceded to himself—stairways that were both straight and five times wider than was proper.

At least there was no need to climb right to the top of the Tower, as he had first feared that they might. But it was still five levels up, an ascent made in armor maybe twice as heavy as his own, and Aldric was only glad to see he wasn't the only person out of breath when at last they stopped. "How—how many levels—are there?" he gasped.

The trooper sent along to guide them—in tunic rather than armor, *he* was in full possession of his breath—gestured upwards. "Fourteen more and then the rooftop, sir," he replied. Politely, for he had been primed or maybe simply warned about the young man with the *hanalth* insignia. "If you're interested, then in daylight and better weather . . ."

"And no armor." The words all came out in a rush as Aldric waved a hand, dismissing the offer. "No, soldier. I'll forego"—and his next hesitance wasn't so much a pause for breath as a meaningful stare at Voord—"the chance for sightseeing. Now, at least."

Any hotter and the spellstone would be raising blisters on his skin! Oh for a moment to himself, a moment's privacy to tug away the glove and look, only to see even if not to understand what the crystal talisman was doing. Apart from hurting him. There was more power contained now in the Echainon stone than at any other time he could remember, it thrummed with it, vibrating down the innermost core of his arm's three bones so that he felt as though the limb itself trembled uncontrollably. Yet a surreptitious look revealed nothing of the sort—nothing whatsoever.

Then the guide trooper paused and tilted his head back as if listening to something. After a moment he shrugged, dismissing it as unheard or at least as unimportant. Nobody else noticed. Except Aldric, for just at that instant he had been leaning against the wall, his hand flat, and he alone knew that what had been heard was less a sound than a vibration in the stone, set aside by the trooper as perhaps snow-slip from a ledge or the

slamming of a distant door. It would take more than
snow, or a bigger door than any he had so far seen, to
create such resonance in the ponderous blocks of which
the Red Tower was built. But something settling on the
roof, something with sufficient mass to well-nigh drown
the fore-deck turrets of a Fleet battleram? That was another matter.

"Fourteen levels to the roof-top, soldier," said Voord
in a voice that was brisk and to Aldric all too businesslike, "but surely Princess Marevna isn't being hel—has
her quarters somewhere more convenient? Where, exactly?" It was a genuine enough question, just the sort
of thing that a man fed up with climbing stairs would
ask, and the trooper read nothing more from it than
that. He pointed along the corridor.

"Fifth on the left, sirs. Will I make your introduc-
tions?"

Voord's smile inside his helmet was more pleasant
than the thought which had prompted it. "No need. I
know the lady, so we'll surprise her."

You should be on the stage, thought Aldric sourly. *Or
on the scaffold.* There was a few minutes of scuffling as
they tugged and neatened their clothing and armor—
brushing away real or imagined dirt, water-beads and
snow-melt smudges, straightening rank-robes, setting
helmets just so. Bruda and Tagen each slid their broad
nasal-bars up through the helmet-peaks and clear of
their faces; but Aldric found it significant that Voord
made no move to follow suit. Indeed, he seemed to have
settled his harness more securely, rather than just making it neat. Aldric nodded imperceptibly; he knew now,
for certain. Voord's actions had confirmed the suspicion
born when Voord—again—had dismissed their honor
guard before they climbed the stairs. So. Aldric too kept
peak and cheek-plates and nasal locked down in battle
position. He didn't trust *Hautheisart* Voord at all—
except where this need for ready armor was concerned.

Then Bruda swore, very softly. Aldric's head jerked
round with a rustle and a click of metal, but saw only a
man emerging from a doorway much further down the
corridor. He turned, stooped and fumbled with keys
until he had locked the door behind him. There was a

cup in his hand—a dainty thing far removed from the beakers Aldric had seen used by the other members of the garrison when they were sitting off-duty in the lower levels, watching him go by—and there seemed nothing dangerous about him. Yet Bruda's face was stamped with a flare of recognition that faded even as Aldric watched to a wary, guarded apprehension.

The man walked towards them, but stared past them, deliberately ignoring them completely . . . until he came close enough to see the glitter of rank badges in the lamplight. Only then did his pace slacken and a certain interest come into his face. It was a thin face, with thin hair and set on a thin body; his only noteworthy feature was the pair of prominent ears which Aldric fancied would never fit inside an army regulation-pattern helmet.

Bruda was less inclined to humor, because he knew this man by brief acquaintance—and more particularly by his reputation. He was well known—or rather, notorious— among several branches of service for what he called "attention to detail" and they more bluntly described as "bloody nit-picking." His gods were the Books of Regulation and Instruction, and one story behind his room-locking custom held that there was a shrine to those gods hidden inside, in a cupboard.

Not even the best-laid plans were proof against such a man, whose life revolved around minutiae and pettiness. He could probably spot some overlooked error from where he stood. All that Bruda could hope was that this encounter was a coincidence and not something far, far worse; and that Aldric Talvalin would keep his mouth tight shut around that obviously non-Imperial accent.

"Bruda? Yes, Prokrator Bruda!" The newcomer laughed as he recognised a more or less familiar face. It was an unmistakable laugh, but it was also unreadable, because Bruda knew already that it would sound exactly the same whether sincerely meant or as a screen for something more sinister.

"Yes, indeed!" Bruda was being as jovial as he could manage, given the circumstances, and was relieved to see that Tagen, Voord and Aldric had all backed away, conscious of the "wrongness" of this situation and—

certainly in two out of the three—ready to respond with total violence should such be required. The young trooper who had been their guide looked from one to another, saw the gathering clouds of a senior-level disagreement and, with a very sketchy salute indeed, made himself scarce.

Aldric watched him go. It was just as well; there was trouble brewing here, even though this new officer hadn't yet seen it and Aldric for his part couldn't guess the reason behind it all. But he was staying well clear of what was only an internal wrangle and nothing to do with him at all. Until the thin man turned to him in all innocence and like the *eldheisart* downstairs asked: "What did you do to earn gold diamonds so young, *hanalth? Hanalth . . . ?*"

Before he could begin to flounder or look otherwise obviously trapped, Aldric caught Bruda's swift nod over the stranger's shoulder. *Go on—tell him,* that nod said. Aldric didn't shrug, or sigh resignedly, although it was a time for doing both; instead he drew himself a little straighter and as he had replied once already tonight, said, "Dirac, sir. *Hanalth Kagh' Ernvakh* Dirac."

Those few words were enough; Imperial officers of such seniority spoke only with the accent of the central provinces—and Imperial officers of any rank at all did not speak with the unmistakable Elthanek burr of northern Alba. The man stepped back sharply, a frown creasing his face; then he swung on Bruda. "What is this?" he snapped.

"Not this—*he,*" Bruda returned simply. "*He* is an Alban."

Shock at the blunt, impossible answer left the man— whatever his name was—speechless for an instant (for a wonder), and those who could see his eyes watched a dozen speculations flicker through them in the brief silence. "And what's he doing here?" No laughter now; no curiosity. Just an angry, tending-to-shrill immediate demand for information.

Bruda glanced at Aldric and allowed himself to smile, because the Alban was ready for anything short of outright murder. It was enough. "Right now? He's going to hit you just as hard as he can manage. *Do it!*"

Aldric's hand had already flattened into a chopping blade and the muscles of his entire body were still tingling with the energies leaking from the overcharged spellstone. So he didn't do as Bruda said and strike as hard as he was able, because feeling as he did now it would likely have knocked the thin man's head clean off. But he hacked down on the close-clipped neck with feeling, right below one of those ludicrous ears, and he certainly seemed to have hit with quite enough force to do what was required. The thin man jolted forward half a step without moving his legs and while still in the process of being utterly astonished, and would have measured his length along the corridor had Bruda not caught him in time. His pretty cup exploded into fragments on the floor.

"I have wanted to have that done," Bruda said, "or do it myself, from the first moment that I met this . . . Well struck, Alban."

"My pleasure." Aldric massaged the edge of his hand thoughtfully and flicked a speculative glance at Voord. "I know what you mean, I've met one or two like that."

"See to the princess, *Hlensyarl*," snarled Voord, nettled despite himself. "We'll attend to this and then I'll be right behind you."

I'm sure you will, thought Aldric. *And alone—but for a* telek. He said nothing aloud, but turned his back and walked quickly down the corridor to the fifth door on the left. Behind him he could hear Tagen being instructed to carry the unconscious man downstairs and have his "accidental" injury attended to. *That leaves you, and Bruda—and me. Well, well.* Aldric unbolted the door, tried the handle, found it unlocked—and went inside.

"Dear God!" gasped Dewan. They had both seen it this time, beyond denial even by the driest of dry humor; seen it as clearly as the swirling snow allowed. A monstrous shape made more monstrous yet by the darkness which surrounded it, vast wings, lean body and a brief bright lick of flame—all landing with audacious ease atop the Red Tower. By now Gemmel and Dewan were close enough to see how a length of parapet broke away under the dragon's weight and went tumbling down and out of sight. Neither of them saw or heard it striking ground.

"How many men in the garrison?" Gemmel had the Dragonwand braced now in both his hands, held like a weapon rather than a walking-staff; that pretence was over, for the energies which it contained and focused were overflowing now, illuminating the snowshot darkness with a fluttering actinic glare like summer lightning behind clouds, the lightning's brilliance muted by great distance—or by the will of he who held that lightning's power in check.

Dewan could hear the sound which emanated from the spellstave; for Ykraith sang to herself with a thin atonal screaming that spoke of nothing less than utter power. The ebb and flow of that high, sweet wail, a song without words, matched every nuance of the arabesques of force dancing along her dragon-patterned length. And both matched the beating of someone's heart. Not Dewan's, for his heart was racing again, pounding the blood through his veins in a percussive arhythmic counterpoint to the spellstave's music; and most likely not Gemmel's either—even if what he was, man-shaped though it might be, had a heart that Dewan ar Korentin might recognise as such.

"I said, 'How many men?' " There was an impatience in the sorcerer's voice, an urgency which spoke of more important things than merely calculating odds.

"Forty, most likely. Maybe more, given the circumstances. But Gemmel, that still makes it twenty-to-one at the very least!"

"Count again," Gemmel reproved. "You're forgetting Aldric—and you're forgetting . . . ." He gestured just once towards the top of the tower, invisible now behind a curtain of snow. "I'd say that evens things a little."

"But what are you planning?" Tactical and strategic studies had never included a scenario quite like this one! "What are you going to do?"

"Diversion. Remember what the Vixen told us? When the alarms go off, the guards should only think of running in one direction. I'm"—his gaze shifted briefly, apologetically, to where Ymareth crouched unseen high above them both—"no. *We're* going to force them to a choice—confuse them with decisions just a little. Let's get closer. I want to hear just when the shouting starts."

They began edging forward, eyes narrowed and squinting against a snowfall that was winding up towards blizzard proportions, until after a few steps Gemmel straightened himself and strode as best he could along the middle of the street, as if he had every right in the world to do so. Dewan stared at him, saw the wizard's outline waver towards invisibility as the white-swirled distance between them increased, and realized what had made him bold. There was no need to hide in *this*.

"I've never seen it fall like this before," Dewan said as he drew level again, "at least not so early in the season. Oh, of course! I'm not seeing it again, am I?"

Gemmel turned to look at him and grinned a grin made vague because white teeth and white beard and white snow were all running into one another. "Snow's easy, if it's already there," he said. "Fog's much more difficult."

Neither saw the cloaked and muffled figure standing with a little group of horses in the wind-lee of the buildings nearest to the wall-gate of the Tower. If they had— and Dewan in particular—then memory and recognition might have stirred a chord. But as the snow fell and danced and whirled across the thick, cold air, not even Gemmel knew that there was someone there.

The room beyond the door was snug and warm, illuminated by scented lamps and by the flickering of a large log fire. Applewood, by the smell. There was a sense of ease and comfort rather than real luxury, but certainly nothing to suggest that this might be a prison cell . . . except for those thick bars across the outside of the door.

But it would have taken far less than that to make Aldric's suspicions gather momentum again. Already there had been too much trickery, too much deception; too many things which had not been as they first appeared. What if the princess was here willingly? Or if he had been unknowingly involved in some internal political power-play? Or if the assassination itself was just another trick?

What if there was no one here at all?

But a book lay on the floor where it had slipped off the arm of a chair, its pages ticking slowly over one by one by one, and there was a tray of honeyed fruit on a nearby table, sweet glaze glistening stickily in the firelight. Beside the tray was a crystal wine flagon and two partly filled—or partly emptied—goblets. *Two?* Aldric's mind yelled in alarm.

Two.

A woman rose from the concealing embrace of one of the deep, padded chairs which faced the fire and rounded on him, dropping a needlework tambour as she did so. There was a sleepiness in her face, as if she had been dozing until awakened by the clatter of his arrival; but that sleepiness did not conceal the expectant look which he had caught in her dark eyes as their gaze first met. It was a look which faded almost at once as she realized he was not the one for whom such expressions were intended, but it worried him. It was wrong. Surely princesses did not carry on liaisons with their jailors—no matter how handsome, or how boring the imprisonment? Although, knowing the Drusalan Empire, such snap judgments were as well avoided.

But even the way she looked, dressed, *stood,* was unprincesslike—to Alban eyes at least. Taller then Aldric, almost as broad in the shoulders—which contrasted dramatically with a neat waist—and plentifully endowed both with curves in all the proper places and aquiline darkly glamorous good looks, this woman was scarcely Imperial. But imperious? There was no doubt about that at all.

"Have you not heard of knocking on a door, soldier?" she demanded. "Or of waiting to be invited into a noble lady's presence? Answer me—then get out!"

"To your questions, lady: yes and yes. To your order: no." Aldric glanced backwards over one shoulder, saw nobody behind him and stepped quickly further into the room. "Where's the Princess Marevna? Not you, I think."

"What are you talking about?"

"I'm here to take her out of this, lady; where is she?"

"And where's your written authority for the move?"

"Listen to me: there aren't any authorities—written, spoken or bloody well sung! This isn't a move—it's supposed to be a *rescue!* If you'd be good enough to let it!" He back-heeled the door shut and looked in vain for bars and catches, finally leaning his weight against it for want of anything better, then glared at the tall woman whom he had now categorised as one of those overprotective waiting-women. Though why she had to look the way she did, he couldn't understand. "And if *you* don't start to move, it'll turn into attempted murder!"

A knife appeared from somewhere in the woman's elaborate clothing, and with that length of bright steel jutting thumb-braced above her fist, she suddenly looked capable of such a crime herself.

Aldric coughed a mirthless laugh. "Not by me, lady— I wouldn't have announced my intentions otherwise; but there's one outside who— Never mind that; quick— boots and gloves and cloaks. Foul-weather travelling gear. And the princess! *Move!*"

"Why so excited?"

Aldric's helmeted head snapped a few degrees right to pinpoint the source of this new voice as the depths of the second chair and whoever was sitting in it—and he saw her: the princess. The one for whom, or against whom, or because of whom, time and money and blood had been expended as if they had as little worth as leaves in autumn. She looked like a princess indeed, the way he had imagined the sister of an emperor should look: small and slight, dressed simply in a pure white robe with silvery patterns embroidered on its back and shoulders, with enormous brown eyes that regarded him gravely from a pale, heart-shaped face. As she stood up and flicked long, long dark hair away from that highcheekboned face, he could sense the dignity that she wore about her like a garment, a measured control which refused to let all she had overheard disturb the way in which she paced forward to look up at him.

Up—because the top of her head came only to the junction of his collarbones. Even Aldric's desperate urgency had to be leashed in the face of such awe-inspiring serenity, for although a failure to comprehend the situation lay behind it, Marya Marevna an-Sherban's vast calm was indeed an awesome thing in one so small. Trained tranquillity; and something which, regretfully, he would have to shatter.

"Chirel," she said across his chest to the other woman, "who is this person? And why is he here?"

"Princess, you were sitting there and you heard me well enough. I came to take you from the Tower. By command of General Goth—and I presume your brother."

"For how long has the Lord General used Albans over and above our own excellent soldiers?"

So she recognised the accent. And wouldn't therefore move without an explanation unless he knocked her out and carried her. But her companion had heard the word *Aalban'r* and moved instantly to shield Marevna with her own body and poised knife. Against a fully armored man it was a useless gesture, but very fine for all that.

"Lady, ladies, it's a matter of politics." Despite the helmet he could hear movement just outside and an instant later the stealthy pressure as someone tested the door. Aldric braced his feet flat and wide apart against the floor and held firm. "Because my king wants to show support—"

He would have kept on talking as persuasively as he knew how had he not heard a sudden, familiar thrumming in the air, felt a tremor in the wood at his back, tasted an acrid flavor both in his mouth and in his mind. All of it too familiar by far.

"Get *down!*" He screamed it, hurling himself forward and sideways, clear of the door and the doorway and the straight line from them to the corridor beyond, but he hadn't even hit the floor before thick timbers and iron hinges and steel bolts all jolted out of their frame in a single mass which was twice the weight of a man and went scything across the room as if flung from a catapult, leaving a swathe of destruction in its wake. Something ponderous plucked at Aldric's shoulder and no more, but all of a sudden a hand's span of the cloak and the rank-robe—and the splint-mail under all—were ripped away and his whole arm struck numb by the impact.

High Accelerator! Aldric almost retched with the shock and with the pain of returning sensation in his arm, but most of all with his own stupidity which had almost lost him the game before he had begun to play. *Voord!* he thought frantically, his mind log-jammed and overloaded with conflicting signals. *And Bruda even told me of his talent!* He glanced sideways even while he still sprawled on the floor, his face gnat-stung by the cloud of sparks exploded from the fireplace when the door's wreckage struck it. The princess was safe; the princess' feet weren't even on the ground for Chirel, the big woman with the knife, had actually plucked up her small and slender charge in the crook of one arm. Marevna dangled there now like a doll, all white robe and long dark hair, all dignity gone. But alive . . . for the moment.

Voices outside, coming closer. Fragmented shouts. Bruda's voice: "Voord, what in hell happened?"

Voord's voice right outside the door: "Don't know! Magic! The princess . . . Treason? Can't be treason—not with a foreigner. Murder?"

Oh, clever, clever Lord Commander, to sow that seed so quickly!

A figure appeared in the doorway, ill-defined through the dust and shadowy because so many lanterns had been snuffed out. One hand a crooked claw, almost useless—but not quite. Aldric could see the hazy shimmering of power around it. How did he gain so much? What bargains did he strike, what promises were made? And in the other hand, half-raised, poised and ready: a *telek*.

"Princess, are you safe?" Voord's voice was loud, full of concern—for other ears to hear. The *telek* spoke silent truth of his intentions. "My lady, where are you?"

"Don't move! You, Chirel—both of you keep out of sight!" Aldric's yell broke into a fit of coughing as he choked on the dust and the stinking smoke from dead lamps and smouldering fabrics and the charred, scattered, still-glowing logs.

Voord snapped sideways out of the back-light at the door, and as he moved Aldric saw the *telek* drop forward to a ready position. The Vlechan said nothing. Yet. Did nothing. Yet. But he waited for a target, any target, to show itself. Alban, Drusalan, male, female. Anything or anyone that he could kill.

Another silhouette filled the space where the door had been, more clearly seen now that the dust was settling. Too tall for Tagen and not broad enough. Anyway, Tagen had been dismissed. Bruda. The Prokrator had a drawn sword in his hand. "Voord?" He spoke cautiously, still shaken by the suddenness of events.

"Look out, sir!" Voord's voice had all the right notes of horror in it. "He's trying to kill the princess!"

"Impossible! Where are you, Alban?"

"Get out of sight, sir! He's got a *telek!*" And as he named the weapon, Voord used it to shoot his own commander at close range.

Aldric heard the slap of discharge and saw Bruda's tall figure stagger back three steps, then fall to the floor. He didn't know where the man had been hit, but even point-blank no *telek* dart could punch through proof armor like this officers' issue they all wore. That left the vulnerable places: face and throat. And both of those were fatal.

But if a soldier of the Drusalan Empire could use a *telek* and sorcery, then how much better might an Alban *kailin-eir* who was also a wizard's fosterling? Aldric tugged free his own *telek* from beneath the layering of garments which had concealed its presence, cocked the weapon quietly, released its safety-slide—then laid it down beside him on the floor. More quietly still he stripped away the glove from his left hand and looked at the spellstone of Echainon, the Eye of the Dragon, as it seemed to look at him. There was still no flare of azure energy; just that cat's-eye pupil at its center, twisting, turning, pulsing to the rhythm of his heart. Pulsing fast; very fast indeed. Aldric slipped it around his wrist so that the stone was snugly cradled in the hollow of his palm, then closed his fist around it as if trying to absorb something of the crystal's power into himself.

"*Abath arhan,*" he said. Light that was as blue and brilliant as a summer sky began to stream between the interstitial spaces of those clenched fingers, painting vivid dapples all across the walls and floor and ceiling, cutting through the smoky air in rods and fans of luminescence that seemed almost solid. The stone was primed now. Ready. Waiting.

And the Red Tower shook to its foundations. Aldric felt the floor beneath him lurch like a battleram's deck and saw more wreckage tumble from the shattered doorframe. He heard glass beyond the window-shutters fragment to shards, and by the half-light of the crushed and dying fire he saw a fresco-decorated wall abruptly crack from side to side and top to bottom. Great chunks of the painted plaster fell away, clogging the air with dust once more. But most of all, there was that sound from outside and above.

Piercing shriek and sub-bass bellow all melded together into a single huge atonal roar and the window-shutters blew in, spraying the room with broken wood and with a whirl of snow made phosphorescent by the flood of light behind it.

Ymareth!

A female voice screamed something, even though the sense of the words—if words there had been—was lost. But the mere sound was enough for Voord. Locating on it, he sent another dart whipping through the air towards the source of that cry. It hit hard, stone or metal amid a shower of sparks, then ricocheted further and drew a shrill yelp of pain from someone. Chirel—or the princess?

"Bastard!" Aldric sent four spaced shots across the most likely target zone in as many seconds; there were more sparks, the clack and clatter of metal missiles hitting stone and the chiming diminuendo of their rebound— then the rewarding soggy thump as a dart hit home, and Voord's voice raised in agony.

But how hard had he been hit? There been none of the thrashing of limbs which normally accompanied a *telek*-strike—nor even the slack, felled-tree thud of a body knocked dead off its feet. Only that single cry. Aldric thought *ruse,* thought *decoy* and cuddled the rubble-strewn floor until he was sure.

It happened sooner than he thought. That hazy, translucent globe of contained force which he had seen perched like a falcon on Voord's ruined hand came surging from the shadows, almost unseen, crossing the room in a flicker of refraction where verticals and horizontals kicked nauseously out of line. It hit the wall over the fireplace, striking square and hard as a siege-ram, and splashed a coruscation of rainbow fire all through the room. The wall slumped downwards, shearing near the ceiling as it folded noisily into the space where thirty square feet of its substance had been ripped into a sparkle of disrupted matter.

Where in hell did he learn that? Even as the thought coagulated in his brain—an organ right now as capable of coherent thought as a bowl of beaten eggs—Aldric knew, knew, *knew* that Voord hadn't been taught that spell or any of the others he might use. They were a gift. Not a gift like the ability to play music, or shoot straight, but the sick, sardonic gift of shoes to a legless man or a beautiful painting to one struck blind. Voord was a channel, a pipeline to this world from somewhere else. Aldric had said it himself: "Where in hell?"

"Fool! Thee has power to match this petty casting—power and more! Why lie ye thus in the dirt, O Dragonlord? Rise up! Rise up and smite!" The voice which burst into Aldric's skull was Ymareth's; but now its background of heard sound was not the metallic rustling hiss which he had—just about—grown used to. Oh, no. This was the draconian equivalent of a yell half urgent and half enraged by stupidity, and it had all the delicacy and subtle nuance of a full-great chord on a pipe organ. It was devastating. What little was left of the window-shutters fell apart with the sheer volume of sound, and the remnants of the fresco wall first crazed with a network of fine cracks then went to powder.

And Aldric stood up; uncertainly, unsteadily, because the floor still quivered beneath the soles of his boots, and because the blast of noise which had been Ymareth's irritation had stunned and almost bled his inner ears so that his balance was none of the best. But he stood, crimson and black in the Imperial Grand Warlord's livery which he had come to hate, with the blue-white fire of the Echainon stone crawling along his arm like some eerie embroidery set into the red-enamelled metal. Yet it was the human weapon, the *telek,* that he extended towards where his enemy must be; a *telek* cocked and ready, loaded with clean steel that was shod with lead for penetration's sake. And at the very back of his mind Aldric wished that he had loaded with pure silver.

"Voord? Voord, you traitor, you mocker of honor, come out!" It was stilted, formal, unreal—but it worked, for Voord emerged from the shadows and stood quite still with both hands by his sides. The other *telek* was still gripped in one of them, but it pointed at the floor and was harmless; Aldric's own ready-levelled weapon could shoot unerringly true before Voord's could rise through enough of an arc to make it threatening. "You failed, Voord—your own worst crime, I've been told. So . . . why Bruda, then?"

"How little you understand, Alban, He's dead. So I'm promoted."

"Why? You killed him."

"Quite. I live—he doesn't. Promotion."

Aldric stared at him, lit by the fires of burning wood and leashed-in power. The words wouldn't take shape in his mouth, wouldn't take their places on his tongue or in his throat. Not in Drusalan, anyway. It was a foul language at the best of times. Alban was better by far and much more appropriate for the formal, age-old declaration. "Then I bring you your most necessary death."

He squeezed the *telek*'s trigger and with a noise like a chisel into grained timber, a dart sprouted just above Voord's right eye. Just clear of the helmet's nasal and just below its peak. At that range—fifteen feet, maybe less—the Vlechan's head was snapped back; right back, so that his skull struck between his own shoulderblades. Even without the dart, that jolt would have broken his neck. The ridge of his helmet-crest grated against the wall behind him . . .

Then grated again as he drew himself straight once more and with a heave which needed both hands on its stubby shaft, wrenched the dart out of his head.

The frontal skull-bone might not have knitted straight

away, but with his own eyes Aldric saw the bloodflow stop and the torn flesh run together like wax smoothed with a hot iron. *Like cu Ruruc!*

"You see, *hlensyarl?*" There was a vile phlegmy thickness in Voord's voice when he spoke now. "You see? You can't hurt me. I'm deathless! Marevna, can you hear me? I'm undying—and I'll come for you again. Enjoy sweet dreams till then, my lady!" He twisted out of the doorway and was gone—and still the power of the spellstone whorled around Aldric's arm, contained, unused. Useless now.

"Does use of this touch over-closely on thy honor, man?" Ymareth's voice was cold, sarcastic, disapproving. "Then hear me this last time and believe, for I shall never speak it more. Honor is mine to judge and thou art not yet wanting; but these ladies are now thine to guard and to keep in safety. How wilt thou, when thou knowest not the place wherein thy foe now hides?"

"Get out of my head!" Aldric wrenched at the straps of the Imperial helmet and pulled it free. He stared at the golden insignia, inverted triangle over diamond over double bars, none of it rightfully his—all of it a lie, all lies lies lies—and flung the helmet away from him in a clatter of metal and leather. It bounced from half-a-dozen things, broken furniture and smouldering logs and sideslipped heaps of crumbling stone, then rolled and came to rest and see-sawed to and fro a moment on the brightmetal comb of its cavalry cresting. Afterwards was very quiet in the room. As quiet as the grave. *Was all this useless?* Aldric thought, fearing for the worst. All the sneaking and the lying and the killing, all wasted by a stray dart of a fallen piece of masonry. "My lady?" He no longer troubled to hide that Elthanek accent of his. "My lady, answer—if you can."

"I can," said Marevna an-Sherban and coughed. She lifted her head and upper body on braced hands and fragments of what had once been a comfortable, pretty room tumbled from her back. "Neither of us is hurt. Much. Thanks to you!"

When both women were on their feet, Aldric was better able to see the extent of that "much." There was a ragged hole through Chirel's upper arm; from the state of her sleeve it had bled heavily until staunched by a torn-off strip of material, and in its triangular *telek*-dart shape it exactly matched the shallow puncture on Princess Marevna's face. Had Chirel's far-from-feminine bicep not been around Marevna's head, cuddling it as she must have done when the princess was a frightened child—or had she been one of those willowy ladies rather than the muscular, capable person she was, then . . . The *then* was obvious.

For the rest there were scratches, bruises, blisters from the sparks and embers flung out of the fire; but nothing worse. Aldric sucked in a deep breath, heedless of the plaster-dust and smoke suspended in it, and felt reborn even as he bent double in an eye-streaming coughing fit. He had known it all along, and had refused to even think about: the possibility that something might go wrong. For if Marevna had come to lasting harm, then everything—all the fear, and the pain, and the lies, and the death—would have been for nothing. Wasted.

"It feels like an hour ago that I last said this, lady, ladies—but I *am* here to rescue you. Dress warmly and follow quickly, please!" Events of the past few minutes had convinced even Chirel far more than his most plausible speech could ever have done, and neither took very long over wrapping themselves in furred garments which were the first sign of real riches Aldric had so far seen. He handed them courteously across the threshold of the room, no longer quite a threshold or even a definite boundary between outside and in; but more particularly, he placed himself and his supporting hand between their eyes and Bruda, for though dying fast the Prokrator was not yet dead. Not quite. He was hanging on to life not to save himself but to do, or say, or pass on something of very great importance. So great that he had held himself away from oblivion for a time which must have seemed far longer than all the years of his life.

His fingers were bleeding, their cracked and broken nails flexing convulsively in and out of his shredded palms as if that little pain could distract fast-ebbing life from its departure through the inch-long rip beneath his ear which had nicked both jugular and carotid, opening them to the pungent air. But not enough for quick release. He still lived—each minute, second, breath marked by the crisp spurt of blood against the floor.

"Talvalin," he gasped as Alaric stepped over him, and in his voice was the sudden fear that this *hlensyarl* with no reason to love either the Drusalan Empire or its Secret Police would walk on, walk away and leave him alone to listen to his last drop of blood as it dribbled out into the Red Tower's dust. But Aldric was already dropping to one knee, heedless of or disregarding the moist dark warmth which soaked through his breeches.

"Tlei-ai, Bruda'ka; mn'aii ch'aschh." "Lie easy, friend, here I am." It was the form of Drusalan which lay easiest on an Alban tongue; amiable and warm, without the strata of rank and separation he always had cause to use before. There was neither time nor place for that now. Not here. A dying Chief of Secret Police on his back in the dust was a dying man first and last. Nationality didn't matter; if there was a way of recognising accent in a wordless sound of agony, Aldric had no wish to learn it.

". . . should have trusted you," Bruda mumbled. "First. Foremost. Last. Honor, you see." The man's hands were already cold as they reached out, and sticky with blood. Aldric caught them; let himself be caught. Like marble: no feeling, no pulse, no color. Nothing. ". . . both betrayed. Me. You. Trust ice in summer first. Voord wanted, wants . . . *has* my place now. My rank. My power . . ."

Bruda was surely rambling, passing into delirium as shadows gathered about him, talking only because the sound of speech was the sound of living and hearing his own voice was proof that he was not yet lost. But for all that there was an uncomfortable reality behind the slurring, broken sentences. Too much so. "You were given to us. For fear—no, in case they got to you first. And I sent Voord!" He laughed, a horrible bubbling sound which brought red froth welling from the corners of his mouth. "But it wasn't right. Wasn't decent. Your king . . . to give an honorable vassal like a slave. Not right to betray . . ."

Bruda's cold hand tightened on Aldric's warm fingers, closing so convulsively that in another circumstance the Alban might have sworn and wrenched away. But not now. Never now. The Prokrator's head and shoulders lifted from the planks which pillowed them, and that strain sent a long spray of darkness splattering across the floor. It seemed wrong that the blood of so educated, so intelligent, so politically aware a man should soak into the hungry dust like an unthinking wave on a beach. "All the honor is yours alone. She is safe. Free. Living." Bruda's eyes opened very wide, blue and ingenuous as the eyes of a child; deceptive to the last. "Go to Durforen, Al'Dirac-*an*. To the monastery. They were expecting us. Hah! You and Marevna should get quite a welcome. Bid Ioen the Emperor live for ever. From me. Who cannot live . . . a . . . moment mor—"

Aldric knew the slack weight of death, cradled in his two hands. He laid Bruda's head back to the floor, very gently, for whatever the man had done and planned to do, he had still died well and it was not for Aldric Talvalin to treat his corpse with disrespect. He closed the fixed and staring eyes and respectfully arranged Bruda's hands crosswise on his chest so that—if tradition spoke truly—he would go with dignity into the Void. Did Drusalans believe in Void, and Circle, and the hope to go from sure melancholy to rebirth and the chance of gladness? He didn't know the answer. But just in case, he did all that was proper by his own beliefs, as he had done once before to a corpse pulped out of recognition. Because fire was clean . . .

Urgency was set aside just for this brief moment, as a respect for that which was an Ending in every faith. Aldric crossed his hands—palms outwards and the stone of Echainon, the Eye of the Dragon, outermost of all. Its fires still rolled upwards, over and around and through his fingers, cool, warm, barely and yet always present. *"Alh'noen ecchaur i aiyya,"* he said, and let those fires wash from the crystal, across all that remained of Bruda, Prokrator, *hauthanalth,* man.

Then he rose, and turned from the low mound of dry gray ash, and walked away.

"Diversion, the man said!" crowed Dewan delightedly, all but clapping his hands. "If that's a diversion, then I wouldn't want to be in the same city as a real attack! Mercy of Heaven, will you just look at that!"

Ymareth was skyborne once more, circling the Red
Tower in a tight, steep constant bank, black and gigantic
against the falling snow and the firelit crimson of the
Tower. Flame plumed constantly from its jaws in great
hot billows that blasted the snow to steam. Around the
Red Tower, it was raining.

All of Egisburg must be awake now, thought Dewan;
no matter how sodden they might be, nobody could
sleep through *this!* That first roar was fit to wake the
dead, never mind the drunken; he had heard windows
shattering all across Tower Square after that brief flicker
of blue light from one very particular window a quarter
up the Tower's grim height. It was then that Ymareth
had roared, and launched with heavy grace into a dive
from the ramparts which had become full flight within a
hundred feet. He had seen that as the wavering curtain
of snow had thinned for just a moment, and then as the
fires began he could see even despite the storm's renewed fury. Still the dragon circled, flaming, and yet,
through all the flames and the roaring, Dewan couldn't
put aside the thought that Ymareth was laughing.

There were no soldiers to be seen. Oh, there had been
plenty and enough to spare a few minutes past, when
they had poured from the Red Tower's doorway like
ants from a kicked nest, but they had kept on running—
through the slush and the deluge of dragon-melted sleet,
out of the perimeter gates, into the white whirl of the
blizzard and out of Dewan's concern. He had seen soldiers run like that before, twice; they wouldn't be back
tonight. Except for Aldric and Princess Marevna, the
Tower was surely empty now.

Gemmel was plainly thinking the same thing. He
scraped snow from his beard and brows, knowing the
gesture to be a useless one, and hefted the no-longer
needed Dragonwand. "Move in," he said.

Directly they stepped forward, the hoofbeats came up
behind them both. Several horses, at the trot. Dewan
drew blade and swung around, dropping to a fighting
crouch—and then relaxed, his moment made perfect by
Gemmel's splutter of astonishment as the wizard saw
Tehal Kyrin approaching them through the snow. She
was leading six horses at a sort of jog-trot: Aldric's black

Lyard and his packpony, her own gray gelding K'schei and three more riding-horses with empty saddles.

"Expecting someone, my dear?" purred Dewan as he bowed low.

"I keep telling you not to call me that," said Kyrin, but her feigned exasperation was half-hearted and lacked spirit; all her concentration was elsewhere, on what was happening around the Red Tower, and Gemmel had to address her twice before she heard him.

"Lady? Lady! Are you also a part of this—or are you acting independently?"

"I . . . You'd be Gemmel. Yes. Who else?" She was still uncertain of how one spoke to sorcerers—cautiously, of course, that went without saying—and twitched him a little bow whose effect was rather lost when K'schei threw up his head and yanked her not only upright but momentarily off tip-toe. "Tehal Kyrin," she introduced herself when she had a little breath back. "And no: I'm not concerned with politics—Alba's, the Empire's or yours. Sir," she added, thinking it prudent.

"That's a relief," said Gemmel, meaning it. He glanced at the sky: Ymareth had swept away from the Tower and was for the moment invisible through the snow, but the old wizard was quite aware of what was going on. The dragon was lining up for a landing run, and in this filthy flying weather was taking plenty of airspace for it. "Now, since we have a moment, Dewan. Explain this young woman."

Dewan did, editing where he thought it wise, but even then wasn't entirely sure what Gemmel thought of it all. The wizard's jewel-green eyes were fixed on him, and if they blinked once during the telling of the tale, Dewan ar Korentin didn't see it. Still there was no reaction— favourable, disapproving or even dismissive—and to break the uncomfortable stillness he looked up and asked, "Where's the dragon?" even though he had noticed it gone before he began to speak.

Gemmel regarded him disdainfully, but forbore to sniff. "Out there"—he pointed downwind—"and coming back." Then with just the merest touch of vitriol, "Any more questions? Or can we actually do something constructive?"

Same old wizard, thought Dewan. He still hadn't really come to terms with what he had learned about Gemmel Errekren, but there were occasional flashes of expression or phrase which were comforting in their familiarity. He shrugged, the movement accentuated both by his furs and by the snow which had collected on them. "Whatever you like. Lead on."

But not even Gemmel was willing to go inside the Red Tower itself. Caution, superstition, a desire not to tempt providence in its present shape of those poised and ominous spiked gates. Or, for Dewan's and Kyrin's part at least, the obvious if unadmitted wide-eyed wonder they both showed as Ymareth the dragon came gliding into view through the very teeth of the snowbearing wind, its flight-path cleared in brief, bright swathes of fire. Heat and the smell of steam washed across them as it settled onto the snowbound earth in a rolling cloud of vapor, and its head swung to regard them as it grinned that long fox's grin, all fangs and tongue and—this time—flames and smoke.

"Many others watched," Ymareth reported, "from doorways and from windows. But I doubt thee will be troubled by their interest." Just to add weight to the pronouncement, its great wedge head turned away a moment and unleashed another blast towards the city proper. Somewhere in the distance, beyond the rushing bellow of the flame, a chorus of doors slammed shut.

"Any s-sign of him yet?" Kyrin managed. Her voice was as steady as she could make it—which meant that it could still be understood. Just about. But then, she wasn't quite so used to the company of dragons as Dewan had become.

"Nothing yet." Less inclined to worries than the other two, Gemmel had wandered a good deal nearer to the Tower, and now he returned with a motley collection of things bundled in his arms or draped across the Dragon-wand. "Just these." He was mystified by the discovery; a helmet, a cloak and an overrobe with rank-tabs on it. "The rest of the armor's back there as well. Looks like somebody wasn't wearing much when they left."

"Looks like they·didn't stop to put these on, you mean. And I can't say I'm surprised." Dewan reached out for the helmet, smiling thinly. A diamond over twin bars, all silver. *Hautheisart.* He grunted and dropped it into the snow, then nudged it carelessly with a boot. "I didn't reach so exalted a rank." There was a touch of bitterness in his voice. "Because I was born on the wrong side of the border. No other reason, even though they always had several— Aldric!"

The helmet, kicked, rolled sluggishly aside and was forgotten as all three—all four, because Ymareth lowered its head to see inside the Tower as well—looked through the gateway to where Dewan had first heard the patter of approaching footsteps and Aldric's voice, trying to make some explanation in two directions at once.

"Another thing," he was saying, "is that one of my companions is, well, different. Don't be frightened; you won't be harmed."

"But how different can he be, if we're—*Father of Fires!*"

"True enough, I suppose; but I didn't say 'he' at all."

It was big, strong Chirel who was most upset by her first sight of Ymareth, reclining in the melting snow and gazing at her through those awesome phosphorescent eyes. She screamed and would have fainted on the spot had not someone—Aldric suspected Kyrin—been ready with a generous handful of snow unsympathetically applied. Even afterwards she seemed seldom far from hysterics.

While Marevna was . . . Marevna. As serene as he had seen her at their first meeting. It was only when he watched closely that he saw how rapidly the white puffs of exhaled breath were pumping from her slack, slightly smiling lips. The calmness, the control, even the smile were all shields to hide behind, just as much as Bruda's mask had ever been. Something with which to fend off reality. But the reality of the dragon for Princess Marevna was a wild, wavering blend of terror and delight; discovering that at least some of the old stories were true was enough to overwhelm anyone.

"My ladies, my gentlemen," Aldric courteously pitched his voice loud enough to include Ymareth in the situation, "I would as soon not wait a moment longer here; we've already outstayed any welcome Egisburg might offer. Mount up, all; let's go." Then more privately to Kyrin, after an embrace that was of necessity both brief and restrained: "I already knew you were beautiful, love; but this goes beyond mere cleverness." He waved a hand towards the horses. "How did you know to bring exactly the right number?"

Kyrin laughed and laid her head sideways on his shoulder—the nearly-bared one that the chamber door had clipped. "Easy enough: your horse, my horse, the packpony—and everything else in the stable." That would have been Bruda's, Tagen's and Voord's mounts, of course. "Although somebody's going to be riding a pack-saddle. I suggest the pretty princess."

"Jealous already?"

"God, no! She's lightest, that's all, and I don't want the horse overloaded," Kyrin walked away, a little distance beyond Dewan, then thought a moment and turned back. "But I did see that piece you had in Tuenafen. Don't do it again . . ."

Ar Korentin, between them, looked with amusement from one to the other. And froze.

"All *stop!*" said Lord Commander Voord.

He stood just at the corner of the Red Tower's gatehouse, his face pinched and bluing with cold, and the *telek* in his outstretched hand wavered with the shivering that racked his body. "I've been waiting for you; listening to you congratulate each other, listening to you feeling so pleased with yourselves! I've been waiting a long time."

Not even the dragon would have seen him, for he was no longer wearing armor, or rank-robe, or cloak. Instead he was dressed in what he must have been wearing under the armor: close-fitting garments of some white material which blended with the snow and made him all but invisible. Too late now, Dewan glanced with all the bright vision of hindsight at the rank-marked *seisac* helmet he had thrown aside. Yet how should he have known?

Other than the white tunic and trews, Voord wore one other thing—itself white now with the sleet and snow which had fallen on it while he crouched in the freezing shadows and waited for his opportunity with that dreadful hatred-fuelled patience, but a thing more usually black as night. A sleeveless vest. A *coyac* made of wolf-skin.

Aldric was the only one to realize what was meant by his wearing of that garment, but the instant he opened his mouth Voord's *telek* lined up on his face. It still trembled, but not so much that he might miss. "Say it," the *hautheisart* invited. "Say anything at all and see how far it gets before this rams it back down your throat."

Nobody spoke. Aloud. But inside his head Aldric heard the dragon's voice, carried on a whisper of metallic sound that Voord would never recognise as speech. "Thou, Dragon-lord, and all of thy companions block my way—else I would roast him to ash and cinders. Move aside." Encharmed with understanding, Gemmel and Dewan heard the words as well and where line of sight permitted, knowing eyes met in swift agreement. Then the sorcerer took a step to one side and Dewan to the other.

Voord glanced at both and smiled like a shark. "Back to where you were," he snarled, "or this one dies!" The *telek* levelled at Kyrin. "Don't think that I'm here and you're there and that thing"—a chin-jerk at Ymareth—"is where it is just by accident. Oh, no. Credit me with that much wit at least."

"W-what do you want?" Marevna an-Sherban was no longer quite so calm as she appeared—unless it was a chillborn shiver that ran the tremor through her voice—but there was still all the dignity of the Imperial line in the way she faced Voord now.

"Want? You, of course, and alive—for the present. And they'll let me take you with me, because then they'll think you have a chance. And because they know what I'll do right now if anybody tries to play the hero!"

"Then do it right now," Marevna snapped, "and at least spare me the delights of your company!"

Voord almost did; his lean face twisted with rage and had he been just a little closer he would have taken pleasure from knocking her to the ground. But discretion returned to him just in time, and with it the realization that any change of position whatsoever might leave him open to a devastating reprisal. "No, lady," he said,

and now it was undiluted fury rather than cold which
was making him shiver, "not until you ask again. Beg.
Without that pride of yours. You'll lose that first, I
promise—because I'm due a reward for all my trouble.
And then I'll make a gift of you to—" He stopped short,
leaving the uncompleted sentence hanging in the cold
air, but his smile remained and that was quite enough.

Kyrin, Dewan and Gemmel had all seen Kathur the
Vixen and all knew exactly what he meant. So did
Aldric—not because of what he had seen, but because
of what he had been told by Voord himself. Those
threats. That "persuasion." He could guess well enough
what the future might hold for Princess Marevna, and
as slowly as the pouring of chilled honey his hand began
an imperceptible climb up and across to where his own
telek was pushed through his belt.

"If I think rightly, *hlensyarl*," Voord continued, staring malevolently at Aldric now, "if I remember things
that I've been told, you've been a thorn in my flesh for
a long time. If I'm due a reward, then so are you. Something suitable." His *telek* steadied as he braced it over
the crook of his left arm and squinted down the weapon's polished, moisture-spotted cylinder. "Enjoy it!"

He squeezed the trigger.

In that instant which joined word to action, Dewan ar
Korentin spasmed sideways from where he stood between Aldric and Kyrin. It wasn't a leap—nothing so
dignified—but a convulsion of muscles, moving his fur-
bulky body from where it had been—

—To where Kyrin was. Because he knew the way a
mind like Voord's would work. And he was right.

Aldric saw it all: saw, and could do nothing. He saw
Voord's finger flex and the *telek* jolt as a dart sped from
it; saw the missile's metal glint as it flew; and saw Dewan
wrenched out of line in midair the way a running rabbit
jerks and tumbles when the arrow hits it square, saw
him flop against Kyrin and bring her down into the
snow. And saw the brilliant spattering of blood that
stained it.

"*No . . . !*"

His hand blurred the last few inches to the waiting
maple-wood stock and tugged his own *telek* free, jabbing

the safety-slide with one thumb while the weapon was still rising, and snap-shot in the flicker that it came on line. The dart, his dart, hit Voord underneath the chin and hammered deep into the soft pale flesh.

And then fell free again, unstained. The Vlechan's outline blurred, altered, contracted in a shape-shift far, far faster than Aldric had expected would be possible—and fast or slow, none of the others had expected it at all.

Between one eye-blink and the next, man became Beast. A huge wolf stood in Voord's place now, its pelt pure white save for the black saddle-mark across its shoulders—as if it wore a jacket. A wolf which, as it turned to flee, ran slightly lame on a twisted, crippled left front paw.

Ravening energies splashed across the ground where it had been as Aldric and Gemmel both unleashed the power contained in Dragonwand and spellstone—but the wolf was already gone. Behind them, Ymareth went for the sky in a single bound and a thunderous clap of wings, passing low above their heads with a huge hot rush from a fanged mouth already agape and flaring. Fire scoured the ground—and snow became superheated steam, the grass and shrubs it shrouded turned to ash and the very topsoil baked to sterile dust from the Red Tower's base to its perimeter wall. But in all that open space, there was no wolf either alive or dead.

"Don't die, Dewan. Oh please, don't die!" On her knees in the snow, Kyrin held one slack-fingered hand in both of hers as if the grip might somehow help; but she had already seen the look in Gemmel's eyes as the old man straightened and she knew her words were worthless. Just air.

Marevna and Chirel stood off to one side, knowing that this was none of their affair right now. Their arms were about one another, for comfort more than warmth, and Chirel did not stir even when Ymareth landed and stalked forward with that grave, pacing grace to spread the vast canopy of its wings above them all.

Dewan's eyes opened and gazed at the three around him. He looked at Gemmel, found a sort of smile some-

where and offered it wanly to the sorcerer. "I thought
my heart might let me down," he said quite clearly. "So
did you. But not like this." His eyes closed again briefly,
a little fluttering movement like a drawing-down of
blinds, and could not open quite so wide next time.
"You didn't tell them how I died, that time on the
beach. He brought me back, then. Now?"

Gemmel said nothing. Could say nothing. He only
shook his head.

"Oh . . ." Again that smile, but fraying fast. "Just as
well. Man in—in my position could get carless without
the fear of . . . It. But . . . hurts, old wizard, old friend.
Hurts!" This time his eyes were squeezed shut and the
lips half-hidden by his snow-caked mustache compressed
to a thin line. "I-I wish it wouldn't do that," he said
again, shakily. "Kyrin, lady?" He forced the hand she
cradled to close a little, enough to squeeze her own fingers with a gentle, reassuring pressure. "Just for me: tell
L-Lyseun I did love her. Really. But tell her, b-because
I never did. I'm cold. I hurt. I . . .

"Aldric? Aldric, where are you? I can't see you any
more. . . !"

"I'm here, Dewan. I'm listening." Aldric's calm voice
belied the tears on his scarred face; cold tears, flayed by
the icy winter wind.

"Nothing of the Empire for me, Aldric. Not now."

"I understand. I know."

"Let me be Alban at the last. Not in the earth. No.
Give me to the flames. Fire is clean . . . and I'm so cold.
So . . . very . . . cold—"

"An-diu k'noeth-ei, Dewan-mr'ain." Aldric said the
words and made the sign quickly, perhaps more quickly
than was proper, and then shook his head violently to
clear his face of tears and his mind of a thought, a possibility that was beyond bearing. That the words of a curse
might just have been fulfilled.

He neither asked for, expected nor would have wanted
any help as he gathered Dewan in his arms, a big body
like a bear in all its furs and leather. But a bear whose
hunting days were done. Staggering a little under the
limp deadweight until he found his balance, Aldric walked

slowly and carefully into the Red Tower. When he emerged a few minutes later, his hands were empty and hanging by his sides but he was still weighed down with grief. "He was my friend," he said. "Whatever he did, he was my friend. And now there isn't enough wood." Aldric turned and stared up and up at the slick red stones which were the color of the blood on his gloved hands. "I wish that I could burn it all."

The voice inside his head was very quiet. "All things burn," said Ymareth. "Just let the fire be hot enough."

Aldric half-turned; looked at Gemmel, who nodded, then at the dragon. "True?" he said. Ymareth's majestic head dipped once, in what could only be another nod.

"True. Only give the word."

"He was my friend," Aldric said again. "He deserves a worthy monument: one that Egisburg and the Empire will remember." He did as he had done once before, and looked straight into the dragon's glowing eyes. "The word is given. Let us get clear—then torch it."

There was no one on the streets of the city as they rode out, and none of those who watched from behind closed shutters made the slightest move to obstruct their passage. It was just as well. Neither Aldric nor Kyrin nor Gemmel were in any mood for mannerly dispute. Two drawn swords were enough to discourage all but the city militia; but the crackling nimbus of force which hung about the riders and trailed tendrils of energy in their wake would have given pause even to the Bodyguard Cavalry at Drakkesborg. *Dewan's old regiment* thought Aldric on the heels of his first notion. He nudged Lyard to a canter and led their way to the gates.

Egisburg seemed content to watch them leave its precincts; but even after they had gone, the city held its breath. Waiting.

"I don't care about the snow," said Aldric as he dismounted, "we're all lying flat. You too." Most of this was to the Imperial women, and particularly Chirel who did not care for his high-handed treatment of the Emperor's sister. "And make your horses lie down as well— like *this!*" He twisted Lyard's bridle in the proper fashion until the big Andarran stallion sank down and rolled onto his side, very black against the snow. "Do it; I'll help."

Gemmel was looking at him strangely. "You seem to know exactly what you're doing," he said.

Aldric glanced towards him, smiled thinly and shrugged. "If that was the case, Dewan would still be alive," he said bitterly. "I know how to be careful; that's all." Then he lay full-length in the snow, his upper body across Lyard's neck and one hand over the animal's exposed eye. His other hand reached out, met Kyrin's and gripped it tight.

"Aldric, do you really think that even Ymareth—" She saw Aldric's face in the dimness and stopped, for though his eyes were still huge and shining with the last remnant of weeping for a dead friend, they also shone with anticipation of what another—yes, another friend—might do as a memorial.

"I don't think," he said softly. "I believe."

Silence. Snow drifting down from the iron-gray clouds. Cold and darkness.

And then—

Light! It scored the sky, a column of fire so hot that its core was tinged with violet, so brilliant that the shadows which it threw were edged like knives, and through the black and purple-glowing flecks crowding his vision Aldric saw the Red Tower. It was more than a mile distant, a tiny pin-sharp image that was as red as blood, as red as murder. And it was shimmering. The crimson that was its true color began to change, shading up through scarlet and incandescent orange to a flaring citrine yellow—and at the last it reached a silvery pink-white which forced him to flinch away.

The air temperature began to climb, slowly at first; then it abandoned so gradual an increase and soared. Falling snow became rain, warm drizzle, and after that stopped altogether as the clouds which carried it were ripped to tatters, seared out of existence by the blast of heat rising from the heart of Egisburg. In the sky above the city, stars appeared again.

And in front of Aldric's eyes two feet and more of snow began to melt, rivulets of water pouring out of it

with the chuckling sound of a brimming stream in springtime. He raised his head a fraction, and through a dancing haze could see the Tower—a structure that he knew
was two hundred feet of stone and iron and massive
timbers—slowly squirming from base to ramparts like a
tallow candle in a furnace. Even that brief glimpse felt
like staring at the noon sun on midsummer's day, and it
was blazing brighter yet.

The earth bucked beneath his prone body in a sudden
convulsion beside which Lyard's terrified thrashing was
like a lover's caress, and Chirel began to scream—but it
was a scream that nobody heard completed. Just as she
reached her highest pitch a noise from the direction of
Egisburg rolled over them, breaking like a great dark
wave of thunder peaked and crested with chain lightning.
The very air howled in their ears with the appalling re-
verberance of that long rumble of destruction, and in its
tingling aftermath they heard, high overhead, Ymareth
the dragon's awesome roar of triumph as its dark wings
scythed across the starlit sky.

"Oh sweet and loving—!" whimpered someone's
voice. "Look there . . . Dear God, *look!*"

They looked. A dome-topped unstable pillar of smoke
and dust lifted into the sky above Egisburg, criss-crossed
with filaments where yet-burning debris was still falling
from the main mass of the cloud. It looked monstrous;
evil and obscene, like some gigantic fungus rearing up to
spread its rotting cap over the ruins of the Red Tower.

Except that the Red Tower was gone . . .

Gemmel stared at the cloud, at its shape, and then
turned to Aldric with all the depths of infinity in his
green eyes. He said nothing, but the Alban thought his
face was that of a man confronted by the reality of an
ancient, long-forgotten nightmare.

"You believed," said Kyrin, still holding Aldric's
hand.

He nodded. "But I'm still learning. There are things
I'm coming to believe in that you and I have never heard
of. And I sometimes wonder if I really want to hear of
them at all." He shivered a little, then turned to help
as the horses scrambled upright, snorting and stamping.
"Princess, I'm taking you to Durforen, it seems. That

was the arrangement with . . . with your brother. We're expected at the monastery."

Marevna an-Sherban gazed levelly up at him with those enormous eyes whose expression he could never read. Framed in the dense dark fur of her hooded cloak, she looked like a little mouse and not like a princess at all. But there was that stillness about her again, that calm which had all the weight of Empire behind it. "Then best go there at once, my lord Talvalin," she said in clipped, accented Alban. For though your company is stimulating, neither I nor the Empire can take much more of it. We have only a limited number of cities, after all."

10

Coda

They reached Durforen at noon on the fourth day out from Egisburg. *Hethra-hamath, de Marhar.* The eighth day of the tenth month. The eighth day of winter and the Hour of the Hawk. All was silent beneath the silver sunlight, without even a trace of wind to move air that was edged like a razor. There was only that chill, glittering stillness; and, three miles up in the icy sky, what might have been a thread of smoke unravelling white against the bleached blue vault of Heaven.

Black on black against the snow, Aldric reined Lyard to a standstill and pushed the hood of a black military rank-robe. Black on black on black, for beneath the robe he was once more wearing his own sable battle armor and the horse he rode had a coat like polished jet. Three days from Egisburg, and halfway through a fourth. Light of Heaven, it seemed so short a time since . . . everything. And yet perhaps it was only right and proper that such a journey should be short, so that he could more swiftly give Princess Marevna into the safe-keeping of whoever, in dead Bruda's words, might be expecting her. And thus more swiftly call a finish to this quest, this exercise in duty to Rynert the King.

It was the discharge of an obligation which had befouled his honor, for all that there were those and one in most particular—he glanced upward with the thought— who still said otherwise; and none could question that it had claimed the life of a man he had called *friend*. Before God, there were few enough with that title; so small a group that he could ill afford to lose a single one.

Aldric could still see, and would always see, the light going out in Dewan's eyes.

He swallowed down a throat suddenly narrower than it had been—that memory was still too recent and too painful—and swept a long stare across the flawless field of white which sparkled back at him as though dusted with crushed diamonds; then his gaze went out and away and up and beyond. And he shivered slightly.

Aldric would as soon have left the Drusalan Empire far behind him; as the old tale said, shaken its dust from off his feet. But he had not, and he would not. Not yet. There were matters—matters of consequence but no affair of Alba's king—which required his attention. Personal attention.

As personal as anything confided by a father to a son.

For in the evenings past, after they had found lodgings at farms and steadings so isolated that gossip regarding their presence would travel slowly if at all in this foul weather, Gemmel had spoken to him. Confided in him. Told him such truths that, though often halfway guessed at already, hearing them confirmed and detailed had shaken him to the soul. There had been times when only the gentle anchorage of Tehal Kyrin—Aldric had refused to send her out of earshot—had kept his mind secured to sense and sanity. And there had been times when her nails had sunk deep into his arm while she too tried to come to terms with what was said.

Those words had changed the way that Aldric looked at his world. *His* world, no longer *the* world; for there were other worlds that were not his. Gemmel had said so. One of those was Gemmel's own. They were words which had fathered, mothered, brought to term and borne those thoughts of enormity, of time and distance beyond understanding, which now made him shiver as he stared at the vastness of the sky. Yet it was not a shiver of fear, not quite. There was awareness in it too; the awareness that comes to eyes newly opened, appreciating for the first time the infinity of light and shape and color which had always lain beyond the limits of their closed darkness. Eyes that now saw a world far smaller than it had been, but a Heaven far, far larger than a man could ever hope to simply dream of . . .

*   *   *

Below the ridge where he sat, thinking vast thoughts and waiting for the others, was Durforen monastery. It was no longer a religious house, but unquestionably a ruin. Not even an especially picturesque one, although the contour-softening coat of snow on its old gray stones had given it a certain charm. But that charm was offset by its present occupants and incarnation, for the monastery was vivid with the scarlet banners and red armor of the host of soldiers encamped there.

Imperial Household troops, thought Aldric. Even at this distance of half a mile, and squinting through a glare of sun on snow that made his eyes smart and his head ache, he could see—if not read—the gold writing on the banners. Those were never seen outside Kalitzim except in one very special circumstance: when the Emperor himself was in attendance.

"Quite a reception, eh?" Aldric said aloud to Lyard and whistled piercingly between his teeth. The horse flicked both ears disapprovingly; he didn't care for such whistles overmuch, for they were too shrill by half and more suited to the summoning of dogs. The Emperor's dogs, this time.

Aldric could see a sudden flurry of agitation in the monastery camp and knew that either his whistle had been heard—not so unlikely in this still air as might appear—or his silhouette had been spotted on the skyline. As other figures joined his own—Kyrin, then Marevna and Chirel close together, and Gemmel as a self-appointed rearguard—the agitation increased and within a few seconds coalesced into a light cavalry patrol heading for them at the gallop amid a haze of churned fine snow.

As the riders boiled over the crest of the ridge in open skirmish order, their line swung through a crescent to a closed circle with the intruders trapped at its center. And then everything stopped, for the "prisoners" hadn't moved at all but merely sat on their own horses and watched the cavalry maneuver with . . . interest and enjoyment? Nor was their reaction the only thing wrong. What the patrol had found was not what the patrol had expected: certainly not two girls, a woman, an old man—and a young man who wore the insignia and the arrogance if not the armor of a cavalry *hanalth*. The soldiers looked nervously from one to another, then at their own officer in hope of guidance; none of them troubled to hide their own confusion.

It was Gemmel who broke the muttering, indecisive stalemate. Perhaps the old sorcerer was lacking patience, or maybe he was just feeling the cold. Nudging his horse forward a step or two, he snapped a very creditable salute towards the patrol *kortagor*—creditable enough for the man to return it—and for some reason he was smiling at some private joke in his own words, even before he spoke. "Take me," said Gemmel, "to your leader."

Goth was here. Of course Goth was here. Aldric might have—and at the back of his mind probably had—expected it; certainly he betrayed not even a flicker of adverse emotion at first sight of the jutting, pugnacious spade beard. Instead he offered beard and general alike a lazy, deep, utterly false bow of respect. And even now, an hour and much talking later, he hadn't yet decided whether or not Goth was glad to see him alive. Or even if he had been troubled by Bruda's murder. It was, as always, impossible to tell what might please or annoy such a man.

Ioen the Emperor, younger, with a freckled milk-pale skin and flaming red hair, was somewhat easier to read. The very presence of this armored storm-column so relatively close to the borders of *Woydach* Etzel's territory was an indication of how he felt about—what? That was the real question. His sister—or the policies which her capture had affected? But either was sufficient reason to make him pleased to see her free and unhurt; and enough to make him wax generous.

"My lords, my lady," he said in stilted Alban—a compliment which, following Aldric's lead, both Gemmel and Kyrin acknowledged with courteous nods—"for this gift of my dear sister, her liberty, gift I in turn gold, land, riches."

Maybe it wasn't just because of those policies after all, Aldric thought; then he saw Goth lean over in his saddle and whisper something which, although he couldn't hear it, was probably an exhortation to restraint. He grinned slightly and made quite sure that Goth saw him do it. "I'm not a poor man, General. Nor particularly greedy. So there's no need to fear for the Exchequer. Not this time."

Goth straightened with a jerk, clearing his throat and pretending that he hadn't said a word. He even had the decency to color slightly—if it was a blush born of decency and not the flush of rage.

"But there are two matters I'd like settled, Majesty," Aldric continued. "One concerns the Jevaiden holding of Seghar."

That name provoked a deal of muttering between Ioen and Goth, so much so that Aldric wondered what he might have started. He was privately relieved to see the beginnings of a smile on the Emperor's freckled face. An absolute monarch with freckles and a schoolboy's face, he thought irrelevantly. Lord God!

"Your concern is for Gueynor-Overlord, rather than the holding itself, yes?" There was an archness in the light, youthful voice that had no place there and could easily become an irritation, but in the circumstances Aldric thought best to let it go.

"Uh. Yes. Put like that, Majesty, yes."

"Concerned with regard to her safety, yes?"

Feeling certain that this was a speech prepared in advance and learned by rote, Aldric nodded silently. He had left Gueynor abruptly, with only a middle-aged demon-queller as protector—he, and the keys to hidden money-chests which gave her power over the long-unpaid garrison. But second thoughts had been suggesting that it might not have been enough. He had to know.

"Then have no fear; she was confirmed as Overlord, with all due rights of rank and privilege within the Empire, two months ago. It pleases me that your wish has been so quickly answered, yes?"

"Yes." Aldric bit the word off short; it pleased Goth as well, apparently, for the width of his grin was such as to put the general's ears in jeopardy. So quickly answered, thought Aldric maliciously—and so cheaply. He coughed in a significant fashion and saw the grin snuffed out. "You forget, General," he reminded delicately, "I said *two* matters. The second involves passes for three to any part of the Empire. *Any*—regardless of current political allegiance. I'm sure that you can think of some clause to ensure that, dear Goth. Yes?"

"No!" Goth was shocked beyond measure. "Never! Of course not . . . !"

Aldric wasn't amused to see how, after his first vehement refusal, the general had to pause and think of reasons *why* not. To cover the workings of that tricky brain, Goth began to bluster about foreigners and lack of rights, and—more dangerously than he knew—duty and obligation. Aldric didn't trouble to hide his grimace of distaste.

But then his attention shifted beyond both General and Emperor, to where Princess Marevna sat side-saddle on a palfrey—red-roan like all the Imperial mounts—and watched and listened. Her simple white clothing had been changed in this past hour to the rich crimson and burnished gold more fitting to an Emperor's sister, but save for that quarter-hour she had heard the whole exchange between the scarlet and the black. Always herself quite silent, not even coughing in the icy air; saying and doing nothing.

Until now.

Now she leaned down to where Chirel stood by her horse's head, tapped the woman on the arm with a slim, scarlet-lacquered scroll cylinder plucked from the long cuff of one glove, and directed that it be taken straight to Aldric.

Aldric himself had seen their little by-play—he was ostentatiously ignoring Goth—and there was already a laugh simmering within his rib-cage as Chirel reached up past his stirruped leg to hand the scrollcase over.

"That should prove sufficient." Marevna's voice, not particularly loud, still cut across all the other sounds—of Goth, of the horses, of the military camp two hundred yards away. But the General and the Emperor jerked round in their saddles, not expecting to hear this little quiet mouse of a sister speak at all. Then they exchanged glances and turned slowly back to Aldric . . .

Who sat, cylinder in one hand, tapping it indolently on the gloved palm of the other as he met Goth's stare with a bland, cool smile. Then, holding the General's

eyes with his own, he held out the little container to
Gemmel.

"I only speak it, *altrou-ain.* Could you do the honors
here?"

Gemmel did so, scanning the high-quality parchment
with its neatly brushed characters and the red-and-black
cluster of seal impressions both at top and bottom. He
didn't read the message aloud, but his indrawn whistle
of amazement—an unfamiliar reaction from him, and
one which made Aldric look round with raised eyebrows—
said more than enough. The sorcerer looked at his fosterling, and at that fosterling's lady, and tapped the scroll
with one long finger. "Citizenship," he said, "while we're
within the Empire's borders. Scholarly passes. Confirming that we are without any political bias. Commanding
aid and protection. Senatorial seals: High, Low and
Priestly." He let the scroll snap shut and returned it
almost reverently to its case. "Go anywhere, do anything, where the law permits. Lady . . ." he bowed very
low towards Marevna, "you have my thanks."

"What point," said the princess, "in having high-
placed friends, if they aren't sometimes of use?"

"You listened," Aldric said, faintly accusing. But
pleased for all that.

"One learns that way."

"Uh . . . true. My lady, Majesty, oh yes, and Goth.
Thanks to you all. For a great many things. Education,
mostly. And now we really must be going."

They went.

Aldric stood up in his stirrups again, scanning a non-
existent horizon for non-existent signs of life, then settled back into Lyard's saddle and exhaled a smoky sigh
of relief. It was now four in the afternoon—the Hour of
the Serpent—and they had ridden constantly since half-
past one, pushing their horses as much as they dared.
Seven horses now; the three additional pack-ponies
loaded with provisions were a token of Imperial generosity and also, Aldric had suspected at first, a means to
slow them up. He distrusted Lord General Goth, who
was the sort of man to overhaul them and take away
their Imperial travel passes, not for any really malevo-

lent reason but simply in order to regain face by having
the power to withhold or return them.

But perhaps he was wronging the General by such a
thought, because there had been no sign of pursuit all
afternoon—and now at last the day was darkening into
twilight once more. Or maybe, Aldric thought with a
quick grin, someone else had suspected how Goth's mind
might work and had forbidden any move which might
resemble an attempt to follow them.

No matter now. All that truly mattered was that there
had been nothing to see and nothing to fear. Only Kyrin
and Gemmel, a little way away, sitting with the horses
in a thin fog of exhaled breath which clung about them
all like the skeins of spider-silk that night glimmer on a
meadow in the first light of dawn. Only Ymareth, high
above where the first cold jewelled stars began to show.

Only snow, and more snow, its once-blinding whiteness shading down now to a silver and smoke-blue in
the shadowed dusk as it flowed out like a waveless sea
towards the cloudless evening sky. Aldric touched heels
to Lyard's flanks and rode forward, eastward, to be with
his companions; the lady lost and regained, and the father more than any parent. At his back, the pale blue
of Heaven was washed with rose and saffron as the sun
set into a distant fringe of haze which was all that
showed where a horizon might have been. Ahead was
that same haze, velvety, darkening to a star-fired night
where the world reached up to touch, to meld with, to
become the very sky itself.

A sky that went on for ever.

The War Lord

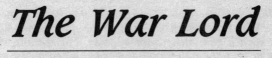

"While being written, I considered this book to be the The War Lord; given the titles of the three books which preceded it, that made a lot of sense. For reasons which I've never fully understood, it was published by the original British publisher as The Warlord's Domain. DAW Books has now done me the courtesy of re-publishing it under its correct title."

For Diane,
This book,
This world,
And all the others.

With thanks to Liza Reeves and Jean Maund for a light hand with the blue pencil.

Preface

". . .thus it happened that LORDE ALDRIC bye his craft and witt did fall in with GOTH, he being Generall of ye Emperor hys Armies.

And being close to this Goth and aware of his counsells secret, ye LORDE did contryve to bee a partye most close unto a plot close-woven by that Generall: whereby he should maken endeavour to preserve and save from close confyne within ye Red Tower of Egisburg that most noble lady MAREVNA, Princess of ye Empyre and very sister unto ye Emperor, and soche dyverse others of her suite that were enprisoned there.

And by soche a deed should he, that most noble LORDE, and so also RYNERT-KING of Alba, be seen to shew their favour unto ye Emperor hys Party. And by soche favour should it be seen and discerned that all support should be ygranten unto ye party of Peaece, who desyred not conquest of other landes. And so it should be seen that those of the WAR-LORDES party had ne prospering of ye Empyre at their hearts, but myght and advancement only for themselves: there being no War, and so ne place ensetten among ye Great for those that did command it, they desyred naught save war against all and any whosomever it may be.

But whenafter ye Firedrake YMARETH had enacted most bravely in favour of LORDE ALDRIC, then he, being still deep within those landes of ye Empyre, was sore betrayed by one in whom he had most placed his trust . . ."

Ylver Vlethanek an-Caerdur
The Books of Years, Cerdor

Prologue

There was a pavement of white marble beneath him, treacherously slick under a covering of trampled, dirty snow, and the wind that slashed at his face and body was edged with such a cold as more fortunate men might only dream of.

Pain, and the gaudy spattering of blood across cracked milk-white marble. Snow falling, drifting, a white shroud across a leaden winter landscape. Out of that stillness, the sound of tears and a buzz of glutted flies. The smell of spice, and incense, and huge red roses. . . .

The marble paving-slabs where he knelt hurt his knees; he didn't know whether that came from the shattered stone or from the crushed and dented armor encasing his legs, and in any case such a small annoyance was entirely swallowed up in the thin, hot pain—both present and anticipated—of the dirk-point which pricked skin a finger's breadth below his breastbone.

"Heart-line," said the voice of Esshau the weapon-master in his ears. "Here, young sirs, in, upward and a half twist of your blade for a quick kill. Or for suicide." Esshau, a stocky, dark, sardonic Prytenek who had been his model and his hero for years, had never dignified the act of *tsepanak'ulleth* with its formal title. He had never called it other than what it was. Esshau had disapproved of waste, and had made that disapproval outspokenly plain. Only his talent with weapons, and in teaching their use had kept him employed at Dunrath. . . .

Why Esshau? He's been ashes ten years now . . . ?

Why not? You'll be joining him soon enough—though he'll not like the way you chose to do it.

Blood runneled between the crooked claws that had
been his fingers; he could see its vivid spots on the marble paving, and soaking into the snow. But for all there
was so much, he couldn't smell it. A deep breath drew
only the winter's chill into his lungs, and riding on it the
unseasonal scent of roses. With snow inches deep on the
ground, there should have been no such smell . . . yet it
was there, impossibly strong, incredibly sweet, a perfume
that made his senses swim like wine.

Issaqua. . . .

A rose as red as blood, thorned with demon fangs.
Hungry. Eager. Vengeful. . . . And waiting for its due
and proper gift of death.

O my lady, O my love. . . .

He dared not look at her, for fear that the sight of
her face would steal away the courage and the small
store of determination he had gathered together, to help
him . . . do what he was about to do. To give a gift
freely, rather than see it stolen. To die a willing victim,
in the full knowledge that with that death others would
have life.

He drove the *tsepan* home, and agony consumed him.

Liquid heat flooded his hand and wrist, making his palm
slippery, preventing him from giving that twist to the knife
which would speed him on his way. For a moment he
could taste his own blood rising in his throat. For a moment he could see her face, shock-white, appalled. *I love
you though I leave you, my sweet lady,* his look said; there
was neither time nor strength for the luxury of a spoken
word. *Think kindly of me now and then. . . .*

And he could see that other face, thin, fine-featured,
pale as the death that had refused to accept him; still
unable to believe, rejecting what he saw even at this
moment when denial and rejection lost their meaning.
That face, all the faces, all the world, slid sideways into
a black mouth that reeked of roses.

*Oh Lord God, why don't they prepare you for how
much a tsepan hurts . . . ?*

And then there were no more faces and no more
thoughts, but only fire and snow and blood and darkness,
and the darkness filled the world, and devoured him,
and he died. . . .

1

Go past the Mountain and through the valley, the old man had told them.

That much was easy. *En Kovhan*, the Mountain, was a huge and shadowy triangular bulk on their right side as they rode south. The sword-hand side, the old man had said. Aldric had thought his tone and choice of words were ominous then—and downright threatening now. Yet the country seemed soft, gentle, its contours smoothed by millennia of slow-turning seasons until it was very different from the harsh outlines of *Glas-elyu Menethen* in Alba. Very different indeed. Even now in the depths of winter an occasional patch of green still showed through the snow; none of those greens were the somber pine-dark of the Jevaiden, and he was thankful for that at least. Thankful that his memories were allowed to rest, this once.

Then Kyrin eased her gray gelding to a standstill and rose in her stirrups, looking swiftly from side to side, and all the old wariness came back to Aldric with a rush. He realized that his hand had closed on his sword-hilt with neither intention nor conscious command. It was enough to make a man embarrassed.

"It's beautiful," she said, turning after a moment to look at him for some sign of agreement. And that was all she said.

"Yes." He made himself say it, made himself relax, made his fingers unwind from Widowmaker's braided leather grip. Aldric grinned a sour little grin. *You're jumpy,* he thought, silently critical. But another, unbidden voice inside his head said, *and with good reason . . .*

They were in the valley now, with forested slopes rising steeply to either side—but Aldric was only too well aware that they weren't steep enough to inconvenience a mounted ambush, nor so thickly wooded that archers would be unable to shoot. He stared suspiciously at it, watching the evening drawing in, stretching out fingers of shadow from the deeper shadows underneath the trees.

"We're going to be late," said Kyrin. There was disapproval in her voice.

"But I sent a message. We're expected. And anyway, it's not my fault." That came out defensively, as a protest, no matter what he might have intended for it. "If we'd had a map . . ." He left the rest unfinished, knowing quite well that Kyrin would add whatever else she felt was necessary. He wasn't disappointed.

"If." She stared at him a moment, then shrugged. "Yes. Quite . . ."

To be called to conference at all during the holiday season was undesirable, and an imposition. To be called to conference at midnight, in winter, with snow on the ground, was little short of scandalous and scarcely to be borne. The Alban Crown Council assembled with poor grace in the corridors of the Hall of Kings, exchanging irritable mutters—and then were shocked even beyond scandal by the words of the very junior officer-of-Guards who appeared before them with discomfort written in large letters on his face.

"My apologies, my lords," he said, ducking a perfunctory bow toward them, "but you must leave your swords with me . . ."

There was silence for perhaps a minute, murmured disbelief for maybe as long; then noisy outrage. Never since the Clan Wars five hundred years before had any Alban royal councillor been asked to give up his blades before a meeting. The right to keep and bear arms in the king's presence was a privilege seldom granted, and one guarded most jealously by those who held it. To be requested, no matter how courteously—though flanked as he was by six fully armored troopers, the young officer's request was no more than a nicely-worded order—

to give up that privilege was tantamount to insult. Alban clan-lords were *not* insulted, even by their king; and that a king would dare the risks—which history had proven to be very real—of giving insult singly and collectively to so powerful a group of men suggested that the matter for council attention was far more delicate than they had been led to believe. The thought occurring simultaneously to several brought a sudden silence to the group.

Lord Dacurre moved first. Old, gruff and well-regarded, he knew that from the instant his age-mottled hand lifted toward his weapon-belt all eyes were on him. That wrinkled, sinewy talon paused for a moment near the hilts of *taipan* and *taiken* as he considered the implications of what he was about to do. Aymar Dacurre had been adviser to three kings in his long life, but a personal friend of only two. This present ruler, Rynert, seemed incapable of either engendering or returning warmth. But he was still the king. Dacurre looked at the other lords one by one, his gaze slow to move away from each face. Just as slowly he unhooked the longsword and its shorter twin from his belt, offering them both, sheathed and horizontal on open palms, to the young officer. "These blades," he said quietly, "are seven centuries old. Respect them as they deserve." Then, over-shoulder to his companions: "My lords, best do it. Then perhaps we'll find out *why.*"

They filed into the great vaulted hall, every man among them irritable and on edge. There was an uneasiness not merely about themselves and the situation, but about the very place in which they were to meet. Its echoing emptiness was not so well lit as was customary, most of the scant illumination coming from the great log fires which spat and crackled in the nine hearths lining the walls, and from the few oil-lamps set along the length of the table whose polished surface was the only bright thing in a hall over-full of shifting shadows. It was a long refectory table of dark, waxed oak, lined with chairs for the twenty-odd *kailinin-eir* and with long-stemmed cups and flagons of wine arrayed across its surface like soldiers on parade. Such furnishings were used for councils in the Drusalan Empire—but never in Alba, where men were presumed able to control their passions without the need to surrender their weapons, or to sit behind a table so that its timbers might serve to keep them from one another's throats. They stared at the offensive gleam of wood with expressions ranging from disdain to unconcealed outrage; it was just another facet of the evening's strangeness . . . and something more to be stored away in the memory of men to whom a reckoning would have to be made, sooner or later.

There was a clatter, loud in the angry silence, as a door was flung open and troopers of the Bodyguard marched in: two files of them, armed, and wearing full battle armor. Rynert the King walked between them to his seat at the head of the table; and he alone of all the high-born in the hall wore a sword. It was a *taipan,* with a faint curve to it which told of great age, and like the dirk beside it at his belt was unrelieved vermeil even to the metalwork of hilt and scabbard. Note was taken not merely of the weapon's presence, but of the color chosen for its mountings. Some of the lords who had been at Baelen Field recalled Kalarr cu Ruruc, and in that recollection found little of ease or comfort.

Rynert wasted no time on preamble; he laid both hands flat on the surface of the table and said simply, "Aldric Talvalin, my lords." And after that he said no more until someone—sitting quite still, he didn't even turn his head to see who spoke—made the necessary request for elaboration.

"What of him, my Lord King?"

"He must die."

Full night was upon them. There were stars overhead, clear and bright in a freezing cloudless sky, but there was no moon. In the starlight, Aldric could see the pale glimmer of Kyrin's face as she turned her head toward him, and the paler cloud of breath that she released in a little sigh of annoyance; but he couldn't see her eyes, and that was probably just as well. There would be accusation in them, and for all that their expression would probably be diluted by the sardonic humor he employed himself on far too many occasions, it was an expression which he didn't want to see at all.

"We're lost." The Valhollan accent made her words come out even flatter than such words usually would.

"We're close. I'll ask someone; they'll be bound to know—"

"—that we're lost . . . ?"

"No!"

"No?"

"No. And besides, we *are* expected."

"Oh, yes, of course. I was forgetting. But I'd feel better about it if you weren't trying so hard to convince me of it. And yourself. But all right—ask. Someone. Anyone. If you can find them awake . . ."

There came at last a time, as the night dragged on, when Aldric's temper began to fray. Despite careful directions from a number of locals—some of whom he had plainly woken from a sound sleep—he was still no closer to finding the steading that he sought.

"If they're making game of me . . ." he muttered between his teeth.

"What if they are?" Kyrin, dozing in her saddle with one knee crooked around its pommel to keep herself from falling, yawned sleepily. "You're the foreigner here. *Inyen-hlensyarl.* Just as much as me, for once, and with as few rights. Maybe fewer. I'm not . . . not an enemy. But even so, I think they're being friendly enough, in a back-handed way."

"?" Aldric made an interrogative noise in the back of his throat that couldn't be dignified as a question.

"I think they don't want to disappoint you. They're telling you what you want to hear—directions to a hold— rather than what they know—which is that none of them have any idea of how to find it."

Aldric looked at her and through her, and this time it was as well *his* expression was hidden by the darkness. But the way in which he spat on to the ground was plain enough for them both.

A few uncomfortable minutes passed in a silence broken only by the slow tramp of weary horses. Then Kyrin coughed politely and pointed; Aldric knew about the pointing, because he could hear the rustle-and-creak of mail and leather as she stretched out her arm, and the glitter of stars reflecting off the metal.

"Now what?" he said, and for the first time in that too-long night, Kyrin heard real tiredness in his voice instead of the increasingly forced bright optimism which had annoyed her before she realized what it was.

"We're passing a gateway," she said, noting absently that her voice was as weary as his.

"Which we're already passed five times tonight, I think. In both directions. So?"

"Don't you think that maybe we should try asking there?"

"I've had enough of. . . ." Then he coughed, sounding just slightly apologetic. "All right. One more . . . just this one. And then I'm sleeping under a tree."

"Or a bush."

"Or the rock I feel as if I crawled from under. But I'm going to sleep somewhere . . ." and Kyrin actually heard him laugh.

The frozen pounded earth of the road gave way to a gravel track which crunched noisily beneath the hooves of pack- and riding-horses. The buildings to which it led were in darkness, without even a doorway lantern, and Aldric reined back uneasily. "I'm not sure about this," he said softly.

Kyrin could detect more than tiredness in his voice this time; there was an uncertainty and a tension which had come from nowhere, for no reason. Leather creaked faintly in the midnight stillness as he twisted in his high-peaked saddle, trying to see her face or maybe only read something encouraging from her half-seen outline. Other than a drift of breath, silver in the light of winter stars, he could see nothing. And she knew it. "Aldric . . . what's wrong? It's just a house like all the others . . . isn't it?"

"I . . . Yes. I think. But I've got—call it a feeling— about this one. There's something not right—as if we're being watched."

"Oh." The pause which followed went on too long. "Are you going to sit on that horse all night—or do you want *me* to hammer on the door?"

"Light of Heaven, no! I'll do it. You stay where you are. And be careful."

"Of what?"

Her question, or maybe his answer, was lost in the crisp double thud as Aldric's boots hit the gravel. He straightened his back, tugging at his furred and quilted clothing to neaten it—and to conceal the half-armor that he wore beneath—then walked to the door of the house and raised his gloved right hand to tap politely on the wood.

Polite or not, the knock never landed. The door jerked back from his descending knuckles, and the glare of a suddenly-unshuttered lantern made him flinch away, shielding eyes dilated by darkness from an amber-mottled purple glare that just now was all that he could see. Even then Aldric might have drawn blade on pure defensive reflex had it not been for the subliminal image which had scorched beyond even the lightborn blindness . . .

The image of a crossbow, leveled at his chest.

There was a cacophony of barking in his ears, and Kyrin's stifled cry of shock far out on the edges of the uproar. Then everything went quiet. Except for the sound of someone laughing . . .

Rynert's statement came out so flat, so unembellished by any intonation, that there were several at first who thought their ears had deceived them. Even when reaction manifested, it was muted by the shock of what they had just heard. If only by default, Lord Dacurre found himself the spokesman once again.

"Mathern-an . . ." Rynert favored him with the courtesy of a swift glance. "Lord King . . . *why?"*

"I am the King: I could say, because I command it." Rynert did not smile as he spoke, and it became starkly plain that there was no subtle joke in what he said. He leaned back a little, steepling his fingers together in the old gesture and studying his silent lords over their entwined tips. "But say rather: because his recent . . . activities . . . have brought us closer to war with the Drusalans than I care to contemplate; because he has

made more free with the Art Magic than any honorable
Alban lord has ever dared to do in all our history. And
because he has caused the death of my own Captain-
of-Guards."

That last stirred them more than anything else had
done, for those whose business kept them close to Cerdor
had noticed Dewan ar Korentin's absence this past
month and more; but had not—given the man's rank
and position—cared to make more inquiries than the
listening to rumor would allow. Those rumors current
had told of a mission for the king; of secrecy; of importance both personal and political. They had told of
enough to discourage the asking of incautious questions.
But they had never told of anything like *this*.

"How . . . how did this happen?" No one councillor
seemed to have asked the question aloud, yet it was so
much to the forefront of every mind that it might well
have taken shape out of the air.

Rynert told them: of the simple task of carrying
friendship-messages which Aldric Talvalin had perverted
to suit his own designs; of his interference in Imperial
policy for as-yet-undisclosed purposes; of the killing of
two Drusalan Overlords at Seghar and the setting up another; of the constant thread of sorcery running through
every report about him; and now the apparent destruction of part of the Imperial city of Egisburg. It was this
which had cost ar Korentin his life: no accurate information had so far filtered through, but the rumors—oh,
there were always rumors—were concerned with the kid-
nap of an important personage under the guise of a rescue, the murder of a highly-placed political figure, and
it seemed now almost certain that in trying to restrain
further such excesses Dewan ar Korentin had met his
death.

Rynert deplored his own lack of foresight in allowing
that particular young lord to be his emissary to the Drusalans, for all Aldric's persuasiveness. He was to blame
for everything, since he should have realized at once that
it would have been tantamount to letting a wolf negoti-
ate with sheep. . . .

. . . And it proved the power of his impassioned rhetoric that not a single one of his Council saw a trace of

the ridiculous in the sprawling and traditionally inimical Drusalan Empire being described as helpless against one young man. Too many of them had memories of Aldric's single-minded pursuit of vengeance, and the blood retaking of his usurped ancestral fortress. Many of their relatives and friends had died in that short, savage campaign, and just for the present they forgot that more had been at stake—for themselves and for all Alba—than one man's personal satisfaction. The only thing they chose to remember, and of which Rynert chose to remind them, was who seemed to gain most profit at the end of it all. The same man who had then apparently washed his hands of his comrades' blood and gone about his own affairs.

Aldric opened his eyes a fraction and at the same time raised both his hands, open and palms outward, to the level of his ears. The laughter continued, breaking off only when a dog—how many dogs, for the love of Heaven?—growled again and was silenced with a sharp word of command.

He was beginning to see them now, through the dance of glowing streaks inside his eyes, and seeing them was not a comfort. Two leggy Drusalan guard hounds sat back on their tailless haunches and regarded him with fanged, tongue-lolling grins which had nothing humorous about them.

Aldric had met Drusalan hounds before; and the memory was not a pleasant one.

"All right," said a voice that was still thrumming with mirth, "I recognize you. Haranil-*arluth*'s youngest. Don't worry; this thing isn't even loaded."

The woman's hair had been steel-gray. It was silver-white now, gilded by the lamplight, and she was wearing a staid and all-enveloping sleeping gown rather than traveling furs and fine woolen broadcloth; but for all that Ivern Valeir looked very little different from the last time Aldric had seen her, in the courtyard of Dunrath when she and her husband had come to sell their fine horses to his father, six years and a lifetime ago.

Except perhaps for the guard hounds . . . and the crossbow.

He swallowed once or twice, trying to clear the constriction in his gullet which felt like his heart halfway between his mouth and its proper place, then endeavored without much success to fit a wan smile onto a face turned white as paper as he gave her the most courteous bow he could summon in the circumstances.

"You invited me, lady," he said, and for a wonder there was neither tremor, nor anger, nor accusation in his voice. "I sent a letter to your husband, asking that I might at last accept the hospitality you both offered, that time in Dunrath when my father paid you for the horses. Unless, of course, I've made a mistake?" That crossbow was still cradled in her arms and Aldric, ever prudent, did not for an instant believe what she had said about it.

"No mistake." She quirked an eyebrow at him. "You were invited, yes. Expected . . . well, call that one *yes* as well. But earlier." Ivern looked up at the sky and rather pointedly—thought Aldric and Kyrin both—at the post-midnight configurations of the stars that glittered there. "Much, much earlier."

"He—*we*—got lost." Kyrin's explanation did not please Aldric much, but he kept his mouth shut and let her talk. "We woke up most of the province trying to find you. And even then the finding was by accident . . ."

Ivern shifted the lamp and looked out into the darkness of her own courtyard. That smile was back on her face as she flicked an amused glance between Aldric and his lady. "Ah. So," she said, plainly trying not to laugh. "I *see* . . ." She probably did, at that; those eyes were like Kyrin's in their ability to look far and deep. "That sort of 'earlier' wasn't what I meant, my dear, although it's true enough. I meant years, not hours—before Ansel, my husband, died." She saw a muscle twitch in Aldric's face, and shrugged to dismiss the matter. "Oh, but that was years ago as well. Now, there are stables and a guest annex behind the house. Once you've settled your animals, come in. You'll have to chop some firewood for the stove, young man, but you look as if you'd be good at that. And then something warm to drink, and a talk, would do us *all* good. Although I think a good night's sleep right afterward would do you two most good of all. . . ."

*   *   *

"There you have it, gentlemen," Rynert said when the tangled, bloody tale was done. The outrage vanished from his voice like frost from glass, so that once again his words came out without inflection, expressing his preferences neither one way or the other. He sat still now, frighteningly so, as immobile as a corpse freshly dug to sit at the head of the table, and with eyes as blank, seeming neither to blink nor to breathe, as patient as a cat waiting at a mouse-hole. But waiting for what? Which of them was the mouse?

Except for the few who had met Aldric Talvalin face to face and refused to believe that the man they knew was capable of what they had been told, there was not one among the councillors who found his behavior other than appalling. High-clan-lords were accustomed to the wielding of power, and to utter ruthlessness if such was required; but—to those who were convinced—this was excessive. To the others it was simply stupid and that, rather than the shocking violence, made it unbelievable. A capability for ferocity, and for the foolishness of impulsive action—that was one thing. This was another. And they all found Rynert's reluctance to give them a lead . . . uncomfortable. Unnatural, and unlike him. Usually he would hint, if only by unconscious shifts of posture and expression, in which direction he hoped his council's vote would take. Not that such hints would have swayed their decision; this was Alba, not the Drusalan Empire, and clan-lords were followers of their own persuasions rather than another man's implicit—or indeed explicit—views. Yet Rynert's blank, uncaring face was so unlike the subtly mobile features which they thought they knew—especially after his first blunt declaration—that private speculation made them feel more uneasy than deliberate, diametric opposition to the king's openly stated, carefully reasoned command. And such a lack of interest as this, in so grave a matter as they had been told of, was most unsettling of all.

"Lord King." Hanar Santon rose and bowed. He was youngest of all the clan-lords present and most recent to his title, his father not half a year dead by formal suicide in the *tsepanak'ulleth* ritual. But he spoke no more than the brief formal salutation, for when he straightened from his bow it was to stare at eyes with no more life in them than wet pebbles, and the other, unsaid words congealed in his throat so that he fell silent.

Rynert gazed at him with a sere, level stare like that of a painted ikon. Lord Santon could have borne a shriveling glare of anger, outrage or condemnation, for that at least would have indicated some emotion. But this . . . was as if he did not even exist.

None of the others tried to speak after that. They were also feeling that their existence had been called into question. Had there been some sort of *feeling* up and down the Council table, one or other of the lords might have felt roused to put some question of his own— the question which had formed in every mind by now: *Why were we summoned here at all* . . . But without that feeling, that passion, that emotion—without *something*—it seemed better to them all that the oppressive silence remained unbroken.

"So." Soft-spoken though it was, Rynert's single syllable had all the impact of a stone dropped into a still pond. Though the king had not moved one iota from his straight-backed posture, there was as much power apparent to all as if he had sprung to his feet and struck the table with a clenched fist. His face, however, was calm.

And if that was *calm,* thought more than one of his lords, then *calm* is what we call a house with all its doors and windows boarded shut.

"If it is your desire, my lords," he continued in that placid voice so unlike his own, "then I give you an hour in which to consider. In private."

There was no mistaking his words and the small movement of his hands for other than a dismissal—and one which was welcomed by many. What seemed to be happening in King Rynert's mind was rapidly becoming both something his lords wanted no part of, and something they wished to discuss among themselves. They rose almost in unison, made their obeisance—and followed the King's Bodyguard out of the hall as quickly as their dignity allowed.

Rynert watched them go, sipping red wine from the

cup before him, then drained the cup at a single draught; and only when the door clicked shut behind the last did he release his held-in breath in a long, slow hiss through teeth that had involuntarily clenched shut. So tightly shut that as he became aware of the reaction and released the pressure, he knew that tomorrow his jaw muscles would ache.

"All alone at last."

The voice came from behind him and though Rynert had expected to hear it at some stage of the night, to have it come without warning from the shadows at his unguarded back was still enough to make him jump. He regained control of the reaction almost at once, and when he turned to face the darkness it was an unhurried, seemingly unworried movement. Even though his hand *was* on the hilt of his sword. . . .

"Where is the other this time?" the voice continued. "Your bodyguard?"

Rynert slid a chilly smile across his face and even as his facial muscles moved, could not have said how much of the coldness was for effect and how much was genuine. "I no longer need him."

"How nice for you." The *taulath* emerged—seemed almost to condense—from the shadows where he stood, dressed in a gray so dark that it was almost black and yet not so dark as to lend his shape a definite outline. Only his eyes were visible; his head was covered by a hood, his hands by gloves and his feet by soft boots that made them noiseless as the paws of a cat.

The Shadowthief held no weapon, and there were none sheathed or holstered anywhere in plain sight—but Rynert knew that this didn't mean the assassin was unarmed. Far from it. . . . The sinister presence was making his heart pound in his ears again, and though it shamed him there was sweat on his brow; he didn't betray its presence by wiping it off, and hoped that with the light at his back the telltale beads would be invisible.

"You came here at my bidding," the king snapped. "So be about your business."

"I came here at my choice," the *taulath* corrected, "and it is your business too, King of Alba." His tone was gently reproving, a deliberate reminder of what Rynert had chosen to forget. "So tell me, what *is* your business this time? Theft? Espionage? Another killing . . . ?"

There was a silence as the king stared at the mercenary assassin, angry—and yet in the circumstances unable to be properly outraged—that an honorless person would presume to guess his employer's intentions.

Rynert let it go no further than a glare, for if this *taulath* was the same one as he had dealt with before, any observation concerning honor or the lack of it would be returned with interest, and the discussion would degenerate into a nasty scene. As for the *taulath* himself, his eyes blinked mildly and his whole body posture radiated unconcern over what Rynert did or did not say and do.

"Yes." The king took his hand from his sword and sat down again, arrogantly, with his back to the hooded man. "Yes, indeed. Another killing. And no mistakes."

"Rynert, Rynert. . . ." The *taulath* padded around so that they were once again face to face, sat down on the corner of the table and nonchalantly swung one leg to and fro, seeming to admire the fit of boot and smoke-dark leggings. His voice and phrase of language were both excessively familiar. "Now really: were there any mistakes last time? Or the time before that?"

Another silence and a glare were Rynert's only replies.

"There. You see. So—who will it be?"

Rynert told him and gave—sketchily—the same reasons he had elaborated to the Council. The *taulath* whistled thinly, whether in feigned or genuine surprise, and didn't speak for several seconds.

"A friend, once," he said eventually.

"How so?" Rynert's question came back with an unmistakable snap to it.

"Simple." Behind the mask there had to be a chilly smile. "You're trying so hard to convince yourself that you're doing the right thing. Too hard."

"When I want your opinions . . ." Rynert began in a soft, dangerous voice, half out of his chair with one hand back on his sword-hilt. The sentence died there, for the *taulath* hadn't moved a muscle, was still sitting there, watching with a calm deliberation that was somehow more ominous than any matching move towards a weapon. As if he didn't care because he didn't need to care; as if he felt certain that he, alone and empty-handed, could take Rynert to pieces any time he chose.

"I offered none. Reasons concern neither me nor mine, except through idle curiosity. Very idle. What does concern me is the fee."

"As agreed."

"Listen to the man. That was agreed before I knew who—and how much—you need . . . ah . . . want him dead."

"What do you mean . . . ?"

"All your understated and yet so passionate concern for the honor of Alba, put in jeopardy by this one man; your fears for the political repercussions of his actions; and your outrage over his use of sorcery and the death of your Captain-of-Guards. Magnificent, Rynert—and meaningless. You forget, I think, our last discussion . . . and the last mission performed for you."

"That has nothing to do with what brings you here," snarled Rynert, slamming his fist against one arm of the chair.

Once again the *taulath*'s voice seemed to smile, although the eyes glittering through the slits in his mask were as cold and humorless as flint. "Let me refresh your failing memory. There was the matter of stealing certain things from the wizard, Talvalin's foster-father—things like that portrait. A simple enough matter, and reasonably inoffensive even if not quite the way to treat a guest in your house. But to give all that information to the Drusalan Secret Police . . ."

"What of it?"

The *taulath* shrugged. "Tell the truth, Rynert, if only to yourself. After what you did, no matter what high-sounding reasons you produce, once he learns of all this Aldric Talvalin will be . . . annoyed. And you're afraid that you know what form that annoyance might take. So you want him killed, before he considers doing it to you. And what's one over-mighty nobleman more or less?"

"And when do mercenaries take it upon themselves to advise a king?" asked Rynert, his voice dangerously devoid of tone.

"Consider it a part of the service. Now, about the fee. Twenty thousand marks, in the usual division: half now and half on proof of completion."

"You're joking!" Even as he uttered the protest, Rynert knew well enough that the *taulath* meant what he had said. Just as Rynert knew that he would pay it. It angered him that a mere hired killer should have given so precise a summation of the truth, and caused him to wonder if any of the councillors had made a similar judgment. If they had. . . . He crushed that line of thought into the back of his mind. Alban Crown Councillors were advisers to the king; but they were also noblemen in their own right and anything which impugned their dignity or honor was likely to be something they would regard as a personal insult. Deliberately or otherwise, Rynert had already offered enough veiled insults tonight for one more to be too many. His chest hurt, a grinding insistent ache that seemed always with him now, no matter what his personal physicians did.

The *taulath* was gazing equably at him when his thoughts came back to the here-and-now. As equably as the blank-masked face permitted, anyway, and with an air of smug satisfaction that neither the mask nor the featureless dark clothing could conceal. "And don't tell me that you've come here without the money, my Lord King; you've never done so before." He slid soundlessly from the table, all business now. "Talvalin. Where can I find him?"

"I . . . don't know."

The *taulath* stared at him, not believing his ears. "If I had known what you were going to say, Lord King, the price would have been far higher still." Then, gathering himself together somewhat: "But you must have some intimation of his last whereabouts, surely?"

"The Drusalan Empire . . . probably," Rynert smiled faintly, "as far from the city of Egisburg as he can get."

"He was involved in *that?*"

"He was directly responsible for it."

"Then small wonder you want him out of the way. If he'll do that to his enemies, who knows what he might do to an ex-friend . . ."

"I told you before—"

"—And I decided not to listen. Oh, I and my people can find him for you, King Rynert—and kill him for you, too—all for the price I asked before I found out how much work was involved. But I'll expect some small favors afterward. Nothing costly; just immunities and pardons. As many as needed, and as often as needed."

"Feel free to leave now."

"Haven't you forgotten something?"

Rynert looked at the dark silhouette, thinking how utterly inhuman it looked, and reached inside his tunic. The *taulath* tensed, relaxing only when Rynert's hand came out holding nothing more aggressive than a roll of treasury scrip. He looked at the sheets of paper as if they were poisonous, then peeled off ten and flipped them disdainfully toward the assassin, with exactly the same gesture as a man might make when flicking something foul off his fingertips.

"These are good?" the *taulath* said, looking at where the scrip-sheets lay at his feet and as yet making no move to pick them up. "You know I prefer coin."

"And I prefer what I prefer. Take them or leave them."

The assassin took them; but lifted each sheet from the floor with such elegance that whatever loss of dignity Rynert had intended was quite absent. "They had best be good, Lord King; I'm not beyond going to work on my own account."

"Get out," said Rynert. The *taulath* watched him for a moment, not moving, then began slowly backing toward whichever window or unguarded door he had used to get in. When the man paused, evidently on the point of yet another dry little observation, Rynert's patience snapped. "Get away from me!" he screamed, springing from his chair and drawing his sword with a rage-born speed and energy he hadn't known that he still possessed.

And on the instant of his scream, the doors burst open and Rynert's guards came running in. Hard on their heels were the noblemen of the Alban Crown Council, all now armed with their newly-recovered swords. Still crouched in a fighting posture that was made foolish by his wide eyes and shock-gaping mouth, Rynert stared at them only to find that none of them were staring back at him but rather at the place behind him where he had last seen the *taulath*. There was a soft laugh from the mercenary, still in plain view for just that instant too many, then silence as he took his leave as quickly and quietly as he had arrived.

"Rynert." Hanar Santon spoke it: just the name and nothing else. He was looking now at the roll of treasury scrip still resting on the arm of Rynert's chair, and had plainly drawn his own conclusions from all that he had seen.

The king colored and his hands clenched into fists. "I have a title, my lord," he said.

"No, not now." Santon shook his head; it was less a negatory gesture than that of a man trying to clear his mind of confusion. "My father took his own life because he felt that he had failed you, yet you repay his memory with this. You have no title, Rynert; you've forfeited that. And duty, and respect, and honor. I defy you, man. I offer you defiance and I challenge you to change my views."

In the dreadful stillness they could all hear how harsh and rapid Rynert's breathing had become. The quick flush of rage had drained out of his face and left it white as bone. "What about the rest of you?" he asked at last.

Heads turned imperceptibly toward the man whose seniority of age, rank and respect made him their chosen spokesman. Lord Dacurre looked at them all, then walked to the King's Chair and leafed through the roll of scrip-sheets. They fell through his fingers to the floor like leaves in autumn. "Lord Santon speaks for us all," the old man said. "You must give an explanation, or—" Dacurre drew the sheathed *tsepan* from his belt and looked at it for a moment before setting it down on the chair's cushion, "—do as Endwar Santon did. The choice is yours, Rynert *an-Kerochan.*"

Rynert the Crooked. No one had called him that in twenty years, and right now it was a name which referred to more than just his twisted body. The king began to tremble; his heart was kicking inside the cage of his ribs like something frantic to be free. Black and crimson spots dancing across his vision all but hid his treacherous, self-seeking councillors from sight, and a stabbing pain was running like hot lead down his left arm. Rynert swayed, then caught his balance with an effort.

"I choose death," he said, steadily and with all the dignity that he could summon. He took a single step forward and the hall reeled about him as agony exploded in his chest. Rynert's sword clattered on the tiles as he dropped it to clutch at the left wrist of an arm that felt on fire. Sweat filmed his pallid skin as he clenched his teeth to hold back a cry that was more shock and outrage than pain. His physicians had first warned him of this long ago, and many times since then; a warning he had ignored, like so much else over the years. A warning he had no more cause to heed . . . not now.

The pain faded, not vanishing but gathering for a fresh assault, and all of Rynert's world narrowed to a single point of focus: Lord Santon's face. It wasn't smiling, or gloating, or satisfied; that he could have accepted and understood. Instead its expression was one of pity and regret, that the illusion of what Hanar Santon had thought his king had been, the lord to whom he had given his duty and respect, should prove to be frail flesh prone to failings after all.

Rynert did not want pity and suddenly hated Santon for daring to consider it. Releasing his throbbing arm, the king bent low and grabbed for his fallen sword, gripped its hilt and cut savagely at the young lord's face. Cut at the expression of pity, to cleave it off.

Santon reacted to the attack as he would to any such, instantly and without conscious thought. He drew his own *taiken* from its scabbard and straight into a simple parry that deflected Rynert's blow—and continued through to a cut of his own. . . .

Rynert's sword-point lowered, relaxing; then his fingers slackened their grip and the blade fell chiming to the floor again as both hands pressed against his belly and the long straight slash now crossing it from one hip to the other. Everything was suddenly so still that it seemed the very night noises had paused to listen. "That was stupid," he said after a moment, although no one could be sure if he meant his own or Santon's thoughtless actions. Blood ran through his fingers and made a glistening puddle on the floor.

Rynert stared at it and then sat down, heavily and uncoordinated, on the steps of his throne, looking at each of his councillors in turn through eyes that were already glazing. "Who will stop the *taulath* now, my lords?" Rynert said, and smiled a horrid smile that let blood dribble from his mouth to make a dark red beard across his chin. "If anybody even wants to. There are the Talvalin lands, after all; among the richest holdings in all Alba . . ." He laughed, a sound like a wet cough. "Protest what you will to each other, gentlemen, but don't trouble me, I pray you. Unless I misread you all most gravely, I leave this land the gift of such war as it has not known for half a thousand years. Make me a liar . . . if you can." Again he smiled and again blood leaked between his teeth. "Now leave. I'm dying and I'd as soon do it in private."

Nobody moved. They stood in silence, watching him.

Rynert watched them in his turn for a few moments with a faint look of amusement on his bloodied face. "I did what I did because I was afraid to die," he said finally. "I'm not afraid anymore. You can only fear what you have a chance to escape. My choice . . ." The mocking humor drained from his face as the last blood and the last remnant of life drained from his body, and King Rynert of Alba fell sideways and was dead.

There was a funereal stillness in the shadowy hall as the lords of Alba's Crown Council stared furtively at one another and at the corpse huddled on the floor, and then there were footsteps as someone at the back of the group turned and walked swiftly away. None of the others looked to see who it was; that would have meant admitting too much, both to themselves and to their erstwhile colleagues: that each man among them also wanted to leave and be about his own suddenly urgent affairs, and that each among them wished that he had been first out of this room with its abattoir smell and its cloud of unspoken accusations.

One by one they left, treading softly for respect or caution, or with the slapping footfalls of those who didn't care what the others thought. At last there was only young Lord Santon and old Lord Dacurre, standing on either side of the blood and the body, one with a sword in his hand and the other with something close to regret on his face.

Dacurre looked at the blade with its smeared stain and shook his head. "He was dying before you hit him," the old man said.

"What do you mean? How do you know?" Santon blurted out the questions, not wanting some sort of worthless comfort just because Dacurre had been his father's friend.

"Rynert was never a strong man. Some illness in his childhood . . . His heart tore in his chest, from rage, or fear, or shock, or a score of other things, I knew it when I saw it in his face. I've seen it happen before; it might well happen to me, now that I'm old. But that," he indicated Santon's *taiken,* "didn't kill him. It just made matters quicker."

"And harder to prove."

"To the others, maybe. Not to me." Dacurre looked up and down the hall, found it empty even of guards and muttered something savage under his breath. "Gone to grab what they can. Bastards!" Then he cleared his throat in irritation at himself. "I'm sorry, boy. Forget I said that. It's their prerogative, when the king dies . . . unexpectedly. Whoever follows might not care to employ them again, so they have to make the best of it . . . Tradition."

Santon looked at him blankly, not really understanding.

"Clean your sword and sheathe it," Dacurre told him, suddenly brisk. "We've got things to do."

"What?" Then understanding dawned. "Oh. Him. Why?"

"Because . . . Because he was the king once, and because he's dead now, and because there's nobody else. Just us. No matter what he was or did, he's entitled to the decencies at least. So straighten his limbs and close his eyes, and find something to clean his face."

The old man bent over the body of his king and tugged at the dead weight with both hands, then swore disgustedly as the corpse made a sound that was half-belch and half-groan; a smell that was a mingling of blood and wine pricked at the air and Hanar Santon jerked two steps backward, whimpering and jamming his knuckles against his teeth. "Come along, help me here!" Dacurre snapped, and then saw how the color had leached from the younger man's face. "Oh, he's dead all right. I just moved him wrongly—squashed out whatever air was left inside him . . . which I wouldn't have done if you'd given me some help. . . ."

Santon shivered, finding himself still unaccustomed to sudden death and the aftermath of slaughter. He had not witnessed his father's formal suicide, and the other two people whose deaths he had attended had taken their leave of life peacefully and in bed. "Will there . . . will there be a war?" he asked, trying to concentrate on something—*anything*—else.

"Eh?" Dacurre rubbed his hands together in a useless attempt to get the blood off them. "I don't know; I truly don't. And to be honest with you, my young Lord Santon, I don't much care. Though I suspect we'll find out. Lift him. Carefully now—I said *carefully!* You opened him up, don't finish it by spilling him all over the floor."

Santon's mouth quirked with nausea at the prospect and he looked away from the gaping wound. Nobody had ever warned him that the culmination of his *taiken* training would result in this. A decorous smear of red, perhaps, but not . . . He shuddered. "What—what about Aldric Talvalin then? And the *taulath?* I mean, with the king dead . . ."

"I don't know how to contact assassins or call them off. Or where to find Talvalin."

"So what will happen?"

Dacurre shrugged as best he could and gestured with a jerk of his chin at the body they both carried. "Something like this, I fancy. Except that I can't guess who it will be. Come on, boy, hurry it up. Dammit, these were my best formal robes once and it feels as if he's leaking again. . . ."

2

The angled shafts of sunlight were golden with suspended dust, but he couldn't see . . .

The warm air was heavy with the scent of mint and roses, but he couldn't breathe . . .

He was trying to break free, but something far, far stronger than himself was holding him down so that he couldn't move . . .

"Aldric . . . *Aldric* . . . *!*"

And there was waking, and sanity; awareness that he was no longer alone, no longer helpless. Awareness that . . .

"It was only a dream, dear heart. Only a dream."

Aldric stared at the fluttering, new-lit candle flame and watched his own limbs as a shudder racked through him. The flame's reflection gleamed back at him from skin entirely sheathed in clammy sweat. The sweat that comes with fear. "A dream . . . ?" he echoed, ashamed of the tremor in his voice, and took three slow, deep breaths to calm himself, making them last so that he wouldn't have to think of anything else for a while.

"I didn't think it was the kind of dream you'd want to continue. By the look of you I was right." There was concern in Kyrin's voice and in her eyes. Concern for more than just her lover scared awake in the night by a bad dream; because both of them knew that Aldric's dreams had an ugly habit of coming true. She had lived through the last part of one nightmare already and had no wish to see another.

Aldric looked at her and recognized the source of her worries. He dragged an uneven smile from somewhere and plastered it across a mouth which didn't want to wear it just now. "You were right. Oh, how very right . . ."

Kyrin was watching him, waiting for whatever he was going to tell her—if he was going to tell her anything at all. There was a cup of watered wine in her hand, and Aldric reached out for it with a hand far steadier than it had any right to be.

"I must have been tangled in the bedclothes," he said and took a long drink, staring over the rim of the cup at the sheets twisted like ropes around his legs. "They were holding me down . . ."

This most private nightmare Kyrin knew already. She alone. He had told her of it a long time ago because he had known, somehow, that she would listen and more, that she would understand. Only someone he loved and who loved him in their turn *could* understand.

When he had been *aypan-kailin,* a teenaged warrior cadet, sex to Aldric and the others of his age was an occasional experiment between the very closest friends, another facet of a complex adolescence in the near-monastic environment of training barracks. Like the other small and private pleasures of which the training and the tutors had no part, it was one with sharing secrets, sharing a purloined bottle and sharing the same miseries as the rough wine wreaked its revenge . . . Until one hot afternoon in the deserted tack-room of Dunrath's old stables when all of that had changed. That was when Aldric, aged sixteen and cleaning harness during a solitary punishment detention, learned the meaning and the pain of rape from the prefect who was supposedly supervising him.

From that time forward there had been no real friends, only "acquaintances" distanced by distrust. There had never been anything approaching love for other than family, who saw nothing more than a quiet, introspective younger son growing even more withdrawn and silent, and sometimes there had been no love even for himself. Not long after the rape he had gone out quietly into a cloudless night and made an oath to the watching stars—and to the One who watched beyond them—that he would never hurt anyone as he had been hurt.

And four years afterward, it no longer mattered anyway. That was when Duergar Vathach's murderous plotting on behalf of the Drusalan Empire had turned his whole world upside down, and his family were gone, and he was first a landless wanderer and then a wizard's fosterling, and the vengeful nature he had fought so hard to keep in check became instead something to encourage. Not merely a spasm of ferocity that was an attempt to make himself feel clean and regain a little of his self-respect, but something to be nurtured as an honorable obligation in a killing matter. They were all of them, all killing matters nowadays . . .

"What have you to say for yourself, *Hautheisart* Voord?"

Etzel, Grand Warlord of the Drusalan Empire, erstwhile paramount commander of half her armies and—until Emperor Ioen had shown himself capable of independent thought—power behind the throne, spoke softly, but his eyes and his face betrayed the anger that his words did not.

"*Woydach,* I did all that you asked of me. I did my best."

"In the past, *hautheisart,* your best has been a deal better than it was this time. Indulge me. Explain in your own words exactly what went wrong."

"The long version, *Woydach,* or the short?"

"Try the short. Save the long for later . . . when I decide if you have a later."

Voord's head jerked up sharply at that, and he stared first at Etzel and then at the two armored guardsmen who flanked the Grand Warlord's chair. It was a high-backed, wide-armed seat, that chair, not a throne for the only reason that no one had yet applied the word to it, and it was set on a raised dais of four steps so that Etzel could look down on whoever was standing in the main body of his audience chamber—or sitting round-shouldered on an uncushioned, uncomfortable wooden stool with his hands clasped between his knees as Voord was doing. There was enough room behind and to either side of the chair for maybe ten guards; that there were only two now was more an expression of Etzel's contempt for the man on the stool than for any more practical reason, even though the pair who remained were among the dozen or so in the Bodyguard who had been invariably seen in Etzel's presence for the past three years. They were his sword and his shield, one to protect him and the other to ensure that those he commanded to die did so without delay.

Voord looked at one and then at the other, at the armor they wore and the weapons they carried, but could see nothing of the faces shadowed by the nasal, peak and cheek-guards of their black and silver helmets. Neither moved to return his scrutiny or even to acknowledge his existence, but stood instead like carven images of war. *And the death war brings.*

"You read my written report, *Woydach.* It was Aldric Talvalin—the one who was the hinge of this stratagem. He was the cause of my . . . my lack of success. His actions were not those anticipated, and consequently the possibility of his behavior was not included in our planning. He—"

"He acted in a fashion you at least might have expected, Voord," Etzel interrupted. "Had you thought about it, which from all the evidence gathered here," he laid the flat of his hand on a thick dossier resting across his knees, "you did not. Careless. Foolish. And potentially ruinous. I dislike having ostensibly secret plans made public, especially when that public includes my enem—, ah . . . political opponents."

"It won't happen again." Voord's voice was still calm and he spoke as though stating an incontrovertible fact rather than the clichéd feeble excuse he himself had heard—and ignored—on so many occasions. "You know me too well." He stared again at the shadowed faces of the guards. "All of you . . ."

"I know you very well indeed," said Etzel, "just as you know me. And you are no longer of much use, Lord-Commander Voord, having lost your place of rank in the Emperor's Secret Police." No threat, not even the delicate threading of menace through the words—just a pronouncement, like that of laws, or policies, or sentences of death. "Deputy to Bruda himself, sir! Do you know how many years, how much gold, how many lesser spies were sacrificed to make you secure in such a position, to make you trusted, to make you privy to the secrets that might be of use to me? I doubt it!"

"Ah, but I did." His pride dented now, Voord straightened his back, planted fists on hips and glared, no longer looking so much like a schoolboy being chastised. "And I worked long hard hours on my own studies, to make all the efforts of others that much more worthwhile." *Platitudes,* said his mind. *Why bother?*

"Yes. Your studies . . . I know about them. Less than I might do, but more than I want."

"You yourself gave me permission—"

"And you overstepped the bounds of that permission. You overstepped so very many things, Voord, that I am at a loss where to begin."

"Try," said Voord.

The *Woydach* looked at him strangely, for his tone was not that of a man with any great concern in his mind. "As you wish. Show him." Etzel made a peremptory gesture with one finger.

His left-hand-side guard stepped down from the dais and crossed to the three canvas-sheeted bundles lying by the wall, bundles which Voord had been carefully refusing to notice since he had first been summoned into the audience chamber a full half-hour past. He was noticing now; indeed, he was staring most intently both at the soldier and at what he had been sent to uncover.

"Proceed," said Etzel. The guard stripped back the first sheet with a flourish and stepped to one side, folding it neatly as he went.

"Books?" said Voord, pushing an edge of scorn into his voice. "You're taking me to task over books? I had thought I deserved better treatment than that!"

"And I had thought, *Hautheisart* Voord, that you were possessed of more intelligence than to meddle with such books as these! Shall I list them?"

"No need; I know their names well enough myself." He did indeed: there was a small fortune's worth of rare volumes strewn every which way across the floor, and their subject matter broke enough of the Empire's stringent sorcery laws to gain him a death sentence twenty times over. Except, of course, that he had been granted

official license to study the Art Magic without penalty,
let or hindrance. Until now, apparently.

"You know the statutes concerning magic as well as
any, Voord," said Etzel softly.

"I was given immunity from the law."

"Show me."

Voord began to say something, then decided not to
waste his breath and showed his teeth instead. There
was nothing else to show. All of the agreements and
arrangements had been made verbally, and he cursed
himself for a fool that he hadn't seen where such an
oversight could lead. "I haven't any written papers," he
said finally, "as you well know. Congratulations on a
well-laid plan, *Woydach*. What now?"

"You're a dangerous liability, Voord. You always
were, but until now you always had a degree of usefulness to offset it."

"Not any more, eh?" said Voord, angry and at the
same time far too cheerful for a man in his position. "So
you're going to dispose of me and pretend I never even
existed. All because of a few books. I'd have expected
more from you, Etzel; I really would."

"If you want more, *hautheisart*, I can show you more.
A great deal more." The soldier who had uncovered the
books turned his head, anticipating the command that
was no more than a gesture of a crooked finger, and
uncovered the other two bundles on the floor.

The things within the bundles were still recognizable as
human, but after what had been done to them, only in
the same way that a roasted fowl can be recognized as a
bird—and for exactly the same reason. It explained the
faint savory smell which had been prickling at Voord's
nostrils since he entered the audience chamber. But it did
not appall him as it did the Warlord Etzel. For all that he
had not expected to see them here, Voord knew who as
well as what he was looking at; they had been beggars,
grubby street urchins whom nobody would miss, taken
and prepared as sacrifices—or would have been, had Etzel
not gone prying into matters that were not his concern.

Voord smiled thinly at the Warlord. "Dinner?" he
said. "Surely not without a table?"

Etzel looked at him as he might have stared at some

vermin which had pushed out of the dirt beneath his feet. "You are a foul creature, Voord," he said, "and my only lack of understanding is in why I failed to see it years ago."

"Perhaps because it was more useful to be blind. And I defy you to deny that I was useful. I did as you bade me do, my lord, by whatever means were in my power to offer to your service; it is no fault of mine that you do not have Alba in your grasp, or Vreijaur, or Marevna the sister of the Emperor. I did as I was able to do, and was crippled for my pains!" He held up the wretched twisted talon which was all that remained of his left hand, flexing what little movement it still had so that the dry skin and the crippled sinews made an audible, anguished creak.

Etzel's shudder was plainly visible. He refused to look at the two cooked corpses that he himself had commanded brought here, and seemed reluctant even to look full at Voord. "Just tell me one thing," he said. "Why this?"

"It was necessary. Required. It was," Voord waved at the heap of books, "written . . . there. I obeyed the writing."

"You're good at obeying orders, aren't you?" said Etzel.

"It was part of my training."

"I see. Then I order you to die. You're a dirty creature, *Hautheisart* Voord, and the Empire which I plan to build will be a better place without you."

Voord looked from one guard to the other, unperturbed. "Another bloody empire-builder," he said quietly, as if to himself. "Soon this Empire will be so full of them that there'll be no room for ordinary people."

Etzel ignored him. "My guards will help you on your way. Goodbye, *hautheisart*. Give my regards to whatever foulness pays you heed."

"Do it yourself, *Woydach*."

"Even in the face of death you keep your insolence. Voord, in another, better life you would have been a fine soldier. You two." The blank, armored faces of Etzel's guards swiveled fractionally, like automata, to regard the man who gave their orders. "Kill him. Here and now."

*   *   *

"Killing matters?" said Kyrin. "You never really need to find a reason. Not from what I've seen."

She was sitting at the foot of the bed, pouring wine by candlelight, and Aldric smiled faintly at the domesticity of it all. If he never truly had a reason before, he most certainly had one now, more even than the requirements of honor. A worthwhile reason. The defense of his lady, as the old songs said—the lady he wanted as his wife.

And then she turned and looked straight at him, and her hand came up in a warding gesture. "Don't say it, Aldric. Don't even try. We had this discussion before, remember?"

"Yes, I remember. That first night, in Erdhaven. But we didn't finish it—at least, not to my satisfaction. And everything that happened between then and now. You left me—but then you came back. That tells me enough. We should finish with all this nonsense, all this running about doing the king's bidding, for God knows he owes me peace and more after what I've done for him this past few months!"

"When we go to Drakkesborg—" Kyrin began to say. Aldric looked at her, then raised one eyebrow.

"What gave you the idea that anyone was going anywhere?"

"You did. It's not the king's bidding anymore, is it?"

"Gemmel-*altrou* is my father, and I have duties and obligations to discharge. Stealing back the Warlord's Jewel for him is—"

"He set a spell of compulsion in your brain, man! To *make* you do it."

"And he took it back. This is my decision, nobody else's. Kyrin, I owe him my life!"

"So you're going to Drakkesborg to look for some blasted jewel that *might* help the old man to go home—wherever home for that one is—even if it might get you killed."

"Yes. But might, not will. The Warlord Etzel doesn't know me, and—"

"I'm coming with you, if it's as safe as all that. We

took our last leave from one another like . . . like a claw from flesh. We won't be parted again."

Aldric, sitting cross-legged, bowed slightly. "Lady," he said very, very softly, "I love you. When you went away, I missed you so very much." He looked at the candle's spike of flame as though he was watching something through a window, then back at Kyrin. "You make me whole, *Tehal'eiyya* Kyrin, my lady, my loved. But understand this. What I'm doing *is* dangerous; it scares me. I would as soon not be afraid for you as well."

Kyrin watched him silently, neither talking nor needing to talk; just looking—at his face, at his eyes, and at what she had seen in them during the quiet times when they lay in one another's arms and looked at each other, as lovers were allowed to do. She had seen then what she was seeing now: the complexities of much troubled thought; an innocence that had never truly left him, despite all that had befallen, despite the mask of weary cynicism that he hid behind; the echo of a loneliness that was all but gone; and the joy when he looked straight at her with that expression in his eyes. Kyrin met that intensity once again, a glowing warmth like the gaze of Ymareth the Dragon, and wondered as she did so—just a little—how darkness could be so bright.

"No. My lady, I want. . . . To turn, and see you. To listen, and hear you. To reach out, and feel your hand in mine. I need you—as I need sunshine, or fire in winter. As I need food, and air. And honor. . . . But wants and needs have to be set aside sometimes and this is one of those times."

Kyrin's slender fingers closed around Aldric's outstretched hand, squeezing hard. "I need you as much as you need me. My good lord and my own beloved, however could I not? When you go through the gates of Drakkesborg to . . ."—she hesitated a little, then made a sound that might have been an unborn laugh—"to be so damned honorable again . . . I'll be with you. You go—and we both go."

Aldric just stared at her, then raised her hand to brush against his lips. "I could almost pity the Drusalan Empire."

Kyrin's fingertips traced the scar running along his cheekbone. "Be more specific: pity the Grand Warlord. I suspect that he'll need all the pity he can get."

The left-hand soldier drew his shortsword and took a pace forward, and the right-hand soldier followed suit—then leaned across the still seated Grand Warlord to stab a handspan of steel into his erstwhile companion's neck, so that the man collapsed with a clatter of armor and a spurting of blood to die on the steps at Etzel's feet.

Voord smiled, a minute quirk of his thin mouth which betrayed as much relief as anything else. He looked weary and a little sick, as any man might who had faced the imminence of his own death so early in the morning and seen it set aside. "Command them again, *Woydach*," he suggested. "Maybe they didn't hear you the first time?"

The Grand Warlord said nothing, but as a horrid suspicion formed in his mind so tiny beads of icy sweat formed on his upper lip. "How long?" he asked, surprised by the calmness of his own voice.

"Hault, it's been four years in the Bodyguard for you, yes?"

"Nearer five in the regiment, lord," said the soldier. "And three of those in the Warlord's personal guard."

"I have always believed in advance planning, *Woydach*," said Voord quietly, "especially when I could never be sure that you might find my past usefulness an embarrassment and myself someone to be rid of in haste and without ceremony. Thus . . . Directly I gained a little power and influence, I prepared this . . . ah . . . insurance against unforeseen events." He nudged the dead guard's fallen shortsword with the toe of his boot. "It seems to me that neither my time nor my money was wasted."

"So you knew all this time that you were safe?" Etzel's mouth curled into a sneer. "It explains your bravado rather better than the unlikely possibility of some real courage."

"Not that you'd believe me, or that I worry whether you do or not, but no—until Hault made his move I couldn't be certain that I was not alone. Not that I need be concerned one way or another . . . not any more. Hault, come here."

The soldier took the few steps necessary to reach his true commander's side and saluted Guards-fashion with a snap of the still-bloody shortsword across his chest that sent a nasty little spattering across the floor. "Sir?"

"Show him. Now."

"Sir!" Hault saluted again, then brought the sword down from the salute and straight out into a thrust. It went into Voord's flank in the soft place just under his ribcage, met nothing more resistant than internal organs and came out the other side as a repellent peak in the *hautheisart*'s tunic that tore just enough to let its point glitter briefly in the lamplight. Voord gasped and went more pallid even than his normal complexion; he gasped again as it was withdrawn, but not loudly enough to drown the sucking sound as entrails reluctantly released their grasp on steel.

There was no blood, and only two small rips in a previously undamaged military tunic betrayed that anything untoward had happened. "Uncomfortable to feel," said Voord, panting slightly, "and unsettling to watch, but having a tooth pulled is more painful."

"Father of Fires . . ." Etzel choked out the oath, then covered his mouth and gagged.

"That One has nothing to do with it!" snapped Voord, suddenly and unreasonably savage. "Or with me!" And then, more controlled and so softly that he might have been speaking to himself: "The Old Ones give me more than stories to believe, and my sacrifices in Their name reward me with more than the stink of burnt beef or the babbled second-hand benedictions of some disinterested priest . . ."

Woydach Etzel looked up at the windows of his private chamber and beyond them to the low, cool sun of winter noon. He knew that he was soon to die, and though the certainty of that knowledge took away his fear of death as he had seen it leave so many at the foot of the scaffold steps, what remained and was enhanced by his familiarity with Voord was a terror of the manner of his dying. And because of that, because nothing he might say now could make his situation worse or better, there were the questions that he wanted to ask no matter how useless their answers might now be. About belief in tales to frighten children, and Voord's strange, twisted fervor; about the why and the how of such sorceries as even the darkest of old stones only hinted at.

As Voord crossed to the books that were strewn across the floor and squatted down as though to begin putting them to rights, Etzel drew breath to ask the first of all his questions, but it caught in his throat when Voord turned to face him. He was holding one of the books, cradling its opened weight like a child in his arms while his mouth silently shaped words from its handwritten pages, and his speculative gaze at Etzel was that of a butcher sizing up a joint of meat. "Hault," he said without looking at the guard, "go outside. Let nobody in. Don't come back until I call you. Understood?"

"Understood, sir." There was something terrible about hearing Hault's relief at being sent away, and about the haste with which he left the room.

Etzel wanted to look after the soldier, to take this one last chance of escape as Hault went through the door and out into the world where none of this had happened and where he, Etzel, was still a man of power and influence, but he was unable to tear his eyes away from Voord's corpse-pale face. The *hautheisart* was muttering something in the hasty monotone of a priest hurrying through the familiar part of a boring litany, but Etzel could still make sense from the slipshod tumble of syllables and that sense turned his belly sick within him.

". . . call upon thee O my lord O my true lord O my most beloved lord O Granter of Secrets I pray thee and beseech thee hearken now unto thy true and faithful servant . . ."

The book was balanced on Voord's right forearm now, leaving his left hand free to creak dryly as he spread the remnants of its fingers, obscenely aping a priestly sign of benediction. ". . . O Dweller in the Pit Jeweled Serpent Flower of Darkness I give now unto thee this offering this blood-offering this life-offering O Lord Devourer . . ."

Voord's voice stumbled on the words of the invocation

and began a gasp he couldn't finish. Some Power beyond that of its withered sinews was straightening his hand, twisting it from the curled and broken claw it had become five months before into a poised fork of bone and leather, twisting it with such violence that it took away his breath and even his ability to scream.

It was Etzel who closed his eyes and screamed, but only very briefly and in a small, lost voice before the thing that had been Voord's hand reached out and pulled his face off.

Woydach Etzel, erstwhile Grand Warlord of the Drusalan Empire and would-be maker of emperors, was grateful for the shock that stopped his heart an instant later and permitted him to die. . . .

When Voord's nausea had faded, all that remained was the tremble of realization that his offered sacrifice had proven so acceptable that the Old Ones had used his hand to take it for themselves. Their gifted power of deathlessness was freshly renewed in his body, the corpse of an enemy lay at his feet and the insignia of still more power glittered about that corpse's neck.

En sh'Va t'Chaal was its formal name in the inventories of State Regalia; *t'Chaal,* the Jewel, so much a symbol of the Grand Warlord that it had been incorporated into the sigil and cresting of the rank. Voord stooped to fumble with the catch of Etzel's collar of office, undid the snap at last and lifted the Jewel from the puddle of blood and slime where it had lain . . .

Then swore at the sudden freezing chill of the thing, stabbing through his leather glove, and all but dropped it again. Glove or no glove, had the Jewel not been crusted almost an inch thick in frozen gore it would have taken the flesh off his hand. Voord's studies had taught him about many objects which radiated such appalling cold, but none of them were things that any Imperialrace Drusalan of the Central Provinces would wear openly around his neck. Cautiously he lifted it higher, and even the slight warmth from his exhaled breath was so different in temperature from the Jewel and its bloody casing that the crust shattered and fell away in tiny splinters of crimson ice. Small wonder that it was mounted in so elaborate a framing of gold filigree and fine velvet,

for no man born of woman could wear such a thing
against his skin. Looking at it more closely, and glad in
his heart of hearts to have something to distract him
from the sights and the smells that went with violent
death, Voord wondered from what mine the gem had
come and how in the name of the Dark it had *been*
mined.

It was rectangular, and small enough to rest comfortably in the palm of his hand had he been fool enough
to place it there; colorless in itself, but cored with green
and a delicate cobwebbing of gold that seemed to lead
out to the minute gold studs which crowded three of its
edges. Voord breathed on it again, watching as the warm
exhalation in that warm room became first cold-weather
mist and then a heavy downward roll of white smoke
that tinkled faintly with the ice-crystals in it. Whether it
was man-made or demon-made was of little consequence
to Voord right now. All that mattered to him was that
he was alive when he had expected to be dead, and that
the confirmation of his ultimate promotion dangled from
his fist.

Securing the collar around his neck was difficult with
only one usable hand—the left had retracted back into
the crippled talon to which he had grown accustomed—
but he managed the task at last. It was heavy, and for
all the filigree and velvet he could feel the coldness of
the Jewel seeping through into his flesh. Nor was the
Grand Warlord's seat as comfortable as he thought it
might have been, when he sat down in it and tried to
relax his nerves from the jangling tensions of the past
few minutes.

And now *he* was Grand Warlord. He had aspired to
the position for years, from the time when his first promotion had proved how one man might rise more
quickly than others equally capable if he was that much
more ruthless—and had the proper support. There would
be no questioning of his right, not once the soldiers of
the *Tlakh-Woydan* regiment had been thoroughly sweetened with gold. Apart from the occasions when they had
themselves seen fit to take a hand, the Bodyguard had
shown small interest in who—or what—carried the title
of Grand Warlord. Just so long as they were accorded

the respect, the privileges and the high pay they regarded as their due, the regiment had as little interest in the political machinations of those who struggled for places at the top of the heap as they would have in the squirmings of a bucketful of crabs.

The air in the chamber stank of blood and sweat and he looked at the mess of death—shivered slightly, wondering: *Was it worth all this?*

The unaccustomed self-doubt startled him. Of course it was. A little killing, something to which he was more than accustomed, and let him become the most powerful man in the Empire, stronger than Lord General Goth and his whelp of an Emperor, backed by elite military forces and by powers that no other man would dare to call upon or challenge.

The question now was, what to do with all this newfound power . . . ?

Voord looked around the room again and knew quite well what he was going to do with it, at least for the next few minutes. "Hault," he called, "get in here."

The soldier came in at once, so quickly that Voord might have suspected him of listening outside the door—except that Hault was beyond all such suspicion since the man would have listened as a matter of course, just as Voord would have done, and had done in similar circumstances. Information gleaned from the wrangling of senior officers could prove useful in all sorts of ways to an ambitious subordinate, and if there was one characteristic shared by the men of the Secret Police on either side of the Empire's political divide, it was ambition. Whoever they claimed to serve, the foremost was always themselves.

Hault would have been well aware that he had been sent away so that he could with perfect truth deny that he had witnessed murder done. He would have been expecting to see Etzel's body on the floor when he was summoned back, for a trooper serving with Lord-Commander Voord—or who was acquainted with any man who had—knew of the *hautheisart*'s predeliction for dreadful violence as the final solution to almost any problem. But from the expression on his face as he rolled the corpse over—an expression fortunately shad-

owed for the most part by the peak and cheek-plates of
his helmet—even he had not expected a response quite
so drastic as *this*. "At your command, sir," the soldier
said in a flat voice meant to conceal what he was
really thinking.

The attempt failed; Voord knew the men who served
him far too well for their collective peace of mind and
now was no exception. "Call some servants, have them
get this garbage out of my throne room, summon Tagen
and five men and take that bloody disapproving look off
your face *right now.*"

Hault flinched. That "my throne room" had not been
lost on him. For diplomacy's sake he went through the
full sequence of an Imperial parade salute and carefully
changed his acknowledgment of the order from "sir" to
Woydach. It seemed to Voord that the man was even
more grateful to be dismissed this time than before. The
notion brought a smile of sorts to the new Grand Warlord's thin lips that would have made Hault hurry even
faster to get out.

*No matter what they said about me then, they'll sing a
new song now. To a tune of my own choosing.* Voord
sat back in the uncomfortable chair, determining privately to have it replaced—or at least reupholstered—
and then closed his eyes and let his mind wander far
away from the here and the now.

They were pleasant memories, perhaps the only truly
innocent pleasure that he still possessed. Voord seldom
indulged in reminiscence; it was a sign of softness, of
weakness—and a waste of valuable time in so busy a life
as he lived now. But just once in a while he deliberately
let the defenses slip, to try to remember how things used
to be. The trying had slowly grown more difficult over
the past year, almost as if those few pleasant recollec-
tions were being rubbed off the slate of his memory.
Maybe the things that he had heard said behind his back
when the speakers thought him out of earshot held more
accurate observation than the veiled insults or crude
jests they seemed. Perhaps he was going mad after all,
losing his mind a piece at a time. It had never been like

this before. . . . Before. Voord took care never to let that thought go any further.

He had been born not far from Drakkesborg, and on clear days the lowering citadel at the heart of the city had been visible on the horizon. His father Eban had served there, first as an ordinary soldier and then, with accumulated merits and good conduct awards, as a sergeant and an officer. One of the images that still remained, one of the very few that were as clear as the very first time, was that of *vosjh'* Eban sitting in the kitchen with his parade harness on the big table in front of him, encircled by the admiring audience of his family as he clipped the paired silver bars of *kortagor* rank in place for the first time. And that was as high as he had gone despite all the other merit marks that he gained in the rest of his career. A short career. Of the wife and four children who had watched him apply the shiny new insignia, not one could have dreamed that in ten more months their father would be dead of the lung fever contracted during urban patrol on a particularly cold, wet night. That he was buried with the partial military honors due an officer who died as a result of duty but not active service was small comfort. Nor was the meager pension due the dependents of an officer dying in such circumstances of any real use to a widow with a growing family. Voord—third child, only son and already listed for entry in the Service—had two long years before he entered barracks to wonder what a bowl of porridge would be like if he had salt and honey and milk to stir into it, enough to taste and even some to spill. Or to eat it only when he wanted to and not because that was all his mother could afford. What was most frightening was the way his mouth forgot the flavors of other food, even that of the thick, rich oatmeal of cold winter nights, and could remember only the dismal taste of the thin gruel. The hungry time had been Voord's first step toward acquiring high military rank, regardless of arm of service or specialization, just so long as its duties did not include late-night patrols in dirty weather. And even now, nine years later, he still loathed the taste of porridge plain and unadorned . . .

*   *   *

The servants who mopped blood from the tiled floor at
Voord's feet and carried out the slack-limbed corpses
were no strangers to the task, since Warlord Etzel and at
least two of his predecessors were accustomed to order
executions in the perfunctory manner of men swatting
flies, and have the killing done at once where they could
see it. They went about their business of swabbing and
lifting and dragging with lowered eyes, taking care not
to see things they were not expressly directed to see, not
even noticing that one of the bodies they took away was
that of Etzel. Any servant in the Warlord's citadel who
noticed such things out of turn was one who was soon
dragged away himself.

Lost in his own thoughts, Voord didn't even see them;
he noticed only that the floor became clean and the
room cleared of all unpleasantness except for his precious books. He looked down at the fat grimoire resting
now in his lap, and stroked it as another man might
stroke a cat. It and the others would soon be restored
to their locked cabinet, and the cabinet itself moved to
the *Woydach*'s luxurious living apartments. *Soon*—his
fingers caressed the sleek black leather of the grimoire's
cover—*very soon . . .*

"My lord?" Hault spoke from the door, reluctant to
come any closer to Voord than he had to. "My lord,
Kortagor Tagen is here."

Voord favored him with a sleepy, heavy-lidded look;
his lazy touching of the black book did not falter by so
much as a single stroke, and he seemed to gain some
sort of comfort from the contact. "Then send him in,
idiot!" he said. "You should know not to keep my close
friends waiting. And Hault . . . ?"

"My lord?"

"What else is on your mind?"

The soldier said nothing, but the corner of his mouth
quirked in a way that might have suggested either
amused surprise or startled apprehension. Had he been
standing closer Voord could have been sure, but the
muscle spasm had at least confirmed as correct what he
had heard in Hault's voice. Certainly it did his own reputation no harm at all . . .

"Yes. Something else. I can read you as easily as this book, friend Hault." His eyes opened a little wider and fixed Hault with an interested stare. "Probably more so. What goes on that I should know about?"

"You have a visitor, *Woydach.* Or rather, there's a man asking for *Eldheisart* Voord. I don't think anyone's corrected him so far, not until you give the word." Hault's bearded lips stretched into a kind of smile, a baring of teeth rather than anything much more humorous. "Though most of those who might tell are already wrong themselves. The news hasn't traveled yet."

"So. Then once I'm done with Tagen, send him in alone."

"He's alone already, lord."

"Ah. What kind of a man is he, then, this visitor looking for me at the rank I held six months ago? Old? Young? Rich? Poor . . . ? Describe him."

"Elderly, my lord—at least fifty years; comfortable, by his clothes. Comfortable, but not wealthy. He looks," said Hault disdainfully, "like a successful merchant."

"I grow intrigued. Go on, go on, let in *Kortagor* Tagen to see me and then bring in your comfortable merchant— but be sure to search him first. Just in case of accidents, eh?"

Hault gave Voord an odd look at that, not understanding such caution in a commander who had proved so graphically that he had nothing to fear from weapons. Watching him as he went through a salute before leaving the room, Voord could see the thoughts and questions chasing one another across the soldier's face. He grinned, quickly and privately, then wiped the expression from his face before anyone might see it and draw the wrong conclusion. No matter that steel could do him no permanent harm, its passage through his flesh still hurt more than he had been willing to show before witnesses, and he saw no reason to risk discomfort for the sake of such precautions as any high-ranked officer would be expected to take; and besides, the habits of the many years before the Gift were hard to break.

Tagen and his five troopers came to heel-stamping attention just inside the doorway and gave Voord the full salute due to his rank with all the precision and cere-

mony of the Bodyguard regiment to which they nomi-
nally belonged. Tagen looked much as the men and
women on Voord's personal staff always did; young,
broad-shouldered and handsome in *Tlakh-Woydan* half-
armor, with the wary eyes and expressionless faces of
those friends considered intimate enough to share in the
secrets of Voord Ebanesj.

He and Voord had been together since Officer-School;
the younger man had recognized even then—because
Voord had explained it to him—that he was in the company of a star determined to rise no matter who or what
was cremated in the process. Impressed, Tagen had remained with him, surviving where others had not during
a meteoric career which had been politically upward and
morally downward all the way. During those chaotic
years they had shared everything—food and wine and
women, bed and bloodshed, advantages and enemies.
Nowadays the advantages were many and the enemies
few—Voord's connections with *Kagh' Ernvakh* had seen
to that—but there were still some names remaining on
the list. In such killing matters Tagen had long since
abandoned the allocation of innocence or guilt. That was
Voord's affair; he just followed orders . . . except when
the matter became personal.

*"Tagen, sh'voda moy. Yar vajaal dath-Aalban'r Aldric
Talvalin?"* Tagen nodded. Of course he remembered.
"Inak dor Drakkesborg'cha. Slijei?"

Tagen's impassive face split in a broad grin. This was
one of the personal matters. Because of Aldric Talvalin,
he had been ordered to kill his very good friend Garet;
Commander Voord had given the command, so he had
done as he was told—but he hadn't enjoyed following
his orders as much as usual. Because of Aldric Talvalin,
he had been promoted only a single grade after the affair
at Egisburg, instead of the three grades he had been
promised; Commander Voord had been very sorry, but
of course Tagen had to understand that since he had
failed in his duty . . . Tagen understood very well. He
understood that he was being made a scapegoat for the
Alban and though he and Voord had made it up later—
because it hadn't been Voord's personal decision to re-

strict the promotion but just something which had to be
done—Tagen had put Aldric Talvalin at the top of his
own private list of names and faces. Work to do in his
spare time, so to speak. To discover that the Alban was
more than just his own concern, that Commander Voord
wanted him dealt with as well, and to be told of it in the
Vlechan dialect which they both shared was a delight.

"*Slij'hah, hautach!* His head only, or do you wish
other parts also?"

"No! No, Tagen. Understand me clearly. All of him . . .
and unharmed. To me, here in Drakkesborg. *Viaj-chu,
slijei?*"

Tagen was disappointed, and didn't trouble to keep
the emotion hidden. It had been just the same that last
time in Tuenafen, when Garet was still alive. For some
reason they hadn't been allowed to hurt the Alban, and
Commander Voord had even kept the woman Kathur
all to himself. It wasn't fair, and it wasn't like the Commander to be so selfish; after he had finished questioning
or punishment, they were always given their turn. Maybe
he was getting soft. Tagen glanced up at him, wondering,
then looked quickly away and squashed the thought
down into the back of his mind where not even the Commander could see it. Or maybe—a happier notion—he
wanted the Alban here to play with him in comfort. Yes,
that would be it. Commander Voord wasn't getting soft
at all; he just wanted to enjoy all the luxuries he had
worked so very hard to gain.

"Yes, sir. I understand quite clearly now. But sir, if
he resists—"

"Then you overcome the resistance."

"I know that, sir. But in Tuenafen when the action
squads went out you gave us drugs to put him to sleep
when we caught him."

"Soporifics, yes, I remember that. Go on. What's the
difficulty? Do you," Voord smiled thinly, "not use drugs
anymore?"

"That's not the problem, sir. You know that."

"Then," and Voord's smile vanished as if it had never
existed, "get to the point."

"Sir, I'd rather he wasn't put to sleep this time."

"I said *unharmed,* Tagen. And I meant it."

"But sir, please, just something for him to remember Garet by . . . Just a few minutes, that's all I'd take."

"We all miss Garet," said Voord wearily, his tone that of a man who had been through all the permutations of this argument before, "and there'll be plenty of time for mementos, but I gave you an order. Obey it."

"Yes, sir." If he had dared, Tagen would have let his voice sound sullen, but he had learned through painful experience that he could not do that to Voord and expect to get away with it. Instead he did as usual, tucking away his anger with all the other thoughts and ideas that he didn't want the Commander to know about, keeping them safe until he could let them out. When that happened someone died, but there were always chances to relieve his feelings in the line of duty, and anyway the people who died were Enemies of the State—Commander Voord always made sure of that. Tagen liked the way the Commander said *Enemies of the State* as if they were written in big letters, because it meant that the people Tagen killed were more important than the enemies ordinary soldiers killed. He knew that because Commander Voord had explained it to him.

"Where is he, sir, and how do I find him? The usual way?" Tagen always made sure to ask that before the Commander told him how; it sounded better when people could hear you had been thinking for yourself. He knew he wasn't clever the way Commander Voord was clever, but he could talk well about weapons and armor and mountain-climbing and feats of strength and all the things that he was good at if he was given a minute to think of what to say.

"The usual way. Contact the *tulathin,* pay them what they want and find out what their spy-net knows. Then go and get him."

"And if he's not alone, sir? The usual again?" Tagen was hopeful, because if he was finding out things from the *tulathin* then this business was a secret, and there was only one good way to keep a secret.

"Yes. Leave no witnesses. Go do it, Tagen. Dismissed."

* * *

The *kortagor* and his squad clanked through another salute before they faced about in drilled unison and left Voord alone again. He was smiling a little, but nothing like the grin which Tagen had been wearing, a happy expanse of teeth similar to those of an attack hound offered fresh raw meat. Voord always felt slightly inadequate when dealing man to man—or man to doom-machine, which was how it often felt with Tagen. The soldier, intimately close and twelve-year-faithful friend though he might be, seemed sometimes no more than a weapon in human form, an intelligent petrary missile to be launched against one's enemies, and no more capable of recall. There had been times before, as there would doubtless be times again, when Voord had cause to wonder what would happen if the need arose to call him off, and whether Tagen would pay heed to any countermand without the presence of the man he had called "The Commander" for eleven years regardless of existing rank. Turning him on was easy; he reacted to the phrase *Enemy of the State* as an oil-filled lamp reacted to a burning taper, but so far as turning him off again was concerned, Voord had no idea how to snuff out Tagen's fire once it was lit.

He relaxed a little, and was wondering whether to call for wine or just get out of this damnably uncomfortable chair and fetch it for himself when Hault reappeared in the doorway. "Engeul Gernai, my lord," the guard announced, stepping aside to let a stocky man into the room and continuing to speak without regard for how this new listener might receive the words. "I searched him myself. He's clean."

The man was indeed as unimpressive as Hault's earlier disparaging description had suggested. He was small and balding and prosperous, if prosperity meant a roll of fat around the waist. For all the fatness there was a haggard look about him, as if he had missed several nights of sleep. But he wasn't the class of person who usually requested to see a senior *Kagh' Ernvakh* officer; more often it was the Secret Police who wanted to have words with people like him.

"Well?" Voord was getting tired of being stared at and he was also growing hungry. "Well," he said, "what do you want?"

"I wanted to see you, sir," the man said hesitantly, plainly afraid of the company he had asked to enter. "I'm a merchant. Of Jouvann."

Voord blinked, bored already. If all this creature wanted was some sort of license to sell his wares, then why in the Name of Darkness had he been allowed to get in here and waste important time which could be spent in doing other things, like eating. He lifted one eyebrow wearily, wondering if the change of expression would be noticed or if he would need something rather less subtle—like having the merchant beaten out of the citadel—and it was as if that single eyebrow was the floodgate that released a stream of babbling.

"I sell wine, my lord." Gernai made the announcement as if it meant something important. "All the wine of the Empire and the Provinces, and some excellent spirits. You may buy from me by the single bottle, or my merchant company can provide for the needs of any gentleman's cellar. At present I can offer you Seurandec, Brightwood, Briej, Hauverne Kingswine—where I can give you both a three-year and a seven-year vintage, one to offer to acquaintances, my lord, and the other to keep for yourself and your friends—red and white Teraneth, and—" The man's flow of words tailed off as Voord held up one hand for silence.

"You don't need to speak to me, Gernai. From the sound of it, the castellan would be more your man. But I'm curious; why did you ask for *Eldheisart* Voord?"

"I used the name and the rank I knew, my lord. Are you not that man? My apologies for wasting my lord's time . . ."

"Your information is several-months out of date, man; several months and several promotions. You address the new Grand Warlord of the Empire!"

"Oh, I see."

The Jouvaine merchant sounded much less impressed than Voord had expected him to be. And there was something else, something niggling that he couldn't place just now. One of those annoying little matters which nag at the back of the mind, evading sleep until the answer comes just before dawn. Voord tried to dismiss it, but the question would neither become clear nor go away.

"But are you the same *Eldheisart* Voord that I was told to find, my lord . . . ?"

The man was persistent at least. "Yes, I am, was, whatever," Voord snapped. "Come to the point of all this before I have you thrown out.' And what *was* the matter with . . . ? His accent, that was it. "You have a Jouvaine name. Why don't you have a Jouvaine accent?"

"My lord is wise—" Engeul Gernai began, prelude to some oily flattery, and was cut short when Voord interrupted with none of the studied courtesy he had been trying to maintain.

"What goes on here?"

"My lord sounds afraid." The man calling himself by a false name made a forceful gesture with one hand and uttered a grunt of effort like someone lifting a heavy weight. Behind him the tall doors of the chamber quivered once from top to bottom and slammed shut with a heavy boom. The double clank as both bolts shot home into their reinforced slots was almost an afterthought in the wake of that huge noise. "My lord is well advised to fear."

"Your accent is Vreijek," Voord said.

"I never had the knack of simulating other voices, Lord-Commander Voord. How did you come by the new style and title anyway? Your usual method? Never mind. I didn't come here to see the Warlord; I came to see the officer who was Imperial Military Adviser to Lord Geruath Segharlin—the man who was so friendly with my daughter . . ."

"Ar Gethin." The crows were coming home to roost with a vengeance.

"Yakez Goadec ar Gethin. Her name was Sedna. She was beautiful . . ."

"Who told you to ask for me?" There was threat here no matter what Hault had said—he would be dealt with later—but Voord was still little enough concerned to have some room for curiosity.

"Another of your women, Voord Ebanesj. Another of the many, boys and men and girls and women, whom you used for your own purposes and twisted up and threw away. Kathur the Vixen sends you greetings, and says you should have killed her."

"So I should indeed." Voord looked at the fat little Vreijek and stretched his mouth into a smile like a snarl. "That error can be remedied more easily than the slut will believe possible."

"Kill. That's all you know, Voord—just as that was all you could think to do when my daughter found out the truth behind your scheming—"

"Scheming? *Scheming?* Yak'ardec ar Gethin, you have a mind like a playwriter! Twisted enough to give challenge to Osmar himself, I think." Voord had been sitting up very straight in the harsh Warlord's chair; now he allowed himself to relax, unconcerned, innocent of whatever accusations this stupid old man was flinging about like seeds at planting-time. "Listen to me, merchant, father and"—a glance at the still shut and bolted doors—"passable sorcerer, I had nothing to do with your daughter."

"Had you not, then? So why is she dead and you alive and higher than you were?"

"I am being patient with you . . . very patient. More patient than my custom with irritating provincials and far more patient than your manners deserve. Now shut your mouth and listen, because I'll say this only once: I did not kill your daughter. I barely knew your daughter. She was the mistress of Crisen Geruath, son of the local Overlord, while I was no more than Imperial Adviser for the Segharlin and Jevaiden Military Districts. There was no love lost and almost no communication between—"

"Liar. *Liar!* I had expected more courage from you, or at least more originality. If you were Imperial anything at all, then why do I find you in a position of such authority here in the *Woydek-Hlautan,* the Warlord's Domain where the Emperor's mandate is ignored? Answer me that!"

"Ah." Voord's slouch of studied relaxation froze as if a poisonous reptile had appeared in the room—or one of those reptilian lesser demons of far-too-close acquaintance. "You prepared your arguments quite well, ar Gethin, didn't you?"

"Yes, I did. It was stopping my ears to what I learned that I found hard. Your name appeared at every turn, and each time it appeared there was more blood on it. Crisen Geruath is dead, his father the old Overlord is dead, Prokrator Bruda who was your senior officer while you pretended to be a member of the Emperor's Secret Police—he's dead, too; Kathur you raped and broke with your fists . . ." Yakez was working himself into a passion that would end in one of two ways; either he would attack with whatever that cretin Hault had let slip through his search—Voord's right hand moved inside his tunic and found the knurled-steel grip of the slender dagger that went everywhere with him—or he would break down . . .

Fingers still tight around the dagger-hilt, Voord watched dispassionately as the old man dropped on to both knees and folded over his own anguished sobs. There was an exposed place the size of a florin coin on the exposed nape of ar Gethin's neck, and Voord was torn between driving his knife-blade into it or using the pommel to stun so that the Vreijek could be sliced to dripping shreds later and at leisure. He debated too long for either chance, because the old man straightened abruptly with more energy in his short fat frame than anyone of such a shape had right to own.

Someone . . . several someones were hammering at the outside of the door, jolting it on its hinges and making the wrist-thick bolts clatter derisively. Apart from the noise, they were producing no effect. Yakez Goadec ar Gethin stood up very straight, and for all that he had to tilt back his head on its thick neck, he looked Voord in the eye. "There are so many things that I would like to do to you," he said, "but all of them would end in death. Kill, die, death, that's all you know, that's your only solution. Voord, I am no sorcerer. I learned only the two spells: one for the door, to let us have this little chat without interruption, and one other. Because I looked at what was left of Sedna when you and the thing you conjured up were done, and I read the books in her

locked library cabinet . . ."—Voord's narrowed, watchful
eyes went wide—"and I decided to be merciful. I decided to take death away from you."

He reached into the money-purse strapped to his belt
and pulled out its lining in a chiming shower of coins.
A lining that was fine, smooth leather, as fine as the
binding of the book that still rested on Voord's lap. The
same leather, even to the grain . . .

"NO!" Voord's voice soared to a scream as Yakez
flung the flap of woman's-leather at him and he felt it
strike his face, felt it stroke against his cheek as warm
and soft as the innermost skin of a lover's thigh. The
scream was drowned by a monstrous crash as the doors,
their bolts snapping back in response to the same gesture
which had first locked them, flew open under the weight
of shoulders pressed against them.

Tagen was first in, his regulation shortsword already
clear of its sheath and lacking only something to cut.
Voord supplied that something; flinging out his hand, he
pointed at Yakez as the small man smiled up at him and
roared, "Take that one!"

Whatever the meaning of the order, no matter what
words were in it, Tagen heard only the words which he
had always heard in a command uttered with that urgency. His balance shifted as he ran forward, the fist
holding his sword swung back, reached the high point of
its swing and came whirring down. He didn't hear what
the small man was saying, or make sense of the Commander's frantic shout, but saw only that his target neither dodged nor ducked, and corrected the arc of his
sweeping stroke as much by deadly reflex as intent.

"And my death will seal—" Yakez had begun to say.
"Don't hurt him, you damned—" Voord had begun
to shout.

But the sound of Tagen's sword as it sheared off the
Vreijek's head made a thick, wet nonsense of all the
words. Blood splattered everywhere, over the steps, on
the newly-scrubbed floor, onto Tagen's armor and all
over Voord's feet as Yakez Goadec ar Gethin's severed
head smacked against the stone between them.

The torso didn't remain upright the way they sometimes
did; it didn't stagger, sway or even reel, but slammed

straight down after its own head under the impetus of the blow. Breathing hard, Voord looked at it for perhaps a hasty count of five and then glared at Tagen.

"I said *no,* Tagen. You disobeyed my direct order."

"Commander, I heard you cry out and I saw this one in a threat position. If I had waited, he might have—"

"Enough. It doesn't matter." *Small use having a perfect instinctive killer like this one and then expecting him to behave like someone normal . . .* "Be about your duties."

The itch was just a tingle on his skin, an irritating need to scratch. Voord's wave of perfunctory dismissal became an unembarrassed raking of his ribs that was such a relief, that felt so good . . . until his fingers sank to the knuckles in the sorcerously healed stab-wound that suddenly reopened in his side. He looked down and saw it, and went chalk-white with shock. Then the pain hit him, all the rending anguish of a sword-thrust in the belly, so that his back arched convulsively and a reflexive jerking in the muscles of his legs sent him tumbling from his seat down on to the bloodied floor.

There was no blood of his own, only the gash with his hand in it and the sickening wash of agony that was worse even than when he gave the use of his left hand in sacrifice to the Old Ones. Voord had thought his maiming was the most terrible pain that he had ever borne until this moment.

He was wrong. Even as he squirmed on the blood-greased tiles, first one hole opened in his head and then a second in his neck; the ragged punctures left by Alban *telek* darts. There was a crater of splintered bone above his right eye, and beneath his chin the clearly visible cartilage of his gullet had been perforated so that even his screaming sounded strange.

Some of the soldiers who had come running to the rescue choked, and retched, and fled, while others remained but clenched their teeth and gazed in every direction but at the man they had thought to save . . . who, pierced by wounds that should have killed him three times over, still writhed and shrieked and tried without success to die.

3

The sword was red oak, straight and smooth and polished, and it had been in his hands since the gray time just before dawn. More than two hours of striking-practice, with only enough rest breaks to prevent his muscles from cramping in protest as they blurred the sword through cut and thrust, parry and block, or brought it to those snapping stops which require as much control as any sweeping stroke.

He had spent years learning how to be lethal with a sword. Years of focusing the force of a strike; years of learning how to bring steel edge and human anatomy together with an executioner's rather than a surgeon's skill; years of learning how to deliver the classic cuts with no thought for what they did.

To face a human being perfect in the eyes of the Power which had made it; and to strike it with a sword perfect in the eyes of the smith who had forged it, in a movement perfect in the eyes of the master who had taught it. From the sum of all that perfection, *defeat* left only food for worms.

And what—or Whose—was the purpose behind such a consequence as that . . . ?

Aldric looked at the wooden *taidyo* braced in his hands. Even now, ostensibly relaxed and with his thoughts turned inward, he had adopted the ready posture of mid-guard-center, a stance from which he could develop three separate killing forms. He breathed out through his nostrils, the breath drifting away in twin plumes like smoke on the cold air, and lowered the weapon's point with slow deliberation to the ground. Only then did his gaze shift to the left, to where *she* awaited his attention; and all at once the winter's chill ground through the glow of well exercised muscle. He shuddered, just once, but with such violence that it brought both rows of his teeth clattering together.

The *taiken* lay an arm's length from where he stood, resting on an austere sword-rack of unvarnished pine. Black lacquer, black leather and black steel, all a stark contrast against the snow and the cross of straw-pale wood.

Isileth.

Widowmaker . . .

The blade, in its many-times-refurbished mountings, was twenty centuries old. Aldric looked at her, as he had often looked before, and wondered again in silence: *How many widows? How many lives? How much blood have you drunk in your two thousand years of life, my cold mistress?*

She would drink his blood, given the chance. Or Kyrin's. Or anyone's. For all the courtesy that they were granted, *taikenin* were never so proud as the men and women who carried them. Whether of prince or of peasant, any death—*all* death—served as their nourishment. He leaned his weight on the *taidyo,* driving it down through the churned snow between his feet and into the dirt beneath, and decided that this morning at least he would leave Isileth at rest within her scabbard.

"Brooding again, are you?"

Aldric jerked sideways to face where Kyrin, well wrapped in a deeply-hooded, fur-trimmed overrobe against the snow that hung in the leaden sky, came stepping delicately through last night's ankle-deep fall. He hadn't heard the sound of her feet, and her voice had made him jump; this in itself precluded any denial of her gentle accusation. Even though he tried.

"I was thinking; that's all."

"Just another word for what I said." She lifted a towel and his black leather jerkin and shirt from where they were draped across the picket fence. "Ivern and her people; they still wonder about you. About us both."

"Let them wonder," he said and returned the *taidyo* to its canvas sleeve among his other practice gear. With it he seemed to set aside his somber mood; or at least return it to whatever locked compartment of his mind he kept it in. "The less that people know, the less they can let slip."

Aldric shrugged hurriedly into his clothes and then—with the merest shadow of a bow—took Widowmaker from her rack and slung the scabbard's strap across his shoulder, but instead of hooking it into a proper combat position on his weapon-belt he left the longsword loose against his hip. The hip farthest from Kyrin.

There were stories about Isileth Widowmaker, and while he was not prepared to credit an inanimate piece of metal with such a thing as jealousy—not even a blade of her profound antiquity, no matter what the stories said—yet he was not about to take foolish chances. Aldric had seen too many strange things for that.

Kyrin looked from his face to the black longsword, and then back. "Still brooding, as I said. About last night?"

"And bad dreams? No. That was in the past."

"So the past doesn't concern you. Aldric-*an,* you're a high-clan Alban. The past always concerns you. I swore an oath once—and as a high-clan Alban you above all should understand how closely a sincere oath can bind—to use my ability and my judgment for the benefit of the sick . . ."

"Are you suggesting that I'm . . . sick?" Something unpleasant hovered in the way he asked it.

"Not sick . . . not like that. But you're hurt; you're in pain. And I don't want you in pain, not ever. I want you rid of the old wounds, the ones that never healed. Time it was done with once and for all."

"I don't need any help."

"No? Not even when you tear at yourself, rip those ancient hurts wide open again every time they have a chance to close? I've watched you do it, Aldric, and it's an ugly thing to see. You're bleeding inside, man—and you're the only one who can't see it!"

"I'm a killer, lady. A killer, not a healer. And all the good intentions in the world won't change that fact."

"So then why blame yourself for Dewan?"

Aldric looked up at her—a sharp, over-quick movement of head and eyes. "Because Dewan died when I was too slow to—"

"No. He died because he'd seen the alternative. He gave himself for . . . for me. And for you. For both of us. Dewan died because he gave his life for ours. At least do him the courtesy of not debating his choice." She had never dared speak to him like this before—but it had to be said. That, and gentler things, like: "How much use would living be for me if you were gone?"

Aldric said nothing for several minutes. There was real anger in his eyes, smoldering there like red coals, and for one frightening moment Kyrin thought that she had gone too far. Then the eyes closed briefly, squeezing tight, and when they opened again the moment was gone. "As little use," he said softly, "as my life would be without you."

"So. You see."

Aldric smiled at her, a wintry skinning back of lips from teeth. "Oh, yes, I see very well," he said, his voice clipped and quiet.

"You were born and brought up *kailinin-eir*. Even if you choose to deny that heritage, the culture behind it is unchanged. Vengeance and blood-feud were—still are—accepted. Traditional. Just as killing *yourself* is an acceptable, traditional thing. *Tsepanak'ulleth*." She was pushing, bringing the unsaid into the open.

"But why haven't you done it, Aldric? All the deaths, all the guilt, all the grieving. Why haven't you rid yourself of them? Why do you . . . not just live with them, but treat them as honored guests in the house of your mind? Because that's the way it looks to me. Why—when you've got your way out here?"

She touched the black *tsepan* at his belt with one finger, a brief, careful contact as if with some dainty, deadly creature that was, for the moment only, tame and safe. "You haven't used it, Aldric. Tell me why not."

Aldric let her hand withdraw to a safe distance, then gripped the lacquered hilt of the Honor-dirk and eased its three-edged spike of blade clear of its sheath. He stared in silence for the longest time at the weapon's bitter point. For so long, indeed, that Kyrin thought he might refuse outright to answer . . .

Or worse, in one of those sudden spasms of fury, try to do what she had so scathingly suggested was permitted him to do. With the shadow of that fear rising in her mind, she reached out swiftly to lay a hand across his wrist. Not restraining it, not yet, but at least reminding him of her presence. He looked at her, full in the face, and again their eyes met; and now hers were worried and apprehensive while his had gone introspective, cold and emotionless as chips of ice.

"Why not?" he echoed, speaking more to himself than to her. "Because I always thought my life was of more use than my death. While I was still alive I could set wrong things to rights. Justify myself to people. To you. To myself." The *tsepan* went back into its scabbard with a whisper of steel and a small, solid click.

Greatly daring, Kyrin reached out and took it from him with an unvoiced sigh of relief. It was only when that dagger was out of his reach that she stared him in the eye and let a little of her fear escape as anger.

"Justify yourself?" The question snapped out, harsher than it might have been, long patience at the end of its tether. "Then why *don't* you?"

Aldric merely inclined his head in the beginnings of a bow. "Because whatever way I chose to do it, I truly had no reason until now."

He pulled the square-faced gold ring from where he had always worn it on his right hand and slipped its warm metal onto Kyrin's finger. "This will keep the place until I buy another just for you," he said.

Kyrin looked at the ring on her finger and felt her eyes sting with the threat of tears. She stared at the *tsepan* in her hand as if she had never seen it before. The time was not long past when she wouldn't have dared to touch the Honor-dirk, much less make observations about the rightness of its use. That she had done so now, like the glimmer of gold on her hand where none had ever been before, meant something.

Didn't it . . . ?

Kyrin glanced back at Aldric, and a half-born word faltered on her lips as she realized he wasn't listening or even looking at her.

Instead he was staring up toward the high hills to the

east where the beams of the late-risen sun speared through a crack in the heavy sky. They were blurred and robbed of their full strength by the falling snow, but there was still enough power in the light to bleach sky and snow together to a blinding glare, like the mouth of a furnace but without any heat at all.

"Company," said Aldric, his voice turned flat and unpleasant. Kyrin followed the direction of his gaze, squinting at the brilliance, and although her vision was shot with streaks and sparkles of phosphorescent purple she could see quite plainly what was wrong.

The six riders on the hill-crest sat very still on their tall horses, long dark shadows streaked across the snow before them, no movement but the white breath of men and animals drifting on the breeze. They were half a mile away with the sun at their backs, but seen without seeing their faces Kyrin doubted that they were dinner guests. "Who are they?" Her words were not so much a question as a wondering aloud, but Aldric answered anyway.

"Not friends," he said, his voice taking on the terrible calm that she recognized from the other times and other places. "If they've got a long-glass, they'll know we've seen them. Is anyone around the steading except us?"

"No—Dryval's up at the farm and Ivern went off to market before I—"

"Good. Into the stable: tack-room first. Saddle up in case we have to run for it. Then get some of my gear—both *telekin* and the great . . . no . . . the short-bow for you. A half-sheaf of arrows should be enough." He squinted at the distant horsemen again and shrugged. "No armor. Not visible, anyway. Willowleaf tips in case there's mail underneath."

"I'll ask you this again," said Kyrin, following him toward the stable door. "Who are they—or who do you think they might be?"

Aldric took his eyes from the still-unmoving riders just long enough to give her a nasty sort of smile that showed far too many of his teeth. "An accurate list would take far too long," he told her, and there might have been just the merest touch of bitterness in his voice as he said it. "Let's just say that if they're looking for Ivern or the others I'll be grateful, and if they're looking for you I'll be surprised. . . . And if they're looking for me without evil intentions I'll be downright astonished. Here they come!"

The horsemen were moving, walking their mounts forward in a leisurely fashion, but after what Aldric had said—and what he had only hinted at—Kyrin would far rather have seen them riding away than coming any closer. Except that they *were* coming closer, and leisurely or not there was something in the way they sat their horses that made her uneasy. Even at such a distance she could see how they rode. She had seen Aldric fork a saddle that same way, menacing and businesslike, straight-legged, feet braced against long-leathered stirrups, spine braced against high, curved cantle, reins gathered together in one hand to leave the other free for weapons.

The stable and tack-room were gloomy at the best of times, and seen through eyes which had been staring straight at the sun they were as black as a wolf's throat. They saddled both riding- and pack-horses more by touch and memory than by sight, and Aldric at least made a few false attempts at it if the sounds of clattering and an occasional oath meant anything. "You can use a bow, can't you?" he asked out of the darkness.

"Yes, I can." If Kyrin's voice had an irritable edge to it, that was probably due more to nervousness than because she had to make an effort to keep her *of course I can* unspoken. The weapon was pushed into her hands a moment later, with an untidy bundle of wooden staves and feathers and leather straps that she guessed—rightly—were arrows and a bow, a shooting-glove and a bracer.

"*Telek,*" said Aldric, looming out of the shadows with a spring-gun in one hand. He broke it and spun its cylinder, then snapped it shut and worked the lever. The weapon's mechanisms clicked and the sear engaged with a small, solid noise. "There. It's loaded and cocked, so don't put a dart through your own foot; that trigger's got a light touch. Inside thirty feet, just point and squeeze."

"I know. I *know!*" Kyrin took the spring-gun and felt its weight dragging at her hand, a crooked shape of wood and metal that was somehow far more sinister that a sword. She hefted the *telek* a few times and looked at Aldric's outline in the gloom. "But what happens if they aren't enemies . . . ?"

"That's their misfortune, isn't it?" he said, his voice deadly calm. The voice of a man who had grown tired of being hunted all across the country by one faction or another. The voice of a man who had had enough.

"So you'll shoot from cover, without warning. Like an assassin?"

"Not like an assassin. Like a man outnumbered six— no, sorry"—she detected the glint of a tight smile in the way he corrected himself—"three to one. And I'll wait until I'm sure."

Kyrin didn't reply, and Aldric could sense her disapproval without needing to see the stare and the compressed lips. He shrugged and laid a hand to the door. "But if you really want, there's one way to find out. I just hope they aren't good shots. . . ."

"That's not fair!"

"All right, it's not. But we have to get out of here anyway, or risk them firing the place. I don't like the prospect of being trapped inside a burning building again . . ."

Kyrin looked sharply at him, wondering about the story behind that "again." Before she could say anything the door kicked at Aldric's fingers as something smacked into it and an instant later dug into the floor, tearing a hole in the planks and letting a narrow shaft of daylight transfix the darkness of the tack-room.

"Of course, there are other ways," he said blandly, "especially if they have crossbows. Convinced?"

"Convinced. They don't have to come in at all, not if they've got enough ammunition?"

"Tell me about it," said Aldric, and nipped a splinter from the pad of his thumb with his front teeth. "Which is another reason why I don't want to stay here."

"But if they can already hit the door—"

"Luck. Or accident. Probably . . ." That hesitation disturbed her more than any further words of explanation. "Or they've moved faster than I thought. Get down. Flat on the floor." He hooked the tip of his own greatbow under the door's hasp, muttered something under his breath and pulled, hard. Nothing happened. Again, and again nothing. A third time, much harder—

—And the door jerked back, flooding the tack-room with light and a heavy swirl of the snow that was falling now in earnest. Five crossbow bolts flicked through the sudden opening and hammered into the back wall with a sound like a demented carpenter at work, almost too fast for the individual strikes to be counted. But not quite. "Go!" yelled Aldric.

Even before Kyrin was clear of the floor, he had stepped into the doorway with an arrow already nocked to his bowstring, spotted a possible target, flexed, drawn and loosed all in one quick movement.

The sound of the arrow's impact was mostly that of splitting timber, and five of the raiders burrowed for deeper cover. The sixth uttered a yell, shot his newly-loaded crossbow into the ground and swung out backward into the yard, nailed through the thigh to the door behind which he had crouched to reload and shoot. He was still yelling, outraged as much as hurt, and with good reasons for both sensations; nobody had thought to tell him that at such close range a wooden door was no obstacle at all even to ordinary arrows—and he was facing armor-piercing points.

Aldric knew the drawbacks of a crossbow: they were murderously powerful, but because of that slow, cumbersome things. He had used them himself in better days, but only for hunting. Against a target able to shoot back, they were a liability during their lengthy reloading cycle without something solid to hide behind. Something much more solid than a door of thin-cut end-grained planks . . .

And then the arrow pinning the raider's leg in place tore free and released him to fall sideways into the trampled show of the courtyard where, fighting forgotten, he used both hands to staunch the outflow of his blood. For all that his clothing was that of a peasant or a forester, unremarkable and instantly forgotten, the wounded man was wearing other garments underneath and had taken the trouble to conceal his features with a hooded mask.

Both the mask and the close-fitting second suit of clothes were of some fine fabric gray as smoke.

Aldric and Kyrin tumbled together into the relative shelter around the corner of the stone-built stable and crouched there, panting. "Oh, Lord God, we're in trouble," he said between gasps. "They're *tulathin*. Assassins."

"*Real* assassins?"

"Professionals."

"We're in trouble." There was a pause, then: "But who hired them?"

"Damned if I know." Aldric was already belly-down in the snow, squirming for a better position, with the seven-foot bow clamped crosswise between elbow-joint and biceps. "I'll ask that question later, if I'm alive to ask or they to answer"—he ducked as sparks and sharp-edged fragments sprayed from stone when another cross-bow bolt probed at their shelter and went humming off at a crazy angle—"because I don't think taking me alive is part of their contract."

A thread of crimson oozed down Kyrin's face from a gash left by a splinter, and she pressed a fistful of snow against it to staunch the bleeding. "Or anyone with you," she said, initial surprise becoming grim belief in all that he had told her these past weeks. All the fears, all the precautions, all the things which she had nodded at and agreed with, if only out loud but never in her heart.

Matters were different now, facedown in the snow with her face stinging, weapons in her hands and the occasional intermittent buzz or metallic smack of passing bolts as a constant reminder that she was going to have to hurt or be hurt. Kill or be killed. Kyrin looked at the coldness in Aldric's face, a coldness which had nothing to do with the snow-melt soaking him, and shivered at the sudden grim reality of it all.

For just a moment she wanted to be sick, right then and there on the ground before her face; then the feeling passed into no more than a clammy shudder in her guts, and she braced her own bow across her arms as he had done and wriggled after him in the crushed snow of his wake.

*   *   *

Ivern's steading might have been designed with defense in mind, and if it had been built in the past ten years there was no "might" about it. Except for the wooden doors, the stone buildings were sturdy enough to absorb a point-blank strike from anything that mounted raiders could have carried. The layout of house, annex, stables and outbuildings was such that there were no positions from which a missile weapon could dominate more than twenty feet in any directions; a range so short that leaden slingshot slugs or Army-issue weighted throwing darts would be of more use than the slow-to-reload crossbows—the kind of range at which Alban *telekin* excelled.

"Our one advantage is," said Aldric quietly as he paused well short of a corner, "that a *telek* doesn't need reloading after every shot."

"So what about the bows?" Kyrin touched her own shortbow with the tip of one finger. "Keep them or put them aside?"

"Keep. We might get a clear shot somewhere. But this"—he indicated the ominous corner with a jerk of his head—"is likely to be *telek* work." He was breathing fast, and Kyrin could see the flutter of a rapid pulse in the hollow of his throat as he half-turned to lean his own bow and bundle of arrows against the wall.

Aldric went round the corner in a half-roll and a flurry of snow, *telek* leveled at where a target might most likely be. There was no one there, but enough footprints marred an otherwise smooth snowdrift to suggest that someone had been, and recently.

"Do you mean we have to kill them all?" whispered Kyrin in his ear. "Couldn't we drive them off?"

"How?" The monosyllabic reply was bitter. Despite his well-feigned confidence he doubted that the pair of them could win unaided against five *tulathin,* let alone chivvy them away like a pack of annoying cur-dogs. Rather than kill all of the remaining assassins, it was more likely that the *tulathin* would kill them. Aldric looked sidelong at Kyrin, at the way her teeth nipped nervously at her lower lip, at the softness of her face, and privately decided that killing would be all that would be done to her—even if he had to make quite certain by doing it himself. He was angry at letting her get involved in this, putting her life at risk because of . . . whoever of the far-too-many in his past had sent this execution detail after him.

"Look there." Kyrin spoke very softly, pointing with her *telek* at what had drawn her attention. A little puff of something that looked like smoke was trailing into view from beyond the hay-barn, and even as they watched, it was joined by a second. "Fire? Or breath?"

"Doesn't matter. It's not one of us; that's enough." A swirl of wind-driven snow slapped Aldric in the face, making him flinch. "Stay here. Mind your back. I'm going round that way"—he jerked his chin at the other side of the barn—"and if he comes out first, kill him."

"What if—"

"Just make sure it's him, not me." He left his great-bow where he had propped it against the wall, winked at her—though that could have been a flake of snow in his eye—and moved quickly out of sight.

Kyrin stared for several seconds into the whiteness, fixing his vague outline in her mind just in case of accidents, then returned her attention to the barn. The snow flurries were dying away into a heavy, steady fall like those she remembered from back home in Valhol, hard to see through and almost hypnotic to watch. She considered the *telek* for a moment, then thumbed its safety-slide into place, shoved it through her belt and set an arrow to her bowstring.

Better the weapon you know than the weapon you just claim to know, she thought with a crooked little smile. At least Aldric hadn't asked her whether she would be able to put an arrow through another human being. Her answer might have shocked him. These people were trying to kill her, and had only themselves to blame for the—

How the man had crept up behind her was all too plain, with the falling snow deadening both sight and hearing, but the only reason why he hadn't shot her in the back must be that he'd spotted she was female and was minded to a little fun before he finished her off.

That was his mistake. For all that he was a *taulath* and a professional assassin skilled at killing people, he had small ability at attempted rape, especially when the subject of his unwelcome attentions was more than just a frightened farm-girl.

He got as far as wrapping his left forearm around her throat and—instead of jamming a dagger under her ribs as the neck-pressure suggested he might do—began pawing at her breasts with the other hand. Mauled, outraged, but still very much alive, Kyrin dropped the bow and its nocked arrow and reached up with both hands.

She snapped his little finger like a twig, then wrenched the pain-loosened forearm from her neck and used it as a lever to hurl her attacker to the ground. The *taulath* landed with a jarring thud on his tail-bone and the back of his skull, an impact that knocked even the uncompleted scream of pain out of his lungs as no more than a grunt.

"Bastard!" hissed Kyrin, clawing the *telek* out of her belt.

"I'll gut you for that, bitch!" the man snarled back with his first regained breath, rolling over with a shortsword gripped in his uninjured hand and already clear of its sheath. Kyrin froze—because the words and the accent were both Alban.

That shocked hesitation was almost enough to kill her, for it let him regain his feet, his balance and enough time to lash out the beginning of a cut with the *taipan* shortsword—also Alban, she could see that now—which would have taken her face off. The pause when time went slow was almost long enough for her to die, but not quite. Her *telek* snapped back on line and jolted in her hand to put a single lead-shod dart into his eye.

Kyrin's heart was beating too quickly and too loudly by far, seeming almost to advertise her presence, and there was an acid queasiness in her stomach which came not from the killing but where the killed man came from. The implications of *that*, already running through her brain, were too ugly to be believed and too urgent to be kept secret for longer than it took to find Aldric again—somewhere out there in the snowstorm, not knowing that the men he stalked were his countrymen, trained as he had been himself and most certainly more ruthless. They were people he might hesitate to kill for one reason or another, as she had almost hesitated, whereas to them he was a job of work, payment on completion and no more.

She was not so panicked that she was about to do something stupid; but whatever she did, she would have to do it fast . . .

The man lying at Aldric's feet wasn't dead, but he would likely wish he was when he came to his senses and the egg-sized lump at the back of his head made its presence felt. Shooting the assassin would have been as easy, but given the chance of choice Aldric had left him alive. Why, he didn't know. But he wasn't about to correct the error by killing a helpless enemy, good sense though that might have been.

Instead, he came very close to killing Kyrin as her anonymous shape appeared out of the falling snow. His *telek* was leveled and his fingers were already putting four of the necessary five pounds' pressure on the weapon's long trigger before he saw just who it was aimed at and twitched the muzzle to one side.

Kyrin's face was pale enough already, and the experience of staring down the bore of a weapon whose power she had had demonstrated barely seconds earlier was enough to leave her as white as the falling snow.

"Doamne' Diu!" he snarled. Alone, things would have been easier, since with Ivern and Dryval and all the others away from the steading, anyone else would have been an enemy and could be dealt with as such. Despite, or maybe because of her courage, Kyrin tied his hands by refusing to hide. But there was another way out, if the snow continued to fall as heavily as it was doing now; a way out in the most literal sense.

"Back to the stables. The horses are ready to go; we'll mount up and get out of here while the weather holds bad."

"You mean *run?*"

"Escape sounds better. We're still outnumbered—"

"Barely! They'll be easier than the others—"

"No, dammit! I know more about *tulathin* than you do. We've been lucky so far—"

"There's no such thing as luck!"

"Then we've—" His patience gave way at last and he grabbed her by the arm. "Argue later, for God's sweet sake. But right now, *move!*"

Kyrin opened her mouth to say something savage; then the focus of her eyes moved from his face to a place behind him and her heel hooked round behind his knee so that they both went tumbling sideways. Two bolts from the three crossbows she had seen in the instant they were leveled went scything through the snowy air where they had stood and exploded sparks and splinters from the hay-barn wall. And that left one.

As Aldric rolled from the fall and back to his feet, Widowmaker came from her scabbard with a whisper of steel on wood . . . and then froze halfway to a guard position as the man with the last loaded crossbow walked forward slowly, enjoying his moment of absolute superiority. Behind him, the other two slung their missile weapons and drew shortswords for what would now be only butchery.

"Aldric Talvalin," said the first *taulath*. He spoke excellent Alban, with a Pryteinek accent, so that Aldric glared hatred. The man's crossbow wasn't aimed, but pointing nonchalantly at the ground . . . for now.

"Keep the girl safe," said the hateful Alban voice behind the hood. "Girls are for dessert."

"Sweets are bad for you," said Aldric, deliberately using the highest form of the Alban language as an unsubtle insult. It was the way a clan-lord would address a beggar, if the clan-lord deigned to communicate with more than just his riding-quirt.

The *taulath*'s crossbow came up, steadied, sighted on Aldric's forehead . . . and loosed. Blue fire exploded unsummoned from Widowmaker's pommel-stone and enveloped her blade in the instant of the missile's flight. The longsword shifted to guard in a flicker of hot blue-white light, and emitted a shrill metallic screech as her edges met the accelerating crossbow bolt and sheared it point to nock in two. Aldric hid disbelief behind a hungry feral grin and whipped the blue-burning *taiken* through to an attack posture—

And then there was a slap of impact and the center of the *taulath*'s hood went explosively concave. As his companions dived for cover, the assassin took a single tottering step backward and fell. Aldric matched his movement with a raking stride forward that slammed his heel square into the center of the masked face, then brought Isileth Widowmaker down with all his force onto the crown of the hooded head.

The *taulath* lay quite still in the snow, split to the middle of the chest, crumpled and bloody and somehow smaller now. The other *tulathin* were nowhere to be seen.

"What—what happened?" Kyrin had spent the past few seconds face downward in the snow, displaying good sense for what Aldric considered was the first time in far too long. "I thought you were dead!!"

"Exaggerated rumors." Aldric's sardonic smile was not a particularly pleasant thing to see, especially since it was spattered with the dead man's blood. "Now, quick, and quiet: to the stables."

"I said what happened?"

"Slingshot." He augmented the laconic answer by turning her hand palm-up and dropping into it what looked like a small egg. Kyrin glanced down—then made a shocked little noise as she realized exactly what he meant, dropped the still-bloody lead slug into a snow-drift and scrubbed her smeared hand hard against the leg of her riding-breeches. The slug had been completely round when it left the sling, but now it was slightly flattened—because a human skull can always put up some resistance, even to a slung lead shot . . .

"Who killed him—not you?"

"I wish . . ." Aldric pushed open the stable door and led the way in with the muzzle of his *telek*. Apart from agitated horses, the place was empty. "No, I just made sure. He shot at me, and then that thing took part of his head off. The other two got out of sight; they're still out there somewhere." He swung up into Lyard's saddle, leaving one foot free of its stirrup so that he could lean sideways, *kailin*-style, along the horse's neck, and looked back at Kyrin. "So are the others, the *tulathin* in white who killed him."

"More *tulathin!* Friends of yours?"

"Just more assassins. They don't want the first squad to kill me—that's the only good thing about them. As for what *they* want, I think it's me again. Alive, this time."

"No encouragement to stay."

"All right, you win." Aldric laughed, a harsh bark of sound with something of a tremor in it even now. "Let's *go!*"

They rode out of the stable and the blizzard closed around them in an icy, impenetrable curtain of white, whirling around black horse and gray, roan packpony and bay. It struck their faces like chilled feathers, enfolded them, sifted across their tracks and bleached the vagueness of their outlines until not even the trained eyes of a *taulath* could have told which mass of white was horse and which was rider, and which was merely drifting snow.

And by the time one or other of the *tulathin* had both time and safety enough to look those looked for were gone.

4

There was confusion in Cerdor.

To those who had lived there during the past thirteen days, it felt as if there had never been anything except confusion in the city, ever since the king had died and all his lords save two had fled back to their own lands. It had little to do with that death anymore, regardless of what the rumors said, but had a far more sinister source that even rumor was reluctant to touch upon: the uncertainty of powerful men.

Granted that King Rynert's death had been the first cause of all the trouble, still it had stemmed less from his passing than the manner of it. That had been interpreted not merely by uninformed second- and third-hand sources but by men who had been there in person as the action of an overly-ambitious and haughty clanlord—Hanar Santon—slighted over some matter by the dead king. That the truth of the matter was very different had no significance now, for the error had gathered its own momentum and was impossible either to disprove or to stop for all that its consequences were already spreading across Alba like plague-marks covering the face of a once beautiful woman.

There had been no meeting of the Alban Crown Council since that night, not even to vote on their establishment of a regency to rule the country—Rynert having failed to leave an heir. Most of the lords present at that last fateful meeting were now watching each other from the dubious safety of their respective citadels, setting to rights the fortifications which long years of peace had allowed to fall into disrepair and mustering en-

feoffed lesser lords to their defense. None would listen
to reason; not since they had seen what they thought
was reason conversing with a hired assassin and moments later slashed open and slain on the steps of his
own throne . . .

"At least there are no declarations of faction yet."
Hanar Santon patted the sheets of dispatch reports together, aligning their edges with punctilious neatness for
the tenth time since their delivery half an hour before.

"Yet." His companion's voice was without inflection,
neither echoing nor squashing Hanar's optimism. "That
doesn't mean anything, either way." If there was cynicism in the statement, it was not the studied art practiced
by younger men. Aymar Dacurre had had many years
of experience in which to get his practice right. The old
clan-lord had as much faith as anyone else in his fellow
men; he simply didn't anticipate it without proof.

"But you heard the names, didn't you? Powerful high-
clan-lords, all of them."

Aymar sighed. *These children,* he thought. *They learn
history, but they never learn from it.* As if the mere fact
of being high-clan-lords was enough to absolve them of
blame for anything. . . . It was all written down in *Ylver
Vlethanek,* and the Book of Years was being echoed far
too closely for Aymar Dacurre's comfort. The same pos-
tures of pugnacious defense had been adopted five hundred years before, and by the ancestors of the same men
who were adopting them today. Those disagreements
had become the Clan Wars, and so far as Dacurre could
see it would require very little force to push the present
situation over into a repetition of the conflict which had
left such a bloody stain on Alban history. But now there
was another factor to take into account, a factor which
the old lords had not needed to worry over and which
their descendants either failed or refused to consider.
The source of the push: the Drusalan Empire.

If what Aldric Talvalin had said was true—and Dacurre had seen no reason to disbelieve the young man's
words whether they were heard at first hand or related
through his foster-father Gemmel—the Empire had been
casting speculative glances toward its neighbor for some

time. What galled most was the reason behind it all; not expansion by conquest, or even simple acquisitiveness, but simply so that a bureaucrat could continue to justify his function.

The military dictator who styled himself Grand Warlord had lost most of his influence in the Western Empire when the new Emperor Ioen had belied his youth and revealed that he possessed a mind of his own, rather than the collection of thoughts and opinions borrowed from the Warlord like so many of his predecessors. The Emperor had negotiated peace—or at least pacts of mutual nonaggression—with all the countries on his borders by revoking the unpopular provincial annexations that were the source of so much unrest. He and his advisers had taken what at first seemed considerable loss of face until it became clear that they had lost nothing. More, they had gained the respect of many on all sides who had grown weary of the constant brutal round of rebellion and suppression in provinces seized for no better reason than that their and the Empire's frontiers ran together for longer than a given minimum distance. But without war, the position of *Woydach* became superfluous, and Warlord Etzel faced redundancy, loss of rank and power and privilege—and the long-leashed vengeance of all those who had survived the trampling of his rise to power.

The danger had become clear almost five years ago, during an insignificant incident which had exploded into scandal and slaughter with the resurrection of a long-dead sorcerer and the butchery of all save one of Alba's foremost high-clan families, the Talvalins. The idea behind that had been for the Imperial legions to intervene, as they had done before in other places, to restore "equilibrium and peace" as the then-Emperor interpreted the term; an intervention whose payment was invariably the province or country which it liberated. That had been the first indication of what was to be a constant threat just beyond the horizon, and one which had lately grown still more significant.

During the course of the past year, after acrimonious exchanges at all levels of the Imperial Senate, the Grand Warlord had split away from the Emperor's "pacifist"

faction and had retired to the old capital of Drakkesborg. There he had set up an Eastern Empire, *Woydek-
Hlautan*—the Warlord's Domain in the guttural Drusalan language—whose political aims were those of the old
emperors of the Sherban dynasty rather than those of
their milksop descendant: bring unity by the swiftest
means. Swiftest of all those means was force of arms and
of course, while the "Empire" was at war, it required a
supreme military commander, a Grand Warlord, once
more.

Alban foreign policy had never been particularly subtle or ingratiating where the Empire was concerned. Lord
Dacurre knew that much even before he had begun
working his way through the archive records of past
Council meetings. He could remember several occasions
when his had been the sole dissenting voice against the
condoning of acts of piracy against Imperial shipping—
and to his shame, the two meetings where he had agreed
that arms and financial support should be tendered to
insurrections in the Imperial provinces now freed by
Emperor Ioen's policy of conciliation. At least he'd been
able to prevent the issue of letters of marque, which
would have been equivalent to a secret declaration of
war on the Ocean-Sea; Cernuan and Elherran privateers
were not the most controllable of auxiliary troops, and
he had said as much, to the great offense of Lord Diskan
of Kerys in Cerenau.

And then other things had started coming to light, like
drowned corpses during a spring thaw and smelling
about as sweet. Aymar Dacurre had discovered things
in the Archive which had never been mentioned by the
late King Rynert, for all that they had been written
down by assiduous *hanan-vlethan'r*—the court recorders
who noted everything of significance for all that their
writings were often edited later. These records were not
edited, and it galled Dacurre to realize that had his fellow councillors seen what had been written there, they
would not now be peering at each other and the rest of
the country over ramparts. What he had seen, and what
he had read, had been the truth behind Rynert's version
of what Aldric Talvalin had been doing in the Empire,
and in Seghar and—most significantly of all—in Egisburg

where Dewan ar Korentin had died. Considering such things, he was astonished that the Imperial threat had not materialized already in the form of warships off the Alban coast, and that nonappearance had given him cause to wonder what Aldric was doing in the Eastern Empire—or *to* it—that might keep its ambitious Grand Warlord so busy.

"Hanar," said Aymar Dacurre, "you are my grandson."

Hanar Santon started very slightly at that. He had known it all his life, but had never heard it spoken aloud except by his mother, Dacurre's second daughter: The explanation for the silence had involved such words as "favoritism" and "respect" and, most of all, "honor," so he had never pursued the matter. To hear it now from the old man himself was something of a shock, for they had moved to first-name terms only in the past ten days or so.

"My grandson indeed," the old man continued, "by an excellent and honorable father. And despite the difference in our ages, my friend. But, Hanar, you are also sometimes such an innocent that I despair of your ever seeing sense."

Santon blinked and licked his lips. He didn't know where this might be leading, but in the company of a fire-eater notorious through three generations of Alban nobility he was ready for the worst. "Sir?" he ventured finally and braced himself for whatever blast he might have provoked. There was none.

"All this talk about high-clan-lords. When you have some free time again"—and Aymar laughed both at the thought of free time and at the expression on young Santon's face, since free time for either of them was less likely than honesty in Imperial politics—"you should go back to your histories and read for yourself how much grief those who style themselves *ilauem-arlethen* have caused down the years. Enough, and more than enough. But first, and now, read this."

The Court Archive skidded down the table and came to a stop almost exactly where Aymar had intended that it should, in front of the younger man. That its passage upset Hanar's painstakingly sorted sheaf of notes and

reports bothered him not a whit; there would be plenty
more of those before the day's work was done and
locked away from prying eyes.

"Read it?" The archive was a good handspan thick,
for all that its leaves were thin and the writing on them
small. "You mean, now?"

"Not all of it, boy. Just look at the pages I marked;
you should find them of interest." Aymar drew across
another bundle of papers and inked his writing-brush
with care, then glanced at Hanar from beneath his fierce
white eyebrows. "But read them carefully. You may well
learn more than your tutors ever taught you . . ."

"Feeling better now?"

Chin-deep in the hot bath-water, Aldric stirred a little
but made no reply other than a faint sigh of contentment. Eyes closed, with a pillow of rolled toweling behind his head, he both looked and sounded asleep.

Kyrin wrapped a warmed towel around herself—there
were plenty more draped over a rack in front of the
fire—and padded across the room to look down at him,
telling herself that she was only making sure whether he
was indeed asleep or just very relaxed, and that he was
in no danger of slipping so far down into the tub that
he might inhale some of the water. For all that, the making sure took several minutes of close study rather than
the cursory glance it might otherwise have required.
"You've lost too much weight with worrying about
things that you can't help, my love," she said quietly in
her own language, and then smiled. "But you're still
good to look at. Very good indeed."

Whatever opinion Aldric might have expressed, the
loss of weight was true enough and beyond argument.
His face was leaner than it should have been, and the
body which in her memory was broad-shouldered, square
and strong was now an incomplete sketch of that remembered image, with all the big muscles defined like a surgical anatomy and ribs and pelvis stark under skin which
lay too close to the bone.

"You need to stop all this errand-running," Kyrin
said. She spoke in Alban now, still reluctant to disturb
him and yet half-hoping he was awake enough to listen.

"You need to stop concerning yourself with all the troubles of the world and find yourself some peace instead." She turned away and shook her head sadly. "I just wish the world's troubles would leave you alone to do it."

"Do what?" Aldric's voice was lazy, an effect of the vast heat recently the water, but lacked the dullness of someone recently asleep.

Kyrin looked at him and raised one eyebrow. "Oh—so you weren't asleep at all."

"I wouldn't dignify it by calling it sleep." He raised one hand to rake back damp hair from his eyes, very slowly and carefully since in water so deep and hot a sudden movement might cause a spill and would certainly cause discomfort. "But I wasn't much awake either. What were you saying?"

"Nothing much."

Aldric gave her back the raised eyebrow—now his own were visible—and added a little to the delivery. "You never let me get away with a response like that, so why should I let you? Tell me about nothing much."

Kyrin exchanged her damp, cool towel for a fresh one, warm and dry, and told him just how very much the nothing much involved. "And neither of us knows," she finished, with anger starting to edge her words, "who those assassins were, or why they came looking, or who sent them. But they tried to kill you all the same!"

"They tried to kill you as well."

"Just because I was in the way, or with you, or a witness."

"Quite. And whose fault is that?"

"Oh, damn you!" Her anger flared and faded like the plume of sparks that billowed up the chimney as a log collapsed in the grate. "If I thought you nitpicked for any reason other than to tease me, I'd . . . I'd. . . ."

"Drown me in the bath-tub?"

"And maybe I will yet." Kyrin glanced at Aldric as he climbed from the water. "We stay here tonight. What about tomorrow?"

"Another inn, closer to Drakkesborg." He lifted one of the towels and scrubbed at his hair for a few seconds before elaborating a little. "I'm in no hurry to get there."

"Then why go at all? Why not go home to Alba?"

Aldric raised both his eyebrows. "The old song, eh? Yet you were the one who said they knew the whys and wherefores of my going."

Kyrin shrugged and smiled faintly. "A girl has to try these things every now and then."

"You don't like Drakkesborg?"

"I've never been to it. I'll go there with you, but . . . but I don't like the sound of the place."

"I do. Imperial Drakkesborg, the City of the Dragon. But with a name like that, I'm biased anyway. And the place does have a few good things about it—theaters, for one." He hitched at the towel wrapped around his waist which was trying to slide floorwards, draped another capewise across one shoulder and an outstretched arm, then cleared his throat in a portentous sort of way and assumed a dramatic pose.

"It pleases me to see the joyful season that is Autumn,"

he declaimed, rolling the words around his mouth like plum-stones:

For it swells the fruit upon the trees
And makes the harvest rich and tall.
And it pleases me to hear the song of the birds
Who make their mirth resound through all the woods.
And it pleases me to hear the song of silver trumpets,
And it pleases me to see upon the meadows
Tents and pavilions planted,
And the flowers of silken banners
And the raiment of fair ladies.
And it pleases me to see ranged along the field
Bold men and horses standing tall
Come from afar to make pretense of war . . .

Then the more important of the two towels gave up its struggle to hold on to Aldric's hips and slithered to the floor despite his frantic clutch, and Kyrin dissolved in helpless giggles.

"Oren Osmar's *Tiluan the Prince*," he explained carefully, trying to keep his face straight. "It's not really like that. At least, not exactly. . . ."

"Nothing else at all?"

"Nothing, my lord."

"Very well." Lord Dacurre looked tired and far older even than his seventy-three years. "You may go. Dismissed."

The trooper saluted crisply—more crisply than he had done before the dead king, and with more respect—then snapped around and walked from the room. Dacurre watched him go. "I appreciate the lasting peace," he said quietly, "but I could almost wish that something would happen. With my fellow lords, or even with the Drusalan Warlord. Anything. Just so that I could do something about it, rather than sit here and do nothing at all."

"You're doing far more than you need, just sitting here." Hanar Santon had sat quietly while the soldier handed over his written report and delivered the verbal observations that went with it. Dacurre—and through his example, Santon—placed considerable value on what was thought and said, the kind of information that seldom passed from a man's mind on to paper, no matter how much of his inmost thoughts he might have tried to write. It was listening to what was said and what was felt that was of real use. Both men had often wished there was some way to glean the same knowledge from within the Drusalan Empire as they were able to obtain from inside the walls of Alba's citadels. "Tell me, Aymar," Santon glanced casually at the new report, then set it aside and stared at the old man, "how much sleep have you been getting?"

"Enough." Even as he said the word, Dacurre knew that he was wasting his breath. Hanar Santon was no more a fool than anyone else who had seen him today, and Aymar knew that trying to deceive the young man was pointless—especially since he had managed perhaps eight hours of sleep in the past seventy, and it showed.

"Of course. Then the reason you fall asleep in your chair must be other than weariness."

"Yes; you're forgetting about boredom." Both men

grimaced at the joke which had long ceased to be funny. The luxury of enough idleness to feel bored was something they had both forgotten in the days since the king was killed.

"Boredom?" It was the standard response, but spoken now in the dull voice of a man exhausted. "What's that?"

"It's like sleep, except you don't close your eyes."

"Oh. Mythic vice." Santon smiled wanly and flipped open the report again, staring at the neat script as if it no longer made any sense. He shook his head like a man walking into a cobweb. "What day is it now?"

One look told Aymar that this was not another joke but a real and rather desperate attempt to regain a faltering hold on reality. "Sixteenth of the twelfth."

Kevhardu tlai'seij, de Merwin, in the formal reckoning. Rynert had been dead twenty-one days now. A lifetime. Long enough for a country to begin to die, except that the threat against its life had done nothing. And neither Dacurre nor Santon could understand the reason why. The old man stretched, trying to ease kinks in his spine which hadn't been there three weeks ago. He wasn't meant to hunch over a deskful of paperwork all day; neither of them was. But with no one else in Cerdor willing or able to do the work, somebody had to. Dacurre wished it didn't have to be him.

The knock on the Council-chamber door brought both men out of their private thoughts with a perceptible jerk, even though neither would have admitted to being startled. Whoever was outside, it was not the usual chamberlain with his diffident rapping, not unless the man had managed to get drunk in the few minutes since he had ushered in the cavalry trooper. This wasn't a polite single knuckle but a pounding fist, and Lord Dacurre knew urgency when he heard it. Caution and the memory of Rynert laid one hand on his *taipan* shortsword, twisting the weapon's safety-collar from the scabbard, before he glanced at Hanar Santon and gave the command to "Enter!"

Both of the big doors were pulled open and seven guardsmen piled into the room with weapons drawn. Their cutting-spears made the spokes of a wheel whose hub, a handspan from each of the encircling blades, was a slim man who wore ragged gray and a tightly-buckled constabulary restraint-harness which dragged his crossed wrists up his back and almost between his shoulder blades. Once his garments might have been a close-fitting suit with gloves, boots and hood all uniform with the tunic and breeches, but now he was clothed more in bruises and tatters than anything else. The guards had plainly borne King Rynert's fate in mind, and had been zealous both in their arrest and the subsequent search-and-subdue procedure.

"Well!" Dacurre covered his astonishment with a monosyllabic exclamation which might have been amuse-ment, or interest, or recognition of a familiar outline. "We would have met before, except that I recall you were in rather a hurry to leave. I think we can chat more comfortably this time, don't you?"

Aymar Dacurre had all the detestations of any high-clan conservative for the *tulathin* mercenaries, and added to that a loathing of this particular specimen of the breed if—and Aymar had no reason so far to doubt it—the battered figure before him was the root source of all Alba's present troubles. "You should not have come back."

"Let me, gran—, my lord!" Santon was on his feet, equanimity and silence washed away by anger. "I owe this *thing* for all the dirt clinging to my name and to my Honor. Let me deal with him myself."

"Hanar, be quiet. You sound like Talvalin." Dacurre's soft-spoken warning was more than most men were per-mitted, and Santon knew it. He subsided back into his seat, glowering and drumming his fingers on the sheathed *taipan* on the table in front of him but saying nothing else aloud.

Dacurre inspected the small bag laid on the table be-fore him by the sergeant commanding squad. It con-tained the results of a stringent body search: small, flat knives, a garrotting-cord, various lock-picks—and a tiny vial of thin glass which the old clan-lord rolled to and fro between finger and thumb, watching the heavy, oily movement of the fluid sealed inside. Then he stared at the *taulath*. "You are already a dead man. And the law

says this: the manner of your passing is in my hands and
not," Dacurre set the poison-vial carefully aside, "by
your own choice."

"Yes, old man, I know the formula." The mercenary
grinned without humor. "I should have had that . . .
choice tucked in my cheek where it belonged, and where
your soldiers hit me. There would then have been no
need for threats and such unpleasantness. But I'd as
soon die an easy death as a hard one. So—what do you
want to know?"

For a moment Lord Dacurre ignored the insolence
and turned his attention instead of the guards. "You
two, bring a heavy chair and secure him in it. You, get
one of the Archive clerks. You, call the steward; have
him bring wine and food. You others, watch this reptile;
if he moves, cripple him." Dacurre settled back, satisfied
that at long last there was activity of a sort, then glared
at the guardsman ordered to fetch food who had reappeared in the doorway and looked confused. "Yes,
what?"

"My lord, the steward wants to know for how many?"

"Two, man! Two—and as many of your guardsmen as
feel dry or hungry. I'll want your names afterward—to
mention favorably when I report this to your commander."

"And what about me?" asked the *taulath*.

Dacurre stared at him, as a cat might stare at a mouse
giving cheek from under the paw that caught it. Then
he smiled, and not the studied smile of cruelty but something strangely tolerant for a man so capable of anger.
"Why not? For sheer nerve alone. All right, guard, get
on with it."

"He was captured in the Hall of Kings, my lord. And
he was limping before we touched him." The sergeant-
of-Guards sounded just a little defensive about the state
of their prisoner; that sort of mistreatment was usually
the prerogative of the Drusalan Secret Police. "Otherwise we couldn't have taken him. He's a skilled fighter,
for all he's one of *them*."

"Do I hear admiration, sergeant?" asked the *taulath*

with an annoyingly arch smile. The soldier glanced side-long at his prisoner and disdained to reply.

"All right," said Hanar Santon, "enough of this. Never mind whether you admire him or not, sergeant; I presume his . . . present condition is a result of that so-admirable skill."

"Yes, my lord. Taking him alive was harder than killing him, but after what happened I thought you and my Lord Dacurre would want information rather than a corpse."

"Commended, sergeant." Santon sipped at a cup of wine and stared at the *taulath*. "Your prisoner, Aymar. I still want to kill the bastard."

"Patience. Now, you." Dacurre returned his full attention to the man strapped in the chair. "What name do we call you?"

"Call me Keythar," said the *taulath*. "In the Drusalan language it means—"

"Fox. Yes, I know that. And it isn't your name at all, is it?"

"Of course not." The man called Fox smiled slightly. "But that hardly matters, does it?"

"No." Dacurre mirrored the smile exactly. "I suppose not. But from your accent you're as Alban as I am—and I'll not speak Drusalan unless I have to, Fox."

The *taulath* shrugged indifferently. "It's a label, nothing more. I stopped caring about such niceties years ago."

"A pity you are what you are; there must have been some good in you once."

"Do I hear admiration, Lord Dacurre?" asked Hanar Santon quietly.

Dacurre looked at the younger man. "No. Regret. You'll recognize it when you're as old as I am. Now, Fox, why did you come back to the Hall of Kings when you must have known the king was dead?"

"Well, that's the question, isn't it? Who says he's dead except those who benefit?"

This was a response that startled not only the two clan-lords but the guardsmen as well, soldiers whose duties required them to overhear many things and react to none of them. Some of these soldiers, however, had seen the ripped corpse carried from the hall three weeks before, and the discovery that a *taulath*—one of those renowned for knowing secrets—was ignorant of just how dead a disemboweled man could be, came as a surprise.

"You really don't know?"

It might have been the tone or the wording of Dacurre's response that brought it home, but all the muscles of Fox's face twisted as he realized just how wrong he had been. "Ah. And I thought that the tales were spread as part of some subtle scheme to provoke unsteady clan-lords into rash action . . . or something like that." He laughed harshly, at himself as much as at the discovery of his mistake. "It would seem, Lord Aymar Dacurre, that old-fashioned directness is something my people must learn to consider all over again. I, they, all of us were thinking in curves and spirals; thinking in straight lines is unfashionable in modern politics."

"You still haven't explained why you came back."

"That one, the guard with the red beard—have him empty the belt-pouch he took from me. You'll find out."

The pouch held what Dacurre had expected it might: leaves of scrip drawn on the Crown Treasury, each with the red and black sigil stamps that indicated a nominal face value of one thousand Alban marks. They were crushed and twisted as if someone had begun to destroy them and then thought better of it. Dacurre unfolded one of the ragged bundles of paper and looked at it, nodding as he saw where the problem lay. "Rynert's authorization," he said. "These are useless."

The *taulath* nodded, and smiled a thin-lipped smile that showed how much he was pretending not to care. "As you both know, I've been out of the country," he said. "One of my people here tried turning that garbage into coin. I found out when I got back. So here I am."

"Trying to get your fee in silver," Dacurre finished for him. "Or get the value of it from Rynert's hide. A pity that he's dead."

"Don't think I wouldn't have done it either," said the *taulath*. "I . . . we . . . have our principles. We don't like to be cheated."

"Not cheated," Hanar Santon corrected. "Outmaneuvered. You should have tried to get your money before you killed Aldric Talvalin, not afterward."

"I said cheated, and I used the word correctly." For all that he was battered, bloodied and trussed like a bird for the oven, Fox was very much on his dignity—as much dignity, at least, as two high-clan-lords would give a mercenary killer credit for possessing. "Talvalin isn't alone and—"

"Tehal Kyrin, too? You cold-hearted butcher!" Santon's voice went shrill with rage and as he came out of his chair his shortsword was slicing from its sheath again. "This time I *will* kill you!"

"Sit *down!*" Dacurre glared at the younger man, then shook his head at the impatience of the younger generation. "Hanar, just every now and then why don't you stop and think before you make a fool of yourself?"

"I don't know what you mean . . ."

"Evidently. Think, I said."

"But you heard him—he said—"

Dacurre sighed. Once again the facts would have to be spelled out for Santon's benefit. It wasn't that the boy was stupid, far from it, but like his father before him once an idea got itself lodged in a Santon mind a team of horses wouldn't shift it. "He said that Aldric *isn't* alone. Present tense; doesn't that suggest anything to you? That perhaps he isn't dead either?"

"Oh. I see . . . now."

Fox had remained quiet while the two lords wrangled, but when Dacurre looked toward him again he shrugged as elaborately as his bonds allowed. "The girl doesn't concern me—and didn't then; she wasn't a part of the contract and I wasn't paid to deal with her. If she'd been in the way, well . . ." Another shrug. "But your dear king said nothing about a bodyguard."

"Bodyguard?" Aymar Dacurre blinked in surprise. This didn't sound like the lethal swordsman he knew—or thought he knew. "Aldric Talvalin doesn't have a bodyguard. Never had one, so far as I know."

"He's got one now: six Drusalans. And you might be interested to know"—the *taulath* Fox smiled like his namesake—"they're just as much *tulathin* as I am."

Santon glowered at him, wanting to believe one aspect

of the mercenary's statement but unwilling to trust the other. Before the Light of Heaven, Aldric was capable of doing such a thing, as he had proven himself capable of so much more, but while sorcery had a certain dark glamour to it the employment of *tulathin* was just dirty. It wasn't part of the Talvalin style. "How do we know that you're telling the truth about this?" he demanded. "How can we believe you about anything?"

"My Lord Dacurre," said Fox, "tell him the reason why."

Aymar didn't turn his head to address Santon directly, even though he could sense that he was being watched for a reply. Instead he gazed at the *taulath*. "Because," he said softly, "you believe me."

Fox nodded. He believed completely and without any of the many doubts his own subtle and tortuous mind could conjure up, because this old, white-bearded, balding man held the dwindling duration of his life by a thread. If Lord Dacurre was unconvinced of anything that he was told, he would go searching for what he thought was the truth with all the means at his disposal. His Honor bound the promise of brief death; that same Honor bound the promise of a death that would be screams and anguish from the beginning to the end of it.

"And because of your belief in me," said Aymar Dacurre, "I choose to believe in you. Hanar, he is speaking the truth as best he can. There are matters here I do not begin to understand, and matters beneath them that I have no desire to understand. Talvalin is alive. Good. But unless, being alive, he is doing something to keep Grand Warlord Etzel safe at home, his life or death is of small importance here."

"Etzel is dead."

The silence that followed on Fox's words was such that all in the room except for the *taulath* might have been struck dead themselves. Hanar Santon and the younger guards had known the name of Warlord Etzel as a kind of bogeyman rather than as a figure with any reality, political or otherwise, and to be told of his death was a greater shock in its way than to learn of the death of a parent. Dacurre was simply relieved. He knew that other and more complex feelings would soon take over, but just for the present Fox's news came as a tonic to offset the weariness of so many, many sleepless nights.

It was only a matter of minutes before the first niggling suspicion cut into his private euphoria. "But how did you come to know this, when you knew nothing about Rynert?" he demanded, and fixed the *taulath* with a quizzical stare. Fox matched and returned it with as much added expression as the reflection in a mirror.

"I heard about it through my usual sources of Imperial information—sources which have little interest in Alba even when they have nothing else to occupy their minds. What occupies those minds right now is the new Warlord's behavior. You might find it encouraging. He hasn't been seen in public since it was announced eighteen days ago that he had assumed the rank and style of *Woydach*. From the commands that issue from the citadel in Drakkesborg he seems more intent on recovering those provinces which have seceded from the Empire over the past few years than in pursuing Etzel's old policy of war against Alba. Either way, he's secure; and so, it seems, are you. Assuming that my sources are correct, of course, and that you can get anyone in this country to believe the word of a *taulath*."

"Never mind that," snapped Dacurre, never at his best when someone else presumed to guess at what he might be thinking. "I'll make them believe."

The *taulath* Fox inclined his head, gazing at nothing in particular; then he smiled a uniquely chilly little smile as if at some private and unpleasant joke. "Of course you will. Alban clad-lords always pay attention to what *tulathin* say, when it comes second-hand from one of their own. Except that they're not paying attention to anything you say at all right now, are they? Oh, and before you think to have it beaten out of me, the new Warlord is a man called Voord . . . late of the Secret Police. You might well know his name already . . ."

Dacurre and Santon looked at one another. They knew the name indeed; they knew, too, how closely Voord's actions in the past few years had intertwined with the military and political fate of Alba—and with the making of a notorious swordsman and sorcerer from the honor-fixated survivor of one of Alba's oldest fami-

lies. When they had at last learned all that there was to
be known about the situation, it had seemed to both of
them that Fate had woven opposites together for the
sake of entertainment: life and death, honor and magic,
Aldric Talvalin and Voord Ebanesj. What the end of the
skein might be, neither man felt qualified even to guess.

The *taulath* who called himself Fox sat still and silent
now. He had said all that there was for him to say, freely
and without the need for violent persuasion, and all that
remained was for Aymar Dacurre to keep his promise.
There was not—nor since his capture ever had been—
any chance of reprieve or escape; the *taulath* understood
that and waited quietly to die. Once the two clan-lords
finished their hasty whispered discussion, the short time
of waiting was over.

Hanar Santon nodded once to Dacurre and stood up,
more calmly now than on the past two occasions when
he had surged out of his chair fired with the desire to
kill. There was no longer hot blood in what he did, but
the vast impartial weight of the law.

"Man-called-Fox," he said, "Aymar Lord Dacurre is
satisfied with your . . . assistance. The law has given us
your life, and even if we were inclined we could not
return it. What we return, by the command of Lord Dacurre, is your choice of means to take your leave of the
life held forfeit. So choose." Santon remained standing,
but said nothing more.

The *taulath* looked at his judges and shrugged. "Why
say, when you both know already." He was staring now
at the vial Dacurre held in finger and thumb. "That
way."

"In wine?" offered Dacurre. It was courtesy, not curiosity, which prompted his question, for by tradition
someone about to die either by legal execution or by
their own hand in the *tsepanek'ulleth* ritual was accorded
more respect than their crime or their rank might have
warranted. It was not, and never had been, a matter
open to question.

"No, just in my mouth. The broken glass cuts, you
see; and the venom enters the bloodstream . . ." There
was a glint of cold amusement in Fox's eyes at the way
young Santon winced.

Dacurre did not afford him that pleasure, but the old man's lips went very thin. Poison had played its part in the shaping of Alba, but it was a part lacking in any honor. "You will forgive me," he said, "if I ask you to put your head back and allow me to drop this . . . this choice of yours from a distance safely away from your teeth and any splinters of glass you might consider surplus."

The *taulath* laughed aloud, very softly but with real rather than gallows humor. He had the look of someone who appreciated the black joke. "If we had met in another place and another time, my lord," he said, "I think I might have liked you—enough at least to grant you the same favor you grant me." He tilted back his head and opened his mouth as a child might when being dosed with medicine, received the pellet and crunched it like a sweet.

"How long?" Dacurre asked.

"My lord, I thought the questions were finished." Fox grinned, and there was blood on his teeth; slivered glass glittered between them like diamonds. "And anyway, I don't know. Nobody does for certain. The herbalist who distils it says 'quite fast,' but he hasn't used it so what does he know?"

Fox chuckled—then gasped, his eyes going wide as his whole body spasmed against the straps holding him into the chair. It passed, and he relaxed enough to grin that bloody grin again. "Perhaps he does know some—" Another convulsion drummed his heels against the floor, and whatever he had been about to say was lost in the chattering of his teeth. There was sweat on his face as the clench of muscles calmed to an irregular tic in all his limbs, but he was still grinning though by now it was more the rictus of a naked skull. "Uncomfortable," Fox somehow contrived to say, "but not really painful. Better than a *tsepan* any—"

His jaws clicked shut and cut the words off short as a final spasm killed him.

5

There was rioting in Drakkesborg.

Its cause was straightforward enough; even in the second-wealthiest city in the Empire—and there were those who quibbled even at that qualification of "second"—prices double and even treble those of bare months past were not to be borne. Such inflations happened every once in a while, the consequence of poor harvests, but never before had the merchants dared such market-place piracy as they were attempting now, and never before had the Grand Warlord allowed them to get away with it once the matter had been brought before him by citizens' deputation. Ironarse Etzel, they called him in the lower city—that and other, coarser things—but it could never be denied that here in Drakkesborg at least he always had time to hear complaints and problems. Until now.

The majority of rumors could be easily discarded; too high-flown for belief, most of them, and the remainder unlikely at best. But the fact remained that *Woydach* Etzel had been neither seen nor heard from for close to three weeks now, and that was where informed speculation took the place of rumor. There were those who said that speculation was just rumor in a finer coat, but they were the same bandiers of semantics who listened eagerly to the latest piece of gossip—or rather, educated opinion—and contributed their own thoughts to whatever the opinion had concerned. All in the most elegantly turned phrases, of course.

The business of these shocking prices, for one thing: nothing to do with poor harvests, at least not this year since the harvest had been if not spectacular then certainly more than adequate. No, the problem this time was the Emperor's intransigence. A mere child, truculently refusing the advice of elders and betters that had been quite adequate for his father and brother. A shame that Ravek had died so suddenly—he would have made a much better Emperor, certainly more tractable than Ioen who was so eager to dance to the tune of his chief military commander. *Coerhanalth Goth,* wasn't it? Nothing but a common soldier. All his fault, probably. Dividing the Empire down the middle like a wheel of cheese, what way was that to run a country? And he was probably responsible for the trade sanctions behind these price rises. A Lord-General, eh? Maybe—but not a gentleman.

And so it went on. Etzel, the story went, was closeted with his own chief military men, organizing a strategy to recover the Western Empire, remove Ioen from subversive influences, and very possibly bring the secessionist provinces back into the Imperial sphere of influence—although this last was scoffed at rather, for Etzel himself had let it be known that if places like Vreijaur and Jouvann were unwilling to remain a part of the Empire, then he would be unwilling to invite them back when they discovered the error of their ways. Although the man really should have taken the time to listen when that company of solid wide-waisted worthies had brought their petition to the citadel, or at the very least come out to receive it with his own hand rather than sending a lackey of no matter how high a rank. To be busy was one thing, and quite understandable; to be discourteous was another thing entirely.

That was what had sparked the riots, more than the prices or the scarcities or the rumor-mongers: the notion, seized on by people of the lower sort, that if they were to gain any satisfaction they would have to find it themselves. Reasonable requests had turned swiftly to demands, then threats, and before anyone with authority to stop it could do anything the stones began to fly. Market stalls were torn down and torn apart, the traders who owned them were pelted with broken fragments and with their own expensive produce—as much of it as re-

mained after the looters were done with it—and though
no injuries more serious than black eyes and bloody
noses had so far been reported, it was only a matter of
time before Authority reacted and someone was killed.
At least, someone among those who were still capable
of dying. . . .

"Giorl, please—none of that matters now. Just do
something . . ." The Grand Warlord of the Drusalan
Empire lay on his back and panted like a dog with the
effort of uttering coherent speech rather than the wordless whimpering which was all his mouth could usually
form during these sessions. The woman he addressed—
or more properly, pleaded with—paid him small heed
and continued her gentle probing of his wounds. If her
hands were gentle, the expression on her face was not.

"I'm doing it, damn you! But I still want to know
what bloody horse-doctor put these bloody stitches in."
The voice was angry, yet curiously dispassionate, that of
a skilled artist outraged by needlessly sloppy work. "And
why they rotted out before the wounds healed. Because
I have to find the fragments, good my lord, before you
start to rot as well. Another. And this one needs to be
cut free, too. Here. Swallow this; all of it." The stuff in
the cup was a liquid mingling of sweet and bitter, she
knew, and knew how hard it was to choke the fluid
down, and how long she had to wait before it took effect.
Not long, that much was certain. *"Schii'ajn nahr kagh-
hui dah . . ."*

Her words became a soft monotone of curses in half-
a-dozen languages as she selected something small and
glittering from the flat metal case beside her. Voord
braced himself, trying to blot out what was about to happen by staring at her clean white browband and the locks
of red hair that feathered over it. He had always found
Giorl attractive—the attraction of the unattainable since,
being married and that unusual thing, faithfully so, she
had invariably rejected his advances with more or less
good humor—and never more so than when he watched
her work. Perhaps because he had never been the subject of that work. Even today, filled with pain and soporific drugs, the sight of her preparations and the first chill

touch of an instrument had brought immediate, blatant arousal. That drained away perhaps three seconds later when, despite the soporifics, he began to scream.

Giorl Derawn knew that she was many things to many people: a good wife with a good husband, rare enough these days; a good mother to her daughters and to the third child on the way which she hoped would be a son; a good—indeed indispensable—servant of the Grand Warlord whoever he, she or it might be; and never mind the good, she was the best cutting-surgeon in the city of Drakkesborg.

She had often wondered why. Most surgeons were men, nowadays, and the old freedoms for working women were being eroded by the military society in the Eastern Empire, but nobody had ever dared to question her skill. Maybe it was her ever-increasing knowledge of anatomy, or her ability to distance herself from the work in hand whatever that work might be—to filter out the reactions and the noises and see only the area of flesh on which she worked—or her lack of emotional concern about the pain involved. It was a part of what she did, that was all, and her customary response to questions, arguments and pleas was simply to remember and invoke what giving birth was like.

At least it was nothing like this. She had seen many, many human bodies reduced to glistening tatters; but she had never before seen wounds that refused to bleed, or heal, or kill. Giorl did indeed want to know which of the Bodyguard's regimental surgeons had cobbled Voord back together; but this had little to do with her anger over what looked more like clumsy sail-making than sutured wounds. She wanted to find out what the injuries had looked like when they were fresh, and she had a suspicion that they had been no different from the way they appeared right now. At least he had stopped screaming.

At last Giorl finished and straightened her back, grunting slightly as her muscles made known their complaint right up her spine. Tweezering out the shreds and fragments of rotted sutures was not, perhaps, as noisy, nerve-racking or downright nasty as many of the things she had done, but she could still think of a great many things that she would sooner have been doing. Caring for her youngest daughter was one of them; the child had been unwell for the past couple of days, feverish and off her food. The instruments clinked faintly as she returned them to their padded clamps in the metal case.

And Voord groaned faintly as she stood up and turned to walk away from him.

Giorl froze in mid-stride, not wanting to believe the sound and yet knowing she had heard it. *"Teii-acht ha'v-raal,"* she swore, very softly. "Father and Mother and Maiden make it not so." The prayer must not have been heard, for when she looked back over her shoulder it was so: Voord was still alive.

Any drug whose purpose was to induce the peace of anaesthetic sleep was a systemic poison which could, in a sufficient quantity, induce the far more permanent peace of death. That had been Giorl's intention, anyway. The poppy distillate which she had given Voord had been of such a concentration that it should have stopped his pain and then his heart in a matter of a few minutes. However, it had done no more than render him a little drowsy, and that drowsiness was already wearing off to let the pain come back. Such a thing was medically impossible; but then, his continued survival of such obviously fatal injuries was just as impossible, and he had survived those for twenty days. Both impossibilities stared at her with agonized eyes and hoped silently that she could do something—*anything*—to help.

Giorl concealed her shrug and returned to Voord's bedside, wondering what in the name of Hell she *could* do. The most obvious thing to do, she had done already; and it hadn't worked. As for the alternatives . . . Giorl looked at the gaping holes in Voord's face and body and wondered what the alternatives might be. And if there were any.

"The stitching helped." Voord's weak and shaky voice cut through her indecision. "When they were closed, the . . . the wounds didn't hurt as much."

"Stitches don't work," said Giorl gently. "You've seen already. If these don't heal—and I've seen they don't— then the severed tissue will just outlast the sutures the way they did today and you'll be right back where you

were when I came in . . . and facing the same prospect.
Your choice." Voord cringed visibly. "But maybe if you
told me how these happened"—inside her head Giorl
was smiling grimly as, like it or not, she slipped into the
surgeon's customary bedside manner—"I might be able
to work out what to do about them."

Voord met her steady gaze for a few seconds, then
very pointedly turned his face away, stifling the moan
that the movement provoked.

"That won't help. Don't forget, I'm good at getting
questions answered." Giorl saw a shudder raise gooseflesh on his naked skin. "I'm good even without using
pressure, so why not talk about it? Eh?" She reached
out one hand and laid it gently on his chest, absently
noting the movements of heartbeat and respiration—
both over-fast—as she did so. "Talking might help for
all sorts of reasons, Voord Ebanesj." The rapid rise and
fall of his rib cage faltered as he held his breath, whether
in reaction to the use of his full name or hearing a voice
that had honest, if merely professional, sympathy in it.
And then the words all came tumbling out.

Aldric and Kyrin rode into Drakkesborg late in the afternoon, through the main gate in the western wall, the
Shadowgate, with the fast-setting midwinter sun at their
backs stretching their own shadows long and dark across
the snow. The guards at the gate seemed preoccupied
with other matters than the searching of baggage, and
after the most cursory of inspections were quite willing
to accept impressively signed and sealed scholarly passes
at face value, without any curiosity as to why two foreign
"scholars" should be so well armed and armored. Or
perhaps the guards knew perfectly well why anyone
would want to have weapons and battle harness close at
hand. Neither the Empire nor its cities were especially
peaceful places, and right now Drakkesborg was no
exception.

After a period of "not noticing" the riots in the hope
that the outburst of initially justified protest would burn
itself out, notice had formally been taken two days earlier
by Authority in the shape of the city's Chief of Constables.
Warnings had been posted after the first day and read

aloud by official criers at the height of the second day's
trouble. Nobody had paid the criers any attention, except
to pelt them with offal and with serious snowballs—frozen,
and cored with chunks of broken paving.

Notice had progressed to action fairly rapidly after
that. Ten squads of troopers from the urban militia had
moved out of barracks at first light, and by mid-morning
they had restored order of a sort in their own inimitable
fashion. It was only because of lenience promoted by
the Midwinter holiday season that no lives were lost, but
there were aching skulls and broken limbs enough to
suppress the fire of civil disobedience in even the hottest
head. So complete was that suppression that by the time
Aldric and Kyrin were cleared to enter the city, Drakkesborg was restored to at least a veneer of normality—
for all that the veneer was not quite thick enough as yet
to make them feel entirely comfortable . . .

"I told you, didn't I?" Kyrin's voice was low; the
things she was saying were not the kind of things she
wanted overheard. "I said I didn't like the sound of this
place. And now we're here, you say that you don't like
the feel of it. Very perceptive, Aldric my love. But just
a little slow."

Aldric smiled to himself at her unease—a thin smile,
without amusement. He had been wondering how long
it would take to come out, and was too much the gentleman to make comment about how she had come to be
in the city in the first place. "At least the passes
worked," he said mildly.

"They got us in, dear. I'd feel happier if I was convinced they'll get us out again."

"Marevna made certain that they showed no bias to
either faction."

"Meaning you get picked on by both, not neither. I
for one would like to get in off the street, with a bolted
door between me and whatever's been going on here."

"Faction fights or something. Tuenafen was like this
and—"

"I don't want to know what happened, Aldric." Kyrin
was growing more twitchy with each passing second, regardless of the way ordinary people went about their
ordinary business around her. Or perhaps because of it,

and because of the way it failed to ring quite true. "I want to find a place where I can avoid it if it happens again. Now, where?"

That was the problem. Neither knew much about Imperial Drakkesborg apart from their own preconceived opinions, and opinions were of small use in suggesting where to stay, much less how much they would be expected to pay for the privilege. Enough, and more than enough, most likely; the cost of a room for the night had increased steadily and steeply as they approached the city, and the risk that they no longer had sufficient coin to live on had become a nagging worry at the back of Kyrin's mind. However, the problem seemed not to concern Aldric.

"I have no idea where. But first we need some cash money." He spoke with nothing like the gravity their situation warranted, and Kyrin looked at him as if he had left good sense behind.

"Just where do you plan to find it? Buried in a snowdrift? Or will you just use the Echainon spellstone to conjure it out of a handful of gravel?"

"Don't be sarcastic, love, it doesn't suit you." As he spoke, his face became an icy mask that warned her she was going just a little bit too far. "And don't mention It. Not here. Just . . . don't. I know the Imperial coinage isn't worth a lot, but there are some limits." Aldric reined Lyard to a standstill and glanced at the citizens walking past, looking for the mode of dress that would indicate the sort of person he sought. "There. That's the kind of man we need."

He indicated a passerby whose noble curve of belly and rich robes might have produced a cheerful demeanor, but whose face had more the appearance of someone who lived on pickled lemons. Kyrin followed the direction of his gesture, then pointedly raised her eyebrows as Aldric dismounted and began a brief, one-sided conversation. He was doing most of the talking—none of which she could make sense of through the background buzz of other people—while the fat man's responses were a mixture of monosyllables and silent head movements. His sour expression had deepened when he was accosted about his presumably lawful occasions by a complete stranger who had both a foreign accent and a sword, but as Aldric continued to speak in what, from his frequent grins, must at least have sounded pleasant, the man's eyes became a touch less flinty. As he pointed out what were presumably directions, Kyrin could see the movement of facial muscles trying to assume the long-forgotten configuration of a smile, but only succeeding in suggesting that the last meal of lemons was fighting back.

Aldric saw the man on his way with a courteous half-bow and an inclination of his head that Kyrin noticed was covering a chuckle, then swung back into the saddle. His grin was very wide and white, and seemed somehow to be stuck in place. "Silly old bastard," he said pleasantly. "You try to be charming and what do you get?"

"Do tell," said Kyrin. The question didn't really need an answer that she could provide.

"Information. Old vinegar-face wasn't exactly chatty, but at least he told me what I wanted—where to find some money." Heeling Lyard into a leisurely walk, he swung the big courser around in the direction his informant had indicated.

"How much money?"

"Enough," he said over his shoulder, "to make the question of what we'll have to pay for a room one we don't need to worry about."

"Are you feeling all right, Aldric?" It was only halfway to a joke, because there was nothing in the baggage they could sell except for the two ponies which carried it, and he knew as well as she how little else they owned that could be turned into coinage. As an urgent heel in gray K'schei's ribs brought her level, Kyrin could see that his wide grin had relaxed to an ordinary smile.

"Oh, yes." He stared over Lyard's ears and kept on smiling. "I feel just fine—and so will you, soon." He flicked one finger at the tooling of his saddle as if chivvying a fly—except that there were no flies in a Drusalan winter. "Listen: once there was a man who was asked to do a favor. It was the sort of favor that—"

"Come to the point, will you! What so-crafty scheme have you got to pull out of your sleeve this time, eh?"

"Not a scheme, and not a sleeve. Scrip and saddle are

the words you need. There's a letter of credit sewn into the welting just here"—again the fly-swatting flick—"and we're heading for the mercantile quarter of the city to find the guild which honors it."

Kyrin blinked, then grinned, then laughed aloud. "You! I should have guessed! Your sour friend was a merchant, then?"

"No friend of mine, love. Yes—and a wealthy one."

"He didn't look to enjoy life much."

"Each to his own delight in life. I've found mine."

"I know." She leaned over, reaching out to touch his hand. "And I'm glad."

Aldric returned the pressure of her fingers, the pinkness about cheeks and ears not entirely a result of the cold air. He could still be very shy, sometimes, about the most innocent public displays of affection; and Kyrin could remember other times when he was not shy at all.

"One thing you didn't ask."

"Mm?"

" 'How much is the credit letter worth?' Unless you're not really interested." With finger and thumb he eased the letter itself from the saddle-stitching—it was superfine parchment, rolled small as a quill—and waved it in front of her nose before tucking it into the deep cuff of his glove.

"Uh, no. I mean, yes. I mean, how much is the credit letter worth?" She could tell already, from the glitter in his eyes, that he wasn't carrying small change.

"Does a value of thirty thousand deniers make you feel a little happier? Because that's what we have, if we need it."

Tehal Kyrin, Harek's daughter, had suffered many shocks and surprises since she took up with this young Alban nobleman, but she had never been the butt of jokes and wasn't pleased at being used as one right now. Then, as he began to explain the system which made the letter work, a system which her own family had used in their foreign trade dealings, she realized that he wasn't joking after all.

"But why so much?"

"No more than a precaution. I'd sooner have more available funds than I'd ever need to call on than be without enough—especially with the direction the Empire's currency has been taking of late." He extended an index finger, then stabbed it toward the ground. "Downward all the way. At least bullion gold is still reliable."

"However did you get so much? I . . ." Kyrin hesitated, not sure how he would take what she was about to say, then ventured the observation away. "I never thought you were so rich."

Aldric seemed to find her confusion funny rather than offensive. "What you mean is that you never dreamed you'd see me with more than a handful of silver to my name. Eh?" Somewhat shamefaced, Kyrin nodded. "Uh-huh. Well, all you need is to remember what my name is . . . and the rank, and the style, and the title that go with it: *Ilauem-arluth inyen'kai* Talvalin. Once in a while it's pleasant to find all of that's worth more than just a point of aim for other people's weapons."

"You're doing this the usual way, with guild authority over existing funds?"

"Only about one-third of what was available." Aldric smiled crookedly. "I didn't want to be greedy."

"Oh, Heaven forbid. But if you've had a falling-out with Rynert the King, then can't he take control of your treasury?"

Aldric shook his head; he'd already considered that risk. It was why his negotiations were with Guild Freyjan rather than with a smaller guild working on a less usurious rate of interest. Guild Freyjan's interest, at least where he was concerned, wasn't merely on him but *in* him. They liked to take care of their investment at both ends of the transaction; and only if Rynert had gone completely insane would he dare locking horns with a merchant guild capable of bringing all trade both in and out of Alba to a dead stop. "He might risk commandeering the gold I didn't pledge to the guild—if the other lords allowed him to set that sort of dangerous precedent—but if he stole what Freyjans regard as their own property until I surrender the credit note, then they'd lay such trading sanctions on Alba that he'd be forced to back down within a week."

"Very clever. I applaud you."

"Quietly, or people will wonder." He reined in and winked at her as he slid from Lyard's saddle to the snow-sprinkled ground. "And we don't want the people in here to wonder any more than they have to already." The elaborate crest of Guild Freyjan worked in brass above the door told Kyrin plainly enough what "in here" was. She nodded at him and patted her gloved palms together very softly, then followed him to the ground.

They secured both pairs of horses to the hitching-rail which Freyjan had so thoughtfully provided for their equestrian customers, dropped a coin or two into the upturned palm of the liveried guild servant whose duty it was to make sure that the animals weren't stolen or their gear interfered with while their owners were away, and went inside House Freyjan. Inside was lit by good quality oil-lamps, and managed to convey an air of un-ruffled efficiency which Kyrin supposed made those who came through Freyjan's doors feel that their money was not being put to flippant use. All that efficiency served only to give everyone they met a few seconds' free time in which to look at them, either with frank curiosity or in the more indirect way that passed for manners. Aldric was long since used to the sidelong glances which people directed more or less covertly at him; the black and silver clothing which he preferred was a statement of faction in the Drusalan Empire, indicating his support for the *Woydachul*, the Grand Warlord's party. The menacing presence of a combat-slung longsword probably had something to do with it as well.

"Sir, milady?" The speaker—he was using Jouvaine, but then in the worlds of art and literature, diplomacy and its bastard cousin finance, who didn't?—was hardly the sort of man Kyrin expected to see in a mercantile house. Mid-twenties like Aldric, or a little younger, he towered over both of them and from the set of his face was torn between curiosity and a definite dislike of the fact that they were both wearing swords. For his part, he was wearing not only a sword but a small repeater crossbow, and half-armor besides; though the fact that everything was marked with the guild crest made it all right . . . more or less.

"Cash conversion," she heard Aldric say, sounding

more authoritative then he probably felt. "Credit scrip to Drusalan florins. Cipher code authority *kourgath*."

"Sir." The word had a definite "so *you* say" feel about it, but the guard was courtesy personified as he gestured them to comfortably quilted chairs set by a table which bore a dish of nuts, dried fruits and other small-foods on the same tray as goblets and a flagon of wine. Aldric glanced at the hospitalities and gave a perfunctory nod which managed to suggest that he had expected nothing less, then settled down to take his ease until whoever was to speak to him came out and did so.

The man who emerged was moving with more brisk enthusiasm than the guard's studied lethargy might have suggested was available in the whole building, but then— small and tubby though he might have been—this newcomer evidently knew what that particular code authority was all about. Gossip travels, even in merchant banks. He bowed nicely to Kyrin, deeply to Aldric, sat down and let it be known that after the customary procedures were complete he was at their disposal for as much cash as they cared to handle. At the usual rate of interest and currency conversion charges, of course . . .

"It seems to me," said Giorl severely once Voord's confession had run its course, "that you're lucky to be even this much alive."

"I don't know what you mean." Exhausted from the pain of injury, the pain of surgery and the soul-wrenching effort of telling everything about his present situation to the one person in the Empire he least wanted to know about it, *Woydach* Voord was content merely to lie still on the thin, hard mattress of sponge-clean leather and be glad he wasn't hurting more than usual.

"I mean that instead of just these mortal wounds which neither heal nor kill you, what about being trapped in a body which had truly died and was decomposing all around your still-living awareness of it? At least you have the good fortune to be reasonably intact." Giorl polished one of her surgical probes on a piece of soft cloth and studied it incuriously. "But from all I've heard, the high stakes in sorcery demand a high price.

I'll stick to more natural skills, thanks very much. Now, about these cuts and all the other mess . . . you say that closing the wounds eases the pain?"

"Yes, damn you, I've said so already!" Voord would have shouted at her had the strain of producing anything above a whisper not begun to squeeze his entrails out of the holes in either flank. He collapsed back again, panting and bathed in sweat. "Yes. Close them . . . please."

"Sutures won't work, the dermal layer outlasts them; we know that much already . . ." Giorl was talking more to herself than Voord, the words mostly medical terms, no more than audible thought and not making much sense to a layman even in his full senses, never mind one who was delirious and almost insane with agony. "Yes, yes," she said after a while, emerging from her muttered reverie, "we could try that, it would at least create no further harm . . ."

"What are you talking about, woman?" Voord stared straight up at the ceiling and tried to control his temper and impatience, because losing one or both did nothing except cause him more pain.

"Silver wire. I could use it to close the cuts and repair the remains of the other damage. It wouldn't rot, and it wouldn't react against your body tissue."

"Silver wire." He repeated the words as if tasting them. "Have you done this before?"

"No." The blunt frankness of Giorl's reply was supported by what else she had to say. "And I haven't tried to heal a man who ought to be three weeks dead, either—just before you ask."

The sound Voord made was like a cat being sick. Only Giorl, more familiar than anyone else in the city with the sounds humans could make under great stress, could have identified it as a laugh. "Do I win the match?" she asked.

"Only half the points," said Voord. "You're forgetting who I am." He grinned at her, a horrid expression like that on the face of a five-day corpse. "The Grand Warlord deserves gold wire at least."

Giorl stared at him, then laughed softly at the determined, ironic attempt at humor. Suffering seemed to be doing something to improve the Voord she knew, changing him inside, maybe even making him into a better person more able to appreciate the difficulties of others. Or maybe not. But it would be an interesting development to watch. "Of course, my lord," she said, still laughing just a little. "Gold wire indeed, my lord. And would my lord also care for little jewels where the ends of wire are twisted together . . . ? Of course," Giorl continued after a moment, "I can't use pure gold wire. Too soft. Where would I find silver-gilt?"

"Send one of my body-servants to the fortress armory. They should have what you want."

"What I want, *Woydach,* is to go home. There are other things that need doing."

"Afterward. I come first."

Giorl kept the obvious comment to herself and spoke to a summoned servant instead. Once the man had gone about her business, she returned her attentions to Voord and to the confidences he had imparted to her. She had never met a sorcerer before, and apart from curiosity had never really wanted to. Giorl disapproved of users of the Art Magic—not in the same way as the Imperial Courts of Law might do, but simply because in her experience there was already trouble enough in the world without bringing in more from Outside. Voord's present situation was a case in point. The thought of living this horrific half-life was enough to make even her skin creep, and the one way to hope for escape was a route along which she would guide him only with the greatest reluctance.

"Have you considered," she said at last, "trying to shake free of this curse by the . . . ah . . . same means as it was laid on you? Have you attempted to reverse the spell?"

"Yes, and no."

"Mother and Maiden, man, why not?"

Voord's teeth showed as his lips twitched back in an expression somewhere between rueful smile and snarl of impatience. "Because," he said, "no matter what it says in children's stories, sorcery is rather more than just the waving of a wand. To grant power, it needs power. And the sorcery I need takes more than most. I couldn't do it and survive the strain, not like this, except that . . . that now, 'not surviving' might mean something worse than death. I'm afraid to die and find I'm still alive . . .''

"There should be enough here to keep us comfortable," said Aldric, hefting a money-purse in the palm of his hand.

"After the trouble they put you through, I should think so." Kyrin was still feeling somewhat ruffled by what had been so lightly introduced as "customary procedures," the way Guild Freyjan had checked and investigated everything to do with Aldric before parting with anything more substantial than good manners, and that he himself had been completely unconcerned did only a little to calm her down.

The cipher code was only the first step. After that, and with the big guard in close attendance, had come comparisons with what was presumably a description prepared and circulated by the Guild House in Alba; comparisons that were ticked off a list like a housewife shopping in the market. Height, weight (there were slight problems with *that* one), eye color, visible scars, seals and similar means of identification and finally, comparison through lenses of thumbprints made on glass.

When first setting up this financial arrangement back in Alba, Aldric had provided two-score and some-odd prints of each thumb on small strips of glass, one for each of the Houses set up by Guild Freyjan to manage their affairs. These had been sent out together with a copy of the identification chart and would be utilized, they had told him, to make certain that the person attempting to make use of Talvalin money was the person entitled to it. He had provided a fresh thumbprint today, on another strip of glass, and they had both watched while one of the Guild's experts in such matters had compared the prints, first side by side and then with the new overlaying the old, looking for points of similarity or difference. Only when that had been completed was Kyrin able to detect real warmth in any Guildsman's smile. And more important still, the guard had been dismissed.

Apart from finally getting to use his own money, Aldric also gained some advice—free, for a wonder; there were few enough things in a Guild House that didn't have some sort of price tag—concerning lodging-taverns in the city. From the shape of him, the Guildsman who provided the information was most likely recommending not only which tavern had the best rooms for the best price, but the best food for any price. That was all right; neither Kyrin nor Aldric had ever known each other to be averse to a good meal . . .

"It's getting late, m'love. Let's get to where we're going."

"Good." Kyrin hunched down into the deep fur lining her hood and watched as a single snowflake dropped like a feather from the evening sky. "He made it sound a good place to stay, at least."

"And eat. I'd say he—"

The woman came running down the street toward them, stumbling, skidding on the snow that traffic had packed down between the cobblestones and screaming, always screaming. Her words were Drusalan, more or less—maybe a local dialect or something of the sort—but whatever the reason, she was ignored. More than ignored: ostentatiously rejected. People returning home on foot the short distance from where they had been shopping in the mercantile quarter of Drakkesborg, merchant families of quality who had town houses hereabouts, actually turned their backs to her, pretending that neither she nor her frantic shrieks existed.

Not understanding anything but the poor woman's distress, Aldric shot a glance at Kyrin; it was returned augmented by a shrug that said plainly *your choice*. Kyrin suspected that she knew only too well why this woman was being treated as an outcast, and if Aldric didn't know now was hardly the time to educate him. That need for a decision, and reasons to help make it, were perhaps what prompted the Alban to knee Lyard sideways, blocking the street. No matter how crazed she might be, the woman was at least sane enough not to attempt barging past a packpony linked by leading-reins to sixteen hands and a good many pounds'-weight of coal-black warhorse.

"What's the matter?" Aldric asked it courteously;

more courteously than he needed, for by her dress the woman was a servant and thus several classes further down the rigid Drusalan social scale than even foreigners. What he got in reply was a slipshod babble of words which, after the first sentence had helped his brain lock into some sort of understanding, were not blurred so much by dialect as by a mind skidding along the edge of desperation-born hysterics.

"Hnach-at, keii'ach da?" This time when he repeated the question it slashed out like a whipcut, in the clipped high-to-low mode that any armed and mounted man could use to a woman on foot, except when that woman was without doubt Princess Marya Marevna, sister of the Emperor . . . or Tehal Kyrin with a sword across her back.

It acted as he had hoped, like the slap across the face of any hysteric, to restore at least a degree of coherence. "Muh-muh-muh," was all the woman managed at first, but that was more a result of her frantic run along the street than anything else.

She clutched at his stirrup-iron, face red and sweaty despite the evening chill, and gasped breath into her outraged lungs. Finally, as calm as anyone might be after such exertion, she looked up into his face and said in better Court Drusalan than he expected to hear, "My lady's little daughter lies dying, lord. I . . . I ask humbly, of your courtesy—help me." Her grip on stirrup and booted ankle tightened as her control slipped a little, and all the forced courtliness of her language dissolved in the anguish of one word. *"Please . . . ?"*

"Oh, God . . . Kyrin? You know more than I do about these things."

"No promises." She spoke softly, and in Alban. "But go with her. I'll—I'll see what can be done." *And,* she looked the thought at him but kept its sound to herself, *what* you *can do, my dear . . .*

Giorl, equipped with pincers and long-nosed pliers instead of her more usual surgical equipment, and feeling more like an armorer than a physician, had almost finished her task when the knock came at the door. Without being told, one of the servants—who took care to

remain well out of earshot when the *Woydach* had
company—moved from his at-ease position to the great
steel bar that ensured privacy, and only then paused to
await instruction.

"Tell him to open it," said Voord. He spoke with difficulty through teeth clenched tight shut, because neither
the mild soporifics nor a large quantity of distilled alcohol had done anything to alleviate the pain of Giorl's
metal-work until she completed her operations on any
given injury. Even after she was done, all he had to be
thankful for was that the wounds once closed faded to
a dull discomfort rather than the white-hot pain when
they gaped open; and now only the sword-stabs in his
flanks remained to be sewn shut.

"The Warlord commands: let the door be opened."
Giorl spoke the few high-mode words over her shoulder
without either turning around or slackening the grip of
her fingers and thumb on the layers of skin, muscle and
subcutaneous fat through which she was threading an
alcohol-doused gilt wire. Any loss of concentration and
it would be all to do again, something for which Voord
wouldn't thank her. It was strange work, more mechanical repair than healing, and despite the pain it was plainly
causing Voord it was like neither of the two skills which
made her so important in the city of Drakkesborg.

Three men came in. They had evidently come directly
from outside the building, for newly fallen snow was still
piled deep on the hoods and shoulders of their Army
overrobes, while inside the military mantles—Giorl paused
in her work to stare until a whimpering groan from
Voord reminded her of the task at hand—they wore the
all-concealing garb of *tulathin*.

Only when the biggest of the trio put back his face-
concealing mask did she feel a little more at ease. He at
least was a man familiar enough to any who had known
Voord Ebanesj in the past few years: the man called
Tagen, who was Voord's closest friend, confidante, bodyguard and some said lover. Certainly his presence indicated that the other two were friendly—so far as anyone
could claim that a *taulath* was friendly.

"Tagen, I told you to take five men," said Voord, and
for all the weakness in his voice he overlaid the trembling

fraility with menace. "I see you and two others. What happened?"

For all that she couldn't see them, Giorl was conscious of the various servants in the room taking as hasty a leave as good manners would permit. Certainly Tagen said nothing until the sound of the great door closing made it plain that he and his people were alone again. She, of course, remained—not only because the work she was performing on Voord's tattered body was not something he would allow her to leave unfinished no matter what the circumstances, but Voord and Tagen were both well aware that Giorl Derawn had already heard so many secrets that one more wouldn't make a deal of difference.

"What happened, sir, was that he wasn't alone."

"The woman?" Voord sat up with a jerk, then lay back gasping as Giorl glared at him and continued to stitch. "I told you about the woman; I warned you before you left Drakkesborg that he wasn't traveling alone, so what went wrong?"

"When we found him, he was being attacked already. You wanted him alive, so we killed as many of the others as we could, but by the time we were finished he had gone. There was snow falling, tracking was a waste of time, so instead of trying to follow we cleaned up our own mess, took the bodies out of sight into the forest for the wolves to deal with and left the steading where we found him as the owner would have wanted to find it. That's what happened, sir. We lost three; the others were very good."

"The others . . . Tagen, what were they? Mercenaries or hired bodyguards who had turned on their employer, or just plain bandits that you interrupted?"

"They were *tulathin*. Just like us."

Voord swallowed this piece of information with as much reluctance as if it was a mouthful of rotten meat, staring at the ceiling and no longer reacting to Giorl's attentions, in a manner that she found unsettling. What she was doing—the same thing that she had been doing this hour or more—was hurting no less; he simply wasn't noticing it anymore. "And what about the target? You said he got away. Surely you went after him when you finished covering your tracks—or had he covered his own too well for that?"

"Sir, I said already—he didn't cover his tracks, the snowstorm did. Even if we had gone straight after him we would have lost him just as quickly as—"

"As you did by doing nothing whatsoever!"

"Certainly he's still alive, sir."

"Oh. And what makes you so sure of that? Knowing it's what I want to hear, maybe?"

"The *tulathin* say so, sir."

"Ah. Wonderful. I'm utterly convinced." Voord jerked and made a whining sound down his nose as Giorl sealed the last-but-one-loop of wire with a quick rotary twist of the pliers. Patient stared at surgeon, surgeon gazed at patient, and no emotion was transmitted either way.

"Almost done," said Giorl. "I could leave the last until you've finished talking . . ."

"No, not when I'm just getting used to the notion of constant pain. Get on with it, and get it over with. I might be needing you for other matters."

"*Woydach'ann,* you told me that when I was finished here I could go home. My daughter is sick. She needs me. She—"

"Can wait. Enough. Finish. Now, Tagen, tell me how this remarkable mess could have happened when I trusted all the planning to yourself and the *tulathin?* What went wrong?"

"They, and the three who died, have worked for you and for *Kagh' Ernvakh* this year or more. But they remain what they first were, *tulathin.* A clannish lot, regardless of their hired loyalties. Most importantly, they have a net of spies and informants all over Alba and the Empire." Tagen walked a little closer, seeming either deliberately or unconsciously to be distancing himself from the two *tulathin.*

"What I suspect happened," he continued in the same careful monotone, "was what someone else wanted Tal— . . . him dead, and hired *tulathin* of their own. Both ours and theirs obtained their information from the same source, went to the same place and . . . well. An unfortunate coincidence."

Giorl finished off all her sutures by braiding a scrap of soft leather into the wires, so that the sharpened ends would not catch on clothing or other skin. She was listening to all that was being said, but without any great attention since there was a feeling about the whole business which suggested she would soon be hearing about it over and over to the point of boredom.

"Is that what they told you?" Voord's voice had lost most of its emotion, as if he had seen sense and regained full control of his temper. "Or was it an opinion you formed yourself?"

"Something of both, sir." Tagen stiffened fractionally, seeing what Voord was driving at. "Though they did take great pains to tell me their view of the situation, and wasted no time about it either. Sir."

"And was that all they told you?"

"Yes, sir."

Voord took a long swallow of the drug-laced spirit that waited in a cup beside his bed. A dribble of the stuff ran like purple blood from one corner of his mouth as his lips quirked in a sort of smile and Giorl, seeing it, knew that whatever suffering had done to him it had not erased the mind-set of the man with whom she was familiar.

"And tell me, Tagen—again, in your opinion—was this *all* that they told you all that they knew?"

"Yes, sir." And then that deadly pause. "I believe so, anyway."

"So." Voord raised himself on one elbow, brows furrowing a touch as the ache of old/new injuries nagged at his nerves but came nowhere near the stabbing anguish of before. "Guards! *Guards!*"

Soldiers sprinted into the room with gisarms at the ready. None of them knew why they had been summoned, just that when it was the new *Woydach* who did the summoning then it was as well not to keep him waiting. They stamped to attention, weapons ready at port-arms, and waited for orders. As usual, they didn't wait long.

"Those two," said Voord, indicating the startled *tulathin* who had just now realized how horribly things

were going wrong, "are to be prepared for stringent interrogation. No, repeat no, preliminary questioning is to
be carried out. By my command. Take them away."

Even through the noises of armored men moving in
formation and the voices raised in protest, Giorl heard
Tagen's breath come out in a sigh of pure relief. His
Commander was evidently in one of those moods where
listening to reason wasn't a priority, and at such a time
not even long-time friendship was a protection.

"My lord," said Giorl, even though she knew already
that it was a waste of breath, "your wounds are closed
to the best of my ability. May I hold you to your promise
and go tend my daughter now?"

"Of course not." Voord swung his feet to the floor
and stood upright unaided for the first time in several
days. He chuckled and reached for his clothing. "Aren't
you forgetting what *I* pay you for, Giorl Derawn? All
this doctoring is what you do for other people. For me,
you extract secrets."

"But I only have my surgeon's instruments!"

"They're sharp; they hurt; they'll do. After all, it was
a leather-working knife that first time. So improvise."

Giorl shrugged. The sooner she was done here, the
sooner she could get home and take care of Mal, because the poor child really was *not* well . . . "All right,"
she said, all brisk now because that was the best way to
be in present circumstances. The small, bright steel
things clinked softly in their sprung clips as she closed
the case and picked it up. "I wasn't really listening.
Those two . . . ?"

"They claim they've told me everything," said Tagen
helpfully.

"Oh, that old chestnut," said Giorl wearily. "Well,
then. Let's see if they're sure . . ."

6

Aldric and Kyrin followed the woman as closely and as quickly as they—encumbered by four horses, and two of those laden with baggage—could follow someone on foot who knew the layout of the busy streets and was moving with a speed born of panic. There was little opportunity to say much either to her or to each other, which was perhaps as well. Once again there was the unpleasant spectacle of other pedestrians looking, recognizing and then deliberately snubbing, and even though Aldric seemed not to notice—or betrayed nothing of it if he had—Kyrin was disliking the situation more and more.

The place to which the woman led them was a town house typical of the well-to-do area of an Imperial city. Kyrin had seen a similar style before, in Tuenafen; it presented to the world the usual featureless outer wall, a wall broken only by the house doorway set square in front up a small flight of steps. There was no stable entrance; those who could afford to live in this part of town could easily afford the rent of space elsewhere for carriage or horses, and had enough servants in the house to fetch conveyance when it was needed. Rather than leaning out over the street in the way older houses did, this—like the others to either side—was set well back. There was a high hedge to either side, thickly capped with snow, to maintain a degree of privacy from even its nearest neighbors. Kyrin pursed her lips and nodded, seeing still more apparent confirmation of her doubts—but like her other private thoughts, she kept this one

quiet; right now, except in the matter of medicine, her
opinions were not required.

The elderly man who came out as the horses clattered
to a halt had evidently been waiting for the woman to
return. It was equally evident as he held the bridles
while Aldric and Kyrin dismounted that he had been
weeping, and his renewed tears and prayers of gratitude
as they went past him and into the house were either
genuine or remarkably well acted.

And the mist of pain met them just inside the door;
it was like an acrid flavor tasted by the mind but not by
any other sense, and it was of such intensity that it made
them both hesitate on the threshold. "Dying of what?"
Aldric wondered aloud for the first time.

Kyrin remained silent. Her own past experience as a
physician's aide had taught her all the odors of a sick-
room, and for all that a deal of this was born of immediate suffering much more of it seemed an echo of older
agony. She glanced at Aldric, carefully sidelong from the
corner of one eye, but saw nothing to indicate that he
detected any of that strata of past pain. What she felt
now merely reinforced what she had seen in the street
and what she had guessed from that sight, seen before
in her own country: people ignoring, people not caring,
people taking the opportunity for a deliberately blatant
insult. Never mind that it was in the better part of town,
never mind its neat, clean exterior, never mind the servants. They were his servants, and this was his house.
The hangman's house . . .

"What in the name of Heaven . . . ?" The servant
woman had run off toward some inner room, leaving
them alone. Aldric had opened a door, looked inside—
and now was staring at the racks of stoppered bottles, the
shelves of jars, the cases of small glittering instruments—
mostly metal, some of glass—all looking wickedly
sharp.

Kyrin peered in over his shoulder and sucked in a
breath between her teeth. She had expected something
of the sort, iron and leather engines of brutality, but
these were too . . . too subtle. Too delicate. Not the
hangman's house, then. Someone more skilled, more so-
phisticated. She felt the fine hairs lift on her arms and

at the nape of her neck as a shudder like an icy needle ran down the core of her spine.

Alba's legal system was unlike that of Drusul and Valhol, having no place for the use of torture, and Aldric plainly didn't recognize the blades and needles for what they had to be—implements not for the relieving of pain but for the causing of it. Kyrin was reluctant to explain, but was drawing breath when hesitation, sense and caution were each and all drowned out by the sound from deeper within the house. It was a scream, thin, wavering and very weak—the sound of a child in pain.

We have to get out now, at once, she thought, hating herself for it, and grabbed at Aldric's sleeve to pull him away in the grace-time while nobody but servants knew that they were there. And then it was too late, for the woman was back and there was a man with her.

He too had been weeping, but now was blotting at his eyes with a cloth and trying to recover something that approximated dignity with which to greet his guests. Kyrin stared hard at him, trying to read from his face, his eyes, his stance, anything at all that would confirm he was an evil creature undeserving of their help or sympathy. She read only desperation and an aching, helpless grief so that no matter what suspicions she still harbored, the fear that they had come too late still twisted deep inside her like a knotted cord drawn tight.

"Of all days," the man said in a voice that was almost flat calm and trembling with the effort of staying so, "of all days for me not to know. Of all days for her to be gone and for me not to know . . ."

He blinked at them, seeing a man in black and silver and a woman in gray and blue, both with sword-hilts rearing above their shoulders, looking in the dim light and their hunched furs more capable of taking life than saving it, and clenched his fists until the knucklebones gleamed white through the tight-drawn skin.

"Sir, madam," he said with that same dreadful calm, "I thank you. I apologize for troubling you. But swords will not . . . not save . . ." His lip quivered, he turned his face away in an attempt to regain the control that was slipping so fast and only one word escaped him: "Help."

Aldric turned his head slowly to stare at Kyrin, wondering why she had already held back far longer than he would have thought her capable of doing in this circumstance. She tried to meet that stare and had to look away. *You took an oath.* The voice in her head was her own, and yet so heavy with accusation that it was not hers at all. *You didn't quibble then. Why do it now? He can't believe that you're just standing here. Tell him why and walk away, maybe he'll understand—or do what you swore to, that night by starlight. But either way, be honest . . .*

Kyrin tugged back her hood, heedless of the snow that fell from it to the floor, and began to walk rapidly down the corridor in the direction from which the man had come. She heard another rustle and thump which told that Aldric had just followed suit, and smiled a swift tight smile which creased little lines into her face. As she opened the door at the end of the passage and saw the bed whose size made the tiny body writhing feebly in it look even smaller and more helpless, the smile went away. "Your servant-woman told us about the child," she said. "Now you tell me. How long has she been like this, and where is the site of the pain . . . ?"

The sight and sound of someone being decisive and knowing—or even just seeming to know—what to do was enough to start the man talking; and once started, he seemed unable to stop until he was rid of all his hopes and fears. Most was just background-noise to Kyrin—she had more important things requiring her attention than to hang on every word—but she listened closely enough to hear symptoms described and thus guess at causes . . . as well as having her own mistaken notions set to rights.

It became plain that the man, Ryn Derawn, was neither a hangman nor a torturer, except maybe of speech. He was a jeweler and goldsmith, a self-styled artist in the precious stones and metals, and a happily married man with a loving wife and two fine daughters. The younger child, Mal, had been troubled with fever and an upset stomach these two days past, and only that morning had been dosed with an infusion meant to relieve it. His wife had given the medicine herself, just before she went out to work . . .

. . . And at first it seemed to help. Then the complaints and crying had turned to screams so harrowing that Ryn had sent a servant with Lorei, his elder daughter, clear across the city to stay with relatives until all was over. One way or another. And still there was no sign of his wife's return . . .

"Why, man. What could she do?"

Ryn smiled wanly. "Everything," he said. "Giorl's the finest surgeon in Drakkesborg."

Kyrin was too intent on the second stage of her examination to waste time or breath on comment, but Aldric could almost hear her eyebrows going up from where he stood. He had already told her what the conventional Alban attitude would be to women who were involved in medical practice, and there was no reason to believe that the Drusalan Empire would be any less straitlaced in the matter. And that was just where physicians were concerned; surgeons, who not only touched bodies but opened them up and rummaged about inside, would be regarded even more askance. Small wonder that the servants from this house were treated as if they were involved in something dirty . . .

She shook her head and dismissed the annoyance to a part of her mind where it wouldn't interfere with the business at hand. That part of her mind was already almost certain about what was wrong here, and just one more test would prove it. Kyrin laid the tips of her fingers on Mal's lower belly, half a palm's width below and in from where the child's hip-bone was visible, and pressed down barely enough to indent the skin. It was more than enough. Mal's eyes and mouth went wide and she screamed. The little girl's shriek of agony had two effects: it confirmed Kyrin's diagnosis . . .

. . . And it provoked Aldric, outraged by the sound, to snatch away her hand with excessive speed and violence, and to snarl something viciously angry at her for causing the child unnecessary pain. Kyrin stared at him, then at the flattened blade of his right hand, and realized with something of a start that the oversight of not explaining what she was about had almost earned her that hand across the face.

Almost, but not quite; and if he *had* hit her Kyrin

knew she had only herself to blame. Ryn had flinched from the scream and the pain which had provoked it, but he was evidently familiar with—or had been told about—this apparently brutal but very proper and accurate test for an inflammation in one particular part of the bowels. Aldric was *not* familiar with it, had *not* been told and had laudably—if barely—restrained himself from reacting to what must have looked like casual and thoughtless probing.

"Thank you," said Kyrin, and if her voice was shaking who could blame her; she knew better than most the power in a focused strike from that particular right hand. "For not hitting me. I should have warned you."

Aldric's hand relaxed now, and he had released his grip on Kyrin's wrist, but he still looked uncomfortable and embarrassed by all that had happened.

"I had to make sure."

"That she was in pain?" There was confusion rather than sarcasm in his voice. "We knew that much already."

"But not why. I know now, and what we can do about it. There's a little tag of tissue, a useless afterthought called an *appendix,* in everyone's guts; not even my master knew what it was for, but he knew what it sometimes did. This." She gestured down at Mal, who had sunk back into an uneasy muttering drowse until the next spike of pain came to disturb her. "This infant's *appendix* has somehow become inflamed or infected, and that test was the final proof. Either we cut it out, or it bursts. And if it bursts, she dies."

"One of the guardsmen in Dunrath fell sick with that," said Aldric, "and my father's physician cut it out of him."

"And . . . ?"

"He lived—long enough to be proud of the scar, and long enough for Duergar Vathach's people to kill him. But he lived. I want this child to live."

Kyrin eyed him thoughtfully, thankful that he couldn't read what was going on in her mind right now. At least she could stand by and take over if she had to—but hopefully that wouldn't be necessary. She took the plunge.

"And I want you to help. Please . . ." The expression on Aldric's face changed and he opened his mouth to protest, then shut it again. "Ryn Derawn, listen to me. I don't dare move your daughter in case her *appendix* bursts, so we'll have to work here. There will be mess. Be ready to change the bed—including the mattress. Order clean linens brought here so that we can wrap the child and shift her out of here immediately we're done. Then go to the kitchen and have water put to boil—lots of it."

"Lady, both the bath and kitchen coppers will be bubbling by now." Ryn gave her a feeble smile. "It is midwinter, after all."

"Better. Then do this: take the biggest pot that has a lid, fill it with the boiling water, have your cook put in salt to four parts in the hundred, then put the lid on and keep it on while the pot is brought up here."

"As she says, there's going to be a mess. But a hot, clean mess." Aldric sounded very brisk, but there was an edge to his voice that Kyrin hadn't heard before.

"Quite so." Kyrin gave him a funny look, but said nothing else until Ryn was out of the room and about his various errands. "Now *kailin-eir* Talvalin, what's biting you? Afraid of a little blood?"

"No. But there need not be any." He unhooked the cross-strap of her scabbard and let Widowmaker slide from across his back, then raised the longsword until her pommel was between them. A thread of blue-white fire coiled deep within the crystal that had been set only recently into the *taiken* hilt, shifting slowly as oil patterns on water. "You're forgetting the Echainon stone."

"I am not, and I was not. But I will not let you use it."

"Why not? You've seen that it works! We both have!"

"On open wounds, Aldric. I haven't yet seen it cleanse foul matter from deep within a body. Because of that, and because of other matters, I can't and won't trust it on this child."

"What other matters?"

"Because of where we are . . . as you continually remind me. Obvious sorcery would not be such a good idea here in Drakkesborg." *And because you place too much reliance on that thing already. That, and the sword it's mounted in. I wasn't happy when you put the spell-stone there. Not happy at all.* "You see?"

"Yes. Yes, I see." He unhooked Widowmaker and wrapped her in her belts, then laid the weapon to one side. "I see much better than I thought. So what do you want me to do?"

"Help me select the proper instruments." Kyrin walked to the door, paused and glanced over her shoulder at him with a smile around her eyes if not quite on her lips. "You might discover uses for sharp steel that not even your weapon-master ever taught you. And better uses than you ever thought possible. Come on."

The place was not the torch-lit stone cavern of an ordinary torture chamber; one of Giorl's predecessors had seen to that when he (or had it been another *she?*) redesigned what was now the citadel's principal interrogation room. There were glazed white tiles on the floor, the walls and the domed ceiling which made the room look like the inside of a skull, and it was illuminated by lensed oil-lamps so that there were no shadows in which the eye could find shelter from the machinery squatting in the center of the floor over an array of inset gutters that could be flushed with clean water whenever they became choked.

Giorl glanced about, making sure that all but her most final preparations had been completed, paying small heed to the two men who had been given over to the embrace of the machines. Behind her, Voord eased himself carefully into one of the observation chairs where the Questionmaker and the Recorder were already sitting, and pressed offered plugs of soft wax into his ears. The acoustics deliberately created by the room's lining of tiles were not something anyone chose to experience. Those who contributed, of course, did not have that choice or any other.

Besides the officials and the subjects, there were two assistants who—with mops and swabs and styptic powder—kept clean the areas where Giorl walked and worked. She nodded acknowledgement at them, and allowed one to help her put on the waxed silk smock and cap, then the apron and the long gloves of fine oiled leather which kept *her* clean.

"My lord *Woydach*," she said, "will you at least send someone to bring back news of my daughter's heath?" It wasn't a demand—she did not make demands of the Grand Warlord—and as a simple request it was refused.

"You should be finished with this soon enough," Voord said flatly. "And then you can go to see for yourself."

Giorl gazed at him, a speculative stare which had unsettled better men than Voord Ebanesj, but then they had not had the twin safeguards of rank and knowledge to protect them.

"Understand me, Giorl, if it was possible I would go myself, but I need whatever information these two have seen fit not to tell me, and if they're left alone now, knowing what they know, they'll concoct some story or—"

"Try to cheat you in some other way, yes." Giorl spoke in the weary voice of one who had heard the same explanation offered on many other occasions to many other people, and hadn't been convinced then either. "Very well. But if you used sorcery there would be no need for all this."

"Aren't you forgetting that sorcery is illegal, and that I've learned I can't trust it, and that if it *was* permitted then there would be no need for you and because of what you know there would be no way in which I could let you leave this citadel alive . . . ?" Voord rattled off the clauses, not threatening her because all the threatening had been done most effectively a long time ago, but just reminding her of her present situation.

"I was not forgetting," Giorl said, and turned from him to her assistants. "That one." She pointed to one of the *tulathin,* fastened naked to an iron chair by neck and waist and thigh, by bicep, wrist and ankle. At present it merely held him fast, but various levers, probes and oil-soaked wicks built into its structure could make it much more than just an ugly, clumsy piece of furniture. The man glared horror and hatred at her, but Giorl had seen worse and in any case intended him no harm just now. "Fit the clamps and the mirror panels. If he can see and understand what I can do," she told Voord over one shoulder, "maybe I won't have to waste much time in actually doing."

Voord said nothing. He was leafing through the small book that always stayed in here, a book as sinister as any grimoire, the accumulated wisdom of generations of interrogators and generations of pain. Various levels of torment were listed in its pages, set out in the language of bureaucrats the world over. Like the neutral titles of the participants in this abbatoir—*Questionmaker, Recorder, Subject*—it was an arid pedantry of instruments and applications and durations intended to place comfortable distance between the reader and the reality of what he read. What Voord read was a handbook of anguish.

Metal clicked and rattled as the clamps were slotted and locked into position. Adapted from a mechanism for performing delicate surgery, once they were secure the *taulath* in the chair could neither move his head nor close his eyes. That effect had been the original intention of the physician who had invented the device, but not in such a circumstance as this. The prisoner could look only at his companion and at what was being done to him, for once the mirror panels were in place even turning away his eyes would show only a reflection of the bloody reality. There was a choking-pear in his mouth, forcing it into a straining gape which at the same time muted any sound of encouragement he might make to a snuffling grunt, and other than what went on inside his own mind he was unhurt.

The assistants stepped back to let Giorl inspect their work. She checked locks and straps and grub-screws with the same dispassionate concentration as she had been giving to the setting out of her own surgeon's instruments—for none of the delicate devices that were her specialty were ever kept down here with the heavy equipment. They stayed at home, and were cared for along with the tools of her other, later trade.

"The questions are decided," said Voord, his consultation with the Questionmaker at an end. "Proceed. Begin with . . ." pages rustled for a moment. "Twelve."

Giorl paused an instant, recalling what Twelve entailed as she might have recalled the steps of a complex surgery, then lifted the medical instrument which most closely approximated to what she would normally have used for torment Twelve, shifted her mind away from any concern for the trembling human being trussed before her and set to work . . .

The two knives, the curved tongs and the three needles—all carefully threaded from a new wax-sealed packet of stitching-gut—which Kyrin had chosen were all laid on a metal tray and covered with a white cloth by the time Ryn and a servant returned with the salted water and the clean bedding. She had also picked out several long strips of a soft, loose-woven cloth and two bottles, one filled clear and one with a straw-colored liquid. From the expression on his face, Aldric had expected her selection to be much larger and more complex, and he seemed almost disappointed with the simplicity of it all. For her part, Kyrin knew that he would soon be grateful there was nothing more elaborate to handle.

With his sleeves rolled up past the elbows like hers, Aldric was watching her preparations with far more apprehension than Ryn; he looked indeed, more like the sick child's father than her father did. "Cheer up," said Kyrin, and saw him twitch, "this is a fairly quick and simple undertaking. You shouldn't be more than a few minutes about it."

"*I* shouldn't . . . ?" His voice, in the Alban language, was no more than a whisper, and it was clear that only force of will was keeping it free of a horror that would have needed no translation. "Just what in hell are you talking about? I can't do this—I don't know how! You're the physician's aide, you do it!"

"Aldric, my loved, I can't." This was the crunch. This was for his health as much as for the child's, but if he learned she was lying to him . . .

"Why not, for all Gods' sake?"

"Because my oath forbids it."

"*What?*"

" 'I will not cut—but shall leave that to those trained in that Art.' " She spoke not in Alban but in Imperial

Drusalan, loudly enough for Ryn to hear what she was saying, and looked to him for confirmation of it. Aldric looked too, but he was hoping more for a denial; he didn't get one.

"I know that oath," agreed Ryn. "A shortened version but the truth, near enough."

Kyrin folded back the cloth from the instruments and moved their tray a little closer. Aldric stared at the tiny knives and didn't move, seeming to the casual or uninformed eye to be considering how to begin. Only she was close enough to see the terror in his eyes; they were fixed, unblinking, watching the bright lamplight shift and glint in the polish of edges and on the points of needles. She knew that he was seeing dead faces reflected back from the burnished metal—faces whose lives he had stolen away with a blade in his hand.

And now, thanks to the hasty planning of the woman he loved and who loved him, he was being asked to cut again, not now for death but for life; and maybe to close at long last the raw lacerations in his own mind. It was a dreadful thing to be wounded so deeply and for so long with a wound that never healed, and if trickery was part of the cure then Tehal Kyrin had a clear conscience about its use.

Moving with the easy speed of long practice, Kyrin set about preparing Mal for surgery. She started by opening the door and all three windows so that a breeze of chill fresh air began to flow through the room, then extinguished all the lamps and angled the bedroom mirrors to reflect light from the door and windows instead. Had he been concentrating on Kyrin rather than on his inner fears, Aldric might have wondered why; except that both reasons were explained the instant she opened one of the bottles and began soaking a cloth in its straw-yellow contents. A heavy, sweetish scent flowed through the room, so intense that it was almost visible, and Aldric shook off his own private thoughts with a jerk of his head and a muttered oath.

"What in hell *is* that stuff?"

"A distillate . . . and an important one. Pungent, poisonous and explosive, hence no lamps and open windows, but this stuff will keep the child asleep and out of pain until you're done." She made a pad of the sopping cloth, folded it once and then again before laying it over Mal's mouth and nose, then removed the stopper from the second bottle, poured clear liquid into a ceramic dish and began washing her hands. The nose-pricking smell of twice-distilled grain spirit mingled briefly with the heavy odor of the sleeping-drug. "Now you wash," she said, shaking drips from her fingertips, "while I clean what we'll need."

Aldric's eyes followed her hands as they lifted the small metallic things that clinked when they were laid into yet another spirit-filled dish until they should be needed, then dutifully scrubbed his own hands and arms up past the elbows with the same chilly, fast evaporating liquid. Kyrin glanced at him, wondering if the slight shiver she saw was a result of the cold breeze or the cold alcohol or what her old master called cold feet. She doubted it of this particular man, but it was so very hard to be sure . . .

Then Mal whimpered even through the drug-deepened shadows, and Aldric's teeth came together with a click that was audible clear across the room; Kyrin had the first knife out of its spirit-bath and ready just in time for his hand to snap out and receive the handle slapped into his palm.

"Where do I cut?" he asked, and his soft voice was without any trace of tremor.

Kyrin breathed a sigh of relief, not caring anymore who heard it, and pressed her fingertips against Mal's neck, counting the beats of the little girl's pulse. Still too fast. "Wait," she said. The rapid fluttering began to slacken its pace, became something like normal for the first time since Kyrin had felt it, then grew slower still. A touch on the eyelashes drew no response. The pad over the child's face was almost dry, and Kyrin moistened it with more of the sleep-drug. She dipped another pad of cloth into a dish of clean grain-spirit and wiped it gently across Mal's belly from hip-bone to navel, waited until the sheen of alcohol had dried and then drew a single marking stripe. "Cut there," she said, "and—and cut as well as you know how."

She saw Aldric's throat move as he swallowed hard.

But she also saw him balance the knife in his hand as an artist might balance a brush, with as much authority as her master had ever shown in all the years that she had watched him work, and as she readied a swab she saw him make the first sweeping cut . . .

. . . The blood felt very warm, tickling Giorl's skin as it wandered over her face in four distinct and separate threads: one from just above her right eye, another down her cheek, a third coming out of her nose and the last dribbling from her slack-lipped mouth.

She moved a little, whimpering because moving hurt. At least Ryn wouldn't be back for some hours yet. She had said as much to Terel, let him know that he had time, just before he . . . She brought one straddled leg under her body and a ragged spike of pain rammed up into her belly, reminding her—as if she needed the reminder—of just what he had done. All that mattered now was that she would have time to clean herself up and think of a credible story before Ryn came home. Clean her body, anyway. Cleaning her mind of the past quarter-hour would not be so easy.

But he's Ryn's friend! she thought wildly. *He's been to our house before, he's eaten here, drunk here, even slept here when he and Ryn were working late. I know him!* Known him, and yet plainly not known him well enough. Oh, wonderful hindsight that let her see now the truth behind his frequent visits to the house, his excessive Jouvaine courtesy with all its kissing and embracing—no matter that he was as much a Drusalan as they were, yet he was a well-traveled man and the affectations had looked well on him. She had treated his over-familiar hands and mouth as ostentatious worldly wisdom, or as the slightly off-color joke it sometimes seemed to be. And oh, the compliments, both private and in Ryn's own hearing, about how lucky her husband was and how jealous he, Terel, was of his old friend, and how if she ever wanted to run away from home she could run straight to him. All with a grin and a laugh. That was all it had seemed to be and perhaps all it was, then; and all it should have remained. Giorl didn't know why the boisterous friendship had turned so sour. Probably no rape victim ever did.

Her bottom lip was split and one of her teeth felt loose. Hardly surprising. She had bitten, until Terel had . . . had persuaded her to play with my daughter, thought Giorl, and went cold inside. Lorei had been five, already becoming beautiful. *But never alone. Never, ever alone, even then. Oh, thank you for that much, Lady Mother, thank you . . .* She had not cried in pain for herself and for her own hurts, but she cried now in gratitude for the safety of her child.

Ryn had been told only of a fall downstairs. Mal was his child, *their* child. She had claimed the three barren years a consequence of the "fall" and Ryn, bless him, had believed. During those years she had made sure to take the proper drugs against conception until she was quite certain that Terel had given her no more than pain and filthy memories . . . and until Terel himself was just another of those memories.

Hatred had brooded in Giorl's mind for those three years, but nothing had come of it until the day when Lorei came in and told how she had met Uncle Terel in the street, and how he had spoken to her for the longest time and had been so nice . . .

For two days Giorl had been quiet and withdrawn. On the morning of the third, she reached a decision. With Ryn off to deliver some finished work, Lorei at her lessons and Mal left with a trusted neighbor, she had gone down to Ryn's toolbox and stolen the leather-working knife he used to cut soft skins into coverings for his buffing-pads. And then she had gone looking for Terel.

He hadn't been hard to find, for all that he no longer visited their house—because of a friendship-breaking quarrel over their shared business which Giorl was certain had been staged just for that purpose. But he had kept his own place on the other side of the city, and opened his own goldsmith's shop as if to prove he no longer needed any partnership. Giorl had thought of dressing up, of wearing cosmetics and letting him believe that she had been taken with his prowess. The thought had been rejected; he was not so much of a fool as to be taken in. And using that sort of deception would leave her no better than the man who had pretended to be her husband's friend.

For all that he *had* been taken in, deceived by nothing more than his own arrogance and pride. Terel had invited her indoors with all the old overblown courtesies, bowing low and kissing the back of her hand like a courtier. He had even started to seduce her, smiling, purring, showing her his house and especially its fine bedroom, plying her with wine the whole time as he had not troubled to do before when brute force had been so much cheaper. That was when she had mashed the wine-jug against the side of his head. He had recovered consciousness tied spread-eagled to the posts of his own ostentatious bed, gagged by the whole apple she had rammed past his teeth and secured with her silk scarf.

Then Giorl had taken out the knife.

She and Terel had learned many things that stinking afternoon: that men plainly knew no natural pain like the pain of bringing a new life into the world; that rape was much more than just an over-rough display of affection—and that it was possible to peel a human being like a ripe fruit . . .

For those few hours Giorl had been insane, and only when the madness and the hatred drained away and let her see what she had done did all the good memories replace the bad. How she and her husband and Terel had laughed at jokes, and gone to the theater, and worried over lack of work then seen it all come right at last. How Terel had made Lorei a little jeweled bracelet for her naming-day, the one Giorl had thrown away and claimed was "lost" and replaced with another gift that had never quite been the same . . .

She was still crusted with drying, flaking blood, still holding the knife and still crying bitterly when some instinct brought two off-duty constables and their drinking companion into the house. The officers had seen only the knife and the mess on the bed, and had arrested her at once, but their companion—much more than another policeman—had been more interested to note that the mess was still alive.

And that was how it had begun. *Either you can do it to them at our instruction, and comfort yourself with the knowledge that they're all criminals anyway—or we'll have someone do it to you and your entire family, because we know you're a criminal, too.*

Ryn had heard it all from the constables' non-police comrade, an *eldheisart Kagh' Ernvakh* named Voord, and though it had taken her lovely husband a long time to come to terms with what his friend and then his wife had done, he had recovered something like equanimity at long last, accepted that she was now in the service of the State and left it all at that. Giorl had just one long-cherished and most unladylike ambition: to be a physician. Now that she was employed in activities far less ladylike than healing the sick, some unnamed person in Drakkesborg citadel spoke words—and likely some threats—on her behalf. It was an annoyance that her success in examination stemmed less from her long, hard studies than from that anonymous patron; and from her extraordinary knowledge of anatomy gained in the bloody chamber.

It was still more annoying to learn that she earned more by carving an interrogation Subject like a dinner joint than she ever would by restoring an operation patient to full health and strength. There was also the small matter of her own expendability. Voord had said it himself: she wouldn't be allowed to leave the citadel alive if *Kagh' Ernvakh* lost their hold on her. Giorl, however, had taken some steps in that direction herself. The insurance, if it could be termed such, took the form of hundreds of sensitive facts filtered from the screams in the questioning room, written down, multiply copied, and held by various people instructed either to open or to forward them elsewhere if Giorl Derawn should either vanish or die of anything other than undisputed old age. It might work, and it might not; there would be no way to tell until the time came to try. And that time was not quite yet . . .

There was less blood than Aldric usually saw when he brought a blade and a body together; but then, there was nothing usual at all about this situation. For all

that Kyrin had talked about the clinical detachment of
physicians, Aldric knew perfectly well that he was
deeply involved in what he was doing. It was as much
a matter of his personal honor as any of the ancient
kailin-oaths.

"Gently," Kyrin said, "as if you were cutting silk on a
table you didn't want to scratch." Aldric nodded silently,
astonished by both the sharpness of the knife's edge and
the steadiness of his own unaccustomed hands.

. A bare touch of the blade was enough. The offending
organ burst from the incision as if it had a life of its
own. Kyrin brushed past him and began to do rapid
things with a length of suture and another of the ceramic
dishes. She stitched and tied, then stitched some more
and drew the stitching tight. "The other knife," she said,
and pointed. "Cut there. Now."

The second knife came to his hand as Isileth Widowmaker came from her scabbard, and he sliced off the
foulness with something of the same grim satisfaction as
delivering a perfect *taiken* cut . . . except that this time
nobody would die.

Kyrin continued to pull the stitches tight. They were,
quite literally, a drawstring to keep the infected and the
healthy separate. .

"Now the water." She was talking to Ryn, who had
done the best and wisest thing he could and stayed out
of their way. "Make sure it's not too hot, then use it to
flush out the wound." Ryn came forward with the pot
of water, cooled by now to little more than blood heat,
and sluiced it carefully into the incision. .

"Save the rest," said Kyrin. "Wash it out some more
as I suture up to the skin."

She was working with the curved needle and length
of gut just now lifted from their bath of alcohol, sewing
membrane and flesh with tiny neat stitches that were
very far from the hasty, clumsy wound-closures Aldric
had seen employed by some military surgeons.

He watched for a brief moment before glancing at his
hands. There was blood on them—but good blood, this
time. Living blood, not dying blood, if the smile Kyrin
had given him was a true judgment. They wouldn't know

for a while yet, but at least he—*he*—had done something with a blade that wasn't part of slaughter.

Kyrin tied off the last suture and wiped all clean with a spirit-soaked pad. All that remained of the incision was an assymmetrical criss-cross of stitches, and those were being covered by a swathing of bandages just as the child stirred. The pad over Mal's face had been dry for some minutes now, and since then she had been breathing the heavy fumes of the sleep-drug out of her lungs without its being replenished. It would be a while yet before its effects had worked out of her bloodstream, and in that time the intrusion of steel and stitches into flesh would be a poppy-muted ache.

"Ryn," said Aldric gently at Kyrin's prompting nod, "wrap up your daughter in these clean blankets and take her somewhere warm."

The man said nothing more than his "Thank you," in a voice so faint that the words were barely there at all. But it was more than enough for Kyrin. She watched through bright-blurred eyes as Ryn lifted and wrapped his limp little burden and hurried her quickly to another bed in another room.

"Will she be all right?" asked Aldric after Ryn had gone.

"Wha . . . ?" Kyrin straightened from her slump against the wall and tried to listen to him. "I hope . . . yes, I think she will. Strong child; healthy. Her mother will check, of course, but I doubt even the best surgeon in Drakkesborg would find fault with how you did in these circumstances. Or any others, damn it! You were wonderful . . ."

She threw her arms around him and hugged him tight, then backed away slightly and looked at his face. "Anything wrong with that?"

"Not with what I did, especially if it works out—"

"Which it will!"

"But I don't like the idea of us being quite this noticeable."

"Ah. I see what you mean."

"This *is* Drakkesborg, don't forget."

"Love, you remind me every few minutes. How *could*

I forget? So you think we should just . . ." Kyrin waggled her fingers in a walking kind of gesture.

"Yes. Very quietly. There's nothing further we can do for Mal now, is there?"

"Not really. She'll heal in her own good time; we can't speed up the process." She glanced at the crystal set in Widowmaker's pommel as Aldric returned the longsword to his belt. "At least, not without attracting even more attention to ourselves, huh?"

Aldric smiled crookedly and covered the spellstone with his hand. He made a small sound of affirmation, nothing more. Now that all the tensions and worries were past he was tired, dog-tired after a day that would have been busy enough without this little side excursion into the world of the cutting-surgeon.

"All right then," he managed at last. "Let's slip away before anyone comes back and wonders who we really are."

"And get something warm inside us," Kyrin suggested.

Aldric's mouth twitched indecisively, halfway between a rueful smile and a quirk of disgust. "I'd as soon not think about warm insides right now, thanks very much," he said; then looked down at his hands, clean now, as if seeing life-blood in the truest sense still on them. "But I deserve a drink, at least."

"You deserve a hero's toast, my dear," said Kyrin, linking her arm through his as they walked softly toward the street. "And I'm buying . . ."

7

"Where is my son?"

There had been a time, an instant ago, when Aymar Dacurre and Hanar Santon had been alone in the Hall of Kings, working over new reports or collating old ones. There had been a time when, except for the crackle of fires in the nine hearths and the rustle of papers, the hall had been silent. That time was past, ended when Gemmel Errekren stepped from the core of a howling spiral of azure flame and dismissed the clamoring blue fire with a single strike of his staff against the echoing floor.

The sound of Gemmel's thunderclap arrival had broken two windows, and the blast of icy air arriving with him had blown a week's worth of paperwork from the desktops and sent it swirling in a blizzard of disorder almost to the ceiling. And it was obvious to both the Alban lords that Gemmel didn't care.

"I ask again," he said, for all that it was a demand instead, "where is my son?" The old enchanter took a step forward, then paused and sent a green-eyed glare up and down the Hall of Kings, a glare that started fierce and finished rather puzzled as he took in the reverberating emptiness, the lack of the usual guards and the white cloth covering the High Seat. "And where is Rynert the King?"

Dacurre looked at Santon; Santon returned the look and added a raised eyebrow to it. "You don't know?" the younger man asked. "Nobody told you on your way here?"

"I wouldn't be asking if I did," said Gemmel irritably.

He smiled an enigmatic little smile. "And I didn't meet anyone on the road I traveled."

"Quite so." Aymar Dacurre was doing his best not to be over-awed by Gemmel's presence, but the overflow of power that sleeted from the dragon-patterned black stave in the enchanter's hands made that exercise in control something of a strain. "You seem . . . well, out of touch with current affairs. Rynert the King is dead. Twenty-three days now. Long enough even for a wizard to learn what goes on in the capital city of his country."

Gemmel gave none of the looked-for signs of surprise at the news of Rynert's death. Instead he repeated his enigmatic smile, the smile of a man who knows more interesting things than he's ever likely to be told. "But Cerdor isn't my capital, and Alba isn't my country. I have been in my home, which I have never regarded as Alban sovereign territory . . . and about my own affairs. Yes, Lord Dacurre, I am indeed out of touch with the events of this world." The way in which he put emphasis on *this* sent icy-footed spiders running up and down Dacurre's back. "Now, my lord, I grow tired of repeating myself, but . . . where is my son Aldric?"

"Son?" echoed Hanar Santon, then quailed as Gemmel stared at him with a gaze that seemed for just an instant as hot and crazy as a goshawk's, sighting down his blade of nose—and down the suddenly-leveled Dragonwand that looked to the young lord more deadly than any more familiar weapon.

"Now don't *you* start," Gemmel warned. "I've had this from better men than you, so . . ."—the old enchanter drew in a long calming breath—"just don't."

"*Ilauem-arluth* Talvalin is somewhere in the Drusalan Empire," said Dacurre. "Doubtless, like yourself, about his own affairs."

"Why . . . ?" said Gemmel; but the word was soft enough for both lords to know that it didn't need an answer, at least no answer that they could supply. And then he struck the black staff against the floor so hard that it drove into ceramic tile as if into a loaf of stale bread. "No." He spoke with the voice of a man denying that which cannot be denied; Dacurre had heard it often enough. "Not the Jewel. Not alone. I released him from that charge . . ."

"Jewel?" Hanar Santon stood up slowly and carefully, not wanting to attract the same level of attention that was still sending after-shock trembles down his limbs. "Gemmel-*purcanyath*, do you mean the . . . the *Warlord's* Jewel? The Regalia?"

"Yes, I do." Gemmel both looked and sounded flattened. "I was going to recover the bloody thing myself—in my own good time. And now he . . . When did you hear of this?"

"Two days ago." Dacurre had put his animosity aside as he might have taken off a garment; he knew well enough that he was no longer looking at a sorcerer but at an elderly man whose son (Aymar glossed over the inaccuracy as easily as Gemmel had done) was unexpectedly going into danger in an attempt to do some favor for his father—though he found Gemmel's use of the word *recover* worthy of curiosity. "If it's any solace, the . . . informant made it quite clear that Aldric is as capable of taking care of himself as he always has been. But may I ask the reason—"

"You may ask," said Gemmel, too shocked to put any snap into what he was saying. His preoccupation with other matters was evident just from that. "At least he's carrying enough documentation to let him travel freely anywhere within the Empire's borders . . ."

"So where's the problem?" asked Santon. "Except of course for the fact that he'll have to steal the Jewel. Voord's hardly likely to hand over the insignia of his rank."

"Voord? What about Voord? What are you saying?"

"You won't have heard," Dacurre said. "It's not even public information in the Empire yet. There's a new Grand Warlord: Voord Ebanesj. We know of this one—he was in the Secret Police, and probably achieved his promotion by the usual method." Lord Dacurre drew one thumb across his throat. "He's been a thorn in Alba's side for a long while, but now he seems more taken up with his own concerns."

"The name is familiar enough," said Gemmel with

venom in his voice. "What worries me is that Aldric won't know of it. And Voord knows him."

"Gemmel-*purcanyath,* Voord has known of the Talvalins for a long time; he was the one who planned Duergar Vathach's spoiling-raid on Dunrath and—"

"Was he indeed? Then damn him for it!"

The Dunrath affair was past, all that Voord *had* done was past and there was no passion in the way that Gemmel spoke of it. All his concern was for what the Grand Warlord might do in the days to come: a concern that was not political, not patriotic, but purely emotional. He had lost the son of his own blood to the Drusalan Empire and its Warlord—he was not about to lose the son he had adopted in the same way.

No matter that Aldric had the same documents as Gemmel carried, declaring them scholars and guests of the Empire, Aldric also had things that Gemmel lacked: enemies who knew him by sight. Enemies among the Secret Police—and now an enemy not only highly placed but in the very place where Aldric would be going. Unless he learned the truth very soon, he would walk all unwittingly into what was an unpremeditated trap.

There was Ymareth the Dragon—but Ymareth was also about its own affairs and no longer obedient to Gemmel's summons. The recollection of the last discussion with his monstrous creation was still something close to nightmare. Maker-that-Was, the dragon had called him, angered by the way he had tried to make use of Aldric by laying a spell into the young man's subconscious so that he would do . . .

What he was doing now, unbidden. Gemmel had lost much honor by that spell, and the removal of it had not been enough to bring his honor back—or his control over the dragon, which amounted to the same thing. A control based on honor was all very well when that being controlled could make no comparisons; but he had also given Ymareth the faculties of reasoning and judgment and that had been his downfall.

Gemmel had attempted to set matters right by commending Aldric to its protection, as it had once been constructed and given life to protect him—but what Ymareth had gained instead was freedom, and freedom of choice. It had provided awesome assistance in Egisburg and seen them safely on their way; then heeled over on one vast wing and flown out of sight. Ymareth was still out there somewhere; but wherever that somewhere was, it was not close enough for Gemmel to dare include the black dragon in the plan he suddenly, desperately, had to put together.

Whatever plan that might be . . .

Giorl's grim talent with blade and pincer was such that it required no more than twenty minutes—during which the unharmed *taulath* in the chair witnessed his companion suffer three full torments and a fourth barely begun— before he made it quite clear, despite his bonds and the choking-pear stuffed in his craw, that he was entirely ready and willing if not yet able to talk. Directly the interrogation assistants made him able, all manner of interesting things came pouring out, the words tumbling over one another so fast that the Recorder's flying pen was barely able to keep pace.

Woydach Voord listened to the stream of secrets and betrayals, editing out the occasional blubbering plea for mercy as being irrelevant. "Quite fascinating," he said, speaking as was customary to the Recorder and the Questionmaker but loudly enough for the *taulath* to hear. "To learn so much so fast, I would have thought we might need something like," he looked toward Giorl, "Thirty-seven."

In response to his cue, she administered Thirty-seven to the other Subject, so that for a short space conversation became impossible. Voord distanced himself from the noises that echoed within the tiled and spattered chamber. He could see only the movement of mouths as both men screamed and begged and spilled out everything they knew in the hope of making Giorl stop or prevent her from shifting her attention. *They aren't breeding* tulathin *as tough as they once did,* he decided. *The hiring-fees should be reduced.* Then the Questionmaker tapped him on the arm and showed a fresh list of questions based on answers to the first set and augmented by various matters which had been revealed unasked.

Voord nodded, there was already enough information to provide excellent leverage on certain of his lords and generals, who until now had seemed pure as the snow and quite free of any handle he could employ to bend them to his will. Not any more . . . He smiled, lifted a pen and marked the questions of particular interest, then looked as the first Subject lost consciousness and the room returned to reasonable quiet.

The Drusalan Empire had long ago considered the various aspects of torture as a means of gathering information; there were those who said that the victim would answer any and all questions with whatever his interrogators wanted to hear, just so long as they would stop. Another school of thought insisted that if a man was put under sufficient stress his mind could no longer formulate convincing lies to protect himself or his associates, and the only thing left for him to tell was the truth. Voord was of a third persuasion: that everything a Subject said, whether pressed or not, should be noted down and collated with known facts, and that pressure should then be applied to discover any deviation from the recorded testimony. It was wryly known as the *let's just make absolutely certain shall we* method of interrogation, and the best way of all was with two Subjects, playing one's pain against the other's fear of it. Of course, even then the information had to be cross-checked—in the appropriate fashion . . .

"Leave that one be for now," said Voord. He glanced again at the list of questions, and then at their ultimate source sitting shivering and immobile in his iron chair. "Get me confirmation of these instead."

As the implications of the Warlord's words sank into his fear-fuddled mind, the other *taulath* began to thrash to and fro, trying impotently to break free of the padded steel bands holding him in place. "I want you to consider Question Seven," said Voord's voice over the rattle of unyielding metal, "concerning what you mentioned about *Hauthanalth* Cohort-Commander Tayr. Help him remember with Chair, ah . . . Chair Three. But don't light the heating-wick until I tell you."

Voord watched with mild curiosity for a few minutes as Giorl's assistants operated screws and levers—he and she both considered Chair torments a deal too crude for her personal involvement—then returned his attentions to the newly-corrected question/answer sheets which the Questionmaker had given him.

He gathered together the various other papers which had resulted from the interrogation and got to his feet.

"Enough for now," Voord said briskly, patting the papers together. "Clean up." He met Giorl's unspoken question without blinking, and nodded. "Yes, and finish up. I'll not need to interview either of these two again."

"My lord *Woydach* . . . ?"

"Yes, Giorl, you're dismissed. And thank you for good work." Voord laid a hand against his side and felt no more than a dull, hot ache. "In both respects, I hope the child will soon be better . . ." But he was speaking only to the assistants; their chief was already gone. He shrugged and followed her out.

"But what about us?" demanded Aymar Dacurre.

"I told you before, my lord," said Gemmel. "This is not my country, and its concerns are not my concerns except in the matter of my son."

"And what of his concerns, Gemmel Errekren?" snapped Hanar Santon. "You seem to forget that he's a high-clan-lord and as such has certain obligations, certain duties—"

"You mean that he should mobilize the Clan Talvalin troops, lock himself up in Dunrath-hold and snarl like a manger-dog at every other lord who dares approach? I doubt he'd see the need to bother."

Dacurre looked at the enchanter and said nothing. Gemmel was right. None of his fellow clan-lords had acted toward Aldric in any way that would incline the young man to return. When Rynert had sent him off to the Empire on whatever crazy mission had been in the dead king's mind—and Dacurre didn't have all of the details even now—those of the council lords who might have taken Aldric's part had remained silent, so that the only voices heard were those of men glad to see him gone. Some of course were merely conservative old men expressing conservative opinions—but there were others, Lords Uwin and Gyras especially, who even then had

had an eye on the Talvalin lands. Scarcely a memory that would make either Aldric or his foster-father look on the present troubles of those lords with anything but a sense of poetic justice long delayed.

He began to wonder, as he had done more and more frequently in the past few days, whether it would not be better—or at least more practical—for himself and Santon to abandon the echoing corridors of the palace where they had done little good that any of them could see, and simply run for the shelter of their citadels as everyone else had done. So far no one had moved to use the situation either for advancement or for profit, but once the last two stable influences joined the rest on the edge of anarchy, falling over that edge would be only a matter of time. Probably their flight alone would be enough, either through misinterpretation or because someone like Diskan of Kerys chose to regard it as deliberately provocative.

If only someone, anyone, had sufficient courage to leave the doubtful safety of fortress walls and come here to talk, that would be enough. But—Dacurre smiled grimly—Aldric Talvalin would be the only man other than himself and Santon who would dare to do it . . . the only man crazy enough. All the others would do just as they were doing now. Nothing. He glanced toward Hanar and nodded.

"Very well then," the young lord said. "Go find him, wherever he is. Go help him. And afterward ask him, ask our friend if he would have helped us had he known. But I refuse to ask for aid from *an pestreyr-pesok'n,* a petty-wizard with no notion of what honor means."

Gemmel's back stiffened. If Santon had pondered for a week he could not have come up with an argument as powerful. His words sounded uncomfortably like those used by Ymareth the dragon, with their accusation of lost or lacking honor and their disdain of everything the enchanter thought himself to be. There had been a time, not so very long ago, when the notion that he might have been swayed by the same arguments these people used on one another would have been a joke, and not an especially good one either. But now . . . To live with them was to live by their rules, like it or not. Each in their own way. Aldric and Ymareth had taught him that much.

"What do you know of wizards and their doings, Hanar Lord Santon?" he asked softly. "Or of what *I* do, and know, and am?"

"Enough to understand what a reminder would do to your so-haughty pride, Gemmel," replied Aymar Dacurre.

"We both of us know Aldric," Santon said. The anger was gone from his voice, as if it had never been there at all—or had been skillfully feigned. "My . . . my grandfather"—Gemmel looked sideways and lifted one eyebrow—"knows him as one lord knows another, and as the last son of a good friend. I knew him less well than I might have done, but enough to understand what kind of man you must be for him to call you *altrou* and *father*."

"So. A nice trap, nicely baited, nicely sprung. A most symmetrical stratagem indeed." Gemmel didn't trouble to sound bitter about it. There was a very pretty elegance about their web of words that he would appreciate—later, when the sting of it wore off. "Very well. You shall have my help. Enough of it, at least, that the country will remain at peace while I attend to . . . shall we say, family matters?"

Dacurre and Santon nodded their agreement to the enchanter's terms, knowing them to be far better than any other proposition of the many they had considered and discarded; but when Gemmel laughed they looked nervously at one another, wondering perhaps too late what they had started. They were not kept long in suspense.

"Understand this," said Gemmel, twisting Ykraith the Dragonwand from where it was embedded in the floor. "If the giving of that help delays me so that harm befalls Aldric or his lady Kyrin, then the civil war you fear will be no more than a soft summer breeze beside the havoc I shall wreak in Alba. And remember for the future, gentlemen: I do not like traps."

Power came roaring from the spellstave in a flare of light and noise, and when it faded he was gone.

* * *

Voord found Tagen waiting for him in the corridor outside, with another bundle of reports. "The riots," he said, saluting, "have been suppressed." Then he glanced at the interrogation room door as it swung shut, catching the muffled sounds of sawing and of running water. "What about them?"

"Suppressed as well. But useful enough beforehand." Voord exchanged the interrogation data for the riot reports, glanced at the topmost page and rolled them into a tight, disregarded cylinder. "Tagen, get that lot to the appropriate people and resurrect Talvalin's picture and description. It should go out at Gold-One priority to the Chief of Constables, the Captains of city guards and of the urban militia, and to the *Eldheisart Kagh' Ernvakh*. Mark it Distribution Code Prime."

Tagen digested the jargon reluctantly. He had small patience with this new efficiency that was no more effective than the old method of doing things. From the way all that would have sounded to a layman, the Commander was declaring war on everything and everybody not inside the city walls; but Tagen knew well enough that when all was said and done, the fancy wording and dramatically colored message pouches that went with it meant no more than the traditional routine of delivering a message personally and leaving a threat of dire consequences if the results were any less than perfect. Still, that was the way the Commander liked to do things, and it wasn't Tagen's place to quibble. Besides which, he could understand Voord's desire to get Talvalin down here for a chat; he wanted very much to be there when it happened.

"You really think he's coming here, sir?"

"Yes, Tagen, I do. Wouldn't you?"

"Sir!" Tagen's chest swelled at being asked for an opinion. "Yes, sir, I do think so. He owes you as much as you owe him, if I may make so bold. And he must think he has a chance, or he'd have run for home once he had the opportunity." Tagen paused as his thought processes ground over another possibility. "But maybe he did run. After all, he ran when we caught up with him, so . . ." The thought ran out of ideas.

"So, I'll have put the city on guard for nothing?" Voord finished for him.

"Not for nothing, sir. I spoke to some of my people in the Regiment and they think . . ." Tagen drew himself up very straight. "May I have the Commander's permission to speak frankly?"

"You have it."

"Sir, the Bodyguard Regiment thinks that you should apply yourself with vigor to matters of state in the *Woydek-Hlautan* before all of the domain goes to rack and ruin." Tagen said it all in a breathless rush and remained rigidly at attention as Voord looked at him with an expression of faint disbelief.

"Most interesting," he said. "Soldiers with political opinions. And who are these opinionated persons?"

"Sir, you said that I could speak frankly."

"But not speak treason."

"It isn't treason, sir."

"It certainly sounds like it, *Kortagor* Tagen. But what word would you employ?"

"Concern, sir."

"Indeed? Explain."

"Sir, the Bodyguard Regiment exists to protect the Grand Warlord—"

"Except when they kill one to replace him with someone they like better, of course."

"Not you, sir. Since you claimed the Jewel, you've been lavish with both gold and honors—none want to see you replaced. And once it's known who or what we protect you against, the form of protection becomes more obvious. In this instance it begins by my bringing you this warning."

Voord leaned back against the wall, wincing just a little as one of his wounds strained against the gilt wire holding it shut. "Bringing me a warning," he repeated. "Of a danger to my life, presumably. Why not simply obliterate it instead?"

"Not even the Bodyguard can kill high-ranking Army officers without permission, sir."

"Ah," said Voord. "So it's that, is it?" The requests that he come out of seclusion and set about being a ruler had increased in volume and vehemence over the past eighteen days or so, during seventeen days of which he had been incapable of coherent thought, never mind ruling the bloody domain. "And what do the Bodyguard's informants think that these high-rankers are planning, eh?"

"Several things, sir. Rumors are vague, but it seems that several would try to take advantage of the Emperor's offered amnesty, to turn their coats and join with him. Some others, supported by their troops, are supposed to be planning to set themselves up as Overlords— petty dictators, really—in the outlying areas of the *Woydek-Hlautan.* Maybe twenty men in all."

"And they really think they can succeed in this?" marveled Voord, smiling slightly.

"Yes, sir. Because first they plan to assassinate you."

Only three weeks previously Voord would have laughed aloud at the thought of the surprise awaiting anyone who tried to kill him. He didn't laugh now. Instead his mind curdled at the prospect of maybe twenty blades ripping into him . . . and neither dying nor healing afterward.

"Congratulate your informants for me, Tagen," Voord said in a slightly unsteady voice. "Tell them there will be gold and high favor for the first man to bring me confirmation of all this . . . intrigue." He cleared his throat. "Tell them straight away. Everything else can wait . . ."

It was full dark and snowing hard by the time they dismounted in the covered stable-yard built behind The Two Towers. A glance from side to side as their horses were taken in hand by the liveried ostlers was enough to give an indication of the clientele the place attracted. Aldric whistled thinly through his teeth at the several town carriages drawn up in a neat row under the sheltering roof of the yard. Some were sedate closed coaches, two others were the sort of transport merchants hired to convey—and impress—business colleagues, but it was the gleaming low-slung two-seater at the end of the line which attracted his attention.

Built as much for ostentatious speed as for comfort, it was a young man's vehicle of the kind only ever built to order, and only ever ordered to demonstrate the style, the taste and above all the wealth of its owner. The coach-building and lacquerwork alone would have taken a craftsman half a year, and the thoroughbred horse-power which drew such elegance was bound to be equally worthy of admiration. More so, to Aldric's mind.

It was inevitable that he would head straight for the stable-block itself, claiming a concern for Lyard's and K'schei's comfort that was in truth no more than one young man's curiosity about another's high-powered horseflesh. He wasn't disappointed, because there was an eight-legged king's ransom munching hay in the wide stalls. Aldric fussed and petted over the pair of softly questing noses for a moment, then let them get back to their eating.

"Content again?" asked Kyrin, watching him rub the hay between his palms and smell it.

Aldric glanced at her. "Good hay," he said.

"Yes, I'm sure it is. And you've checked to make sure there's nothing in here that matches Lyard."

He grinned at her. "That obvious?"

"Every time. At least you're feeling better."

Aldric dusted the hay from his fingers and smiled. "I'm getting my appetite back, at least. But I'll still hold you to that drink. Let's get in."

There was some sort of clerk seated inside a booth under the sweeping curve of the main staircase, who sniffed disdainfully at the sight of the inn's latest guests. Certainly they looked disreputable enough: the big gilt-framed mirror that formed the entire side wall of the entrance lobby reflected a couple wearing long furred and hooded overrobes, black with soaked-in meltwater except for the places where there were still solid snow. There was slush-mud on their boots. The battered saddlebags slung over their shoulders—money had changed hands and the stuff from the pack-horses was being carried for them—weren't exactly the richest or most stylish form of luggage, and both they and their bags smelt faintly of wet horse.

"Yes, can I help you?" the clerk said, not troubling to stand up and at the same time conveying the fervent hope that he wouldn't be able to do anything of the sort.

"A room, a private bath and hot food and drink, all for two," said Aldric, pushing back his hood with his free hand. The clerk said nothing straight away; instead he looked pointedly at the heap of snow which had slithered to the floor and now sat there, melting fast. Aldric cleared his throat equally pointedly. "Is there a problem?" he asked.

"I really think that you should read our list of charges, sir," said the clerk, staring hard at the state of their clothing. He pulled a board from beneath his counter and held it out, not quite between finger and thumb but managing to convey that impression successfully enough. "And . . . these are fixed charges, sir. That means no haggling; The Two Towers does not encourage haggling."

"Oh." Aldric took the board and looked at it, then said, "Oh," again.

"The tavern on the corner of Bridge and Central will probably be more to your liking," said the clerk with an air of finality.

"Why?"

"Well, sir, the prices are—"

"Higher? I doubt that."

"No sir, quite the rever—"

"Don't assume, my son," said Aldric, feeling suddenly very much older than the puppy snapping from behind the safety of his desk. "It can affect your health and job prospects." Reaching inside his overrobe, Aldric pulled out the Guild Freyjan money-purse and held it for a moment with the Guild's unmistakable crest an inch from the end of the clerk's nose, then dropped it with a crude but highly satisfying slam and a puff of chalk-dust into the middle of the charge-board. "Hard cash," said Aldric, his face expressionless. "Want to find out just how hard?"

The clerk looked at the purse, then opened it and peered inside. He blinked twice and swallowed, not daring to try biting one of the coins, if indeed that was what had been meant, and he was inclined to doubt it, then summoned up a sort of smile. "Uh," he said. "No. I mean yes. I mean thank you, sir, but you can pay when you leave, sir. Enjoy your stay in Drakkesborg, sir . . ."

Everything the Freyjan Guildsman had said about The Two Towers was true—including his warning about the prices. Kyrin was able to understand more clearly why Aldric had acquired such a quantity of cash, for their accommodation and meals for the next week would take a sizable bite out of it. At least they were getting what they paid for. She had never seen such luxury, not even when they had been hauled into the presence of Alba's King Rynert that time in Erdhaven. His home-from-home and part-time palace had been furnished in the classic Alban style of understated elegance, whereas there was nothing understated about The Two Towers. It shouted opulence at the top of its voice.

There seemed to be a competition between the bedroom and the bathroom as to which could shout loudest; the bathroom probably won on grounds of sheer sybaritic exuberance. Kyrin had thought the tavern three nights ago had come close to crossing the border between elegance and excess, but it seemed either that the Towers had never heard of any difference between the two, or had forgotten it superbly. There was no nonsense here about wooden tubs, no matter how fine the wood might be, or water-coppers heated by the same fire that warmed the room. The water for *this* bathroom, they had been informed in proud and enthusiastic detail, came from the cellar furnaces that kept the whole inn warm, and in unlimited supply. The center of the floor was all bath, sunken into it and ringed with baskets holding sponges and fine soaps in block form and in handsome ceramic jars. Its fittings were either solid gold or some other metal so heavily gilded as to make little difference, and for those who preferred steam-baths in the fashion of the Eastern Empire and—Kyrin grinned and made straight for it—the far North, there was a timber cubicle and an iron rack loaded with sleekly riverpolished granite rocks that could be heated in the room's own fire. Aldric, of course, tried both; and when they emerged from their respective baths they tried the bed as well.

Whether or not it was the brief altercation with the clerk downstairs or any of the various other distractions of the past hour, Aldric was quite recovered from the stomach-flutters born of his first venture into surgery by the time a liveried servant brought the night's bill of fare for their inspection. There was fish, both fresh and smoked; five meats; two sorts of roasted bird; vegetables fried, boiled, steamed, and baked in a sour-hot sauce; pastries with two savory and three sweet stuffings; four soups; seven cheeses; and a sufficient variety of different wines to leave even Aldric lost for choice.

After making their decisions during a lengthy, amiable wrangle with each other and the servant—who had opinions of his own and was not afraid to share them—they changed from their rakishly-wrapped towels into fresh clothing and sauntered down to the tavern's dining-room, set comfortably far away from the noise and smoke of the public common-room. Aldric nodded equably to the clerk as they passed him, pausing long enough to make some softly-spoken inquiries before arranging to rent a carriage after dinner.

"What for?" Kyrin asked as they took their places at the quiet corner table Aldric had requested. There was a bottle packed in snow already waiting for them; it seemed that the desk clerk was apparently trying to put right his earlier mistake by being more than just knowledgeable and obliging.

"After-dinner entertainment," said Aldric, lifting the chilled bottle and pouring wine for each of them. "And behaving entirely as two wealthy people such as we appear *would* behave." He swirled his own glass thoughtfully under his nose and sipped; then seemed to forget what he was about to say, gazing instead into the middle distance with a dreamy expression on his face. A moment later he shook himself just a little, and gave the shy half-smile that might go with learning all was well with the world after all. "Anyway, we're visiting the theater. And this is as fine a Seurandec as I've ever drunk. If it's a bribe from that clerk, I think we'll forgive him."

Kyrin, amused, had watched his little byplay with the wine, well aware it was for the benefit of various watching eyes. No wine could be that good. Except that this wine was . . . "Which play—as if I had to ask? *The Prince,* wasn't it?"

"Of course. And that's *Tiluan the Prince.*" He glanced sideways as plate-bearing servants made their way toward the table. "Oh, God be thanked. Food!"

By mutual consent all attempts to talk were suspended for the next few minutes, at least until the first fine edge of a noble hunger had been blunted. Dinner began with a dish of several smoked meats and fishes, arranged in a handsome pattern and then glazed with a thin piquant jelly of red wine and bitter oranges; then came the grilled freshwater crayfish tails, the veal in cream and white wine sauce with morels, the bacon-stuffed potatoes roasted in herb butter and the half-dozen other items they had ordered. Both were grateful that they had thought to make an additional request—for small portions to offset the variety of the food.

It was Kyrin who first broke the companionable silence with more than the softly-voiced exclamations of pleasure that might occur at any dinner table and so scarcely qualify as conversation. "Aldric," she said, "what plans have you made? Or haven't you made any at all?"

The wine-glass lifting to his lips paused for a beat and then returned untasted to the table. He smiled, the sort of pleasant smile that would be adequate response to almost anything; except that it went no further than a mouth which shaped it by a deliberate movement of muscles and left his eyes cold, cold, cold . . .

"Hit," he said flatly. "One point to the lady. How long have you known?"

"Since now." Kyrin shrugged. "It was no more than a guess."

"Best you know . . . so you can start to understand."

Aldric tried another smile and still his facial muscles seemed unwilling to carry the expression. He pushed his plate aside, appetite fading as fast as the smile. "I've been hoping for some wonderful idea. I hoped that maybe coming here, starting to make all the proper moves, playing the part without a script, would produce some flash of brilliance, something foolproof." He shook his head, pressed fingertips to head in imitation of deep thought and grinned, a wry expression that seemed much more at home than anything humorous. "Not a damned thing—except such a bloody case of the shakes I'm surprised you never noticed."

"Not such a bloody case as you thought. You covered well. You think terrified, but you don't act it. And you tried—you did your best." Kyrin stretched luxuriously; despite the intensity of the murmured words, they were both taking care to maintain the pretense of a young couple with too much money, enjoying it and all that it could bring. There was a deal of released tension in that stretch, but she wasn't about to say so here and now. "Now we can leave."

"Without the Jewel?"

"Let the Warlord keep it. Let Gemmel get it back himself. When he put that spell into your head he took away whatever duty you owed him, and when he took it out he gave you back your free will. You don't owe anybody anything anymore." She stopped talking abruptly and took a mouthful of wine, trying to cool the angry heat that was building in her words. "Except maybe . . . you owe yourself a life. Start living it."

Aldric sat quite still for a long time, and it seemed to Kyrin that she could see the thoughts swim in his eyes like fish—except that these thoughts were black fins cutting through gray water. Then he blinked and the image was gone. "Tonight," he said, "we'll go to see the play." He got to his feet, drawing Kyrin up with him. "And then tomorrow we'll go home."

Lacework patterns of frost obscured the windows' leaded panes, and icicles hung from the snow above them in a ragged fringe, like fangs in a gaping white-gummed mouth. Dark clouds drifted across the moon.

Inside was colder still, and darker. *Woydach* Voord could feel the blood thickening and freezing in his veins despite the charms of warmth and nourishment and guard that ringed him. The candles had gone out, choked in their own stinking grease, and he hadn't dared leave his protective circle to relight them. Voord had seen what happened to people who were rash enough to make that mistake, and had no desire to experience the same rending at first hand. His own hand hurt him, throbbing alternately hot and cold along the marks of its mutilation. All the other injuries had faded to a background murmur of discomfort, but here in this place the old wound pained him as if newly inflicted. Voord was on his knees at the center of the circle, a weaving of curves and words, of angles and symbols and letters inlaid in black in the white marble floor of his most private chamber. In the intermittent, frost-muffled moonlight, it lay on the surrounding pavement as stark as ink on paper. Slow coils of spicy incense smoke echoed the shapes that made the circle . . . . then, shifting subtly on unfelt currents in the icy air, made mock of them instead.

There was a heavy droning that filled all parts of the room, a sound like bees in summer—or flies around a ten-day corpse. It swelled and receded in slow waves of sourceless noise, then faded slowly, slowly, until it was gone. Voord stayed where he was for a long time, making absolutely sure, sweating even as he froze. At long last he stood up—a movement that seemed more like one long shudder—and looked about him. There had been starless void beyond the circle, and Presence. Now he was alone in a circle at the center of the room, hemmed in by shadows and by smoke-skeins that smelt of spice, of incense . . . and of roses.

Voord raised his hands with their palms pressed together—or as near together as the talon of his crippled hand allowed—then parted them, stepped across the circle's outermost perimeter and closed his hands again. It was a simple enough charm, to preserve the integrity of the protective patterns—and forgetting it had killed so many sorcerers that Voord was determined not to be the next unless he was quite sure that death was permanent.

And It had told him death was not . . . not yet, anyway. If he expended more power, then perhaps . . . If he gave It more gifts and sacrifices, then perhaps . . . If and perhaps; that was all he heard, nothing more certain than *if* and *perhaps*. Neither was enough for Voord to gamble the little power he still had at his disposal. He husbanded that, spending it as frugally as—Voord thought of his mother, years dead—a widow trying to feed her children. *If and perhaps.* Too many ifs for one uncertain perhaps. Get the equation wrong . . . and learn what Hell is really like.

He bowed toward the empty darkness, always mindful of his manners even when nothing was there—or seemed to be there. The courtesies were due, witnessed or not—but once they were completed Voord didn't linger. There was always the risk that until it had completely dissipated the aura of sorcery—and more especially of Summoning—lingering in the small dark chamber might attract things other than it was intended to, like wasps to honey. Now that he was outside the circle, if something like that were to happen he would as soon be out of the room as well. And preferably the city, the province and even the Warlord's Domain itself . . .

And once again, Tagen was waiting for him outside the door. Voord closed it, locked it and secured the key on its chain around his neck before he said anything at all. An awful jolt of fright had gone through him at the sight of the bulky silhouette backlit by the lanterns in the corridor outside, for with the smells of incense and roses still in his nostrils it had been only natural to think for just an instant that Something *had* been attracted . . . and even recognition didn't take away the fear at once. Tagen was a friend, a companion, a confidante, all those and more; but there was and always had been an air about him which suggested the not-quite-natural, the sensation felt by others that was inadequately defined when men earned the title *Terrible*. Then Tagen saluted, and smiled, and the image was gone.

"I thought my orders were that I was not to be disturbed when in my workroom," said Voord. "Wasn't I clear enough?"

"Sir, I know that. So I didn't disturb you at your work; I waited."

Voord looked at him, then up and down the corridor. It was icy down here, for except the lanterns there was no other source of heat; and the still more intense cold flowing out of his workroom had left long glittering fans of frozen air around and under the door—one of the reasons why a sorcerer didn't leave his spell-circle until certain it was safe to do so. However, Tagen's comfort was not his foremost concern: it was what the man might have heard. "Did you wait long?"

"Until you were done and came out, sir. Your orders said *under no circumstances,* and that means never."

Voord shrugged, dismissing the matter with the realization that whatever his henchman might have overheard, it would have been done by the Commander and that would make it all right. Tagen was slow rather than simple; but disciplining him for the normal small infractions or too-literal interpretations of commands—which would be done without a second thought to any other soldier—seemed always too much wasted time. As well discipline a dagger when it cut one's finger. "All right. Explanation accepted. Now, *why?*"

"Good news, sir. Two guards—they were on the Shadowgate duty shift between the hours of Hawk and Serpent this afternoon. Hault has them upstairs. In the Hall." Tagen shouted the last words, because Voord was already running for the stairs.

"Yes, soldier, I know about the description sheet, there's no need to describe it," said Voord impatiently. He stared at the two troopers, wanting to grab them by the fronts of their undress tunics and shake what they had to say out of them, rather than waiting while they took turns at making the most of their brief importance. At least their chattering had given him the chance to get his breath back; but now he'd had enough. "I was the one who had it sent out, remember? Get to the point."

"Yes, sir. A little before the bells struck for Serpent, Karn and me, we went off-duty at Dog; we were going for a drink and then to see the play, but he'd left his smokes behind."

The soldier Karn held up a pipe and drawstring pouch for proof—then saw the expression in the *Woydach*'s face and gave his companion an elbow-nudge of warning. Voord noticed it and smiled thinly, a smile that was all teeth and cold, cold eyes.

"You're very right, Guard-trooper Karn. Because if I need to order Guard-trooper Volok to hurry up just one more time, I'll forgo the command and have the information beaten out of you. Do you both understand? Good. I see you do. Now talk! *Sch'dagh-veh hoh'tah!*"

Trooper Volok's face had drained of any color given it by the drinks he and Karn had consumed before going back to the Shadowgate to find Karn's forgotten pipe. He jolted through a rapid full-honors salute and slammed to rigid heels-together eyes-front parade attention before daring to say another word. All the stories told in barracks about *Hautheisart* Voord had taken on a new edge with the discovery that he was now Grand Warlord, and Volok was very scared indeed.

"Sir! We-admitted-two-people-who-might-be-the-state-criminals-on-the-recent-warning-sheet-they-are-now-in-the-city-and-have-not-left-it-to-the-best-of-our-knowledge-at-least-not-by-the-same-gate-they-came-in-by *Sir!*" he said all in a single breath.

"Very observant," said Voord, not troubling to keep the satisfaction off his face. "I'll remember both of you." The troopers managed to maintain eyes-front—just—but there was a hint of a flinch about the way Karn stiffened his back like someone waiting to be flogged. Voord chuckled, feeling in rather better humor. "Favorably, that is. Hault, pay them a bounty of ten florins apiece; it might remind them that it's worthwhile keeping their eyes open—and their mouths shut. Dismissed."

When Hault and the two troopers had gone out, Voord glanced at Tagen. "State criminals?" he asked.

"I didn't know what other charge to use, Commander. And they're your enemies and you're the State, so . . ."

Voord concealed his groan behind a cough. "Yes, of course. Well done, Tagen. And thank you for the compliment." He stood up, feeling the wounds ache again and not caring just this once. "Turn out the Guard. Clear the gates and seal the city. Start a search from the walls inward . . . and bring what you find to me . . ."

8

" *Tiluan the Prince,* now. How could you be sure of finding a performance? There must be lots of other plays playing in a city as big as this . . . ?" Kyrin adjusted her balance against the slight sway of the coach and quirked her brows quizzically at Aldric.

"It's the size of the city that counts. At this time of year there's bound to be some company somewhere playing *Tiluan* as well as all the others."

"Time of year? Surely it's not a religious play? Not with men in towels, dropping them everywhere . . ."

"That performance was by me. Just me."

"Mmmm. I still like the bit with the towel; they should put it in the real play."

"Ask them and maybe they will."

"I might. I just might . . ."

In a city as large as Drakkesborg, Aldric had known there would be at least one theater performing the seasonal dramas, and the clerk of The Two Towers had directed him to the most well-known and splendid and now the most modern as well, the new Old Playhouse, recently refurbished and made *New* at great expense to house the Lord Constable's Men. He and Kyrin spent the short journey looking through the sheaf of pamphlets and handbills which all the theaters printed at this time of year to entice customers through their doors. Comical; historical; tragical; and all the subgenres, admixtures and complicated bastard children that resulted from combining them together.

" '*The Claw Unsheath'd,* by Reswen and Lorin,' " read Kyrin, laughing as she made sure to give a good delivery

to all the emphases, " 'being a very Pretty Fine new
Fantastical Satire, where Cats are shewn large as Men,
with Marvelous new Masks and Costumes *never before
seen!* Also Musick, Songs and Dances wrought *for this
play only!!*' " She fluttered the sheet of paper at Aldric
and grinned. "This has to be a joke!"

"No. But it *is* a sequel . . ." Aldric unfolded another
pamphlet, this one with four pages and colored illustra-
tions, all very splendid—which to a cynical mind might
suggest that the play it advertised needed all the support
it could get. "Whereas this . . . !" He seemed unable
to decide between wry amusement and genuine anger.
" 'Count your country and yourself fortunate. *Lord Urick's Revenge,* or *The Alban Tragedy,* by Gaufrid ar
Meulan.' "

"What's wrong?" Kyrin was making a very good attempt at keeping her face straight, but it wasn't really
working. "Did you *know* this Urick person?"

"Hardly; it's not even an Alban name—though I'll
concede it's close, very close. The enticement, I'm afraid,
continues at some length. " 'A Play play'd in the True
and Actual Costumes of that Land with Swords, Harness
and etcetera all recreat'd in the Barbaric Splendour of
the People. Together with such Musick, Songs and Dancing as are us'd commonly in that Land, played by Proper
skill'd musicians, brought Here with their very Instruments at Much Cost and No Small Peril to the Company.

" 'There will be in this Drama three strong Castles
besieg'd with Real Siege-Engines, to be seen upon the
Stage shooting Fire as in Life; a Battle of Two Hosts; a
great Sea-Storm, with Thunder-and-Lightning made by
Herran d'Win, Thundermaker to the Lord Constable's
Men; Lord Urick's Concubines, seen clad in the Flimsy
Garments of such Lewd Females and play'd by Real
Women; and many other Delights.' "

"Is that what they really think of you . . . ?"

"It's the popular image, which counts for the same
thing in the long run." Aldric looked once more at the
pamphlet and its gaudy woodcuts, then folded it up and
creased the folds down to a razor edge with nails that
were far more ready to tear the offensive thing to rags
and tatters. "Never mind. We're not going to see that,

regardless of the 'Real Women in Flimsy Garments.' At least Osmar uses words instead of—he spat the word like an insult—"spectacle."

"The Playhouse, sir, milady," said the coachman. "Play's not started yet, so no need to rush."

Translated as, no need to hurry off without giving me a few coins extra, thought Aldric without malice as he helped Kyrin back into her furred overrobe. *And why not?*

"Well driven, man," he said aloud, dropping an extra couple of coins into the coachman's hand. "Now get yourself into a tavern and have some ale to keep out the cold, then collect us here after the play."

"Sir, yes sir," said the coachman, saluting with the butt-end of his whip but quite unable to take his eyes from the soft golden glint of the two quarter-crowns resting in the palm of his glove. Whoever or whatever his passenger might be, he had just been tipped maybe half the value of the whole carriage for one short ride. The coachman fought a brief and silent battle between avarice and conscience, before conscience—reluctantly—won. "Sir, you've given me—"

"What I meant to give you. Just don't talk about it, in case the lady's . . ." Aldric gave him a conspiratorial wink. "Ahem. Never mind that. Go get your drink, and be here later."

"Yes *sir!*"

"Why?" asked Kyrin. She had seen the gold change hands where silver would have sufficed and was understandably curious.

"Because," he said. "That's all."

Kyrin smiled. "That's enough—for me at least."

Aldric glanced sidelong at the departing coach, not smiling. "And for him, I hope. Shall we go in?"

The good citizens of Drakkesborg had long been used to soldiers on their streets. The city was not only the capital of the Warlord's Domain but had for a long time been a garrison town in its own right, so that the sounds of drum and trumpet and the business of military routine went almost unnoticed . . . until the routine changed. As it was changing now.

Because of the many barracks within the walls and the consequent need for a degree of both security and military discipline, Drakkesborg's gates had always been shut at night from the striking of the hour Fox at ten o'clock to the hour Horse at six the next morning, but those with the proper papers could still enter and leave without restriction through the smaller posterns. Except that this night, the great iron siege-screens were in place and locked before the halfway strike of Dog at seven, sealing the entire city like a corked bottle. Neither papers nor bluster nor bribes were enough to obtain entrance for those outside; and use of the same methods by those trying to get out resulted only in quick, quiet arrest.

After the rioting earlier in the week, followed only this morning by a vigorous restoration of order, no one was concerned by the presence of the constables or the urban militia, even though both now wore light armor beneath their uniform tunics and carried hardwood truncheons in full view as a deterrent to anyone thinking of resuming such nonsense. If anything they were a comfort to the law-abiding majority, a reminder that their right to walk the city streets without harm was being protected, but the men who joined them as the evening drew on were not a sight that held the least reassurance.

Some were in the full battle harness, and bore gisarms instead of staves. They had shortswords, still sheathed but with the red tapes of their peace-bindings unsealed, and their armor bore the mailed-fist insignia of the Bodyguard, down from the citadel itself. Elite troops to be sure, but still only soldiers. It was the others who sent people hurrying to clear the streets: those whose rank-robes showed no rank at all, only the jagged black and silver thunderbolts that marked them as *Kagh' Ernvakh.*

Getting behind a door and locking it was of little use, for as the formation of armed men moved forward in an iron ring that encircled the city perimeter, every building that they passed was searched. The regular law enforcement officers had all their entry warrants ready, and somehow contrived to leave the places that they had examined as neat if not neater than when they came in;

but the Bodyguard and the Secret Police went in where they pleased, whether that was through a door or through a window—or even through a wall if the notion struck them as amusing—and left devastation in their wake.

Privilege was no protection. The most privileged person in Drakkesborg was the Grand Warlord who had commanded this operation, and neither rank, money nor the names of friends in high places were of any use. Occasionally such attempts were made to sway the intrusive troopers, but as at the gate those making the attempt were either ignored or put under close arrest on any one of half-a-dozen charges.

No matter how ruthless they were, it was a slow business. Drakkesborg's position as first- or second-wealthiest city in the Empire might have been subject to question, but that it was by far the largest both in buildings and in population had never been in doubt. Slow or not, progress was made and small successes scored; the suddenness of the security raids caught several criminals red-handed in the middle of their preferred crimes, and with no need for a court to judge a guilt which was apparent to all, justice was swift and bloody.

It was, as young *Tau-kortagor* Hakarl of the Secret Police observed to his men, a bit like lifting up a rock and finding something nasty underneath that needed to be squashed. His squad did its own fair share of squashing before they reached the Merchants' Quarter and Hakarl thought to find out what the Guilds themselves might know . . .

Oren Osmar's *Tiluan the Prince His Life and Triumph* was recognized as a classic throughout the Drusalan Empire, and was perhaps the most enduringly popular of the Vreijek playwright's works. Because most of its action took place during the Feast of the Fires of Winter when the days reached their shortest and began to lengthen again, it had been performed at the Winter Solstice since its writing almost three centuries before, in guises varying from masques to musicals.

According to the pamphlet in Aldric's hand, this present revival was based not on Drusalan translations but

on the Jouvaine-language original. Having read that
same original some two years earlier, and knowing the
current state of political turmoil within the Empire, Aldric doubted this production's vaunted "accuracy" at
once. In the present climate an Imperial audience would
hardly appreciate either the plot or the sentiments it
expressed—all about fealty to a lord rather than to his
chiefmost lieutenant—and especially not this audience.

Their entry vouchers had been assured by a runner
sent from the Towers, and as they were shown to their
seats another sheet of paper was pressed into Aldric's
hand to keep all the rest company. This, on a superior
quality heavy paper, carried the usual things that wealthy
theater-goers might want to know: the names of the
Lord Constable's Men and of their characters, a useful
if over-lengthy synopsis of the plot, a briefer and more
restrained description of the effects that had been lev-
ered in between Osmar's words—though the program
didn't express it in quite that way—and where, from
whom and for how much food and drink could be
acquired.

There was an unsettling number of soldiers in the audience, wearing either undress uniform or their best civilian clothes, but all labeled clearly by their neatly—if
excessively—close-cropped heads. Aldric's own hair was
not long recovered from just such a military crop, and
though Kyrin either didn't notice them or made a point
of not registering their existence, he felt uneasy until it
was clear that both their seats—while commanding an
excellent view of the stage—were shadowed by a pillar
and by the balcony above it. The nasty sensation of
being watched was probably a result of nothing more
than hindsight-aided wariness; but this was augmented
by the idle glances turned towards him by so many of
the Empire's military, any of whom might through the
workings of an unkind fate have recognized him from
past events. He didn't feel truly comfortable until the
house-lights were hoisted into their dark-shades and the
play began.

Events on stage were more than enough to distract
anyone's attention, with plenty to entertain the senses
as well as—Aldric sniffed, exchanged a pointed glance

with Kyrin in the gloom and smiled thinly—*ymeth* and other substances in use to dull them.

The audience's own small entertainments aside, *Tiluan the Prince* had been brought up to date with a vengeance. There was one scene, the Betrayal, which should have been restrained and intimate, as terrifying as a whisper in a darkened room. Instead it took place during the gold and scarlet glitter (the Emperor's colors, a fact not lost on any of the audience still in possession of their senses) of a court ceremony, contrasting outward splendor against inner corruption. The overt political comment did not go unnoticed, drawing whistles and jeering laughter as the scene reached its conclusion— which, to Aldric's mind, suggested it had worked quite well enough.

Trumpets in the wings and among the musicians blared an elaborate fanfare as first the lamps and then the curtain opened up again. Figures in armor fantastical as that of insects strutted to and fro beneath their gilded banners, declaiming the famous well-known speeches that each drew their own separate applause:

It pleases me to see the joyful season that is Autumn.

the actor playing Overlord Broknar was saying,

For it swells the fruit upon the trees
And makes the harvest rich and tall.
And it pleases me to hear . . .

Gibart d'Reth had been a Guildsman for forty of his fifty-seven years. He enjoyed it; there was a certain sense of satisfaction in watching, helping and, as time passed, controlling the extraordinary sums of other people's money that gave a merchant guild its power. The power rubbed off. Few men were as respected as those of Guild Freyjan's House in Drakkesborg. There was a degree of amiable rivalry between his House and its opposite number in Kalitzim, but on the whole Gibart felt that he was the senior Master in the Empire. Certainly he saw more money in the form of cold, hard cash than Ascel in Kalitzim could ever hope to do. If he wasn't bound by the near-religious secrecy of the Guild, he could tell such tales . . .

Drakkesborg was like that. There was enough luxury for any man to enjoy, especially if like Gibart d'Reth he was a bachelor as well as wealthy, but beneath the surface the city was simmering with plots and intrigue. Senior officers in all the arms of service had far more gold to hand than on their rank insignia, and were working busily to have it moved away from any area of trouble— which in the present climate meant right out of the Empire. And then there were the ordinary matters of business, which were sometimes far from what a layman merchant would regard as normal practice. Gibart smiled at the thought and closed his last ledger of the night. He put it, with all the others, into an iron safe with powdered clay packed tightly between its double skin as a protection against fire, and turned the first of the three keys. This was a ritual performed every night, more important by far than simply locking away the Guild's gold. There was not sufficient gold in all the Empire to buy those ranks of dull blue covers—or more precisely, the transactions recorded between them. He put the second key to its lock—

—Then dropped it at the sound of a crashing in the corridor outside. The key made a sound like a tiny metallic laugh as it bounced under the immovable mass of the safe, something that would normally have made Gibart swear at the prospect of the grubbing about with a bent piece of wire which usually followed such a fumble, but he was past worrying about such petty everyday annoyances. Sounds of violence in a Guild House after dark meant one thing only.

The door of his office was kicked open, so hard that it was vibrating like a drum as it shuddered to a halt, and three men stepped inside. Or rather two men, dragging what looked like a side of raw beef between them. Gibart came surging to his feet, mouth open to yell something about the outrageous liberty of entering a Guildsman's presence in this fashion; but he froze halfway as he recognized the side of beef.

It—*he*—was Kian, Guild House Drakkesborg's chief guard; and the horrified Gibart could identify him only by his size and by the Freyjan crests marked on his tattered gear. Not even the man's mother would have known him. Gibart could only stare wide-eyed and realize for the first time what that saying really meant.

"He didn't want to let us in," said one of the two men bracing Kian by the elbows, and as he spoke both of them removed their support. The guard swayed forward and his head struck squarely in the center of Gibart's desk before he rolled limply to the floor. "Even though we told him that this was official business."

"What the hell are you doing here?" roared Gibart d'Reth, finding his voice at last. "And who gave you the right to act like—"

The riding-crop of plaited leather that slashed a weal across his cheek was just one more of the several shocks Gibart had suffered in the past few seconds; but it was the first one that really hurt. He clutched his face and flopped back into his chair, too stunned by the impact and the anguish and the suddenness of it all even to protest.

"I told you," said the man who had spoken before; he was very young. "Official business. That means the *Woydach* himself gives us the right." He grinned, his teeth very white against his tan and the shadows within his helmet, and reached out to stroke the tip of his crop lightly across the other side of Gibart's face. "You don't object to that, now, do you?" Gibart said nothing; only his eyes moved, following the crop as it weaved to and fro before them like a plaited leather snake.

"Wise," said *Tau-kortagor* Hakarl gently. "Now," he pulled a crumpled sheet of official-yellow paper from the cuff of his glove, smoothed out the creases more or less and held it up for Gibart to see. "Read this description and then tell me: have you seen this man . . . ?"

> . . . *the song of the birds*
> *Who make their mirth resound through all the woods* . . .

"Broknar" was over-acting just a touch, his gestures too flamboyant and his voice too determinedly thrilling, but at least it cut through the chords of exciting music so that everyone could hear what was after all the best known speech in the entire play.

Just so long as he doesn't sing, thought Aldric with a mirthless smile. The smile faded almost as soon as it appeared, for he was beginning to hear something very wrong in the treatment of this crucial speech—something very wrong indeed, and a wrongness that was of a piece with the unsubtle use of colors on the stage.

Tiluan's colors were the red and gold of the Emperor— that much he had noticed already, and thought no more than some satirical observation; but "Broknar," leader of the group of lords who seized the country from its prince, not only wore the Grand Warlord's black and silver but was speaking the words of a hero.

The historical Broknar had been a usurper who with his companions had misruled the land and brought it to the edge of ruin before remorseful suicide had restored order, and had been treated as such in Osmar's original play. Here he was portrayed as a wise, experienced military man who had *rescued* the land from an immature and willful tyrant. The whole play was a propaganda for the *Woydachul,* and for a policy of war. Just the sort of thing that would appeal to the young hot-heads amongst the lords and officers of the Warlord's Domain; they wouldn't object to a war, no, not at all, for the sake of its drama, its romance, its excitement—and the rapid promotion that comes with filling dead men's shoes.

Aldric stared at them, actors and audience both. He still remembered—how could he forget?—riding past the battlefield of Radmur Plain, not quite nine months ago. *Righteous Lord God, was it really so short a time?* Enough to begin a new life of his own, but not enough and never enough to restore the tens of hundreds of lives cut short on those bloody pastures.

It had been before the burial parties started work and he had seen a mile-wide meadow strewn with men and horses, all bloating in the warm spring sun. He had smelled them, too. Even the mere memory of that ripe stench was enough to make him wrinkle his nose. A whiff of it here would drown out the scent of *ymeth* and of perfume, and put paid to such nonsense as was being ranted from the stage. Or would it . . . ?

And it pleases me to see ranged along the field
Bold men and horses armed for war.
And it pleases me to see my foemen run away,
And I feel great joy when I see strong citadels besieged,
The broken ramparts caving in among the flowers of
* fire,*
And I have pleasure in my heart when I behold the
* hosts*
Upon the water's edge, closed in all around by ditches,
With palisades of strong stakes close together . . .

Kyrin's mouth quirked in distaste and she turned to look at Aldric to ask if this was really, truly, the rest of the speech she had heard him quote with such good cheer and laughter. Her question was never asked, because the expression on his face provided her with answer enough.

And once entered into battle let every man
Think only of cleaving arms and heads,
For a man is worth more dead than alive and beaten!
I tell you there is not so much savor
In eating or drinking or sleeping
As when I hear them scream . . .

Aldric stared coldly at the rest of the audience, not feeling superior but just more bitterly experienced. Though most were drinking in the ringing words, several—the more imaginative—were looking apprehensive, and one or two almost queasy. *Oh Light of Heaven I would love to make you sick,* he thought savagely. *All of you. You might be less enthusiastic for this sewage then.* The images were there, rising unbidden from the dark corners of his mind like drowned men in the first thaw: a raven with an eyeball on its pick-axe beak; the putrid seethe of maggots; gray wolves whose pelts were slimy with the juices from some mother's liquefying son.

" 'I would speak to thee of all the glory that is war,' " quoted Aldric softly.

"You've seen it, haven't you?" Kyrin said. "You know what it's really like."

"Yes, I've seen that *glory.*" He seemed almost to be tasting the flavor of the word. "Duergar Vathach used

the Empire's way to making war; he brought it to Alba
with him. Burnt villages, dead children and the sound of
women weeping. Crows and buzzing flies and the air so
thick with death that you could taste the stink. Sweet,
and sickly, and foul." He knuckled tiredly at his eyesock-
ets, all the warmth of wine and food quite gone and only
a leaden coldness left behind. "I know indeed. All too
well. Kyrin, when this scene ends, we're going—back to
the Towers, to pack our things. I want to leave the city
at first light tomorrow."

"To go home?"

"Home. Or wherever. I just want away from here."

"Sir, may I speak privately with you?"

"Not now, Holbrakt." Hakarl paused on the threshold
of The Two Towers, a mink baulked at the door of a
chicken-run, and glanced back at his sergeant. The man's
expression—what could be seen of it—was worried. "Or
is it as important as you make it look?"

"Yes, sir. I fear it is."

"Damn you!" Hakarl's voice was calm, controlled,
without animosity in the curse. "All right, then. You,
you and you," Hakarl pointed with his crop, an odd
accoutrement for a foot soldier but one he found most
useful nonetheless, "get in there. If he's there, call me *at
once.* If he's not, ask—nicely, at first." The *Tau-kortagor*
smiled so that his men could see it. "But don't stop
asking until you get an answer."

He left them to their own devices, however inventive
and worth watching those might become before the information was obtained, and turned back to Holbrakt.
The sergeant still looked like someone with griping in
the guts, far from comfortable with whatever it was he
had to say.

"What's the matter, man? Your belly hurt?"

"No sir, my neck. As if there was a headsman's axe
resting across it." Hakarl watched him but said nothing.
"I mean, sir, the Guild Houses and what was done in
them."

"I did wonder . . ."

"Four Guilds will hold you responsible, *Tau-kortagor,*
sir. They will—"

"Do nothing." Hakarl cocked his head sideways and listened as the thuds and grunts and cries of an impromptu interrogation reached his ears. "Particularly when I bring these criminals before the *Woydach*. That's the way to be forgiven, Holbrakt; forgiven for anything." The rhythmic thudding from inside the inn stopped and there was silence; then a sound of breaking glass and an instant afterward a high, shrill scream suddenly cut off.

"But you killed two Guildsmen and tortured three—"

"I sergeant? Why all this *you* that I keep hearing. What about *we* and *us,* or did I merely imagine seeing you and all the others? You didn't falter when there was a chance of finding gold coins piled up on the shelves. Was that what you expected, sergeant?" Hakarl flexed the whippy crop between his hands and smiled. "Was that why you didn't make your little speech until now, eh? Well, they don't keep their cash like that these days, as I could have told you had you asked."

Holbrakt took a step backward, skidded on the frozen snow beneath his heel and almost fell. *Tau-kortagor* Hakarl laughed at the man's discomfiture. "That's right, sergeant. There's no sure footing anymore, and we are all of us in this together . . . which some realized before you chose to say it." He tapped the crop against his boot and looked pleased with himself. "That's why Meulan needed only a suggestion and not an order before he went back to fire all the Guild Houses that show . . . ah . . . signs of interference. Rioters and looters, Holbrakt; they always take advantage of any confusion in the city. Am I not right . . . ?"

"Yes, sir." The words came out grudgingly, but they came out nonetheless. "You are, sir."

"Then remember it. Ah, good." Hakarl turned to face his three troopers as they emerged from the inn. One of them was flexing his fingers and blowing on bruised knuckles, the others were wiping blood-smears from their truncheons. "What news?"

"Sir, we have him. Both of them. They're in The Playhouse even now—watching *Tiluan,* if you please."

"I do please. Very much. Because the play's no more than halfway done by now, and because we've loody got them . . . ! Well, come on, *move!*"

And when I hear them fall among the palisades and
*   ditches,*
Little men and great men all one on the bloodied grass,
And I see fixed in the flanks of the corpses,
Stumps of spears with silken streamers,
Then I have pleasure in the downfall of my enemies!
Great Lords and soldiers of this great Empire,
Pawn your mansions and your cities and your towers
Before you give up making war upon all who
*   oppose you!*
Swiftly go now to the great Grand Warlord and tell
*   him*
He has lived in peace too long!

As the scene intensified the stage lights dimmed as tinted
shutters were drawn across them; but as the symbolic
darkness fell Aldric stiffened in his seat and his eyes
went very wide, trying to make use of the remaining
glimmer of red light and thus make sense of what they
saw. His stare was fixed on one man's face, an Imperial
officer glimpsed in profile just as the stage beyond went
black. There had been something about those adze-
carved features, a strange familiarity that sent a nervous
shivering all over his skin, as if God had spoken his
name and not with favor. It was a face which raised
questions, the kind of questions that needed urgent
answers.

"Up," he snapped to Kyrin. "Up and out, right now."

"Now? You said at the end of the—"

"Don't argue with me. Do it."

Kyrin's eyes went wide and her face paled, for though
she had heard him use that flat and deadly tone of voice
before it had never, ever been directed at her. It was
only when she saw how the anger and mild disgust on
his face had been replaced with something very close to
fear that she began to understand. They got to their
feet quickly, quietly and with minimum inconvenience
to those around them.

"Play faint," Aldric whispered, fanning Kyrin with the
playbill as he laid a comforting—and concealing—arm
across her shoulders to force her head downward and

out of sight. "I'll help you out." They managed to work their way clear of their own seats and along the row for a few feet—and then the scene ended, and so did their escape.

Neither Aldric nor Kyrin had expected anyone else in the Playhouse to stand up just as they did, clapping their hands and shouting for a reprise of the most raucous part of the speech. Although there was enough applause to cover the movement of a troop of horses, there was also enough movement in the audience itself to prevent that troop of horse from taking more than two steps in any direction. They managed those two steps as the cheering died down a little, only to be trapped again when the actor playing "Broknar" returned to the stage.

The man held up his hands for silence, and waited patiently during the few minutes while the mannerly resumed their seats and went quiet—then for the few minutes further while they shushed their less courteous or more drunken neighbors.

"My lords, my ladies and good people all," said "Broknar," making his obeisance to all into a single splendid gesture, "I pray you, let the play continue to its true conclusion; for the company do promise that they shall both reprise and re-enact while yet in costume when all the action's done, being certain that more will be demanded than just the words of this poor player. Enjoy our play—and of your mercy, make way for the lady that she may recover and return ere we begin again."

Aldric flinched and felt his stomach give a lurch like something pushed abruptly off a roof; but, trapped too far away to return to their seats, somehow they both contrived to remain within their roles. Kyrin put one hand to her face and forehead again, concealing any expression that might betray her, while Aldric inclined his head to acknowledge the actor's thoughtfulness—and to conceal his features from whoever might find them of interest. But neither, now the focus of benevolent attention, moved quite fast enough.

The Imperial officer Aldric had spotted as the last scene ended glanced once incuriously in their direction;

then again, far more intently, and stood up to see them
better. Aldric saw his eyes and his mouth move, and he
knew that what the man had said was *"You . . ."*

Aldric was able to go one better, if "better" meant
having a name go howling through his head rather than
vague sounds of recognition forming on his lips. Warship
commanders needed shore leave as much as lesser mor-
tals, and it was likely that most would try to spend the
winter holiday somewhere they could be assured of
entertainment—like the capital of whichever region of
the Empire had their allegiance. But whatever had
brought *Hautmarin* Doern of the battleram *Aalkhorst* to
the Playhouse on this night of all nights, Aldric hoped
that it was choking on the laughter of its dismal joke.

There was no real enmity between Doern and himself,
but after their last and so far only encounter the *hautmarin* would want to know what business brought the
man he knew only as a mercenary—and a sorcery-
enraveled one at that—to the heart of the Warlord's
Domain. It wasn't every battleram commander whose
ship had helped destroy one of the flying demons known
as *isghun,* and even the wildest optimist wouldn't dare
to hope he had forgotten it already. Aldric was not an
optimist—at least not in a situation such as this. The
only hope he entertained was that Doern had read only
blank non-recognition from his face rather than the startled concern that was really there—and it was a hope
dashed almost at once, when the *hautmarin* yelled, "You
there, *stop!*"

That Doern would know nothing of which he could
suspect them was never any obstacle to an Imperial officer; flight was guilt until proved otherwise, and their departure from the theater would already have seemed
flight enough. At the same moment they broke free of
the audience who hemmed them in, and ran. Kyrin,
aware of it as much as Aldric, was playing her part to
the hilt in an attempt to give their haste another reason.
With one hand to her forehead and another flat across
her stomach, she projected such an impression of a pa-
thetically sick lady of quality that the crowd who might
have tried to block someone with a sword parted to let
her through.

Hautmarin Doern and the two other men who were presumably his First and Executive officers were trying to follow, but like all the other military men in the Playhouse they were in civilian clothes. It was a small point, but where the people around them would have scattered in obedience to the orders of a Fleet uniform, now they merely continued to resume their seats or even actively obstruct the passage of a trio whose actions they regarded as being no more than rude. Sparing a second at the door to glance behind him, Aldric saw just enough of Doern's difficulties to create a sort of smile. Then Kyrin's hand was pulled from his own as she was seized, dragged through the door and out of sight. Aldric's smile dissolved in an oath and he kicked the closing door wide open, plunged outside . . . then froze.

There were eight men standing across the entrance of the theater, all in the thunderbolt-slashed black of *Kagh' Ernvakh,* the nominally-Secret Police. A ninth lounged nonchalantly against one of the uprights that supported the entrance awning, tapping a riding-crop against his booted leg and looking very pleased, for all that he and his men seemed out of breath. "You see, Holbrakt," he said smugly to the tenth and last man, the one standing beside him who was holding Kyrin by the elbow, "I knew that we should double-time it here before the end of the play. And once again, am I not right . . . ?"

"Yes, *Tau-kortagor* Hakarl, sir." From his tone the other soldier didn't seem especially happy to make the admission. "You are, sir."

"Well said. And you"—the junior officer Hakarl straightened himself and leveled his riding-crop at Aldric—"are the man the *Woydach* wants."

Aldric ignored the threat implicit in the crop and stared instead at its wielder, not much liking what he saw. So this was the face of the new order in Drusul, the face of the New Imperial Man whose destiny it was to rule and be obeyed. It was scarcely an appealing prospect. "Why me?" he asked.

"Because the *Woydach* said so should be good enough for you, *hlensyarl.* Good enough for you and your woman both."

Hakarl's words made Aldric shiver; this was becoming

too much like the episode of Ivern's steading. It required
a conscious act of will to keep his right hand away from
Widowmaker's hilt. No sense in starting trouble yet;
there would be time enough for that when the moment
came. "And why the rough handling? We're guests in
your city, *Kortagor,* not criminals."

"My orders say otherwise." Hakarl made a quick motion of encirclement with the thonged tip of the crop.
"Take him."

Isileth Widowmaker came out of her scabbard with
the sort of eager metallic singing that gives even the
most battle-hardened soldier pause for thought, and
these men were not combat troops no matter how the
term was stretched. Their more usual opponents were
unarmed men and women, confused beyond the capability for rational thought by being woken from a sound
sleep in the small hours of the morning by the noise of
their house doors being kicked in. The sight of a
longsword poised in the hands of someone who looked
all too eager to use it produced an immobility that made
nonsense of Hakarl's order.

"Sh'voda moy, Kagh' Ernvakh," said Aldric, and for
all that he spoke softly there was a deal more authority
in his voice than there had been in Hakarl's. Widowmaker leveled in exactly the way that the young officer
had leveled his riding-crop, her gleaming, bitter edges
giving extra weight to the gesture. Aldric tracked her
point from face to face, slowly, as if he was letting the
blade have first sight of her prey. *"Hlakhan tey'aj-hah,
ya vlech-hu taii-ura! H'nach-at sliijeii keii'ch da?* Or as
we say at home, who's first?"

"The woman!" snapped Hakarl and chopped his
hand downward.

There was another quick scrape of drawn steel—then
Holbrakt shrieked hoarsely and fell over as Tehal Kyrin
put the sergeant's own stolen shortsword through his left
lung. She stepped back, whipping blood from the blade
with a quick sideways slash that—deliberately—sent a
spatter across Hakarl's glossy boots, and said, "Not
quite. Who's next?"

"What are you going to do?" asked Hakarl mockingly.
"Fight the whole city garrison?"

It was a question that had occurred to Aldric and
Kyrin already. Before blood was spilled they might have
had a chance to talk their way out of this situation, although with the Warlord's personal involvement—if the
young *tau-kortagor* spoke truth at all—that was always
unlikely. Now, with one of the Secret Police choking in
the snow, it was downright impossible . . .

Then everything happened at once. Hakarl, still not
convinced that what Kyrin had done was more than
lucky accident, snapped the lash of his crop at her eyes
with one hand and with the other ripped his own sword
from its sheath into a thrust at her throat; the theater
door burst open as Doern and his two companion officers finally reached the exit and jerked back into the
Playhouse again as three feet of *taiken* split the still-
swinging door in half from top to bottom; and in the
momentary shift of Aldric's concentration all eight of
the remaining troopers leapt at him . . .

Straight into the arc of a longsword's focused strike.

The snow went scarlet and began to melt as blood
gouted streaming across it from two troopers whose concerns were more immediate than their bad landings. Two
more, crumpled at the end of long smeared skid-marks,
were no longer concerned by anything at all. The four
who remained fell back in confusion at losing half their
number to a single cut.

Aldric snarled silently at them. There was the pain of
what felt like a pulled muscle in his shoulder, brought
on by the strains and stresses of the impact, but otherwise nothing at all—no reaction to killing two men with
a single blow and most likely mortally wounding two
others.

That would come later, when he had time for it. Right
now his training and his reflex responses were all that
mattered. More of this and he and Kyrin might—do
what? Fight the whole garrison indeed? Run? Hide?
Where . . . ?

During the brief lull he had enough time to glance
across to where Kyrin matched cut for cut with Hakarl.
She skidded for one heart-stopping instant on the snow,
only to flick out her free hand and rip the riding-crop
from his grasp before snapping it back across his eyes

in a reflection of his own opening attack . . . but a reflection that moved slightly faster than the original. Hakarl's screech at his blinding was a muffled squawk, gagged by the wide blade that rammed up underneath his chin and almost took his head off.

Aldric saw her pull the shortsword free and look down at the corpse a moment, then turn toward him. He saw her eyes go wide and her mouth open in a cry of warning . . .

. . . But he didn't see *Hautmarin* Doern, or the makeshift cudgel descending on to the base of his skull. And after that all the world's lights went out.

9

A storm-wind came shrieking out of nowhere into the Hall of Kings in Cerdor, and a spout of blue fire sprang up before lashing itself into oblivion; when all was over and silence had returned, Gemmel leaned against Ykraith the Dragonwand and smiled a little wearily. "It is done," he said. "There will be peace in Alba, at least for a little time. Now the matter of how long it lasts will rest with both of you, and all of them, and what you have to say to one another."

Lord Dacurre said nothing, merely inclining his head a touch in gratitude and more relief than he was prepared to let the enchanter see. Lord Santon, younger and if not more skeptical then certainly less controlled and infinitely more curious about the ways of wizards, leaned forward across his table and its carefully weighted paperwork and stared. "How? You can't have spoken to all the lords in Alba! You were only gone a day!"

Gemmel and Dacurre glanced at one another and, their differences temporarily set aside, exchanged the sort of rolled-eyes look of despair that all old men with youthful relatives must employ at some stage if they wish to keep their tempers. For all that Hanar Santon was a high-clan Alban lord, he was also the same age as Aldric Talvalin—but lacked Aldric's four years of experience in why people shouldn't ask users of the Art Magic just that sort of damn-fool question.

"The *how* is my affair, my lord, and so is the time I took to do it." Gemmel's hesitation just before he spoke made it quite clear that what he was saying now was not what had first crossed his mind, and Dacurre was grateful for the other man's restraint—such as it was. "I much regret that talking to full-blown Alban clan-lords—that is, of course, *other* Alban clan-lords—is never something I prefer to take long over. They're all so . . . honorable." He said it as if the word was a sticky sweetmeat lodged in a hollow tooth, and for all that Aymar Dacurre knew that he, too, could take offense if he so desired, the old man hid a smile behind his hand instead.

"What did you say to them?" Dacurre asked when his features were once more under some control. "And what did they say to you?"

"Respectively, a little and a lot," said Gemmel. "And none of them offered me a chair, nor a drink, nor anything to eat despite the distance I had traveled . . ."

Dacurre went somewhat pink at having to be reminded of the oldest obligation due a lord of any standing—that of hospitality to guests. He rang the small bell on the desk in front of him with quite excessive vigor, and when the ringing was answered by two sentries and three servants—all of whom gaped to see Gemmel somewhere he shouldn't be without their knowing it—issued a rattle of orders that sent all five of them scurrying in different directions.

While Gemmel took first his seat and then some food and wine, Dacurre leafed through his files to find whichever papers might prove useful. There were very few. Alba's past rulers had made few provisions for being assisted in their work by the dubious class of wizards, sorcerers and enchanters. At least, unlike the Drusalan Empire, there were no laws on the statutes involving guilt for actually talking to one of them—and if there were, neither Dacurre nor Santon had seen them, and right now did not wish to.

Though he hid it better than the younger man, Dacurre was as curious about Gemmel as Santon seemed to be—a curiosity that today was based on something rather more solid and immediate than the whys and wherefores of the Art Magic. Aymar Dacurre was more concerned with the enchanter's clothes. On the few other occasions when their paths had crossed, Gemmel had been dressed in commonplace Alban garments—shirt and tunic, boots and breeches, jerkin and over-mantle—

quality work and weave, but none of them worthy of a second glance and certainly not the fanciful robes that sorcerers were supposed to wear. Only the ominous presence of the Dragonwand had ever marked him out as different before; that was, until today. Now, under the furred overrobe that was the same concession to the season made by everyone, he was wearing what Dacurre could only think of as some kind of uniform—and one which, colors apart, was too like that of the Imperial military for comfort.

There was a high-necked shirt beneath the tunic, and he was wearing boots and breeches; but though the garments could be named, their austere cut and their material were unlike anything Dacurre had seen before. Everything was a blue so dark that it was almost black, with insignia in a silvery metal at the shoulders, cuffs and collar; except for the leather of boots and belt which *were* black and of an impossible glossiness. There was a flapped weapon-holster on the left side of the belt, supported at a cross-draw angle by a strap that ran across and down from the opposite shoulder, and at first glance it appeared to hold nothing more outlandish than a *telek*. Then Dacurre got a slightly better look and realized he wanted to know neither what the weapon in the holster really was, nor where it had been made.

"You came into the presence of *ilauem-arluthen* dressed like that?" Always, always, Santon could be relied on for the unsubtle question. Dacurre flinched slightly, more from personal affront than out of any fear of Gemmel's reaction, and quelled the younger lord with a glare.

For his part, Gemmel sipped his wine and studied both of them over the rim of the glass. "It's almost like having Aldric here, don't you think?" he observed mildly. "And in answer, Lord Santon, yes I did. Since I was making a formal call, so to speak, I chose to dress formally; it's only polite." He set the wine-glass down, considered refilling it, then pushed both glass and carafe aside, sat back in his chair and made a steeple of his fingers in a mannerism unsettlingly reminiscent of the dead King Rynert.

"As both of you are probably well aware, the so-haughty members of the ex-Crown Council were not exactly pleased to be addressed with the words I felt that all of them needed to hear. Words not unlike those you used to me, Lord Santon, and which proved so . . . effective." Gemmel didn't smile; he wasn't making a joke, and had neither forgotten nor forgiven the way the younger lord had trapped him with a net of words into performing this mission when he had so many other things to do. "Especially when those words were spoken by the *pestreyr* sorcerer who had obtained the fealty—some two or three who thought themselves witty said fouler things—of Aldric Talvalin by some sort of wizard's trick. Lord Ivan Diskan of Kerys was one who thought to elaborate on what an unmarried older man might want from one much younger." This time Gemmel did smile and Dacurre, seeing it, would have preferred that he had not. "His sight will return, in time. And in the meanwhile, Lord Dacurre, he has developed something of a willingness to talk about peace. So have they all, even the ones who didn't . . . ah . . . provoke me."

Gemmel stood up and closed his overrobe about him, hiding the strange uniform and the stranger holstered sidearm. "Their couriers are heading for Cerdor even now, and I am heading for the Empire."

"Where?" asked Dacurre, rising from his own seat. "Maybe we can help you . . ."

"You, help me?" That Gemmel didn't laugh out loud was only out of courtesy. The mocking laughter glittered in his eyes just the same. "No. I shall start at the center, in Kalitzim, and work outward from there. The Emperor's sister owed Aldric the favor of a life and I intend to collect the debt. Just remember this. What I said before holds true: I lost a day thanks to the pair of you, and if that lost day has hurt me and mine then I shall hurt you and yours. Revenge, my lords. You Albans know the word, I think . . ."

There was a sound like thunder and a blue-white flash like lightning that made both clan-lords blink; and then there was a short sharp bang as air rushed in to fill the space where Gemmel Errekren had been . . .

* * *

Voord had achieved something like a sound sleep for the first time in many nights, only to be woken from it by a polite, persistent rapping on his bedroom door. Two seconds before he became sufficiently aware to mumble, "Yes, what?" in a tone of entirely justified irritation, there was a shortsword out of its scabbard and in his hand. At times he wondered what it had been like to sleep easily and to awaken unafraid; but even the recollection of those times had been forgotten long ago.

It was Tagen again. There had been a time when Voord would have expected him to be there, but he had tired of handsome young men with heavy muscles and was growing still more tired of finding this particular example of the breed lurking outside his doors at all hours of the day and night. Indeed, he was growing simply weary . . . of constants: constant fear, constant plotting, constantly keeping two steps ahead of the knives that sought his back whether they were simply political or real steel. And most of all he was weary of being in constant pain. Giorl had done her best, but that best was based on ordinary medicine rather than the ailment which infected him. As he sheathed the sword and beckoned Tagen in, Voord realized that what he wanted most from life at this moment was an ending to it. The one thing that he was denied . . .

"Good morning, sir," said Tagen. "A very good morning indeed. We have them both."

Voord blinked, the significance of the words eluding him for a moment. Then he remembered and made himself smile, since that was evidently what was expected of him. Yet he knew that just now he didn't care. There had been nights when he had lain awake beside the sleeping body of whoever had been sharing his bed, staring at the ceiling and wondering what his imagination could create for Aldric Talvalin if and when there was ever the opportunity for such a diversion. There had been nights, too, when his lovemaking or his sleep had been sweetened by those same dreams of atrocity-to-come. But this night, with the opportunity for making dreams reality placed in his grasp, all that he could think of was trying to recover the stillness and the rest that Tagen's arrival had stolen from him.

"Then have them placed somewhere secure. I'll see them later in the morning."

Tagen stared, plainly astonished at this lack of eagerness. Voord returned the stare with a gaze as blank and expressionless as that of a lizard on a stone. Right now he was unwilling—no, unable—to share Tagen's bottomless capacity for violence. The gilt wires twisted through his flesh were hurting him, and the cuts and gashes they held shut were hurting him, and even his head was hurting him as well. Looking more speculatively at Tagen, he wondered whether spreading the pain would not in fact reduce his own—or at least take his mind from it for just a little while.

"Do as I command, Tagen," he said. "Then come back here." The thought faltered, faded, and one hot and hurtful memory was replaced by another just as hot, just as painful, but far more recent.

"No. Instead of that, I'll come with you. Help me dress. This is supposedly official business, so it had best be uniform." Voord sat up, slid sideways and got out of bed, moving as carefully as an old, old man for fear of ripping open one of his wounds. The burnt flesh of his legs stung him as if to emphasize his recollection of what had brought them to such a state, and he glanced down at the wrapping of ointment-smeared bandage which had been all Giorl could do. There had been Dragonfire and raw, unfocused power in the courtyard of Egisburg's Red Tower. He had been within an instant of becoming no more than a silhouette etched into the stones at the base of the Tower, but with shape-shifting and the speed that granted him, he had escaped . . . all but the pulse of force that leapt from the spellstone in Talvalin's hand, blue fire, white fire, heat and light and noise . . . and, inevitably, pain.

"What about their gear? Was everything brought here?"

"Everything; even their horses are stabled in the Guards Cavalry block."

"Good." Voord spoke with the neutrality of mild interest, taking care not to betray what was forming in his mind for fear that Tagen would object and, given sufficient time, work out some way to thwart the plan. "And them: have they said anything yet?"

"The girl, Kyrin, alternates a sullen silence with inventive oaths. The man Aldric is still unconscious."

"Unconscious? I said that neither was to be harmed."

"There was a brawl during the arrest, sir." Tagen began talking much faster; he knew of old that coldness in Voord's voice, and had no desire to be the recipient of his rising anger. "The Alban had a sword with him, and the woman stole one during the fight. By the time he was knocked out four *Kagh' Ernvakh* men were dead and a fifth isn't expected to last the night."

"Just now I don't care about *Kagh' Ernvakh!* The clumsy fools had their orders. Which of them hit him?"

"A Fleet *hautmarin* called Doern, sir—in the city on leave over the holiday. He was in the Playhouse where the arrest took place. It seems he knows the man Talvalin from somewhere else; he's been asking questions . . . and mentioning the use of sorcery."

"Has he indeed? All right." Voord stamped into his boots and waited while Tagen knelt to buckle them. "Then this afternoon I'll have this quick and observant *Hautmarin* Doern presented with a fat bounty and a promotion for assisting in the capture of a dangerous enemy of the state. That should convince him how important a catch he's made; and how pleased with him *I* am."

"And once he leaves the fortress, he's to be 'robbed and murdered,' sir?"

"Not this time. It would look overly suspicious." Voord hesitated, considering, then glanced down at Tagen and patted him on the head as he might have done a dog or a precocious child. "All the same, put someone on to him while he remains in Drakkesborg and have them report back twice daily. If Doern finished his leave and returns to his ship, well and good; but at the first indication that the gold or the rank-tabs haven't shut his mouth, I promise that I'll let you kill him."

"Sir!" The boots dealt with, Tagen sprang to his feet and saluted, all bounding energy and quivering eagerness. Had he a tail, he would have been wagging it. "What about Talvalin and his woman, sir . . . ?"

Good dog, Voord thought, coming very close to saying it aloud. "In my good time, Tagen. I'll let you know when that time will be, never fear. But I think I should take a look at them first, don't you?"

Kyrin had drifted in and out of an uneasy doze since they were brought to the fortress. Between cat-naps she stared through the gloom of the poorly lit cell toward the pallet where Aldric had been laid. Shackled by one wrist and one ankle to the bed on the opposite wall, stare was the most that she could do.

Kyrin had had only the briefest chance, in the snowy bloodstained darkness outside the theater before the pair of them were dragged unceremoniously away, to make sure that his skull had not been fractured. Certainly there was a lump the size of her fist, and without light there was no opportunity to check for pupil dilation or any of the other signs of concussion. Aldric's head was notoriously hard—he had said as much himself—but Kyrin doubted it was hard enough to take the sort of impact that Doern had delivered and still remain intact.

What concerned her most of all was the gentleness with which they had been treated. After the deaths of four of their comrades, she had feared rough handling at the very least from the remaining Secret Police. Instead, the worst that it could have been called was unmannerly. It suggested either that they, or more probably Aldric, were being held as bargaining counters for the Empire to gain some sort of concession from Alba—or that there was much, much worse to follow.

The cell door opened and two guards carrying lanterns came inside. Now that there was light, she was surprised at how spacious their confinement really was.

Apart from the massive door and the wrist-thick bars on the little green-glazed windows, it didn't look too much like her idea of a prison cell. No chilly damp, no sodden straw on the floor, no stinks except for the smell of oily metal that wafted from her manacles every time she moved and a faint, sourceless almost medicinal odor; and no rats. That, too, wasn't much of a comfort, and for the same reason; after all this softness, how hard would the truly hard become?

Their lanterns hooked to metal fixtures in the wall on either side of another door she hadn't seen before, the guards glanced toward her and as they went out again exchanged some remark that made them both laugh. It was an unwholesome laughter, the sort that went with the image of several drunken men meeting one woman in a lonely alleyway. Kyrin shivered and tried to put the thought out of her head by wondering what was behind the other door; only to discover that the sort of suggestions her mind was putting forward were even worse than thinking about the laughter.

"I bid you welcome to Drakkesborg, Tehal Kyrin," said a suave voice, "and I bid you welcome to my house."

Kyrin's head jerked up to see two other men standing in the doorway of the cell; she had been so lost in her own thoughts that she had neither seen nor heard them come in. One was a young man, big and broad-shouldered, with a face she would have called handsome had it not been for the shuttered eyes that gave his expression a disturbing vacancy. It looked not so much as if he was concealing what went on inside his head; rather, that nothing went on there at all except what he was ordered to do. And the most likely source of those orders was standing right beside him.

"I know you," said Kyrin softly, trying not to be frightened of the man she had last seen aiming a *telek* at her face: the man who had killed Dewan ar Korentin that time in Egisburg, when Dewan took the dart meant for her. The man Aldric had called Commander Voord, and therefore the same man who had—Kyrin was suddenly very conscious of the bed beneath her—raped Kathur the Vixen two months past in Tuenafen.

"Good," said Voord, and pressed one hand over his heart to give her a small mocking bow. "I have a certain reputation; it pleases me to see it spread."

"Your reputation!" Kyrin's mouth twisted in a sneer she didn't even try to hide. There was most certainly nothing she could do to make their situation any better, and probably nothing to make it any worse. "As a murderer and a traitor—"

"And most recently as Grand Warlord." Voord was

unruffled by the insults, and even smiled faintly at her recitation of what he probably considered virtues. "Which makes all the rest a little insignificant." Then he turned from her and looked at the big man who stood at his side. "Tagen, you told me their gear was brought here, too. Where is it?"

"Sir, he's an Alban *kailin-eir,* one of their clan-lords and for four years before that he was an *eijo,* a landless warrior who lived by his sword. Until we check every piece of clothing and equipment for concealed weapons, I don't dare take the risk of leaving anything where he might—"

"That stuff doesn't concern me; where's his sword?"

"That would be the worst thing of all to—"

"Enough. I ask again, where is it?"

"In the armory with everything else. It needs checking too, just in case there's more to it than just a sword."

Voord's head snapped round and as his eyes met Kyrin's, he smiled. She had betrayed no reaction at all to his words, but evidently he had sensed something . . . or it amused him to let her think so. "I don't know about the rest of it, but you may well be right about the sword. Have it brought in here."

"Here? Now . . . ?" Tagen was aghast. "But sir, you know what this man is like! Bringing a weapon anywhere near him would—"

"Tagen, shut up. He's unconscious and hardly likely to stir for a long while yet. So do it." Voord glanced around the cell, considering. "Bring one of the armorers with you—and whatever materials he might need to fix the weapon to that back wall."

Tagen hesitated for maybe one whole second, as close to disobedience as he had ever been, then shrugged instead of saluting and left the cell. As Voord watched him go Kyrin could see an odd expression on his face: anger that his authority had been challenged, mingled with shock that the challenge had come from this of all sources.

"What's wrong, Commander Voord? Was your dog threatening to bite?"

Voord shot her a quick angry look, but paid no further

heed to the remark. Instead he walked over to where Aldric lay and gazed thoughtfully down at him, then put out his hand—the unmaimed right—and laid its wide-spread fingers across the Alban's face.

"Leave him alone, you bastard!" Kyrin yelled, jerking forward to the full length of her chains and lashing out at Voord with one futile fist.

"Make me," said Voord, and smiled. "Did he ever tell you about a certain use for the drug *ymeth?*" Kyrin glowered but said nothing. "To get inside a man's mind, to learn what he knows, what he thinks—and what he fears. Useful things like that. Nothing held back, nothing hidden, nothing lied about. I need no drugs, not when he's like this." Voord took a deep breath and his fingers tightened until they seemed about to sink into the skin of Aldric's face.

Kyrin had been expecting Aldric to cry out, or to try to pull his head free, or to do *something.* Instead he did nothing; even the quick, shallow rhythm of his breathing remained unchanged. Voord, however, turned his own head and gazed at Kyrin with such lascivious amusement that she blushed scarlet and looked away. "Yes, indeed," said Voord. "Nothing hidden." Then he glanced back at Aldric with the suddenness of one finding exactly what he was looking for, and laughed as he released his grip. "Good," he said softly. "Welcome to your nightmare . . ."

Tagen was back in a matter of minutes, with Widow-maker held in both hands and slightly away from his body as if he didn't want even the scabbarded blade to come too close. The armorer was at his heels, a stocky, silver-bearded man in a leather apron with a canvas bag of tools and equipment hanging from one hand as though a permanent part of his anatomy. He glanced incuriously from Voord to the shackled prisoners and then back, plainly seeing nothing until he was told what he was supposed to do.

"You brought all you need?" asked Voord.

"I did, my lord." The armorer fished noisily in his bag for a moment before holding up a piece of forged metal for Voord's inspection. "Two of these clamps, three strips of steel, ten masonry spikes and my best hammer. Do you wish the weapon capable of being drawn, or not?"

"Emphatically not. I want the whole thing immovable. But also I want as much of it on view as can be managed—you understand?"

"I had already suspected as much, my lord. Hence the clamps, one for point and one for pommel, and the steel stripping to hold the crosspiece and the scabbard snug."

Voord looked quickly at Tagen, but guessed that wherever the armorer had gleaned his information it hadn't been from that source. Tagen was still looking too worried about the whole proceeding to have realized yet what was in Voord's mind. But the woman knew; she was glaring hatred at all three of them, blue eyes venomous as those of a basilisk. Voord smiled back at her, quite unaffected by her gaze. "Yes, my dear," he said. "Expressly to frustrate the pair of you . . . and especially him." He jerked his head toward Aldric, and his smile went thin and nasty as he patted the innocent blue-white crystal that was the *taiken*'s pommel-stone. "This . . . Ah, this sword's the only thing that makes him what he is. We'll see how he fares when he can see it and speak to it, but can't get at it . . ."

Aldric's eyelids fluttered, squeezed tight shut and then ventured open. "I think I'm going to be sick," he announced in a fragile voice, and abandoned any attempt to sit upright.

He closed his eyes to blot out the sight of two of everything, wishing fervently that he hadn't opened them at all. It didn't seem to matter that he was lying flat on his back and looking nowhere except straight up; the entire world appeared to be making a slow spiral progress through his throbbing head, with exactly the same effect as watching the real world do the same thing from the deck of a heaving ship. It made him want to heave as well.

There was a sound like little bells jangling in his ears and mingling most unpleasantly with the thumping of his own heart, every beat of which sent another dull spike of pain jolting from the back of his neck to the backs of his eyes. There were a few minutes just after he moved when he thought that he might die; and then a few more when he fervently hoped he would.

"You were hit on the head," said a voice like Kyrin's, sounding very far away and almost drowned out by the noise of those damned bells. "I suspect that you have a concussion."

"I suspect nothing of the sort," said Aldric. Even his own voice sounded far away, and he had to pronounce each word carefully to make sure that it was the right one. "I *know* I have a concussion . . . and that I was hit on the head. It's happened before. Either that or the Playhouse fell on me."

"Aldric, we're in trouble," said Kyrin's voice, sounding frightened as she began to explain exactly what the trouble was.

He listened to the words without really hearing them, trying instead to track the swirling world and make some sense of it. Although he had passed into something more like deep sleep within two hours of Doern's cudgel-blow, the brain-rattling effects of the impact required rather more time than just a night's sleep before he shook them off. Shook off, indeed, was scarcely the proper word, since Aldric knew from past experience that if he tried to shake off even a speck of dust tickling his face, he would regret the sudden movement for a long time afterward. Only the name *Voord* managed to pierce the purple fog filling his mind. It was a name he knew from . . . Dizziness or not, his eyes snapped open.

"Say that again; the last part, about Voord." Aldric didn't want to hear it, because that would mean it had to be true and wasn't just another part of the foul fever-dreams that were troubling his sleep.

"What I said was, Voord has somehow become the Grand Warlord. And he's the one who had us both arrested." She looked over at him again, lying quite flat and still as if posing for the carven effigy on a tomb-lid. After the arrest, *Kagh' Ernvakh* troopers had searched them both. They had found three small knives on Aldric: one strapped to his left wrist, a second down his boot and the last—a tiny push-dirk—hung from two loops at the back of his tunic collar. After that, they had taken away all outer garments made of fabric thick enough to hide a blade. For the first time in her memory Aldric was in total black, without the touches of white or silver or of polished metal which had been his—conscious or otherwise—nods in the direction of melodramatic dress. That somber uniformity of non-color, and the blow against his head, gave his face the bone-white pallor of someone two days dead.

Aldric closed his eyes again and this time not just through sickness, unless it was a sickness of the spirit. Without the life and movement granted by those eyes, his face became that of a corpse; it was an image and a premonition that made Kyrin shiver.

"I'm sorry," she said.

"Sorry? For what?"

"For coming here. For getting involved when you wanted me safe. I'm sorry for all of it. But I told you: where you go, I go. To the end of all things."

The fetters clinked as Aldric moved his hand slightly, dismissing the matter. He smiled wanly up at the ceiling and shook his head, both sadly and with pride that anyone should think him worthy of such love, then lay quite still and shivered as that head-shake brought the nausea quivering back into his stomach.

"I know how much you want to hurt him, Commander, and I know how much he deserves to be hurt. But what I cannot understand is why you would do anything so dangerous as putting his sword in with him. Putting it *into* him would be—"

"Too quick, Tagen."

Woydach Voord finished his breakfast, a syrup of white poppies in brandy and a piece of bread, then pushed the cup aside while his mouth twisted at the taste of the stuff on which he had been living for what felt like years. He looked enviously at Tagen's mug of beer and at the fried blood-sausage on his plate. Voord's nostrils twitched; there was thyme in it. *All forbidden now,* he thought. *One more reason not to stay here longer than I have to . . .*

"Much too quick—although I appreciate the irony of it all. And I have another use for Talvalin. What do you think that he would do if he got loose, knowing who I am and what I've done to him and his in the past few years?"

"Sir, he'd try to kill you!"

"And do you think that he'd succeed?"

"Not while you're under my protection. Otherwise . . . almost certainly. Except that you can't die of wounds anymore; they only hurt you."

"They always hurt me, Tagen."

"I wish that I could do something to help, Commander— but all I know is killing."

Voord looked at him for a long, silent moment. "You could help me, Tagen," he said, "by not killing."

"Sir . . . ?" The big man was confused; it was as peculiar a request as Commander Voord had made of him in all the years that they had known one another, and Voord was well aware of it. "*Not* killing, sir? I . . . I don't understand."

Voord had hoped, uselessly it seemed, that Tagen would take his meaning straight away. Evidently not; the leaving-alive of an enemy until that enemy has done what no friend could was far too subtle for this particular *kortagor* of Guards. As well expect an arrow to understand why it must remain in the quiver.

"Talvalin," said Voord, slowly and carefully so that his meaning was quite clear, "must remain alive until after he has killed me."

"What?" Tagen came out of his chair so hard and so fast that beer and sausage both went flying. The clatter attracted accusing stares from all across the Food-Hall for the half-second needed to recognize who had made the noise—and who was sitting with him. After that the only thing that it attracted was servants to clean up the mess and to replenish Tagen's plate.

"After you are certain I am dead, you can kill him as slowly and in whatever way you wish."

"Commander, are you drunk? Or would you rather I called a physician?"

"No to both. I haven't been well drunk in over a month; I don't dare for fear I fall and do myself yet another irreparable mischief, and I'm sick of the constant need for a physician within call. Do you understand

me at last, Tagen? Do you begin to realize how my days
are no longer anything to live, but just to be endured?
Do you?"

Tagen sat very still; what he knew and what he understood was that when Voord's voice took on that particular shrillness, it was safer to be somewhere else—and he
had nowhere else to go. As Voord watched him, he
could see a kind of comprehension beginning to form in
the big man's mind as he tried to relate the Commander's trouble to the sort of life he led himself.

Not to take a woman now and then, because her bites
and scratches would never go away; not to ride a horse
for fear of the broken limb that wouldn't heal or the
broken neck that would leave you still alive but useless;
not even to fight someone for the joy of it in case they
killed you and you didn't die . . . He broke off his nervous, submissive stare at the table, straightened his back
and looked at Voord instead. "Yes, my lord *Woydach*,"
he said, using the new and proper title for the first time,
"I understand completely." He rose, saluted and
walked away.

Voord watched him go, wondering just how much
Tagen really understood at all. Had he been fully convinced of that understanding he might have asked the
big man—the only person in the whole world whom he
could trust—to take Talvalin's sword and do the necessary killing himself. But only if he could have been
sure . . .

Because if the sword alone couldn't do it, then the
spellstone certainly could. Voord recalled the thrill of
mingled shock and pleasure he had felt when he discovered barely half an hour ago that someone—Talvalin
most likely—had put the two together into what should
be a single, supremely potent weapon. And tomorrow,
the twentieth day of the twelfth month, was the beginning of the Feast of the Fires of Winter, when night and
darkness were at their most powerful. By the twenty-
first, the Solstice itself, he would know if his planning
had been successful—or more hopefully that success
would be manifest in his knowing nothing anymore. Now
that Tagen had been dealt with—and it had been both
easier and much more difficult than he had expected—

there remained only the prime mover: Aldric Talvalin himself.

His own reflection, his image in a smoking mirror. That was one of the many, many reasons why Voord hated the young Alban so very much. Mirror-reversed from right to left though it might be, and invisible to others, Voord could see it. What Aldric Talvalin was, Voord Ebanesj might well have been . . . except that he was not.

They were most alike in one very particular characteristic, the one that was most useful to Voord now. Give either sufficient reason to do so, and they would rip the world apart to gain requital for an injury. Voord's methods were crookedly subtle, but Aldric Talvalin could be just as implacable and far more savagely direct in avenging any violation of his personal honor-codes. It was a matter confirmed by written records, both here in the Empire and most likely in Alba as well. That vengeful streak was a quality of which Voord approved, though he himself had never let something so abstract and valueless as honor control the way he acted.

There was just one risk: that if Talvalin guessed how he was being manipulated, and that killing his enemy would not be vengeance but a kindness and a gift, then he would be just stubborn enough to withhold the final cut. Therefore he would have to be brought to such a white heat of hatred that the risk did not exist.

Voord reconsidered the word *violation,* and liked it.

Aldric and Kyrin had learned at last where that other door led to, and Kyrin's worst terrors were made manifest in the white-tiled room beyond. Some of the equipment there was so elaborate that they could only guess at operating principles, but the function of each and every device was invariably plain enough. They had been designed and built solely to bring pain, or to hold securely while the pain was brought by someone else.

They sat on opposite sides of the room, leather straps around their wrists and ankles holding them in wooden chairs that were far more ordinary than the ugly, ominous metal seats which squatted empty here and there. Not all were empty; one held the clerk from The Two

Towers, or what the past two hours had left of him. No
questions had been asked, none of the babbled confes-
sions to various petty crimes had been paid any heed,
for that was not the function of this particular exercise
in cruelty. Before it had begun, the gloved and aproned
chief torturer had studied both of them dispassionately
as they were strapped down and informed them that
Voord had ordered an entertainment for their benefit.
"I am Giorl," she had said. "The *Woydach* orders me
to show you what it is that I do." And she had said
nothing more, but had shown them far more graphically
than any words.

It was sufficiently appalling to learn that what they
were witnessing should be done to another human being
merely to impress them; the revelation that the principal
architect of this fleshly dissolution was a woman came
close to unmanning Aldric entirely. It was grotesque beyond belief; torturers were hooded, hairy, subhuman
brutes, not a pleasant-faced woman who looked more as
if she should have been at home with her children than
here putting a near-surgical skill to this perverted use.

"Enough," said Voord's voice from the door. "Finish
with him."

The woman Giorl glanced over her shoulder as if to
ensure the identity of the speaker, then nodded. "As
you command," she said, and extinguished what life remained with a single incision underneath where her Subject's right ear had been. "The rest of you, clean up,"
she said to her assistants, stripping off her stained gloves
and dropping them into a waiting hand. "My lord, if you
no longer need me I'd like to go home. Until she regains
her strength I want to be close to my daughter."

Aldric and Kyrin gaped at one another across the
room as this ultimate obscenity sank in. That the woman
should do this was bad enough, but that she should then
wash off the blood and slime and go home to a child
with the smell of someone's excised guts still warm in
her nostrils . . .

"All right, Giorl. And thank you for coming here at
such short notice." Voord gave her a perfunctory salute.
"How is the child, anyway?"

"Improving. Whoever did the surgery lacked finesse,

but I'd have thanked a pork-butcher for doing it then, just so long as it was done. Good day, my lord."

"Just one last thing, Giorl . . ."

She hesitated, watching him, waiting for whatever was in his mind this time. Voord moved aside so that the exit was clear and inclined his head a little, manners as polite as any Jouvaine courtier.

"The rest of this is all for me. Don't come back until you're called—do you understand me?"

Giorl glanced at her recent and most definitely captive audience, then back at Voord. Her face was devoid of all expression. "My lord, as always, my understanding of your wishes is quite perfect." She bowed, brushed past him and was gone.

Voord watched her go, appreciating the delicacy of her snub, then gestured with both hands so that the four Bodyguard troopers behind him came into the interrogation room. "Take them out of those chairs," he said, "and put them back to bed." He was immediately conscious of the effect his choice of words was having on the two prisoners, and augmented it with a slow, lecherous smile at Kyrin as he reached out to cup her chin in the claw of his left hand. She spat at him, then flinched in anticipation of a slap as the hand jerked back from her face. Instead Voord merely patted her cheek in light reproof of unladylike behavior, although Kyrin would have preferred the slap; there was something dreadfully promissory about this uncharacteristic gentleness, and she had seen what had been done to Kathur—an employee rather than an enemy—for far less reason.

"This is between you and me, Voord," said Aldric, trying to keep his voice quiet and reasoned while at the same time struggling uselessly against the buckled straps that held him down. "Let her go. She has nothing to do with either of us."

"Oh, but she does. You love her. When I hurt her, I'll hurt you, and when she's been all used up, why then I'll still have you. I am the master here—time you both began to learn it."

"Then you'd best learn this as well." Kyrin and Voord both recognized the terrible calmness with which Aldric spoke, but only Voord was truly pleased to hear it. "The whole of this world isn't big enough to hide in. There'll be nowhere far enough for you to run."

"Fine, stirring words, Aldric Talvalin—but slightly misplaced, considering your present position. Get them into their cell."

The guards carried out his command with all the swift economy of movement that comes with long practice. Both Aldric and Kyrin gained the negligible satisfaction of landing a few telling blows with fists and feet, but against men wearing half-armor and heavy leathers it was mostly wasted effort. The order executed, all four soldiers saluted and left the cell without needing to be dismissed. There was a distinct impression that Voord had told them in advance that he was to be left alone, which to Kyrin's mind meant only one thing. The bed beneath her felt more like a torture-rack with every passing second, and as she stared at Voord like a rabbit confronted by a weasel it took all her force of will not to be sick.

"Well now," said Voord, folding his arms and leaning back against the door, "this *is* cozy."

Aldric, flung unceremoniously face-downward on his pallet and chained that way by the one guardsman who had taken knuckles in the face rather than on the helmet, said something venomous that was muffled by the crumpled bedding and then coughed as dust caught at his throat.

Voord stared at him. "I don't know why you want me to go to Hell, Aldric; this is Hell enough. Except that all of it's for you. I can't begin to explain how long I've waited to offer you just this sort of hospitality. And I can't begin to explain how much of a thorn you've been in my flesh these past years. First Duergar—" —Aldric choked on another cough and stared in disbelief—"then the Geruaths, and finally Princess Marevna. Oh yes, I was involved in all of those, and every time you blundered in and ruined subtle plans you sometimes didn't even know existed. I could forgive a little if you were a true opponent—but not when your interference was driven by nothing more than your pretty personal motives! Father of Fires, that a stratagem three years in the making should come to nothing because of some sword-swinging Alban lout who hadn't the grace to be killed with the rest of his clan of bloody barbarians!"

Voord's voice had risen almost to a yell, but stopped just short of it as he shook his head and pulled himself back under control. There were flecks of spittle on his lips, and his face was red. "But then, I can attend to that unfinished business at my own pace now," he said more quitely, panting slightly. "And in my own fashion. Slowly . . . slowly and with imagination."

He looked briefly at Kyrin, caught her staring at the gilt wires twisted through the flesh above his eye and below his chin, and straightened up so that the metal strands glinted in the light of the lanterns. "You wonder about these?" he said in response to a question no one had dared to utter. "Another memento. Your lover is very good at causing pain. Even I could learn from him—and he will learn from me." He walked over to one side of Aldric's bed and stood there for a long while, staring. Then he reached down with his crippled hand and stroked it slowly and gently down the entire length of Aldric's spine.

His free hand pressed against the back of Aldric's head, pushing his face down into the pillows for a long and choking moment before releasing him to gasp for air. "The learning starts now." Voord spoke with an Alban accent which had not been there before, a careful, deliberate simulation of someone else's voice from long ago and far away. He could as easily have handed over one or both of them to Giorl the torturer, but his subtle mind with its fondness for equally subtle stratagems had seized on this as being far more effective.

The *Woydach* gazed at him through hooded, unreadable eyes, and though nothing could be taken from Voord's still features, the manner in which he now spoke was enough to set Aldric's skin crawling as the more brutal threat had been unable to do. It was too . . . He crushed the memory at once, but still wasn't quick enough.

It was too familiar . . .

"Yes, indeed," said Voord, and smiled. "Welcome to your nightmare."

*   *   *

It was over. Voord was gone, the cell door slammed shut and locked behind him, but not so soon that the laughter from outside hadn't drifted in. All that remained was pain, and shame, and the feeling of being unclean.

And the tears on Kyrin's face that said how much she understood . . .

10

"Why did you do it? Why not just give both of them to the torturer?" Tagen was intrigued by what he had watched through the spy-hole in the cell's outer door, so much so that just this once he had set aside all the respect he had for Voord and gone straight to the point with his questions.

Voord sipped at another cup of the brandy-and-poppy tincture, no longer caring about the taste. His exertions of the morning had strained several of the wired wounds, so that the flesh had been cut like cheese and several wires were beginning to unravel. There was another session with Giorl in the offing, and while he didn't relish the prospect he no longer cared very much. Not when he felt so pleased with himself. Voord was glowing.

"Talvalin was expecting torture, his woman was expecting rape. What I did was the only thing neither was prepared for; neither had their defenses ready." Voord's eyes widened and he clapped one hand to his side, holding it there and whimpering. An ooze of fluid darkened the fabric of his shirt, and the sharp ends of a length of wire poked through the weave in the middle of the stain. When the spasm passed, he drained his cup at a draught and refilled it from the green glass bottle on the table. "And it was a private horror of his own. Oh, there were all the other fears, of loss and pain and death—both his own and the woman's, which is worth bearing in mind—but this was special. It might have been a pleasant memory of his youth for him to look back on"—Voord grinned viciously and raised his cup in a mocking toast—"except that someone he thought he knew took it and him and turned the whole thing foul. And now neither of them know what to expect from me, except that it will always be far worse than anything they can imagine. I think that Talvalin will be more than ready to take any chance we give him . . ."

Tagen muttered something under his breath, still far from happy with this death wish of Voord's even though the reasoning behind it was plain enough even to him. "Then what about the woman, sir?" he asked. "Will she be left until . . . until afterward?"

"Mostly." Voord's eyes were a little glazed as the drug and the brandy began working their brief effect. The respite would be short—it always was, and had been growing shorter with each passing dose. Giorl had warned him that the poppy-syrup liquor was known to be addictive, but for any one of several reasons Voord felt he had no need to worry about that risk. He shook his head to clear away the mists that threatened to fill it completely, and looked back at Tagen. "Mostly, but not altogether. You and your four men go down to the cell and move our two guests back into the interrogation room." Tagen got up, eager to begin, and Voord rapped the table for attention. "You will not, I emphasize *not,* harm either of them just yet."

"But sir, you said—"

"Move them. Nothing else . . . yet. But you can make it plain to both that she'll be next. When I give you permission, you and the others can do whatever takes your fancy—but only when I allow it. And I don't want her killed, or disfigured, or permanently maimed, otherwise escaping will lose its appeal for both of them and Talvalin won't try as hard as he might do when there's everything still to gain. Do you understand what I mean?"

"Yes, sir. I think so, sir."

"Then go do it—and remember, only threats and promises until I say otherwise. Dismissed."

"Sir!"

Voord watched as Tagen hurried off, wondering what the big man would say if he knew that his Commander was even now considering which of the Bodyguard troops were least efficient and most expendable. After Tagen's squad had done to Kyrin whatever it was their unpleasantly fertile minds could conjure up, Voord's plan was that Aldric alone be moved back to the cell— by two guards of sufficient clumsiness for his savage efforts to break free to have a better-than-ever chance of success. And after that . . .

Voord had seen the Alban in action before, and knew well enough that once loose and with a weapon—any weapon—in his hand, he was more than a match for any but the most capable swordsman in the Guard. Neither of the soldiers that Voord had in mind was anything like good enough. There was another matter needing some attention in the little private room near the interrogation chamber; the room with the spell-circle set into its floor. And after that, it would be only a matter of waiting for his release to come through the door.

He swallowed more of the pain-easing drink as the effect of the last mouthful began to fade and the lines of fire began once more to mark out his wounds, and thought of how good it would be to end the hurting once and for all. He would welcome oblivion as any other man would welcome recovery from sickness, smile at the Alban as he swung his sword, open his arms to embrace the descending blade. And then Voord thought of the way that Aldric had looked at him, and despite his eagerness to die he shivered . . .

"Aldric . . . ?" Kyrin spoke the name for what had to be the hundredth time, and again heard no response other than the too-quick, too-shallow rhythm of his breathing. He hadn't moved since Voord finished with him and went out, not even to rearrange his clothing because with hands shackled at shoulder-height and ankles secured to either upright of the cheap little bed, there was no way in which he could have reached. All that he could do, and all that he had done, was to lie still to avoid the pain of moving and stare at the wall with an unreadable expression burning behind the eyes which blinked too slowly.

Oh my love, thought Kyrin, *oh my dear one, I wish*

that you would say something. Anything. Not just lie there and watch it all inside your mind, over and over and over again.

She began to speak, very softly, not calling his name anymore but telling one of the old stories of her people as she might have done to a child awakened frightened in the night. Kyrin didn't know what good it would do, whether he was hearing what she said—or even whether she was doing it not for his benefit but for her own, to take her mind away from the time when the door would open and it would be her turn.

"Long, long ago and far, far away in the frozen Northlands, there was a hunter who went out one day to hunt, and as he wandered near to the shores of the cold Northern Sea he heard a crying and went to see what made the sound. And there among the rocks and the grinding bergs that surged up and down on the icy swell, he found the cub of a white bear and the bear's mother dead and drowned beside it. So the hunter thought at first to kill it, but it cried so sorely that his heart was touched and instead he took the little furry creature home to be a pet and a companion if it lived . . ."

She spun the tale out and out, weaving into it shreds and threads of other stories so that it grew more fantastic and seemed to take on a life of its own. That had always been the way with the old tales, so that a traveling storyteller could spin an entire evening's entertainment— thus ensuring his bed and board for the night—from a single original idea. But unlike the storytellers back home in Valhol she was not to be allowed to finish without interruption, because she was only three-quarters through the tale when the cell door clanged open and Tagen's squad of guards came in.

Aldric turned his head just enough to look at them, but his blankness of expression did not alter; he remained shut up within himself, seeming neither able to see nor to hear anything except whatever was going on within his head, refusing to react to the crude hands dressing him or the cruder jokes made while they did so. As they hauled him upright, Kyrin got her first chance to see his face in other than shadow—and by comparison with the man she knew he looked like a house where nobody is at home. And then she saw the quick, almost imperceptible glance that he shot toward the back wall of the cell, and toward the *taiken* that was shackled there just as securely as he had been shackled to the bed.

There was just the glance and nothing more; it was gone again almost at once, and if she hadn't seen it so clearly Kyrin would have doubted that the somehow shrunken figure who slumped between the soldiers had such a speculative, calculating look left in him. She wondered what hope or plan or seized chance lay behind it; and indeed, as the guards dragged him from the cell into the torture chamber next door, whether there would be enough left of either of them to make use of any granted opportunity.

They came back for her a few minutes later, all hot hands and stale breath and hungry eyes as they unlocked the chains and told her what it was they were going to do once *Woydach* Voord had learned whatever it was he wanted to know. Kyrin shut her ears to the stream of dirt; most of it was coarsely repetitive and not overly original, and the fact that they kept using the word "later" allowed the tremulous flutter of her belly to relax a little. That "later" would be respected, if only out of fear, for only one of the five dared more than an elaborate fumble around her crotch while setting the chains aside, and he was promptly snarled at by the big *kortagor* called Tagen.

And then they were alone again, strapped to the only ordinary chairs in the interrogation room that was empty of everything but the hulking inanimate machinery of pain, left no doubt to think of the last time they had sat in these same chairs and what they had witnessed. Left to wonder when Voord would come in, and what would happen the next time the door opened. And to wonder whose turn it would be then.

Ryn Derawn filled his wife's glass with distilled grain-spirit for the third time in ten minutes and watched uneasily as she stared at the clear juniper-scented liquid like a wise-woman reading futures from a bowl of water, then—also for the third time in ten minutes—drank down the potent stuff in a single swallow.

"I'm still not convinced," said Giorl to her husband, "no matter what you say. If I was wrong, then the consequences for you, for me, for the children, for all of us . . ." She shook her head, dispelling the images, and held out her glass for yet another drink.

"No. You've had plenty for now, and I haven't had half enough for this to make any more sense." Ryn put the tall stoneware bottle to one side and smashed its stopper into place with the flat of his hand. "Giorl, no matter what you do up at the fortress you've never needed to hide behind this stuff before. These two new prisoners . . . You must have *some* suspicions, or you wouldn't even have mentioned them."

"All right. All *right!* So I'm wondering." Giorl looked at her empty glass one final time, then thumped it down onto the table and stared instead at Ryn. "And I'm scared to give room inside my head to what you've just suggested. Whoever they are and whatever they did, they're his now. Voord's . . . to do with as he pleases. And there's nothing I could—or would dare—do about it!"

"If they're the ones I think they saved Mal's life—you said that yourself. If they hadn't been there she would have died long before I could have found you." Ryn sat down beside her and put one arm around Giorl's shoulders. "That wasn't all you said. Do I have to remind you—or didn't you mean any of it at all?"

"Oh, you bastard . . ." Giorl's taut features crumpled, she leaned her head against him and Ryn felt the first sob go jolting through her as she began to cry. He felt wretched too, wishing that neither of them had brought the matter to discussion; but he knew also that he would never have looked at his beautiful, kindly, learned, lethal wife in quite the same way again if he had kept silent.

All he wanted was for Giorl to take him inside the Warlord's citadel for sufficient time to see the two captive foreigners that she had spoken of. Nothing else. Just so that he would know enough for his own peace of mind. Ryn hadn't yet decided what he would do if they really were the young couple with the talent for impromptu surgery. He almost hoped that they were not— that he could look, and shake his head and go away again . . . and try to forget what it was that awaited them. He knew little enough about what was done in the Underfortress when Giorl wasn't acting as consultant surgeon to various high-ranking personages, and that little he had discovered had been more than enough to prevent him from trying to learn more. For her part, Giorl didn't talk. That was what had made her outburst today so startling, when she had come through the door of the house shaking all over—and not from the cold—and had drunk down the first of those brimming glasses before trusting herself to speak.

Not that his response had calmed her down. When she described the people for whom Voord had ordered a demonstration—and Ryn was grateful that she hadn't described what *that* had involved—she had been hoping for a denial. He knew her well enough by now to read something so simple from her face, and he was angry now that he hadn't told a lie; except that she knew him just as well, and would not only have been in her present state but also something worse because of his attempted deceit. Truth, Ryn decided, was the least painful of the several painful courses open to him. Assuming that *Woydach* Voord did not become involved . . .

"Put on your outdoor boots and get your overmantle. We're going to the fortress." There was still the thickness of recent weeping in Giorl's voice, but once she had straightened her back and wiped the tears from her face all other traces of uncertainty were gone. She had spoken calmly, with determination and the serenity born of a decision made and now unshakable. Almost unshakable; for when Ryn hesitated she smiled minutely at him and make small shooing movements with both hands. "Do it, love. Quickly. I'm running just a step ahead and if we don't move now, at once, it'll catch up with me."

Ryn looked at her quizzically but received no further elaboration. He stamped into the fur-lined boots and pulled on his heavy, quilted overmantle without asking anything aloud, and it was only as they left the house and walked out into the slowly falling snow that the question moved out of his eyes and became words.

"What are you running from?" He thought that he knew the answer already, but he had to hear it from her just so that he could be sure. The silvery mist of Giorl's exhaled breath was between their faces and she glanced at him and then turned her head away, still smiling that same small fixed smile, and Ryn knew his guess had been right.

"My own fears," she said softly, and looked up toward the gray clouds as though a shadow had passed across the unseen sun. "Of course . . ."

The candles in the ice-encrusted room were burning blue, their flames stirring the sluggish drifts of incense smoke and sending them in spicy-scented tendrils up to the crystalline ceiling. There was a buzzing, the sound of glutted flies, and there was the sonorous rise and fall of words from where Voord knelt once more at the center of the circle and spoke to That which listened to him only through lack of any other worshipers.

". . . O my Lord O my true Lord O my lost beloved Lord O most favored Bale Flower O Issaqua Dark Rose Dweller in Shadows I pray thee and beseech thee hearken to thy faithful servant who begs most humbly take away this Gift of life from me and grant me peace . . ."

He could smell the roses now, an overwhelming perfume which blurred his mind in a way that the poppy-syrup never could. The candle-flames began to shrink and for all that it remained snow-shot day beyond the shuttered, curtained, frozen windows, a darkness deeper than mere nightfall flowed like ink into the room. Voord began to hear the sweet, sad, wordless music that was the Song of Desolation, and with that hearing he began to tremble. The warning words of the charm written into one of his grimoires came back to haunt him; but he had ignored that warning so many times now that the haunting was little more than one ominous memory among many.

Issaqua sings the Song of Desolation
And fills the world with Darkness . . .

In that Song there was a loss and a betrayal, the sense of being discarded that was all part of the smashing of altars and the tearing down of shrines, or worse, their re-consecration in the names of other Powers with no right to dwell there. When his dabbling in sorcery began, so many lost years ago, Voord had been delighted by the ease with which demons responded to his Summonings; it was only as time passed and he learned more that he discovered the truth behind their eager attention. The deities of an older race were reduced to the demons of the new, diminishing thus down through successive generations until they were forgotten. For all their past majesties, they were often as pathetic as lost children—grateful for any attention at all, even idle curiosity, rather than re-consignment to oblivion.

Issaqua the Bale Flower hung before him in the icy air, a wavering nimbus of reddish-amber light—like that from heated iron—that formed unstable curves suggesting the whorled petals of a monstrous rose. He bowed very low, stood up and stepped out of the circle without any of the precautions he had always been so sure to take before. They were redundant at this late stage; and in the Presence of Issaqua, there would be nothing of a lesser stature that he needed to fear. The light throbbed slowly behind him, illuminating nothing but itself, and Voord felt his boots crunch in the hoarfrost that had formed from the moisture in the air as he walked to the door. The dry coldness ground into him, searing his mouth and nostrils as he breathed, chilling the metal wires that held his flesh together until they seemed to burn instead.

Tagen was outside, standing at parade-rest a diplomatic distance down the corridor. As Voord emerged in a pearly cloud of freezing vapor, the *kortagor* came to attention and saluted. Voord nodded acknowledgment, then sagged backward against the rimed timbers, exhausted. *Soon now, very soon . . .* he thought, looking at the big man through eyes that refused to focus properly. *A long race, but almost run . . .*

"I was coming out to tell you—"

"That we can attend to the woman, sir?"

Oh eager, eager, my hound. "Yes. I will be in here, Tagen . . . waiting. Make certain that Talvalin knows. Now go. Gather your squad. And, Tagen . . ."

"Sir?"

"Be thorough."

*   *   *

"Ryn? Well, tell me."

Ryn Derawn backed slowly away from the small shuttered peephole let into the door of the interrogation
room. It was only when Giorl touched him that she realized how her husband had begun to tremble. He stared
at her and his lips moved, but no sound came out.

"It's the pair you thought, isn't it?" she hissed, shaking him, trying to restore some sort of coherence. Ryn
nodded. He had gone chalk white, not so much with fear
of where he was or recognition of Aldric and Kyrin,
but because of his look within the harshly white-tiled
environment where his wife did most of her work. He
had never seen a torture chamber before, except in old
woodcuts, and hadn't been prepared for the air of cold
efficiency that flowed from the place like mist. Most of
the apparatus was too mechanically defined for him to
guess its purpose without explanation, but there had
been enough pieces whose operation was all too obvious
for his stomach to turn sick.

"Yes," he managed to say at last. "I was hoping not,
but . . . there they are: the ones who saved Mal's life."

"And what are we going to do? Let them go and
end up where they are now?" Giorl was always deadly
practical where cause and effect were concerned, and
never more so than when the matter in question was
serious. This was a serious as any in her life, and already
she regretted giving way to Ryn in the first place. "We'll
have to get out of here before someone sees us," she
said, the hand which had touched his shoulder in comfort tightening to pull him away. "There isn't anything
that we—"

"Cut them loose," said Ryn. He shrugged free of Giorl's grasp and turned toward her. "We needn't help
them escape—but we can give them the same chance at
life that they gave Mal." He grinned crazily. "Cut, and
go away, and let them survive if they can do it by themselves. Please, love! Do it—it's only right!"

Giorl stared at him and at the wildness in his eyes.
This wasn't the Ryn she knew, but a man fired by a
purpose. She had seen many such, whose various Purposes had brought them no further than the room be-

yond the door and to what was done there. Then she
shrugged, a quick dismissive twitch that agreed with
none of his reasoning and just barely with his plea, and
went past him into the interrogation room.

Though his face somehow managed to remain immobile
and unreadable, Aldric's stomach turned over when the
woman torturer Giorl came through the door, lifted a
knife from on of the wall-mounted clips and walked
toward him. He stared at her for just a moment as she
approached, then through her and behind her as if she
did not exist. At least Voord wasn't here yet; though
doubtless he would arrive before the show really began
in earnest, grinning and wearing that self-satisfied expression Aldric wanted so much to shear right off the
Woydach's face. It seemed as though he would no longer
have the chance to do it—not in this life anyway.

Then Ryn Derawn stepped quietly into the torture
chamber just behind her and pulled a second knife from
the same row of clips. Aldric made a supreme effort to
keep any giveaway flicker from his eyes, wondering first
how Ryn had got in here and second if he knew exactly
where to plant the knife. When Giorl said, "Hurry up,
for the Lady Mother's sake," and said it unmistakably
to Ryn, he thought for just one horrible instant that his
mind had given way.

*If you go mad, is part of the madness in not knowing
it?*

He had asked that question years ago, so many years
that he couldn't remember if there had been an answer.
Certainly there was no answer now, only utter confusion.
Seeing the two of them together made no sense, especially when the man he recognized and the woman he
feared—and feared enough to admit it even to himself—
not only knew each other, but set about the same hurried task of sawing through the heavy bull-hide straps
that held his wrists and ankles to the wooden chair.

Cutting was the quickest method, or at least not the
slowest. The buckles securing each strap had been
threaded through with heavy wires which had been plier-
twisted shut, like gross copies of the little golden threads
that he had seen—and felt—decorating Voord's face and

body. Unpicking them would have needed armorer's tools and more time than Ryn and Giorl seemed to be willing to take. Aldric flinched once or twice when the blades, designed to cut through less resilient skins than these, skidded on the leather or the wires and sliced him instead. He made no sound the whole time, not so much through stoicism as not trusting himself to speak, because by then he had seen the looks and the quick nervous smiles that his two rescuers exchanged—and they were the same looks and smiles which passed between himself and Kyrin . . .

It was impossible to bear, and when his right hand came free with the sting of another accidental cut that became the rending snap of whittled leather giving way, he resisted the first and still near-reflex reaction—which was to seize Giorl by the throat and not let go until she had at the very least thrown away her knife—and merely asked, "Why?"

"A debt," said Giorl, gasping slightly as she had to saw with a delicate instrument whose edge was now quite spoiled with all this clumsy work. "You're owed one life."

"Whose?" He looked at Ryn. "Your daughter's?"

"Our daughter's." It wasn't Ryn who said it but Giorl, and the laconic statement shocked Aldric far more than if she'd run one of her spiked probes into his ear instead of speech. Again his stomach did that violent shocked somersault and with as much or better reason.

Maybe going insane is just a way to make the world make sense, he thought, and almost giggled. *Because I don't want to take much more of this* . . . The bubble of crazed laughter welling up inside him turned to a sob that was actually painful; but then he ached all over anyway, thanks to Commander Voord. The cold-eyed, long-jawed face smiled down at him in his imagination, and with the pain was quite enough to jolt him back to something like sobriety, where giggles had no place and sobbing was for later.

The only sound that Aldric wanted to hear in the next while was the liquid ripping of Widowmaker's blade in flesh . . .

"Yours, too?" he said to Giorl in a voice that surprised him with its calmness. She nodded and continued cutting. "Then that means he's your husband?" Another nod, more impatient now; the strap on his left ankle was giving trouble and by now her knife was just a flattened piece of metal with no indication that it ever had an edge at all. "And that means you," said Aldric to Ryn with all the pedantic are of a child getting some fact explained just so, "are married to the chief torturer of Drakkesborg." Ryn nodded. "Why didn't you mention it before?"

"Was it so important?" Ryn said defensively. "Would it have made a difference to what you did for the child?"

"I . . ." Aldric began to say and stopped, suddenly unsure. The tugging and hacking at his bonds continued and across the room—half-hidden by one of the more elaborate machines—he could see Kyrin trying to get a glimpse of what was happening. *Of course it wouldn't have made a difference* was what he would like to have said, but wondered now if that was true. A sick child was a sick child, in any language of the several he knew; but to know what one of that child's parents did for part of a living—let alone that it was the *mother,* for sweet pity's sake!—and to guess, as he guessed now, what sort of cutting might have been keeping Drakkesborg's best cutting-surgeon from doing something to help her own daughter . . . He shrugged, not caring now that the movement would hurt scratched and bitten shoulders, and told the truth. "I don't know. Probably yes, if I'd known beforehand. Neither of us would have gone near the house. But we didn't know, and," another shrug, "it wasn't so very important anyway."

"A very pretty confession, Alban," said Giorl, ripping away the last shred of leather strapping from his leg by main force rather than with the useless knife. "I couldn't have got a better out of you myself."

Aldric looked at her for a few seconds, then curled his lip. "That was a poor sort of joke," he said.

Giorl looked at her knife, made the beginnings of a motion to throw it disgustedly away and then slipped it into a pocket of her overrobe instead. "Someone might notice," she said to herself, then glanced at Aldric with a far from humorous quirk to her mouth. "I don't joke about my work . . . any of it."

"Then you *are* a surgeon—Ryn wasn't just using—"

"An imaginative figure of speech? No, he told the truth. The acceptable half of it, anyway."

"But *why?* Why do you . . ." Aldric was at a loss for some way to phrase his question that would not be dangerously rude; he hadn't forgotten that there was still a belt of wire-reinforced leather holding him to a chair far too heavy to be lifted, that Kyrin was still strapped into another chair, and that the woman he spoke to had obviously been persuaded to come here by her husband and against her own better judgment. The combination of factors made for a deal of delicacy when it came to choosing words, and he was grateful when Ryn came to his rescue in a manner just as real as the cutting of any number of restraints.

"It's a job; someone has to do it. My wife does it." The man was smiling, but it was a mechanical curving of the lips that came nowhere near his eyes. "Maybe sometime soon she won't have to do it anymore . . . and then she'll be able to stop. Satisfied?"

Aldric nodded silently. He hadn't missed the emphasis Ryn had laid on certain words, and though there was certainly an interesting story behind how a pretty woman, a mother and a much loved wife would become what Giorl had become, it was no story that he had any wish to hear. He lifted his hand free of the halves of the last strap and stood up; then brought both hands together and bowed, giving honorable obeisance to them both for any number of reasons. He watched as the couple took up new knives and went to free Kyrin, waiting just long enough to see the relief wash the uncertainty out of her face . . .

Then he turned, forcing down any reaction to the pain which lanced up into him at every step, and walked back as quickly as he dared toward the cell . . .

Isileth-called-Widowmaker hung upon the wall of the cell, with her weapon-belt wrapped interlacing-style around her scabbard. That style, *hanen-tehar,* showed proper respect for the ancient longsword; but it was respect shown only to mock for instead of being laid across a sword-stand she hung vulgarly point uppermost, crucified upside down.

Aldric looked at the steel strapping and the hammer-forged clamps that were as thick as his own wrists. She was as securely shackled as he had been, and as helpless to resist the hands which had left the smeary marks of fingers everywhere; but she was eager to be free and about the business for which she had been made.

He could feel the killing-hunger radiating from the blade as he might have felt heat radiating from a fire; it might have been his own feverish imaginings, but Aldric doubted it. This *taiken*'s name and reputation had not come from daydreams, and his own respect had always borne the merest unadmitted thread of caution. Many things might happen to a weapon in twenty centuries, and most of them had happened to this sword; but it was widely believed that no good could come from a blade with so ominous a name as *Widowmaker*. Aldric had stopped caring what was said; what the faceless, nameless *They* said, and always had to say, about a hundred disparate matters that were not and never had been any of their concern. Four years now he had slept with this cold mistress by his side to guard him, and she had never failed him yet.

Aldric reached out one hand to Widowmaker, and felt the familiar cool harshness of braided leather and black-lacquered steel solid and reassuring against the calluses of his right palm. He closed his hand around the grip, feeling the hilt-loops squeeze against that familiar angle-joint on the index finger where it hooked over for better control. But she remained where she had been placed, not even moving in her irons, fulfilling the function of that placement, teasing and frustrating him like any object of desire held tantalizingly just out of reach . . . but not quite far enough.

Had she been truly out of his reach, as she had been before, Aldric would have been more concerned; had he been stronger in both mind and body, it would have concerned him less. But he had outrage instead of health, anger instead of caution and fear not only for

himself but for the others outside instead of any cause
more just. Those substitutes for rightness, as so often
happened in this far from perfect world, would have to
suffice. Their less worthy cousins, vengeance and hurt
pride, had been enough before.

"*Abath arhan,*" said Aldric quietly, the words familiar
as his own name now for all that he still had no memory
of learning them. Warmth of hand and words of power
wound together on the longsword's hilt and worked their
magic. There was a sound, a sonorous thrum so deep
that it was more felt in the marrow of the bones than
heard, and the Echainon spellstone that he had set as
pommelstone into Widowmaker's hilt left off its pretense
of being no more than a polished dome of crystal and
came back to life.

It began as no more than a thread in the heart of the
stone, twisting like a flaw come to life; and then the blue
flames spilled out in a great globe of cool radiance that
flung Aldric's shadow up and across the farther wall and
ceiling. Fire licked upward from the *taiken*'s pommel,
lapping his fingers and Widowmaker's hilt with lazy
tongues like those of sleepy tigers. Aldric brought them
fully awake.

"*Alh'noen ecchaur i aiyya, r'hann arhlaeth.*" The words
of the spell, if spell it was, came from his mouth in a
tangle of syllables that bore no relation to Alban or any
other language spoken in the world of men, and the
spellstone and the sword responded.

The blast alone should have killed him, for it ripped
stones from the walls and tiles from the floor and flung
them like catapult missiles from one end of the cell to
the other, leaving Aldric standing in a scoured space that
smoked and spat as though just drawn from the heart of
a furnace. It had been a furnace hot enough to melt
proof steel, for the straps and clamps and rivets which
had held Widowmaker to the shattered wall glowed rose
and white and fell in thick trailing drops like honey to
the blackened floor as they let the sword come free. The
light that filled his vision faded down through purple and
orange to a dazzled near normality, but as the reverbera-
tions of the contained thunderclap became no more than

a jangling echo in his ears, Aldric heard the slam of a door flung open and then the shouts of angry men.

He drew in a breath and turned, feeling the smooth slide of joints and muscles which no longer hurt. The breath came hissing out again through teeth close-clenched in a feral snarl as he heard a voice he knew among the babbling outside. Voord's henchmen Tagen was out there, making threats. Aldric buckled Widow-maker's weaponbelt around his waist and stalked out of the cell.

Kyrin hadn't believed her eyes when Ryn came through the door behind the torturer. She hadn't believed her ears when he told her what was going on. But she had believed her sense of touch when the brutally tight strapping on the chairs began to fall away. She let no surprise show on her face at the revelations of how strange the family of Ryn and Giorl Derawn seemed to be, disarming Giorl's own terse and acid observations with equally sharp comments of her own. It made the interrogator-surgeon look oddly at the knife she held, then stare at Kyrin even more oddly still.

"Ryn told me about you both," she said. "Not just about what you did, but about what you were like. He was wrong about only one thing: when he said your gentleman friend didn't talk much." Without a smile, or indeed the slightest hint from her emotionless features, it was difficult to decide if Giorl had made some sort of joke, or was expressing irritation, or was merely passing the time of day until she was done and could leave.

"We can't, and won't, help you to get out of this fortress," she continued, slicing efficiently at leather and with less success at metal wire. "That's your problem and his. I have a family to take care of, and playing some sort of hero isn't part of it. At best you'll get away; at worst, find yourselves a cleaner death than the *Woydach* has in mind. Because if you're back on those frames when I come in to follow orders, I'll do exactly as I'm told to do. I can't do anything else. Understand?"

Kyrin shivered slightly and made a vaguely affirmative noise. She understood exactly. Giorl had the classic sur-

geon's mind: too classic by a long way, if the opinion of
an ex-physician's aide was worth anything—which it was
not—and if she dared to offer it aloud, which she didn't.
To Giorl, work was the bringing together of metal implements and human flesh, to heal on one side and to hurt
on the other. She had managed to lock away the different end results in some dark place at the back of her
mind, and now regarded what she did as something more
akin to mechanics: removing a part that no longer
worked, closing an accident-created hole . . . or testing
until something cracked.

"Understood. Thanks for telling me. I hope—"

Whatever it was she hoped was lost in the vast wash
of light and noise that blew the fragmented, burning access door of their cell clear across the torture chamber.
And then the other, outer door slammed open in the
ringing silence after the blast, and *Kortagor* Tagen
came in.

He was not alone. There were three other men behind
him, all in the undress uniform of *Kagh' Ernvakh* and
all wearing expressions in which shock shared equal
space with the vast vestiges of lust. Tagen hesitated in
the doorway for a heartbeat's duration, and in that brief
time whipped sword from scabbard with such speed that
his right fist seemed to sprout steel in the instant of his
clenching. There was no shock on his face, and while
his expression might have passed for lust it was a lust
for slaughter.

"Treacherous bitch," he said to Giorl, and he said it
in a calm, pleased voice. "You and your husband, both
traitors. Both helping enemies of the state. The *Woydach*
will want to deal with you personally—but we'll have
the rest right now . . ." He grinned and started forward,
with the rest of his squad close on his heels.

"I think not," said Aldric's voice behind them, and
the door of the torture chamber shut and locked with
clicks as small and final as a coffin-lid coming down. "In
case you're wondering," he continued, as Widowmaker
sheared off both key and handle, "the only way out is
through my cell. You're all welcome to try."

There was an interesting silence during which the
loudest noise was the echo of the severed key falling to

the tiled floor, and then Tagen lost his temper. Had he paid any attention to Voord's carefully explained lessons in pressure and leverage, he might have earned himself and his companions some few minutes more of life by trying to hold Kyrin as a hostage for their release.

Instead he leapt at the young man who was only another victim after Voord was done with him, an enemy whose time to die had come at last—and who smiled coldly as he sidestepped Tagen's rush to let him meet a blur of blade instead . . .

"Hai!"

Tagen's leap continued straight into the wall, but the top of his head and most of its seldom used contents were already all over the floor behind him.

Aldric snapped blood and a few flecks of brain-tissue from Widowmaker's blade, quite well aware that the movement sent a sinister swirl of azure fire up and down his hands as he brought the weapon back to low-guard center. "Next?" he said. The first wild flaring of rage had died away by now, enough at least to let his skill return; but his anger remained, fueling the skill and giving him Voord's own potential to be cruel. Raked, banked fires burn hottest, and the heat within him was such that none of the Warlord's Guard would leave alive while he lived to stop them.

None did.

Giorl and Kyrin looked at the bodies, and the contents of bodies, and the pieces of bodies, and listened to the blood that was already dripping audibly down the torture-chamber's drainage gutters. Ryn was staring at the wall behind him, and had already been sick twice. It had taken perhaps three minutes, and that only because Aldric had been in no great hurry.

He wiped Widowmaker clean with a strip of cloth torn from the front of Tagen's tunic, which through the manner of his dying the big man had not soiled, then picked his way through the carnage as delicately as a cat in wet grass. The *taiken* glinted as he raised her blade in salute to Giorl and her still-nauseated husband. "If not for you," he said, and didn't trouble to say the rest. They had all seen, and all heard, and anyway words whether of thanks or of thanksgiving seemed somehow inade-

quate right now. "Lady," this to Kyrin, "are you
unhurt?"

She held up a wrist nicked twice during the freeing of
it and shook her head. "Nothing else. You?"

"Not even that. You know the spellstone well enough
by now." Widowmaker whispered thinly as he slid her
back into her scabbard, and he glanced around the
chamber looking for other things than the ragged
corpses. "Where does Voord go to play, if not here?"
he wondered aloud, and gazed equably at Giorl.

She met him stare for stare, and after a few moments
smiled. "If he's dead, I'm free," she said, and smiled an
honest smile which looked a little clumsy through lack
of use. "Look for him in the room under the gallery.
There'll be no guards anywhere in this wing of the fortress, not now. Not after . . . whatever it was exploded
in the cell. When something like that happens—and it
does, now and again, thanks to the *Woydach*—those who
want to live long clear out until they're told it's safe.
Down the corridor outside, then left, left again and
down. And when you cut his heart out, do it slowly, just
for me."

Aldric blinked, his own feelings about Voord seeming
mere annoyance beside the coldly cherished hatred of this
small woman. Again he found himself wondering what story
she could tell, and again, despite the lack of compunction
with which he had executed the Guardsmen—there being
no better or more appropriate word for it—he didn't want
to know whatever nasty truths were there. Instead he
stepped back to let Giorl get past him, acknowledged
Ryn's feeble smile with one equally half-hearted, and
watched as they made their way to the cell's side-door,
and through and out of sight.

"Kyrin," he said as she peeled the last pieces of cut
strapping from her arm and leg, "there was something
said about the rest of our gear in the armory. In the
corridor outside. If she's right, the place should be deserted. Help me arm."

Tehal Kyrin, Harek's daughter of Valhol, stood up
and dusted herself down, then looked at her lover and
her husband-to-be. "Only," she said, "if you then help
me . . ."

                    *   *   *

Giorl had been right: the corridors and passageways of
the Underfortress were deserted. Aldric and Kyrin found
their gear strewn about the armory in various stages of
disrepair, but it had been the kind of articles—like
clothing—most easily pulled to pieces which had suffered the greatest damage. There had been little mere
"investigation" could do an *an moyya-tsalaer*. The Alban
Great Harness had evolved over centuries to withstand
more than the curious pokings and proddings of Drusalan Secret Police. There were no secrets to be extracted
from the gleaming black-lacquered metal, other than
that a man encased in such carapace was safe from all
but the most determined attack.

Aldric felt a deal more comfortable once he was inside
it; and more at ease with himself, in a far more subtle
way, when his *tsepan* Honor-dirk was back in its proper
place pushed through his weapon-belt, rather than hanging from straps as a self-preserving imitation of less worthy weapons.

The black dirk had not been beyond arm's length
since he had received it from Lord Endwar Santon more
than four years ago, except for those times when it had
been taken from him by force. All but one of those
thieves were now dead. Santon was dead too, in the
honorable act of *tsepanak'ulleth* before witnesses, to
atone for his failure in the campaign against Kalarr cu
Ruruc. He had been a grim, courteous man who had
conducted his entire life as if knowing that the fixation
with honor that ruled it would also govern its ending.

Aldric had been one of the witnesses to Lord Santon's
suicide, and for all his own respect for the old Honor-
codes and no matter that he wore his own dirk as a
mark of rank, he was secretly glad that within himself
there was nothing so—fanatical was the only word for
it—which would make him put his *tsepan* to its ultimate
purpose. It had threatened often enough: to preserve his
own endangered honor, to resolve the intolerable conflict facing him while on task for Rynert the King—when
to obey was to be shamed and to refuse was to be
dishonored—even to reprove Rynert for the stupidity of
his actions. But there had always been a way out that

kept the dirk's blade from his chest—provided he looked
hard enough. His dark moods aside, Aldric loved life
too much to regard the leaving of it with anything but
reluctance.

He was conscious of Kyrin watching him as he picked
up the *tsepan,* and was half-inclined for the sake of her
already-jangled peace of mind to slip it down inside his
boot, or give it into her keeping, or do any of the number of things which would be consonant both with honor
and with giving her a crumb of comfort. He shook his
head, a gesture only for himself and imperceptible inside
the helmet. That would have to come later, after he had
dealt with Voord. And after that both sword and dirk
could be retired to a handsome weapon-rack on the wall
of some small house, and he and Kyrin would forget
their duties owed to honor and to vengeance and to the
simple requirements of keeping alive when they moved
in such lethal circles as this, and they would live their
lives for each other instead of for everyone else. That
was a dream, indeed; but he and she both had seen so
many nightmares become real that there was no reason
to doubt reality might have some room left over for the
small and ordinary. He hoped so, anyway; it would be a
sick world otherwise.

"Ready?"

"Ready." Kyrin piled up her hair inside one of the
Empire's own *seisac* helmets and settled it until it felt at
least not actively uncomfortable. "If being ready is being
scared sick."

Aldric glanced at her and smiled coldly, knowing exactly how she felt. "It is," he said, and meant it.

The room where Giorl had told them they might find
Voord was itself easy to find, whether he was inside it
or not, and the look of the door alone was enough to
raise Aldric's armor-protected hackles. Its timbers—on
the outside—were sheathed in a finger's thickness of
clear ice—and there were wide white fans of frost on
floor and walls around its edges. Neither of them cared
to think how cold the room itself would have to be.

Kyrin stopped in the corridor outside, well away from
that sinister portal, and was reluctant to take a step

closer until someone with the authority to do so told her
on oath that it was safe. One look at Aldric's face was
enough. He might have had the experience and the consequent authority, but he wasn't about to start telling
any lies.

He had talked a little—surprisingly little, for a man
who tended to be garrulous in company he liked—about
some of his previous encounters with the Old Magic and
with the High. It had made uncomfortable listening, and
Kyrin had been grateful not to have a part in any of the
stories . . . until now, and the still more comfortable
discovery that she was a part of this encounter with the
darkness whether she liked it or not, unless she turned
and walked away right now, and came to terms with
staying away for always.

She was in love and filled with joy at being so—but
she was human enough, and frightened enough, to weigh
what she felt for Aldric very carefully in the balance
against the chance of such a death as she dared not
imagine. Then she drew her Jouvaine *estoc* from its scabbard slung across her back and poked thoughtfully at
the ice, and said. "Well, how do we get in?"

The way that Aldric looked at her, and the crooked
smile he gave to her bold words, made Kyrin wonder
briefly just how much of her hurried calculation had
been visible across her face. "I have a key here for all
locks," he said, and leisurely unsheathed Widowmaker.

Her blade came from the lacquered wood with a soft
whispery song of steel and arched over into one of the
ready positions Kyrin had seen him practice with nothing
more dangerous than a length of polished oak. It was a
length of polished metal now, and the lanterns in the
corridor flashed back blue-white from the weapon's edges.
"Isileth'kai, abath devhar ecchud," Aldric said to the
sword, focused for the taking of a single breath and
swung full force at the door.

"Hai!"

Widowmaker smashed into the nailed, ice-encased
timbers in the downward diagonal cut called *tarann'-ach,*
striking thunderbolt. The door boomed its bass reply to
the high vibrating shriek of the *taiken*'s impact and
then—perhaps made brittle by the intense cold—made

a harsh high crack unlike the rending of wood and exploded into a shower of burned and burning splinters. The few smoking fragments which remained on the hinges swayed slowly to and fro like hanged men, and there was the scent of lightning on the icy air.

Lightning . . . and roses.

Voord Ebanesj stood quite still in the center of the pattern at the center of the floor, and waited. He had waited for a lifetime, if a lifetime is how long it takes to suffer more pain than a man has any need to bear. His shirt and trews were stained with foul matter which had been leaking stealthily out of him since the silver-gilt stitches of his injuries had pulled through the flesh and left each wound like a mouth—mouths that smiled with ragged open lips, and exhaled the heavy stench of gangrene.

It had begun when he had been preaching his theories to Tagen and feeling so very pleased with his own cleverness. Why then, he didn't know; all need to know the reasons behind happenings was lost in the limitless world of pain caused by the happenings themselves. Voord had cried with the agony at last, made all the noises he had heard in the white-tiled bloody chamber, even pleaded for release to a tormentor three weeks beyond hearing him. Yakez Goadec ar Gethin had gone willingly and open-eyed into the darkness to give his sorcery such power, and there was nothing on the breathing side of the gulf of Hell that Voord knew could stop it. Except perhaps for the spellstone of Echainon, mounted in the pommel of Aldric Talvalin's hungry sword.

The door of the chamber blew apart in a billow of smoke and sparks and slivers of charred wood went skittering across the frozen floor. The smell of burning fought with the perfume of roses and mingled briefly in an amalgam that was like the scent of funeral cremation.

Aldric stepped across the threshold, and his sword was burning blue.

Voord looked at him, not making any move. He had never seen the Alban in his own armor before, only that loaned to him by the Drusalan Empire, and had never realized just what an air of menace the Great Harness gave its wearer. Talvalin was just a silhouette against the doorway, blacker than the shadow that stretched out before him, but as the candles within the chamber were caught and flung back from the lacquered surfaces of helmet and plate, mail and lamellar cuirass, he glittered in the darkness as if coated in frost.

The Alban paused just inside the room, his breath pluming grew in the cold air, and looked from side to side as if searching for something. "No guards, *Woydach?*" he asked. "Now that was most unwise."

Voord looked at him, not making any move. He could hear the soft lament of the Song of Desolation, and sense the coming of Issaqua as a man might sense the sun's position through an overcast of cloud. And he could sense that Talvalin was not especially impressed; instead the armored man was reacting with what looked like familiarity to the ikon of the misty rose that hung in the air at Voord's back.

"Oh, Voord, Voord, you'll have to do better than *that.*" The too-controlled voice with its hateful Elthanek burr was mocking him and making light of everything he held in esteem. "I've pruned roses before, in Seghar. You might know the place . . ."

Voord's mouth quirked at the inference. Sedna ar Gethin again, no matter how distant the connection. He stared balefully at Aldric. "I know it," he said, "as I know you."

"As you know your own reflection," said Tehal Kyrin, stepping into view behind Talvalin, unharmed, armored and carrying a bared sword. "Because you and he are each other seen in a dark glass. But he had all that you lacked—and still does. That's why you hate him so, Commander Voord. Deny the truth, man."

Voord glared hatred at her and shrugged in resignation though the movement sent agony lancing through him. "What truth?" he said. There was a buzzing in his ears as the Song of Desolation faded, becoming no more than the sound of an insatiable hunger waiting to be fed with what he had promised it. "The only truth is that which brought you two here with weapons drawn. Killing is truth. So kill me."

It was an invitation which needed no repeating. Voord saw the black-hilted longsword shifted from a single- to a double-handed grip, and he saw, too, the expression on the Alban's face as he took three steps forward and one to the right. The pupils of his eyes were as wide and dark as those of a hunting cat, and there was no mercy in them.

"As you wish," said Aldric. Widowmaker rose to poise behind his shoulder for an instant, and then came scything down.

"Hai . . ."

Aldric snapped one step sideways and froze in low-guard ready position for an instant, then relaxed. The form *achran-kai*, the inverted cross, comprised two strokes—one horizontal through the target's upper chest and the second a vertical directed at the crown of the head. He had never yet needed to complete the second cut, and he did not need it now. If the horizontal sweep connected, it was not a cut from which opponents walked away.

Its impact had thrown Voord off his feet so that he lay on his back, arms and legs widespread. For all that he had been opened like a sack of offal there was hardly any blood on the *taiken* blade, as if the dead man's body had none left to spare. Only a small and stealthy puddle formed beneath the Warlord's body as it stared through sightless eyes toward the ceiling.

And then Voord's corpse reared from the bloodied floor and screamed a dreadful blubbering scream that came less from its mouth than through the huge straight slit across its chest. Issaqua the Bale Flower expanded with that awful undying striek as a man's chest might expand upon inhaling some sweet scent, and as its own reeling perfume flooded the icy air the demon rose swelled out to the monstrous proportions Aldric had seen before in Seghar.

Almost as if it's feeding on his pain . . . The Alban stared grimly from devourer to devoured, then shook his head and spat sourness from his mouth. *No, not almost. Of course it is . . .*

He staggered as the marble pavement underfoot rose and fell in a motion like that of a massive wave, flexing the inlaid tiling under it shattered. Part of the chamber's outer wall cracked across and across, then fell down with a slithering crash so that snow came swirling in. Two great chunks of stone tumbled in as well, looking like gross snowflakes until their impact against the armor guarding Aldric's legs—for no snowflakes could crush proof metal quite like that. He barely noticed, for the perfume of the rose grew more and more intense until their senses swam with it as though with *ymeth* dreamsmoke . . .

Voord continued to scream. Aldric looked once, then winced and turned away. And still the screaming went on, and on, and on . . .

"He's dead!" Kyrin's voice came hard to his ears, fighting through a sound like a million buzzing flies. "He's dead! You *killed* him—so why won't he die . . . ?" She was near to screaming-point herself. "*Aldric!* Leave him. Take me away from here!" She tugged at the icy metal that sheathed his arm, trying to drag him toward the door. Great white flakes of snow slapped against her face, and Voord's howling hammered at her sanity. "Finish it! For sweet mercy's sake, kill him and get us out of this place!"

Aldric remained where he was, staring at Issaqua, the scent of roses in his nostrils and the sounds of dying in his ears. "Kill him?" he said, the words more read from his lips than heard. "How? With what? Widowmaker can't. Not then, not now. He's a toy now, for that *thing* to play with. It needs to have a death . . ."

Kyrin saw the pallor in his face within the shadows of the helmet, saw the anger and the revulsion and the shame, and suddenly she was afraid—afraid for herself, but most of all afraid for him. "Use the sword again, and this time use the spellstone too," she said quickly and too loudly. "Do it now."

"No." Aldric swung Widowmaker up from where her point was braced against the snowy floor, and stared somberly at the weapon's long blade. "Not that way, and most especially not with this." The gray menace hung about the *taiken* still, flowing like a chill air from her bitter edges, a need for slaying that was at once terrible and yet no more than a sense of purpose and an awareness of function.

"Enough killing for you," he told the sword gently,

regretfully. He went down on one knee and braced
Widowmaker flat across the other, closing his left hand
on her naked blade span down from the point. The
edges bit at once so that his own blood, steaming slightly
in the winter air, mingled with Voord's on the shining
steel . . . as if they were becoming brothers rather than
merely reflections of each other.

As he leaned into the work and the blade arched back
on itself, whatever else he might have said was changed
to a quick, shallow gasping. Widowmaker twisted in his
grasp like something living, something trying to break
out of a strangling grip. Like something trying to stay
alive . . . Aldric's face went white as bone, and sweat
dripped from it almost as swiftly as blood ran from the
sword.

Then Isileth, called Widowmaker, snapped in two.

Aldric tried to release the broken shard of blade
locked in his fingers, biting back an anguished whimper
as sinew and tendon refused to obey him anymore. The
palm of his left hand had sheared clean away, and all
that remained of his Honor-scars spattered blood across
the broken milk-white marble of the floor. While the
remnant of the hand . . .

Had become a twisted claw like Voord's.

The piece of sword-blade came free at last and fell
with a harsh belling to the ground near his feet. It was
a clumsy, messy, painful business trying to open laced
lamellar armor with one hand, but he managed at last.

Voord's screams were growing ragged now, but there
was still no sign of an end to his long dying, if while
Issaqua remained there would ever be an end to it.
Worst of all, he was denied even the refuge of insanity,
for there was still intelligence in his bulging, bloodshot
eyes when Aldric steeled himself to look that way.

Enough intelligence at least to recognize what the eyes
saw, and enough skepticism not to believe it.

Kyrin believed it. She saw the black *tsepan* leave its
sheath and Aldric kneel awkwardly in First Obeisance
on the churned, snowy, bloody floor, and believed im-
plicitly not only in what she saw but that it would be
carried through. She began to cry the bitter tears of loss,

yet made no move to prevent Aldric from completing what he had chosen to do.

"It needs to have a death," he had said, and without needing explanations Kyrin guessed his hope—that a death offered willingly would tip the scales. He had taken responsibility for Voord, for what had happened to him and—for all she knew—for what the *Woydach* had done to them both. It was his choice, and his right.

The *tsepan* went in beneath his breastbone at a steep angle, and Aldric's face was wrenched into a grimace of pain. Blood poured out through his fingers and as he coughed, darkened his teeth and chin. He swayed a little, and only now that strength of will was of no more account did he look toward Kyrin, pouring all into the look that he would have said aloud had he been able.

Voord's screaming stopped abruptly.

In that silence, Aldric Talvalin smiled at some small private victory; then he slumped on to his side as gently as if falling asleep, and lay still . . .

I miss her. I wish she was here, too. But you always pass the door alone.

Alone and naked. Aldric wore nothing but the marks collected over the course of a quarter-century. Most were not even welted scars, merely the pale traceries of wounds that were all the spellstone of Echainon left in the wake of its healing. Only the puncture beneath his breastbone was worthy of note, and that because it was where his life had drained away.

Nothing can ye bring, and nothing bear away; skin was thy sufficient dress in the beginning and sufficient shall it be at the end; naked come all into the world, and naked all depart . . . And it was in the face of this truth, written in the oldest of old books, that the corpses of dead clanlords were clad in their finest before their bodies were committed to the fire . . . Aldric would have laughed aloud except that laughter in this place seemed less than proper.

It was dark beyond the door, that Door which the books said only ever opened in one direction, only admitted and never released. The air, if air it was, felt neutrally warm against his bare skin, and still, and very quiet. It was the sort of place where if voices were heard at all they would be mannerly murmurs and nothing louder. But there were no voices. No other people. Only himself . . . and one other.

That other's eyes were squeezed tight shut, so that he might as well have been alone. Aldric wondered why. He thought that he might know this other man, if he could just recall his name, and any companionship would be better than none at all. By the look of him he would have tales to tell; the long straight slash of a sword-stroke had ripped his bare chest from one armpit to the other, there were other brutal scars on face and body and something had mangled his left hand until it was no more than a claw of bone and leather.

Just like Aldric's own . . .

"Voord," he said, remembering at last. Remembering all of it. The *Woydach*'s eyes opened and Aldric smiled at him as calmly as he would at his best friend. Or at Kyrin herself. *Oh God, how I miss her. But she understood what it was I had to do. She understood me. That's why I miss her so much.*

"Talvalin . . . ?" Tentatively the smile was matched and mirrored, until at last it reached Voord's eyes and warmed them as they had not been warm this dozen years. All at once those eyes flinched away from Aldric's steady gaze, as if embarrassed—or ashamed. "Talvalin, finish with me. Do it now . . . while I have the courage."

Aldric's left hand, crippled now and cradled in his right, was clenched shut in an attempt to contain the blood-flow in his fist. It wasn't successful. When he reached out to touch Voord's forehead with fingertips that left dark smears in their wake, there was no mockery in what he did. It was simply that there was blood everywhere. His blood . . . this once, his blood alone. "*Woydach* Voord," he said, not caring that titles of rank were no more carried here than the badges and regalia that marked them, "I think it's been done already."

Voord stared in disbelief at the blood and the evidence of pain. "You . . . you did this. For *me?*"

"Voord," Aldric said softly, not knowing his once-enemy by any other name and here no longer needing to know, "it counts for very little. What value is a fight that's easy to give? Killing has been the easy way for both of us; it always was. Living in peace—with the memories we share—would have been the hard part. That alone would have made it worth doing . . . for both of us. A pity that we missed the chance."

No matter what Kyrin had said, while they lived neither would have been able to accept the other as a brother beneath the skin. There was too much hatred and brutality between them for anything that might have led to understanding or forgiveness. And now, for all the words that might be said concerning dark and light, right and left, good and evil, none of it had any value anymore.

There was a smell of lancemint leaves in Aldric's nostrils and just for a moment that clean astringence made his gorge rise, made him—almost—thrust Voord away as the memories of lancemint-sweetened breath and the last time he had smelled it came flooding back, heavy with pain and self-disgust and loathing for the man who might have been a friend. Then he saw the tears streaming down Voord's face and the old hurts twisting at his features, and knew that this time and for always he had won.

Lancemint leaves. And roses . . .

As that too-sweet, too-rich perfume cut sickeningly through the sharp scent of mint, Aldric blinked rapidly and for the first time paid some small attention to what surrounded him.

At first there was nothing. Utter nothing. No shape, no color, no sound, neither above nor below nor before, nor behind, nor to either side. Only the stillness and that cool warmth which was neither pleasant nor unpleasant, no more felt against his skin than skin is felt against the flesh beneath it. Skin which for no reason at all was hackling like the back of a frightened cat . . .

And then the reason became all too plain. Voord began to scream again, and this time his screaming was edged with the knowledge that he was beyond even the release that comes with death . . .

Kyrin cradled the body on her lap and stared down at its still face. There were no more tears, not now; she had been shocked beyond weeping when the *tsepan* drove home, when the blood flowed, when Aldric really, truly gave up his own life as honor's price for an enemy's clean death. There had always been the hope that the gesture alone would be sufficient, right up to the moment when he fell over and the quick, shallow movement of his breathing fluttered to a stop.

Aldric's eyes were closed and his features without expression, almost conveying the illusion of sleep until illusion was destroyed and the reality made plain by the black dirk jutting from his chest. Already he was growing cold and there was no color in him; all the color had leaked out on to the floor, as red as . . .

As roses . . .

Kyrin pulled the borrowed helmet from her head and flung it clattering clear across the room. She would hate the color and the scent of roses for the rest of her life. As grief gave way to awareness of the eight guards staring through the still-smoldering doorway, she realized that *the rest* was measured now in seconds. Their lord was slain and his assassin was beyond their reach, but whether impelled by loyalty or by more mercenary motives these were men who wanted to kill someone—and she was the only one not dead already.

Her own long stabbing-sword was belted at her hip, but at first Kyrin gave it only passing thought. The cooling dead-weight across her thighs had taken away whatever desire she might have had to prolong an inevitable and now enviable end. Kyrin was not fond to live. At long last, and too late, she began to understand Aldric and the Albans.

Without the helmet they could see she was a woman, but at least there would be no nonsense this time about keeping her for later, "for dessert." They were too enraged. They would carve her as the main dish on revenge's table, and it would be quick—perhaps too quick even for pain, although in her heart she knew that thought was foolishness.

Kyrin closed her eyes and shook her head. Nothing made sense anymore, and shaping a decision from the confused whirl within her mind was as lifting some great weight. Oblivion. Peace. To go where Aldric was. To die . . . that would be good. But to die well. Maybe it would be better to go out fighting after all. She owed these bastards so much—they and what they represented.

"Soon, my loved," she said, letting Aldric's body slide gently to the floor as she came to her feet and unhooked the sheathed *estoc* from her belt. "Very soon. Wait for me . . ." Kyrin raised the sword level with her face, one hand about its hilt and the other on its scabbard. The guards fanned out, watchful and suddenly uncertain, eager to slaughter her and at the same time reluctant to make the first move. There was too much of death and desperation in this room to leave any space for error. Kyrin could feel it.

She forced herself to smile at them across the *estoc* blade as she slowly drew it from its scabbard, and saw at least one flinch as she dropped the empty scabbard to the ground beside the empty husk which had been her lover. That one had made the connection, and knew she had neither reason to live nor fear of dying. In his career he would have seen many such, and none left free to swing a blade would have gone alone into the darkness. Kyrin met his eyes, concentrated on him and made her forced smile grow tight and cold and predatory. He was afraid . . . that left seven who were not.

The seven poised their swords and came for her in a single rush.

The release that was death gave only a surcease to the pains and terrors of the flesh. Those were past and done with, an ugly memory and no more. What remained for Voord was worse. Far, far worse, he had died in debt, with what he owed still barely collected . . .

And dying was no escape from demons.

The cool un-warmth on Aldric's skin was suddenly swept away by an iciness that ground through to the marrow of his bones and the very core of his spirit. Darkness became dawn, and was flushed by an unwholesome light that was the livid color left by blood settling through the tissues of a days-dead corpse. All of that dark untrammeled world contracted in upon them, until the boundary of what had been infinity was the inside of a mirrored sphere as wide as the gulf between the living and the dead.

Issaqua crossed the boundary, following its prey.

For all that the demon was hunger incarnate, it still smelled of roses. The perfumes carried with it a reeling drunkenness that even here set the senses swirling like strong wine, but that was the last remaining trace of the Bale Flower which Aldric had seen twice before. In the here and now beyond death, where all was made naked and unadorned, there was no place for the foul-fair semblance of a monstrous blossom. No need for anything at all but truth at last—a truth that was reason enough to set Voord screaming.

Issaqua's shape had warped from the softness of rosepetals into a thing of fangs and drool and chitin, the glistening armored bulk of its first, worst child. It was a shape that Aldric knew of old, from dreams that lurked beyond the gates of sleep and from a reality that was worse than any dream. It was a shape that he could name: Warden of Gateways, Herald of the Ancients. *Ythek'ter auythyu an-shri.*

The Devourer in the Dark.

Ythek Shri swung its eyeless armored head to study them, and Aldric felt that unhuman consideration sweep over him like gust of winter wind. There was a promissory recognition in the demon's gargoyle glower, a recollection of the Devourer's last meeting with this puny scrap of living meat which had dared give it defiance—and worse, had won. It stepped forward with that raking grace he knew so well, stalking on triple-taloned claws across its own curved and distorted reflection that was thrown back and back again from the mirrored limits of the world. Aldric held his ground and returned the demon's regard with as much composure as he could summon. He had made no pacts, owed no debts, and the Law of Balance that lay behind all things extended even here. Ythek Shri could not harm him.

Voord . . . was not so lucky.

Kyrin stared at the oncoming swords with less fear than she would have believed. They glittered coldly in the wintry light streaming through the shattered wall, and were for all that threat no more than her keys to the door that kept her from Aldric's side. Sharp keys, and painful, but of no more concern to her now than any of the other means to an end that she had employed in her brief life.

She laughed, a grim sound that was more than half a sob, and met them halfway across the room with the cut that the Albans called *tarannin-kai*, twin thunderbolts, a horizontal figure-eight that jolted either side in flesh and sent someone's fingers pattering across the floor. The charge broke, guardsmen scattering in every direction— and Kyrin pirouetted like a dancer, cut backhanded and felt first impact and then a spray of wet heat. She was not fencing in the Jouvaine style she had been taught but fighting for her life—or at least a good death—in the ruthless Alban fashion which Aldric had favored, where any move that failed to draw blood was wasted. A return cut clashed on the forts of her sword, and as the force of the stroke glissaded uselessly against her hilt she counterthrust hard into an unguarded shoulder. The meeting steel rang and grated. It was not the harsh wild belling of Widowmaker's hungry blade, only the shrill chime of common metal—but metal that was hungry enough without two thousand years to teach it appetite. Kyrin's boot slammed up to drive the air from a guardsman's lungs before her sword ripped out the little that remained. For that first frenzied minute their fear of her desperation was as good as a weapon—and then a blade bit into her side and all fear and hesitation vanished.

Kyrin cried out, a sound that was more shock and outrage at the violation of her flesh than any reaction to pain—the pain of such an injury would come later, had there been a later. She clapped her hand against the spurting wound, missed her balance for an instant and almost at once took another cut that opened her thigh from hip to knee. This time, Kyrin could not help but scream as she reeled sideways and fell down onto the broken marble paving of the floor.

Everything went black and when her senses came wavering back, the first to return was taste as the tang of blood and oily metal flooded her mouth, dribbling from the smeared sword-point resting against her lips. Kyrin

stared up at the soldier whose boot was under her chin.
There was no pity in the man's face, nor in those of his
companions. As the blade pressed downward and clicked
against her teeth, Kyrin clenched them uselessly and shut
her eyes.

Aldric watched with revulsion as Voord cowered in the
presence of his nemesis, then turned, screaming—always,
always screaming—in an attempt to flee. It was useless;
here, where all places were the same place, there was
nowhere for him to run without the glinting black bulk
of the Devourer there already, waiting. As the once-
Warlord stumbled to a terror-stricken halt for the tenth
or the hundredth or the thousandth time, Issaqua the
Shri grinned at him with a mouth that was the mouth
of Hell.

It made a slavering noise, and its great triangular head
split wide apart like the petals of a flower—except that
no flower possessed such a ragged infinity of dreadful
teeth. The spikes and blades of those fangs dribbled glu-
tinous saliva as they ground together with a sound like
shears, and strings of vile slime dripped onto Voord's
upturned face. His shrieks rose to an incoherent squeal
that was beyond screaming as Issaqua stooped down
from its fifteen feet of height and opened its crooked
claws in a rending embrace that ended when Voord
came to pieces . . .

And was restored, to do it all again for as much of
eternity as the demon desired.

Aldric stared in horror for a long second while the
mangled fragments which had been Voord became
Voord again and tried to escape. Except that here there
was neither escape by flight nor escape by insanity any
more than there was escape by death. Issaqua's talons
clashed shut on nothing, mocking him by missing as he
flinched frantically aside, then opened wide and reached
for him again.

They jarred to a halt as Aldric blocked the way.

He had seen what had happened to Voord—what
even now was happening again to Voord—and was consumed with a fear that was as far beyond earthly terror
as he was now beyond life. Fear and honor had fought

together for the longest of times, and yet it seemed only the barest instant before honor won. Aldric had not driven his *tsepan* into his chest, had not given up that life, freely and without bargains, to preserve Voord from torment only to see it happen now.

The Devourer's monstrous head jerked backward as if it had been burned. It reared up hissing to its full height and snarled like torn sheet steel. There was intelligence in that sound, but it was not the sort of intelligence which could be bargained with. Voord had made that mistake and was paying for it now. He had forgotten that Issaqua was a demon and its processes of reasoning were uncluttered by pity, or mercy, or remorse. There was only the Law of Balance, a logic cold and hard and unforgiving as a razor's edge. Cause and effect, action and reaction. Guilt and punishment.

It was all that kept it from doing to Aldric as it had done to Voord, and somehow, from somewhere, he knew. The icy aura of fear which hung around Ythek Shri did not fade, but rather it ceased to chill his flesh. Voord was behind him, cringing on his knees like a beaten dog and whimpering so that Aldric's stomach turned sick inside him. There was nothing now, neither fear nor threat nor past hatreds, that would make him step aside and allow Issaqua to reach its prey, for all that the prey was lawful and condemned to this by his own actions. To do so would make his death a worthless gesture and no freely-given gift at all.

The Devourer's fanged maw gaped, drooling, and made a softly bubbling hiss that was heavy with malice. Only the Balance stood between Aldric and an eternity of anguish, the Law that not even one of the ancient powers could flout with impunity. And yet, for all the bindings and restrictions that hedged it, Ythek, Issaqua, the Herald, the Devourer, was subject to at least one all-too-human failing: a failing Aldric had seen too many times, in himself and others. It was rage, that very special single-minded rage which comes from being flouted, mocked, denied, defied. The rage that makes fools of the wise and strengthens the weak. The black and brooding fury that blinds to all thought of consequence.

The pallid, deathly light began to fade, taking on the

colors that Aldric had seen once in the petals of a rose—
crimson and black and purple as a bruise. Issaqua's
spiked and jagged bulk melted back into the shadows as
night returned to the world beyond death's door. Yet
the demon was so much darker than the darkness that
Aldric could still see it as a silhouette, a hole ripped in
the very structure of things through which all light and
hope of rebirth were leaking out. The heavy reek of
roses clogged his nostrils and the sound of the Song of
Desolation was in his ears—and in his head, repeating
like some grim litany, were the words of the prophecy
he had read in Seghar; only words then, but a threat
now. Or a promise.

> *The setting sun grows dim*
> *And night surrounds me.*
> *There are no stars.*
> *The Darkness has devoured them*
> *With its black mouth.*
> *Issaqua sings the Song of Desolation*
> *And I know that I am lost*
> *And none can help me now.*
> *Issaqua comes to find me*
> *To take my life and soul.*
> *For I am lost*
> *And none can help me now.*
> *Issaqua sings the Song of Desolation*
> *And fills the world with darkness.*
> *Bringing fear and madness*
> *Despair and death to all . . .*

From out of the darkness, in a blur of fangs and claws
that were as black as a wolf's throat, Issaqua came for
him.

Kyrin lay on her back with a boot across her throat and
the point of a sword in her mouth. Fresh blood, her own
blood, was trickling from the cuts the guardsman's sword
had made in her lips, but its point was still poised on
her teeth and no further. All it needed was a little pressure and the blade would come crunching down, but that
pressure was withheld. She still lived.

A hot wind burned one side of her face, and its source became a glow of light that she could see even through her closed eyelids. Someone swore, and all of a sudden the blade was gone from her teeth. Kyrin's eyes snapped open. The soldiers still surrounded her, but she was no longer the center of their attention. She took the only opportunity that she was likely to get and rolled frantically sideways toward her own discarded *estoc* as fast as her wounds allowed. Aldric had always said that there were good and bad ways to die, and what had threatened her was one of the worst. He had not lived long enough to make her Alban by marriage, but rather than be butchered on the floor she could at least be Alban enough to die in their way—quick and clean on her own sword's point.

The rings and bars of the *estoc*'s hilt rattled as she grabbed at it, reversed it—and then blade and hilt together clashed against the broken flagstones as a foot clad in a long black boot kicked the weapon from her hand and stamped it tight against the floor.

"No need for that," said Gemmel Errekren. "No need at all." He lifted his boot from the sword and reached down to help Kyrin to her feet, driving the Dragonwand into the stone floor for her to lean on but never once taking his eyes away from the guards. None of them had moved: the manner of his arrival amid fire and lightning had seen to that, and his appearance now was enough to confirm their caution. Kyrin glanced sidelong at him and herself felt the beginnings of that very special skin-crawling unease which comes when the familiar turns strange. She had barely grown accustomed to him as a sorcerer, even one who refused to dress the part; she had no terms of reference at all for whatever he was now.

What Gemmel wore now was without doubt a uniform, and one which by its cut and color was intended to be ominous, but more ominous by far was the weapon he had cross-drawn from a flapped holster and now held in his right hand. Her first glance made her think it was a *telek*, but her second and all other glances told her that it was nothing of the sort. It was more massive than the Alban spring-guns, and tiny lights glowed red and blue and green like jewels against the steely sheen of its metal. Gemmel's thumb shifted something, two of the red lights turned blue and the sidearm began to sing a faint, high, two-toned song to itself, a thin humming that was to Kyrin's ear as sinister a sound as any demon-born Song of Desolation. "Is that magic?" she ventured.

Gemmel glanced at the thing in his hand as if he had never seen it before. "No," he said. Then he looked from beneath his brows at the guards and smiled crookedly. "But whatever happens, *they* won't know the difference."

There was a shimmering exhalation of waste heat from the black fins running the length of its heavy barrel, but other than that haze-dance there was no suggestion of movement. Gemmel was holding the weapon as if shooting in formal competition at a target, shoulder and arm and hand all one straight line, but the barrel remained as unwavering as if clamped to a bench as it swept across the five guards who were still a threat.

The soldiers looked at one another, then at the elderly man and the injured girl who was as good as dead already, and without saying a word began to fan out. Gemmel watched them in silence, but there was a glitter of cold amusement in his eyes as he saw his firing arc grow slowly wider. *"Teyy'aj hah!"* the enchanter said at last. It was a simple, blunt command to stop, but a half-hidden something in the back of his voice made the Drusalan imperatives more brutal than even they normally sounded. *"Kagh telej-hu, taii'ura!"*

The guards only grinned and began to move faster. One of them raised his sword and poised it behind his head for a downward stroke. "I suggest you don't," said Gemmel. His voice was bleak, and Kyrin felt the hackles rise on her neck at the sound of it.

"Listen to him, you fools!" she snapped desperately. Even though she knew that she was the last person the soldiers would heed, the warning was something she had to give. The attempt to save lives had to be made.

Gemmel's hand came down lightly on her shoulder. "Save your breath, lady," he said, "and your concern. This is their choice."

"Their choice," echoed Kyrin softly, and shivered. That was when the guardsman farthest to the left made his move. The man might have been nettled by the sound of two victims expressing a sort of pity for their slayers, or he might just have reached that one point of the floor from which his attack could best be launched. For whatever reason, he raised his sword and charged with a guttural war-shout—that became a scream in the instant he realized that he would never reach the old man fast enough.

Gemmel's arm came around with all the smooth speed of a battleram's turret mounting, and the weapon at the end of that long arm matched the soldier's scream with a screech of its own. Focused energy blasted across the intervening space in a sweep of heat and light that ripped into the man's chest and flung him backward in smoking pieces.

The sidearm had begun to fire an instant before it came on target, and Gemmel had held its trigger-grip closed right through the weapon's traverse. By the time he released it, a long horizontal stripe of the wall was glowing white and the rough-hewn granite all along that line of heat had slumped out of shape like wax in a furnace. The air was darkened briefly by a billow of greasy gray smoke that smelled horribly of burned pork, and when it cleared Gemmel had the undivided attention of everyone in the room.

He stared at the surviving guards and tracked the shrouded muzzle slowly across them just to make sure that they understood. The men went white and the sound of four shortswords being dropped to the flagstones might have been confirmation enough, but it was only when they picked up their wounded companions and scurried from the room that Gemmel let his hand and its lethal burden drop back to his side. Slowly he returned the sidearm to its holster and secured the flap. His face was without expression, as blank as a sheet of paper, but Kyrin had seen it in the first instant that Gemmel had let himself look full at Aldric's body, and at the black *tsepan* hilt jutting from it, and she knew . . .

"So you killed yourself." Gemmel dropped heavily on to one knee and put out one hand to touch the cold face. "No one else could." The hand was shaking. "Why, my son? Oh, why . . . "

"For Voord," said Kyrin miserably. "He did it to let Voord die."

Gemmel's head jerked up and the glisten of unshed tears in his green eyes hardened to the brilliance of flawless faceted emeralds. He drew a quick, deep breath and came to his feet in a single movement, no longer a grieving old man but a sorcerer fired with hope. Kyrin felt a surge of new strength in the hands which came out to grasp her upper arms. He managed not to shake her in his eagerness, but all the energy of that shaking was contained in a single softly spoken word. "Explain . . ."

There was nothing left of Aldric's world but the promise of pain in a glitter of talons and teeth. Without thought and without hope, his instincts took over and his empty right hand lashed out at the heart of the hungry blackness in an attempt to block. Without a sword in that hand the gesture was useless, but long years of practice had made some kind of defensive counter as much a reflex as pulling back from a fire.

And then the hand was empty no longer. A light that was the hot transparent blue of an alcohol flame ran down his arm from where the cut was born, up in the heavy muscles of shoulder and back, almost as if the power that would have propelled a sword had become visible. It flared out from his fist and formed a blade— no more than the shadow of a blade, as all things here were shadows—but when one unreality slashed across another in a sweeping stroke that left an arc of fire in its wake, Issaqua the Devourer reeled back screeching.

Aldric glanced quickly over-shoulder, making sure that he still stood between Voord and the demon. The once-Warlord was on his feet, watching wide-eyed as the Alban who had been his enemy defended him from the demon which had been his ally. From the expressions fighting for precedence on his face, the Vlechan's confusion was absolute.

None of Voord's old certainties made sense anymore. That any man should willingly have died for his sake was hard enough to comprehend; that it should be *this* man,

and that the gift should go on beyond pity and into forgiveness, was almost more than he could bear.

Aldric knew; he had been there, seconds and a lifetime ago, when he had knelt and drawn his *tsepan,* and
realized not only what he was finally about to do but
why. It had been the last of all the reasons he had ever
considered and yet, strangely, the most honorable of
them all.

He shook his head, then stared at his own poised right
hand; the arm, his whole body, were naked no longer,
but instead were encased in a familiar metal skin, *an
moyya-tsalaer,* his own Great Harness. It was as it had
always been, jet-black, so that as he moved his limbs
they glittered darkly. Like Ythek Shri. Too much so for
comfort. For all that the armor looked to have been
wrought of smoke instead of steel, he had no doubt that
it would be just as effective as the sword.

That, too, was still gripped firmly by his mailed fingers,
and its shape was without doubt that of a *taiken.* It was
as if Isileth Widowmaker, being broken, had come with
him into death and had waited only to be summoned to
his time of greatest need. The long-sword or—by its
color—the Echainon spellstone set into its pommel.
Both, maybe. Singly and together they had preserved his
life often enough, had been almost as much a part of
him in the past year as his own heart and hands. Why
not then preserve his soul from harm . . . ?

Aldric watched Issaqua coldly from beneath the shadowy peak of a shadowy helmet. What was, was. Thinking
grimly that it would have amused Gemmel to see him
dismiss the mystery, Aldric questioned no longer, did not
pause to wonder any further about the *why?* or *when?* or
how? but instead closed the distance in three swift steps
and cut again.

"Hai!"

Teeth glistened amid a webbing of saliva as the
demon's maw gaped wide—then went on gaping, wider
and wider as both of its lower jaws fell away. Issaqua
bellowed, vomiting up a thick silvery blood like molten
metal as it scrabbled at the ruined mask of its face, trying
to restore the smashed pieces to their proper configura-

tion. In some dispassionate part of Aldric's mind it seemed strange that the Devourer could so easily repair its careful dismemberment of Voord so that it could pull him apart again, and yet could not heal itself.

A strange hope began to take shape, that instead of fighting this long fight down through eternity he might actually finish it—finish with Issaqua once and for all and finally be at peace. Kill it, if killing was possible here beyond the door of death. Maybe it was. Maybe this was the only place where the unkillable could truly die. Slain by the already-slain.

Aldric laughed harshly through the wild whirl of his own thoughts. His sword had twice cloven the demon's substance, yet when the great hooks of its talons came raking toward him they were blocked by something more than just the smoky carapace that was the memory of armor. That merely gave an outward form to his true protection. He was already dead—and unlike Voord he could not be harmed or torn or tormented, because even now in his willing defense of a helpless victim he had done nothing to deserve retribution.

It was Issaqua's attempt to rend him which had broken the Law and upset the Balance, and he held the bladed consequence burning blue in his right hand. Aldric hefted the un-weight of the shadow sword and watched the Devourer rear up to its full height, more than twice his own. The coldness of its hatred burned him and despite his confidence all the old fears came whimpering back. If he had misjudged, if he was wrong about this, if *auythyu an-shri* laid hold of him—then eternity would be a long, long time to scream.

There was a flickering of half-seen movement. Too fast. Far too fast. Aldric snapped around and the sword came up, but long before he even saw what it was something had seized his left arm in a grip like white-hot metal. And behind him, with the sound of despair that comes only when hope is offered and then snatched away, Voord began to shriek . . .

Gemmel was working with a feverish speed that Kyrin had never seen before. He had taken Ykraith the Dragonwand out of her hands and spoken to it under

his breath in that quick, slipshod monotone which always
made her think of priests babbling over-familiar litanies,
then thrust its spike into the stone floor beside Aldric's
body. As Kyrin watched, he repeated the procedure with
Widowmaker's hilt-shard, driving the broken blade into
the marble flags with an ease that gave the lie to its
impossibility.

"Why can't you let him be?" she said wearily. "This
is a waste of time."

Gemmel straightened up with a jerk and stared at her,
and for just an instant Kyrin discovered what it felt like
to receive a flicker of real rage from those deep-set emerald eyes. She flinched as if he was about to strike her,
then the old enchanter forced a smile on to his face and
the moment was gone. "Then it's my time to waste, lady.
Isn't it?" He stepped back from the corpse and beckoned her closer. "Come here. Now."

She stood at the crown of Aldric's head, looking down
at him. Gemmel had withdrawn the *tsepan* and returned
it to its scabbard, and had rearranged his dead son's
limbs and clothing so that the ugly wound was hidden.
Had it not been for the ivory pallor of his skin, Kyrin
might still have believed that Aldric was only sleeping
and might be wakened by the touch of her hand. Gemmel watched her for a moment; then he said. "Call him."

Kyrin was not in the habit of swearing, especially at
people so menacing as Gemmel Errekren, but she swore
now—bitterly and with the tears newly stinging at her
eyes. For all that she called him filthy things which would
have drawn a reaction even from Aldric himself, the
enchanter took her oaths without a flicker of response.
"Call him."

"He's not asleep," wailed Kyrin softly, "he's *dead!*"

"I know." The flat response silenced her as nothing
else could have done. "But you told me the reason and
the manner of it. There is a Balance in these matters,
Kyrin, and for these few moments it's still weighted on
his side. So do as I bid you and *call him!*"

"I . . . Yes." Kyrin stared at the pale, still body and
tried to forget that she had seen a knife go into it and
all the blood and life go out. She put from her mind all
but the times when he had dozed off fully clothed, all

the times when he had looked as he did now, all the
times when a word or a touch was all she needed to
make his eyes open and his mouth smile. "Aldric. Oh
my loved, can you not hear me? Aldric, dear one, come
back to me . . ." Gemmel was beside her, watching, and
she turned to him in despair and hope of sympathy. "It
isn't working. Nothing's happening. It isn't working . . . "

"Hush, now. You wouldn't have brought him back
from the corridor outside, and he's farther away than
that. Call him again and keep calling him until . . . until
I tell you to stop."

"And then . . . "

"And then watch, and learn, and become wise. *Abath
arhan, Ykraith, hlath Echainon devhawr ecchud. Aih'noen
ecchaur i aiyya.*"

Kyrin felt the air turn thick, like honey. Power
thrummed in it so that little sparks ran crackling down
her hair and sleeted from the tips of her fingers. The
spellstaff and the broken *taiken* became the uprights of
a doorway, one that had no lintel and no door save only
a slow rippling like the near-invisible haze that rises
from a heated surface. It was quite transparent, yet
things seen through it were not quite the same as things
seen around the sides. They were . . . changed. A whirl
of snow from the darkening sky outside gusted through
the shattered wall and roof, and Kyrin saw the doorway
fill with stars. Then there was only a scattering of snowflakes that settled on to Aldric's face and had not heat
enough to melt.

"Take his hand," said Gemmel. There was the sound
of effort in his voice, and it took on an edge of urgency
as Kyrin bent toward the cold hands crossed on the cold
breast. "No! Through the door. Reach out and bring
him home."

Kyrin did not hesitate, but extended her hands toward
the shimmer and into it, and through it. The hand vanished from sight as if she had thrust it into ink instead
of a surface that seemed as clear as glass. The junction of
wrist and doorway was as straight-edged as the stroke
of a razor, and there was a freezing instant of horror as
she realized this was what an amputation would look
like. Then something solid and metal-cold brushed against

her fingertips, something laced and buckled. She closed her grip on what could only be the wrist-plates of an Alban lamellar battle armor. There was a sudden wrench of resistance and Kyrin cried out, pulling with a desperate strength that had no thought for what else might be brought as well . . .

His sword was halfway through a savage downward sweep when Aldric wrenched the descending blade to a dead stop, for what was locked around his armored sleeve was no demonic claw but a human hand and wrist which had pushed through a shimmering shear plane in the very air itself, a hand that burned but only with the heat of living blood. He felt his throat thicken and tears sting at his eyes as he recognized the ring on its third finger: heavy gold, with a square face that was plain except for the chequered diagonal of a clan-lord's youngest son—the ring that he had set on Tehal Kyrin's finger as a love-token until they could find a better.

Kyrin's hand began to pull him through the walls of death and back toward the living world, and in the same moment Issaqua took a single raking stride forward. Once he was gone, it would have Voord all to itself. The *Woydach*'s renewed wails of terror dinned in Aldric's ears and made his skin crawl. Everything was going to be worthless after all. Unless . . .

His left arm had been drawn through almost to the shoulder when Aldric threw himself against the slow, steady pull and lunged toward Issaqua. It lacked all grace and control and was more the limb-flail of someone falling from a horse, but it brought him just close enough to cut *tarann'ach,* a vertical stroke with all his focused force behind it that split the universe in two blue-blazing pieces. His whole body jolted, and he didn't know whether it was with the impact or with being brought up short in his tracks by a frightful jerk on his outstretched left arm.

The demon's armored shape stood quite still for a long second with only its great crooked claws flexing like a spider's legs—glowering, unhurt, as impossible to dismiss as a bad dream.

Oh God, what does it take to kill you . . .

A silvery line as straight and precise as a geometric exercise appeared down the center of the demon's huge triangular head. It slumped a little and ceased to be symmetrical, then sagged sideways and fell apart in two sheared halves. Issaqua, Ythek Shri, the Devourer in the Dark, quivered once all over and toppled silently forward in a long, long fall that flared into hot blue light and drifting ashes and never reached the bottom . . .

Kyrin's hand came back through the doorway with a sudden rush, and the haze between the lintels winked out of existence. There was nothing now except a staff carved with the outlines of a dragon and the black hilt of a broken sword. Nothing at all . . . her hand was empty. She stared at it, not wanting to believe that what her eyes said was the truth. The ring on her finger, Aldric's ring, glinted coldly in the cold light and mocked her hopes.

Gemmel was watching her. He did not speak, and Kyrin was glad of it. There were no words left to him that would mean anything more than the most feeble of excuses. She tried not to blink, for fear that the tears would start again. "I told you." Her voice was quiet, without any hint of blame. "Can we go now, please?"

"Not without my son."

"I would have carried him," said Kyrin simply, "but you can help me, if you want."

"No." Gemmel made no move. "Wait!"

Kyrin felt anger at the old man's stubbornness boil up slowly through her grief. She could understand how Gemmel felt—did she not feel the same?—but not why he persisted in this useless charade once they had both seen how he had failed. There had to come a time when he accepted what she had known in her heart all along, that Aldric was dead and no sorcery or talk of Balance set awry would bring him back. To do otherwise lacked dignity, and that was all Kyrin had left. "Wait?" she echoed. "You've done all that you thought you could, old man—more than that, you made me believe it, too. You made me see him die all over again . . ."

"Did I? Then I ask your pardon for it." Gemmel

shrugged, dismissive more than apologetic. "But had you trusted more and doubted less, it would not have happened. Look, Kyrin . . . look again—and see him live."

Kyrin looked . . . and at first saw nothing. Aldric lay as still and pale and dead as when she laid his body on the ground. Then something moved, a thing so small that at first she did not realize what it meant. No more than a bead of water on his brow, as unremarkable as sweat or rain . . . or a snowflake that had only now begun to melt.

Aldric's eyes snapped open, then as quickly shut to squinting slits until they grew more accustomed to the winter dusk that was a blinding glare after the blackness beyond the gate. For long seconds after that they stared unfocused at the ceiling, while vague dark figures moved to and fro and voices spoke through the ringing silence in his ears. The breath came back into him in a single long shudder and he tried to sit up; then let that first breath come gasping out again as the hurt muscles of his stomach suggested *not just yet*.

There was more pain in his left arm, a silver needle of it stabbing up from the hand he had braced against the floor—a hand whose palm he was suddenly afraid to look at. Now that memory came rushing back like the spray of that wave of pain, he was more than willing to lie still and try to make some sense of what had no sense in it at all. "I was dead."

"You were dead." That the first voice he heard should have been Gemmel's, and agreeing with him, was of a piece with the rest. That it should have been edged with irritation in an attempt to hide any softer emotion was also quite in keeping. "Pig-headed self-sacrificial tradition-bound honor-fixated . . ." Gemmel paused, clearing his throat with unnecessary vigor. Seen upside-down, his smile was a peculiar thing, but even so it went a long way toward taking the sting from what he said. "Don't make a habit of suicide, Aldric. It's usually permanent."

Always give as good as you get, when you're able . . .

Aldric grinned the tight little smile of someone receiving unnecessary advice. "I'll bear that in mind, *altrou.*"

Gemmel snorted and stalked around to stand beside him, where he leaned on the Dragonwand and stared down critically. "Can you stand?"

Aldric thought about it. "I think so."

"Then take my hand."

"I . . . Your pardon, Father, but there was another hand—the hand that brought me back. Please. Kyrin was here."

"She still is, my love." Kyrin knelt down beside him on the shattered marble of the floor among the snow and the blood, and reached out as she had done before across an infinitely greater distance. "I told you once, Aldric: where you go, I go. We go together, or not at all."

Aldric looked at her left hand—long-fingered, ringed with gold and perfect—and shuddered when he thought of the claw that Isileth's edges had made of his own. At last, reluctantly, he raised it. There was no claw. The hand on his wrist showed hardly any sign at all that its palm had been carved off—except that where the Honor-scars had been was now all new, unblemished, slightly tender skin.

Kyrin had seen the look and the hesitation, and knew why. She took his hand in hers and helped him to his feet. "They're gone. All the duty and the obligation went with them." She touched a fingertip lightly to his chest, and to the small white triangle where a *tsepan* had gone home to the full length of its blade. "The only Honor-scar that matters now is here."

"Now, and later," said Gemmel. "Much later, and well away from here." He bounced something on the palm of his hand, a thing of gold and greenish crystal which Aldric had known for several months by no more than a description, before he saw it clasped around the neck of *Woydach* Voord. The Jewel, that had been the cause of so much grief. "Before he wants this back."

Aldric and Kyrin gazed distastefully at it and then, as the import of the enchanter's words sank in, stared at the place where the Grand Warlord's corpse had been. Voord was standing up . . .

"These things happen," said Gemmel, very dry. "But then, I understand you couldn't kill him anyway?"

"I tried." Aldric shrugged, watching the unsteady figure in the sword-slashed clothing. "But I couldn't."

"You tried to help him die . . . and instead helped him to live."

"You know that well enough," said Kyrin, and gave the old man a warning look from underneath her brows.

"I do. Yes, indeed. But I'd as soon not put too much pressure on his gratitude. Not after this"—he tucked the Jewel into one of the pockets of his tunic and out of sight—"and especially not now that he owes you what can never be repaid. I doubt he takes kindly to the debt."

"He's got his life back," said Kyrin, "and ought to be satisfied with that."

They walked carefully together toward the ragged hole that sorcery had torn in the wall, breathing the cold clean air of winter as it gusted through, and then Aldric hesitated. "What about Widowmaker?" he asked.

Kyrin glanced sharply at him, and for a second her expression was that of a woman whose lover asks after the health of an old mistress. "It's just a sword, and a broken one. Leave it."

"It still deserves better than to be left here."

"I don't . . ." Kyrin shrugged and smiled briefly, dropping the dispute. "Go and get her. We'll," with a warning look at Gemmel, "stay here."

As he searched for the point-shard, meaning for safety's sake to replace it in the longsword's scabbard, Voord watched him through glazed, hooded eyes. The *Woydach* was breathing, but as Aldric reached out carefully for the still-sharp blade it occured to him that Voord was somehow different, as if he had not been restored whole and entire. There was a lack of luster about the man, as if some inner spark was missing; he might be upright, but he was still dead inside.

Aldric's fingers closed on the length of chilly metal, and he realized that Widowmaker, too, was changed. There was no longer the tingle of hungry menace which he had associated with the *taiken* for so long. It was as if all the killings of the past two thousand years had never happened. She had returned to what she had been in the beginning: Isileth, "Star-steel," an elegant weapon

made by the finest swordsmith of all swords in all times
and places from metals that had fallen from the sky,
for no other reason than to test his skill. Kyrin would
like that.

Aldric heard the scuff of feet behind him, overlaid too
late with Kyrin's cry of warning. Something massive hit
him in the back, punching through the lamellar armor
as if it wasn't there and doing something to his lungs
that made him cough. He staggered forward into arms
which had not been close enough to save him. There
was perhaps two feet of steel in Widowmaker's hilt, and
by the feel of it most had gone inside him. There was
no pain, only a dull sensation of being pulled off-balance
by the long blade standing out between his shoulders,
and a sickly awareness of his own stupidity as he turned
his head.

Voord was smiling now, as he had not smiled before.
It had been brooding hatred which had made him seem
so dull and dead—hatred at being saved, which was bad
enough, and saved through pity and an enemy's sense
of honor, which was far worse. Only with requital for
that ultimate of insults had the spark of his life returned.

"Burn the bastard!" Aldric heard Kyrin spit the words
in a voice so vicious that it had almost ceased to be her
own. For the first time in her life she had learned what
it must be like to suffer Voord's soul-spoiling hatred for
any other living thing. He felt Gemmel draw his sidearm
from its holster, and his ears filled with the high shrill
whining that meant death.

"No . . . " He grabbed for the weapon and weakly
tried to pull its muzzle out of line, but might as well
have tried to bend a bar of iron.

"No?" Gemmel plainly did not believe what he was
hearing.

Aldric coughed blood-spots on to the old man's im-
maculate uniform. "No. Didn't go through . . . all of
that—not just so you could kill him. D-dying isn't *that*
much fun."

He saw understanding in their faces, felt the pistol's
long barrel drop from aim and smiled with relief. His
head lolled forward as if it weighed a thousand pounds,
then dragged upright again as he shook the encroaching

darkness from his vision and grinned savagely back at Voord. "Poor sort . . . of revenge anyway," he said, taking care to speak distinctly. "No imagination anymore."

Woydach Voord glared at them in loathing with all satisfaction drained out of his face, knowing beyond doubt that whether Aldric lived or died the sweet taste of his victory had turned irrevocably sour. He began to screech something that none of them bothered to heed. Kyrin and Gemmel heard only the frightened urgency in Aldric's voice: "Like death. N-not worth repeating. Once is . . . is enough. But I'm dying, Father . . ."

"Easy, my son," said Gemmel. "I know." He raised the Dragonwand above his head and braced his newfound children close against his side. Power blasted down from the spellstaff and swirled about them so that they stood at the heart of a twisting column of ice-blue flame. "I know. We're going where I can help you. Home . . ."

Aldric watched their faces, heard their voices, until all faded. All sound was lost. All sight was swallowed up. All the world faded; and went black.

The fire faded and went out, and they were gone.

Glossary

achran-kai. (Alb.) "inverted cross"; a double cut in *taiken-ulleth* in which the blade, often striking from the scabbard, follows first a horizontal path at chest or eye level and then a vertical downward path, both to strike a target directly in front. If the first cut is delivered with proper force, focus and accuracy, the second is not usually required.

altrou. (Alb.) "Foster-father"; also a title given to priests.

an-sherban. (Drus.) Patronymic of members of the Sherbanul dynasty, present rulers of the Drusalan Empire.

arluth (Alb.) "Lord"; ruler of lands or of a town.

aypan-kailin (Alb.) "Cadet-warrior"; a youth undergoing training in the military skills of sword, horse and bow.

coerhanalth (Drus.) "Lord General"; Commander-in-Chief, most senior of all Drusalan military (as opposed to political) ranks.

coyac. (Jouv.) A sleeveless jerkin of fur, leather or sheepskin.

cserin. (Alb.) Child of a clan-lord, and in line of succession to the title.

cymar. (Alb.) Long overrobe for outdoor wear.

eijo. (Alb.) "Outlier"; a wanderer or landless person, especially a lordless warrior.

eldheisart. (Drus.) "Commander"; Imperial military rank.

elyu-dlas. (Alb.) "Color-robe"; formal crested garment in clan colors.

erhan. (Alb.) "Scholar"; especially used of one who travels in the course of his/her studies.

eskorrethen. (Alb.) The coming-of-age ceremony at age twenty, when a warrior is confirmed in his status and in any ranks, styles or titles to which he may be entitled. His hair, grown long for the purpose, is tied back in a queue (originally the handle by which his severed head was carried if he fell in battle); oaths of loyalty are taken before religious and secular witnesses; and if he is *kailin-eir* (q.v.) and thus of a rank to warrant it, he is given a *tsepan* (q.v.) which is used to cut the Honor-scars in his left hand. These three scars are a permanent reminder of his blood-oath of honor and duty to Heaven, Crown and Clan. From that time forward the *tsepan* must always be within arm's length, and when in public his hair must be tied back in a queue.

estoc. (Jouv.) A sword with a slender single-edged blade, sometimes slightly curved but more usually straight, whose fencing style makes more use of thrusting than does the Alban *taiken* (q.v.)

glas-elyu Menethen. (Alb.) The Blue Mountains, a range in North-Western Alba.

hanalth. (Drus.) "Colonel"; Imperial military rank.

hanan-vlethanek. (Alb.) "Keeper-of-Years"; a Court archivist.

hautach. (Drus.) "Sir"; literally "High One," used when acknowledging the commands of a superior officer.

hauthanalth. (Drus.) "Over-Colonel"; Imperial military rank.

hautheisart. (Drus.) "Lord-Commander"; Imperial military rank.

hautmarin. (Drus.) "Ship-captain"; Imperial naval rank equivalent to *hautheisart.*

hlensyarl, hlens'l. (Drus.) "Outlander"; a foreigner or stranger. This can mean someone from a different province, city or even village, but is always a person of whom to be suspicious.

ilauan. (Alb.) "Clan"; a noble family, linked by name and bloodline. All members of a clan are related to a greater or lesser extent, but only the *cseirin-*

born(q.v.) may rule, and then only in line of succession.

ilauem-arluth. (Alb.) "Clan-lord"; the head of a noble house, ruler of its lands and commander of its forces.

inyen-hlensyarl. (Drus., from *hlensyarl* q.v.) "Alien-foreigner"; someone from another country, and therefore always considered a potential enemy. The present political situation within the Drusalan Empire has done nothing to amend this, and increasingly the word has taken on the connotation of insult.

kagh' ernvakh. (Drus.) "Honor's-Guardians"; the Imperial Political and Secret Police.

kailin. (Alb.) Warrior, man-at-arms, especially when in service to a lord.

kailin-eir. (Alb.) Warrior nobleman, of lesser status than *arluth* (q.v.)

kortagor. (Drus.) "Lieutenant"; Imperial military rank.

kourgath. (Alb.) The Alban lynx-cat, proverbial for ferocity out of all proportion to its size; also a nickname.

margh-arluth. (Alb.) "Horse Lord"; one of the Alban warrior nobility whose clan lands are found mostly in Prytenon and Elthan.

mathern-an arluth. (Alb.) "Lord King"; literally "lord above other lords"; formal title of the King of Alba.

matherneil. (Alb.) "Kingswine"; the sweet white vintages of Hauverne in Jouvann, rare and expensive in Alba because of small vineyards and restrictive export tariffs.

moyya-tsalaer. (Alb.) "Great Harness"; full battle armor, with helmet, lamellar cuirass, armored sleeves and leggings. Shields are uncommon, normally carried only during formal combats.

pesoek. (Alb. dialect, Cernuan and Elthanek.) "Charm"; a lesser spell, or a conjuring trick performed without true magic.

pestreyhar, pertrior. (Cernuan, Alb. dialect.) "Wizard" or "sorcerer"; literally, one who creates power with words.

pestreyr-pesok'n. (Cernuan, Alb. dialect.) "Petty-wizard";

a conjurer, one incapable of using true power, an employer only of insignificant charms or sleight-of-hand. (*pesoek,* q.v.)

purcanyath. (Cernuan, Alb. dialect.) "Enchanter"; literally a spell-singer.

seisac. (Drus.) A distinctive form of helmet with (usually) a high, conical crown, deep neck-guard and cheekplates and a peak through which may be slid a nasal bar.

slijei? (Vlech.) "Understand?"; interrogative imperative of an officer completing the issue of an order to subordinates. The word carries an element of promisory threat.

slij'hah! (Vlech.) "Understood!"; standard response to the interrogative imperative.

taidyo. (Alb.) "Staffsword"; a wooden practice foil, usually of oak or a similar hardwood.

taiken. (Alb.) "Longsword"; the *kailin*'s classic weapon, a straight, double-edged cut-and-thrust blade in a hilt long enough for both hands but sufficiently balanced for only one. When in these trained hands, a properly forged and polished *taiken* (the word "sharpened," with its suggestion of prior bluntness, is not encouraged) delivering a focused strike can shear through most forms of composite armor. The body of the armor's wearer has never been considered an obstacle.

taiken-ulleth. (Alb.) Generic name for all schools and styles of *taiken*-play.

taipan. (Alb.) "Shortsword"; a short, sometimes curved, often richly mounted weapon which is usually restricted to wear with the formal *elyu-dlas* (q.v.)

tarann'ach. (Alb.) "Striking thunderbolt"; a cut in *taiken-ulleth* in which the blade follows a diagonal downward path to strike a target directly in front.

tarannin-kai. (Alb.) "Twin thunderbolts"; a cut in *taiken'ulleth* (q.v.) in which the blade follows a horizontal figure-eight to strike two targets at right and left.

tau-kortagor. (Drus.) "Under-lieutenant"; the lowest Imperial military rank.

taulath. (Alb.) "Shadowthief"; secretive mercenaries,

available for hire through devious routes for the purpose of spying, sabotage, blackmail and assassination; they perform all those politically necessary duties forbidden to *kailinin* by their codes of Honor.

telek. (Alb.) "Thrower"; a personal-defense sidearm which projects lead-weighted darts with considerable force (over short distances) from either a box or rotary magazine by means of powerful springs.

tlakh-woydan. (Vlech.) "Lord's-Protectors"; the Grand Warlord's Bodyguard Regiment, stationed in the Drakkesborg Barracks.

tsalaer. (Alb.) "Harness"; the lamellar cuirass worn without armored sleeves or leggings, often under clothing as a concealed defense. (All parts of *an moyya tsalaer* (q.v.) may be worn separately, as need dictates.)

tsepan. (Alb.) "Small-blade"; the Honor dirk of Alba was originally a weapon carried into battle by its owner as a mercy knife, for others or himself. (It was and still is considered dishonorable and vulgar to finish off a fallen *kailin* with a *taiken,* for all that he may be killed outright with one while still on his feet.) As the requirements of honor, duty and obligation came to be observed with ever-increasing stringency, the *tsepan* became instead a means whereby a warrior could recover lost honor (or at least evade the consequences of its loss) by killing himself. This was an acceptable form of self-punishment, and meant that other penalties, notably forfeiture of lands or titles, were withheld. With a few notable exception, the practice has fallen into disuse.

tsepanak'ulleth. (Alb.) The act of ritual suicide.

vosjhaien, vosjh'. (Vlech.) Father, "papa."

woydach. (Drus.) "Grand Warlord"; while the title appears exclusively military, it also carries political connotations. The Grand Warlord of the Drusalan Empire was originally responsible for foreign affairs, frontier security and the overseeing of any policies of expansion put forward by the Emperor. More recently the post has been that of military dictator, with the Emperor as no more than a figurehead.

woydachul. (Drus.) The Warlord's faction in the Empire.

woydek-hlautan. (Drus.) "The Warlord's Domain"; all those provinces of the Empire which through policy or conquest regard the *Woydach* rather than the Emperor as true head of state.

ymeth. (Drus.) "Dreamsmoke"; a common recreational narcotic, used also as a soporific before surgery and as an adjunct to certain forms of sorcery.

Irene Radford

"A mesmerizing storyteller." —*Romantic Times*

THE DRAGON NIMBUS
THE GLASS DRAGON
0-88677-634-1
THE PERFECT PRINCESS
0-88677-678-3
THE LONELIEST MAGICIAN
0-88677-709-7
THE WIZARD'S TREASURE
0-88677-913-8

THE DRAGON NIMBUS HISTORY
THE DRAGON'S TOUCHSTONE
0-88677-744-5
THE LAST BATTLEMAGE
0-88677-774-7
THE RENEGADE DRAGON
0-88677-855-7

THE STAR GODS
THE HIDDEN DRAGON
0-7564-0051-1

To Order Call: 1-800-788-6262

Melanie Rawn

"Rawn's talent for lush descriptions and complex characterizations provides a broad range of drama, intrigue, romance and adventure."
—*Library Journal*

EXILES
THE RUINS OF AMBRAI	0-88677-668-6
THE MAGEBORN TRAITOR	0-88677-731-3

DRAGON PRINCE
DRAGON PRINCE	0-88677-450-0
THE STAR SCROLL	0-88677-349-0
SUNRUNNER'S FIRE	0-88677-403-9

DRAGON STAR
STRONGHOLD	0-88677-482-9
THE DRAGON TOKEN	0-88677-542-6
SKYBOWL	0-88677-595-7

To Order Call: 1-800-788-6262

DAW 33

Tanya Huff

The Finest in Fantasy

SING THE FOUR QUARTERS   0-88677-628-7
FIFTH QUARTER   0-88677-651-1
NO QUARTER   0-88677-698-8
THE QUARTERED SEA   0-88677-839-5

The Keeper's Chronicles
SUMMON THE KEEPER   0-88677-784-4
THE SECOND SUMMONING   0-88677-975-8
LONG HOT SUMMONING   0-7564-0136-4

Omnibus Editions:
WIZARD OF THE GROVE   0-88677-819-0
(Child of the Grove & The Last Wizard)
OF DARKNESS, LIGHT & FIRE   0-7564-0038-4
*(Gate of Darkness, Circle of Light & The Fire's
Stone)*

To Order Call: 1-800-788-6262

DAW21

Rod
561 266 7503